Den Of Nightmares

CURSE OF FATE OMNIBUS

SAMANTHA BARRETT

*This omnibus is dedicated Ryan Knox,
Without Ryan I wouldn't be where I am today or even an author
so, thank you miss Knox for all that you have done for me and all
the doors you opened.*

Dream
CURSE OF FATE BOOK 1

Chapter One

RYAN

I wake in the woods again, wearing the same white summer dress I always am. I didn't need to call out—I knew he would be here. He always is. Glancing over my shoulder, I lock eyes with him. I know it's a dream, but God, it feels so real. The raw sexual attraction between us in the air is almost like a fuse to a bomb. The closer we get to each other, the closer we are to detonating.

"Hello, love." His voice is pure sin and virulent masculine sexiness.

"Hi," I can hear the lust in my own voice, making it husky and soft.

He looks at me like I am his last meal. It sends shivers down my spine and liquid pooling between my thighs.

"Come here, love." I saunter over to him, admiring his beauty. He towers over me at six foot three. He wears jeans that hang low on his hips, showcasing that beautiful V. He's sans shirt, as always. My eyes travel to his face, his beautiful full lips turned up at the corners in a smirk. Those eyes are so captivating and the deepest violet in color. Yeah, I know no one has violet-colored eyes, but this is my dream, and I'll have what I want. His jet black hair is slicked back, like he has just run his hand through it.

I stand in front of my dream man, so close I can feel the heat radiating off his body. He pulls me flush against his chest, and I gasp at the contact. The heat from his body is making me burn, in the most delicious way.

"You're so beautiful, love. I could never get enough of you." My dream man always knows the right things to say. Before I can respond, he stops my reply with a kiss of such force that it steals my breath.

I wrap my arms around his neck, and he slides his hands down my thighs and lifts me off the ground. Instinctively, I wind my legs around his waist. We never break our kiss. He walks us a few steps forward and lowers me to the grass.

"I can smell how wet you are for me," he whispers against my lips.

I need him inside me now. I need his mouth on mine like I need my next breath. He pulls the thin straps of my dress down each arm, exposing my breasts. I don't have small boobs, but they aren't large either. What is it they say? "More than a handful is waste." He moves his head down to my breast and starts to suck hard, just the way I like it. I sigh in pleasure as he continues to suck and bite my nipples. His right hand slides my dress up to expose my lower half—I never wear panties in my dreams. He slides his hand between my soaking wet folds, and as soon as his fingers graze my enlarged nub, I scream out. I am so close to coming already, and he knows it. He withdraws his hand and mouth from my body and leans back, peering down at me with a smirk. He knows what he is doing to me and he loves every second of it.

I lean forward and unbutton his jeans, pulling them down so I can expose his cock. When it springs free, I smile. It always takes my breath away. He is so large that his hard length nearly hits his navel. I start to stroke him roughly, and he hisses through clenched teeth.

He wiggles out of his jeans then pushes me back down so I'm lying flat on my back, his hard body hovering over mine. The heat of his kiss makes more liquid gather between my legs. I am so fucking wet for him. He positions himself between my legs, then slams into me. I swear I can feel him hitting the back of my womb, and the combination of pleasure and the slight sting of pain forces a moan from me.

"Scream for me, love," he whispers in my ear, while driving into me. I can feel how I close I am already, a moment later he has me screaming out.

"I'm coming, Nico! God, don't fucking stop," I scream, clawing at his back like a possessed woman.

"Come on my cock, love. I love feeling your pussy clench my dick." His words are my undoing, and I come almost violently while screaming his name to the heavens.

But he isn't done with me yet, and he wrings another orgasm from me before he finds his own release. Once he's spent, he collapses on top of me, both of us panting like we have just run a marathon. It feels like we have. Once my breathing is under control, I open my eyes to look at Nico.

"I know this is all a dream, but God I wish you were real." As soon as the words leave my mouth, it all goes dark.

RYAN

I woke panting and out of breath, my hair sticking to my forehead and cheek. My steamy dreams always left me this way, but I wouldn't change it for the world. In my dreams I was strong, confident, and sexy—and adored by my men. I was none of those things in real life: I always second-guessed my decisions, and my long hair was plain Jane brown. I had strange eyes that seemed to unnerve people. They were a bright shade of green, and there was a ring of yellow around my pupils. I was not adored by anyone in real life. My mother beat me throughout my childhood, and my father left with my twin sister just after we turned five.

My mother would tell me that she was preparing me for when "the others" would come. I never knew what that meant, and if I tried to ask, she would simply say I needed to toughen up. That was always her excuse for beating me and locking me in my room for days on end. "A weak bitch can't lead anyone," she'd yell when I begged her to let me out, "You will die after a day, if you don't suck it up." She told me there come a time when I would be caged, and I needed to learn how to cope.

Shaking myself from my inner thoughts, I peeled the covers

off my sweat-laden body and went to grab some clothes from my bag so I could have a quick shower. I had stopped at a hotel the night before, too tired to drive the full distance to Stevie's house.

I still had a long drive ahead of me to reach my sister, and we still had a lot to get ready in the two days before we left on our big trip to Alaska. My life was finally my own and not ruled by my mother, and I was going to enjoy every moment of it, with my sister by my side.

I was almost bouncing in my seat with excitement as I arrived at my sister's house. There were two cars in the driveway; I knew one was Stevie's beat-up old Mini, but I had no idea who owned the other.

As I got out of my truck, I heard the front door swing open. My sister came running out to greet me. She looked as beautiful, as always. She was the better-looking twin, with long brown hair and hazel eyes—with no weird yellow ring around her pupils. She had a slim figure with curves in all the right places, and even in a plain white V-neck shirt and a pair of worn-out jeans with tears in the legs, she still looked like a Victoria's Secret model.

"Sissy!" she screeched as she pulled me in for a bone-crushing hug.

"Hey, Stevie," I murmured, hugging her back.

"How was your drive? You must be tired. Come on, let's get your bags and get inside. I'm freezing my balls off." I couldn't help but laugh at my sister, who continued her chatter as we pulled my two bags from the trunk. She never had a filter— not that I was any different. My mouth always got me in trouble with my mom, but I just couldn't help it. I am who I am, I guess.

"So, do you want to tell me who that car belongs to? Or do I have to guess?" I asked. She always had boys falling all over her, so it wouldn't surprise me if it belonged to some guy she knew.

"Oh, you will just have to wait and see when you get inside. It's a surprise! I'm sure you'll love it," she said with a wink.

Now I was on guard. My sister was always one for the dramatics. You never knew what to expect when she said she had a surprise for you. I just hoped it was nothing like the surprise she sent me for my sixteenth birthday. I have never hated a gift more. She had one of our cousins—Chase—show up at my high school and bring me flowers and chocolates and act like he was my new boyfriend! She did this because my ex had recently dumped me in front of the whole football team. They all laughed their ugly asses off. Needless to say, don't ever tell Stevie when a guy dumps you.

As soon as we passed the threshold of the front door, I was grabbed from behind lifted off my feet.

"Put me down!" I yelled, trying to wriggle around and see who the hell had grabbed me.

Once on my feet, I swung around to see my cousin Chase hunched over, laughing his ass off. He looked up with those sky blue eyes, and I couldn't help the grin that tugged at my lips. Once he stood to his full height, he was over six feet tall.

"I can't believe you still scream like a girl," he said, still chuckling.

"That's because I am a girl, you jackass," I huffed.

"Now, now, you two—cut it out. You know you love him still, Ry, even if you did fake break up with him in eleventh grade," Stevie said, grinning like a fool.

Chase gasped. "Oh my God! Yes! Stevie, you still owe me

for that. Ryan nearly punched me in the face that day for telling her friends I was her boyfriend."

I narrowed my eyes. "I hate you both."

Just as I turned away from their giggling nonsense, I was grabbed again and let out another screech, sending Chase and Stevie into howls of laughter once more.

"Holy shit, she sounds like a cat that got its tail stepped on," Chase said between guffaws.

Once I was put back on my feet for the second time that day, I looked up to see my other cousin—Chase's older brother, Alex.

"Alex!" I pulled him in for a hug. I hadn't seen Alex in years. Chase and Alex were my uncle's sons, from my dad's side. I was never allowed to visit them, and Mom had told me that my uncle hated me because I lived with her. I found out after Mom went missing that my uncle didn't hate me—it was just Mom trying to turn me against Dad's side of the family.

"Hey, squirt, how are you? It's been way too long. I see you finally grew into your big head," Alex joked.

I smiled sweetly at him. "Aww, it must run in the family. You finally grew into your ears." Looking at the beautiful man that now stood in front of me, it was hard to believe he was the same kid who was called Dumbo on the playground. He still had his coal black hair and baby blue eyes, though. He was a bit taller than Chase, but not by much, with a strong jaw line and high, defined cheekbones. He could have been a model—heck, maybe he was. I didn't know very much about these boys anymore.

In spite of Chase's sandy blond hair, the brothers looked very much alike. They also looked like they spent every spare minute they had at the gym.

"All right, enough of the pleasantries, family. Ryan's had a long drive, and I am sure she would love to take a shower and rest before dinner." *Bless you, Stevie, for reading my mind.*

"I would really love a shower. I feel icky after the long drive." Chase and Alex started giggling like schoolgirls. I pinned them both with a glare.

"And what the hell is so funny now, you two goons?" I snapped.

"Well, for one, no one outside of first grade says icky," Chase said with a snort, trying to cover his laughter.

"Shut up. Lots of people say icky," I argued.

"Oh yeah, like who, squirt?" Alex was grinning at me now.

"Well, I can't think of anyone right this second, but..." I was cut off as all three of them started laughing their asses off at my expense.

"Okay, okay. Chase, you start getting the meat on the grill. Alex you can make us all some drinks while I take Ryan up to her room. Once you're done with the drinks, Alex, can you bring Ryan's bags up?" Stevie was like an army general barking out orders to everyone.

Both the boys gave a nod and went about their tasks. On the way up the stairs, I paused to look at the many photos that lined the wall, almost all of them of Stevie, from her first day of school to her graduation, and photos of her on her birthday—well, our birthday. The one that got my attention had Stevie, Dad, and me in it. We must have been about 4 years old, and one of us was perched on each of his knees and smiling. I wished I could have gone with my Dad and Stevie when they left, but my mom wouldn't let both of us go. Truth be told, she only wanted to keep one of us so Dad had to pay her child support.

Stevie noticed I had stopped following her up the stairs, and she came back down and wrapped an arm around my shoulders. She knew it was hard for me to see the photos. She had the happy childhood and a loving parent. I had neither.

"He never stopped loving you, and he talked about you all the time."

"Then why did he never fight for me? He never came back *once* after you left, Stevie, He left me with her! I would have given my firstborn child to have been with you and Dad. I never had a choice."

I knew she wouldn't have let me go with them, no matter what Dad said, but it still hurt to have been virtually abandoned.

My sister looked at me with such pity in her eyes, but I didn't want her pity or anyone else's. I had no intention of letting my mother's abuse define me. I am not a victim; I am a survivor.

"I don't know, Ryan. For years I asked him if you could come for holidays or if I could go visit you and Mom. He always said no to me visiting you. He rang Mom a few times to ask if you could come here. He told her it wasn't healthy to keep us apart. She would always tell him he could see you again when he got over himself and came back to her."

There wasn't much to say after that, so I just sighed and started my trek up the stairs. Once at the top, she opened the second door on the right. The room was beautiful, with painted pink walls and a queen-sized bed in the middle of the room. There was a unicorn plushie perched on the bed, even. I used to love unicorns. There was a single dresser on the far wall with little snow globes on top. I made my way over to inspect them further, only to be distracted by a note on the side table by the bed that was addressed to me. I raised a brow at Stevie in question.

"The letter is from Dad. He wrote it to you the week he passed. It was like he almost knew what was coming. Dad always said one day you would come back here. He never gave up hope, Ry. He wanted his girls back together. This was supposed to be your room."

I looked to my sister, my mouth hanging open. Her words set an ache in my heart. I had dreamed of a room like this when I was little, instead of the dirty mattress on the floor with no sheets. Mom never spent money on things that weren't an absolute necessity. She always told me I should be grateful it wasn't the floor.

"If he wanted me to come back here so bad, why didn't he open the front door and let me see you when I came here, Stevie? I don't understand any of this." I was trying so hard to hold back the tears. My sister looked at me with utter heartbreak in her eyes, and I forced myself to swallow down the pain. I couldn't take that look from her.

"Don't worry, Stevie. I just want to grab a shower and relax. It's supposed to be a happy time. We're finally together again, and no one is here to tear us apart this time. We'll deal with all this other crap later."

She smiled, but it didn't reach her eyes. She simply took my hand in hers and squeezed it tight once before leaving me in my pink room with my unicorn and my grief.

Chapter Three

RYAN

After having a long, hot shower, some of the stress from my drive and the memories of my childhood start to ease. I was thankful for that; I didn't want to spoil this time with my sister and cousins by living in the past. While brushing out my hair and staring at myself in the mirror, I thought about how different mine and Stevie's personalities are. She has such a carefree spirit, and I always worry and over-think things. She has so much confidence and could hold her own in a room full of beautiful people, where-as I would sit in a corner, hoping no one would notice I was even there.

I leave the bathroom quickly and change into my favorite pair of jeans, which had tears in the knees. I grab the first shirt I can find: it's a Harley Quinn and Joker printed T-shirt. What can I say? I loved their crazy, unorthodox love. It made me want to find someone who would love all *my* craziness. I loved how they both changed to fit together as one. I wanted someone to love me the way the Joker loves Harley—but with less homicide.

As I started to descend the stairs, I could hear raised voices. I wasn't planning on listening to their conversation, but when I heard my name, I couldn't help it. I crouched on the stairs and listened intently.

"What do you mean, Ryan doesn't know?" Alex snapped.

"Keep your voice down, Alex, I haven't had a chance to tell her, and Dad never got around to it. He thought he had more time." I could hear the hurt in Stevie's voice when she mentioned our dad.

Our father died suddenly, three months after Stevie and I turned eighteen. I did not attend his funeral, as I thought he wouldn't want me there. I would learn later that was not the case at all, and I would forever regret not attending and saying goodbye to my dad.

"She has to be told who she really is and what she is capable of, before she hurts herself or someone else, Stevie." Chase sounded annoyed at Stevie's reluctance.

"I plan on telling her when the time is right. She has been through a lot, and just being here, in this house, is hard for her. She didn't grow up like us, with a loving parent. She has built all these walls up around herself, and I don't want to drop this on her and risk her having a breakdown." Wow, clearly it was something big if she thought I would have a breakdown.

I couldn't quite understand what this big secret was that they were keeping from me. I mean, I know we didn't all grow up together, but we always found ways to talk on the phone. When they came to visit, I would sneak out after Mom fell asleep or passed out. She only caught me sneaking out once, and let me tell you, I couldn't sit for a week afterwards. She whipped me like a dog, splitting the skin on my rear open. I screamed so loud I thought the neighbors would call the cops. Hell, I wanted them to call them. After getting whipped twelve times, I was locked in my room for the next two days, with no food or water, just my mattress and a bucket in the corner.

"You need to tell her soon, Stevie, or Chase and I will. She has a right to know, for God's sake. She could have protected herself from your mom, if you or your dad had just told her," Alex whisper-shouted. This was getting more interesting by the minute.

"Don't you fucking think we wanted to, Alex? We tried to tell her so many times. We went to their house *six times* and got turned away by my so-called mother. She said if we ever came back, she would out us to the humans! What do you think we should have done? Kept going back? Risk being exposed to the world? That drunken, drugged-up bitch would have sung like a bird, and you know it!" Stevie had so much hate in her voice when she mentioned our mother.

I was done listening to their conversation *about me*, which was happening *without* me, my fury building as I heard about things for the first time. Unfortunately, as I turned to go back upstairs, my foot caught on the stair tread, and I fell, letting out an involuntary shriek as I bounced and rolled. I was waiting for the last bang, when I knew I would connect with the tile floor, but suddenly I stopped. When I opened my eyes, I saw my sister and cousins in the kitchen doorway, mouths hanging open and eyes wide. I looked down and realized my body was levitating a few inches off the floor and emanating a blue light. I let out another scream, and my body dropped the remainder of the way to the ground with a thud. Within seconds, the others were on either side of me, barking questions.

"Are you ok, Ry?"

"How did you do that?"

"Are you hurt anywhere?"

I couldn't think, let alone answer questions. I lay there for a few moments, mind whirling and body groaning, before finally answering.

"I'm fine, and no, I'm not hurt. I have no idea what the hell that was. I'm a bit creeped out by it, to be honest."

I caught a glimpse of pride in my sister's eyes before she quickly masked it. Why would she look at me like that? I have never levitated before, but I have seen the blue light a couple of times. I've never told anybody about it, because first of all, who would believe me, and second, I didn't quite believe it myself.

"Well, it was cool, but let's not dwell on it. Dinner is nearly ready, so come on, up you go, Sissy." Stevie was already pulling me up before she finished speaking.

Chase and Alex both exchanged looks I couldn't quite read. I thanked them and followed them into the kitchen. It was slightly dated, with vintage cabinets lining the walls, but there was a massive, stainless steel gas stove. Alex and Chase were both sitting at the breakfast bar on two of the four bar stools. Stevie was on the other side of the bar, assembling a salad. I sat next to the boys, still reeling at what the hell had just happened, when Alex nudged me.

"What?" I asked

"Didn't you hear what Chase said?" Truth be told, I hadn't heard a word.

"Ummm...No, sorry, can you please say it again, Chase? I was off with the fairies there for a second." I forced a smile with my words, so they wouldn't worry about where my head was at.

"Totally understandable, but I was just wondering how your last day of school went, and did you hear anything more from the cops?" He looked like he was scared to ask the last part. I knew all of them were wondering the same thing, so I thought I may as well get it out of the way now and just be open and honest with them about Mom's disappearance.

"I haven't heard anything from the detective who was the lead on Mom's case. They said there isn't much more that they could do, as she did leave a note, and I'm an adult. To them, she willingly left and that's not a crime."

"What note? You never said she left a note." Stevie looked

annoyed, and I winced. The reason I never told her was because the contents of the note were spiteful.

"I never told you about the note because what she wrote was not nice, Stevie. She said a lot of stupid shit in it. None of which is true, so to save you the hurt, I never said anything. I'm sorry for keeping it from you."

"I know you just want to protect me, Ry, as I do you, but you don't have to. I'm a big girl. Can you please just tell me what the note said?"

"She said that now that Dad is dead, she doesn't get paid for me, and wasn't going to stick around to raise the bastards that still to this day are mistakes that should never have happened. Also, she wished she had left me years ago."

The words in the note hurt more than what I wanted them to. Part of me always wanted my mom to love me. I guess you always want the love of your parents, no matter what they do to you. She was all I had. I knew she had a drug and alcohol problem, and I tried to blame her abuse and neglect on that, but I knew deep down that it wasn't.

"Damn," Alex and Chase both hissed in unison.

"I don't really know what to say to that, to be honest. I knew she had issues with having us young, but I never thought she would hate us like she obviously did. I mean, we never fucking asked to be born."

I knew where Stevie was coming from—I felt the same way. "She should have kept her fucking legs shut if she didn't want us. I am glad to be here, though." She said the last part with a cheeky smile and a squeeze of my shoulder.

"She has a lot of demons she needs to work out on her own. I think I'm just glad that she didn't try to kill me before she left," I said with a nervous laugh, which betrayed the bitter truth of my admission.

"Don't say shit like that! It's not funny, Ryan" Alex scolded with a stern look.

"I'm sorry. I didn't mean it; it's just it was hard to live with her. She used to say she would end me before she let me go. I'm sorry. I didn't mean to bring the mood down. Can we change the subject and talk about something else, like what you've been doing?"

"Okay, fine. We'll let it go *for now*. We still have to get shit ready for our trip. I'm so excited! I cannot wait to get the hell out of this town and go on a trip with my three favorite people. Oh, that's right, Ryan! I forgot to tell you that part of the surprise is that Alex and Chase are going to be coming with us." My sister was just full of surprises today, wasn't she? But I was super excited that my cousins would be taking this trip with us.

"Well, that's just awesome. I'm so glad you two are coming with us. It wouldn't be as much fun without you both," I said, nudging Chase.

"I'm as keen as a jelly bean to go on this trip. Alex and I have been looking forward to this for months now, and I'm glad we don't have to keep it a secret anymore." Chase said all this while looking my sister directly in the eye, almost as if hinting that now would be a good time for the big reveal. I have to admit, I am dying to know what Stevie is hiding from me.

"I second you there, my brother," Alex said while grinning at me and waggling his brows.

"We need to get the house in order before we go, so let's have some dinner and then get packing and sorting this house out." My sister always loved to boss everyone around. We did as she asked; it was easier than having to deal with the bitch fit she would throw if we didn't.

Chapter Four

RYAN

The two days flew by as we packed, cleaned, and locked the house up. My aunt (Alex & Chase's mom) would be checking on Stevie's house while we were away. It was really nice of her to do that, as we would be away for three months. I couldn't freaking wait to finally ride on a plane and have adventures with my sister and cousins, something that had been impossible until now.

I hadn't had any of my dreams since arriving at Stevie's; I was really starting to miss my dream guys. I know it sounds silly, but Nico and Kai made me feel so alive. Oh yeah, I forgot to mention, Nico wasn't my only dream sex god. I had another god-like man in my dreams. His name is Kai, and he is just as yummy as Nico. I had been trying to dream of each of them for the past two nights, but it was like they weren't at home, which had never happened before. I was a little worried, to be honest.

Stevie and I were dragging our bags down the stairs, when we heard Chase yell out.

"Yo! Cab's here! Move your asses, ladies; we need to go."

Stevie and I glanced at each other, grinning in anticipation.

We hurried the rest of the way down the stairs to the front door. I followed Alex out with my suitcase trailing behind me, and Stevie stopped just outside the door. I turned to see her holding her hand over the door handle whispering something, and then I saw her hand glow. I gasped and almost tripped on the path by the taxi. I thought I was the only weird one—a freak, as my mom used to say. Stevie began to walk toward me with her bags in tow, eyebrows raised as she saw my expression.

"Ry, why do you look so shocked?" Stevie asked.

"Your hand! I saw what you did. I saw your hand glow," I screeched.

Stevie shared a look with the boys before bringing her eyes back to me.

"I don't know what you're talking about. You did bump your head the other night, so you could be seeing things. Now hurry, before we miss our flight."

Stevie continued on to the cab like nothing had happened, but I know what I saw. There was no way I had imagined that. The strangest part was that her hand had glowed like mine had done a few times when my emotions got out of control, my glow was blue, but Stevie's was purple. This obviously wasn't the time to get into all that, though, so I shook it off and decided to corner my sister on the long plane ride.

We arrived at the airport twenty minutes later. Once all the bags were out and the driver was paid, we all made our way into the airport to check our bags and go through security.

Once seated on the plane, I finally started to relax. I was

actually going on my first-ever plane ride! My first trip abroad –
I was beyond excited to be leaving New Zealand.

Once the plane took off, everyone started to get comfortable.
We had a long flight ahead of us: sixteen hours to Los Angeles
and a further seven hours to Anchorage, Alaska, followed by an
almost five-hour drive to Wonder Lake, to reach our destination.
It was going to be a long-ass few days of travel. The first part of
the flight went quickly. I watched a few movies and caught
some shut-eye. I couldn't relax during the last leg. I needed to
talk to my sister about what I saw back at the house. She was
asleep beside me, but it was about time for her to wake up,
anyway. I gave her a few shoves to wake her.

"Now would be a great time for you to drop the act and tell
me what that really was, back at the house."

She looked at me like I had three heads, but the look on my
face told her I wasn't going to let this go.

With a long exhale, she finally responded.

"I promise you, Sissy, when we get to where we are going, I
will explain everything. I can't do that now—there isn't enough
time for the answers you seek. So please, just wait."

"I can't let it go for that long! I don't even know where
Wonder Lake *is*. All you told me is how long it takes to get
there."

"I know, Ry. Can you just wait, please?"

"Can I ask one thing?"

She sighed. "What is it, Ryan? I will answer it if I can."

"What I saw back at the house, how your hand was glowing.
I can do that too, can't I?"

"I am so sorry, Ryan. You should have known about all of
this so long ago. We couldn't get near you. We tried to come for
you, Ry, I swear we did. Mom wouldn't let us. She is such a
bitch for denying you the right to know the truth of—"

I cut her off —I had zero interest in this wait-and-see game. I just wanted a straight answer from her. The longer she took, the more anxious I got. I just wanted the truth, for once in my damn life.

"Truth about what, Stevie? I have a right to know. Just answer me, for God's sake."

Alex leaned across the aisle and eyed us both. "Now is not the time for this conversation, cousin. If you both could please keep the noise down, so we don't attract any more attention from the other passengers, it would be appreciated." As he finished, he shot Stevie a warning look that look shut us both up.

We spent the remainder of the flight quiet, occasionally making small talk with each other. I was still feeling antsy, needing answers from my sister. After the plane made its descent into LA, we left the aircraft to search for the boarding gate for our connecting flight to Alaska.

Once aboard the aircraft, we found our seats. Due to it being a smaller plane, we sat apart. Alex and Stevie were seated next to one another, with Chase and I a few rows behind. Once we got settled in our seats and fastened our belts, I leaned back in my chair and closed my eyes, intending to get some shut-eye. After the plane was in the air, Chase leaned over and whispered, "You will get all the answers you seek, cousin, once we get to Wonder Lake. I promise if Stevie does not tell you, I will."

I opened my eyes and moved slightly so I could look my cousin in the eye. There was no deceit behind his words; I knew Chase would spill the beans if Stevie didn't. I appreciated Chase so much in that moment.

"Thank you, Chase. I just don't want to be lied to anymore. I deserve to know." He gave me a warm smile and nodded. We spent the remainder of the flight in a comfortable silence. I couldn't stop thinking about what I had seen my sister do. I would glow blue if my emotions got the better and I never understood why. I need my sister to help me figure this all out and soon.

After departing the plane, we made our way out to the parking lot. Stevie had organized a hire car for our time we were here. We stuffed all our bags in the SUV then headed out for the long drive. We were a couple hours into our journey when I dozed off. I could feel the pull of my dream land awaiting me.

Chapter Five

RYAN

I walk through the woods, smiling up at the sky, when I felt the sensation of being watched. I stopped walking and scanned the area. He was here. I could feel him. I can't explain it, but I could always tell when Kai or Nico was near in my dream.

"I know you're out there, Kai. Why don't you just come out?" I turned when I heard a bush rustle behind me, then I saw him.

One of the most beautiful men I had ever seen in my life was stalking toward me. His skin was flawless, his body a work of God himself. He was shirtless, and had the kind of abs that men spend years trying to achieve. On him they just looked natural... meant to be. He had the most perfect set of teeth on display, and as I looked up to meet his gaze, I was drawn in by the most beautiful gray blue eyes and was unable to look away. His hair was rumpled, a rich mix of brown with hints of blond.

"I have missed you, mi amor," he said as he lowered his head to kiss me. I opened for him immediately, like I always did, and he slipped his tongue inside my mouth. He pulled away after a few minutes with a smile on his face, leaving me breathless and panting. The sexual tension was palpable; I could feel my body heating with the need to have him inside me.

"That's one hell of a hello, Kai."

"I have missed you and have not seen you as much I would like." My dream guys were always so demanding. I never understood why—I mean, they were just dreams, after all, but it was so nice to feel needed and wanted by someone. Nico was the dominant one who always demanded my submission, while Kai was gentle and soft.

"I'm sorry," I said, feeling silly for saying that to someone who was just a figment of my imagination, but compelled to apologize all the same.

"Never be sorry, mi amor. I will take whatever time you give me."

I smiled at his sweet words. "Now that I am here, what would you like to do?"

"I wish we had time, mi amor, but you are nearly at your destination now, and I must get back. I will visit you soon and explain everything, I promise." What the hell was wrong with me? My dream guys were always weird, like they actually had somewhere else to be. Sometimes I wondered if my subconscious was trying to make them seem more real.

"Okay Kai, sure thing. Next time I want less talking and more body action." I would never say stuff like this to a real guy —I wasn't that kind of girl—but with my dream guys, I let my inner vixen out to play.

"Believe me, there will be no talking just you screaming my name, mi amor." His words sent shivers down my spine. He bent down and kissed me with such hunger that I swear I could have come just from kissing him. I put my hands around his neck and gripped the back of his hair, moaning into his mouth. I wanted him right here, right now. I needed him inside of me. I lowered my hands to undo his jeans, but he grabbed them and pulled away from me.

"There isn't enough time for that, mi amor, but rest assured I *will make it up to you next time." the smirk on his face telling me he knew what that kiss had done to me and he loved it.*

"Fine, but next time I might be the one playing hard to get," I said while still pouting at him.

"Go now, my love, and I will see you soon." Before I could respond, the darkness started to overtake me, but before I was fully out of my dream land, I heard Kai whispering, "Please try to understand and forgive me."

I wake to Stevie shaking me, a worried look on her face. I looked around and realized I was lying on the ground,

the car parked haphazardly nearby, with Chase and Alex on either side of me with similarly anxious expressions on their faces.

"Why are you all looking at me like that? And why the hell am I on the ground?"

They all shared a look that I couldn't read. I felt once again as if I was being left out of a secret.

"You were shaking, and we tried to wake you, but you wouldn't wake up, so we got worried and stopped. What the hell happened?" Chase asked.

"I fell asleep." Geez, I didn't know being a deep sleeper was a crime. I didn't understand why they were freaking out.

"No, Ryan, you weren't just sleeping. You were shaking and glowing. What the hell happened when you were asleep?" Stevie demanded. Shit, I needed to figure out what the hell this glowing thing meant. It normally only happened when I was really angry or scared. I was actually starting to get worried, but I couldn't tell the others that.

"I was just having a weird dream, okay?" I obviously couldn't tell them that I was trying to seduce one of my dream lovers. I could feel the heat rising to my cheeks even thinking about mentioning such a thing.

"Tell me about the dream, Ryan, please," Alex pleaded, none the wiser as to the reason of my heated state.

"I would really rather not, but thanks for worrying," I said, hoping they would drop it.

"Ryan, come on" Chase urged.

"It was my dream, and if I don't want to tell you about it, I don't have to."

Chase let out a huff of air then looked me straight in the eyes.

"Well, when you start *glowing* in a public area, it then becomes *our* problem, but this isn't the place to talk about it, so let's get a move on and get to the cabin."

I nodded, knowing they weren't about to disclose any information they had on the whole glowing thing until we got to the cabin, and I was in no position to argue, given my refusal to discuss the dream, so I reluctantly got into the car.

Once we arrived at the cabin, the boys started unloading our bags and supplies, and I stood on the porch for a moment, taking in the view. To get to the cabin, you had to go along a dirt road that if you didn't know it was there, you would never find it. Thank God I wasn't driving. The cabin was surrounded by dense woods and very isolated; it would be the perfect place for someone who needed a break from real life.

The cabin was old, but sturdy by the look of it. It was a

faded brown color, with dark green porch columns much like the color of the trees surrounding the house. The small porch on the front held two old rocking chairs that would be perfect to sit in and watch the sunset. I loved being here already and smelling the fresh air that the mountains and trees offered us.

As I was taking one last look around before heading inside, a shiver ran down my spine. It was that same feeling I had in my dream, of someone watching me. I felt a shiver run down my spine. I looked around the wooded area and saw nothing. Even so, I high-tailed it inside to find my sister and cousins.

As I entered the cabin, I was awestruck. The outside may have looked run down, but inside was like something from a magazine.

The entryway was decorated with antlers hanging on the wall, and just past that, the main living area held a beautiful set of gold and cream armchairs and a three-cushion couch. Next to that was the dining room and kitchen. The dining room was huge, with a long table fit for a castle, flanked by bench seats on either side.

"Close your mouth before a fly gets in there, squirt," Alex said with a laugh.

"Sorry, it's just I didn't expect it to look like this inside! You know, since the outside could use a refresh."

"Don't judge a book by its cover, cousin. All is not what it seems."

"Yeah, you can say that again. So, which one is my room?"

"Third door on the left, and there are towels in the hallway closet. Each room has its own en suite, so at least we don't have to hear you two girls fighting over the mirror," he said, smirking.

"Shut up, Alex, but thanks."

"You will love your room, it has a daybed and a great view of the landscape."

"How do you know that?" Alex looked around the room,

searching for the others I assume. He finally pulled his gaze back to me and sheepishly replied.

"I saw it, when I put your bags in your room." *Okay*, I wasn't convinced, but I would let it go for now.

I set off down the hallway to find my room and wash away the couple of days of travel residue I could feel clinging to me. The room that was mine for our stay was the nicest room I'd ever stayed in. It had a massive, four poster king-sized bed in the middle of the room, with a bear skin rug at the foot of it. I had a beautiful view of the mountains, and right below the window was the day bed Alex had mentioned. I loved this place already. Tearing myself away from the view, I grabbed some clothes and headed into the bathroom for a quick shower. After that I was hunting down the others to get some answers and food. I needed both as soon as possible.

Chapter Six

RYAN

As I was leaving my room, I heard the others arguing, so I quietly shut my door so I could sneak down the hall and eavesdrop on their conversation. This was becoming a habit.

"She is going to want to know the whole story, Stevie." I could hear the irritation in Alex's voice.

"I will tell her everything she needs to know, especially if he is visiting her in her dreams now," my sister replied.

"We don't know for sure it is him she is dreaming of. But we can get the protection of the coven and the pack to keep her from him. But if he knows she is alive, he will be coming for her Stevie, and we all know that it's not an *if*, it's a *when*. So we need her to know now," Chase snapped.

"Keep your damn voice down. I have no idea how he would even know she exists. Dad made sure no one knew about her to keep her safe. I wonder how long he has been visiting her, if it is him?"

Alex butted in. "Long enough for her to feel the need to protect him from us. She doesn't want us to know that he visits her, and she doesn't even know who he is."

I came around the corner then, having had enough of all this talk behind my back. They needed to start telling me the truth, right now.

"I need to learn what? And who the fuck is coming for me?"

They all spun around in shock. Stevie pursed her lips, obviously annoyed that I had been listening in on their conversation, but I didn't care about her feelings right now.

"Why don't you have a seat, and we can start from the beginning and work our way up to the why and what, okay?" Chase was looking at me with pleading eyes, so I nodded and took a seat at the table next to Chase while Stevie and Alex sat on the other side.

"Okay, Ry, so you already know that we have been keeping something from you, but it wasn't because we wanted to. It's just that we didn't know how to tell you. It's not something you hear every day, and to be honest, it's not easy to explain either, so please just let us get it all out and then you can ask all the questions you want."

I nodded slowly. "Okay, I guess I can do that for you."

Stevie looked to both Alex and Chase, and they each gave her a nod. She let out a loud huff of air and then began.

"Ryan, you and I were born with...gifts, we'll call them, for argument's sake. I grew up knowing about mine, and how to use and channel my gift, because Dad taught me how."

"Wait—Dad knew about this? All of this glowing hands shit?" I exclaimed, cutting my sister off.

"No interrupting, I said! But yes, Dad did know. I am just going to come out with it—we're witches. Not like ride-around-on-broomstick witches...like cast spells kind of witches...we have powers."

Finally stunned speechless, I sat quietly, trying to put the pieces of my odd life together with the information I'd just received. Alex eyed me warily then nudged Stevie. She sighed, then asked.

"Are you okay?"

"I don't know what to think, or what I'm supposed to say to all this, Stevie. Alex, Chase—are you both witches?" I asked.

Alex and Chase both scoffed then pinned me with a glare.

"We are not witches. We are warlocks. Only women are called witches, Ry," Alex responded haughtily.

I nodded and rolled my eyes at their drama. As if being accidentally called the feminine version of something was a grave insult. Chase waved me off and Stevie gave me a sheepish smile.

"So, what does all this mean for me then?" I asked the group.

"It means that you have gifts and abilities, Sissy. They can help keep you safe. I know that this must be a lot to take in, and you should have been told about this a long time ago." My sister had an aura of sadness around her.

"Why was I never told about any of this? If Dad told you about all of this, and showed you how to use these *gifts*" I said with air quotes, "Why the hell was I kept in the dark?"

"Ryan, we tried to tell you..." Stevie started before I cut her off.

"Well, you didn't try hard enough! If what you say is true, then I could have protected myself, from her and all the bad shit she did to me! Instead you and Dad just gave up and left me with that fucking monster!" I screamed.

I stood to leave, when Chase tried to put his hand on my shoulder. I shrugged him off and walked to the front door. I needed some air. I couldn't process what they were saying. Part of me couldn't comprehend any of it, but then the other half of me knew on some level that it was true. Whenever I was glowing, I always felt like I was a live wire. When my emotions got away from me, things would happen around me, things I couldn't explain—like the walls would rattle or the ground would shake, and things would go from one side of the room to the other.

Before I could continue with my thoughts, I heard a branch snap. I stopped dead in my tracks and realized I had walked so far into the woods that when I turned around, I couldn't see the cabin anymore. When I started to take a step toward the direction I came, a deep, husky voice froze me in place. Fear washed over me as I slowly turned to see who that voice belonged to.

"Hello," he said. He was huge, with intense brown eyes that stared at me so directly I wanted to look away. His hair was disheveled, and a few strands hung over his forehead. It was a light brown. He had this whole lumberjack look going on—he even wore a red and black flannel shirt with faded blue jeans that hugged him in all the right places. I didn't feel scared, like any normal person would have.

"Umm...hi?" It sounded like more of a question than I meant it to.

"You look lost?"

"I'm not lost. I was just taking a walk."

"Lie."

"Excuse me?" I snapped.

"You lied. Your heart rate picked up."

"What the fuck?" Is this fucking guy for real? How the hell could he hear my heartbeat?

"I'm sorry, I didn't mean to upset you Miss...?"

"Umm...Ryan. My name is Ryan."

"Well, Ryan, I did not mean to upset you, so I apologize."

"Thanks, that's okay. Look, I'm sorry. I shouldn't have cussed at you. It's just been one hell of a day, and I should really be heading back. The others will be getting worried. It was nice to meet you Mr...?"

"The pleasure was all mine, Miss Ryan, I'm sure I will see you around town sometime. Best get moving, it's getting cold."

He turned on his heel and walked back into the woods, heading away from my temporary home. I started walking back the way I came, thinking about the strange encounter I just had, and the fact that he hadn't answered my question about his name. After ten minutes, I emerged from the woods to find the others sitting outside on the porch. I approached them with my head held high. Chase and Alex stood from the two chairs on the porch, while Stevie remained seated on the steps. I exhaled loudly before addressing the group.

"I'm sorry I took off. I just needed to get some fresh air and clear my head. That was a big info dump."

"We understand," Chase replied with a sad smile

"No, you don't. This is hard for me to even believe, that you guys have grown up knowing all of this and being taught what you are. I have not had that luxury, and I wish I had. Stevie, I'm sorry for yelling at you. I know it wasn't your fault. I just feel like my life could have been so different if I had known. Maybe, if I did know, I could have protected myself. I always felt like a freak. Whenever my emotions would get out of control, I would glow, and I never knew why, but Mom hated it."

"I wish you had known, Ryan. I wish I knew what I know now, so that I could have come for you or tried to help you. I didn't know my specific gifts back then; if I did, I could have gotten you out. I am so sorry for what you have endured throughout your life. If I could have swapped places with you, I would have! I promise you, Ryan Gene Knox, that we will teach you what you need to know, so you never feel unprotected again. We will show you how to channel and harness your power. You are stronger than you know, Ry. So much stronger."

I looked into my sister's eyes and saw hope. She was proud of me for making it through my childhood with our mother. She didn't know our mother that well, but she had heard the stories I would tell her when I would sneak out to meet her.

"Stevie, it's not your fault…" I didn't get a chance to finish before Alex cut in.

"We have company."

Chase moved to stand in front me, as if to shield me from our visitor. Stevie and Alex stood on either side of Chase, their bodies coiled tight with tension. I didn't hear a car or even footsteps.

"Well, well, the infamous Knox family has returned." The man's voice sent shivers down my spine, and not in a good way, either. "Tell me, Miss Knox, where is your father? Surely the great Ralph Knox did not let his prized daughter come here alone, unprotected?"

The man's voice had a harsh edge to it, and you could tell from the condescending way he spoke my father's name that he hadn't liked him. I didn't understand why. This was the first time Stevie had been here, so how did he know her or my dad? Before I could think on it more, my sister spoke.

"Randall Cane, what an unpleasant surprise. What brings you to my family's land? You know your kind is not welcome here without invitation."

Wait, what did she just say—our family's fucking land? I'm missing something here, and I do not like it one bit. As soon as this Randall guy left, my sister was getting an earful from me. I was fucking done with the lies and the secrets. What else was my sister hiding from me?

"The fact that my clan was not notified of your return is what brought me here, young one. You would be wise to watch your tone. I do not care for smart-mouthed youth," he snapped. "Where is your father? We had an agreement, and your kind have not kept their end of the deal."

"My uncle is no longer with us, Cane. So watch how you speak of the dead!" Alex roared. I could feel the tension rolling off my three family members.

"My apologies, I did not know of his death. I meant no disrespect, young ones. Your father was a great man, Miss Knox. He brought peace to all the communities, but I am afraid that peace may not last much longer, given recent events." Randall sounded like he was trying really hard to project sincerity, but he failed miserably to pretend he wasn't also happy our father was dead.

"What do you mean? The peace treaty has had no problems as far as we are aware. Our coven has been keeping tabs on the witches and warlocks in our region," Chase stated.

"Then they have misled you, Mr. Knox. I can assure my kind and the packs have been under attack for the past three months. We assume it's the coven, as it's not my clan or the pack. If you cannot reel your coven in, we will take matters into our own hands."

"Is that a threat, Cane?" Chase snapped, stepping off the porch stairs, heading toward Randall. His fists were balled at his sides, with a purple light covering them. No sooner had Chase moved—and I came into view—did the strange man take a step back, almost like he had seen a ghost. He looked scared.

"It cannot be! You cannot be alive—she said you were dead!" I was meant to be dead? Chase stopped in his tracks and peered over his shoulder at me, clearly no better informed than I about this development. I shrugged and decided to ask Randall myself. I wasn't going to hide anymore, or be lied to and kept in the dark.

"What do you mean *I'm supposed to be dead*? And who is this 'she'?"

He shook his head before he answered; it was as if he was trying to clear his mind of what he was thinking. He was not a tall man—Chase and Alex towered over him. He had blond hair and blue eyes, and his build was stocky. If he hadn't been projecting malice and rage like an antenna, I might have even described him as attractive.

"Forgive me, I am Randall Cane, king of the Alaskan Vampire Clan," he said with a bow.

My mouth charged ahead before my brain could catch up. "What the fuck did you just say? Vampires? Are you kidding me?" Randall turned to Stevie with eyes sparking in outrage.

"My sister is new to all of this," Stevie rushed to add, giving me a sharp look. Her irritation pissed me off. How dare she? It wasn't *my* fault I didn't know about this shit.

"Sister? Well that explains why you look alike." he said dryly. "Why have I never heard of her before? Ralph never said he had two daughters."

"That is not of your concern, Randall!" Stevie's voice was like a knife, razor-sharp.

"It *is* my concern when I signed a blood treaty with a man who lied to me, and told me he had one living heir, not two!" he roared.

"You will watch your tone when you address the coven heir, Cane. If she says it is not your concern, then it's not," Alex bellowed and took a step forward.

"You will watch how you address me, Mr. Knox. Do not forget your place here. I will end you if you push me too far, boy!"

"You lay one hand on my cousin, and I will kick your ass to kingdom come, buddy. I may not have the witchy voodoo shit under control like they do, but I am a black belt in karate," I snapped at the vampire king. Nobody was talking to my cousin like that in my presence.

All heads turned in my direction. Stevie looked shocked, while Alex and Chase were suppressing smug grins.

Randall guffawed, which sent my blood pressure rising.

Once his fit of giggles finally stopped, he looked to me and spoke.

"There will be no need for that, Miss...?"

"My name is Ryan."

"Well, I guess your father was telling the truth. He said your mother really did want a boy." The sarcasm was thick in his tone.

He was actually right about that. My mother hated the fact that we were not boys. She said girls were always trouble, and boys were easier, because they could never come home with a baby growing in their womb.

"Well, surprise! I'm a girl, just like my sister, tits and all," I replied, with a wink and fake smile.

"You have the mouth of a sailor to boot. It's a pleasure to meet you, Miss Ryan. I hope you will be staying in town for a while? I would love to get to know you better."

"That's not going to happen. If you want to talk to her, then you can do so in front of all of us." Chase's tone left no room for argument, and his glare would have sent me back a step or two if it had been directed my way.

"Well, if that is the case, I would love for you all to join me this evening at my home. I am having a little get-together. The pack will be over for a meeting regarding the treaty, so it would be beneficial for you all to join us."

"Wait! What do you mean *pack*? As in, like, a werewolf pack?" I said, laughing. Next thing you know, they're going to produce Santa Claus at this meeting.

"I do not understand why you think the pack is funny. They are hairy, ugly creatures, but they are no laughing matter." Randall seemed bemused by me, tilting his head to the side.

"Holy fuck, you're for real. There is a wolf pack?" I can't believe this; my mind is reeling with all the shit I have learned today. This was some *Twilight* shit, was Randall going to sparkle in the sunlight?

Stevie turned to me and murmured, "We will explain everything, Ry—we just haven't had the chance yet." Stevie then turned back to Randall. "We accept your invitation, Randall."

"Excellent. Please arrive no later than seven this evening. Until then, I will bid you farewell, Knox family." And with a slight bow, he turns and is gone like a flash of light. I scan the yard, unable to believe my eyes. It was like he just vanished into thin air. I didn't even notice Alex approaching me, I was so stunned by Randall's vanishing act.

"How you holding up, squirt?"

"I feel like I should be in a looney bin," I deadpanned.

"With padded white walls?" Chase teases, a playful smirk on his face.

"Yep," I agreed.

"I know you must have a lot of questions for us, and we want to answer them all. For your own wellbeing, though, we can't right now. We have to get ready for this evening's event. Can you handle waiting a little bit longer?" Alex asked.

I didn't really know how to answer that question. I wanted answers, and I had so many questions, but I needed time to process what I had just learned today. So I simply shrugged and nodded in agreement. With that, we all went inside to begin getting ready for an evening with vampires and werewolves—whatever that entailed.

Chapter Seven

RYAN

While standing in the shower, letting the water rinse away the day, I couldn't stop my mind from going over all that I had learned, not only about myself, but my family and even the world as I knew it. I would never have thought that a family could keep such secrets from each other. I finally gave up on trying to piece the puzzle which was my life together, and sighed and got out of the shower. I put my robe on and left my hair in a towel, deciding it was best to worry about my unruly mane later. As I was going through my bags, I realized I didn't have anything suitable to wear. Or at least I didn't think so. I'd never been to a party with witches, warlocks, vampires and werewolves. I was just working up the nerve to go ask about the dress code when someone starts knocking on my door. Without waiting for an invitation, the door opened and my sister poked her head in.

"Jesus, Stevie, I'm not even dressed yet."

"Oh please, Sissy, we're identical twins. I see what you have every day when I look in the mirror!" She snorted at my prudishness, and I let out a huff and waved her in.

"I have nothing appropriate to wear to dinner, Stevie. I don't think I can go in skinny jeans and a T-shirt."

"No, you probably can't, but you can wear this," she said, handing me the most beautiful dress. It's a deep blue, with a plunging neckline. It had two slits down the sides that stopped just below your panties. When she turned the dress around, I saw that it had no back, and realized that underwear would not be an option in a dress like that.

"Stevie, there is no way in hell I can wear that. I'm not you. I can't pull off a dress like that."

"Shut up, Ryan! I don't want to hear that shit come out of your mouth. You are beautiful, and you will wear this dress. Don't knock it til you try it on. I bought it a while ago and never had a chance to wear it, so I want to give it to you." I knew by the look in her eyes I wasn't going to win this argument.

Sighing, I got up and took the dress from her, heading into the bathroom to change. Once I finally got the dress on, I refused to look in the mirror, knowing that if I saw what I looked like, I might take it off. When I finally emerged from the bathroom, I looked to my sister, and her mouth was hanging open. A blush started burning its way up my neck. I never wore things like this in real life—only in my dreams.

"Is it really that bad? I told you I couldn't pull it off, Stevie." I was about to take the damn thing off when Stevie grabbed my arm.

"Don't you dare! You look beautiful, Ry, and I mean it. I just can't believe you don't see how beautiful you are."

Her words brought tears to my eyes; my mother always said I was hideous. The only time I ever felt truly beautiful was when I was in my dreams with the guys. They made me feel like a goddess. I only started to view myself as something more than trash when I started to have dreams with Kai and Nico in them.

They would always tell me I'm beautiful and my beauty shined from within me.

"When you grow up hearing how ugly you are all the time, you start to believe it," I whispered, my head hung low. Stevie grabbed me by the chin and lifted my head so we were eye to eye.

"You will never look down at yourself again, do you hear me? I will not have it. You are a fucking coven heir, Ryan! You look down to no one. –Tonight you will hold your head high and handle yourself like the royalty you are. Do you hear me? If you don't, they will see you as weak, and you will become their prey. Always keep eye contact and never let them know how they make you feel."

"I don't understand what you're saying, Stevie."

"If they know you are scared, they will prey on that weakness. The Knox coven is the strongest in the world, and we cannot be seen as anything other than that. If you have to fake it til you make it, that's what you will do. Randall may seem harmless, but he is not, and neither is the pack. We must show strength in the eyes of our enemies—you understand?"

It was clear there was a lot more to what she was saying than what I knew, but I was going to try the whole "fake it til you make it" thing, starting now. I gave my sister a tight smile and nodded.

"Okay, now let's do your hair and makeup!" She said with a clap of her hands. Dear Lord, save me now.

An hour later, we were walking out of my room to get the boys and be on our way to Randall's little gathering.

"Yowza! Look at you two. Ryan, you look absolutely beautiful." Chase was such a charmer, but his words gave me a small boost in confidence. I refused to let my family down. I was going to make them proud tonight.

"You both really do look great, but if we don't hurry up, we're going to be late, and that will be a problem," Alex said while holding the front door open.

After a forty-five minute drive through forest and gravel roads, we approach two massive iron gates held up by huge brick pillars. On top of the pillars sat two gargoyles whose grimaces were just plain creepy. Alex pulled up next to an intercom and hit a button. After a moment, a man's voice came over the speaker.

"Cane Manor."

"Alex Knox, from the Knox coven. We have been invited here this evening by Mr. Cane." I can hear the distaste in Alex's voice when he says Randall's name.

"Yes, sir, please drive through."

No sooner had the man finished speaking then the gates opened and we drove through. The driveway has trees lining the drive all the way up to the house. As we get closer, I saw a fountain in front of the house, its presence creating a roundabout for drivers. The fountain itself is a beautiful work of art. It had four horses rearing up, almost like they were fighting. The horses were shooting water from their mouths, spotlights were pointed at the fountain. It was clearly the center piece of the front yard.

The house—I mean, it wasn't even a house, more like an estate—was huge; it reminded me of the White House. It had the same four big pillars out the front, windows were scattered all over the front of the mansion, there was an American flag placed on the roof as well. The White House seemed more welcoming than Randall's mansion though. The entrance to the home had guards stationed outside of it. Or at least I assumed they are guards. I was a bit nervous about coming here before, but now I was about to burst out of my skin from nerves. I mean, who has armed guards at the door besides pop stars and presidents?

Alex finally eased the car to a stop, and he and Chase started to climb out. I grabbed Stevie's hand.

"Why are there guards?" I whispered.

"Because he is the vampire King, not just *a* king—he is *the* king." My face must look like a mask of horror, as she gives my hand a reassuring squeeze. "We're here with you, Ry. You are not alone. No one will harm you. If they even look at you wrong, let us know, and they will be taken care of. We may be young, but we are not weak. *You* are not weak."

With that, said she slipped out of the back seat to join the boys. I took one last deep breath and did the same. Chase offered me his arm, and I linked mine through his and gave him a nervous smile. He patted my arm and gave me a wink. Alex and Stevie led the way. As we approached the stairs leading to the front door, I start worrying I might trip and break my ankle. I was never any good at wearing heels, but Stevie insisted I wear them because, "Converse were not acceptable to wear with a dress." I felt like everything was on display: my back was bare; my breasts were just barely covered. The slits up the sides were making me worry if a gust of wind came, everyone would be able to see the G-string I had on.

As we reached the top of the stairs, Alex gave the guards a curt nod. The guards opened the two massive wooden front doors, and immediately I am assaulted by classical music and voices and laughter. I don't know what I was expecting, but this wasn't it. The foyer is beautiful. There are wooden floors throughout, with stunning furs lying on the floor. I had a brief pang of sadness for the animals that had worn those beautiful skins in life, and hoped they had not been killed simply for their fur. I loved animals and found value in all life.

As we neared the end of the hall, Alex and Stevie made a left turn into the main area, where the people had gathered. As Chase and I rounded the corner, I stopped dead in my tracks. There were people everywhere! The women were in ball gowns that looked like they were from the 1800s, but they made them look so glamorous and relevant to this era. And though the dresses were elaborate, no clothing could dull their radiant beauty. They were flawless.

The men wore tuxes like Alex and Chase, but there were cravats and elaborately embroidered vests and all manner of colors and fabrics. The men were just as beautiful as the women in their own way. They knew it, too—you could tell by the way they sauntered around the room like they owned it. A server passed by with a tray full of champagne, and I grabbed one, thinking the alcohol would calm my nerves. Just as I was about to take a sip, a hand snaked around me and nabbed the glass right out of my hand. I froze, and the stranger came around to face me—it was the man from the woods.

He stood there, calmly sipping my champagne, a smirk on his unreasonably handsome face. My breath caught in my throat. He looked delicious when I saw him earlier today, but now, done up in his tux, he was a whole meal. Gone was the lumberjack-looking hunk and hello, Mr. Sexy. His hair was slicked back out of his face, and my God, those chocolate brown eyes! They could peel the clothes off any woman. He had a five o'clock shadow marking his jawline, and he made not shaving look like a new trend. His tux fitted him like a glove and showed his well-defined muscles. Chase broke the tension-filled silence.

"Jax. What can I do for you this evening?" Irritation was clear in his voice. Jax. I was irrationally pleased to have a name for my mystery lumberjack.

"Chase, I didn't realize you were in town. Did any of the others return as well?" he asked, his eyes never moving off me.

"We're all here, Marshall, so I suggest you take a step back from Ryan and remove your eyes from her, before I do it for you," Chase snapped.

"So, she's yours then?"

"That is not of your concern now, is it?" I could hear the underlying threat in Chase's voice. Why did my cousin not like Jax?

"When you bring a stranger onto my lands and you have no claim on her, it becomes my business. She doesn't smell like one of you." My hackles rise as they continue to speak about me like I'm not even here. Rude much?

"As you can see, jackass, she is Stevie's twin sister. If you can't know that from looking at her, then you're more fucked in the head than I thought. She has just as much right to be here as you do, pup."

"Pup?" Jax let out a throaty growl. "Boy, I am no *pup*, I can assure you of that."

I knew things were getting out of hand when Chase grabbed my arm and started pulling me behind him. I don't know why he felt so much anger toward Jax, and I didn't think now was the time to ask. I yanked my arm from Chase's grip and stepped between the two brooding males that looked like they were about to tear each other apart.

"My name is Ryan. As you already know, Chase is my cousin. I don't know why you two don't like each other, and at this point in time, I don't give a shit." I then turned to Chase and said "Dial it down a notch, big guy. We just got here, and I don't want to get kicked out. Let's go get me another glass of something to help me get through this, okay?"

Chase gave me a stiff nod while still pinning Jax with a death glare. Just as we were turning to walk away, Jax put a hand on my shoulder.

"I'm sorry, I didn't mean to ruin your evening. It's just that you don't have the same scent as the others. You are different, and in this world, different can be dangerous."

Chase was standing beside me, seething, ready to throw the first punch if Jax didn't let my arm go. Noticing Chase's discomfort, Jax let his hand slide off my shoulder.

"Look, dude—"

"My name is Jackson Marshall, but my friends call me Jax," he said, smiling.

"Okay—*Jax*. I just got here, and I don't know a lot about what the hell the others do, okay? So, if you could just back off and stop freaking smelling me, that would be great." With that said, I turned on my sky-high heels and headed out to find my sister. Tonight, was going to be a damn long night if this shit kept up.

Chapter Eight

RYAN

After leaving Jax and finding another server, Chase and I grabbed a glass each this time and made our way out to the back patio in search of Stevie and Alex. I couldn't help but stop and take in the yard. It was like a fairy tale. There were candles along the ground, lighting up the pathways. A fountain sat in the middle of the yard, a twin of the one out front.

Small shrubbery bushes lined the paths, and a dream-like white pergola sat at the end of the pathway. I never thought vampires would have a yard like this. I spotted Stevie in the pergola with a few others. I could only tell it was my sister because she was wearing an off-the-shoulder yellow dress—she stood out like Big Bird. That was Stevie—she loved being center of attention.

As we were walking toward the pergola, I once again had the sensation of being watched. I scanned the yard, but no one was looking our way. I knew there were lots of people here, but I just couldn't shake the feeling that a predator was lurking in the shadows.

"There you two are! We lost you as soon as we got here," Alex said, shaking me out of my inner thoughts.

"We got stopped by that dick Jackson Marshall," Chase grumbled, still tense from the encounter.

"What the hell did he want?" Stevie snapped.

"To ask about Ryan and why she smelt funny."

"Shut up! I don't smell! He's just weird. Hot, but weird." I swear I heard a growl coming from the forest as I spoke. This paranoia was ridiculous.

"Stay away from him, Ry. His kind doesn't like us." Alex always had to be so cryptic.

"Actually, that reminds me—you told him your name and then said 'but you already know that.' How would he know that, Ry?" Chase asked.

"I met him earlier today, when I took off to clear my head. He was in the woods," I replied sheepishly, feeling like I had done something wrong. How was I supposed to know who to talk to and who not to?

"That fucker was on our land? What the hell?" Alex hissed.

Stevie shushed him. "Now is not the place to worry about this. We don't know how far Ry wandered; their lands do back onto ours. She could have crossed the boundary. We need to find Randall and sort out whatever he has to tell us, and then let's get the fuck out of here," Stevie said with a grim look.

With that done, the four of us went in search of the vampire king.

After making our way back inside and maneuvering through the crowds of people, Stevie lead us down the hallway near where we entered. We stopped outside a large wooden door. Alex knocked and we waited to be invited in.

"Enter!" a voice shouted from behind the door.

Alex opened the door, and we all filed in. The room was decorated in rich browns and maroon, with oil paintings in elaborate gilded frames. The fire was lit, and above the mantle there was a portrait of a woman in a lavender gown, with a small hat atop her head. Her face was fanned with black curls and her skin was luminescent, even in a painting. She had the most rich and vibrant violet eyes. They reminded me of Nico's. I heard someone cough and turned to see Randall standing behind a massive oak desk. Behind him were floor to ceiling windows that perfectly framed the view of the forest and mountains. He waved us over to the other side of the room, where there were two couches and two single chairs that looked more like thrones than living room furniture.

"Please take a seat, and we can discuss some matters," Randall instructed I let out a snort when he took one of the single chairs at the end. Stevie shot me a death glare, so I quickly masked my snort by coughing.

"What are the matters you would like to discuss, Mr. Cane?" Alex asked, adopting a blasé tone.

"First, why was I not notified of your uncle's death? And why was I never told that Ralph Knox's other daughter survived?"

"I was planning on telling you my father had passed, once we arrived and got settled in. Rest assured, Mr. Cane, we were not leading you astray. Also, my sister was not raised with my father and me, so he thought it wise not to let anyone know that she was alive, since she was not under his protection. She lived with our mother," Stevie stated.

Randall sat on his throne, scratching his chin like he was deep in thought. He turned his eyes to me, and I forced myself to meet his gaze, head up, as Stevie had demanded.

"Did you know of any of this, Miss Knox?"

I didn't know how to answer that question appropriately, so I thought telling the truth was the best option.

"Mr. Cane, this is all new information to me, like my sister just said. I was raised by our mother. I had no idea about any of this"—I waved my hands around— "magic stuff, until this morning." He looked like he had just won the lottery. That wasn't creepy or anything.

"I understand, Miss Knox, I really do. However, your father should have told us about you. It changes things with the treaty, you being alive and present in our midst." I was about to respond when the door swung open and Jax strolled in. What the hell was he doing here?

"Sorry I'm late! You forgot to let me know the meeting was starting." Jax was pinning Chase with a death glare. Chase just smiled.

Jax took a seat on a couch and asked, "What did I miss?" Randall filled him in, and Jax seemed to have trouble hiding his shock at my ignorance.

"Why were you kept a secret?" he asked me.

"I wasn't a secret, as far as I knew," I told him with a shrug.

"Ryan was not raised with us, so she was not mentioned for her own safety," Stevie snapped.

"Just because she grew up somewhere else does not give you and your father the right to LIE TO ME!" Randall roared. I sank back into the couch cushions and started counting the possible exits.

"No one lied to you, Randall. We were all children when the treaty was renewed. None of us were involved, so if Ryan's existence being kept from you is a problem, we cannot help that. The one who could answer that question is now dead," Alex fired back at Randall.

"Look, we're all a bit on edge having your cousin here. Having two heirs is unheard of, so you can see why we are a bit upset about all this," Jax said, looking sympathetic.

"What's so bad about having two heirs?" I asked to no one in particular.

Jax shared a look with Randall, and then they both looked to my sister and cousins, as if waiting for one of them to answer my question. With a sigh, Stevie finally answered.

"An heir is someone who is next in line to rule. In our case, being an heir means one of us is in line to rule the Knox coven. Because you do not yet know how to wield your powers, I will step up to rule our people until you are ready. Then we can sort what happens next." I could tell by the look on my sister's face that she was eager to take on that leadership role, which was fine by me. I knew there was more to it, Stevie was withholding information. Once again I was being put in a situation I didn't understand, by the people who supposedly loved me.

"You know what? I never asked for this shit, Stevie, any of it! And I don't want it." As I stood up to leave, the office door opened once more, and in walked the last person I thought I would ever see in life. I couldn't breathe. I couldn't move. Then it all went dark.

Chapter Nine

RYAN

As I was coming to, I braced myself for the inevitable pain from hitting the floor, but it never came. My head was resting on something soft. I heard the others fussing around me, wondering if I was okay. As I opened my eyes to try tell everyone I was fine. The first thing I see, Is beautiful blue-gray eyes, I know those eyes they belong to Kai. My dream man was real. He was holding me in his lap. My breaths were coming out in short fast pants; I thought my heart might jump out of my chest. I tried to open and close my eyes a few times to make sure I wasn't dreaming, but he stayed right where he was.

As he was leaning his head down to look at me, I realized my head was resting within an inch of his manhood. I couldn't help the blush that spread across my cheeks. I tried to sit up, but he put his hand in the middle of my chest to stop me, and in the quietest whisper, he spoke to me.

"I would never let you fall, mi amor." Holy fuck, he is real. I couldn't wrap my head around that. He called me 'mi amor,' so that must mean he was really in my dreams, right? But how?

I looked at him, at a loss for words which was a rare thing for me. I had been dreaming about this man for years and now here he is, holding me.

"Thank God you're okay," Chase breathed, kneeling down beside me. He started to slide his hands under my arms so he could lift me up, but my beautiful dream god growled. I snapped my head back toward him and gaped—he had his lips pulled back and his fangs out. Yes, I said fangs! My dream guy was real and he was a...vampire? I am clearly fucked in the head. The dude has fangs, and I'm sitting here swooning over him.

He looked down at me, and his eyes told me what he couldn't. He was ashamed of himself and his actions. He clamped his mouth shut, as if to hide his fangs, and turned his head away. Out of sheer instinct, I reached out and turned his face toward me so I could look him in the eyes.

"Don't hide from me," I said firmly. He had nothing to be ashamed of. I mean I'm a fucking witch—so what if he is a vampire? Before he could respond, my sister spoke.

"Let go of my sister now, enforcer. If you harm her, I will end you." Stevie had so much hatred in her tone that it made me gasp.

I was about to say something to protect my dream man, but before I could, Kai had me on my feet in a flash. He had his hands on my hips to steady me, but it also felt like he didn't want to let me go. I couldn't help but remember my dreams— were they real? I tilted my head back so I could ask him the one question burning a hole in my head.

"Who are you?"

"My name is Melakai Cane, Miss Knox. I am the head of the vampire king's enforcers." He had a look of regret on his beautiful face. He was being so formal. I didn't like it. Where was my relaxed sex god, who always made me laugh?

"Kai, step away from her now, before you do something you will regret," Jax warned Melakai, taking a step toward us.

"You take one step closer, Jackson, and you and I will finish what we started years ago—right here, right now," Kai growled at Jax.

"Melakai, son. Step away from the girl," the king ordered. Son? Wait, did that mean Randall was his dad?

With a final look at me to make sure I was okay, he took his hands off my hips. I felt instantly cold without his touch to warm me. I didn't want him to let me go. I wanted him to hold me forever. He was real, and I needed to know if he was really in my dreams. I have never been one to be like this toward a guy, but I just couldn't help the pull I felt toward him, like my life force was telling me to hold onto him. I have never felt safe in my life except when Kai was holding me. After stepping away from me, Kai made his way over to stand by the king. Stevie came rushing over and gave me a bone-crushing hug.

"What the hell was that, Ry?" she asked, looking me over for injuries, I guess.

"I don't know. Sorry for worrying you. I should have had something to eat before having that glass of champagne, I guess." I couldn't tell her the truth about Kai being one of my dream guys. I don't know why, but I felt like Kai being in my dreams was something I needed to keep private. Glancing over at Kai and seeing the look on his face, I knew I made the right decision.

"Now, can we all have a seat and try this again? I would like to finish our discussion," the king barked.

"Sounds good to me, but why is he here?" Jax asked, nodding toward Melakai.

"He's my heir and my son." Oh, so he *is* the king's son. "He has every right to be here, Mr. Marshall. Do not ever question my leadership or my sons again. Do I make myself clear?"

Randall said, pointing a stern look Jax's way. Kai had a look of disdain plastered on his face, but he quickly masked it. That look was pointed at Randall, not Jax.

With a nod of his head, Jax took his seat and the rest of us followed. The door opened again, and in walked a huge man, around the size of a big bear. He had a ginger beard, shoulder-length red hair, and brown eyes. He wore dark jeans, a black button-up shirt, and my God, was the shirt tight! If he flexed his biceps, he would tear the shirt. He gave us a nod and smiled at my sister then went to stand beside Jax.

"Since your second-in-command is here, I thought mine should be as well. Everyone, this is Tyler. He is my Beta," Jax told the group. Stevie couldn't keep her eyes off Jackson's Beta. I gave her a nudge so she would close her mouth.

"Pleasure to meet you all," he said with a bow of his head.

"No, no the pleasure is all mine," Stevie said with a wink.

I couldn't help it; I started laughing my ass off. Alex and Chase joined in as well. The king gave me a dirty look, but fuck him and the stick up his ass. Stevie punched me in the arm to shut me up, but Melakai didn't seem to like that. He took a step forward and pinned my sister with a glare.

"You would be wise to never lay your hands on her again, Coven heir," Kai spat.

I stopped laughing immediately, as did the others. Stevie stood up to square off against Kai. Oh no, this wasn't going to end well.

"You would do well to know your place, enforcer. Do not ever interfere in my family business again. It's coven *queen* now," she hissed. I felt like I was missing something here. Everyone seemed to have ill feelings toward Kai, and I didn't understand why.

"Why doesn't everyone stop hating on the poor guy and get on with this talk, so I can go and get something to eat." Kai had a look of pride in his eyes that look sent butterflies to my tummy. He could always set my body on fire with just one look in my dreams, now he could also do it in real life.

"Tyler and I can take you ladies out for something to eat after this. Their kind doesn't eat real food." I could hear the dig in Jax's voice—he clearly only said that to piss Kai off.

"You will not be going anywhere with her, dog," Kai snapped back.

"Is that a threat, you leech?" Jax sneered back. Both men took a step toward each other. I quickly stood and jumped between them.

"Thanks, guys, but I'm a big girl, I can make my own decisions, and I'd rather just go home and eat there. So let's get this show on the road." I couldn't tell everyone the truth, that I would rather go out with Kai.

Both men then stepped back, and Jax took his seat. I took my seat next to Stevie. Chase and Alex had smiles on their faces. I shot them both a dirty look; I knew what they were smiling about. They knew I was attracted to Kai.

"Now that the pissing contest is out of the way for Ryan's attention, let's talk about the treaty," Alex said, still grinning. I went beet-red from embarrassment; he was *so* getting punched for that comment when we leave.

"I would like a new treaty drawn up with new terms," the king stated.

That was it. Everyone stood up and started shouting over each other. The whole room was in uproar. Before anyone knew what was happening, the door burst open, and guards came piling in. One grabbed Stevie, and Alex went to lunge for him, but was caught mid-air by another guard. Chase went to help his brother, but was restrained by another guard. These guys were coming out of nowhere. Jax went to grab my arm and was stopped by a fist to the face—Kai's fist to be exact. Then they were all-out brawling on the floor. Tyler couldn't help Jax as he was subdued by three guards.

I was trying to help the others when a guard grabbed me from behind. I screamed, and Stevie started shouting threats at the guard to let me go or she would tear him limb from limb. I don't know what happened: maybe it was the rush of fear I was feeling, but my body felt really hot, and then out of nowhere, blue light shot from my hands at the guard that was holding me. He dropped to the floor. Stevie had a look of utter shock on her face.

I looked around the room and realized everyone had stopped fighting—they were all staring at me. My hands were still glowing, and I felt like a live wire.

"She is the one," the king said with awe in his voice, almost like he had found the missing puzzle piece.

"Ryan, look at me. Relax, Sissy, just breathe, everything is going to be okay," my sister said, trying to shake out of the guards hold. He reluctantly let her go and took a step toward me, but I stepped back out of her reach.

"How the fuck is this all okay, Stevie? I'm a freak! Look at me! I'm fucking glowing, and I just hurt SOMEONE!" As I screamed the last word, a blast of blue light shot out from me. The force was so great it shattered the windows and blew out the fire in the fireplace. I couldn't control the rage coursing through my veins. All the feelings I had bottled up, and the anger I had pushed deep down inside of me, from the years of torture as a child, were trying to break free. It brought everyone in the room to their knees— except for Kai.

Melakai made his way over to me, pushing against the power I was pulsing out. I could see the strain on his face as he struggled to get to me. When he finally stood in front of me, he cupped my face in both his hands and spoke so softly.

"Mi amor, it's okay, you are safe. Just breathe. Let me help you. I can make it stop. Just let me help you," he begged. I knew in that moment I could trust him to make it stop, so I nodded. He closed the sliver of space between us and pulled me into a tight embrace, whispering, "Sleep, mi amor." With his words, everything just stopped and went dark.

Chapter Ten

RYAN

I awoke on the edge of the lake. Sitting up, I looked to my side, and sure enough, Kai was sitting next to me. This was our other dream land. The lake was so beautiful and calm. It was my favorite place to be, surrounded by trees and mountains. Knowing Kai is now a real person and not a figment of my imagination, I felt shy and unsure.

"Where are we?" I asked.

"At Lake William, mi amor."

"I got that part, Kai; I mean is this place even real?"

"Yes."

"Are you going to tell me where this place is located?"

"You can find Lake William hidden in the mountains in Alaska. I found this place many years ago, with my brothers." I was determined to find Lake William now. I didn't want to waste any more time talking about the lake.

"So you're real?"

"I am as real as you are."

"Okay...so how are we here, and why are we here?"

"I brought you here so your mind could relax. I know this is your favorite place, so I thought bringing you here would help.

Your power was too much for you, and you couldn't control it. So I helped you."

I remembered that he had offered to help me after I hurt that guard and blew the office apart.

"I hurt that man and destroyed the office. I didn't mean to hurt him. I don't even know how I did it! It just happened," I wailed.

"He's a vampire. He will heal fast, and he will not die."

Thank God for that. I don't know if I could live with myself if I had killed him. At the time, I didn't care what happened. It was like I wasn't myself.

"I'm sorry, I lost it back there. This is all just too much for me. Finding out I'm a witch and then that you are real. I mean, holy shit—like, this is mind-blowing stuff." Kai leaned over and tucked a tendril of hair behind my ear. I felt my body starting to heat from his touch. His voice distracted me from my thoughts.

"I can't begin to try and understand what you are going through, but just know I will be here to help you along the way, mi amor. I am sorry for letting you believe I was not real."

"What happened in my dreams—" He cut me off before I could finish.

"All of it was real, all of it," he said with a devilish grin.

"Oh my God!" I started blushing, feeling so embarrassed about everything that we had done and the things I had said to him. "I'm a virgin," I blurted out. Fucking smooth Ryan, real smooth. Kai started laughing.

"I beg to differ, mi amor," he said through breaks in his laughter. His laugh was like music to my ears. I loved that sound so much.

"How is this possible? Are you telling me that my dream sex is all fucking real?" God strike me down now; this has got to be the most embarrassing moment of my life.

He tilted his head to the side and pressed his lips in a tight line, like he was trying not laugh at me again.

"Yes and no. After all, it is still just a dream. Your physical body has not been touched by a man in the real world, just in your dream world."

"Why didn't you tell me you were real? After everything we have done and the things I have said, you could have told me." I couldn't look him in the eye. I behaved like a ravenous hussy in my dreams.

He laughed at me, again! I couldn't stop the smile that spread across my face. He looked so relaxed and carefree. I didn't really know the real him, but in person he seemed like the type that was always serious and on guard. I wanted so badly to know the real him and what made him happy.

"I'm glad that my embarrassment amuses you, Mr. Cane."

He immediately stopped laughing, all traces of humor wiped from his beautiful face. I didn't know what I said to upset him so badly.

"Please don't call me that; I do not wear that name because I have a choice."

"I'm sorry, I didn't mean to offend you." I hung my head, not wanting him to see the confusion on my face. I don't know why his name upset him, but I didn't want him to be angry with me.

"Never turn those eyes away from me, mi amor." I snapped my eyes back up to him. His voice had such a command in it that I knew not to defy him. He always demanded eye contact when we had sex in my dream. I loved staring at him while he pounded into me. Oh God, I needed to stop thinking of that right now. Judging by the smirk on his face, he knew exactly where my mind had drifted. His eyes were burning with desire, and I couldn't look away. My nether region was getting slick, just by the way he was looking at me. He raised his hand to my face and pulled me close. I could feel the sexual tension building between us. I closed my eyes, waiting for his lips to crash against mine. I wanted him to take me right here, right now. Instead, he pulled back and dropped his hand. I snapped my eyes open, not knowing what the hell made him stop. I needed him to relieve the ache between my thighs.

"We must go, mi amor. The others are awaiting our return." Before I could answer, he grabbed my hand, and I felt a whoosh of wind—then nothing.

Chapter Eleven

RYAN

I feel someone shaking me, and hear my name being called. I don't want to wake up. I was having the best dream ever. Then I realized it wasn't a dream; Melakai was here and I wanted to jump his bones again in my dream. Holy fuck! I was acting like a hussy. I got so turned on in my dream that I could feel the pool of liquid between my thighs. I had to find a way to not dream anymore—to block him out somehow. I snapped my eyes open to see Stevie leaning over me with worry lines marring her face.

"Thank fuck, Sissy. I was about to stake his vampire ass if he didn't bring you back from wherever the fuck he took you," she said. I'm a terrible person. Here's my sister, worried about me, and I'm in a dream trying to screw Kai.

"I'm okay, Stevie, I swear." Well, except for the fact that I was feeling needy and hot, thanks to Kai.

"You smell like you're more than okay to me," Tyler retorted, a look of disgust prominent on his face.

"What the fuck is that supposed to mean, jackass?" Chase snapped.

"Ask your new coven queen—she knows," Tyler smugly replied.

I could feel all eyes on me in that moment. Surely he didn't mean he scented my arousal, right? Judging by the look on Jackson's face, I was starting to think they *could* smell my arousal. Before the tension-filled silence could continue, Kai spoke.

"She needs to be trained—her power is too great for her to control."

"Well, that's what we're here to do, Captain Fucking Obvious," Stevie tartly replied. She stood up and leaned me a helping hand, so I could get to my feet. I didn't want to talk about this anymore. I just wanted to go back to the cabin and sleep and deal with all this shit tomorrow. It felt like my head was going to explode.

"We still need to finish our discussion." Would Randall ever shut up about this fucking treaty?

"I think Ryan needs rest after what just happened," Jax answered, looking over and giving me a kind smile. I nodded in return. I felt like Jax could see I was at my limit for the day.

"You do not tell her what she does and does not need, dog," Kai roared, and before another fight broke out I quickly intervened.

"Look, guys—I have had a hell of day and night. If you have to talk, fine, but I'm going home. I'm wiped out." With that said, I started walking to the door, only to be stopped when Kai suddenly appeared in front of me. I screamed. What I can say? I startle easily.

"Forgive me, mi amor. I did not mean to scare you," he said, placing a hand on my shoulder. His touch sent shivers down my spine. In this moment, I would kill to have had his hand or mouth somewhere else. *What the fuck is wrong with me?* I can't do this with him anymore. He's a real person and not just part of my imagination. A part of me felt so betrayed that he lied to me. How would he have told me he was real, though—would I have believed him?

"Take your hands off her. We will discuss this tomorrow. My sister is tired, and we will be taking her home now," Stevie announced to the whole room. Kai was gone in a flash. I looked over my shoulder to see him standing by the king. I guess being a vampire meant you were super-fast. They all started discussing when and where to meet tomorrow. I tuned out of their conversation, not wanting to worry myself with more details that would make my head spin. I started for the door again for like the tenth time tonight. When I felt a hand land on the small of my back, I knew who it was before I even saw him; my body reacted to his touch like a paper to a flame. I turned to face Kai.

"Hey, I'm sorry if I got you in trouble."

"I'm fine, mi amor. I'm more worried about you."

"I'm fine; I've just got a lot going on in my head at the moment."

"I would love to try and help you figure out some of those things," he murmured.

"I need my sister and cousins to help me figure this power thing out, and I need you to tell me how you can get into my dreams." I really wished he could be the one to help me sort out this whole power thing, but at the moment I felt like I couldn't trust him.

He lied to me. He was real this whole time and never told me. The things we did together in my dreams...God I feel like such a fucking fool. I was also so ashamed of myself. I behaved like a hussy in my dreams. I mean, my first-time having sex in my dreams was with Kai.

"You would be surprised how much I would be able to help you with your power."

"What do you..." Jax, who stood just off to the side of me, interrupted before I could finish my sentence. He had a strange look on his face.

"We will meet again, Ryan. I'm sorry we couldn't talk more, but we will get another chance soon."

"Um...that's okay, and it was nice to meet you to Jax," I said with a forced smile.

"Tyler and I will come by the cabin in the morning to discuss some matters with you and your family." Just as he finished speaking, Kai pulled me in front of him and gripped my hips with both hands. I gasped at the contact, and he rested his chin on my head. Jax was growling like an angry dog. I knew what Kai was doing...he was telling Jackson that I was his and to back off. I wasn't his or anyone's, and I was about to tell him that, but he spoke first.

"If you plan on going past in the morning, I think I might make a point to join you all as well. I'm sure Ryan doesn't mind, do you, love?"

"Umm...no, you can come." Oh fuck, I just said that out loud. "I mean come to the cabin." I could feel the blush creeping up to my cheeks. I hung my head down in shame when I felt Kai shift and wrap one arm around my stomach, with the other lifting my head. He then whispered in my ear.

"Never look down, mi amor. Your eyes are far too beautiful to be hidden."

I blushed harder at that compliment. When he said stuff like this, it made me so confused. He lied to me, but then he could say a few words and I was eating out of the palm of his hand. Jax stepped forward and spoke through clenched teeth.

"There is no need for you to attend, enforcer...these matters do not concern you."

"Let's not start another pissing contest over my cousin's affections, okay, dickheads? Now get the fuck off her, Melakai, so we can go home." Chase looked disgusted, seeing how Kai was holding me.

Reluctantly, Kai let me go. I somehow knew it pained him to

do so. I'll admit, it pained me as well. When he held me in my dreams, I felt safe and protected. I needed time to think. If he was real, then did that mean Nico was real too?

"How do you do it?" I asked Kai.

"Do what, mi amor?"

"How do you come to be in my dreams?"

"Ahhhh, Melakai, please do tell her how you acquired your gifts," Jax sneered at Kai.

"That is a story for another time, mi amor." Kai had a distant look in his eyes as he replied, like he was lost in a dark memory.

"Come, Ryan, let's get you home," Alex said, putting his arm around my shoulders and pulling me to him. With a final look at Kai, I let Alex lead me out of the office.

Chapter Twelve

RYAN

We finally arrived at the cabin. I was too exhausted to worry about answers for my questions. I decided to get a good night's rest and drill the others in the morning. With a final bid good night to my sister and cousins, I retired to my room.

After a quick shower, I slipped into a pair of sleep shorts and an old T-shirt. I climb into bed with a heavy feeling on my chest. When I wake up tomorrow, more shit in my life was going to change. I decided right there, in that moment, that I was not going to throw myself a pity party any longer. I was free from my mother and her abuse. I may not have gotten to see my father before he passed, but none of that would hold me back any longer. I was stronger than that.

Come tomorrow, I would take whatever came at me and demand the answers I needed to make sense of my life. I hated not having control of things in my life. I lived too long with no control, and I would never, never have that taken from me again.

I was a grown-ass woman now, not some meek kid that could be bullied or hurt. I turned on my side to try and get some sleep and my eyes landed on the letter my dad wrote me, still sitting on the nightstand. I wasn't ready to read that yet, so I did what any grown women would do: I rolled back over and went to sleep.

I awoke to the feeling of the warm sun on my face. I smiled to myself. I was never allowed to sleep in. Mother forbade it; she would tell me weird stories about strange things, and I would have to repeat them to her, so she knew I was listening.

The only reprieve I got from her was when I was at school or she was drunk and passed out. Refusing to let my thoughts consume me, I climb out of bed, stretching my arms high above my head. After finally being satisfied with my stretch, I made my way to the bathroom to quickly brush my teeth and wash my face. I wanted to meet the others for a nice quiet chat and get some answers, but that was not how it happened.

After exiting my room and making my way down the hall to the kitchen, I stopped dead in my tracks at seeing Tyler leaning against the front door, a smirk on his face.

"What the fuck is funny? And why the hell are you here?" I snapped putting my hands on my hips.

"I guess I'm not the only one standing up this morning," he said, wiggling his brows. I tilted my head to the side, not understanding what he meant. Then I heard a cough and looked to see the others at the dining table.

"You might want to put a sweater on, Sissy. You seem a bit cold, if you know what I mean!" It hit me then what Tyler was laughing at: my fucking nipples were on high alert. I forgot to put a bra on before I left my room.

I quickly covered my chest and pinned Tyler with a dirty

look and turned to go and change, when I heard him yell after me.

"I do love the little piggy sleep shorts you're wearing too, though, princess!" I groaned, could this morning get any worse? I wanted to slap that smug bastard Tyler.

I heard a growl come from the kitchen that I could only assume it was Jax trying to tell Tyler to shut his fat mouth. After quickly getting changed into a pair of skinny jeans, Ugg boots and a long-sleeved V-neck shirt—with a bra on this time—I left my room to re-join the others. Once in the kitchen, I made myself a quick cup of coffee and joined Chase at the table.

"Nice of you to join us, squirt," Alex quipped.

"Your mouth is as annoying as your face, Alex, so please shut it, would you?" I said with a devilish smile.

"Well, I guess you're still not a morning person, then, eh, Sissy?" Stevie remarked with a snicker.

"Guess not, Sissy. Anyway, I want answers, and you are all going to give them to me. But first—Jackson, why are you here?" I saw a look of hurt flash past his eyes before he regained himself.

"I'm here to help you, Miss Knox, and to also discuss the treaty."

"Okay, no offense, but I don't give a shit about some treaty. I just want to know what the fuck I am and if I can give these 'gifts' back. I don't want and never asked for them. I just started to get my life back on track, and now all this shit comes out. I mean, can a chick catch a break?" I was flinging my arms in the air like a mad woman, but I didn't care. I just wanted them to understand that I didn't want any of this. They may like what they are, but I don't—not after last night, anyway.

"The day-walking leech is here, Alpha," Tyler sneered. Jackson just growled.

He didn't knock before entering; he just walked in like he

owned the damn cabin. He nodded to the others and smiled at me. With a huff, I stood and shouted at no one in particular.

"Let's just invite the whole fucking neighborhood over, shall we? I mean, it's only Ryan who is the odd one out and doesn't know shit from dick, right? I stood by and listened while you all talked shit last night about shit I don't even know about, and now you want to do it again before I can get any answers! Hell to the mother-fucking-no!"

They all looked at me like I had just grown another head. I was pissed. Jax, Tyler, and now Kai are here? How am I ever going to get any answers, if all they wanted to do was talk about some fucking treaty?

"You a bit hungry, squirt? There's bacon and eggs in the microwave. You were never pretty in the mornings or when you're hungry," Chase said gently. I deflated a bit. He was right. I was a bitch in the mornings, and I was even worse when I was hungry.

"Only you know the way to my heart, cousin." I gave Chase a wink as I made my way to the microwave. Once I got my plate and sat back down at the table, I plopped a bit of bacon into my mouth and moaned—it was so good.

"I feel like I'm watching food porn" Alex joked while making a funny look with his face. With my mouth full of eggs, I replied.

"What can I say, food turns me on, baaabbbyyy." I heard Kai's sharp intake of breath and Jackson growl as soon as I finished speaking.

"Ryan, don't be a goddamn pig, we have guests!" Stevie's a party pooper. After swallowing my mouthful, I turned to my sister and tartly snapped back.

"Well, since my outburst, no one has even made a noise, so I forgot they were here, and it's not like we only just met. One stalks me in my dreams, the other follows me into the woods, and that one"—I said nodding my head in Tyler's direction—"just checked out my rack, so we may as well be besties, if you ask me."

Everyone laughed at that comment, and now with the mood lighter, Kai came and took the seat next to me. Tyler took the seat next to his alpha, on the other side of the table. I don't know why I was feeling nervous, but I started twisting my hands in my lap, waiting for someone to break the silence. My food was long forgotten now. Suddenly, I felt Kai's hand on mine, stopping them from fidgeting. I looked up and he gave me a reassuring smile, like everything was going to be okay. I don't know why, but that small gesture made me feel reassured.

"Okay, Ryan, we owe you that much. What would you like to know, squirt?" Alex asked, while leaning his elbows on the table.

"How am I like this? Like, how did I get this power or gift or whatever you call it? Why did you all freak out when I had that dream, in the car ride up here?" Kai gave my hand another reassuring squeeze. I felt better just with him touching me, like he would protect me from all the bad in the world. I was still pissed that he lied to me, but right now I needed his support while I dealt with this conversation.

Stevie cleared her throat and leaned forward to rest her forearms on the table.

"I don't know how else to say this, so I'm just going to say what I think, okay? All the fairy tales about witches, vampires, werewolves, fae, and so on are true. Our grandfather was the one that founded the treaty with Randall Cane and Jackson's father, to keep peace among the races. You're a born witch from the Knox coven, descendent of Marcus Knox, who was the leader and founder of the Alaskan coven."

"Okay, but why did you freak out, about the dream?"

"Because, we knew then that Melakai was coming for you" I

was shocked at Stevie's reply. I didn't dare look to Kai; I wanted to hear my sister's reasons.

"What do you mean, coming for me, Stevie?"

"As you know, Melakai has certain gifts. We learned long ago that when he enters a mind, he can persuade a person to do his bidding, or the King's."

"Okay, I'll process that later. So I'm a witch, you're a witch, Alex and Chase are warlocks. Jax and Tyler are werewolves, and Kai and Randall are vampires. Who the fuck are the fae? I haven't heard any stories about them."

A look of pain passed over Jackson's face. He shook his head as if to clear his mind of the thoughts he was having. My heart ached for him, as the pain was so clearly written on his face. I could tell from that look he hated the fae. He spoke with such malice and hatred in his tone when he answered my question.

"The fae are vile creatures that prey on the weak and care for no one but their own kind. They are cruel, heartless beings and need to stay on their side of the veil. If they dare to step foot this side again, my pack will stop at nothing to eradicate their kind from this earth."

I felt like there was a big part of this story that I was missing. I don't know how, but I knew everyone was keeping something from me.

"Why do I feel like you all are being very cagey and not telling me the full story? I want to know all of it. Don't lie to me, please—you owe me that much, Stevie," I said, pinning my sister with a stern look. Stevie wasn't the one who answered my question, though.

"We have our suspicion that the fae are the ones who murdered your father, Ryan." Wait a fucking minute! I thought my dad died from a sudden illness. "We have no proof, as of yet, but when we examined your father's body, there was a strong stench of magic on him. Every magic user leaves a trail. Witches have a certain scent, and once you have that scent, you will be able to tell who that scent belongs to. The one on your father was not from any witch. The only person or persons that could leave that scent are the fae," Alex said with a look of remorse on his face, like he never wanted to burden me with that secret.

I didn't know what to say. I felt so much guilt for my sister and my dad. I wasn't there when he passed, as I was so mad at him for leaving me with Mom. I should have been there for my sister, but I was too selfish and wouldn't listen to Stevie when she said she needed me to be there the day that he was buried. She never told me Dad was murdered.

She let me think he died of illness. I was angry all over again that she lied to me, but I needed to put my feelings aside for now and be there for my sister.

"Stevie, I am so, so sorry. I wasn't there for you when you needed me. I was so selfish." I hung my head in shame, knowing my sister had to deal with our father's funeral and burial on her own.

She shook her head and leaned over the table, her hand extended to me. I pried one of my hands from Kai's and grabbed my sister's. She looked at me with sadness in her hazel eyes.

"I forgive you, Ry. You had no idea what had happened, and I couldn't tell you all of this over the phone. We didn't want to tell you any of this at home, as we had a feeling they were still watching the house. That's why we left so soon after you arrived. We needed to get here and alert the coven and the pack, as well as Randall. If the fae are waging a war, we will need all the help we can get."

"I will help you all in any way I can. I will not let them get away with hurting our dad, Stevie—I swear."

"If what you say is true, why would the fae return now after so many decades of peace, and why only target your father?" Kai asked no one in particular. He seemed like he didn't believe that the fae were to blame, and that made me suspicious. Why is Kai defending these people, when he just heard that they killed my father?

"We have no idea. That's why we came here to seek answers we could not get at home, and to train Ryan. We fear that they now know of her existence and will come after both her and Stevie," Chase said, looking Kai directly in the eye, almost like he was challenging him.

"We must all prepare our people. The coven will want revenge for their king being killed at the hands of the fae. As their queen, I must honor their wishes." Stevie was pinning me with a look that implored me to understand what she was saying.

"You mean you want to *kill* the person that killed our father?" I couldn't murder someone in cold blood! We had a justice system for a reason.

She just nodded. I couldn't believe what the hell she was saying.

"You can't just go around fucking killing people Stevie, that's wrong—it's murder," I said, in shock.

"I can and I must— blood must have blood. That is our way, sister, and you will soon learn that." She snapped, anger lacing her words. What the hell is wrong with my sister?

"You are not the only coven queen now, Stevie," Jax retorted.

"I am the oldest, therefore the role is mine, not my sister's," she snapped back at him.

"That may be the case, but she can challenge you to a duel for the crown, can she not?" Jax asked.

I felt all eyes on me in that moment. I didn't know how to answer that, so I said the first thing that came to my mind.

"Let's talk about my dreams and how Kai is in them," I said, looking to anyone for answers before my eyes finally settled on Kai. With a sigh, he answered my question.

"Because of my gifts."

"What kind of gifts?" I asked.

"The kind of gifts that let me enter people's minds. I can alter their moods and emotions, if need be. I am the king's secret weapon." Well, not so secret anymore, dumbass.

"So that's why you were there last night? To get my sister and Jax to agree to change this treaty thing?" I heard the others gasp. Were my feelings for Kai real? Or were they part of his emotion control power? Jax stood up, leaning on the table, with a glare on his face. He was growling, and his eyes were changing color. They weren't chocolate brown anymore—they were yellow. Holy shit, I think Jax might be changing into a wolf right in front of me.

"You son of a bitch. She's right, isn't she? That fucker was trying to con us by using your *gifts* to get us to agree!" he roared. Tyler put a hand on Jackson's shoulder to calm him, but he just shook it off. Kai stood and leaned over the table so he and Jackson were nearly nose to nose.

"I have to follow orders and what my king wants, whether I think it's wrong or not. I must do as he asks." Okay, that's a bit weird. So Kai didn't like doing what Randall wanted all the time? That's good to know.

"Bullshit, Melakai. The enforcer is back in full swing now, ladies and gentlemen. You would have tried to kill us last night if we didn't agree, wouldn't you? That's why all those guards were nearby—in case all hell broke loose when you tried to take us out!" Jackson did have a good point with that.

"What is done cannot be un-done, Alpha, so there is no use worrying about what has not come to pass," Kai said, with annoyance thick in his tone.

Jackson couldn't take it anymore. He jumped across the

table and grabbed Kai. It all happened so fast. I could see arms swinging left and right. Everyone was trying to break them up and shouting directions and threats. I grabbed hold of Kai's arm, but just as I gripped him by the elbow, he spun around and grabbed me by the throat. As soon as he realized it was me, he instantly dropped his hand, but it was too late. Jackson hadn't stopped. His fist connected with Kai's jaw, and I heard a crack. I was sure his jaw was broken from the force of Jax's punch.

I couldn't watch any longer. Kai was hunched over on one knee, a hand on his jaw, and was struggling to stand. I jumped in the middle, before they could continue to harm each other, and pinned each of them with glare of fury.

"Would you two learn to use your fucking words?" I shouted.

"That fucker deserved the punch he got for laying hands on you, squirt," Alex snapped. I looked over my shoulder to glare at him—he was not helping the situation.

"Not helping, Alex." I then retuned my focus to the two brooding males. "Both of you need to cool off and come back when you can apologize to each other, okay?"

With a reluctant nod from each of them, they left the cabin, letting us know they would be back later to discuss the treaty, again.

Chapter Thirteen

RYAN

After Jax, Tyler and Kai left, Stevie and I told the boys we were going to go for a walk to catch up. They feigned hurt feelings, but truth was, they didn't care, and they wanted to watch some game that was on TV. Boys will be boys.

Stevie and I walked at a moderate pace through the woods, down a well-warn path that clearly had been used by animals and humans.

"Dad used to bring me up here all the time as a kid. I loved coming here—it always meant I could stop hiding who I was and be free. I couldn't do that back home." Stevie spoke with a faraway look in her eyes, like she was reliving a happy memory.

"Why didn't you and Dad just move here then?"

"He would never move a country away from you, Ry—even if it did feel that way to you growing up. We tried to come for you, Ry, so many times. But Mom got tired of our pleading and said if Dad came by again and tried to take you from her, she would expose what we were to the humans. Humans can never know we exist, Ry. They can't handle what they cannot control. They would exterminate us. That is why the treaty is so important—it keeps all the supes in the world in line."

"I never knew you tried to come for me. I just assumed Dad didn't want me. Mom always said Dad only wanted you. I guess I just believed her; I gave up waiting for him to come save me, Stevie. I know I shouldn't have, but I did."

"I never knew how hard it was for you until the first time you managed to get a hold of me and we finally saw each other after so many years. That's when I got a glimpse of how bad it was. I saw the bruises, Ryan, no matter how hard you tried to hide them, Sissy. I am so truly sorry, from the bottom of my heart, that I couldn't get you out. I was scared and weak, but I swear I will never fail you again, my sister. I am not scared or weak anymore."

I knew she was telling me the truth. I could hear the conviction in her voice. I knew, no matter what life threw at us, we would always stick together and fight for each other. We were two halves, but together we were whole.

"I know, Stevie, and you don't need to be sorry. It wasn't your fault. We were children. We didn't know any better." I gave her a playful bump with my hip to lighten the mood, which made her laugh. I was glad; I hated seeing her so sad.

"So anyway, enough sad shit. What's the deal with you and Melakai? I know Jackson Marshall is into you, as well. I can see the way they both look at you." I shook my head at her —she was so wrong.

"I don't know. Jax is nice and very handsome, but I don't know what to think about him, really. It's so confusing. Melakai, on the other hand, the day we came here, and I had that dream, I didn't even know who he was. I didn't know he was real. Now I'm more confused, because I can't tell if my feelings for him are real or are they part of his control over people's emotions."

"I get what you are saying, I do, but Jackson would be the better choice, if you ask me. Melakai seems so doom and gloom all the time. Would the guy's face break if he smiled? As for the emotion control…I have no idea, Ry. That is something you will have to ask him."

"Don't be mean. I don't want to jump into anything; I have way too much going on as it is, and a guy would just make things ten times worse." Changing the subject, I asked. "Why Alaska though Stevie?"

"Because this is where, dad was born." That was news to me. I thought dad was born in New Zealand, like us.

"I didn't know that. I guess it makes sense now why we are here. Why did dad leave?"

"He was sent on an overseas trip or something like that, some witches were going rogue in New Zealand and dad had to clean up the mess. While he was in New Zealand, he met mom. I guess he decided she was worth giving up his place here, to be with her."

"Were our grandparents okay with that?"

"I don't know to be honest. Dad never talked about his parents much." Oh, that's strange.

"Are they still here, in Alaska?" Stevie had a look on her face that I couldn't read.

"I don't actually know, I have never met them. I assumed they died because I have never seen them at the coven. Dad would always change the subject if I asked about them." Why would dad do that? What was he hiding?

We chatted about more mundane things as we walked through the woods, finding our way back to the cabin as dusk was approaching. We needed to be ready for the wolves and vampires when they came to discuss the treaty—and I now understood why it was so important.

Chapter Fourteen

RYAN

When we arrived back at the cabin, the boys had dinner ready, so we quickly ate and then I headed to my room to have a shower before everyone arrived. Stepping back into my room with a towel wrapped around my hair and another around my body, I stopped dead in my tracks when I saw a man sitting on my bed.

He had blond hair that fell to his shoulders, blue eyes like the ocean, and a strong, tall frame. His shirt wrapped perfectly around his large arms. He was hot! He stood with his hands held up, as if surrendering. I don't know why I didn't scream for the others to help, but I felt a sense of calm wash over me, so I stood rooted to the floor.

"I do not mean to frighten you, Ryan. I am here because I need help, and you are the only one I believe can help me. Will you hear me out, please?" I couldn't speak, so I just nodded. He took three steps closer to me. There was only a foot of distance between us. His scent hit me hard—he smelled of wild flowers and trees. I loved wildflowers. He chuckled, as if he knew what his close proximity was doing to me. What the hell is wrong with me? I seem to be getting turned on by every damn guy, I need to get my shit together.

"My name is Simon. My people are being framed by one the clans, who are a part of your treaty. My people had nothing to do with the death of your father."

Holy fuck, he was fae.

"You're a fae, aren't you?" I asked him. He nodded. "I don't know why you are here, asking me to believe you. I don't even know you, and from what I understand, it's pretty obvious who killed my father."

"I had nothing to gain from your father's death. He was a fair ruler and a good king, but more than that, he was a good man, Ryan." He spoke as if he knew my father.

"Did you know my father?"

"Yes I did. I helped your grandfather gather the intel he needed to create the treaty, so we could all live in peace, and my people would stop being hunted. Many lives were lost in the last war between all the supernatural kinds."

"So, you knew my grandfather as well then?"

"Yes."

"Why are you telling me this and not my sister? I don't know much about all this supernatural stuff. I just found out I was a witch yesterday."

"Ah, but you are so much more than just a witch, Ryan. Ask your precious vampire Melakai. He knows the truth." There was anger behind his words, and I couldn't imagine why.

"What do you mean?" And how does he know about Kai?

"I'm afraid our time is up. Please heed my words. My people are not to blame." I could hear it in his voice—he was telling the truth, and that confused me even more. "I will find you again, Ryan."

He turned and just vanished. I had no time to ponder what the fuck had just happened, because my bedroom door flew open, and Jax and Melakai barged in with feral looks on their faces. Melakai came to me and put his hands on my shoulders, leaning in to sniff me. He bloody sniffed me!

"What the hell do you both think you are doing in here?" I snapped, yanking my body out of his hands, just now noticing that I was half naked. I gripped my towel tighter.

"Who was in here with you Ryan?" Jax asked, with an agitated look on his face. I don't know why I lied, but I knew if I told them what just happened and who was in my room, all hell would break loose.

"No one was in here." They both gave me a look that said I was full of shit.

"I can smell someone else was in here, Ryan. I can't place the scent, but it is familiar to me. I know you weren't alone," Jackson said, taking a step forward.

"So, you're calling me a liar then?"

"I can tell when you lie, love," Jax replied with narrowed eyes.

"I heard you talking to someone, tell me who it was," Kai demanded.

"One—don't fucking tell me what to do, and two, get the fuck out, both of you—NOW!" I shouted. How dare they fucking barge in here.

With one last look at me, they both turned and left my room. I finally released the breath I didn't realize I was holding, and quickly got changed into some leggings and a long-sleeved shirt. On my way out, I grabbed my Ugg boots and slipped them on. I felt like we needed to hold off on blaming the fae. I didn't understand why I trusted what Simon said about his people not having anything to do with my father's death, but I did.

Chapter Fifteen

RYAN

Upon arriving in the kitchen, I saw that everyone was seated, waiting for me to join them. I saw a space between Alex and Melakai, but after what had just transpired in my room, I did not want to be anywhere near Melakai. I walked over to the table and nudged Alex over so I could sit between him and Chase. Alex looked confused, assuming I would be more than pleased to sit next to Kai. Yeah, not right now buddy—he's on my shit list.

Once seated between my two cousins, I addressed the group.

"Sorry for keeping you all waiting. I was rudely interrupted by two overbearing jackasses, which delayed me." I delivered this with a fake hostess smile. Chase was giggling beside me, and Alex coughed to mask his laughter.

Stevie pinned us all with a disapproving look that had us sitting up straight and wiping the smiles off our faces.

"Don't worry about it, Ry. We all just sat down," Stevie said. "Now that we are all here, let's discuss the treaty, shall we? Ry, just to fill you in a bit, every time a new leader is appointed, the treaty needs to be re-signed, so that all parties are up to date with what is expected of each coven, pack, vampires and fae."

"Do all the vampires, packs, covens and fae all over the world have to obey this treaty?" I asked.

"Yes, they do, as we are the head of all of our kind. If any witches step out of line and judgment must be passed, they are brought here to stand trial before our coven elders and king, while now it's queen. Same as for the wolves and the vampires, I don't know how the fae do things. They do have an elder council like the rest of us though." Stevie answered. I nodded my understanding. I guess since everyone hated the fae at the moment, they wouldn't be signing the new treaty.

"Okay. Now that Miss Knox is up to speed, may we continue?" Randall Cane asked.

"Yes, why don't you start, Randall, and tell us all why you want to change the treaty and what your reasons for the changes are?" my sister asked.

"I want the fae realm completely sealed so that they may never enter this realm. In order to do that, I need the witches to try seal it and the pack sign off on it," Randall said, like we were all supposed to agree with him.

"If we do that, Farrarie will die. You know it needs to be stabilized by Earth," Alex said, with a look of shock on his face, as if he couldn't believe Randall had just said what he did.

"I am well aware of that, Mr. Knox, but I do not care. Their kind has done enough damage, don't you think? And if what Melakai has told me is true, I would think you would be open to this idea, given what they did to your uncle." It was clear what Randall wanted.

"That cannot happen. You will kill innocent fae women and children. We cannot condemn a whole race for the actions of a few. That's inhumane!" Chase bellowed, pounding his fist on the table.

"WE ARE NOT HUMAN, BOY!" the king shouted, rising to his feet.

"Watch your tone and how you speak to my cousin, king," I sneered, coming to Chase's defense. How dare he yell at my cousin, the old prick! King or not, he would not speak to my cousin like that.

"You should not speak of matters you know nothing about, little witch. Be seen, not heard," he shot back.

I stood, fists balled at my sides, ready to give him a piece of my mind, when I felt Kai place his hand on my shoulder, as if to sit me down. The king had a smile on his face, like he thought Melakai could settle me. I shrugged his hand off my shoulder with a vicious twitch.

"Don't fucking touch me, douche bag. You're on my shit-list at the moment." A look of hurt passed over his face, but he quickly gathered himself and masked it. I pointed my finger at the smirking king. "Do not ever speak to me or my family like that again! I don't give two shits who the fuck you are. You don't know me or what the fuck I have been through - if I want to say something, I will."

My sister stood, fire blazing in her hazel eyes, but her anger wasn't directed at Randall. She was angry with me.

"Enough, Ryan, sit down! Cane does have a valid point. The fae have caused so many problems in the past, and given what had happened to our father, I would have thought you would have been more on board with this."

"Are you serious? You haven't heard a word Alex or Chase has said, have you? You would wipe out a whole race like the shit under your shoe, just to help you sleep better at night?" I snapped back at my sister.

"You know nothing, Ryan. I must do this for my coven. Blood must have blood, no matter the cost. If wiping them all out is the answer, then so be it! I am the queen of this fucking coven and I decide—not you! Do I make myself clear, sister?" There was so much anger in her voice, and her words hurt me more than I could say. I fought to keep the tears at bay. I climbed off the bench seat and headed for my room, when her words stopped me. "You do not get to walk away from me. I am your queen. You will answer me when I ask you a question. Do you understand me, Ryan?"

I peered over my shoulder, staring at my sister, tears running freely down my face. I saw Jax's eyes soften when he looked at me. Both Alex and Chase had looks of pity on their faces. Kai looked hurt—not for himself but, for me.

"If following a queen means killing innocent people just to please her desires and selfishness, then I want no part of that queen's coven. If you do this, Stevie, you are a monster! You are no better than her!" I spat those words at my sister like they were acid on my tongue. A look of hurt quickly morphed to anger on her face, and her eyes went blank for a moment before she regained control. She climbed off her chair and came toward me.

I turn to face her head-on, using the back of my hand to wipe the tears away. I was waiting for the verbal abuse, but that never happened. Instead, she slapped me right across the face. The force was so great, I lost my footing and fell to the floor. I touched my cheek, which was now stingy and pulsating. I look up at my sister with utter disbelief; the girl staring down at me wasn't my sister. The person looking at me was full of rage and disgust. If looks could kill, I would be dead.

"You will never speak to me, your queen, that way again, Ryan, do I make myself clear?"

She looked so power hungry. I couldn't believe what she had just done, and what she was now saying to me. She promised me just hours ago that she would never let anyone hurt me again, and now she was the one doing it to me. A surge of anger shot through my veins, and I stood up to face my sister. I was done having people lie to me and hide things from me and treat me like I was nothing. I was not going to let another person hurt me ever again.

When we were face to face, so close that our noses were nearly touching, I heard Tyler say from his seat at the table, "Oh fuck, shit's about to get real now, boys."

I looked my sister directly in the eyes, and I couldn't see the loving, caring person anymore. I only saw a power-hungry girl, trying to prove she was woman enough to lead, even if it meant killing innocent people.

"I am not that weak child who you can use as a punching bag, like Mom did, Stevie. I will not let you do to me what she did. I will not stand by and allow another person to dictate my life. I don't give a fuck if you are some coven queen. You will never be my queen, sister, if you do this. I will never follow someone who murders innocents, sister or not." I brushed past her and headed to my room to pack my things. I couldn't stay under the same roof as a person who thought it was okay to treat me the way she just did.

Once in my room, I slammed my door shut and sat on the edge of my bed. I couldn't stop the sob that crept out. After everything I had been through in my life with my mom, the one person I thought who would understand my need for change and a new life was Stevie. I was so wrong. She was exactly like Mom; she just hid her monster better. I saw the look she had in her eyes—it was the same look Mom had when she used to beat the devil out of me.

I didn't hear my door open over my sobs, and I jumped when I felt a hand on my shoulder. I could tell Jackson was upset about what had just happened, and I didn't want him feeling sorry for me. I was sick of being pitied by people.

"I know we don't really know each other well, but Stevie had no right to do and say what she did, Ryan. What she did was out of order."

"I don't know what I am going to do now. I cannot stand by and watch a whole race be destroyed because of my sister's rage, Jackson. That's not who I am. I will not follow a queen who is prepared to sacrifice the lives of innocent people just to satisfy her own blood lust. I'm not like her," I said though my tears.

He shushed me and started rubbing his hand up and down my back, trying to soothe me, in a bid to stop my crying.

"I know you are different from your sister. I can see it in your eyes. You have an innocence about you that is so captivating to see and very rare to find in our kinds. The world we live in is so different to the one you were raised in, Ryan. We answer death with death. That's all we know. We were never taught any different." His voice was so soft and smooth, and it made me feel calm. The tears slowly stopped falling. I pulled away to rest against the headboard, and Jackson sat at the bottom of the bed.

"Can't you all change the way you view things?" I asked, my throat scratchy from all the crying.

"I wish it was that simple, but so much has happened between the supernatural races, Ryan. The vamps, witches, and wolves came to an understanding many years ago that ensured peace to all our people. The fae have upset that balance. The fae king, Nicholas Stone, signed the same treaty as my father and Randall. Your father also signed that same treaty. The fae king agreed to the terms that were stated. The king and his people would remain in Farrarie and never step foot on Earth as long as we left the portal open, so that their world wouldn't die."

"Why did the first war start?"

"The fae killed my father." Oh my God, so that's why Jax hated the fae. They killed his dad and broke the treaty. That's why they were all so anxious to write a new one and cut the fae out.

"I'm so sorry, Jackson, I didn't know." I grabbed his hand and held it, giving it a squeeze.

"It's okay, Ryan." His words had no conviction in them. They were hollow.

"How many treaties have there been?"

"Two. The first was with my father, Randall, your grandfather, and the fae king. The second was signed by Randall, my father, your father, and the fae king. The one we are trying to discuss now will be the third."

"How come a new one was never signed when you became Alpha?"

"Because your father helped me protect my people from other supes, who wished to challenge me for my throne. It is my birthright to be alpha of my people. When the time came for me to sit on the throne, I had grown strong, and that was thanks to the aid of your father. He trained me and taught me how to be a good and fair king to my people. He put off the signing of the new treaty til he knew I understood what I was doing. When the time came, it was too late—he was gone. That's why Randall is pushing so hard now. Stevie and I are both new leaders, and we both must sign."

Holy shit, I never expected that. My dad was that kind of man. What he did for Jackson spoke volumes of the kind of a man he was. Instead of trying to kill Jackson and take over his pack to gain power, he helped him and kept putting off the signing of the treaty until Jackson was old enough and strong enough to rule on his own.

"I'm so glad my dad was there for you and helped you out, Jackson. I'm sorry that I pulled you away from the treaty meeting. I know you need to be out there, so you can go." I felt guilty for taking up so much of his time.

He cupped my chin and lifted my head so he could look me in the eyes.

"Never look down, Ryan. You are royalty and have every right to the throne as well. You can challenge your sister for the throne, you know, and rule your people in the way you see fit." His eyes held so much hope that I couldn't get any words out. He took that as his cue to lean in. Just as his lips were about to touch mine, a knock sounded at the door. Startled by the noise, I jerked back and tried to get my breathing under control. Shit, I was about to let Jackson kiss me!

My bedroom door opened to reveal Tyler.

"The meeting has hit a stalemate for now. We will continue the discussion tomorrow at the king's manor, so all parties can go over what has been said." Jax gave Tyler a nod and stood up to leave.

"I hope we will see you tomorrow, Ryan. Until then, please take care of yourself, and if you need anything, just call me." He handed me a card with his number on it. I thanked him and wished them both a good night.

Once they left, I settled down in bed and shut my eyes, thinking I would just have a minute's rest before packing my bag and leaving this place for good.

Chapter Sixteen

RYAN

I must have fallen asleep, as when I awoke, I was in my dream woods again.

As soon as I realized where I was, I called out to him, knowing he wouldn't be far away.

"I know you're here Melakai—you may as well just come out!" I shouted, turning around in a circle until my eyes landed on the shirtless vampire. Yummy.

"You catch on fast, mi amor," he said, walking toward me.

"I'm a quick study, what can I say," I drawled, sarcasm thick in my tone. I didn't want to be here. I wanted to wake up so I could get my shit together and get the fuck out of the cabin and away from my sister.

"I am sorry if I upset you tonight. That was not my intention." I could hear the sincerity in his voice.

"Look, don't worry about it. It's just been a long day and night."

"Will you walk with me?" he asked, his hand extended toward me. I didn't have enough fight left in me to refuse, so I placed my much smaller hand in his and let him lead me through the woods. We walked a few minutes before he stopped us at the *lake and he sat down. He looked at me, asking me with his eyes if I would sit. With a loud exhale, I sat down reluctantly.*

"Will you let me tell you a story, mi amor?" I could see he was torn on whether or not to tell me this story, so I nodded. I mean, curiosity did kill the cat.

"Many years ago, the supernatural races used to be at peace. Until one day a greedy king fell in love with a woman of a different race, who was of royal blood herself.

She left her people to live with the king in his realm. They married soon after, and they spent many happy years together, so in love with one another. The king—slowly over time—became so obsessed with gaining power that he hurt many people and took many lives to get what he wanted. He wanted to rule all the races and be the king of all the supernatural kind. The queen couldn't stand by and let him continue to hurt others for his own selfish gain, so she tried to stop him.

"He saw her act as treachery and sentenced her to life as a slave. She was beaten, raped, and made to work as the king's personal handmaid. The queen was very powerful in her own right, but she could not access her full power because the king had a witch cast a spell to keep her weak; he worried that she would be the only one in his realm strong enough to kill him, so he took precautions to ensure that never happened.

"What the king did not expect was for her to fall pregnant to some warlock that was one of the many to defile her. The king could never sire children himself; he was sterile. He was enraged by the sight of her and the knowledge that she was carrying some other man's child within her womb. He locked her in the dungeon, planning that when she gave birth he would kill the child while she watched, as a punishment. The queen could not let that happen to her child. She saved what little magic she had left so she could portal the child out of the castle as soon as the child was born. She was almost starved to death by the time the

child came; the king was hoping that if she wasn't fed enough that the child would die in the womb, but that never happened. The queen gave birth to a healthy baby girl. She knew she didn't have long before the king came to kill the child, so she quickly teleported the child out of there, but she didn't have enough strength to take herself. She chose to save her child's life over her own. When the king came to collect the child, he was so angered at her defiance that he killed the queen with his bare hands.

The king never found the child, no matter how long and far he searched. What he didn't know was that the queen had cloaked the child so that no vampire may ever find her or harm her.

You see, that child would be one of the most powerful children to walk the earth; it was part witch and part fae—no one could ever match the child in strength or power. The only curse the child would bear from her mother was that she could never access the power herself, only her offspring.

Blinded by rage, the king unintentionally started a war by killing the queen. Her people wanted his blood for what he had done, and the king could not win a war against her people on his own. He needed the other supes to stand with him. He knew they would not stand by his side, for it was his own stupidity that started the war, so he needed to think fast.

And so he killed one of the leaders of another supernatural race and pinned it on the queen's people. He got what he wanted in the end—all the supes rallied to his aid. He told them that the queen's own people had killed her and tried to blame him because they wanted to start a war.

After the king had won the battle against the queen's people and banished them to their lands, he went in search of the child once again only to finally find the child and realize that the child had no powers of any kind. She was as human as they came, and the king went about his business, confident that she would live and die, as all weak humans did, not knowing that this human would pass on the power she inherited through her children.

And so it came to pass that the queen's daughter gave birth to twin girls, but only one child could receive the power of both fae and witch: the child with the purest heart, received those powers."

I had been listening carefully to his tale, making sure I had the details straight, and so after he finished I sat there quietly, trying to piece together the story. Then it suddenly hit me. I jumped to my feet.

"Wait—so you're telling me that my mother is the daughter of the fae queen, and my sister and I are half fae and half witch?" I screeched.

He stood and placed both his hands on my shoulders, almost like he was keeping me grounded for the bomb he was about to drop.

"No, mi amor, your sister is full witch. You are half fae and half witch. Only the child with the purest heart could wield the powers of both races."

Holy fuck.

"No. No, that can't be. My dad was a warlock, and my mom was human. I'm not who you think I am, and if what you say is true, what is the fae king to me?"

"Yes, in a way your mother was human, but only because her powers were inaccessible to her. The fae king is of no relation to you, as he was only king of the north and east at that time. The queen was the princess of the south and west. She would have been queen of fae realm had she not left to marry the king. During the Great War, her father died, so now Nicholas Stone rules the north, east, south, and west. They are all one kingdom now."

"Wait—who the fuck is the king, the one the queen married,

then?" I had a good idea who he was going to say, but needed him to confirm it.

"The Vampire King Randall Cane," he said dispassionately. How the fuck could the queen marry that asshole?

"Holy shit, he was the one that killed Jackson's dad, not the fae..." It was more a statement than a question, but he nodded anyway. "The fae didn't kill my father, did they? Randall Cane did, didn't he? He's still trying to take the leaders out so he can rule all the supernatural kind."

"I cannot be sure of that, but I do suspect it was him, and yes, he is still trying to take over, but he didn't account for Jackson surviving the war. He started trying to rule the wolves after the war had ended, but your father protected Jackson, and Jackson's people were loyal to him. They knew he would take the throne and responsibility that came with it when he was strong enough. By then it was too late."

"Why are you telling me this, Melakai?"

He had a look of regret on his face, like he was about to dump the world on my shoulders, and in a way he kind of was.

"Your sister and the king have decided to seal the fae realm, which means Farrarie will die, and if that happens, that means all the fae will die."

I knew the point of the story now—if the fae realm was closed, and if I am half fae, that would mean I would die along with them.

"I get what you are saying, but what the hell am I supposed to do about any of this? You saw what happened last night; my sister will never listen to me."

"You need to try, mi amor, for if they succeeded in doing what they plan, your people will die, as will you." He leaned down to look me in the eyes while placing his hands on my hips, and my body temperature skyrocketed. My body had a mind of its own whenever he touched me.

"They are not my people, okay? I will try to help them, but that does not mean I will ever accept being part fae, if it is true." With a nod of his head and a large exhale of air, he spoke.

"I can accept that and I thank you for helping"

There was one thing I couldn't quite get though, how the hell did he know all of this and how did he know so much. Was he a fae, no he couldn't be because he was a vampire an un-dead so to speak? I had to ask him, I needed to know but I had a sinking feeling I wasn't going to like his answer.

"How do you know all of this, Melakai?" I watched his face closely for the truth.

He tensed slightly and tried to cover it up as fast as he could, but it was too late—I had felt it.

"I knew the fae queen," he said, dropping his head in shame.

"Wait, so you were there when all of this happened?"

"Yes."

"Are you Randall Cane's son?"

"Yes and no." Vague much?

"Which is it, Melakai? And I want the goddamn truth," I said, pulling away from his grip so I could have a few feet of space between us. I couldn't think straight when he was so close, and he knew it too.

"I am his son through a blood oath, but not by blood."

"Explain, please." He sat back down on the grass and once again patted the spot next to him in invitation. I relented with a huff and dropped down beside him.

"When the fae queen first came to live with the king, I made sure I was the best and most trusted enforcer. I was assigned to escort the queen everywhere and guard her with my life always. I did this for many years, until the king banished her to be a slave, and even then,

I would look out for her. She was a kind and caring woman. She loved everyone and everything. It was just who she was. I thought the warlock that impregnated her had raped her like the others,

so, I ended his life. What I could never have foreseen was that the queen and the warlock had a bargain: she would bear him a child if he helped her open a portal back to Farrarie to her people, where she could get help. I killed the only hope she had for her freedom. I tried in every way I could to help the queen to escape, but all attempts proved futile.

Once the child was born, I tried to delay the king as long as I could to give the queen time to teleport her child out of the dungeon and into its new life. I never thought the king would kill the queen, and I was too late to save her. I made a vow in that moment to never let anything happen to the queen's child."

"So you knew this whole time where my mom was?"

"Yes."

"How?"

"The spell the queen cast was to cloak the child from any vampire that wished to harm her. I did not wish to harm her, therefore I was able to locate the child." His matter of fact responses were raising my ire.

"Why do you seem like this isn't a big deal? You knew where the fae queen's child was this whole time and never told the king? How do you know the king killed Jackson's father?" If he had helped the king commit these crimes, I would find a way to end him and the king both. I could never trust Melakai again if he had helped kill my father.

"I followed the king every night while the queen was locked up, to see what he was doing and if he would visit the witch that had blocked the queen's powers. I saw him lure Jackson's father away from his people on a false pretense of spies in his pack, swearing him to secrecy. That was how the king killed the pup's father. I told you I have no proof he was involved in your father's death; I only suspect that he did, because he's done it before."

I was trying so hard to keep up with what he was saying when a thought suddenly struck me.

"You saw, didn't you?" He tilted his head to the side, a look of confusion on his face.

"Saw what, mi amor?"

"What my mother did to me. You saw it all, didn't you?"

A look of pain, anger, and heartbreak crossed his face before he hung his head in shame. He didn't need to reply—his face and body language gave me all the answer I needed. I jumped to my feet and couldn't stop the words from pouring out of my mouth.

"You gutless, spineless, son of a bitch!" I screamed at him. He jumped to his feet and tried to grab me, but I side-stepped him and continued my rant. "You have the nerve to stand before me and claim to want to protect me from harm, when you let a monster abuse me for years, when you could have saved me from all of it. You just stood by and watched her beat me and starve me and tear me down to nothing. How do you look at yourself every day, knowing you could have saved a child from a lifetime of misery? You're a fucking coward!"

I slapped him so hard across the face that my hand developed a pulse. I couldn't stop screaming at him, calling him every name I could think of while pacing and swinging at him wildly. After a few minutes he finally had enough and grabbed both my arms and spun me around so my arms were locked behind my back and my back was to his chest. We were both breathing fast and hard. After he gained his composure, he spoke.

"I tried to help, Ryan, and I made it fucking worse okay, I confronted your mother while you were at school —you must have been eight or nine. I told her the truth of who and what she was. She didn't believe me at first, until I showed her my fangs and what I truly am. She screamed at me to leave and never come back, or she would kill you. She was mentally unstable. I couldn't trust that if I came to you and told you what you were, that you wouldn't tell her you had met me. I saw what happened that night when you came home from school, and I am so sorry, Ryan, for my part in making matters worse, I truly am." That was the first time Kai had ever called me by my name.

I was still trying to calm myself after hearing what he had said. I knew which night he was talking about—that was the night everything changed for me and my mother. She threw me down the stairs, and I hit my head so hard that I needed stitches and had a concussion. It didn't end there. After getting home from the hospital, she used the belt on my ass until I passed out from the pain.

Now I knew why she had done it: she hated me so much after finding out what I was that she was trying to beat the magic out of me. She was jealous of me.

"Get your hands off me now and let me go. I want to wake the fuck up now, and I want you to stay the hell away from me, Melakai Cane!" As I spat that last word out, I felt him flinch behind me, and I knew it was wrong to blame him for what my mother had done, but I didn't care. I was angry and hurt and even ashamed, and I wouldn't spend a minute longer with someone who watched my abuse and did not stop it.

He released my hands, and I spun around to look at him. His eyes betrayed his surface calmness; they had a storm brewing inside them. He finally gave up the staring contest and nodded.

He turned to leave, but stopped and looked over his shoulder and whispered, "I am so very sorry, mi amor; I wish I had done more. Just know that I was there, even if you do not remember." I had no idea what the hell that meant. I gave him a curt nod of my head and then everything went dark once more.

Chapter Seventeen

RYAN

I woke the next morning feeling more exhausted than when I went to sleep. I was in no rush to leave my room this morning, knowing I would have to face my sister. That was a conversation I was more than happy to put off.

I dragged myself out of bed and hopped in the shower, hoping it would release some tension in my body. After showering, I towel-dried my hair and put on a pair of my most comfy sweats and paired them with a plain black singlet, I threw a red and black checkered flannel shirt over the top. After changing, I went back into the bathroom to finish doing my hair, and when I looked at the mirror, I was shocked by the person I saw.

My eyes seemed more greenish-yellow, and my hair was shinier and richer in color. I looked more a woman than a girl. The changes wouldn't be noticeable to anyone other than myself, but I felt a surge of confidence shoot through me, along with an ember of hope that maybe some man might be able to love me for me someday. I quickly pushed those thoughts aside, because I had enough to worry about without adding man problems.

I ran a brush through my hair and tied it into a high ponytail. I needed to think about how I was going to tell the others what I had learned without making myself look like a crazy person. Easier said than done, if you ask me. Knowing I couldn't hole up in my room forever I pushed myself off my bed with a sigh and went to search for the others.

The boys were kicked back on the couches in the living room, watching TV. I bid them a cool greeting and went to the kitchen to find my sister. She was at the bench, staring out the window. I cleared my throat to get her attention.

She snapped her head my way, looking at me with eyes that I didn't recognize—it was like the light had been sucked out of her. She shook her head, and then her eyes changed from the dark green I had just seen back to their normal hazel-green color. I couldn't explain it, but something was not right with my sister.

"Morning," I said.

"Hi," was her frosty response. Wow, she thought she had a right to be pissed at me? Other way around, Stevie—you fucked up, not me.

"Look, I need to talk you about something," I said while taking a seat on one of the bench chairs.

"Unless it's an apology, I'm good, thanks."

"Are you fucking kidding me right now?" I couldn't believe this. She wants me to say sorry after she hit me? Bitch much? I was stunned.

"No, I am not. The way you behaved last night, and the way you spoke to me in front of the other leaders, is unacceptable Ryan. If you want to talk, apologize first, then we can work something out from there." I snorted, and she narrowed her eyes at me.

"You may think I am in the wrong here, but I am not, Stevie. You need to hear what I have to say, or it will be on your head when the treaty goes to shit," I said, my fury rising.

"The treaty is none of your concern sister; I signed it this morning when Randall came by."

Holy shit, she just sealed my death warrant and the whole of Farrarie with what she has done. I walked right up to my sister so we were eye to eye; she needed to see the truth in my eyes.

"You stupid fool; you have no idea what the fuck you have done. You are a murderer, Stevie! The blood of every fae will be on your hands, and *so will mine*." She just stared at me with a blank look on her face; I had nothing left to say to her. She wouldn't listen to anyone but herself; she thought what she was doing was right. I pushed passed her and went back to my room to think of a new plan, one that involved saving my life and the fae realm.

I went to sit on the day bed right by the window; it was such a beautiful sight to see the snow falling and watch the ground be blanketed with white. The sun was out, and there was a slight breeze outside.

It was a beautiful day. It helped raise my spirits a bit. Just as I leaned back on the pillows and closed my eyes, there was a knock at my door. Not bothering to open my eyes I told whoever it was to come in.

"Hey, squirt, we need to talk to you." I opened my eyes immediately to see both my cousins standing in the doorway; I waved them over and told them to have a seat. Chase closed the door and sat on the edge of the bed while Alex leaned on the wall beside the window.

"What's up, guys?" I asked, curious as to what they had to say.

"About last night..." Alex began but I cut him off.

"Don't cry over spilled milk, Alex. I'm a big girl, and I get it that you guys can't stand against her because she's your leader. It's fine. I don't blame you or have any ill feelings toward either of use for it," I said with a slight smile on my lips, hoping to ease their guilt.

Alex shook his head. "We do not condone what Stevie did to you, Ryan, nor do we agree with her decision to sign the treaty and seal the fae world from ours. A whole race cannot be accountable for the actions of a few."

"So what does this mean?"

"It means, squirt, we want to try stop her, and something you said caught our attention earlier," Chase answered.

"What did I say?"

"That your blood would be on her hands if she signed the treaty. What did you mean by that?" Alex asked with a quirk of his brow. You could always count on Alex to listen to every word someone said.

"It means that if she seals the portal to Farrarie off, she will kill all the fae, me included."

They both exchanged a look of worry and confusion, but Chase was the one who spoke first.

"Ryan, if you're thinking of taking your own life to prove a point, there are other ways! We can help you through this." He looked so broken in that moment, like he wanted to lock me away where no one could harm me and I couldn't harm myself. An inappropriate giggle burbled out of me before I could stop it; it was a nervous habit.

"This isn't fucking funny, Ryan. We're serious," Alex said, annoyance thick in his tone; I stopped laughing and answered him.

"I am not going to harm myself in any way, I promise you that. I have to tell you both something, but you may want to take a seat; it's a long-ass story." They both nodded and made themselves comfortable. "Where's Stevie?"

"She went out to see if she could get Jackson to sign the

treaty. He said he needed time to think about it, which I guess is a good thing," Chase said.

"Well, listen up." I recounted Melakai's story about the vampire king and fae queen to them. Their expressions morphed from awe to confusion, then hatred and anger. I could relate to how they were feeling, but rather than getting heated and being irrational, we needed to come up with a plan—and fast. If I know my sister like I think I do, she will be trying to get this plan done by whatever means necessary.

Alex leaned forward, placing his forearms on his thighs and asked, "Wait, so if the queen had a kid, and then that kid had twin girls, we need to find them and protect them from the king?"

"If he finds the child that inherited both witch and fae powers, we are all royally fucked," Chase said, exasperated.

I stared at them both, astonished at their failure to connect the dots. "Well, boys, we have already found the girls."

"Where are they, Ryan? We need to go get them now!" Alex demanded while pacing the floor. And to think Alex was the brainy kid of the family.

"One is out there, and the other is in here," I told them, Okay, maybe I was enjoying having the upper hand on Alex for once.

"What the fuck does that mean, Ryan? Stop being cryptic and spit it out. Their lives are in danger!" Alex retorted. I let out a loud huff of air before standing and looking at them both.

"Stevie is the first born twin, and I am the second born!"

"Dear God," Chase said, placing his hand over his mouth.

"I fucking know that, Ryan, but where—" Chase cut Alex off with a growl.

"You are not listening, dipshit; Stevie and Ryan are the granddaughters of the fae queen. Stevie isn't the one with both fae and witch power—*Ryan is.*" Chase turned to look at me, and he looked scared, but not for himself. Alex stopped pacing and stared at me in disbelief.

"Holy fuck, Ryan. This isn't good at all. If they seal the fae realm off, you'll die?" Alex asked

"Yes, Alex, if she goes through with this, I will die. We need to figure this out fast, but I don't know how to stop this. Stevie has gone so power hungry that I don't even recognize her," I said.

"I can agree that the power has gone to her head a bit," Chase said, shaking his head.

"We need to try talk to her tonight, and if she won't listen, then we're on our own," Alex stated grimly.

We all agreed to talk to her tonight at dinner. We all hoped she would see reason and stop this madness, but a part of me knew my sister wouldn't listen. The look in her eyes told me enough this morning.

After the boys had left my room, I went through my bag and pulled out my favorite book, *Night Flame,* by Catherine Hart. I sat back in my chair by the window, prepared to spend the rest of the afternoon reading, when a shiver ran down my spine. I jumped out of my seat and spun around to see a pair of yellow eyes glowing in the corner of the room. As those eyes drew closer to me, I realized that it was Simon, the fae that came to warn me the other day.

"Hi," I said, keeping my voice low so the others wouldn't hear.

"Hello, Ryan, may I speak with you, please?"

"Sure, hang on one sec, okay?" I dashed over to the other

side of the bed and grabbed my iPod so I could plug it in to the speaker. With that going, if anyone went past my room, they wouldn't hear us talking. As I set the iPod to play, the song that started was one of my favorites, Frankie J's song, "Obsession."

"Clever you are, my dear," Simon said as I walked back to take my seat. I waved to the bed so that he could sit, and he did. I looked at him, thinking that he reminded me of someone, just the way he moved and how he looked at me, but I just couldn't think who it was.

"What can I do for you, Simon?"

"I have been keeping an eye on things here in this realm regarding the treaty. I see your sister is still out for blood, as is the vampire king."

"Look, I've tried to talk to her but she won't listen. My cousins and I are going to try to talk to her tonight again."

"If she won't listen, what then?"

"Then we come up with a plan B." He looked at me skeptically for a moment.

"What are you?" I didn't know him well enough to share the truth, so I lied.

"I'm a witch," I said, looking him in the eyes. He tilted his head to the side and looked me up and down with an intensity that was deeply uncomfortable.

As an awkward silence settled between us, and then in a blink he was standing right in front of me. If I pursed my lips, I would kiss him. I took a deep drag of air through my nose; his scent was almost intoxicating. It was turning me on, and I felt my body heating.

Holy fuck, snap out of it, Ryan! You're acting like a hussy! I mentally bitch-slapped myself out of my thoughts.

"Next time you want to lie to me, try to do a better job of keeping your breathing steady and your heart rate normal. You're not very good at deception, are you?" He was looking me straight in the eyes, and I was rooted to the spot. I had to keep reminding myself to breathe. I couldn't speak, so I just nodded. He smiled; he knew what he was doing to me, and he loved it. Simon is attractive, don't get me wrong, but something just felt off, like it wasn't him I was feeling these feelings for. I couldn't explain it. "I must return to my people now, but I will be back soon. If you find yourself in trouble or in need of my assistance, just say these words."

He handed me a card with what appeared to be gibberish, smiled, and then he was gone. I put the card in the pocket of my sweats for safe keeping and prayed I never needed it.

After Simon left, I lay on my bed, thinking of everything that had happened. A week ago, my life was normal—or as normal as it could be. I was so bothered that things had changed so much.

After arriving in Alaska, everything went to shit pretty much straight away. I started learning about my family's secrets, only to wish they had stayed hidden from me. My sister had changed so much; she wasn't even the same person anymore, and after the other night, I found it hard to imagine how we could ever have a loving relationship again. We had only seen each other a few times over the years, but we always talked and texted as much as we could. I thought that not having Mom around would mean we could finally have a normal relationship —how wrong I was.

I needed to figure what the hell was wrong with my sister. I couldn't survive the loss of another family member; she kept me sane through so much of my life with our mom.

She would talk to me on the phone for hours when Mom was drinking or gone on a bender for a few days. Stevie would tell me, "Everything's going to be okay, you will be eighteen before you know it, and you can leave and come and stay with me." And that was the first thing I did when I turned eighteen and Mom vanished.

A knock sounded at my door and pulled me from my thoughts. "What?"

Alex poked his head in the door. "Dinner's ready, and Stevie just walked through the door. We have to try to convince her, Ry. I don't want to go against her, but if it has to be that way, so be it." His voice was just a whisper so the others couldn't hear our conversation.

I gave him a nod and stepped out of my room, trailing him down the hallway to the kitchen. As I entered, I saw Chase plating up the food, which smelled divine. I didn't notice how hungry I was until my stomach growled.

"Easy, tiger, dinner's nearly ready," Chase said, giving me a wink. I took a seat on the opposite side of the table to my sister.

Once I was seated, I looked at her and gave her a shy smile, which she returned. That helped relieve the tension in the air a bit. Alex took a seat beside Stevie, while Chase served each of us our plates. He had made an amazing spread: steak, potatoes, and a crisp green salad. I couldn't wait to dig in.

We all ate in relative silence. Every now and again, the boys would try to bring up stories from the past, trying to engage my sister and me into the conversation, but it never worked. After we all finished our meals, I pushed my plate away and exhaled a breath. I cleared my throat and looked my sister in the eyes as I began to speak.

"Stevie, I need to tell you something, and you must listen to me, because what I have to say is life or death."

"Like what, Ryan? Please do tell me what is so important." I gritted my teeth, not wanting to take the bait and engage in a fight with my sister.

"What you are doing with Randall Cane is wrong, and deep

down you know it. The fae didn't kill Jackson's father or our father, it was—" She cut me off before I could finish.

"You think you have the right to tell me what I am doing is wrong? What would you know about this world we live in? You are new to this life and know nothing of what lurks in the shadows. I am the leader of this coven, and I say what we do and don't do, am I clear?"

"If this coven is so great and powerful, how come I have never seen or met any of them then?" Stevie glared at me before answering.

"Because I have not allowed it. I will not take in someone who cannot respect the orders of their queen or someone who will embarrass our family. When you get over your insubordination and the victim act you play so well, then you will be welcomed into the coven, and not until then."

I was so shocked by her words that I couldn't answer her straight away; I kept opening my mouth and then shutting it.

"You have no right to speak to her like that, Stevie, and you know it. What you just said was a low blow and uncalled for. What the fuck has gotten into you in these past couple days? This is not you." I looked up to see Chase on his feet, chastising Stevie for her behavior.

"I am finally seeing clearly, cousin. Maybe you need to open your eyes and see what is going on around you. We are on the brink of war with the fae, and all you and Alex are concerned with is coddling my sister. If she chooses not to side with her people, then she does not belong here." Fuck that hurt, to hear my own sister say that I didn't belong. I was trying so hard to fight the tears that were threatening to fall.

"What are you saying?" Alex asked Stevie.

"She's saying that if I don't agree with her sealing the fae realm off, and start obeying her every command as my queen"—I said that last word with air quotes—"that I have to get my shit and leave, and I will not be welcome here anymore." I couldn't hold back my tears now.

"Stevie! You cannot do that; she is your sister, and you two just got each other back after all these years. You need to listen to her and hear what she has to say." Chase was trying to appeal to my sister, but it was clear her mind was made up.

"I have heard enough. Either she is on our side or she is against us. They killed my father, Chase!" Stevie screamed, and I could hear the heartbreak in her voice. My own heart hurt for her, but she was so wrong. The fae didn't have anything to do with our father's death.

"No they didn't! Randall fucking Cane did, Stevie!" I yelled back at her.

We were both standing at this point, staring at each other; her eyes were filled with disbelief and anger. Her eyes seemed darker, they were a dark green now.

"You're lying! Randall has done nothing of the kind. Ever since Jackson's father was killed, he's been the only one to see the fae for the blood-hungry monsters, and now that I am queen of the coven, I will be joining our forces with the vampires to ensure the fae never return to this realm."

My anger was reaching breaking point, and I could feel my magic rising inside of me. I took a few calming breaths to try to tamp down the magic burning inside of me; I didn't want to hurt anyone again.

"If you seal the fae realm, you will not only kill the fae, but you will also kill me. Randall knows this. He wants me dead, because he's afraid I'm the only one that can kill him." My sister just scoffed and pinned me with a death glare.

"And why, dear sister, would it kill you? And why in God's name would Randall be scared of someone like you? You have no control over your powers and cannot wield them. You are untrained and weak as a baby."

"Fuck you, Stevie. He wants to kill me because I am part—"

I was cut off before I could finish. The front door swung open and in walked Randall Cane and his enforcers, at least eight of them.

"What the hell do you think you are doing, Cane?" Alex roared.

"Keeping peace among our people," Randall said with a smug look in his face.

"What the fuck does that mean?" Chase snapped.

"It means that you are either with me and my decision, or against me," Stevie answered.

"Against you for what Stevie?" I asked.

"You either respect my decision and help us close the fae realm, or you are against me. I have the right to detain my enemy until I can figure out a punishment for disobedience," she snapped back at me.

"How could I be against you if I am not even part of your coven?" I tartly replied.

"Don't play coy with me, Ryan. CHOOSE NOW!" she bellowed.

I couldn't believe what my sister was doing. She was out of her mind, and there was no way in hell I was going anywhere with Randall. I looked at my cousins, seeking an answer as to what the hell we were going to do. Chase gave me a nod and a small smile; he was with me whatever I decided. I looked to Alex for his decision. He looked torn as to what he should do, but then he took a deep breath and gave a stiff nod. Alex would stand against Stevie, if it meant doing the right thing.

"I cannot let you do this, Stevie. I may be new to all of this, but even I can see what you are doing is wrong. I am begging you to reconsider." I looked to my sister, pleading with her to change her mind, silently begging for her not to do this and tear us apart. I just got Stevie back and now it seemed I was about to lose her again.

"You do not understand what you are asking, Ryan. I must do this for our people. It is our law—blood must have blood. You need to learn the ways of our people and fast. You will go with Randall until I can think of what to do with you."

"She's your fucking sister, Stevie! You can't do this. It's wrong and you know it," Alex said, exasperated with how my sister is behaving.

"Just because she is my sister does not mean the rules don't apply to her. She dares to defy me and thinks she can go unpunished!" she yelled.

At the mention of punishment, I could feel the magic coursing through my veins, and no matter how many deep breaths I was taking, I couldn't tamp it down. My anger was too strong. It was fueling the magic, and I couldn't stop it. One of Randall's men made a move toward me after receiving a nod from my sister, and as soon as his hand touched me, I exploded.

Blue light shot out from my hand, and he went flying back, landing unconscious on the floor. Two more men started toward me, and without thinking, I stretched my arms out toward them and they went sailing back, as well. One hit the wall with a cracking of plaster, and the other went through the window, sending glass shooting across the room.

"Stop now, Ryan, before you do something you cannot come back from!" Stevie shouted, but I was too far gone.

"Fuck you, Stevie; I will not let another person try to lock me away!" I spat at her. I was distracted for that brief moment, and when I felt two hands clamp down on my arms with a vice like grip. I screamed with rage. Alex rounded the table and shot a purple light from his hand, and my captor went sailing, unfortunately with me still in his grasp. Luckily, when we landed, he broke my fall.

"Run now, Ry!" Chase yelled while fighting with two of the guards. I looked to Alex, who was fighting another with magic. I went to make a run for the front door when Randall came out of nowhere and hit me hard in the face. I landed on the ground with a thud, hitting my head. I was stunned by both the blow to my face and knock to my head. I put my hand up to touch my head, where the thumping was happening and the shock of pain made me flinch. I pulled my hand away to see blood on it.

"You smell so good my dear," Randall sneered, hunger giving his voice a disturbing edge.

"Don't you fucking touch her!" Chase yelled from across the room. He and Alex were trying to get to me, but the guards wouldn't let up; they were all still fighting. I tried to bring my magic back by getting angry, but I couldn't feel it—it was just gone. Randall was on top of me in a flash, and I was pinned on my back, held captive by his weight. He leaned in close to my ear, his lips brushing my lobe, and whispered.

"I will not end you quickly. I will drink from you until you are within an inch of your life, then I will feed you my blood to heal you. I have a vast arsenal of ways to inflict pain on you. I have been waiting for you for *four* decades, and I plan to make you pay for all the years I was searching for you." He pulled back slightly so I could see his face, then he lunged like a cobra.

I screamed as soon as his fangs pierced my skin. He had a death grip on my head. I couldn't move. I heard my cousins shouting out my name, but I couldn't answer them. My eyes rolled, searching for help, and landed on my sister, who stood by, watching Randall drink, a smile on her face. The look of satisfaction on her face broke my heart. She wouldn't have to wait long for my death; I could feel my head getting light and my eyes getting heavy. I could feel the pull of death, and I welcomed it. Just as I convinced myself to let go, there was a whoosh of air, and Randall was gone.

I couldn't get my eyes to focus, and I was drifting in and out of consciousness. I felt an arm at the back of my head and then one under my legs. Someone was carrying me. I was trying to fight to open my eyes, but they refused. The harder I fought, the faster the darkness came, and eventually I couldn't fight any longer and darkness won.

Chapter Nineteen

RYAN

I could feel the heat of the sun on my face; it was so bright I could see it from behind my eyelids. I smiled to myself, thinking it was going to be a beautiful day, when I was suddenly hit with the reminder of what happened the night before.

I opened my eyes to see I was on a bed—but not my bed. I peeled the duvet off my body and flung my legs over the side. It was then that I noticed that I was not in my own clothes. I was in a silk nightgown; it was a low cut one to. Who the fuck changed me?

I hopped of the bed and walked over to the window. I had no idea where I was. I was surrounded by trees and open land. I turned away from the window to further inspect the room. In the middle of the room was a beautiful king-sized bed that I had just climbed out of, two flanking side tables, and a rug at the foot of the bed. The room had antlers on the walls, and a small open fireplace at the other end, with two single chairs positioned in front of it.

I was making my way over there when I heard the door open. I stopped dead in my tracks and looked to see who it was. I let out a large exhale of relief when I saw it was my two cousins. My smile dropped when I saw who walked in behind them: it was Melakai and Jackson. What the fuck were they doing here?

Chase rushed over to me and pulled me into an embrace, I had to tap on his back a few times before he got the hint that I couldn't breathe. He pulled away to look at me, as if to make sure I was really here. I was then yanked away by Alex, who pulled me in for another bone-crushing hug. He managed to let me go before I had to tap on his back. We all stood there staring at each other for a moment before Jackson finally broke the silence.

"I am very glad to see you are okay, Ryan." I gave him a small smile in return.

"What happened last night?"

"You nearly died," Alex stated with a look of anger on his face.

"I thought I was going to die to be honest, I couldn't get him off me" A shiver ran down my spine thinking about how close I had came to dying last night. Randall wanted me dead and my sister never lifted a finger to help. I could feel tears welling at the back of my eyes, I felt so betrayed. Chase put a hand on my shoulder and gave me a gentle squeeze.

"We thought we were going to lose you last night until Melakai came and knocked Randall off you, He helped us hold off the remaining guards and escape with you. If it wasn't for him, you would be dead and we would be Randall's prisoners right now." Alex said with a look that was begging me to understand what Melakai had done in order to save us. Obviously Kai had told them that I might not welcome his presence.

He went against his king and his people to save me and my cousins. I looked past Alex and Chase to meet Melakai's gaze.

"Thank you for saving me last night and for saving my

cousins. I am forever in your debt, Kai." I couldn't hold the tears at bay any longer. Kai saved us, even after I rejected him.

"I couldn't help you when you needed it most, mi amor, but like I told you, I will always protect you from now until my dying breath." I could tell he meant every word; he really would lay his life down for mine.

"Where is Stevie? What happened to her?" They all exchanged uneasy looks, but Alex was the one to answer.

"She got away. By the time we took the remaining guards down, she was gone." My sister is a coward. The next time I laid eyes on her, the gloves were coming off.

"Where are we?" I asked no one in particular.

"We are at my home," Jackson answered.

"Why are you helping us, Jackson?" I thought werewolves and witches didn't get along.

"Because what your sister is doing is wrong, and I cannot stand by and watch her hurt innocent people. My pack is divided at this time; some want me to agree with her and the king, the others do not wish death on innocent people." I could tell he was conflicted.

"I am sorry that this is all happening to all of you. I wish I had more to offer but I don't. All I can offer you is my help." Each of the guys gave a smile and a nod.

"The first thing we need to do is try find a fae, or a way to talk to one, so we can get some answers and warn them about what is going on," Chase said

"I think Ryan may be able to help with that." Jackson was looking at me with knowing smile; dammit, he knew all along I had been talking to a fae!

"What is he talking about, Ry?" Alex asked.

"She knows one of them. I could smell it on her the night we came to the cabin to sign the treaty." They all turned to me expectantly, waiting for my answer.

"Okay, so maybe I have talked to one a couple of times, that doesn't mean I *know* him," I sheepishly replied.

"HIM?" Jackson and Melakai boomed in unison. I rolled my eyes at their reaction.

"Is there something you want to tell us, Ryan?" Chase gave me an accusing look.

I let out a large exhale and told them everything that Simon had told me. Their faces morphed from stunned to angry as I spoke. I knew they would be upset, but I never expected them to be that mad just because I had spoken to a fae. Melakai and Jackson seemed to be sharing a look of understanding between each other, but I didn't have long to ponder that look before Alex spoke and disrupted my thoughts.

"So this Simon that you have been speaking to, is there any way you can contact him?" I went to feel my back pocket for the card he had given me and remembered I wasn't wearing my clothes anymore.

"Where are my clothes?"

"We can get you some clothes soon, but answer my question, Ryan!" Alex snapped.

"I need my fucking clothes, Alex—it's the only way to contact him." With a nod of his head he turned and left the room, coming back a moment later holding my sweats and top, both of which were spattered with blood. I grabbed them off him and retrieved the card from my back pocket.

"He said that if I ever need his assistance or help that I should say the words on the card." I told the four men in the room, and they all nodded and told me to go ahead.

"I think it's in Latin or something. I'll try my best. *Azarah metronia openinga portass!*" As I finished saying the strange words, a strong wind picked up in the room. Chase grabbed my arm and pulled me across the room to stand by Melakai and Jackson, and Alex followed us.

The wind started swirling into a circle, and it grew larger, almost to the width of a car, and it was growing taller than Kai. The wind was so strong it pushed all five of us into the corner of the room. Then as abruptly as it started, the wind died down. On the other side of the portal I could see a beautiful castle and a large expanse of open land so bright and vibrant that it took my breath away. Before I could get too lost in my thoughts, Melakai spoke.

"It's a portal to Farrarie. If we wish to speak to this friend of yours, I think we must enter his realm."

"Are you crazy? We have no idea if they know about what our kind is trying to do to them. They may want our heads on a spike," Chase retorted.

"If we don't go, they could all die! This may be our only chance," Jackson snapped.

"The portal is shrinking. We don't have much time. We must go," Kai said, taking a step toward the portal.

"I'm with you; I just need to let Tyler know he is in charge and that I will be away."

I huffed. "We don't have time for you to do an errand, Jackson, and we won't be gone long."

"I can speak into the minds of my pack, love."

"Come on, it's closing" Kai said, grabbing my hand and leading me toward the portal. The others followed close behind us.

As we passed through the portal and made it safely to the other side, we all looked back to see the portal closing and the room we just came from disappear before our eyes.

"I don't suppose he gave you a get-home-safely card, did he?" Chase asked, and we all chuckled at his attempt at a joke.

"I think we need to make our way to the castle," I told the guys.

"We cannot go there; that is where the king is." State the obvious much, Jax?

I had felt pulled toward the castle the moment I stepped through the portal. I just knew we had to go there.

"I can't explain it, but we have to go," I said, not waiting for them to start walking.

"Fine, but the first sign of danger, we high-tail it out of there and try find a way home," Jax retorted. He and Kai both seemed more agitated than the rest of us, but I didn't have the energy to figure out what their problems were.

"Agreed, and do not touch anything. Everything can pretty much kill you here, according to the books I have read," Alex said.

"Nerd alert, nerd alert!" Chase whisper-shouted, and we shared our first genuine laugh in a long time. And as a group, we began our trek.

After walking for an hour, we came to a small moat. We were trying to work out how to cross it in order to get into the castle when a drawbridge came down. Two guards came out from behind the bridge with swords drawn. I couldn't fucking believe it. I thought we had gone back in time; these guys were in armor, like in the medieval days.

Melakai put his arm in front of me and started taking slow steps back the way we came. Just as we all turned to run back the way we came, a whole fucking army emerged from the trees we just walked through. We were trapped.

"We can't fight them all," Jackson snapped.

"Chase and I don't have enough magic to even wipe a

quarter of them out, and Ryan doesn't even know how to use hers to help us," Alex snarled in reply.

"We protect Ryan or die trying," Melakai commanded. I was going to respond when someone cleared their throat behind us. I spun around and the boys turned to the side, not wanting to turn their backs on the army behind us. I could tell they were all pissed that none of them sensed the army hiding in the woods. The throat-clearer was a beautiful young woman. She must be my age or slightly younger.

She had pale blue eyes and beautiful white-blonde hair that was so long it was past her ass. She had curves in all the right places, and her skin was a pristine white, but it didn't look sickly.

"The king wishes to speak to you all, if you would please follow me?" she said and turned to walk back in the castle. We exchanged a look between ourselves, trying to figure out what to do. "You could always stay out here and take your chances with the king's army, I suppose. No harm will come to you, I swear it. The king just wishes to speak to you, and then you may leave." With a nod of my head, I started to walk toward the drawbridge. The others followed behind. I could feel the tension in the air—they were pissed that they had zero options other than to follow this girl.

Jackson and Alex shot in front of me, while Chase and Melakai fell in step behind me. They were boxing me in to protect me, and my heart swelled at the gesture. No one had ever wanted to protect me in my whole life, and now these four men were going to fight or die trying to get me out of here.

We followed the girl down long, winding corridors that were lined with big wooden doors on either side, none of which were open. The walls were made of stone, and no paintings hung on the walls. The only light we had were the fire sconces on the wall. Clearly they were not set up for electricity.

As we rounded the fifth corner we came to a stop at the end of the hall, where there were two huge wooden doors that were guarded by two hulking men. They wore the same armor as the two men from the drawbridge. I swallowed loudly and felt a hand squeeze my shoulder—it was Chase. I gave him a small smile; he knew I was scared, and he was trying to assure me that we were going to be okay. If a fight broke out, I would not stand on the side and watch them fight for me. I would fight for all of them.

"Open the doors. The king wishes to speak with the trespassers," the girl said to the guards.

The two men opened the doors, and we followed the girl into what appeared to be a throne room. It was huge, with a long black carpet that ran down the center of the room right up to the foot of the throne. The benches flanking the runner were filled with people. It was like the whole town had come by to see the circus.

I looked up to see a huge chandelier suspended from the ceiling, lit with hundreds of candles. There were six guards on both sides of the room positioned against the walls. The girl led us up to the end of the aisle and told us to wait.

We all stood stock-still, looking around the room. The people who had gathered were gawking at us right back. I saw a small girl with brownish hair and green eyes watching me curiously. When we made eye contact, she smiled, and I gave her a small wave.

"Rise for the king!" cried a voice from the room.

I leaned forward a bit so I could take a peek between Alex and Jackson's shoulders. When I saw him, I couldn't fucking believe it. The lying bastard played me like a violin, and I fell for it, because of his good looks and the way his voice made my body burn with need. I am such a fucking idiot. I watched as he stood before his throne and commanded his people to sit. Once they were all seated, he turned his attention to our group. He had a sly smirk on his face that made me want to punch him square in the jaw.

"I scent witches, a vampire, a werewolf, and something else I can't quite place," he said, amusement thick in his tone. I snorted, knowing my cousins would hate that he referred to them as witches and not warlocks. "Ahhhhh, the halfling does not agree. Why don't you both step aside so I can see her?" he said.

"Over my dead body!" Alex snapped.

"You either move, *witch*, or I will move you, the choice is yours."

"You can try, king, and its *warlock!*" Alex said with disdain in his voice.

"Have it your way, boy. Guards, remove them, and if they resist, kill them," he bellowed.

We all looked side to side to see the guards coming our way, Melakai drew his sword that I hadn't even noticed was strapped to his hip. Alex and Chase's hands started to glow, and Jackson started growling and snapping his teeth at the approaching guards, and his hands turned into claws. I could feel my magic well up inside me and my hands were glowing. I spoke for the first time.

"You touch any of them, and I will kill you all, mark my words. Your king will not save you from my wrath. We did not come here to fight; we came here to help you." I just hoped that they believed me. I don't think I could even kill a fly intentionally.

"Stand down!" the king shouted, but I could hear undercurrent of amusement in his voice and it pissed me off. It felt like he was laughing at me. "Come forward, little one." I put my hand on Alex's shoulder to tell him to step aside, and he looked at me, his eyes communicating the fear he felt on my behalf. I gave him a small smile and nudged him to the side.

"Hello again, love," the king said once I had stepped out from the cover of the others. I looked up to see those to beautiful violet eyes staring at me with amusement and desire, just like the last time I saw him.

"Hello, your majesty—or should I say Nico?" I asked the king. I could hear a collective sharp intake of breath at my words echoing through the room.

RYAN

The people in the room must think I have a death wish for addressing their king so informally. I turned to look over my shoulder at the others, whose expressions ranged from angry to confused. I guess both my dream boys are real—just fucking great.

"Hello, my love. I was wondering when I would see you again. I never thought you would have to use the card I gave you, but I would be lying if I said I wasn't glad you did. I just wish you had come alone," he said with a wide smile. Wait— what did he mean *give me the card?*

"Well I wish I could say that I was glad to be here, but then I would hate to lie to the king himself, even if he thinks he can lie to others." I heard more gasps, but I ignored them. "If I came alone then they would have hunted me to the end of the earth until they found me, so I thought it better to bring them along. Saves us all the hassle, you know. And what card are you talking about?" I said.

"Oh, my love, there is so much for you to learn. We fae can glamour ourselves." I must have had a look of confusion on my face, because he explained further. "It means we can change our appearance." With that said he changed right before my eyes and became the man I knew as Simon, the fae that visited me in the cabin back in Alaska.

"Oh, for fuck's sake, you lied to me yet again? What a fucking champ," I snapped.

"You will address the king in a respectable manner or lose your tongue, mutt," one of the guards boomed, stepping forward. A wall of four men closed rank in front of me, tense looks on their faces.

"You come anywhere near her or lay a finger on her head, I will end your life slowly" Jackson growled.

"Is that a threat, dog?" the guard snapped. Jackson moved to toward the guard but stopped dead in his tracks when the king spoke.

"You will close your mouth and not speak unless asked to, Cyrus. How dare you insult my guest," he snapped.

"Forgive me, sire," Cyrus said stiffly before resuming his position against the wall. The king stepped down off his podium and walked toward me, and Jackson growled. Melakai came to stand beside me.

"If I wished to harm her, Kai, I could have done so many times. I am of no danger to her," Nico murmured. They stood staring at each for a minute before Melakai finally stepped aside and let Nico near me. He stopped directly in front of me, and his scent was so overwhelming that I had to take a step back. I looked up to see him smirking; he knew what he was doing to me and he loved it. Judging from the growl Kai let out, he knew what Nico was doing to me as well.

"All of you will leave us now," the king shouted, never breaking eye contact with me.

"But sire..." said Cyrus, who clearly couldn't keep his trap shut.

"I SAID NOW!" Nico roared.

Everyone got up and quickly scurried out of the room. Nico never took his eyes off mine, even after we heard the big wooden doors close. Chase interrupted our staring match by clearing his throat.

"Do you mind telling us why the fuck you gave Ryan that card if when she uses it you intend to kill us?" Chase asked. Nico finally looked away from me to stare at my cousin.

"Because the card was only meant for her, not for all of you," he said without an ounce of remorse. I cut Chase off before he could even reply.

"Why did you lie to me, Nico?"

"I never lied to you, love. You just never asked me what my full name was. Also, the glamour was for my protection, as well as that of my people, in case you chose to side with your coven or tell your sister I had visited you," he said with a shrug.

"What a dick," I muttered under my breath. I heard Melakai cough to try to hide his laughter. Alex, Chase, and Jackson did nothing to try to hide their amusement. I was angry and embarrassed at the same time. I couldn't believe that both the men I have had sexual encounters with in my dreams had deceived me.

I thought I had made them up in my own head, but they were both real and willingly entered my mind without me knowing the truth. Nico just scowled at me and let out a huff of air before he spoke.

"My name is Nicholas Stone, but I go by Nico. Simon is just a persona I created," he said, shaking his head, like he didn't like having to explain himself. I'm sure he wasn't used to it either. He was a king—royalty never had to explain themselves, I suppose. I gave him a stiff nod in response. I was still pissed at him.

"Why the grand display of power when we arrived, *your majesty*?" I asked. He rolled his eyes at me for calling him "your majesty" but he couldn't very well say anything about it, because he was. Suck it up, buttercup. I have a lot more sarcastic remarks coming your way.

"When my scouts tell me that there is an unauthorized portal opened in my land, and that two warlocks, an alpha, and vampire walk through, with a being that scents as a witch but also scents as a fae, I go on high alert. What can I say?" Nico says while smiling from ear to ear, fucking arrogant prick.

"So you did all of that for show? Gather your people here just to show them how powerful you are?" I sarcastically ask.

"Well, no, they were already here, as I was briefing them on the coming war. You just happened to arrive at the wrong time, my dear" he drawled.

"We have important matters to discuss with you," Melakai said to the king.

"Well, well, look who finally got off the leash from his daddy," Nico replied. Kai stepped toward the king until they were nose to nose.

"Watch yourself, Stone. You may be the king, but you are not invincible," Kai snapped. Jackson caught Kai's arm and reeled him back to our group.

"You two need to grow the fuck up and put your past shit behind you," Jackson said to them both. Alex, Chase, and I all exchanged a look of confusion. They were acting like they knew each other—what the fuck is up with that? But before the other two could reply to Jackson's statement, they were cut off.

"Are we missing something here?" Chase asked the three men, who seemed to have some very big secrets.

I moved to the side where Alex and Chase were standing, making my allegiance clear.

"I guess I'll tell them then, but first, let's go to my study. It's a long story, and I'm going to need a drink to tell it," he said, heading toward the back of the room behind the throne. Jackson and Melakai followed him, while Chase, Alex, and I walked slowly behind them. Once we reached the back of the room, Nico opened a door and ushered us in.

The room was huge—it had stone walls with lit sconces, a large lit fireplace on the side of the room, and four couches set up at the back with a plush red rug in the middle. A huge oak desk was positioned on the other side of the room, but it was clear of papers.

Nico made his way over to a small table near the couches and motioned for us to sit. He poured himself a drink and offered one to the rest of us. I declined, but the four other men accepted a drink. I sat in the middle of one couch with Alex and Chase on either side of me. Jackson sat on the couch to our left, Kai sat to the right of us, and the king sat directly in front of me on the remaining couch.

"This is a long story, and no one else knows this story besides the four of us," Nico started.

"Wait—four? What four?" I asked.

"Yes, there is someone else, but we will get to him soon. Let me tell you how we all came to know each other first. Many years ago, there were two young boys who loved to run away from their duties and escape to the Earth realm for some fun and to watch the other supernatural kinds.

They wanted to get a look at what the others could do—how they could wield magic and how they could fight. Also so they could go to a pub and get drunk." Nico and Kai both laughed at that. "One night the two boys snuck out of the castle and went to the pub. The two boys were drinking beer when they heard a fight just outside of the pub. When they got outside, they saw two young teenage boys being attacked by at least twelve humans. The boys could tell by their scent that the two getting beaten were supes, so they helped the two boys and ran off the attackers. Once all that was done they all stood staring at each other, not sure what to say or do, until one of the boys that was getting beaten said—" Nico was cut off before he could finish.

"Hi, I'm Jackson, and I'm going to be alpha of the greatest wolf pack the supernatural world has ever known," Jackson said, shaking his head while laughing, Nico smirked at him and then continued.

"One of the other boys from the other realm said—" He was cut off again.

"Nice to meet you, Jackson. My name is Melakai, but my friends call me Kai, and I am the right-hand man to the prince of the fae." My jaw hung open at Melakai's admission. I looked to my left and right, and felt a little comfort that both Alex and Chase had similar looks of shock on their faces. The king continued.

"The other boy that came with Kai then said, 'Hi, my name is Nico, and I am the prince of the north and east castle in Farrarie.' All the boys then looked to the other one that was standing next to Jackson and he said—" The king was once again cut off, this time by a whoosh of wind, and then out of nowhere, a man appeared. I yelped and dove behind Alex and Chase, who stood and blocked me from the view of the strange man. I could see through the gap between their bodies that the man had a cloak on, with the hood up so you couldn't see his face.

"Hello, my name is Dominic. My friends call me Dom. I am a hybrid, the first of my kind. My mother is a fae, and my dad is the alpha of the New York wolf pack."

"How the fuck did you get in here?" Alex asked the man.

"Clearly you weren't listening to the story, young one; I am the fourth member of this group, I guess you could call it. I was just filling in my part of the story; the others got to say their part, so why shouldn't I get to do mine?" Dominic asked, tilting his head to the side. "Now if you both step aside, I would like to see the young woman that has been causing so much trouble with my brothers."

"Why don't you take the cloak off and stop scaring her, then she might be more forthcoming and her 'boys' might step aside for you." The sarcasm was thick in Jackson's tone, but Alex and Chase both shook their heads stubbornly. I stood up behind them and pushed through the middle of their bodies. Chase grabbed my arm as I made it to the front of them.

"Take your hand off her now before I remove it for you," Melakai snapped at Chase.

"You need to mind your own fucking business, Cane. We cannot trust any of you with all the lies you have told, and especially your new friend that has just arrived," Chase retorted, I cut them both off from any further arguing by speaking for myself.

"I have to agree with my cousin. We cannot trust any of you. I trusted you, Nico, and you played me for a fool. The same goes for you, Melakai. You both have lied to us, and now you expect us to stand here and listen to more of your bullshit? I don't think so. Nico, thank you for allowing us here, and for the story, but we want to go home now! Also, new guy, nice to meet you, and hope you have more luck with these jackasses," I said as I headed toward the door. I looked over my shoulder to make sure Alex and Chase were following, and just as I turned back around, a figure appeared in front of me. I screamed.

"I did not mean to scare you, little one. Please do not leave just yet. You have not heard the rest of the story" Dominic said.

I had to take a few calming breaths to try to slow my heart rate. I felt Alex and Chase bristle behind me; they did not like our exit being blocked. I didn't even know how we were going to get home, but we would have figured it out, I'm sure.

"Why should we listen to anything you all have to say? All they have done is lie to me since I met them. Why would that change now?" I asked Dominic. He smiled and leaned down to whisper in my ear.

"Because, my dear, they will tell you the whole truth. They could not do that before, but they can now because we know which side you are on." I could feel the power radiating off of him... it was like a drug.

"Please let us explain further, Ryan, and it will all become clear. If you are not satisfied with the truth we tell you, I'll transport you back to the Earth realm and leave you be, I swear." Nico was pleading with me, and I saw the truth in his eyes.

"This is the last chance I will give the three of you; if any of you lie to me again, we are done. Do I make myself clear?" All three of them nodded and took their seats. I gave Alex and Chase a smile as I passed them to take my seat on the couch we occupied before. They followed suit. Dominic sat beside Nico on the couch in front of us. Once he was seated, he pulled his hood back, and a gasp escaped my mouth before I could stop it.

He was beautiful. He had silver-colored hair that was short on the sides and long on the top, but that wasn't the part that got my heart fluttering. It was his eyes.

He had eyes that could see into your soul; they were magical, and the color was a beautiful violet color like Nico's, but brighter. His skin was so tanned that it looked like he had been kissed from the sun. His hair color and skin color made his eyes stand out like beacons. He leaned forward and placed his forearms on his legs. The cloak he wore did nothing to hide the muscles underneath.

"Would you like to hear the rest of the story, or should we just go on a tour and I can show you my room?" Dominic said with a wink, Nico leaned over and slapped the back of his head.

"Excuse Dom, he tends to think with his other head ninety percent of the time," Nico said while scowling at Dom.

"What can I say—when I know what I want I go for it," Dominic said with a smirk at me; I shook my head and laughed.

"Well anyway, before I was rudely interrupted for the third time—after all three boys introduced themselves, they went back to the pub to have a few beers and chat. None of them knew much about the other races, only what they had learned in books. The boys continued meeting secretly for many months, and they quickly became the best of friends. They even swore a blood oath to each other, which lasted for many years—until everything changed. Did you each want to tell your sides, or should I tell the rest?" Nico asked, looking from Jax to Kai and then to Dom. Melakai spoke next.

"I stayed with Nico for many years. I know we may all look young, and we have let you think that, but in truth we are all far older than you may comprehend. Jackson is the youngest of us," Kai said looking at me to see my reaction.

"If you were here with Nico growing up, does that mean you are a fae?" I asked.

"I was a fae until I was turned into a vampire."

"Why were you turned into a vampire? How did you come to be with Randall?"

"When the fae queen started seeing Randall, she thought no one knew. Nico and I started following her to the Earth realm and learned of her affair with the vampire king. We knew she was going to flee Farrarie, so I was tasked to follow her and guard her by Nico—she was his intended bride, after all. Neither of them wanted the marriage, for they never loved each other; they were only to wed for the purpose of merging both the kingdoms together.

I followed the queen to your realm and guarded her until I was ambushed by a group of vampires one night and nearly killed. I didn't know at the time that the queen had begged Randall to save me, as she and I had become close friends in the time we were in the Earth realm. Randall did as she asked, thinking I would not survive the change, but to his utter dismay, I did. The reason I can walk in the daylight is because I was turned with fae blood in my system, and after Randall learned this, he would feed from the queen and draw some of her blood to feed his most trusted guards."

"Oh my God, so that's why you hate the name Cane?" I asked, finally understanding why he hated me calling him that.

"Yes and no. I hate the name because he forced me into the blood oath that I could not refuse, thereby making me his heir to the throne should he ever fall. It ensured that I would never be able to rise against him if there should be a war between the vampires and the fae."

"What did he have over you, Kai, to make you go against your people? And why can't you rise against him in battle?" I asked.

"He used the queen's life as a bargaining chip. I failed her and my best friend," he said, anguish plain on his face. "It is written in the blood oath that I cannot rise against him. I am bound by blood to honor that or I will die. Me being here isn't going to break the oath, but if I try to harm the king in a fatal way, the oath will take its pound of flesh."

"Wow, I never expected that. I just thought you were his loyal solider," I said, feeling guilty for assuming the worst of him.

"It is not your fault, mi amor; I gave you no other reason why you should think differently of me."

"But if you all broke the blood oath to each other, how can you not break it with the king?" I asked. Dom was the one to answer my question.

"The blood oath was broken when Kai turned. Technically he is dead; he has no heartbeat, so upon his change the oath broke between us, and more things changed." All four of the guys had solemn looks on their faces.

"Please fill in the blanks for us. How did you all stop being brothers or whatever you want to call it?" Chase asked.

"There were many factors: the fact that Kai chose being next in line to the throne instead of his brothers, and the fact that the fae killed my father," Jackson stated flatly.

"I never killed your father, nor did my people. I swear it to you, Jackson, if you would have just given me the chance to explain when this all happened none of this would have come to pass," Nico said, with such conviction in his voice that you just knew he was telling the truth.

"I never chose the throne over any of you. I never wanted it. I just made Randall believe that I did so I could better protect the queen and Sophia," Melakai said, looking Jackson in the eyes.

"But you failed, didn't you, Kai! She died anyway, and you still get to be prince of the vampires! The only reason he keeps you around is for fear that the queen's blood supply will run out, and then he'll still have you, a willing fae blood donor," Jackson spat at Kai. I saw Kai flinch at Jax's words; they were harsh and hurtful, and Jax meant every one of them.

"I never helped him kill the queen! I tried to SAVE HER!" Melakai shouted. Jackson stood from his seat, and Kai did the same. They were staring into each other's eyes, a silent battle of wills to see who would break first.

"That's what you say, but where were you when my father was killed? None of you came to my aid...not one of you. So much for brothers," Jackson snarled. He was making his way to the door when Dom spoke.

"The fae didn't kill your father, Jackson—the vampire king did; Kai has been working with Nico and me to try to bring him down." Jackson stopped dead in his tracks and spun around.

"How the fuck do you know that, Dominic?" Jax snapped.

"Because I followed him and saw him do it, Jackson. I cannot do anything to harm him, therefore I could not tell you outright—not that you ever gave me the chance," Kai answered.

"Okay, guys, can we cool down for a minute? Because we are not getting anywhere with this story," Nico said while motioning for Kai and Jackson to take their seats again.

"I will finish the story if no one else interrupts," Dominic said, and we each gave him a nod and he continued.

"Not long after Kai was turned, we all felt the snap in the line, so to speak, when the blood oath broke. I was here in Farrarie with Nico. We knew neither of us broke it, so we traveled to the Earth realm to check on the others. We saw Jackson with his pack when we snuck onto his lands, so we knew it was Kai who had fallen. We traveled to the manor of the vampire king, and what we saw through Randall's window was almost impossible to believe. Kai was on his knees in front of Randall, and we saw him drink from a chalice full of blood and watched his eyes change color. We knew then that Kai was not dead, but had been changed into a vampire. We waited for Kai to meet with us like we normally did every month at the pub, but he never showed. We couldn't contact him or see him. We tried to plan a raid to steal Kai from Randall and bring him back here, so we could have our brother back. We never expected that the night we raided the manor that Kai and Randall wouldn't be there. That was the night Jackson's father was killed."

Chapter Twenty One

RYAN

"So you guys all knew who killed my dad?" Jackson roared.

"No, we did not. We suspected that the vampires were behind it, and when we tried to come to you and tell you this, you tried to kill us both!" Nico yelled.

"Because there was fae scent all over him! How the fuck do you explain that? But you, Melakai, you have betrayed me the most. You knew and never said a word," Jackson shouted at Kai.

"I tried to tell you and the others, but you would never listen. You all hated me ever since I was turned. You never let me explain what my reasons were for the change. You just assumed I turned my back on you all," Kai shouted, his face a mask of anger. All these guys were so quick to judge each other and turn their backs, when all they had to do was just open up their ears.

"We all tried to tell you, Jax, but you were not ready to hear what we had to say." Dom spoke with such sympathy; you could feel how heartbroken he was for not being able to help his friend in his time of need.

"So that explains why Kai and Jax fell apart from you all,

but what happened between you two?" I asked, motioning between Nico and Dom.

"Nothing. Dom and I remained close. We tried for many years to help our brothers, but they rejected us many times," Nico answered.

"So when I told you all who the fae was that I was talking to, you knew who he was? And the reason you didn't want me to go to the castle when we arrived is because you knew who lived here, right?" I asked, looking at Jax and Kai.

"Yes," they both said in unison. At least they had the decency to look ashamed of themselves.

"Well, that explains why they were super uptight about the whole thing," Alex said with a chuckle. Jax and Kai shot him a death glare.

"Shut up, Alex. Why did you both come here, then, if you knew we were bound to see Nico?" I asked.

"Because I would follow you through the fires of hell, mi amor. I wanted to protect you. I thought Nico would punish you to hurt me," he said with a sigh and looked at the floor. I knelt down in front of him and placed my hands on either side of his face and lifted it so he could look me in the eyes. I didn't miss the growl that came from Jackson, or the snickers coming from the other four males in the room, but I chose to ignore them and focus on the broken man in front of me.

"Thank you for wanting to protect me, even if it meant fighting your brothers. I now understand why you did what you did when I was younger. You stayed away, hoping that one day I would be free of her and be able to live a normal life. You just never banked on me seeing my sister, did you?"

"I am sorry, but yes, that was my wish. I wished that Randall would never find you, because he would use you and then kill you." I could tell Kai was ashamed of his involvement in all this, and I hated that he felt like this.

"What do you mean *use her*?" Alex asked, always so observant.

"Her blood is the key to allow all vampires to walk in the daylight."

"Why her blood?" Nico asked Kai.

"Because she has the power of fae and witch, which means her magic is stronger than even Dom's," Kai replied.

"Holy fuck—so that's why he killed the alpha. He wanted to take the blood of all the leaders, so when he did eventually find the child, he had the most powerful blood to feed himself," Dom said with a faraway look in his eyes, like he was watching the pieces all fit together in his mind.

"Wait, if that's true, then that's why Randall is pushing the treaty, so he can crown the two new leaders. It was never about sealing the portal to the fae realm; he used Jackson and Stevie's hate for the fae to push them into agreeing with the treaty, and then he was going to kill them," I said, finally putting all of my puzzle pieces together as well.

If Randall took out all the leaders and drank their blood, that would make him one of the most powerful supes ever.

"Fuck, you could be right, Ryan. I am sorry that I doubted you, my brothers. I was too overwhelmed with my own grief and the loss of my father to see the truth; will you all ever be able to forgive me?" Jackson asked, looking to each of his brothers. They all nodded and shared tentative smiles.

"Melakai, I ask your forgiveness, as well, my brother, for I should have never tasked you with the job of keeping the queen safe," Nico said, looking Kai in the eyes, with his hand outstretched. Kai looked at his hand for a moment then stepped around me and put his hand in Nico's. I took a seat on the couch next to the spot Kai had just left.

"You are forgiven, my brother," Kai said while pulling Nico into a bro hug.

"So, this whole time, you three have been working together, trying to bring Randall down?" Jackson asked. They all nodded their heads.

"Why have you all waited this long to try take him down?" I asked, feeling like it was the obvious question.

"Because Randall has something that belongs to us, and I need it back before we can take him out. He is the only one that knows where it is." Nico had so much sadness in his voice that it made me want to take him in my arms and make the hurt go away. *Where the fuck did that come from? I need to get my head back in the game.*

"What is it?" Alex inquired.

"Something of great importance to me, and I need it back." What could be so important to a king that he had to have this *thing* back before he went to war?

"So why don't you just ask him or make a trade? I'm sure he would give whatever it is back to you for the right price," Alex reasoned.

"No, he won't. I have tried for many years. What he has ensures that I will not attack him, even if he starts this war against my people."

"Then you are a coward, if you let your people suffer," Chase snapped.

"No, he is not. What he is doing is the right thing. You do not understand the circumstances," Dom snapped at Chase.

"Then tell us so we understand. We came here to help your people, Nico. My cousins have gone against their coven, and I have gone against my sister, who I love more than anyone else in this world. I gave her up for the life of your people.

We have given so much up for the sake of you and your people; the least you can do is be honest with us!" I shouted. I was shaking, my anger rising. I couldn't stop it. I could feel my magic bubbling up. If they didn't start being honest with us soon, I was going to lose my grip.

"You need to calm down, Ryan, you're starting to glow," Jackson warned, taking a step toward me. As soon as I raised my hand to motion for him to stop, a blast of blue light shot from my hand and sent Jackson flying back into the wall.

"Holy shit, Ryan, stop!" Alex shouted

"I didn't mean to! I swear, it was an accident!" I snapped at him. I pushed my way past Alex and Chase and ran to Jackson. Dom, Nico, and Kai were already bent down beside him. I bent down near his head and lifted it so it could rest in my lap. I couldn't stop the tears from falling. I was a monster who hurt people, and I hated myself for it.

Jackson's eyes fluttered open, and he groaned as he tried to sit up. Dom placed a hand on his chest and told him to lie still for a few moments more. I bent over him so he could see my face and spoke softly.

"Jackson, I am so sorry. I didn't mean to hurt you, I swear. I am so damn sorry."

"Shush, it's okay. It's not your fault, Ryan. I know you didn't mean to do it. Now if you could back up so I can stand, that would be great," Jax said, looking to his brothers, who nodded and moved back. Once on his feet, he leaned down to offer me a hand up. I accepted it and let him pull me to my feet and into a tight embrace.

"You can let her go now, Jax," Nico said, irritation clear in his voice. Jackson let me go and stepped back, but his hands were still on my shoulders. I looked into his eyes and saw raw desire; it set my heart racing, but not for the reasons Jackson was thinking. Don't get me wrong, he was hot—but I didn't feel for him what I felt for Kai, and if I'm being honest, I didn't feel for Jax the way I did about Nico, either. Fuck my life.

Someone cleared their throat, which derailed my train of thought, thank God.

"Now if you two love birds would break apart and stop picturing each other naked, that would be great." Dom didn't apparently have a filter. I looked out the corner of my eye to see Nico slap the back of his head yet again. I moved away from Jackson and sat on the couch Jackson was occupying before I sent him flying. Dom took the seat next to me and everyone else took the same seats from before.

"I think you need to tell us what Randall has over you, king, before we risk our lives to save your people," Alex said.

"My sister. Randall Cane has my sister." Well that was a fucking game changer, now wasn't it?

Chapter Twenty Two

RYAN

"It all makes sense now; Kai couldn't come back after the queen died. He stayed with Randall so he could try and protect your sister. You sent your best friend into the lion's den to try to infiltrate Randall's enforcers, which he did. What you didn't expect was how far said bestie would go to protect the queen and then your sister. You have not retaliated to Cane's threats for fear of him hurting your sister. Kai followed us here with an agenda of his own, didn't you, Kai—you needed the king to think you came to Farrarie for me and not to tell Nico what you had learned," I said breathlessly. I knew I was right; I could feel it in my bones.

Dom started clapping beside me, and I turned to see the biggest smile on his face.

"They seriously do not deserve you. I swear, you are smarter than what anyone gives you credit for." Dom had such awe in his voice as he spoke. Wait—did everyone think I wasn't smart?

"What he means is everything you just said is right, all of it, actually," Melakai responded.

"Why did he take your sister?" Alex asked.

"Because she is my half-sister. Her mother was a witch, and Cane thought she was the one, but she isn't. Ryan is the one with pure blood," Nico said, looking at me with a sad smile on his beautiful face.

"So what does this mean for Ryan?" Chase asked

"That she can never fall into the hands of the vampire king, or a war will break out that might very well be unwinnable. I have no idea what the blood from you will do to his strength." I had forgotten all about Randall drinking from me until Kai just mentioned it.

"We need to make a plan, and fast. I will teach Ryan how to master and control her powers. I believe I am the only one strong enough to do that, and she needs to be ready, if her blood is supercharging Randall. We need a weapon of our own to beat him," Dominic said while giving me a devilish smile. That guy seriously had a huge ego and no regard for serious situations.

"But first we must send you all back. Dom will accompany you, and I will get to you as soon as I can." Nico didn't seem worried that my blood could potentially make Randall stronger then all of us. He just wanted us to go home. What a dick!

"Why do we have to go back now?" I asked, looking to the four alpha males in the room for an answer.

"Because I need to go back and explain my actions for saving you, so I can stay on the inside of Cane's manor. I also need to locate Sophia, before this war breaks out. Jackson needs to get back to his pack and prepare them for war. Dom will stay with you and your cousins to help you train. Nico needs to remain here and to prepare his people for battle," Kai said with a somber tone.

"Hang on a second—you just said she was your half-sister? And Dom said he was the first hybrid?" Alex asked the group.

"I am the first, because I can access both sides of my blood-line; I can change into my wolf form as well as use magic. Sophia can only use her witch magic, not her fae, so she is just a low-level witch, essentially." Dominic's answer seemed harsh, but it was the truth.

"I see. So does that mean I will be able to access both sides of my magic?" I asked no one in particular.

"Yes, you will be able to use both sides, with training. You have already shown how strong you are, but you are only using your witch magic, not your fae magic. That is why I will accompany you and your cousins home, so I can train you to use both sides," Dom answered.

"Thank you, I will try not to let you down," I said with a sheepish smile on my face, I looked over to Nico, only to see him trying to avoid looking at me at all cost.

"You will not let me down, sweetheart. I have faith in you, and we know you can access both sides already because you don't glow purple. That's the dead giveaway," Dom's answer explained why I didn't have the same color as my sister and cousins.

"We all have faith in you, mi amor. You just need to have faith in yourself," Kai said with such gentleness that it made my heart swoon a bit.

"How can you all be so sure? You guys don't even know me that well, and you are putting so much trust in me to save a world I didn't even know existed until a few days ago." I started pacing . These guys are putting so much pressure on me and what if I let them down, I would never be able to forgive myself if I let a world fall because I wasn't up to the task.

"Because I have been told that you will save Farrarie, I know someone who can see things. The fae realm will make it, with your help love." Nico seemed so confident that I could do this.

"I was just a normal teenaged girl a few weeks ago, and now here I am about to fight the only family I have left in this world —well, aside from Alex and Chase. But still, Stevie is my twin." I couldn't help the rising pitch in my voice as I thought about my sister. I was holding it all together as best as I could, but it was getting too much for me to hold in. I needed to get my shit together before my magic exploded out of me and I hurt someone else.

"Ry you are the strongest person I know. You have been through so much, and yet here you are, still standing strong and still trying to help others, even when no one helped you," Chase said, looking ashamed.

"Chase is right. Ryan, you are strong, wise, and selfless. You can do this. I know you can, because the cousin I know doesn't quit, and she sure as fuck isn't a pussy who runs away when shit gets hard! I know you are scared, and we all are too. We are about to take on the most powerful clans in the world, and the only way we are going to be able to even have a chance at winning this thing is if you man up and get your ass training so you can master your powers and help us win this thing." I looked Alex in the eyes and could see he believed every word he said, bolstering my confidence. With a curt nod and smile on my face, I gave both my cousins a hug and thanked them for their kind and empowering words.

"I feel like as long as I have your faith and support, I can do this. I think," I told the group with a forced laugh. "All joking aside, though, let's get the heck out of here and get our butts home and start training. If I know my sister, which I do, she will already be getting her soldiers together to shut Farrarie off from Earth."

I don't like the idea of fighting against my own coven, but I had no choice. They were loyal to Stevie, and they had no idea who I was, or that I even existed.

"Then we need to move fast. We need every minute we can get to train you, Ryan. It will be hard, and you will hate me each and every minute of it, but it will be worth it once we win the war." Dominic had a look on his face that I couldn't quite place, and it started to raise the hairs on the back of my neck. There was something these guys weren't telling me. A quick glance at both my cousins they looked like they were wondering the same thing. Before I could even ask the question burning in my mind, Chase voiced it for me.

"What aren't you telling us? And don't bullshit me either."

"It may not even come to pass," Nico protested.

"Whether or not it does or doesn't happen, we have a right to know whatever it is. After all, we are planning to go to war against our own coven for your people." I agreed with everything Chase had said; I want to know what these guys are hiding.

"Tell her, Dom," Nico ordered with a sigh.

"You may be king, brother, but you are not *my* king, so watch the way you speak to me! If your sister does not surrender, Ryan, we will have to take out the threat by any means necessary." Dom cast his eyes downward, clearly anticipating my unhappiness. My blood started to boil, and my hands started to glow blue. Alex and Chase jumped back, and before I knew what I was doing, I raised my hands at the four men in front of me and blasted the whole lot of them across the room. Nico crashed into the far wall, and Dom smacked into the door and then crashed to the ground with a groan. Jackson was blasted through the nearest window, and Melakai hit the book shelf and collapsed the shelves, sending books cascading down on his slumped body.

"Holy fuck, Ry! You just smashed the shit out of them without even trying," Chase said with his hand raised in the air, trying to give me a high five. I just glared at his hand and he quickly dropped it and stepped away. I turned back to face the four men I just blasted; they were all standing now and dusting themselves off. At least they all had supernatural healing, so if they were hurt it wouldn't last long. I did feel bad about what I had just done, though, and at the same time I also felt good about it.

If they really thought I would let them harm my sister, they were badly mistaken. I would never let anyone harm my sister, no matter what she has done or will try to do.

"We are sorry for upsetting you, mi amor. That was not our intention. What the others were trying to say is that we understand that Stevie is your sister, but if the choice comes to stop your sister or save a whole world, would you be willing to make that sacrifice?" I knew what Kai was trying to do, and he was right, but it still made me angry that he would even ask me that question.

"How am I supposed to answer that, Kai? Save a whole world or kill my sister—those are my only choices?"

"Ryan, we know that she is your sister, and that she is all you have left, but we are here too, and we are your family. I know it's not the same, but if it comes to it, you have to make the right call. Stevie knows what she is doing by siding with Cane, and that is on her, not you! She has made her choice, and now it is time for you to make yours, cousin." Alex was right; I needed to pull my big girl pants up and make the choice, but I would never harm my sister if I could avoid it, and that right there might just be my weakness.

Chapter Twenty Three

RYAN

"Now you all must go through the portal so I can seal it. Dom will be the only way to contact me until I unseal all the portals. I cannot take the risk that your sister or Cane will send an army through to kill my people before we are even ready. They won't make it far if they do, but still I don't want them here."

The only portal that would be left open was the main portal to Earth that kept Farrarie alive.

"I will go first to make sure that it's safe." Kai gave me one last look before he stepped through the portal, followed by Dom, then Jackson.

"I'll go ahead of you both." With a nod from Chase, Alex stepped through. As I was about to walk through the portal, Nico grabbed my arm. I looked up and saw those beautiful violet eyes pleading with me. I felt anger rise inside of me at the lies he told. He knew he was real when he came to me in my dreams, and he knew I was real, and never did he or Kai tell me the truth. I felt like such a fool; I gave them both so much of me in those dreams, and they lied.

"I know this is hard for you, but please believe me when I

tell you I never meant to hurt you, love. I had always intended for us to meet, but not like this." I couldn't bring myself to feel bad that he was feeling like shit; in fact, I thought he deserved to suffer. He and Kai both deceived me; they're not the ones who are feeling foolish, only I am, because they knew the truth all along.

"Now is not the time for this, Nico. I already have so much on my mind and so much to wrap my head around...the last thing I need is for you to fuck with my head some more. I will train and help you win this war, but as far as everything else, it's finished.

Don't ever come to me in my dreams again. Do I make myself clear, *your majesty?*" I could hear the anger in my voice as I told Nico how I really felt. The worst part is that most of it was lies. I missed having fun with Nico and Kai in my dreams, and how they made my body feel. But now it just felt like what we shared was tainted by their betrayal.

"Yes, Ryan, you made your point. Just please promise me one thing?"

"What?" I said with an eye roll.

"When this is all over, will you give me a chance to explain why I came to you and why I kept the truth from you?"

"I'm not making any promises I can't keep, Nico, so if there is nothing else, I really think we should be going before the others get worried."

"Very well, love, be safe and look after yourself, please," he said before leaning down and placing his lips on my forehead. The touch of his lips sent a shiver down my spine. I could feel the heat creeping up my neck and into my cheeks. The bastard had a satisfied smirk on his face when he pulled away and I itched to send him flying once more. I couldn't fight my body's reaction to his touch, even though I hated it.

Chase clasped my hand, and we walked through the portal. I never looked back, but I could feel Nico's eyes burning a hole in the back of my head, and that put a smile on my face. Once Chase and I entered my bedroom at Jackson's house, it was exactly the same except for the three alpha males and Alex standing against the far wall. I felt like I was a piece of meat in a lion's den, the way three of them were looking at me. We were stuck in a staring match until Alex cleared his throat.

"Now if you three are finished eye-fucking my cousin, you filthy pigs, let's get to work on a plan, aye?" Alex had so much anger in his voice that I think I even flinched a little. Chase had a glare plastered on his face, as well. It was no secret my cousins didn't like the men standing in front of us, but in order for this to work, we all had to get along, or try to, at least.

"I know each of you have issues with each other, but that needs to stop for the time being. I am not going to put up with you all squabbling like a pack of school girls."

I made sure to look each of them in the eye as I spoke so they knew I was serious. They each gave a nod, agreeing to what I asked.

"I think we should start with the history of each race first thing in the morning. Take the rest of the afternoon to chill." Dom was looking at me as he spoke, and I gave him a thumbs-up. Not so mature, but I couldn't formulate the words right now. I was nervous as fuck.

Kai walked over to me and gave me a quick hug, like he knew I was breaking down inside and just needed to be reassured that we were going to be okay. He gave me a small smile and I couldn't take my eyes off his mouth. I wondered what it would be like to kiss him in real life. I used to fantasize about Kai and Nico being real...what it would be like to finally have someone who would love me and protect me. And now here they were, and things were so complicated that none of my dreams could be reality. A throat-clearing shook me from my depressing thoughts.

"Well, now that we got that sorted…it's been a long-ass day, and I think we could all use a bath and something to eat." Trust Chase to be the one thinking of food, but he was right—I was hungry and wiped out. Kai stepped back and faced Jackson.

"I will stay here with Ryan tonight to make sure she is safe." *Uh, a bit presumptuous, don't you think, Kai?*

"Oh like fuck you are. I will stay with her, not you, *enforcer*," Jax snapped.

"Now, now, ladies. I will be the one to stay with her, since you two can't get along," Dom said while winking at me. *What is up with him and winking?*

"Piss off, you horny bastards! No one is staying with my cousin. Chase and I will be the ones to stay with her," Alex shouted, motioning them to the door. I was getting pissed now—they were all talking about me like I wasn't even in the freaking room. That was about to stop right now.

"All of you can kiss my ass! I don't need a babysitter in my room, and do not ever talk about me like I can't make my own choices. I am a grown-ass woman, and no one will ever take away my freedom to choose what I want again! Do I make myself crystal fucking clear?" I was seething, and I know I went over the top, but I couldn't hold back. Control was my trigger button.

"Oh, Ry, I'm sorry. I never meant to upset you, I promise." I could see Alex meant every word he said when he looked at me; he was never a good liar—his eyes always gave him away.

"The only reason we want to have someone in the room with you tonight is because we're worried about your safety. Your sister or Randall could ambush you, and it would just give us peace of mind if someone was here to watch out for you.

Please consider it." I never thought about it like that, and deep down, I knew that Dom had reason to be concerned. "You can choose who you would like to stay with you, if that helps, and just so you know, I am an outstanding big spoon." Oh my God, he was relentless. I sent him a glare in return, and he just laughed.

There was no way I was choosing Dom; he would never sleep on the floor, and judging by the way he was eyeing the bed I had slept in, he was thinking the exact same thing. I couldn't choose Jax, 'cause that would just hurt Kai, and the way Jax looked at me, I knew he wanted in my bed. There was only one man here I had eyes for, and I couldn't choose him either, because we had a lot to work out. Which meant my "choice" wasn't much of a choice at all.

"Alex, would you and Chase be okay with staying with me tonight?" My cousins both had a satisfied look on their faces, like they knew I was always going to pick them.

"Of course we will, Ry, we wouldn't have let you stay with any of these predators." Chase seemed pleased with himself after saying his piece. He walked straight past me and collapsed on the bed with a huge exaggerated sigh, just to rub it in the other's faces. Jackson gave Chase a look of utter disgust and growled. Before I could even comment on it, Dom slapped the back of his head.

"Dude, you really need to chill out. We all have to work together, and trying to kill Ryan's cousins isn't going to help anyone, now is it?"

"Since when did you become so mature, Dominic? Do not forget where you are," Jackson spat back at him.

"Well! Before this gets out of hand, we should all get cleaned up and then grab something to eat and work out a plan for tomorrow." Alex to the rescue—he was always the level-headed one of the family.

"Very well. I will send Tyler to get the three of you in an hour. He will escort you to the dining hall." With that said, Jax, Kai, and Dom exited the room. I made my way over to the bed and plopped down next to Chase. I was so exhausted. I really just wanted to hide under the covers in this beautiful soft bed forever. Alex made his way over to where I was lying on the bed, pulling me to him and wrapping his big arm around my shoulders. I leaned my head against his chest and let the tears fall. Alex held me while I cried, and I could feel Chase shift on the bed behind me and then he was rubbing my back, trying to soothe me.

"I am so sorry that you have to go through this, Ry. I wish there was something Alex and I could do to make this better."

"Thanks, Chase, but we can't run from this or hide from it. I need to woman up and get my shit together. I just don't want to hurt my sister. I still love her more than anything." I was sobbing more now just thinking about having to make a choice between my sister's life and the survival of Farrarie.

"Shhhhh, it's all right, Ry. Chase and I will always be here for you, and we will help you get through this." I was so blessed to have two such amazing cousins. They went against all they have known to help me. I sat up straight and turned on the bed so I could face both my cousins.

"I just want to say thank you to both of you, for all you guys have done for me over the years, and for what you are doing for me now. I know this can't be easy for you guys, and I just want you both to know that if either of you should want to return to your coven, I would totally understand."

"That will not be happening, Ry. We stand with you." Chase gave me a small smile which didn't quite reach his eyes.

"Chase is there something you aren't telling me?" He looked to his brother, as if asking permission to answer my question, and now my interest was piqued. Alex gave a small nod for Chase to continue.

"My family—I mean myself, Alex, Mom, and Dad—have had doubts about Stevie for a while now, even before your dad passed away. Stevie started to change over the last six months, almost like she is a whole new person. She stopped hanging with us and wasn't home whenever we would go visit her and your dad.

Your dad was starting to get worried about her too—they were fighting all the time over him needing to step down as coven king so he could pass the title onto her."

I was shocked to hear this; Stevie had told me Dad was her best friend. "I know this is gonna be hard to hear, and for you to even believe us, but what I am about to tell you is the truth. Will you let me finish explaining before you go off your rocker?"

"I will keep my trap shut until you are finished Chase." I gave him a small reassuring smile, and Alex leaned over and grasped my hand and gave it a quick squeeze.

"Three weeks before your dad died, Alex and I went with our parents to your dad's house so we could discuss coven business. When we got there, the front door was open, so we all just walked in. We could hear shouting from the kitchen. Your Dad and Stevie were screaming at each other. They were so wrapped up in their fight that I don't think they even heard us come in. Stevie was out of control. She said, 'Mark my words, Dad—if you do not step down and let me take over, you will regret it. Ryan isn't even half the witch I am, and if you give her the crown, I will take her out as well.'"

I gasped, I knew where this story was going, and I didn't want Chase to tell the rest of the story, but no words would come out of my mouth. "The next week, Mom and Dad met with your father in private, and he told them that he was going to get you back from your mom and bring you home, so he could train you and pass the crown onto you." I couldn't sit still a moment more. I stood up and started pacing the room, mulling over everything Chase had just said. One question came to mind. I stopped and turned to both my cousins, and Alex must have read my mind, because he answered before I could voice it.

"He wanted you to have the crown, Ryan, because he never trusted that Stevie would do right by our people. He knew she was power-hungry. She even told us that she wanted to be the most powerful witch and rule all the races. She tried to convince your father to go to war against Jackson and Randall so our coven could rule."

Chase chimed in then.

"Oh and let's not forget about the whole marriage thing."

"Wait, what marriage thing?" I asked.

"Well, Stevie wanted to rule over all, so she thought that if she could get your dad to pass the crown onto her after he took out Jackson and Randall, she could then approach the fae king and offer an alliance through marriage." I was boiling now, and I could feel my magic rising. How dare she think that she could go and marry *my* Nico!

"What the fuck do you mean, *my* Nico?" barked Chase. Oops. With a sigh, I began to explain how I knew Nico.

"You know how Melakai came to me in my dreams?" They both gave me a nod, so I continued. "Well Nico use to come to me in my dreams, as well; that's why I knew who he was when we went to Farrarie."

"Wait—so if Melakai and Nicholas Stone have come to you in dreams, does that mean Jackson and Dominic have too?" I could tell Chase was pissed, knowing that not one but two supernatural's have been visiting me in my sleep, but before he could get me more upset, I answered.

"No, just Kai and Nico. I swear I didn't even know who Jackson was until I met him in the woods the day of Randall

Cane's party—and I met Dom the same time as you guys did." They both seemed less tense after that.

"So anyway, back to Stevie—are you saying that because my dad wouldn't take out the other races and agree to give my sister the crown, she killed my father?" My voice rose to a high pitch when I reached the last part of my question.

"We don't think she did it herself, but we do think that she organized for someone to take him out." Alex wouldn't look me in the eye while telling me this, and I could tell from the tone of his voice that he regretted not intervening over Stevie sooner. I went back to pacing, trying to sort all my thoughts out.

I didn't want to believe anything that my cousins were saying, but what would they gain out of lying to me? I knew my sister had a thirst for power; I could see it in her eyes when we arrived in Alaska. To have our father killed, though—that was extreme. I needed proof. If I did find out that Stevie had our father killed for her personal benefit, I would go after her with everything I had, trained or not.

Chase, Alex, and I took turns getting cleaned up after our conversation. The shower here was to die for; I felt like I had washed all the bad away. Jackson had someone drop by with clothes for us to change into, which I really appreciated.

Tyler turned up a short time later to lead us to the dining hall, which was just a short walk from the room we were staying in. I could hear loud noise Dom and voices coming from the double doors just ahead of us.

"My people don't take kindly to your kind, so stay close and we shouldn't have a problem." He had a satisfied smirk on his face that I just itched to slap right off. I knew Tyler didn't like us because we weren't wolves, but how fucking dare he judge us? Before I could retort, he pushed the two double doors open, and we were hit with the smell of roasting meat and the sound in the room amplified, almost as if the doors were acting as a sound barrier.

No sooner had I entered then the room went completely silent—I mean, you could hear a goddamn pin drop. I never liked being center of attention—hated it, actually—and right now I felt like I was a prized filly on show. I ducked my head down to avoid their stares, but I could feel their eyes burning holes into me.

"Put your head up, Ryan. If you want these people to believe in you, then you need to show them that you are strong." Chase murmured, and I knew he was right. These people were about to go to war because of my sister, and I was here in their home, asking them to fight with me to save a world that wasn't theirs. There were long tables and bench seats spread out through the huge room. I could see men, women, and children, and a broad variety of ethnicities represented. Before I could see more, a man shouted.

"The Alpha's bitch is a half-blood! Why would we help some low-level witch that can't even use her own magic?" I could hear the hatred in his voice; he didn't want me here, and I couldn't blame him for that—he didn't have any loyalty to me. But who was he to call me a bitch?

"You say anything like that again to my cousin, you hairy piece of shit, and I'll pummel your fucking face in!"

I loved Chase for sticking up for me, but we were outnumbered here, and I didn't think for a second we could actually win if a fight broke out. I mean, there must be at least sixty people in here.

"What are you gonna do about it, witch, huh?" The angry

voice belonged to a huge mountain of a man…I mean, this guy must be nearly seven foot, and he was all muscle, with shaggy black hair that just touched the tip of his ears and eyes they looked so dark they were almost black. We were about to find out what color they really were—he was making his way toward us, pushing people aside, to get to me and my cousins. By the looks of things, no one in here cared if he killed us.

I looked to Tyler for help, but he was just standing by with a smirk on his face. I made a promise to myself that if we got out of this hall alive, I was going to punch that asshole in the face. Before the hulk could make it to Chase, I jumped in front of him and put my hand out to tell the hulk-man to stop. Unfortunately, between the fear and adrenaline, I must have sparked my magic, because the hulk went flying across the room and landed on top of a table, which collapsed instantly from the weight of him. It was like it took everyone in the room a second to catch onto what I had just done, then the room erupted: the screaming was deafening, and some of them started throwing things. I put my hands over my head so I didn't get hit in the face by a plate that some lady just threw at me.

Chase pulled me into his chest and spun around so that he could cover me, but just as quickly as the roar started, the room fell silent once more. I peeked out from Chase's arms to see Melakai standing in front of us, fangs out, and body coiled tight, ready to fight.

"The next one of you that comes after Ryan will have me to deal with. If any of you so much as even looks at her disrespectfully, I promise you, your shifter healing will not be able to heal you fast enough." Melakai's words sent a shiver down my spine; I could feel he meant every word he said. Now I understood why he was the head of the king's enforcers—he was freaking scary when he wanted to be. And fuck me sideways if the lethal tone of his voice wasn't making me so hot and wet for him.

"What makes you think we're scared of you, vampire prince? You may have a reputation of being a killer, but even the great Melakai Cane can't take on forty adult male werewolves by himself," jeered a woman with long shaggy brown hair and dull brown eyes.

"Ahhhh, Jessica but he isn't alone, love. He has me and two warlocks, as well as the strongest being alive on his side." God bless Dom and his power to just appear anywhere; he was standing right beside Kai. I straightened and stood on Kai's other side with my head held high, looking her dead in the eyes, daring her to make a move against us. If she had the power to kill someone just by looking at them, I would be dead. Chase stepped up beside me and Alex stood beside his brother, the five of us against all of them. I didn't like our odds, but I knew we would all go down swinging.

"Don't make me laugh, half-breed! You think that bitch standing there is the most powerful thing in world? Give me five minutes with her! I bet my life I would kill her in the first thirty seconds." A few people started laughing with her, and I felt my magic rise with my anger.

"You make one more threat like that, Jessica, and not even your father will be able to save you from my wrath!" It was Jackson who spoke, striding through the double doors. By the look on his face, he was pissed off at what had just transpired. "How dare you disrespect my guest like this?" He was screaming at her, and everyone in the room was bowing their heads.

Kai whispered in my ear, "All wolves must follow their alpha's orders. They are bowing their heads to show Jackson that they are submitting to him and don't want to fight. If you look an alpha or any wolf in the eye for too long, it is seen as a challenge."

"I have looked Jax in the eye a lot, and he has never tried to attack me or challenge me," I whispered back, but Kai didn't get a chance to respond as the plain girl spoke up.

"They aren't even pack, and you invite them into our home! You even let an enforcer in, the leader of the vampire king's army, not to mention two warlocks, a mutt, and a halfling," she said with a lip curled in distaste. I hated this girl already. She had no idea who I was or what the fuck I had been through in my life. I was done holding my tongue—this bitch was going down.

"How about I show you what this halfling can do with no magic?" I took a step forward to go over and slap that smirk off her plain face when Kai reached out and grabbed my arm. Jax let out a growl—who was he growling at, I wasn't sure. At that moment plain girl started laughing, and it had an edge to it that I couldn't understand.

"Oh my God, this is too good! The Alpha has finally found his mate, and she doesn't even shift. Does she even know that she is your mate, alpha, or have you not told her, in case she fancies the enforcer more then you?" I jerked my eyes to Jax and he tried to quickly mask his expression, but it was too late—I had already seen it.

"Do you wish to challenge my leadership, Jessica?" Jax was looking her directly in the eye, his tone icy cold. Plain girl went pale; she knew what Jax was doing. He was issuing her with a challenge, and by the looks of things, it was one she wouldn't win. She lowered her head and submitted to Jax.

"That's what I thought. If you ever disrespect me like that again, I will exile you from this pack." I heard gasps and murmurs around the room, but I couldn't take my eyes off Jackson. "I don't give two shits if your father is an elder and is on the council—he will not be able to save you from exile or my wrath. Do I make myself clear?"

Plain girl didn't move or speak for a moment; her head was

still down, and then she finally nodded and pushed past a few people blocking her way so she could leave the room. When she got to the double doors that we came through, she turned back and shot me a vicious glare. I gave her my biggest smile and waved. She screamed and slammed both doors open and made her exit. I know it was childish to taunt her, but I couldn't help it. After all, she did start it.

Chapter Twenty Four

RYAN

Jax lead us all to a table in the far corner. I sat down between Alex and Chase, and Dom, Kai, and Jax were on the other side. Dom was sitting directly in front of me and wore a sly smile on his face. I couldn't help but grin back at him—his carefree, mischievous attitude was infectious.

Tyler returned carrying some plates and was trailed by a small, frail-looking girl who must've been about my age. She had long blonde hair that was past her waist and the most striking blue eyes that were so pale they almost seemed white. She was absolutely beautiful, and I totally had a girl crush going on. Tyler set three plates out in front of the three guys opposite me, and then the girl set mine and my cousins' plates in front of us. That's when I noticed that my cousins couldn't take their eyes off her, either. Just as she was about to turn to leave, I felt an internal push to talk to her, one that I couldn't ignore.

"Hi, I'm Ryan, and these are my cousins, Chase and Alex." I pointed out who was who, and she gave each of them a shy smile and then finally looked at me.

The moment her eyes landed on my face, her pupils went

completely freaking white. Alex and Chase jumped out of their seats and reached for her, but Tyler threw an arm in front to stop them.

"You cannot touch her when she is having a vision, it could harm her." I had no idea what the hell Tyler was saying, and the look we were giving him must have prompted him to explain further. "Aurora is a seer. She can see into the future and the past—it is a rare gift to have, and it is unheard of to be able to do both, so she is one of a kind." Just as Tyler finished explaining what was happening, Aurora spoke from behind him.

"You can move now, Ty, I'm fine, I promise." He reluctantly moved aside so we could see her, and sure enough, her eyes were back to being a beautiful blue. "I am very sorry I gave you all a fright. Sometimes my visions come on so suddenly." Alex stepped up and held his hand out for her to shake.

"Hi, I'm Al—" Aurora cut him off with a smile.

"I know exactly who you are, Alex, and I also know who you are, Chase," she said. "I have seen you both many times in my visions; you both play a huge role in Ryan's rise." Alex and Chase both looked at each other and then looked back to the blonde beauty standing in front of them. I pushed my way between the two of them so I could see her clearly.

"Hello Ryan, I'm Aurora." I stuck my hand out to her, and when she placed her hand in mine, I went icy cold, head to toe. I couldn't see anything for a moment, and then it was like a movie was playing: I could see my life from when Stevie and I were born, and then when my dad left with Stevie. I could see my childhood with my mother, and all the horrible things she used to do to me. I wanted it to stop, and I was screaming and begging, but the memories kept playing.

I could hear yelling in the background, though I couldn't make out the words, and I knew I couldn't take much more of this. The look of disgust in my mother's eyes was splintering my heart. I never wanted to see that look again. Just when I thought I couldn't go on, it cut off, and I could see the room again. I tore my hand from Aurora's and pushed past her, running toward the exit, tears streaming down my face. I was sobbing so hard I could barely breathe. I heard the guys yelling out to me to stop, but everything in me said to run, and I did.

Once I was out the double doors, I turned left and ran down the hall. Everything was a blur, and I was turning left, then right, then left again, until I finally found a door that looked like it led outside. I swung it open and spilled out into the yard. I ran right into the woods that flanked the yard. I don't know how long I ran through the woods, but I finally slowed when a creek came into view. My arms and face were stinging from scratches from branches that had slapped me as I'd ran.

I sat down on the grassy bank, buried my face in my hands, and cried. I was crying for the shit mother I'd had, and my crappy childhood;

for my dad dying before I ever got a chance to get to know him. For the sister I just got back and then lost again. It seemed like there was always someone who wanted to hurt me, from my mom, to my sister, then Randall, and now the wolves. I just couldn't understand how I could be so disposable to everyone.

I was sobbing so loud I didn't realize people had arrived until one of them put a hand on my shoulder. I didn't know who it was, and I didn't care. Let them kill me and allow me to be done with all this. I just kept my head buried in my hands and continued sobbing.

Strong arms came around me and lifted me up. I moved my hands away from my face and saw that it was Jackson that had come for me. He didn't say anything, he just sat down and held me in his lap while I cried. His big, warm body was comforting, and before long my tears dried, and I was left feeling embarrassed that Jackson and the others had seen me break down. I couldn't see them, but I knew Kai and Dom were sitting on either side of Jackson. I could just sense their presence.

"I'm sorry for running out, I...I...I just couldn't... I mean, I needed air and I—" I couldn't form a coherent sentence. I was still hiccupping from crying, and Jax saved me from further embarrassment.

"You don't have to explain, sweetheart, I don't know what happened back there, but it must have been bad, because you ran out one door and Aurora ran out the other." I knew Jax was worried for both me and Aurora; I could hear it in his voice.

"Did you want to try telling us what happened back there, love?" For once Dom wasn't being a smart ass. He actually sounded really worried, which made me pause and look toward him. I could see the worry lines etched on his face. I glanced to my other side to see Kai giving me the same look. These three badass guys were brought to their knees by a woman crying. If this wasn't such a serious moment, I think I would have laughed. It was then I realized how I was sitting—I was right between Jackson's legs, with my back against his chest. I went to move so I could sit somewhere else, but Jackson wrapped both his arms around my waist and pulled me flush against him again. At this point I must have been as red as a tomato.

"I don't think so, little miss. You will remain right where you are until I am certain you won't take off on us again." I heard the smile in Jax's voice, and it made me relax a little.

I let out a long slow breath and begun to tell them what happened between Aurora and I.

"When she touched my hand, everything went dark and then all of a sudden my entire life was all I could see, and it was like a movie. I mean, I could see from the time I was born all the way up to now. The memories I saw are things that I have been trying to forget for years. It was just too much to handle." I didn't want them to know what happened to me at the hands of my mother. Kai already knew some, at least, but I didn't want to share that with the others.

"What happened in your past does not define you. It may have shaped you into the person you are today, but that does not mean that you are your past. What you went through made you stronger and smarter in ways that no books would ever be able to teach you. You are like a phoenix, so you need to rise above the ashes of your past and sort through those horrible memories, because they are not you, Ryan; you are a badass halfling and heir to the most powerful witch coven in the world." I couldn't help but snap my head in Dom's direction—it was the first time I have ever heard him speak seriously. I felt Jackson turn his head that way as well, and from the rustling behind me, I suspected Kai was staring too.

"Oh, for the love of God, don't look at me like that. I can be deep and meaningful at times, just like the rest of you." Dom seemed sheepish after we all focused our attention on him, but his words meant so much to me. He was right. I wasn't who my mother said I was. I wasn't worthless, I wasn't a nobody. Mom wasn't around to hurt me now, but I kept letting the memories of what she had done to me define who I was. I knew I was changing and trying to make myself stronger by not letting others make decisions for me, but I was still a long way from being the strong independent woman I wanted to be. I still had nightmares every few nights, and I would wake crying and searching every corner of my room to make sure my mother wasn't there. I snapped out of my thoughts when I felt Jax rub his hand up and down my arm. I looked to Dom again and reached out to grab his hand; he let me hold it and gave me a faint smile. It was the first time I saw behind the cocky, arrogant façade Dominic projected.

"What you said—I...I... I want to be that phoenix; I want to rise above my past. But I think it will take me a while to fully get there."

Dom gave my hand a reassuring squeeze and leaned forward to tuck a strand of hair behind my ear with his free hand. A part of me expected to hear Jax start growling, but he remained silent. Dom's hand lingered longer then it needed to, and part of me didn't want him to move his hand away, but the other part of me knew it was wrong having him touch me like that while sitting in another man's lap. Dom finally let his hand drop with a reluctant sigh, and I pushed myself off Jackson's lap. I started pacing up and down the river bank, with the guys sitting there watching me, looking slightly amused at my repetitive path.

I had no idea what I was going to do, but I knew I had to at least try and learn how to use my powers in order to help Nico. I wasn't going to run anymore; I was going to stand and fight for once in my life. I was tired of always being scared. It was time for me to be the person my father clearly thought I was and fight for what I know is right.

"Okay. I'll do whatever I need to so I can be ready to help Nico," I said to all the guys.

"Oh, so you're just helping Nico, doll?"

"What are you on about, Dom?" I asked, confused by his question. I was trying to help save a whole world not just one person.

"Well, love, you said just NICO, not Farrarie, so I was just thinking maybe you only wanted to help for Nico's sake." Dom was laughing now, I mean full on belly-laughing, and here I am trying to hide my shame. I knew I was blushing; there was nothing I could do about it though, so I just glared at Dom.

"Shut up, you idiot!" Jax slapped the back of Dom's head "You need to learn how to filter shit before you say it, dumbass." He turned back to me. "We know you want to help the whole of Farrarie and not just Nico, love. Ignore Dom, he's an idiot."

I appreciated Jax so much in this moment for turning the attention away from me that I walked right up to Jax and gave him a hug. I felt him tense for a second then relax, and he circled his arms around my waist and buried his head in the crook of my neck.

I could hear Dom mumbling about Jax being a suck-up, but that's not what stopped our hug—it was Kai. Kai pulled Jax away from by the back of his shirt with enough force to throw him on the ground. I was shocked by his display of anger. I could feel the jealousy rolling off him in waves.

"Unless you want me to put his fucking head through a tree, I would restrain from touching him again."

Jax was on his feet and furious. "You ever fucking touch me like that again, you blood-sucking leech, and I will tear your fucking heart out. Well, what's left of it, anyway," Jax sneered. Kai spun around and stepped toward Jax, and I couldn't suppress my short scream of frustration.

"I am no one's, Melakai—do you understand me?" Both Kai and Jax shifted their attention back to me. "I am standing right here! You have no right to tell anyone they can or cannot touch me. That is *my* choice." I was shaking now, and I could feel my anger rising higher and higher the longer I looked at Kai.

"Ry, sweetie, you need to calm down. You're starting to glow." Dom was right, I realized. I could see my hands were glowing. "Deep breaths, babe, in and out. Just focus on me, okay? Just look at me, Ry." I did as Dom said and kept my eyes on him, breathing in and out for a few moments to regain my composure. "Good girl. Do you feel better now?" I gave Dom a curt nod.

"I think we need to head back now." Jax had a look of pure torture on his face—something was wrong.

"What's wrong?" I asked Jax.

"Nothing, we just need to head back, is all." *Liar,* I think to myself. The walk back to the compound was silent, all of us lost in our thoughts.

Once we got back to the compound, Jax lead us on a winding path through the biggest building and stopped at a set of massive oak doors. Jax ushers us all into the room, and I nearly gasped when I got inside. The room was huge, and lined with bookshelves floor to ceiling, complete with a sliding library ladder. There was a huge wooden desk in front of beautiful bay windows that overlooked a section of the forest, and a lovely sitting area with enough seating for all of us and then some.

"Please have a seat. I will get one of my pack members to bring in some drinks and food." Bless you, Jackson Marshall, you read my mind; I was so hungry my stomach actually ached. Jackson led the way over to the couches and took a seat at the far end, closest to the fireplace. Dom sat on the same couch as Jax. I sat on one of the couches that Kai was occupying, but I made sure to sit all the way on the other end.

"Right, well, let's get down to it, shall we?" Jackson always sounded so businesslike; he needed to let loose a little.

"Well, we can't attack Randall without rescuing Nico's sister first." I couldn't help thinking of what this poor girl has gone through at the hands of Randall Cane. "Second, we have to stop Stevie. We cannot let her help Randall destroy a whole world. We must try to reason with her first, before other drastic measures are taken." I knew Jax was right, but hearing him talk about "other ways" to stop my sister was very unsettling.

"Are you okay, mi amor?" I could hear the concern in Kai's voice.

"Yes, I'm fine, thank you." I couldn't look him in the eye; he would know straight away that I wasn't okay, and I didn't want anyone's pity, nor did I need it.

I took a deep breath and shoved everything I was feeling deep down inside of me. I would deal with all of that later; there was no time for me to even try sort through everything I was feeling. Before we could continue with our discussion, the door opened and my cousins walked in. They both sat on the couch opposite Kai and me, and we filled them on what we had just discussed.

"I think the first thing we need to do is start training Ryan and get her familiar with her powers. Then we need to get everyone else training and preparing for the war that is to come. We won't be able to call on other clans, as the witches answer to Stevie. We can't call on any vamps, either, as Randall will find out." Everything Jackson had said only highlighted the struggle ahead for us.

"I can call on all the packs, as they answer to me. I will call the elders here for an emergency meeting to ask them for their help; it will be no easy task to sway them, so we need to make sure Ryan is able to showcase her powers for them, to be able to believe that she is indeed the chosen one." Wow, no fucking pressure then. "We will also need to make lodging arrangements for the packs willing to fight for our cause. I am not like Randall; I will never force my people to fight a battle they do not wish to fight. I ask that you all show some respect to those who wish not to take part in this war."

"How long do we have to get her ready?" Alex asked.

"You have about two weeks." The whole room erupted, everyone was shouting and yelling to the point I couldn't understand a word any of them were saying. I was about to walk out of the room when suddenly everyone stopped yelling and looked to the door. Aurora was just standing in the entryway; she looked so small and fragile, with her hands clasped in front of her and head slightly downcast, yet she was still so lovely. Jackson stood to make his way over to her, but then she spoke, and her words stunned us all.

"The time frame you have given is long enough; you will all be ready. But none of you will be training Ryan right away. She has another path to take before then, I have foreseen the struggles she will face. It will be hard on her, you will want to quit Ryan. Just know that the struggles that are coming will end, please remember that. My vision also tells me she must marry in order for her powers to truly be unstoppable—only by uniting two worlds will you be able to stop the war from ending all supernatural's." I swear to God that you could have heard a pin drop in the room.

I looked around the room, almost wanting to laugh at the stunned looks on the faces of the men, but when I looked back to Aurora, she had a look of such pity and it sparked my fury.

"I know this is hard to hear, bu—" I cut her off, not wanting to hear what she had to say. Hasn't she already said enough?

"You have no idea what the fuck I am feeling, and I don't know how to believe you after that trick you pulled on me today."

"You may not think so right now, but believe me I *do* know how you feel. Like you, my future has already been planned for me. I will marry someone I do not love either, Ryan, but for the greater good I will do what needs to be done. You can either fight me on my vision, and we all die, or you can try to understand that marrying to save lives rather than for love will be the only way we all live."

What the fuck was I supposed to say to that? "My brother is not thrilled with my future outcome either, and chooses not believe it will happen, but I have never been wrong. I am asking you to please trust me and let me guide you through this, as I am the only one in this room that can help you unlock the other half of your powers." Before she could continue, Dom interrupted.

"How in God's name do you know how to help her unlock the other half of her powers?" Everyone was waiting for her answer.

"Because I know who put the lock on her powers, and he also showed me in the vision from the past how to unlock said gift, if the time ever came."

"Wait—you said he?" Trust Kai to only hear the "HE" out of everything she said. I rolled my eyes at his nonsense.

"Yes, Mr. Cane." Aurora was looking at me like I should know who "he" was, but I had no idea who she was talking about. Then out of nowhere, the answer hit me.

"It was my dad, wasn't it?"

"Yes, Ryan, it was the last gift he gave you." I wanted to drop to my knees at the thought. "He also left you a message, I don't know how he knew that you would meet a seer, but what he has to say will hurt you, so you must be prepared." I didn't think I would ever be ready for anything my dad had to say to me; I still haven't opened the letter he left for me. I left that letter in my room at the cabin, I may never know what he had written now.

I sighed. "Okay, Aurora, let's do this." I wasn't sure why my dad would put a lock on my powers, but I knew he would have only done it to protect me.

"You all need to back up, please, so I can begin. Ryan, I need you to relax and take a few deep breaths and just try to open your mind. I know it's hard, but if you could just try it would make it a lot easier and less painful for you." I tried to ignore the feeling of being watched and concentrated on clearing my mind and letting Aurora in.

"Ryan, I'm going to touch your hand now, and I need you to try not to resist or it will hurt you. It won't be like before." I didn't understand what she meant. "I'm trying to show you a memory, not read your thoughts, so it's a bit trickier." Dear God, what the hell have I gotten myself into? Before I could ponder that thought at any length, I felt a stabbing pain in my head and a cry tore out of my mouth. I heard a commotion, but I couldn't move—I couldn't even open my eyes; it was like my body was frozen in place.

"Ryan, I know you're scared, but just breathe and try to relax. I'm going to try and push the memory into your mind again. Don't try to resist or it will hurt. Just breathe and try to let me in. If at any time you want me to stop, just say so." I took three big gulps of air and tried to relax as much as I could, focusing solely on letting my mind be blank and open.

I didn't feel a thing this time, I just saw it. Once again it was like a movie was playing in my mind, but this was one I hadn't seen before. All I had to do was focus and I could hear and see everything, and then that's when I saw him. I saw my dad.

Chapter Twenty Six

RYAN

I could see him! I could freaking see him, and I burst out crying. He was right there in front of me like I could touch him. His brown hair was the same as I remembered, long on the top and short on the sides, and his eyes had so much love in them. I remember those big beautiful green eyes; when he looked at me as a kid, I always knew I was loved. His eyes told the story that he couldn't. I don't remember this ever happening—I must have been like eight or nine. My mind went blank then, and I was transported back to the time this memory occurred.

I couldn't believe it! Daddy had come to see me. I hadn't seen him in so long, and I missed him so much. Daddy picked me up from school early and took me to get ice cream, and we went to the park. I never got to go to the park; Mommy always made me go straight to my room when I got home. I shivered thinking about what Mommy does when she's angry with me, but I didn't *want Daddy to know that Mommy hurts me. It might make him mad at me too*

I was sad that Daddy didn't bring Sissy to play, but he said he wanted to spend time with just me. Daddy pushed me on the swings and watched me play on the slide and helped me on the monkey bars. I was having so much fun, and I never wanted this day to end. I was playing in the sand pit when Daddy called out to me. He was sitting on the picnic table that was under the really big tree.

"Ryan, come here a minute, sweetheart. Daddy wants to talk to you." I quickly got out of the sand pit and ran over to Daddy, climbing onto the bench seat opposite him.

"I need to talk to you, sweetheart, and I need you to listen to Daddy. I know it will be hard for you to understand, but when you're older, a seer will show you this."

"What's a seer, Daddy?"

"You will find out when you're older. For now I need you to just listen to Daddy, okay?" I nodded my head so he would continue. "You are a very special girl—one of a kind. You and Stevie may be twins, but you are so very different. One day when your older you will feel like there is something missing or that there is a part of you that needs to be set free, and when that times comes, that is when you will know that you are ready to unleash the other half of you that's waiting inside. I hope when that time comes, I will be here to help guide you, but just in case, I'm telling you now.

Your sister isn't like you; she is not strong enough to hold both influences. I will continue to try to guide her, but I feel that she is already too hungry for power. I know this all sounds mixed up and confusing, but I promise it will all make sense one day." I didn't know what Daddy was saying—it was all so hard to understand—but I didn't want Daddy to think I was dumb, so I just nodded my head like I knew exactly what he was saying. "One day you will have to make a choice, Ry, and that will be the hardest choice of them all; what you can do is so extraordinary but also such a burden. Your blood is the key to seal a world. It is also the most potent power enhancer in existence. Anyone that drinks from you will become virtually invincible. If that day should come, only you will be able to stop it—well, with the help of a bloody fairy." Daddy didn't sound like he liked fairies at all. I was shocked; I loved fairies.

"What I'm trying to say, Ryan, is you need to learn how to harness and control what you are. Your gifts are tuned to your emotions, so if you have a meltdown, it could really harm a lot of people unless you learn to control it. I have seen that in the future you will meet a group of men who can help you, but only one of them can help you unlock who you really are.

When that day comes, it will be so overwhelming and so hard to control, but you must try, okay?

No matter how hard or how painful it is, you must try to push through it. You need to control the power inside you, if you don't it will consume you.

Stevie will not be there to guide you; I have seen it, and it hurts me to know that my two girls will be on opposite sides of the war to come. You need to save your sister, Ry. She will need you more than ever. Promise me that when that time comes to pass, you will do everything you can to save your sister. Promise me, Ryan, that you will save Stevie!" I was scared. I didn't know why Stevie would need saving, but I loved my sister, she was my other half, so of course I would do whatever it took to keep her safe.

"I promise, Daddy. I will always protect Stevie, no matter what." The look in my father's deep green eyes was so sad that it scared me. I didn't understand why he would look like that.

"If there is ever anything you need to know, go to a man named Nico. He is a friend of mine. When you get older you are

destined to meet. He can answer the questions you will have. I will always hate myself for the way things ended up. I know what your mother is like, and believe me, I wish I could take you away from her."

I could see the look of defeat on Daddy's face and I hated he felt that way. I knew then it was best that Daddy never know what Mommy had done to me. I leaned across the table and grabbed Daddy's hand. *"I wish with all my heart that you could remember this day and this talk so that you would know that I have always been here watching over you and loving you since the day you were born. I will always be here for you, and when the time comes, I will be here to help you understand what you are and where we come from. Your mother doesn't understand what we are and doesn't want to. I tried so hard and for so many years to help your mother, but nothing I did could get through to her. She has so many demons inside her mind that she is trying to fight."* I knew better than Daddy did about Mommy and her "voices"—she said they always told her that I was evil and needed to be put down.

"I love you Ryan, that's why I need you to remember that the key to unlock what you need is within you. You will need another to help balance the power; you need to merge two worlds to unlock your gifts. Just remember to focus and harness it, and most importantly embrace what you are, because you are strong and smart. You will know what to do. The answers you seek are within you. I love you, my baby girl. My princess."

Chapter Twenty Seven

RYAN

I came back to the present with tears rolling down my face. I never remembered that talk or that day—God, I wish I did remember. That would have been the last time I saw my father properly. I couldn't hold the sobs back; the tears just kept flowing. I knew as soon as I opened my eyes I would see so many pairs of eyes on me, and I wasn't ready to face all the questions. I felt strong arms engulf me, and I knew straight away that it was Kai, and as much as I hated to admit it, his embrace made me feel so grounded, like I could get through this and find whatever the key was inside myself. If my dad thought I could do this and unlock the power inside me, then I would, do it for him as well as for Farrarie.

"I've got you, mi amor." I couldn't speak past the lump in my throat, so all I could do was nod my head against Kai's chest. He didn't push me for an answer or ask what happened; he just held me, and it meant more to me than he would ever know.

"Aurora are you okay?" Oh my God, in my selfishness I completely forgot about her and the toll it must have taken on her showing me the memory. I pulled away from Kai and started to dry my eyes.

"I'm fine, just a bit tired, Jax."

Kai reluctantly pulled away from me with a sigh and stood up to move out of my way. I saw Aurora sitting on the chair directly in front of me. She looked exhausted. I was so absorbed in my own drama that I didn't even think about the toll it would take on her.

"Thank you, Aurora. You have no idea what a beautiful gift you just gave me." I felt more tears threatening to spill, but I forced them back. Now was not the time or the place for me to break down.

"It was my pleasure, Ryan. You are so much stronger than you know. You will be our savior, and if what I have seen comes to pass, you may change my future as well."

"What do you mean *I can change your future?*" She just responded with a sweet little smile. A smile is not a fucking answer, woman! Give me a little something to work with. I could see Alex and Chase sitting nearby with worried looks. I knew I would have to explain what I saw to everyone, but I just wasn't ready. Kai, Jax, Dom, and Tyler were in the corner having a private conversation that I just knew was about me.

"If you guys want to stand in the corner like school girls and talk shit about me, at least say it to my face," I said loudly. All four guys had the decency to look guilty.

"Forgive us, love, we were just trying to figure out what we should do from here." Trust Dom to come up with the million dollar questions of the year; I couldn't answer his question so I just shrugged.

"Ry, I understand that what you saw must have been hard, but if there is anything you need, or want to talk about, Chase and I are here for you." Bless Alex—I would be so lost without my cousins.

"Thank you both, but I think the only person who can answer my questions is Nico." I saw the look of shock cross everyone's faces—except for Aurora, obviously she knew why I needed Nico.

"Why the hell do you need that dick?" Chase grumbled.

"Because Dad said I needed Nico." I saw a flash of anger cross Kai's face, almost like he felt betrayed, but I couldn't bloody well help that Nico knew my dad, now can I?

"Well, I did not see that coming"

"I don't think any of us did Dom" Jax started pacing, and I had no idea why he was anxious. I should be the one up and pacing, not him. "If Nico knew your dad then that means he lied to us again."

"How can you be sure? Maybe he was sworn to keep a secret for an old friend." Trust Dom to be the voice of reason and on Nico's side.

"I knew he would never change," Kai growled.

"How do you know that, Melakai? Maybe he was trying to protect the girl's feelings." I never thought I would see the day that Tyler ever stuck up for the king.

I knew he hated other supes. I don't think I was the only who thought that either by the looks on everyone's faces, they were all thinking the same thing. "Why are you all looking at me like that?"

"Oh my God, Ty, because no one ever thought you would care to defend any other supes ever!" Aurora responded with exasperation.

"Don't make a big deal out of it, okay? It won't happen again, trust me." I couldn't help but laugh at Tyler's red face, he was embarrassed. I had never seen the big wolf blush before. Everyone else joined in and was laughing, and Tyler was getting so pissed at all of us. "That is the last time I try and be nice to anyone other than my kind" with that said Tyler turned and stomped out of the room like a child. Not letting Tyler's departure deter our group from the main problem, Alex spoke.

"Okay, well, we need to get Nico here and have a chat with him." the only one who could get a hold of him was Dom, so it was all resting on Dom to get Nico here so I could demand answers.

"Okay, I'll see what I can do. I'm going to need some time, as he has sealed all the portals. I can open one, but Nico will have to allow the portal to open in Farrarie."

"What do you mean allow you to open a portal?" Chase took the words right out of my mouth.

"Nico needs to allow my magic into Farrarie, because if I just force it then I could end up shattering the magic he has sealing the other portals. It's hard to explain but it will be easier if I just reach out to Nico with my magic and he just accepts it and lets me have access to Farrarie so I can bring him here. No one can know Nico is here—I mean no one." Dom was starting to make me worry, so I had to ask.

"Why can't anyone know Nico is here?"

"Because if by some chance there is a traitor in our midst, then they will know that Farrarie is unguarded by the king, or they could come here and try and fight to take Nico. Nico would give up his life to save his people, and I don't want my brother dying anytime soon, Ryan." I gave Dom a stiff nod; it wasn't very often that Dom was serious, so I knew he meant business.

Everyone left the room to give Dom time to prepare whatever he needed to in order to get Nico here, agreeing we would meet back in Jax's office in an hour.

With an hour to kill, I decided to ask Aurora if she would take a walk with me. I needed time alone with the seer to pick her brain about this whole marriage thing. The guys were reluctant to let us go wandering around by ourselves, so I said that we would go to my room and talk there. They were hesitant but eventually agreed. Once we were safely inside my room, the questions just came pouring out.

"You need to help me understand some things. Why do I need to marry? *Who* do I have to marry? How long do I have before I have to get married? It's some old weird man, isn't it?" I had to take a few deep breaths and try calm down. Aurora just looked at me with a smile and waved me over to sit next to her on the bed.

"I cannot tell you what you want to know, Ryan. All I can say is that I know your heart belongs to one another, even if you don't want to admit it to yourself. The man you must marry has a lot of trust to build back with you, but he is the one you need. He may not be the one you want right now, but he will be everything you have ever wanted, if you just give him a chance." God this is so frustrating. I hated not knowing who "he" was. A knock sounded at the door before I could ask Aurora anymore questions.

"Come in," I shouted, and Kai walked through the door a second later. The look on his beautiful face had me immediately jumping off the bed to stand in front of him. "What's wrong— why do you look so sad?"

"Because the time has come for me to leave you. I need to go back to Randall and explain why I helped you. I need to cover my tracks, he needs to think I was doing it so I would gain your trust. I'm sorry mi amor but I must make out like you mean nothing to me." I forgot all about Kai needing to leave; I didn't want him to go, if making out like he didn't care about me save his life, I was okay with that.

"I don't think it is safe for you to go back there, Kai. He could hurt you"

"The only person that could hurt me is you, mi amor. Don't worry, I will be fine, but I will probably be gone for a few days, so don't worry if I don't come back straight away. The others will watch over you and keep you safe." I didn't want to say goodbye to Kai, and the words I wanted to say wouldn't come out, so instead I let my actions speak for me. I leaned up on my tip-toes and pulled Kai's face down to mine and kissed him.

He was stiff as a board for a second, as I think I caught him off-guard, but then he snapped, grabbing me by the waist and pulling me flush against his chest, and I couldn't stop the moan that slipped free. Our tongues were intertwined and fighting for dominance. I needed more of him, and I went to put my hand under his shirt when a throat cleared and broke the spell that I was under. Kai reluctantly pulled back. That kiss was amazing. I looked over my shoulder to see where the noise came from, only to remember Aurora was still in the room. Oh my God, how embarrassing. I knew I was blushing, I could feel the heat in my cheeks.

"Well, I don't mean to interrupt, but I feel like a bit of a third wheel here." Kai and I both started laughing at Aurora's admission. I don't know what came over me. I'm a shy person—except for in my dreams, of course—and just with that thought I started blushing even harder.

"I must go now, mi amor, but stay safe. I shouldn't be gone long. If by any chance I don't return, you must carry on with your training and defeat Randall. You must promise me this." I could hear what he was saying, but I didn't want to think of the possibility that Kai might not come back. "Promise me, Ryan. I can see the fear in your eyes. I don't want you to be scared for me; I will be fine." I looked deep into his eyes and could see the desire he had for me, but I could also see that he meant every word; he wasn't scared for himself, and just knowing that gave me the strength to answer.

"I promise I will carry on training, but if you don't come back, just know that I will find a way to get you back and I'll burn Randall's fucking mansion down to get to you if I have to."

With that said, I embraced Kai once more and held onto him like my life depended on it. I reluctantly let him go after a minute and watched him walk out the door. I felt like a part of my heart was leaving with him, and I had a feeling of dread in the pit of stomach, like something was going to go horribly wrong. I needed Kai to return so I could tell him that I loved him. That I had always loved him.

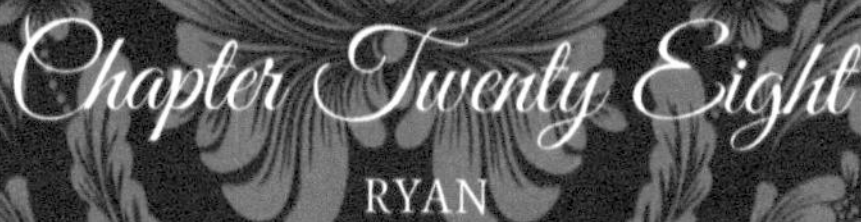

Chapter Twenty Eight

RYAN

Aurora and I made our way back to Jax's office to meet with the others and hopefully be able to talk to Nico. I needed the answers he held like I needed my next breath. I had to know why he kept this from me. Nico hiding this from me hurt, I trusted Nico. I confided in him and Kai in my dreams- never thinking they were real. They knew so much about me and I knew virtually nothing about them. I was more upset with the fact that I had such strong feelings for them both, what the hell was I going to do?

Once we were all inside and seated on the couches in Jax's office, I watched Dom in awe. He had these crystals that he was placing in a circle. Once they were arranged to his satisfaction, he went into the center of it and sat down with his legs crossed and head bent down, he began speaking in some foreign language.

"Portaly openinga feylinga realmy!" Once those words left his mouth, yellow sparks began flying from his outstretched hands, and then within a minute, Nico was standing in front of Dom. Dom quickly stood and gave Nico one of those man hugs.

Nico looked around the room, taking us all in, and then asked Dom.

"Why am I here brother?" I didn't let Dom answer, I was too pissed and wanted to get this show on the road.

"Because I need answers from you, and I want to know why the so-called king fucking lied to me." The sharp intake of breath from the others could be heard but I didn't pay them any attention. Nico and I were in a staring match.

"What answers are you wanting, love? And I also don't believe I have lied to you." Smug prick...I swear I never wanted to hit anyone so much in my life.

"I want to know why you helped my father lock away my powers, and why you fucking lied to me about knowing my father." His expression was unreadable.

"I never lied to you, love. You never asked me directly. We fae cannot lie; we may skirt around the truth, but if you ask us outright, we cannot lie."

"So answer my fucking question then! Why did you not tell me you knew my father?" I didn't realize I was crying until Nico walked over to me and wiped a tear from my cheek.

"I told you when I came to you in the cabin, as Simon that I knew your father." Nico looked around the room at the others, and then said. "Perhaps you might want to have this conversation in private, love. I don't believe it will be pleasant for you."

"We are not going anywhere, Stone." Trust Jax to be the first to speak; at least he wasn't growling this time.

"I want to stay; watching Ryan get pissed is so hot." Dom really needed to learn to filter his mouth. I could hear Tyler chuckling at Dom's comment, but I chose to ignore it. Nico was standing so still you would swear he was actually made of *stone*.

"I just want answers, Nico. Please, I need to know why you kept this from me." I couldn't keep the hurt out of my voice; I felt so betrayed by Nico once more. A look of anguish crossed his face before he quickly masked it.

"Fine, you might want to sit down, then, because it's a long story." if you wish for the others to stay then fine, but you all will remain quiet" Nico looked to everyone and gave them all a look that dared them to try defy him, no one did they all nodded and sat down, Nico and I both followed. I sat in the middle of Alex and Chase while Nico sat between Jax and Dom, Aurora sat on the single high back chair and Tyler stood behind her like a protector. Nico looked me right in the eyes before sighing; I had a feeling I wasn't going to like how this story went.

"When you were younger, your father sought me out. I do not know how he came to find me or how he even knew who I was. I lived in a different realm, after all, but I did come here every so often to keep an eye on Jax and Kai, even though we did not speak. I needed to know they were okay."

I felt a sense of respect for Nico in that moment; he didn't need to come and check on them, but he did it anyway. "One visit back here, I came alone without Dom for the first time. I decided to stop at the pub that we all used to go to and have a beer, for old times' sake. Once I was seated at the bar, a man came up to me and said, 'I've been waiting a long time for you.'"

"I had no idea who this brown-haired, green-eyed man was, but I knew he wasn't human. I automatically went on alert; I thought he was there to ambush me. Before I could attack him, he raised his hands and said, "I'm not here to hurt you, son. I'm here to ask for your help. You may not know me, but I know who you are, your majesty, and I believe that I can help you get your sister back if you just listen to me.

"I was shocked, but then anger overtook me. I didn't know how this man knew who I was or how he knew my sister was taken. I did the only thing I could think of—I told him to follow me outside, which he did. Once we were out front and around the corner where no one could see, I grabbed him by the throat and slammed him against the wall. I'm sorry, Ryan, but I was going to kill your father." I gasped; I couldn't believe Nico openly admitted he was going to hurt my dad, but before I could yell or scream at him, he continued. "He raised his hand at me and sent a blast of magic so strong it knocked me back several feet. I was going to charge him again, but he raised his hands in surrender and said, "I told you I'm not going to hurt you and I meant it. I'm here to ask for your help. Please—my daughter is in danger, and I don't know who else I can turn to.'"

"'Who the hell are you?' I asked him. 'I am Ralph Knox, head warlock to the Knox coven. You are Nicholas Stone, king of the fae. I mean you no harm, your majesty. I just need your help please, I believe my daughter is the key to eternal power, and she has the blood to seal the fae realm from Earth.'" My dad knew I was the key, he spent his life trying to help me. I would forever live with regret if not saying goodbye to my father.

"I didn't believe him at first, but the look on his face showed me he was genuinely scared for his child. I wanted to walk away and not help him, even if he was telling the truth that his daughter was the key to kill my people. Then I thought of Dom, Jax, and Kai, how we could be friends and trust each other, even though we were from different clans.

Maybe this man could be trusted too. I agreed to meet with your father at a later time, as I had to get back to my realm. A week later I met your father at the same pub, but this time was different. I was keen to hear what he had to say, as I had done some research on what all the elders believed to be the key to power, and low and behold he was telling the truth—the blood of a witch-fae halfling with a pure heart is the key to seal the fae realm from Earth. Ralph and I spoke for hours about you, Ryan. God, he loved you so much he was willing to risk his life to find me just so you could live." I couldn't stay quiet anymore; I had to know.

"Why did my dad find you, though, and not someone else?" Nico gave me a sad smile, and I knew I wasn't going to like his answer.

"Because I am the only one strong enough to remove any fae's powers." My mouth dropped open at that. I mean, what the actual fuck? Dom scoffed, clearly not impressed that Nico said his magic was the strongest.

"So you knew when you sent us back here that I could never learn how to control my powers, because I didn't even have all of them!"

"It's not that simple, love. Let me finish the story and you will understand why I did what I did, okay?" I gave him a curt nod to continue. "I told your father that before I was willing to strip someone—even a child—of their gifts, I needed to see for myself that this child did in fact have both witch and fae powers. I was there that day when your father took you to the park. You never saw me, but I was there." Creepy, but okay. "I watched you and saw that you had no evil whatsoever in your body. I just saw light, and I was awestruck by your gentle and forgiving nature. You were abused so terribly by your mother, but you never let the darkness consume you.

"You are strong, Ryan. Do not ever forget that your strength grows within you every day. All I did was put a block on your powers—I never stripped them. I couldn't strip them, if I'm being totally honest."

"Why couldn't you strip them?" Alex asked.

"Because she is too powerful. She possesses even more power than me and Dom." Holy shit balls! I could tell by the look in Nico's eyes that he was telling the truth—he really thought I was that powerful. "Also I didn't even want to try, because there was a chance you might die, and I wasn't willing to take that risk."

"Why did you do it, though? I don't understand why you would help my dad when you just said you didn't trust him. Why not just kill me?" Nico started looking around the room, almost like he didn't want the others to hear the answer to my question.

"Because I felt a connection to you that I can't explain. I know that doesn't make much sense to you, love, but I just knew one day our paths would cross again, and you would need my help. So I did the only thing I could think of, which was to block your powers, so when the day came that you would need to access them, you would have to come find me. I could never hurt you, Ryan." I don't know why, but his admission had me swooning a bit, in spite of the fact that the look in his eyes told me there was more to this story. Nico was still hiding something from me, and I wanted to know what it was.

"Now that you're done eye fucking my cousin *your majesty,* can we get back on track here" I couldn't help but blush at Chases' statement, everyone in the room just saw me melting all over the Fae King. To break the awkwardness I cleared my throat and asked.

"What happens now then?"

"That's the tricky part, love; unlocking your powers is going to be painful."

"Why would it hurt her?" Bless you, Jax, for asking the question I was too scared to say out loud.

"What I mean is that when I unlock the other half of Ryan's powers, it will be like letting a caged animal run free for the first time. Her powers have been locked up since before she hit puberty, so it will burn through her, so to speak. We will have to manage it as best we can and try to help her control it, or she could seriously hurt someone or even herself." I was sucking in huge amounts of air—I mean, it sounds like I was about to burn Jax's whole compound to the ground, and the last thing I wanted to do was hurt anyone. "Well, it'll be best to do this outside, where no one is around, so maybe in the woods?" I don't know who Nico was directing his question to, but Dom was the one to answer him.

"We'll go to the woods, when everyone is at dinner, and I'll put a ward around us to try control the damage to the area."

"Why would we need a ward? You're making it sound like she's going to blow up!" Alex snapped.

"There is a chance that there could be a huge blast. Like I said, Ryan is very powerful, and with me unlocking this side of her powers that she has never had to deal with, it could cause her to lash out to stop the pain. She won't know how to control all the power coursing through her veins." Well, Nico was shit at pep talks, wasn't he?

"I will be there to help guide and train her to harness the energy," Aurora chimed in. I was glad that no one had mentioned me getting married. I was really hoping that they had forgotten that bit; I didn't want to marry anyone. I was too young for that, Nico never said I had to marry in order for him to release my powers. I was counting that as a win.

I tuned everyone out while they made plans for what was to happen this evening, I couldn't take the pressure, so I walked out of the room and headed back to my temporary bedroom, somewhat amazed I found my way back there. Once inside, I plopped down on the bed and covered my eyes with my arm. I just needed to be alone and to think. But that wasn't apparently an option, because almost as soon as I had the thought, there was a knock on my door.

"WHAT?" I bellowed.

"Do you mind if we come in?" At the sound of Jax's voice, I quickly sat up. It wasn't just Jax, though—he was followed in by Dom and Nico. They all stood awkwardly at the end of my bed, but given that I'd left them for peace and quiet, and they're the ones who came to my room, I wasn't going to be the one to talk first.

"I know this is a lot for you to take in, but we're trying to help and make this as easy as possible for you," said Dom.

"I know you guys are, it's just hard to process the amount of mind-boggling information I'm getting hit with. I don't want to hurt anyone and I sure as shit don't want to hurt myself."*Or get married.*

"We're not asking you to hurt anyone, love— were just asking that you let Dom and Aurora train you to allow you to get some sort of control over your powers, so when the time comes, maybe the reality that your enemies know you know how to harm them will scare them enough to back down." I wish what Jackson was arguing could happen, but we all knew that Randall Cane wouldn't back down without a fight.

"Okay, I'll agree to Dom and Aurora training me, but you all have to promise me that no matter what happens, none of you will harm my sister." They all exchanged looks with one another and agreed.

"I've also been wondering—Randall drank from me at the cabin. I guess that means he's going to be strong and powerful now, right?"

"No, Randall will be the same strength as he normally is. Your fae side isn't unlocked yet, so he only drank your witch blood, so to speak." Nico's answer made me feel slightly less fucked, which was a pleasant surprise.

"We must begin the training as soon as we can. I have a feeling Randall won't sit by much longer; he's chronically impatient, so something must be wrong if he is not attacking us already." Dom sounded so sure, which made me worry even more for Kai. What if something happened to him? What if they knew he was helping us? Would they harm him?

"Do you think if Randall found out Kai was helping us, that he would kill him?" They all shared an ominous look, which gave me the answer to my question. "By the looks on your faces, I'm assuming that's a big fat yes." Dread filled my stomach. I couldn't explain it, but I just knew Kai was in trouble and needed our help—I could feel it in my soul.

"Look, Kai is strong, and he is a great solider. The best there is, really. Randall has known for a while that Kai hasn't been himself. Kai is loyal to a fault, and if Randall has sensed that his loyalties are shifting, he will try to take him out." Nico wasn't sugar-coating the truth.

"I can't explain it, but I have the worst feeling that Kai is in trouble and needs our help. I feel like he's trying to tell me something, but I don't' know what. I felt this pulling sensation, like I do in my dreams but nothing is happening. Could that be Kai?" Dom's face went from calm to serious in half a second.

"Ryan, sweetheart, I need you to lie down, okay? The only way Kai can come to you from a distance and without touch is if you are asleep." I did as Dom asked without question and shuffled up to the top of the bed. "Okay, I'm going to do a sleeping spell, love, which will take you to Kai and—"

"I'm going under with her, in case it's a trap." Nico was looking me straight in the eye, and I knew by the look on his face that he wasn't going to take no for an answer, so I just nodded. He climbed on the other side of the bed, linking his fingers through mine, and I felt like a zap of electricity had shot through my arm just from that small contact. I always felt a spark when Nico touched me.

"Okay, well, I guess I'll be putting you both under then, Jax, and I will stand watch to make sure you're both fine. If anything happens, pull her out straight away, Nico." Nico gave Dom a firm nod and closed his eyes, I leaned back and closed my eyes as well and listened to Dom chanting in another language. I didn't feel anything happening for a while, and then all of a sudden everything went dark.

Chapter Twenty Nine

RYAN

Being here at the lake with Nico felt wrong; this was my and Kai's place—well, one of them. We would meet in the forest or at this lake. It was beautiful, with serene water that mirrored the surrounding forest and mountains. The silence here is what made this my favorite place on Earth.

Never have both men been in my dream at the same time. I knew I loved Kai; I've always known that, at least subconsciously. The more I am around Nico, the more I'm starting to feel things for him. I love Kai, but I love Nico too. My heart needs to stay out of this. I have no right falling for either of them. Shaking myself out of my thoughts, I call out for him.

"Kai?"

He always came when I called. This time it felt different, like something was off. I can't explain it but, I just felt it. I heard a branch break, only to find Nico, not Kai, which was slightly worrying.

"Where is he?"

"I don't know. He's always here, Nico—he never makes me wait."

Nico came over and wrapped an arm around my shoulders.

I appreciated the gesture; I didn't feel so alone in his embrace. I was thankful to have him here with me, now. I was scared for Kai, I just knew something was wrong, I could feel it.

"Kai, please come out! Nico and I are here."

My bad feeling about Kai was getting worse. I felt cold, and I never felt uncomfortable in my dreams. I always felt warm, like in springtime. I heard some branches snapping and quickly spun toward the noise. Nico and I both gasped at the sight, my heart sank.

Kai limped towards us, only to stumble, and grab a tree trunk before he could fall to the ground. Nico rushed over and caught him, then eased him down carefully on the ground by the side of the lake. I rushed over and knelt down beside him. His face was covered in blood, with black bruises marring his beautiful face. He only wore a pair of shorts, and his legs were covered in wounds. I noticed his fingers and toes had no nails.

"Oh my God, they're torturing you, aren't they?" I started to cry. Kai was in so much pain, and I could tell he was trying to mask it for my benefit. He tried to lift his hand to wipe away my tears, but he didn't have the strength to even do that. He turned away from me and looked to Nico.

"I have fulfilled my vow to you, my brother. Your sister is free and making her way to Jackson's camp as we speak." Nico jerked back, obviously shocked by the revelation. "You must warn Jackson that his second in command is a traitor. Randall knew I was coming and that I was helping Ryan."

"How?" Nico snapped.

"Tyler and Stevie are working together, and he has been feeding her information." Kai turned toward me then. "You must not come for me, mi amor, no matter what. " I started to protest, but Kai cut me off. "It is a trap. Randall knows you will come for me, and by the time you get to me, I will already be dead." I started sobbing in earnest now, holding onto his face and smoothing back his hair. "I don't have long left—I can feel my life force fading now."

"Don't cry, mi amor, I am grateful I got to have any time with you at all. I need you to listen to me now." I nodded so he could continue.

"Your sister is not coming back from this, Ryan" I started to shake my head; I had to believe I could save Stevie. "She is the one torturing me with Randall, and she enjoys it so much more because she knows that hurting me will hurt you." Rage like I had never known surged within me. How could she do this to Kai? I could hear Kai's breathing start to shorten, and I knew deep down he was dying.

"Nico, please you have to help him, I am begging you, please!" Tears were streaming down my face. I couldn't lose Kai. Nico looked sick with grief. "Why the hell aren't you helping him, Nico? He's your fucking friend! Cast a fucking spell or something!" I shouted. He just looked at me with tears in his eyes.

"I can't heal the dead, Ryan. There is nothing I can do." I wanted to argue with him, but I could see he was just as angry and heartbroken as I was. I tore my gaze away from Nico and looked down at my strong and courageous vampire. I couldn't stop the tears falling.

"Do not cry for me *mi amor*, I will see you again" he sounded so certain, almost like a promise.

"I love you, Melakai. I always wished you were real. And when I finally got my wish granted, I wasted so much time. I am so sorry, Kai. I swear on all that is holy in this world that I will avenge you and make anyone who hurt you suffer. You have my word." I leaned down and kissed his cold, chapped lips. And then it all went black.

I awoke next to Nico on the bed. Before anyone could say anything, Nico grabbed me and pulled me into his embrace. I started crying—great heaving sobs. The dream ended because Kai was gone. She fucking killed him.

"I am so sorry, we couldn't save him," Nico stuttered out.

"Wait, what the hell do you mean? You couldn't save who, Nico? Where the fuck is Kai?" Dom was shouting at Nico, I could hear in his voice he knew the answer to his own question, but he didn't want to believe it.

Nico had to answer for us. "We couldn't save Melakai. They killed him."

I drew in a steadying breath. I could feel the lump in my throat and had to push past it. "We need to unlock my powers and I need to train. We are going to war, and we are going to kill every single one of those fucking sons of bitches, and my sister is at the top of the list."

Epilogue

NICO

I held her sobbing form for over an hour. I understand her heart is broken for the loss of my brother, whom she thinks she loves. She has no idea what she wants, but I will be the one to show and guide her through all this. Now she is finally sleeping, her beautiful long brown hair fanned out behind her. Jackson and Dom haven't left the room. They each sit in the single high back chairs, their eyes glued to my girl. Their grief clear on their faces, they are hurt by the loss of Kai. We all are, we just lost our brother.

"Jackson, I need a favor." Jackson reluctantly pulls his stare from Ryan.

"What do you need, Nico?"

"I need some of your men to find my sister. Kai set her free." I can hear both Jackson and Dominic's sharp intake of air. Neither of them expected those words to come from my mouth, especially not after learning of Kai's death. I don't know how Kai knew where she was or how even set her free, I owed Melakai a debut. He fulfilled the vow he made to me seventeen years ago.

"You have my word. I'll go myself and make sure she is okay."

"Jax, I'll go with you," Dom said. I thanked both my brothers as they exited the room and shut the door. Now I finally have a moment alone with my girl.

"When you wake, I will tell you everything, my love. You are so much more than you even know."

I move my free hand to my back pocket and feel the outline of the envelope. I stole the letter her dad wrote her.

I never opened or read it, but I couldn't leave it there when I snuck into her room to see her. I am no thief, but I also didn't want her bitch of a sister getting her grubby hands on it. This letter may contain information that we can't afford Stevie to have. Before I can continue my train of thought, the door opens and Aurora walks in.

"Have you told her, Nico?"

"No, I will tell her when the time is right."

"You need to tell her immediately. She deserves to know the truth."

"Her heart is broken right now, and if I drop this bomb on her, she will hate me more than she already does."

"Stop being so selfish, she has a right to know!"

"That is not your fucking secret to tell!" I'm shouting now; I need to calm down and keep quiet or risk waking Ryan.

"Tell her the truth, and do it soon, or I will, Nico."

"I'll tell her as soon as you tell Jax that she isn't really his *mate.*" I hear her gasp, and her pale blue eyes turn stormy.

"I'll tell Jackson the truth as soon as you tell Ryan you are her future husband. You can also tell her the truth about where her mother really is, while you're at it. I'm sure she would love to know how *close* she is to her abuser."

Oh, fuck. I am so fucking screwed.

Fate
CURSE OF FATE BOOK 2

Chapter One

RYAN

"You have to do the spell; the boys will know what spell to procure. Trust in yourself, you can do this."

"How can you be so sure?"

"Because you are stronger than you know. He will need to play his part—you must do this spell."

I drifted out of my daydream and sighed. Yeah, I wasn't just dreaming while sleeping now.

I sit in my room, gazing out the window, not really seeing anything. The doubts of what I am supposed to do are creeping in. Kai's gone. He's actually fucking gone.

I feel the tears starting to build again. Taking a steadying breath, I push my emotions back down. I can't give into my grief when there is a chance the tears will be wasted. I've spent the past three days in this room, planning and plotting.

Losing Kai was a hard pill to swallow; I didn't even get the chance to really get to know him. I shake myself out of my thoughts. I need to get my head back in the game and stick to the plan if I want vengeance for Kai.

I take my first shower in who knows how long and slip on the clothes Aurora brought me. They fit like a glove, but even if they didn't, beggars can't be choosers. I quickly brush my hair and teeth and, taking a deep breath, I brave leaving my room.

I try to make my way to the mess hall, where I assume everyone will be. I haven't seen Dom, Jax, or Nico since I awoke after losing Kai. I'm anxious to see them.

Guilt has me stumbling. I lied; I'm not anxious to see *them*, I'm anxious to see *him*. When I found out that Kai was real, I knew there was a slim chance Nico was too. Kai may be dead, and here I am being a worthless piece of shit, pining after his best friend. Now that I know the truth, I shouldn't feel guilt for my feelings toward Nico, but I do.

I refuse to let my mind wonder anymore. I need to find the guys and make a plan. After turning down many different hallways and then retracing my steps because I went the wrong way, I finally got to the mess hall. I can hear muffled sounds coming from inside the hall. I know people are going to stare, but before I can talk myself out of it, I push the doors open and enter.

As soon as I walk in, all conversation stops. I can feel so many pairs of eyes on me. I hold my head high and make my way to the food station. It takes all of ten seconds before both my cousins are beside me.

"Squirt, you don't have to be here." I count to three in my head and then address Alex.

"I know, but sitting in that room and feeling sorry for myself isn't going to help anyone, is it?" I don't mean to sound bitchy, but I need to keep up my act that I'm grieving. I need to make sure to keep my answers vague in front of Jackson or he will know I'm lying.

"If you need to be angry, then do that. But don't let any of these assholes see you hurting. We're here with you every step of the way, cousin." Chase's words helped ease some of the tension in my body. I kept my head held high, grabbed my food, and followed the boys back to their table.

I feel it the instant his eyes lock on me; I feel a sizzle zapping down my spine. I avoid eye contact and take the seat between Alex and Chase. No one speaks for a long moment. I push the food around my plate, not having much of an appetite due to someone's gaze burning holes in me.

"It's good to see you, Ryan." I don't need to look up to know its Aurora that spoke. Again, I count to three in my head before lifting my eyes to hers. The look on her face is nearly my undoing— so much pity shines within them. "We're all here for you."

How am I supposed to reply to that? I know Jax and Dom are waiting for me to acknowledge their presence, but in order for me to do that, I would have to see *him*. And as if sensing my inner struggle, *he* speaks.

"I know you are hurting." God, the sound of his voice is making me feel things. Things I don't want to feel right now.

"We need to speak with you, privately." I don't voice a reply or lift my head. I simply nod. After a minute or so, conversation around the table continues, and I zone out, lost in my own thoughts.

"Ryan, did you hear me?" I turn toward Chase, staring into his sky-blue eyes. I shake my head.

"I just said, if you are done eating, we should go to Jackson's office and *talk*." I nod and stand, following the group to Jackson's office. Once we enter the room, I move to the couch and sit down on the far end, so I don't have to be seated between anyone. I don't make eye contact or speak to the others as they all find their own seats. Someone clears their throat; I look up and quickly scan the room. Jax, Dom, and Aurora share a couch. Chase is beside me and Alex beside him. *He* sits in the lone chair in the middle, and I don't make eye contact. I pretend he isn't even there. It's easier if I pretend my feelings for him don't exist. My heart has no place in this war, plus I can't trust him. He has no idea I know about his lies and secrets. It's crazy that after everything he has done, I still want him to hold me. I want him to tell me we'll be okay and we can make this work. I quickly shake my thoughts away, and ask the pertinent question.

"So, what do you all want to talk about? Please don't treat me like I am made of glass." I'm quite proud of myself; my voice is strong and steady.

"We need to make a plan to move forward with unlocking your powers" There it is, the reason why everyone is so tense. Did they think I would back out?

"I agree, when should we start?" Jax looked shocked. I agreed with him so easily. They were all giving me strange looks now, almost as if they expected me to have a tantrum and let a world die. I would never do something like that; I gave my word and I will not go back on that promise.

"Ahhhh... Okay, I thought that we were going to have to convince you, Squirt. I guess the next question is what do we do now?" Oh, Alex, if only you knew the full story.

"Before all this happens, we need to make sure that you are ready for what comes next, love." I wish they would all stop beating around the bush.

"Just say it, Dom." I made sure to keep my face blank of all emotion. I couldn't afford for them to see beyond the mask I was wearing.

"Okay, Love, are you ready to take your sister down?" Dom asks, never breaking eye contact. Looking into his violet eyes was almost hypnotizing.

"Yes, I will do whatever needs to be done to ensure the safety of the fae realm. My sister will pay for what she has done." I meant every single word; I waited for the sting to come, knowing that I had just vowed to destroy my sister, but I felt nothing. I was numb. Stevie made her choice, and I have made mine.

"Tonight, we will need to head toward the northern border. It's far enough away from the pack and humans." Jackson's concern for his pack and the humans in the area was touching but unnecessary. My powers wouldn't be unlocked tonight—not that *he* would tell the group why that is. I needed to keep up my act by playing along like I didn't know the truth.

"What happens if you can't control the blast, Dom?" I asked, and judging by the looks on the others faces, they were all wondering the same thing.

"I will try my best. I have never had to contain something like this before." I appreciated his honesty. "If we are far enough away from the pack and humans we should be fine." Dom then turned to *him* and asked, "You would have more of an idea than any of us, brother—what do you think?"

"I think what Jax has planned is the best option. I don't know exactly what the blast radius will be." His voice was like music, a beautiful tune that you didn't want to stop. "I think we should start tonight." Before he could continue to torment me with his song, Aurora started to shake and her eyes went white. Dom and Jax quickly jumped from their seats, followed by Alex and Chase. Alex went to reach for her but Jax slapped his hand away.

"You cannot touch her! If you do, it could cause her harm."

After what felt like hours but was only minutes, Aurora finally stopped shaking, and her eyes returned to their normal pale blue color. No one spoke. We were giving her time to sort her thoughts and gather herself. Jax made his way over to his desk and grabbed the bottle of water that was sitting there; he returned and handed it to Aurora, who thanked him and took two big sips.

"I'm sorry, I didn't mean to scare you all. I think you should all sit down. I didn't see anything good, I'm afraid" Aurora gave me a strange look. I was starting to panic now—what if she saw and knew the whole truth? I couldn't risk them finding out now, not yet. I just hoped that she only saw what *he* wasn't telling the group.

The four guys take their seats, all eyes turn to Aurora, waiting. Shaking her head and taking a few calming breaths, she spoke, looking me dead in the eyes. *Oh God, please.*

"Ryan, you can't unlock your powers. I had a vision, obviously. If you attempt to unlock your powers, you will die, and—" Nico cuts her off before she can finish.

"That can't be! I put the lock on her powers"

"Yes, but what you don't know is Ryan's father changed the key to unlocking her gifts. Ralph only needed your help to lock her fae power down. He couldn't risk you wanting to claim the greatest weapon."

"Okay, so Ryan's father changed this *key*... What happens now? How does she unlock her powers?" Oh, Alex, you are going to be so pissed.

"She will need to merge with her intended."

"What the hell does that mean, Rora?" *Rora?* Since fucking, when did Chase give her a nickname? I didn't realize they were besties now. Aurora turns her gaze back to me.

"Remember I told you that you would need to marry?" I give her a stiff nod. "You need to marry so your power can merge through you both and not kill you. I know this isn't what you want to hear but..." I cut in, not wanting to sit here and hear her continue to beat around the fucking bush. Steeling my spine, I turn to face Nico and look directly into his eyes for the first time.

"So, when should we get hitched, future husband?"

Chapter Two

RYAN

What the hell!

How did she know? She's looking at me with so much anger and mistrust. Did Aurora betray me? Everyone is staring at me, and Jackson looks like he is two seconds away from wringing my neck.

"Well? Are you going to answer me or sit there like a fish out of water?" I gulp, I know Jax heard. I think that's the only reason why the hateful look he is aiming at me is starting to fade from his face.

"I...I...how?" I sound like a blubbering idiot, but she has me stumped. She is loving every minute of this, judging by the smirk on her beautiful face.

"Oh, you mean how did I know you and Aurora are both lying assholes? That's easy, I have a secret power for sniffing out bullshit!" There is so much venom lacing each of her words. Aurora has a hand clamped across her mouth in shock. So she didn't rat me out after all...who did, then?

"What secret power? And what the fuck is going on here, Squirt?" Her cousin is clearly pissed that he was in the dark about the little bomb she just dropped. She pulls her hateful stare from me to face Alex.

"I can't tell you, Alex. All you need to know is when Aurora dropped the bomb about me needing to marry, she meant I had to marry *him*." Alex spins his stare from Ryan to Aurora, an unmistakable look of hurt on his face. Ah, the young warlock has a crush.

"Why would you hide this from us? You have had so many chances to come clean. I think you need to start telling everyone the fucking truth!" Alex is pissed. Aurora is shaking; she hates having to lie. She looks my way, waiting for me to give her confirmation that she could tell the others the truth. It was time they all knew. I give Aurora a small nod.

"Okay, let's start from the beginning then. I wasn't lying when I told you that in order for your powers to become unstoppable that you needed to marry. What I didn't know at the time was that your father added a failsafe to be sure no one could do this without your consent." I didn't like where she was going with this. "You cannot be forced to marry; you must *choose* to marry. You must also *want* to unlock your powers"

If there was more to her explanation, we wouldn't know, because as soon as she said the last part, everyone was shouting and talking over each other. It was fucking madness. All at once the conversations stopped, and everyone turned to Ryan. She was glowing, staring my way, pointing an accusing finger.

"You bastard! You planned this, didn't you? You knew the whole fucking time that I would need to choose you. That's why you never fought Kai; you always knew I had to *choose* you in the fucking end." Before I could even respond I was blasted from the chair and sent sailing through the air. I hit the back wall with a thud and dropped to the ground. Fuck, that hurt like a bitch. Groaning, I used the wall as support to get me to my feet. My legs were shaky and protesting. That blast she sent had a punch packed within it; she intended to hurt me.

Once on my feet, I pushed away from the wall and turned to face the others. All of them have a look of shock on their faces, except Jackson. He looks smug. Ryan is still glaring daggers my way.

"If you really thought that, you wouldn't be this angry. I never fought my brother because I thought you might be better off with him than with me. I swear to you, love, I didn't know your father altered the key. As far as I knew, all I had to do was remove the bonds I had on your power. I knew you had to marry, but I didn't find out you had to marry *me* until recently." I was praying she could hear the truth in my words; I would never lie to her about this. Did I want her to choose me? Of course, but not like this, where she didn't have a choice.

"Nico is telling the truth. The vision I had showed me what your father had done, afterward." How the hell did Aurora keep getting visions and messages from Ralph Knox? Also, why the hell was she not telling anyone? Something more was going on with this seer, and I am going to find out what it is.

"What exactly did my father do? Don't fucking lie to me, Aurora." Aurora flinched at Ryan's tone, and I don't think she was the only one.

"He added a spell to Nico's. If Nico lifts his bonds, your fae power will surge through you and burn you on the way out. No blast radius, just your death. I have no idea how Ralph knew you would meet a seer, especially one who can see the past and the future."

Jackson butted in before Aurora could finish.

"She cannot marry him, she is my mate!"

I was about to answer, but Ryan beat me to it. She made her way over to Jax and knelt down in front of him. Placing both her hands on top of his, she looked directly into his eyes.

"Jax, I am not your mate." Jackson sucked in a big gulp of air."You were tricked into thinking that I was. I'm sorry, but I am not your mate." No one spoke for a long while, tension-filled moment. How the hell did she know that? Dom looked from me to Ryan, then to Jax and Aurora. I saw the moment when Dom figured it out; he knew what we did. Dom glared at me.

"You have pulled some shit in the past, brother, but this takes the fucking cake. Why? Why would you do this to him?"

"Because it served his endgame! He knew what he was doing. Didn't you, Nico? You like to fuck with people's lives, lie to them, then tell them you love them." I couldn't look Ryan in the eyes; her words hurt more than she would ever know. "Answer the fucking question, Nico. Why did you do this to him?" I didn't get a chance to answer, Aurora answered instead.

"Because I asked Nico to cast the spell."

"What fucking spell?" Jax was pissed, and it was all my fault. I never meant to hurt him; it wasn't supposed to go this far.

"To conceal who your true mate is. I asked him to find a way to deceive you and throw you off the scent of your mate." Jax snapped his head in Aurora's direction, the tension was rolling off him in waves.

"Why?" That one word sent dread sliding down my spine.

"Because I was trying to stop the future from happening."

"What the fuck does that mean, Aurora?"

"It means *I* am your mate, Jackson. I don't want to be, though; that's why I asked Nico to help me. He never meant for you to think Ryan was your mate, your attraction to her led you to think she was your mate, I think." Jackson fell back into the couch, like someone had slapped him. Ryan clutched his hands tighter, offering her silent support to her friend.

"You don't want to be my mate? So you decided to trick me, hurt me, and lie to me. Why not just come clean and tell me the truth, Aurora? Why go behind my back and ask that piece of shit—who is supposed to be my brother—for help?" Aurora looked to me for assistance. I knew that it was time for the whole truth to come out. Clearing my throat, I addressed the whole room.

"Aurora came to me and told me about the situation, and I offered to help. The only reason she lied to everyone is because—"

Aurora interrupted. "If you mate with me, Jackson, you will die. I have seen it, and I want to change your future. I have never interfered with my visions before, but I cannot let you die. I told you all once that I would have to marry someone I didn't love; that someone is you, Jackson." I was proud of her for voicing her deepest secret.

"Wait! Jackson is not fucking dying." I could hear the alarm in Dom's voice. He wouldn't lose another brother.

"If he mates with me, he will. I am born from wolves, and yet I cannot shift; I am a seer. Jackson is alpha to all wolf packs, and our offspring would be hybrids. No one will understand, and the packs will turn on Jackson. The pack is in uproar now, as they believe he has mated with a witch. No wolf has ever mated outside of their race before." Chase, Alex and Ryan were deathly silent; Dom was trying to remain calm. Jax, on the other hand, just looked defeated.

Chapter Three

RYAN

I can see the look of heartbreak on Jax's face. He's devastated. He thought I was his mate, only to be told that I wasn't, and to make matters worse, his true mate has rejected him. Jackson's expression changes from heartbreak to betrayal. The woman he trusted so much has lied to him and broken his trust in the worst way possible. No one says a word as we wait for Jax to process the information and all its ramifications.

"I think we should forget about this conversation and move on to figuring out how to help Ryan." I was grateful for the subject change, but at the same time I would love to slap Chase for bringing the attention back to me. So, I did what any grown-ass woman would do in that moment—I stalled.

"I think we should all take a break and reconvene tonight. It seems like we could all use some time to ourselves." Everyone quickly agreed and started shuffling out of the office.

Jackson stayed behind, claiming he had pack business that he needed to attend to. Honestly, I think he just didn't want to face anyone right now. I couldn't blame him for that. I made my way back to the bedroom I was currently occupying. Once inside the room, I shucked off my shoes and headed for the bed.

I needed to close my eyes and let my mind go blank. Just as I was starting to relax, and my mind finally stopped running away with all different kinds of possibilities, someone knocked on the damn door. Fuck me! I was so damn close! Not bothering to sit up, I called out.

"Come in." I heard heavy footsteps and then the door clicked shut. Peeling one eye open, I turned slightly to see who had entered and groaned.

"What do you want, Nico?" I didn't want to be alone with him; it wasn't a good idea for either of us.

"I just want to explain and talk to you. I know I don't have the right to ask this, but I had my reasons for skirting around the truth." Oh, this should be good. Apparently fae can't lie but Nico manages to navigate around this rule perfectly.

"You have five minutes." I was already doing the countdown in my head. He made his way over to the single chair near the window, resting his forearms on his knees. The T-shirt he was wearing was stretched to its limits. Fuck, he was huge, and he could pull off a plain white tee and jeans like no other.

His beautiful, jet black hair was slightly longer now. I was glad he wasn't looking at me, his deep violet eyes are like a vortex, they would suck me in and I would crumble.

That sounds so cliché, I know, but Nico had a hold over me; it was like there was a string constantly pulling me toward him. It was so hard to fight it but I had to, he lied to me and hurt me. Now that my mind was finally clear after years, I felt so much more for him than I should. I wanted to hate him but I couldn't.

"I'm sorry I deceived you." He was off to an okay start. "I never should have, but I was only trying to protect you from getting hurt. I had no idea your father put a failsafe spell on you after I locked your powers. I swear." I could hear the truth in his voice, but he wasn't getting off the hook that easy.

"You knew I had to marry you, though?"

"I only found out a few days before you came to my realm."

"Aurora came to Farrarie?" I saw him tense and then take a few deep breaths. I could tell he didn't want to tell me, but he knew if he didn't I would kick him out.

"I went to Aurora, she and I would meet every month to re-do the spell masking her scent. She told me then." What the actual fuck! He and Aurora had been doing this for months? Poor Jackson.

"Why let Jackson think I was his mate, then?"

"It was never meant to end like this. Aurora just needed some time to figure out another way. She wanted to find a powerful witch and see if they could break the mate bond. She knew it would be a challenge; if she and Jackson mate, she will need to carry an heir, and if she does that, she will no longer be a seer. She wants to keep her gifts so she can monitor Jackson's future." Oh, I didn't know that part.

"She said in Jackson's office not long ago that she didn't love the man she was supposed to marry. But what I saw today was the total opposite."

"You're right, she is in love with Jax, that is why she will not mate with him." Go figure, how bloody confusing.

"What makes her think she has to carry an heir? They can adopt." As soon as I finished speaking, I wanted to slap myself. Of course they couldn't adopt. Jackson was a fucking shifter.

"Forget I said that, I had a brain fart." Nico started laughing, and I sat up to glare at him, but paused. He looked so carefree and relaxed. I was taken aback; he never looked like this, except when we were having sex, in my dreams. Just thinking about that made me blush. I looked to Nico, who stopped laughing immediately, and the way he was looking at me made me think he knew exactly where my mind had drifted.

Clearing his throat he asked, "What is a brain fart, love?" Screw my life, he had to bring that up, didn't he?

"It's where your mind goes blank for a second, okay? Let's never mention me saying that again, please." He gave a little chuckle, then his face went serious again. I turned so I wasn't looking directly at him; his beauty always distracted me.

"Aurora keeps the pack safe. She sees what will happen and when. If she were to mate and become pregnant, she would lose that advantage. She loves Jackson enough to never endanger his safety." My heart kind of hurt for her. She would give up Jax for him to live.

"That is the stupidest thing I have ever heard; Jax wouldn't care. I am so annoyed that you both felt the need to lie and then cast a spell to trick him. He was just starting to forgive you, Nico. Now you have gone and fucked that up again." I saw him flinch at my words, but I don't feel sorry for him. He knows how I feel about lies, and yet he still felt the need to do it, again. I know this wasn't all his fault, but he could have come clean at any time. Poor Jackson.

"The spell was never meant to make him think you were his mate. I think his initial attraction to you made him feel all of the things he would feel toward a mate. I will not get involved anymore, I swear— she is going through enough as it is."

He's not wrong. Her brother is a fucking rat and a traitor. Tyler was Jackson's right-hand man, his beta. We only found out that he betrayed us when Kai told us the truth.

Kai. Oh, my heart hurt just thinking about him. Kai was so beautiful. He had the most striking gray-blue eyes that I swear could see into your soul. He had light blond hair that you wanted to run your fingers through. I loved Kai, or I thought I did, but he was never mine to love. My twin sister killed him, with the help of Randall Cane, king of all vampires.

I learned recently that my heart needed to stay out of all this mess. My sister would use my love against me and hurt those I cared about. Shaking myself out of my thoughts, I ask Nico the question that has been bugging me for days.

"Did you know that Kai tried to make me fall in love with him so that I would never choose you?" I heard him gasp; clearly he didn't know. I was hurt by Kai's deceit. His betrayal burned like acid. I thought I loved him, and that makes me more angry. I understand why he did it, though. I can never tell the others how I am getting my information—not until the time is right.

Nico never got a chance to answer: my bedroom door flew open and in walked a goddess of a woman. She was rocking a navy crop top and skin-tight white jeans. She had beautiful, long black curls that were past her waist; full, kissable lips; and violet eyes like Nico. Oh God! It hit me like a freight train— she's Nico's sister, but she is also the lady in the painting that was hanging in Randall Cane's office.

"Melakai was never yours to love. Your feelings are what clouded his judgment and got him killed." There was so much venom and hatred lacing each and every one of her words, but I couldn't stop staring at her, wondering why a portrait of her was hanging in Randall's office.

"Sophia, that's enough. Ryan didn't cause Melakai's death, you know this." Nico addressed his sister like she was a young child.

"Do not try to soothe me, brother, your *pet* knows what I say is the truth." Did she just call me a fucking pet? That's it, she didn't know me and she sure as fuck didn't get to stand there and pass judgment and blame me for things that were not my fault.

I had enough guilt over Kai's death, I didn't need her rubbing salt in my wound.

Standing from the bed, I make my way over to her, only for Nico to jump to his feet and block my path. I glare at the beast of a man. Being this close to him made me feel things I shouldn't; his proximity made my head go cloudy. He was like a drug to me. I wanted to touch him and let him hold me again. I wanted him to kiss me. I couldn't go down that road, so I leaned my head around his shoulder so I could look his sister in the eyes.

"I don't care if you are some fucking princess from a different world, you do not get to come in here and blame me for Kai's death. He would never have been with Randall if it wasn't for you getting your ass kidnapped." She recoiled at my harsh words, and Nico flinched, and I regretted the words as soon as they flew out my mouth.

"I'm sorry, that was harsh. I should never have said that."

"Don't ever apologize for saying what you think; you will be an honorable queen and good match for my brother." This woman is fucking crazy! One moment she hates me and wants to kill me, and now she is looking at me with respect. Clearing his throat, Nico spoke.

"Ryan meet Sophia. Sophia meet Ryan. I wish you both had met under better circumstances, but I guess luck was not on our side." Ignoring his introduction, I asked Sophia, "Why did you say Kai was never mine to love?"

"Because you were always destined to be Nico's, not Kai's."

"How could you know that?"

"I have premonitions."

"So you're a seer, like Aurora?"

"No, she can see future events and past events. I can only see people's love lives. I know, it's a crap gift to have, but it helped Nico." I pull my stare from Sophia to look at Nico, gauging her meaning from him. He gives nothing away, as usual. His eyes are burning with desire, and I would be lying if I said that one look didn't make me feel like melting on the spot.

"So, I guess I will just see you guys later then."

Nico and I don't acknowledge his sister's departure; we just stand there staring at each other. I don't know how long we stand there rooted to the spot but he is the first to pull his gaze away. I make my way back to the bed and sit down, trying to calm my racing heart. Nico reclaims his seat by the window.

"My sister is...she...she can be a lot to handle. Her time away from the fae realm has changed her." I could only imagine the horrors that Sophia went through at the hands of Randall Cane. Randall was a disgusting, vile man, and to make it worse, he now has my sister by his side. She and Randall want to use my blood to seal the fae realm. My blood is also the key to allow vampires to walk in the daylight. Unlike full fae blood, where you have to constantly top up, one drop of my blood is all it would take for a vampire to walk in daylight for eternity.

The only way to defeat Randall and my sister is to unlock my fae side, I'm an anomaly, half fae and half witch. Randall killed Jackson's father and drank his blood, the blood of an alpha.

We think he was the one to kill my father, for his blood as well. Randall drinking the blood of the alpha and the blood of my dad—a great warlock king and the best damn king the Knox has ever had.—means their power would run through his veins, making him stronger than almost everyone, except for me.

"I could only imagine the type of horrors she has had to endure at the hands of the Vampire King." Nico has a faraway look in his eyes, almost like he is reliving the torture of not having his sister by his side. "Nico, I need you to tell me the truth, please. Why were you so mad when you found out about Kai coming to me in my dreams?" With a deep breath, he looks me dead in the eyes and shatters me with his words.

"Melakai was never supposed to have a relationship with you; he was supposed to kill you."

Chapter Four

NICO

I see the moment she processes my words—her face falls and her beautiful hazel eyes with the peculiar yellow ring start to glisten. I fucked up big time, and I know I have just broken her heart more than any person has ever done before. I just told her that the man she *thinks* she loved was meant to kill her, not love her. She was never his to love, and he fucking knew it; he betrayed me by seducing her and making her love him. My blood starts to boil as I think about his conniving ways, and I clench my fists, trying to control the rage coursing through my veins.

"Thank you." What the fuck is happening here? Did she just thank me?

"I don't understand? Why are you thanking me?"

"Because for the first time, you haven't lied or given me half-truths. You were honest. I appreciate your honesty, even though it hurts me. Can you please explain why Kai was supposed to kill me?"

This strong, beautiful woman has endured so much in her life, and yet here she sits, accepting every burden placed on her. She is the most beautiful creature I have ever met in my life. Her long brown hair is falling over her shoulders, I would love to tuck those strands behind her ear and whisper sweet nothings to her. She deserves my honesty, and I must do what I can to earn her trust back, before I break it again.

"I wasn't lying when I told you that I could never harm you, personally. Dom had gotten a message to Kai not long after I met with your father that day in the park; we told him about your blood and what it could do. We knew, no matter what we had all been through, Kai would never let our world die or let Randall and his vampires get your blood so they could walk in the sunlight. If vampires were allowed to roam free at all hours, they would cause mass havoc on the humans. So he offered to take care of it for us. Kai made a vow to your grandmother that he would protect her child, but he never vowed to protect the child's children. When Kai realized it was you who had the blood to seal my realm, he went rogue. He got a message to us months later saying the job was done and the problem was solved. Years went by, and by the time I figured out what this nagging feeling was in my chest, Kai had already made his move on you."

"I was sixteen when I first met Kai, and in the vision Aurora showed me, I must have been eight or nine. So Kai watched me for years."

"Yes, I only figured out what the feeling was in my chest because you and I are linked."

"Wait, we're linked?"

"Yes, love. I bound your powers so part of me remains inside of you." She opened her mouth, but I raised my hand to stop her. "Let me explain, then I will answer any questions you have, okay?" She gave me a stiff nod and I stifled a grin. My little spitfire didn't like to be silenced.

"I felt your fear and then I felt your...*need*, when Kai first came to visit you. I am aware that Melakai didn't attend to your *needs* until years later. I can feel when your emotions are heightened or when you are being..." I couldn't bring myself to finish the sentence.

"You mean to tell me you could feel every time Kai and I were *intimate*?" I couldn't form the words, so I just nodded. She blushed immediately, pushed up off the bed, and started pacing. I was coming to learn that she did this a lot when she was stressed or overthinking. "What am I supposed to say to that, Nico?"

"Nothing at all, love. It was never meant to happen. I didn't even know that it could happen until it did."

"What the fuck does that mean?"

Obviously I sounded like a blabbering idiot. I needed a second to collect my thoughts so I could explain this better. After a moment of silence, I felt composed enough to continue.

"What I'm trying to say is I didn't know I would feel your emotions or anything else. I only realized I could when you were scared or hurt or..." I knew the moment it clicked—she whipped around, glaring at me. I hung my head in shame, unable to meet her eyes.

"Stop, I don't want to hear anymore."

"I'm sorry."

"You're sorry. You're fucking sorry?"

She continued pacing, and I knew she wasn't done yelling or being angry with me. She had every right to be pissed; I knew and had done nothing. I left her there, when I could have saved her. I was a coward. I sat on the sidelines and watched, never once intervening, fearing that if I helped her she would eventually turn against me. She has the power to kill my people, and I left her to suffer at the hands of her mother because I was scared of what she could do to me. If she was this angry now, learning this, she was going to light me on fire when she found out what I had done *recently*.

"All the times I felt like I was being watched, I thought it was Kai. It wasn't, though, was it? It was you this whole time. When I felt like I was being watched at Randall's manor, it wasn't Kai. That was you." I nodded.

"You saw my mother and me, didn't you?" Again I just nodded. "Why, Nico?" I don't know if she meant to voice her last question, she whispered it so low, but I heard.

"Because I am a coward. I thought if you didn't know who you were, you couldn't hurt my people. Then things changed."

If this was a cartoon, steam would be blowing out of her ears. She stood directly in front of me now, hands on her shapely hips. I slowly raked my gaze up her luscious body until I landed on her eyes.

"What changed?"

"My feelings for you."

She laughed, I mean a full-on fucking belly laugh, with tears streaming down her face. I was stunned. Her reaction was not the one I expected, that's for sure. After a minute or so she finally got herself under control, glare firmly back in place, and I knew she was about to rip me a new one. My balls may have shriveled up in self-defense.

"Your feelings for me? Don't fucking make me laugh. If you felt anything for me you would have helped. You're right, Nico, you are a fucking coward. Did you like watching her beat me?"

I growled in response. I fucking hated every minute of seeing her being hurt, but I still did nothing to stop it, so I have no defense. "Did you like it when she couldn't pay and got her dealers to beat me? How about when she would lock—"

I couldn't take it. I jumped to my feet, and to her credit, she didn't shrink away or flinch; she stood her ground. We were so close I could feel her heat. She was so tiny the top of her head only reached my chest. She craned her neck back so she could look me dead in the eyes, and those full, beautiful lips were calling to me like a siren. I wanted to capture her bottom lip and nibble on it like I had done so many times before in her dreams. I reached my hand out and clasped the back of her neck. She tried to hide the effect I had on her, but she failed—I saw her eyes roll slightly and felt the shiver that went down her spine at my touch. She may be angry with me, but she also knew my touch could relieve the tension in her body and make her mind relax for a while.

Chapter Five

RYAN

His touch was like fire, and my body felt so hot and needy from his close proximity. I couldn't think with him being this close to me. I was hurt, *so hurt,* from what I had just learned. Looking into his violet eyes made me feel things I shouldn't feel. Kai had just died, and here I am begging Nico with my eyes to kiss me or fuck me. I was trying to shake myself out of my thoughts and pull away, but I couldn't.

I was a prisoner, and he had the key to release me. His eyes kept jumping from my mouth back to my eyes; he was contemplating whether or not he should kiss me.

I wanted him to kiss me. If he did, I could escape my thoughts for a while. I knew I could get lost in Nico; he constantly hurts me with his lies, but he was the only one who could mend me.

Nico was slowly leaning down, so close I could feel his breath on my lips. I snaked my tongue out to moisten them and his eyes followed my movement, his eyes turning so dark they were almost purple.

I knew that look, Nico was turned on. He closed the gap

between us with no hesitation and began exploring my mouth; as soon as his tongue entered, I let out a moan.

This was my first *real* kiss with Nico, and holy shit did it put my dream kisses to shame.

We explored each other's mouths, and for the moment, nothing in the world seemed to exist except for the two of us.

He ran his hands down my arms and to my hips, pulling me even closer. I gasped, but he didn't let me break the kiss. I could feel his erection pulsating against my stomach, and a sense of pride flowed through me, knowing that I was the one who had done that to him. This god of a man was turned on by little old me. His hand continued down to my ass and then to my thighs. He gripped the back of my legs, lifting me, and I instinctively wrapped my thighs around his waist and circled my hands around his neck. Holding him like this, and him holding me, felt right. I felt safe and protected, which was ludicrous considering he just said he watched me be beaten for years.

Nico started walking us back toward my bed, I wanted him inside me for real, it was all I could think about right now.

A throat clearing made Nico stop in his tracks. We both pulled apart and turned toward the bedroom door, where Dom, Jax, Alex, and Chase stood. I could feel the heat making its way up my neck to my cheeks. Fuck my life—my cousins looked pissed, Jax looked hurt, and Dom looked happy. There was an awkward silence for a beat until Dom spoke.

"Since you don't want to put her down, caveman, can I join you?" Nico started growling at the same time Jax smacked the back of Dom's head.

"Put her down now, *Tinkerbell*." I could tell from the tone of Chase's voice that he was mad I was in such a compromising position. I tried to wiggle out of Nico's hold, but he wouldn't budge, instead gripping my ass harder to make sure I couldn't move. I placed both my hands on his cheeks and turned his face so he could look me in the eyes.

"Let me down, big man." Nico didn't release me; he just continued to stare and nuzzled his face more into my hands.

"Yeah, put her down now, *big man.*" Chase was being a sarcastic ass. When Nico didn't immediately put me down, I saw, from the corner of my eye, Chase taking a step forward. Nico quickly put me down and then pushed me behind his back, shielding me from the others. A part of me swooned at his protective instincts, while another part was pissed he wanted to protect me now, and not before.

"Take another step closer and you will regret it, *witch.*" He did not just threaten my cousin. I tried to move around him, but he just kept blocking my path.

"Move away from her now, *Tinkerbell.*" Oh God, did Chase really just call the king of Farrarie a fairy, *twice?* The others started laughing, but Nico didn't find it funny, judging by the way he went stiff as a board and stood even taller, if that was possible. I needed to defuse this situation now before we had a brawl on our hands. While Nico was distracted—glaring at Chase, I assume—I quickly stepped around him, only for him to reach and grab my arm and haul me back into his chest.

"Let her go Nico, now!" This time it was Dom, and I've never heard him use such a harsh tone before. Nico reluctantly let me go after a moment and then slumped down into the single chair. I didn't have time to process his actions before Chase was barking at me.

"What the actual fuck, Ry? Him? Seriously? Of all the fucking people, you go for Tink."

"Chase, please stop. I don't need to justify my actions to you."

"Yeah, I'm just here to worry about you when he breaks your heart like the last one did. Guess what, though? This time it will be worse, because you have to marry that piece of shit." Shocked, I reeled back like Chase had just slapped me. Chase didn't wait for a reply; instead he stormed out of the room like a fucking toddler. His words hurt. I didn't mean to piss my cousin off. This was all so confusing, and it was fucking with my head. One minute I hated Nico and then the next I was grinding on his dick while he carried me to bed.

"He didn't mean it, Squirt. He's just worried about you, and doesn't want to see you get hurt. I'll go talk to him and meet you later for our meeting." I gave Alex a forced smile before he left the room, shutting the door on his way out. I stood rooted to my spot, head spinning. Guilt was starting to eat at me now. Chase was right; Kai is gone, and here I am trying to jump Nico at the first opportunity. I felt someone place a hand on my shoulder and looked up to see it was Jackson. He held so much warmth in his chocolate brown eyes. He looked so young, but he was nearly triple my age. Being a supernatural had its perks, I guess.

"Take it from someone who thought he had a mate, but was tricked by his real mate. Love is complicated, and both of those boys love you dearly. Seeing you so torn up about Kai, and you shutting them out, has been hard on them. They just want to be there for you." I felt like a complete asshole now; Jax was right—I holed up in my room since learning about Kai and never once have I given any thought to how my cousins would be feeling. I was such a selfish bitch.

"You're right, Jax, I'm gonna go see if I can find them and talk to them." Jax gave me a gentle squeeze on my shoulder and then released me. I nodded to Dom as I exited the room, but I didn't utter a word or turn back to Nico. I was confused and ashamed at the way I had just acted. What the hell is wrong with me, and why can't I fight this pull I have toward Nico?

As I walked down the hallway, I turned right and found both my cousins arguing. When they spotted me, they stopped their bickering immediately. I didn't have any words, so I just walked right up and engulfed Chase in a hug. It took him by surprise, and after a beat, his arms came up and wrapped around me. He rested his chin on the top of my head.

"I'm sorry, Ry. I didn't mean what I said, it's—"

"Shh, Chase, it's fine. I know you are hurting, and I know a lot has changed for both you and Alex. I am the one who is sorry; I let my grief cloud my judgment." Chase and I pulled apart and I hugged Alex, as well, telling him how sorry I was. They both waved away my concerns and we made our way toward the game room; it had pool tables, air hockey, ten-pin bowling and TVs. We wandered over to one of the many couches and took a seat.

"Squirt, we are here because we want to be and not because we have to be. Chase and I could have easily gone with Stevie but we didn't. We believe she is wrong." I appreciated what he was saying. It meant a lot to know that they chose to come with me instead of having to.

"I just want you both to know that I am so thankful to have you here with me. I couldn't do any of this without either of you." Chase looked like he swallowed a lemon; I could tell he wanted to ask me something. "Just ask whatever you want to know, Chase"

"How did you know Tink was lying, and how did you know he was the one you have to marry?" *Shit.* Taking in a few deep breaths, I unburdened myself and told them the truth and what my *secret power* really was. I needed to trust in them, that they would have my back. This was new for me. I have never had anyone who would risk something or was even willing to choose me before.

Chapter Six

NICO

I didn't look up when Ryan left the room. I couldn't. I could tell Jax and Dom both stayed behind, but I couldn't look at them either. If I did, they both would know the truth.

"She's your *hugacko,* isn't she?" Trust Dom to put the pieces together. I heard Jax's sharp intake of breath. Well, now they both knew.

"Does she know?"

"No, I haven't told her. I don't want that to have any sway in her decision." I knew as soon as the words left my mouth they were both going to be pissed.

"You need to fucking tell her, Nico! She has a right to know."

I stood and marched over so Dom and I were toe to toe. I needed him to see the look in my eyes.

"It is my burden to bear, not yours."

"So you're just going to lie to her *again?*" Jackson needed to learn how to keep his big mouth shut for once.

"This is none of your business. Stay out of it Jackson. I mean it."

"Or what, Nico? She has been through enough, and I have

had enough of your shit. I was just coming around to forgiving you, but after the stunt you pulled with switching Ryan for Aurora, I want nothing more than to rearrange your fucking face." I sighed and scrubbed a hand down my face, then made my way back to the chair and dropped down. Jackson was right; I was fucking everything up because I was scared. I would never admit that to them, though.

"What do you suppose I do then, Jackson? I never meant for my spell to make you think Ryan was your mate. I would never trick you like that; it was only supposed to mask Aurora's scent."

"I understand why she asked you to do it. I'm still pissed that you did it, though. You both could have come to me."

"No, she can't Jax. You know as soon as the spell wears off and you scent her, you will want to claim her. She doesn't want to be claimed; she's not a wolf." Dom was right, every wolf that scents their mate is overpowered by the need to claim and mark them as their own.

"Enough about me and my fucked-up love life. We should go grab a bite to eat and then get ready to meet the others." I was not looking forward to this meeting. I somehow had to convince Ryan that she *wanted* to marry me.

After getting something to eat in the mess hall and catching up with a few of Jackson's pack members, we started to relax in our chairs. It was just the three of us now, and I started feeling nostalgic. We used to hang out all the time and just talk shit and have fun, and now our foursome is a threesome. It was hard to wrap my head around Kai being gone. I was angry as hell at him; he had no right to go behind my fucking back and trick

Ryan. She had no right falling for him, either; her heart needed to stay out of it when it concerned him. She was mine, whether she knew it or not. Kai was the safe one, and I was the one you took a gamble on. I would never be the one to hold your hand and make you think everything was okay. I am the one who will push you and tell you to just do it. Snapping out of my somber thoughts, I turned to face my brothers, ready to try mend things, until my sister ruined it.

"Why are you three sitting here like there isn't about to be a war?"

"Sophia, what an unpleasant surprise, as usual."

"Dominic, be seen not heard. No one wants to hear your bark." Sophia and Dom were always bickering at each other, even before Sophia was taken by Randall. Now they didn't even try to hide their loathing for each other; They used to be so close, and now they couldn't be in the same room without trying to hurt the other in some way.

"Cut the shit, you two. What do you want, Sophia?"

"Nothing, Jackson. I just wanted to make sure that I wasn't going to be left out of the meeting you are planning with the half-breed." Jackson started growling at my sister, and I had to defuse this before she went hurricane Sophia on their asses. My sister had a temper on her even before her ordeal.

"How do you even know about that, sister?" No one knew about the meeting except for us, Ryan, Alex, Chase, and Aurora. My sister was always sneaky, it seems over time she has honed her skills.

"I have my ways, brother. I want in on the meeting." Before I could even answer, Dom did.

"No, you're not invited."

"I'm not asking, and if you want information about what Randall is planning, then you will have me there." *Shit,* she had us there. She turned before any of us could respond and left the mess hall.

"Well, I guess Sophia is coming to the meeting." Dom didn't look pleased at all about my sister joining us, but I didn't have time to dig into what was wrong with him.

We made our way to Jackson's office, and as we rounded the corner, I spotted Ryan, Aurora, Sophia, and Ryan's cousins leaning against the wall outside of Jackson's office.

"I thought I told you not to be here." Who the hell was Dom snapping at? Dom was the most chill and relaxed one out of all of us. To see him so uptight and angry was slightly unsettling.

"Oh, Dominic, since when have I ever listened to a word you have said?" Sophia had an evil smirk plastered on her face, and her eyes were shooting daggers at Dom. Dom marched right up to my sister, leaving barely an inch of space between them, I tensed, ready to intervene if things got out of hand. I would not let anyone hurt my sister, no matter how difficult she was. She has been through enough.

"How about you start listening now, little dove?" *Little dove?* Since fucking when did Dom have a pet name for my sister? He and I would be having a little chat about that after this meeting. Sophia flinched at the nickname.

"Dom, that's enough. Sophia has information we need, hear her out." At Aurora's words, Dom took a reluctant step back from my sister, muttering something under his breath about *pain in the ass* and *never listens.*

We all entered Jackson's office, each taking a seat except for Soph, who stood staring out the window. No one spoke for a good minute or two; I avoided eye contact with Ryan as best as I could. The tension in the room was stifling. No one wanted to push Ryan, but we were running out of time. Before I could get lost in my thoughts any further, Sophia spoke.

"How long before her powers are unlocked?"

"The *her* is sitting right here, thank you very much," Ryan snapped. She hated people talking about her instead of to her.

"Okay, everyone chill out. We're all on the same side here, and we all need to work together." Alex the know-it-all told us off like we were children.

"Well, since you clearly have it all figured out, little Knox, why don't you fill us in?" I knew I was being a condescending prick, but I didn't give a shit. Alex was annoying.

"Actually, Nico, I do have it figured out. Since it is a binding ceremony of two races and two members of royal bloodlines, all leaders will need to be present for this, including Randall." What the fuck—since when? How did I not know about this? I looked at both Dom and Jax, both of them had the same look of shock, so I'm not the only one who didn't know then. "Judging by the look on all your faces, none of you knew about this"

"Don't be smug boy, it's unattractive" at least Sophia found her voice because Dom, Jax and I were still in shock. I looked over and saw Aurora with her head down and shoulders bunched, something was wrong.

"Aurora, are you okay?" she looked up and tried to hide the fear etched across her face, now I was really worried. What the hell happened to put that look on her face.

"I.....I...um...I" she couldn't even string a sentence together. Jax got up from his seat and rushed over to her kneeling down in front of her. He tried to grab her hands but she snatched them away. He fell back on his heels but didn't move.

"Aurora, can you please tell us what happened?" I had never heard Jax speak to anyone like that. He was so calm and soothing, like he was trying not to spook an injured animal. He knew Aurora was his mate, but because the spell hadn't worn off yet, her scent was still masked. Everyone knows it's only a matter of time before Jax pounces on her. She took a few deep breaths and then looked directly into Jax's eyes.

"If Randall has to attend the wedding, then so does Ryan's sister." I heard Ryan's sharp intake of air. She didn't want to face her sister, yet. "Tyler will come with them as well." Ah, so this was about her traitor of a brother. Tyler betrayed us all when he decided to help the enemy, but I imagine his betrayal crushes Aurora worse than anyone.

"I know this must be hard for you, love. Tyler made his choice. No one blames you."

"Everyone hates me! the whole pack has turned against me because of my brother. I was already an outcast because I can't shift, and now this?" Jackson was growling and starting to shake; he needed to get his emotions under control before he shifted and hurt Aurora, being that close to her. Dom and I jumped to our feet at the same time and rushed over to Jax, while Ryan was pulled to her feet by both her cousins and went to stand by Sophia. I placed my hand on Jax's shoulder. *Worst mistake.*

Chapter Seven

RYAN

Jackson turned and snapped—I mean, full on went to bite Nico. Nico quickly jerked his hand away and stepped back. Jax was shaking and trying to take deep breaths. His hands were turning into claws. I gasped. Jax spun toward us and his eyes had turned yellow. He started growling again. He took a step in our direction, and I froze. Nico jumped in front of Jax, shielding us from his view.

"Brother, you need to calm down. Aurora is safe, and she's here with you now." Jax didn't reply; he just stood there, staring at Nico. Hair burst from the pores of his arms, and long gray hair was present on his legs, too. Jackson was going to shift, and I felt like I was going to piss myself. "Aurora, you need to talk to him; you're the only person he is going to listen to at the moment."

Aurora raised from her seat, no sign of fear on her face at all. She didn't even seem nervous. She made her way over to face Jax, and Nico stepped aside so she could take his place. She tentatively reached out a hand and placed it on Jax's cheek, and he looked down at her. I felt like we were witnessing a private moment between two lovers.

"Jax, sweetheart, I'm gonna need you to calm down and take a deep breath for me." At the sound of her voice, Jax started to relax, the fur on his arms and legs lying down and beginning to retract. I swear Aurora is an animal whisperer. No one moved or spoke for fear of setting Jax off again. Aurora took a step back from Jax once it looked like he had himself under control. She took the seat she vacated and tapped the spot next to her for Jax to join her. He didn't hesitate; he made his way straight over to her and plonked down, sniffing her and rubbing his cheek against her head. Dom gestured for the rest of us to take our seats and we did, except for Sophia, who remained by the window. I was seated between Alex and Chase, Dom took the spare spot next to Jax, while Nico took the single seat.

"I'm sorry for my outburst, I normally have better control of my wolf," Jackson said, voice still gruff with wolf. I felt sorry for him; you could see in his eyes he was embarrassed for his loss of control but pleased that Aurora was now tucked firmly into his side.

"Don't worry about it, brother, we all lose control some-times." Dom seemed to always know the right things to say, bless him.

"Let's move on and get down to business shall we?" Clearly Nico was sick of the interruptions. I couldn't really blame him, because I want to get this over with as well—the suspense is killing me.

"What are the first steps for Ryan?"

"The first step Chase is that Nico and Ryan need to marry." Well, Aurora doesn't beat around the bush, does she? I couldn't help my next words—sarcasm is my go-to in serious situations.

"Yay, I'm going to be a teen bride, how cool." I felt at war with myself over this situation: part of me felt sick for being forced into marriage, but another part just felt...numb. Resigned to follow a path I didn't choose. I don't know how I'm supposed to feel, honestly. Nothing has gone right for me in the past few weeks. My sister has gone rogue, my dad died—murdered, though I didn't know that originally—and Mom is fuck-knows where. I don't have a home anymore. The only thing I do have is my truck, which is still parked at Stevie's. I have no idea what the hell I'm supposed to do. I didn't notice Nico had moved until he knelt down in front of me. He didn't touch me but just stared into my eyes. And for a moment, I got lost in the depths of those beautiful violet eyes.

"I know this all must be hard for you, love, believe me. I have been around for a really, really long time, and I have never married. This is all new to me too. I don't know how to be a husband, or if I will be any good at it, but you have my word I will try my hardest, and when that isn't enough, I will try even harder. I will treat you like the queen you are and cherish you daily. You will be loved by me and want for nothing."

Nico's words stirred something in me. I didn't know what this feeling was. It almost felt like hope. I knew Nico meant every word he said, and call me a fool if you like, but I believed him.

A thought entered my head at that moment, telling me I was lucky it was Nico I had to marry and not some weird old guy in a suit.

I leaned forward and placed my hand gently on Nico's cheek. I don't know if he meant to but he pushed into my touch, almost like it soothed him. I was scared and unsure, but deep down I knew Nico wouldn't let me fail or fall. As much as I tried to deny it, he really was the same man I spent hours laughing with and talking to in my dreams. I did know Nico. I just didn't know him properly, while I was awake.

Taking a deep breath to steady my nerves, so I wouldn't fumble my words when I spoke, I said, "I hear everything you are saying and I believe you will do all of those things. I just need you to be patient with me. I will do my best to be all the things you need me to be." I feel like I should tell him that I know his secret, but then I would need to answer his questions of how I know and I wasn't ready to reveal my answer yet. Both my cousins knew how I was getting my information.

"Okay, well, now that Nico is on one knee and just proposed, I think we can start planning the Faeling wedding of the year!" Dom seemed excited for this wedding, and that made me feel uneasy. I could tell he was up to something.

Nico stood and offered me his hand, and I hesitated for the briefest moment before gingerly placing my hand in his, letting him pull me to my feet.

There was a small gap between us, and I could feel my body wanting to gravitate toward him. It took a lot more restraint then I wanted to admit to stay where I was and not close the gap between us.

Looking me in the eyes and never breaking that contact, Nico asked the others to give us a minute alone. Everyone except Chase and Alex readily agreed.

Those two bozos left the room grumbling about jackasses and rich-dicks. When the door clicked shut behind them, Nico led me over to the window Sophia had been staring through earlier.

The view from Jackson's office is stunning; you can see the forest and mountains that seemed like they went on forever. I could sit here gazing out at Mother Nature all day; I found it so calming. Jackson told me the compound was built in the middle of their lands so that no one ventures near their living quarters. I guess it wouldn't be a good idea to live close to town, in case humans saw them in their wolf forms. Nico's homeland was beautiful as well, and also a wooded retreat from the world. At

Nico's loud exhale, I snapped from my thoughts and turned so I could see his face. He was still looking out the window.

"I shouldn't even be saying this, but you can still turn around and run, love. You owe my realm nothing. You owe *me* nothing. I'm a selfish bastard, I admit that, but I would never force you to marry me. Do I want to marry you? Yes, I do. But you're so young and have your whole life ahead of you. If we marry, you will be expected to return to Farrarie with me and rule by my side. You will be Queen."

Fuck, I didn't think of any of that. I would have to leave my realm and live in his. Though, it's not like anyone here would miss me, aside from Alex and Chase.

I would have to leave everything I know and move to a whole different world. Part of me was scared shitless and another part was longing for the adventure that move would bring. It would be a new beginning for me, a fresh start where no one would know of my past. I could start over.

"As scared as I am with this whole unlocking my power thing and marrying you, I could never let innocent people die due to my own fear. I don't want to have to do this, Nico—any of it. In a short amount of time I have lost two people I care about, one is dead and the other might as well be. The point is I will not let my fear overshadow what I am supposed to do. If I have to marry in order to stop my sister and Randall, I will. I promise you, your world will not die because of me. I will do everything I can to protect your people, and I will try to be the best queen I can be." I could see pride shining in his eyes at my words; it meant a lot to see that look and made some of the tension in my body dissipate.

"Hearing those words means a lot to me, love. I will help you with training and be there with you every step of the way." I knew he meant every word. Nico grasped my hand and led me over to the couch, where we both took a seat and quietly sat with each other, hands clasped. I don't know how much time passed, but we were both pulled out of our moment when the others re-entered the room. No one said a word, but I did notice both Chase and Alex were apprehensive at seeing me sitting with Nico instead of rejoining them. They took their seats on the other couch, with Sophia now taking my normal spot between them. Dom sat on my other side, and Jax and Aurora each took one of the single seats.

"Right, so let's get down to business. I'm guessing by the way you're holding his hand now, Ry, that you are okay to go ahead with this sham of a wedding." Before I could snap at Chase, Alex did it for me.

"Brother, if you can't support our cousin and the great sacrifice she is making, then you need to get the fuck out of here." I have never heard Alex or Chase speak to each other like that; to say I was shocked is an understatement. Judging by the look on Chase's face, he was just as surprised. He kept opening and shutting his mouth like a fish out of water. I could tell he wanted to say something, but no words would come out.

"I...I don't know what to say to that."

"You're not supposed to say anything, Chase, you're just supposed to nod your head and agree with me. I know this is hard, but we need to support our cousin. She needs us." Hearing those words from Alex gave me a rare feeling of belonging. I would miss these two the most when I left for Farraric.

"Thank you, Alex. Nico and I have decided that we will continue on with the wedding. Our feelings about this mean nothing in comparison to a whole world dying." Nico gave my hand a squeeze, letting me know that he supported me, which was good, because I was going to need his support to get through all of this.

Everyone then launched into plans for the wedding. It wouldn't be anything huge, just something small and intimate.

We didn't have enough time to plan a huge wedding, anyway, and we didn't want a lot of people there in case Randall or Stevie tried something stupid, which seemed likely. We agreed the wedding would take place in four days' time.

After a couple hours of planning, we all decided that we were happy with the outcome. Everyone had their own jobs to do in order to make this wedding happen. We would be run off our feet for the next couple of days, that's for sure. Nico and I haven't broken the news to my cousins that after all this stuff with Randall and Stevie, that I would have to move to the fae realm. I was not looking forward to *that* conversation. I knew my news would hurt them and they would worry. We all decided to make our way over to the mess hall and grab some dinner. After that I planned to retire and enjoy a nice long soak in my claw foot tub in my en suite.

You could hear muffled sounds of everyone talking and laughing as we neared the mess hall. Thank goodness that room was sound proof I could only imagine how loud the noise would be if it wasn't. Jackson was leading our group, so he was the one to push the doors open for us to enter.

As soon as we did, everyone's laughter and conversation stopped. Awkward much? Sophia didn't seem to notice, or she just didn't care—she pushed past us and made her way over to the buffet counter and started to dish her food.

Alex and Chase followed. Nico rested his hand at the small of my back and gave me a gentle push toward the others. I felt like his hand was burning through me, the way his touch set me ablaze. Trying to push my focus away from the feeling of Nico touching me, I started counting in my head how many steps it takes to get to the counter. Conversation seemed to resume once we had taken our seats, and no one approached us, which I was thankful for. I ate as quickly as possible and excused myself with the explanation that I was tired, but I really just needed to dream.

Chapter Eight

NICO

I know she is hiding something, but I can't figure out what. Her cousins know her secret, I'm sure of it. They never questioned her exit, and they *always* questioned her whereabouts. I needed to figure out her secret; she knew things she shouldn't. Before I could get more lost in my thoughts, a bread roll hit me in the side of the head, snapping my gaze to the left and glaring at the asshole who dared to throw anything at me. I wasn't surprised to find the asshole was none other than Chase. The prick had a smug smile on his face that had my hand itching to slap off.

"Now that I have your attention, your *majesty*, what do you really have planned for your wedding with my cousin?" He's a smart fucker, I give him that, but I couldn't let on that I had ulterior motives for my wedding day.

"I have no idea what you mean, little witch." His playful expression dropped immediately and his eyes turned dark. That's right; let your magic out to play, young one, so I can teach you a real lesson.

"You may think you have my cousin fooled, *King*." I was getting sick of having the words *king* and *majesty* thrown at me like they were vile terms. "But you are wrong; we are already two steps ahead of you. You are the one playing catch up to our plan." Alex stood and placed a hand on his brother's shoulder, and Chase reluctantly stood and followed his brother out of the mess hall. To say I was confused was an understatement. I knew she was up to something, but if Dumb and Dumber were that cocky about their plan then she must be planning something big.

"Was it just me or did they just say they have a plan of their own and we are not privy to any of it?"

"I hate to say it, but I think you're right, little dove. I believe our little Knox coven has their own plan." Sophia and Dom were right; they are the best at finding out secrets. They always have been. It is a hidden talent of theirs. Apart they are good at solving mysteries, but together they are unstoppable. My little witch and her cousins are hiding something big from us, and we need to find out what it is.

"I think we should..." I couldn't even finish my damn sentence before my sister cut me off.

"No, whatever you are thinking, it is wrong. Aurora and I will go and speak with the witch alone. She will not disclose anything to you, brother. You have lied and hidden things from her, and she needs allies. Aurora and I will be that for her." Dom and Jax both looked apprehensive about this plan, but we really didn't have a choice. Sophia stood and nodded for Aurora to follow her. Both of the girls exited the room without even glancing back or waiting to see if we agreed or not.

"I guess I'll say it, then; those women have you both by the balls."

"And So-So doesn't have you by the balls, Dominic the Great Sorcerer?" said Jackson. *Wait a fucking minute.*

"You have feelings for my sister?" I was burning a hole in

the side of Dom's head with my glare, but he wouldn't tear his gaze from Jax's. I slapped my hand on the table, which garnered the attention of the others in the room, but I didn't give a fuck at this point.

"Answer me now, Dom!"

He finally pulled his gaze from Jackson's to meet mine, and we sat there staring at each other for a long moment. Dom wasn't giving anything away; he was the hardest person to read. Jax was an open book—his eyes told you his emotions. Dom hid his better than anyone I knew.

"Of course I care about her, Nico. She is like a sister to me. Do not ever question my affection for her; you know as well as anyone I love her. I have always cared for her as much as you." I felt like there was a double meaning to his words, but shouting broke out across the room and distracted me.

"Alpha, the traitor is at the border! He wishes to speak with you." Jackson, Dom, and I all jumped to our feet and rushed toward the young man who had shouted the news.

"Is he alone?" Jax had his alpha voice on now; he wasn't asking for the truth—he was pulling it from his pack member. Jackson is one of the strongest alphas I have ever met in my time, with the exception of Dom.

"No, Alpha. He has four vampire guards with him."

With a curt nod from Jax, the young man turned and hustled out of the hall. We followed Jax outside and toward his border, at least twenty other pack members following us. They would never leave their alpha, and if Tyler tried anything on Jax, the pack wouldn't hesitate to take Tyler out. Once we neared the border, I could see Tyler and four others, like the young boy had said, but the four of them were carrying something big. My heart dropped when I caught sight of the item they were carrying.

"You are either stupid or suicidal for coming back here, *Beta.*" Unsurprisingly, Jax was still bitter and angry about Tyler's betrayal. Tyler winced at Jax's words.

"I have not come here to fight or to die, Alpha. I have come to return something that belongs to you, and then I will leave."

"Why would you come here, knowing that we could kill you?" His behavior seemed inexplicable.

"Because, your majesty, not everything is as it seems. I mean you all no harm—I just want to do the right thing." The four vampire guards stepped forward to hand over the huge, rolled-up carpet, and four of Jax's pack members stepped forward and collected it for us. Tyler turned to leave when Jax stopped him with his words.

"Aurora's my mate." Tyler didn't turn or tense.

"I know, Jax. I've always known. So has she. You will make her strong, and she will make you stronger. Treat her well and love her like she should have always been loved. Trust in her and prove to her that you are worthy of her, and I promise you she will give it up to stand by your side." Jax stood there gaping at Tyler's retreating form, clearly lost for words. I think we all were. Aurora has clearly known she was Jax's mate longer than she let me believe.

After Jax finally gathered himself, we made our way to the compound and to one of the spare rooms. Once inside, we made our way over to the bed, the carpet was unrolled and the contents were revealed. I owed Tyler for the return of my brother's body. Looking at Melakai, lifeless, covered in bruises and cuts, nearly brought me to my knees. His fingers were broken and nails were torn off, and his ankle was snapped and laying at an odd angle.

"I will fucking kill them for what they have done." I could feel the anger radiating off Dom, the need for vengeance thick in the air.

"None of them will make it out of this unscathed, brother—I vow that to you." Jax was right. Anyone who had a hand in doing this to our brother would not live.

"We will avenge our brother." We would make every one of them pay. Just then the bedroom door burst open and all three of us spun around, shielding the intruder from being able to see Melakai.

"You have five seconds to move, all of you, or I will make you." How the hell did Ryan know we were here, and how did she know we had Kai?

"How did you know he was here, love?" I'm glad Dom asked the obvious question, as I was still too shocked to form words.

"I told you all before, I have a secret power." Her cousins, my sister, and Aurora then filed into the room as well. My gaze shot to my sister, who just nodded, telling me to give Ryan what she wants. Reluctantly, all three of us stepped aside to let Ryan see Kai.

There was no look of shock, or any emotion at all, which was worrying, to say the least. She stepped forward and made her way around to the side of the bed and perched on the edge, gently placing her hand on top of Kai's battered one and using her other hand to caress his cheek. Due to my little bond with her, I could feel her sorrow and heartbreak.

"I'm glad you got here safe. Now I think it is time for me to tell the others the truth." Jax, Dom, and I looked to the others, and they seemed to be clued in on what was about to happen, which set me on edge. Chase, the smug prick, smirked at me. I tore my gaze from him and focused on Ryan. I needed answers, and she was about to give them to me, whether or not she liked it.

"What is the truth, love? What are you hiding from us?" *From me.* She took a few calming breaths before she answered.

"I will tell you everything, Nico."

Chapter Nine

RYAN

After I left the mess hall, I made it back to my room in record time. I quickly made my way over the bed and grabbed the small vial Alex had given me. Without hesitation, I drank it and laid down. A short while later I was being shaken awake. I blinked a few times, trying to get my eyes to focus, and when they did, I saw both my cousins standing by the edge of the bed.

"Did you do it? Is it done?"

"Yes, Alex, he's coming to us now."

"Okay, we need to be ready. Are you ready to tell the others the truth?"

"Yeah...I think so, Chase. I understand a lot more now, and when he is woken he can help me understand more. He is a key piece in this war; I needed the others to think I was scared and uncertain about marrying Nico blindly or else they would have asked too many questions. Nico is very bright, and he would have caught on to my lie, or Jax would scent the lie or some shit. I know you don't like it, Chase, but I do still have to go through with this wedding."

Chase didn't comment, just nodded his head. He didn't like

Nico and that was okay, but I did need him to be cooperative while we fought this war.

A few minutes later there was a knock at the door, and before any of them could answer it, the door opened and in walked Sophia and Aurora. These belonged on a runway, they both had bodies to die for. To say I was shocked that they were in my room, would be an understatement.

"Yes I know, I'm the last person you thought would come to see you. Just know that Aurora and I both know what is about to happen. She has seen it and I was the one who cast the spell, I didn't know if it would work but clearly it has."

"Wait, you knew this whole time and said nothing?" I could hear the shock in my own voice.

"Yes, it wasn't my story to tell. I owe Melakai my life; he saved me from the torture I endured every day, and he knew setting me free would cost him his life. I did the only thing I could." Wow, color me purple and call me Barney! Sophia has more fucking layers than an onion.

I could feel him. I knew he was here. I told the others it was time. None of us said a word on the walk to the room where the guys had brought Kai. Aurora led us there, knowing which room Jax would use to hold the body of his fallen brother.

I slammed the door open—nothing like a grand entrance—and strutted into the room. All three of them were staring, their faces slack with shock. I felt pretty fucking cool to be the one surprising them for a change.

"You have five seconds to move, all of you, or I will make

you." My words were harsher than I intended them to be, but time was of the essence.

"How did you know he was here, love?"

"I told you all before, I have a secret power." It was the only answer I could give Dom at the moment. I moved past them and made my way over to the side of the bed. I ignored all of Kai's injuries and placed my hand atop his cold one, my other hand caressing his hollow cheek. He was so cold and stiff; I hope I wasn't too late. "I'm glad you got here safe. Now I think it is time for me to tell the others the truth."

"What is the truth, love? What are you hiding from us?" What Nico really meant was what am I hiding from *him*.

"I will tell you everything, Nico—after." I knew the guys deserved an explanation but right now, I didn't have the time.

"Later, brother. Alex, you and Chase get her what she needs. Aurora, draw the blinds and close the door." A moment later Sophia was sitting on Kai's other side, holding his other hand. "Thank you" was all she whispered. A little while later the door opened, and Alex and Chase came in with the dagger and spell. They made their way toward me when Nico blocked their path.

"You are not going near her with that blade."

"If you don't step aside, *Tink,* I won't help her save the dirty leech." I flinched at Chase's words. Kai wasn't a dirty leech; he was a good man. Kai may have led me astray for years, but his reasons were noble, in a way. Dom pulled Nico out of the way, and the boys quickly made their way to my side. I grabbed the dagger and the spell paper from them. I have never in my life cast a spell, but the boys assured me I could do this. I *had* to do this. He told me to trust him, and I did. We needed Kai alive so he could fulfill his role in our plan. I hope Kai didn't hate me when he learned I had double- crossed him. I knew it was wrong of me to do this, but

I had no other choice. I just hoped Kai saw it that way, as well.

"Wait, what are you doing, Ryan?" Blowing out a breath, I turned to face Jax and answered his question.

"I'm going to try and bring him back." I heard Jax, Dom and Nico all gasp; I know this must be hard for them to believe.

"You can not bring back the dead, babe. He won't be the same, trust me." I know Dom is scared, but he didn't understand.

"He isn't dead, per se." Dom snapped his head toward Sophia.

"What the fuck are you talking about, little dove?"

"I cast a spell. I didn't know if it would work, but apparently it did. That's why Ryan is trying to revive him with her blood and the spell she has in her hand." I mouthed a silent *thank you* to Sophia for explaining what I couldn't; the lump in my throat was preventing me from saying anything at the moment.

I gripped the dagger in my left hand and pressed the blade to my right hand, slicing my palm. I winced at the pain. I have never cut myself on purpose before, so I was shocked at the pain. I placed my right hand across Kai's lips, letting my blood drip into his mouth, and began to chant the words written on the paper.

"*Revivera ma soulty inuguta, revivera ga parsona. Revivera ma soulty inuguta, revivera ga parsona. Revivera ma soulty inuguta, revivera ga parsona.*" I kept chanting, over and over. Minutes went by that felt like hours. When Alex placed his hand on my shoulder, I snapped my lips together and turned to face him. His beautiful baby blues held so much pity in them, and my eyes began to fill with tears. I could feel the tension in the room rising. The spell and my blood didn't work! I thought it would work, and banked on it working so Kai would be with us again. I failed. I failed Kai, and I failed everyone. I removed my palm from Kai's mouth and placed it on his hand, not caring that my blood was still dripping everywhere. I looked at Kai's beautiful, ashen face and whispered a final goodbye. I stood, ready to leave, when my right hand was gripped. I spun around and saw Kai's hand covering mine. No one spoke or even moved —we just stood there and watched for a moment. Kai's eyes started to blink ever so slowly. I held my breath, praying he would come back to us.

"Holy fuck, he's...he...I think he's waking up." I assume it was Dom who spoke. I couldn't tear my eyes from Kai for even a second to check. I didn't want to miss seeing him come back to us. After a few minutes, finally Kai opened his eyes, and I had never been happier to see those beautiful gray-blue eyes in my life. I gently sat back down beside him and rubbed my hand across his cheek. He turned his head slightly my way and our eyes locked. I could feel his love for me pouring through his gaze. *Oh, you really would have been the better choice.*

"I just contacted the pack healer. He's on his way, and I got another bringing in some blood bags." That is so cool that Jax can communicate with his pack through their mind link. Focusing back on Kai, who hadn't taken his eyes off me, I spoke.

"Welcome back, big guy. I thought we had really lost you there." Kai tried to speak but ended up in a coughing fit and groaning in pain. The healer arrived at that moment, pushing us all out of the way and barking orders at the two ladies with him.

"Hello, Melakai. I am Dr. Jeremy. I'm going to take a look at your wounds and try to see what I can do to help. I'm going to give you some painkillers and run an IV of blood, then I need you to try and relax." Kai grunted in response. Two men I haven't seen before came and made their way over to the doctor. "I need you both to hold him down while I realign his ankle."

"He's a vampire. He can heal on his own." Dom was right; I forgot vampires and shifters could heal on their own.

"The spell that was cast must have slowed his healing abilities. I need to reset the break before it heals at an incorrect angle." Oh, okay, that made sense now. But it sounded awful. We all left Kai's side to allow the doctor to do his job. Everyone spread around the room and sat in chairs or on the floor. Occasionally one of us would pace to pass the time, and the others would chat among themselves. Hours passed, but none of us would leave the room. We didn't want Kai to be alone. I could feel Nico's gaze on me, but I was a coward, and I couldn't face him. I knew I had a lot of explaining to do, and I knew he would be angry with me for keeping this from him, but now everything made sense for me. My feelings for Kai were never my own, but my feelings for Nico, they *were* all my own. I still loved Kai, but just not in the same way I used to, more like a brother or best friend. Ugh! I shouldn't say brother—that was fucking gross, considering the shit we did together in my dreams.

It was late by the time the doctor was finished with Kai, and I was fucking exhausted and needed sleep stat. The doctor treated all Kai's wounds and dressed them with gauze. His ribs needed to be wrapped, as he had broken most of them.

His ankle was in a splint and resting atop a mound of pillows. The Dr said he should be fully healed by the afternoon. That would be great, as my wedding was fast approaching.

We still had so much to do. Jax had tasked his pack members with making the necessary arrangements for the ceremony, Nico was bringing a fae minister from his realm, and Aurora was organizing my dress. Alex and Chase were saddened that the Knox coven wouldn't be attending one of their heir's weddings, but I couldn't help that. Stevie was their queen, and I was just a stranger to them.

I was shaken from my thoughts when I heard the bedroom door close. The doctor and all his helpers were gone; it was just us now. Jax, Dom, Nico, and Sophia made their way over to Kai. Aurora and Chase followed them. Alex offered me his hand to help me to my feet, as I was sitting on the floor. I gladly accepted, and we followed the others over to Kai.

Kai already looked better and had some color back in his face. The blood bags must have really helped; the cuts on his face and arms were already starting to heal. I reached out gingerly and ran my fingers through his beautiful blond hair. His eyes fluttered open at my touch. His gaze zeroed in on me and remained there. I smiled, trying to reassure him without words that he was going to be okay and that I have forgiven him. One day soon I would be the one asking for his forgiveness.

"I'm glad you're okay, big guy. I'm sorry it took me so long to cotton on to your messages."

"You have nothing to be sorry for, mi amor." His voice was scratchy from disuse. The torture he endured at the hands of my sister and Randall made me sick to my stomach. How my sister could change from being one of the most caring people to a monster still baffles me.

"It's good to have you back, brother." Kai pulled his gaze from me so he could look at Jax.

"Thank you, brother, it's good to be back. I didn't think the spell would work, but I'm glad that it did." Kai turned from Jax to Sophia. "Thank you So-So, I owe you my life." Tears started to cloud in Sophia's eyes, but she quickly blinked them away. Sophia didn't seem like the type of woman who cried or let anyone see how she was really feeling. I admire that about her.

"You owe me nothing, Kai. After everything, I would say we are even." Dom and Nico shared a look and judging from their expressions, they hated not knowing the full story of what happened to Sophia. Nico's eyes told me that there was so much rage simmering beneath the surface. He wanted revenge for what happened to his sister. I could be wrong, but Dom was giving me the same vibe.

"I'm glad you're back, Kai, but I have to know how this is even possible." I knew Dom was trying to be patient and not push Kai for an explanation straight away, but there was only so much he could handle. Dom was one of those people that had to know the full story about everything. Before anyone could speak, I answered for Kai.

"Why don't you guys grab some seats and get comfortable. It's a bit of a long story." Everyone settled themselves around the bed, waiting for Kai and me to explain.

Chapter Ten

NICO

I'm sitting here, staring at her and the way she is running her hand through Kai's hair. Since when did she stop being angry at him and when the hell did they become friendly like that? I knew they were *close* in her dreams, and just thinking about Kai having his hands on *my* woman made my fucking blood boil. I hate the way I'm feeling, like I'm some insecure child. I have never felt like this before about anyone. I hated Kai just for having her hands on him.

"Could you stop fucking touching him? He's alive, yay! That doesn't mean he needs you to constantly fucking pat him like he's your pet." I snarled, shocked at my own outburst. I saw the others staring at me with wide eyes. Dom and Jax both looked like they wanted to laugh. I narrowed my eyes at them until they looked away. I returned my stare to Ryan and found she was glaring at me. The look she was giving me told me that she was about to lose her shit. Oh, great, here we go. I'm about to get my ass handed to me, again.

"Get off your fucking high horse, Nico. You have no right to tell me what to do. We may be getting married, but make no mistake—this is a business transaction and nothing more." Fuck, her words hurt more than if she just stabbed me. Schooling my features so she couldn't see how much she hurt me, I went to answer her when Jax spoke.

"Don't kid yourself, love, you know I can tell when you're lying." She went beet red. I forgot about Jax's secret talent of being able to detect lies. His little talent would come in handy for this conversation. She was glaring daggers at Jax.

"Tell them everything, mi amor, they have a right to know." She moved her eyes from Jax to me and I saw her swallow. Time to fess up, baby.

"Okay, after Nico and I returned from the dream where we saw Kai die, I thought the same as all of you, that he really was dead. After I awoke that day, I was alone, but I started hearing a voice. I honestly thought I was going nuts, but then I was pulled into a daydream. That has never happened to me before with Kai or Nico." She was blushing. Aw, my little spitfire was embarrassed. I hated hearing her mention that Kai was present in some of her dreams as well.

"I only see the guys in my dreams at night. Anyway, once I was in my day dream, I saw Kai. Needless to say, I was shocked and happy, because I thought even if he was dead, I could still see him, you know." I couldn't help the growl that slipped out. It pissed me off to know she was still seeing him when she clearly had feelings for me. "Easy, tiger—it's not what you think."

"What is it that you think I am thinking, love?"

"If you let me finish, Nico, then you will understand," she snapped, like I was a petulant child. "Back to the story then. I saw Kai, and he told me he was still alive. I didn't believe him, of course, I thought it was my subconscious playing tricks on me. After talking with him and hearing his explanation, I started to hope. He told me a spell had been cast to slow his healing, so that it would appear like he had actually died. Kai also told me that Randall would want to gloat about killing him, so he would make sure that his body was returned to you guys."

"That doesn't explain how you knew that your blood and that spell would bring him back." Dom hated not having all the answers, and right at this point in time I couldn't agree with my brother more.

"When I cast the spell, Kai asked me to make Ryan's blood the key to return to the living. The spell to revive him was passed onto Alex and Chase by Kai through Ryan."

"You don't have enough power to cast a spell like that, Sophia." I didn't mean it as an insult, but from the way my sister stiffened, I knew that was how it came across.

"You have no idea what I am capable of, *brother*. The trials that I have had to face have made me stronger. I am no weak half-breed anymore." The conviction in Sophia's voice was slightly unsettling, but I didn't have time to sit here and pull her words apart.

"So-So, that's enough." I turned to glare at Kai. How dare he speak to my sister like they were long-lost siblings! She wasn't his sister, she was mine!

"You do not get to butt your nose in my affairs, Cane, she is my sister, not yours!" I saw the look of hurt cross his face before he quickly masked it and nodded.

"Don't you dare sit there and throw around insults like that! You may be a king in Farrarie, but you are not in your realm now. You do not get to speak to people like they are trash. Do I make myself crystal fucking clear, brother?" Everyone in the room stopped and turned their gaze to my sister. I was as shocked as the rest of the group. Sophia has never, I mean never, spoken to me like that before. I wasn't angry at her for her outburst—on the contrary, I was fucking proud that she had found her spunk or backbone or whatever you want to call it.

"Well, fuck me sideways till Sunday, babe. That little

outburst was so fucking hot!" I leaned over and slapped Dom up the back of the head. "Dude! What the actual fuck was that for?"

"That's my sister you are fucking flirting with. You are never to talk to her like that," I hissed.

"Calm down, King. She is a grown-ass woman and can decide who she wants to spend her time with." I was about to slap the stupid smirk off that dumbass warlock Chase's face.

"Calm down, everyone! All of you need to shut it and listen! We do not have the luxury of time. You and Ryan get married in three days time." With that reality check from Aurora, everyone shut up and sat back in their chairs and gave Ryan their full attention.

"The reason I could be the key to bring Kai back is because his blood still lingered in my system. After the blow up at the cabin and Randall biting me, Kai gave me his blood to help heal my wounds—" Melakai cut Ryan off before she could finish explaining.

"I asked for Ryan's blood to be the key because one, I knew that she would be with you all. Two, I trusted her to return me to the living. I am sorry, brothers, but with how things have been between us, especially between you and I, Nico, I didn't know if you would want me to wake up. There are a lot of sins I must atone for, but I am ready to move forward."

"But you said you could never go against the blood oath you have with Randall." The know-it-all warlock Alex had a point.

"The spell Ryan asked you to acquire is a death spell, as well as a reviving spell. What that means is the spell kills me then restarts me."

"What exactly are you saying, Kai?"

"What I am saying, So-So, is I could never make you the key to bring me back, because you would never have completed the spell Ryan did. You are far too loyal; you would never have gambled with my life."

"You knew he could have died and you still fucking did it?" My sister was angry, and she started to make her way over to Ryan but was stopped by Dom. How the fuck did he move so fast?

Dom was right in front of Sophia, blocking her path. She didn't try to move around or make a sound, just simply lifted her hand and placed it on his chest.

Dom flinched.

Why was he flinching at her touch? Before I could ponder that thought any more, a bright yellow light shot from the hand she had placed on Dom's chest, and he went sailing across the room before he smacked into the wall beside the bed, cracking the plaster. Jax was quick enough to move out of the way so he didn't get crushed. Everyone was on their feet, trying to find a safe place to stand for the presumed show-down. Dom was quick to recover and was back on his feet. I quickly jumped in front of her, trying to stop this battle between her and Dom.

"Enough, Dominic, you will not hurt my si—" I couldn't even finish what I was saying before Dom fucking used his magic to freeze me. I couldn't move or speak. I was lifted by his magic and placed to the side. He must have done the same to everyone in the room because no one was moving or speaking. I could see him making his way over to my sister, but she didn't move or cower. She squared her shoulders and lifted her chin. Fuck, she really has changed. The sister I knew would be hiding behind me, crying, begging me to save her. Dom's eyes were glowing a bright purple; they only did that when he was really pissed off. Sophia knew that and I'm guessing that's why she is smirking at him.

"You think it's funny, little dove, to launch me—me, of all

fucking people—across the room? If you were anyone else, Sophia, I would fucking end you."

"But I'm not just anyone else, am I, Dominic? Oh, that's right. We don't talk about that, do we? You just hide behind your power and lie through your fucking teeth!" What the fuck is my sister talking about? "You deserve so much fucking worse. You're a fucking coward, Dominic Silver."

I could immediately sense the change in Dom. He never really shifted anymore; only when he absolutely had to. His wolf was huge and a born alpha. Jackson and Dom had tried to shift together many times, but every time they did, their wolves went at it. Jax was an alpha by birth, and Dom was the son of an alpha. Dom is stronger than any wolf I have ever met. He and Jax are both evenly matched, and if Dom shifted now, I guarantee Jax would shift also. They would both be slaves to their beasts in the fight for dominance, and they would tear this room apart. Dom was shaking and taking deep breaths, trying to calm down so he didn't shift. He must be focusing hard on trying not to change into his wolf and putting all his energy into that, because we suddenly found ourselves able to move again and speak. I rushed over to my sister to grab her and move her out of the way. I was just about to grip her hand when she pulled it away. She never broke eye contact with Dom while she spoke to me.

"If you touch me, brother, he will shift and try to kill you. You need to move back with the others and stay there until he calms."

"I am not leaving you, So-So, never again. Slowly move toward me and then stand behind me." Dom was growling now, I could see his eyes had changed from violet to gray-silver.

"Touch her and I will fucking kill you, Nico!" Dom growled through clenched teeth.

"Nico, move away from me now. If you don't move, he will

shift and take you and Jackson out. He hasn't shifted for months; his wolf will go rogue and block our Dom out." I was torn; I didn't want to move in case Dom hurt her, but then I didn't want to make the situation worse by not listening.

"Nico, can you please come here and listen to Sophia?" I turned to Ryan, who was pleading with her eyes as well as her words. She was a siren to me, and I had no choice but to listen and move away from my sister. I made my way over to her and stood beside her, at the head of the bed, next to Kai.

Chapter Eleven

RYAN

I was standing between Nico and Kai. Kai was trying to sit up to assess the situation better. I placed my hand on his chest and shook my head. With a huff, he laid back down and didn't try to move again. Sophia and Dom were still standing in the same place. Jax, Aurora, and my cousins were standing on the other side of the bed. Jax was standing slightly in front of Aurora, ready to shield her if Dom did shift.

"Deep breaths, Alpha, I don't want to have to throw your wolf around as well." Dom laughed at Sophia's words, which is what I guess she was hoping for, as some of the tension in his back and shoulders started to ease. He wasn't fully calm yet, but a lot calmer than he was a minute ago. His laughter stopped abruptly, and tension returned to his body.

"You're right, Soph, I deserve so much worse. I will spend my life making it up to you, I swear." Wow, since when did Dom have a remorseful side?

"I can't forgive you, Dommie, I have tried for years."

"Forgive him for what, Sophia?" Nico had his big brother voice on now, and fuck, it was hot. Shit! I had to get my head out of the damn gutter. Sophia turned her gaze to her brother while Dom seemed to stiffen.

"It doesn't matter, Nico. It was a long time ago."

"It matters to me, little dove."

"Why the fuck do you keep calling my sister *little dove*? What the fuck is going on between you two?" Nico was pissed. Anyone with eyes could see that there was something going on between Dom and Sophia. When they thought no one was looking, one would stare at the other. Nico was so blind to not see that there was history between his best friend and his sister. You could tell neither of them wanted to discuss this, so I did the only thing I could think of.

"How about we table that debate for another time and get back to planning a wedding and talking to Kai?"

Everyone agreed and started to situate themselves around the room again. Well, everyone but Nico, who still stood and glared at his sister and Dom. Jax brought a chair over for Nico so he could sit, but Nico ignored his friend's gesture. I sighed and grabbed Nico's hand, and that seemed to have shocked him out of his glaring match.

"Come on, big guy, sit down." I gently pulled my hand from his and pushed on his chest till he was sitting. I turned to head back over and sit with Kai, but before I could move an inch, an arm snaked around my waist and I was pulled backward till I was sitting on Nico's lap.

I turned to glare at him and tell him what I thought of his macho man display. The words died in my throat when I saw his eyes. He was battling his anger and trying to control his control freak urges by not demanding answers from Dom and Sophia, and if me sitting on his lap was what was going to help him calm down, I would endure this torture. Well, I would make him think it's torture. Inside I was swooning like a schoolgirl at the close contact. I loved having Nico's hands on me. I felt safe and secure. I loved when he would whisper sweet nothings in my ear when we were in my dreamland. A throat clearing had me snapping out of my thoughts and looking straight at Jax.

"Um...shifters have great noses, love..." I didn't know what that meant. Nico was chuckling behind me, and now Dom was too, but at least he was trying to hide his laughter behind a fake cough.

"Okay?"

"I mean we can scent when people are happy, sad, angry, hungry, turned on..." Oh fuck no. Nico and Dom both started laughing, I turned beet red and looked to Kai for confirmation. He nodded. Oh my God, they could smell my arousal. I went to quickly stand but Nico tightened his grip, his laughter stopping immediately.

"I could have gone my whole life without knowing that my cousin was turned on, fuck you very much, jackass." Kill me now. I couldn't even look toward Chase; I was embarrassed enough without having to hear his comment.

"I think Ryan has suffered enough, let's move on, shall we?" Bless you, Alex.

"I have to say, at least we know she will be okay with consummating the marriage," Dom commented, and Jax slapped the back of Dom's head. "Dick, would all of you fuckers stop hitting me? It's fucking starting to piss me off."

"Stop saying dumb shit and then no one would hit you," suggested Kai, and we all turned to stare at him. He hasn't weighed in on this discussion much, so I think we were all shocked to hear from him. Everyone started laughing, which helped lighten the tension in the room and make everyone feel more comfortable.

"I'm sorry I lied to you all, I couldn't risk telling anyone except for Alex and Chase. I needed them to handle the spell for me." I was lying through my teeth. I told them to grab the piece of paper from my room; it had the spell *he* told me to use on it, not the one Kai said to use.

"I would like to continue to move ahead with the wedding planning and making sure everyone is on the same page with Randall and my sister being here." At the mention of the vampire king and my sister, everyone seemed to tense up and sit straighter in their seats. I knew my time was running out on avoiding my sister.

"Mi amor, you can do this—" Nico cut Kai off.

"I think Ryan and I need a moment alone with Kai, if you guys don't mind." Alex and Chase didn't move an inch, Dom and Sophia seemed reluctant to act. Jax and Aurora watched the lack of action with interest.

"Why would I leave my cousin alone with both her stalkers?" Fuck, Chase was exactly like Dom, they both needed to filter their words.

"Because soon enough she will be my wife, and I won't be asking next time, I'll be *telling you*." The balls of Nico to speak like that to my cousin! I turned so he could get the full effect of my glare.

"Do not treat me or speak about me like I am some property to be owned! I will not let you dictate my life, married or not."

"I will make any call I see fit for your safety and what is in your best interest, with or without your permission, love. I won't ask for forgiveness or permission. That is not in my make-up. I am King. It is my right."

Hell to the fucking no! He did not just pull the *I am King* card! I've had enough of his bullshit. Just when I think he is starting to understand me, he goes and does some stupid-ass caveman shit like this. I have been controlled my whole life, and I will not let anyone control me again. I pushed his hand away and stood, but of course Nico couldn't let me have the dominant ground so he stood as well. We were chest to—well, his chest to my head, so I had to take a step back and tilt my head to glare at him. He was glaring back.

"You are a stubborn-ass bastard is what you are, Nicky boy, and I have had enough. We all know what needs to be done to prepare for the wedding, so I suggest we all should hop to it before I kill the fucking groom!" I turned away from Nico and made my way over to Kai, pecking a kiss to his forehead and ignoring Nico growling behind me. I told Kai I would come back later and check on him, thanked the others for their help, and left the room. I didn't spare Nico a glance on my way out.

Once again, I walked down so many different hallways that I got lost. This place was so freaking huge it would take me years to learn its layout. After another five minutes, I finally found a door that led to the backyard, where there was a beautiful garden. There were beds of roses and wildflowers. The garden seemed like it went on forever, so I began to walk to try clearing my head. I had so much going inside me that I didn't even know where to begin. The first thing I knew I had to do was talk to Nico and tell him everything about what happened with Kai and how I came to know certain things. Part of me felt like I finally got some form of closure with Kai, now that I knew the truth. Yes, it sucked to hear it, but it helped me move forward from what I thought I had with Kai. I knew, deep down, from the moment I found out Nico was real, he would be my future. I have never admitted this to anyone, or even myself, but if there was a man I would want to marry, it was Nico.

I loved who I became when I was with Nico. I felt stronger and brave. I have never stood up to anyone the way I stand up to Nico; he pushes me to want more and to strive for better things. I decided right then that after my walk, I would find Nico and we would talk this shit out. I wouldn't marry him while we were both angry at each other. As I was rounding a corner, I stopped in my tracks when I heard very familiar voices bickering.

Bending down, so I could peek around the corner of the building, I saw Dom and Sophia arguing. I know I shouldn't be eavesdropping, but I wanted to know what the deal was between these two. The chemistry between them was off the fucking charts, and the sexual tension was even worse.

"How many times do I have to say I'm sorry, Soph?"

"You can say it a thousand times more, Dominic, and I still won't forgive you."

"I tried to find you!"

"You didn't try hard enough!"

"I fucking went ape shit, Sophia, I hunted through the whole of Farrarie and Earth for you. I didn't know that asshole had taken you until Kai told us."

"Don't you dare blame this on Kai! He was the only one who fucking helped me. You have no idea what that son of a bitch did to me every fucking day. He knew hurting me would hurt my brother. He never loved Ryan's grandmother; he is *incapable* of love. He let his own wife be beaten and raped by his men. What do you think he let happen to me, the sister of his greatest enemy? I was used and tortured more than you can even imagine. Do you know—"

"Stop! I can't...I...*please!* I will fucking kill him, Sophia. I swear to you, I will make him pay."

"I will be the one to put a stake through that fucking pig's heart!"

I quickly turned so I could sneak away but I ran straight into a solid wall. Before my scream could come loose, a hand clamped over my mouth and I started to panic.

"Shhhh, love, it's just me." I relaxed instantly at the sound of Nico's voice. He removed his hand from my mouth and then placed it on my lower back, guiding me back toward the way I came. When we were far enough away from Dom and Sophia, he asked, "How much of that did you hear, love?"

"More than I should have," I answered honestly. He grunted but didn't comment on me spying on his sister and Dom.

"I want to take you somewhere, if you will let me."

"Nico I appreciate the offer but I just…"

"Give me an hour, please." It wasn't often Nico said please. Interesting.

"Since you said please…" We both chuckled at my reply. "Where are we going?"

"It's a surprise. I'm going to open a portal so we can get there faster." I didn't argue, and we continued to walk toward the woods. A couple of minutes after we reached the tree line, we came upon a clearing. Nico removed his hand from my back and stood in the center of the clearing. He was whispering words under his breath and then a portal appeared. I don't think I would ever get used to this whole magic thing, it was always a sight to behold. Nico reached a hand out to me and I placed my hand in his without hesitation and stepped into the portal. It felt like we were being sucked in by a Hoover! Once we stepped out the other side of the portal, I gasped.

Nico had brought me to my favorite place on Earth, the *real* Lake William.

Chapter Twelve

NICO

I heard her gasp as the portal closed behind us. Was that gasp because she was happy I brought her here, or was she pissed off because this was the place Kai had brought her, and where she thought he died?

"Nico, I...I—" Dammit, I made a huge mistake bringing her here. I bowed my head, feeling defeated, letting my black hair hang over my face, shielding my eyes. Nothing I do seems to make her happy. Instead I have a knack for pissing her off.

"I'm sorry, I'll take us back now." As I turned around to open another portal, she grabbed my hand. My eyes shot to hers. She had a beautiful, shy smile on her face, and her eyes told me what she could not. She was glad to be here, but unsure what her next move would be.

"I'm shocked you brought me here. I have never been to Lake William before. Well, of course I have, but only in my dreams. I didn't even know this place was real until recently."

I couldn't stop the grin that crept across my face. I made her happy by bringing her here! I am going to take that as a big win. She grasped my hand and led me along the small trail toward the lake's edge. Once we got to edge, she let go of my hand, kicked her shoes off, and shuffled closer to the edge of the bank, easing down and letting her feet dangle at the water's edge. I followed her lead, though I must say I can't remember ever doing something so mundane. There is little time for such things when you are a king. We sat in comfortable silence for a while, just gazing out at the lake and the mist-wreathed mountains. I can see why she loved this place so much. Alaska was one of the most beautiful places here in the Earth realm.

"You know how I knew about Jax not being my mate?" I turned to look at her; her long brown hair was hanging like a curtain, shielding her face from me. I leaned over and gently tucked it behind her ear so I could see her profile. She sucked in a breath at my touch and smirked. I loved how my touch affected her.

"I have an idea," I answered.

"If your idea is that Kai told me, you're wrong." I stiffened.

"I don't understand, love. If it wasn't Kai, then who was it?" She took a deep breath and then turned so she could look me in the eye.

"My dad. He's been coming to me in daydreams as well."

"How long has this been happening?" Randall Knox was dead. The only way for him to be able to come to his daughter was if his remains were never properly consecrated back to the earth, or so I have been told.

"Since we arrived in Alaska."

"Why didn't you say anything?"

"I didn't know what it was at the beginning. I only started to think they were real and meant something when I met Kai and then you. After we left you in Farrarie, I started to pay more attention to my daydreams, in case they were real, you know?" She turned and focused her attention back on the lake, and I did the same.

"I understand what you are saying, love. So when Kai came

to you and you realized that he was still alive, you thought that maybe—?"

"That maybe my father was alive?"

"Yeah"

"I really wished that was the case, but my father told me that there was no way he could come back. The thing with Kai coming back is a once-in-a-lifetime kind of deal. He also told me that Kai would play a big part in the coming battle." I reached over and grasped her hand in mine, locking my fingers through hers. I knew that reality had to hurt even more after losing her sister.

"Have you told any of the others about your father coming to you?"

"No, I wasn't ready to share this with anyone. I didn't even tell Kai or my cousins." Knowing that I was the one she trusted with this information meant so much to me.

"Thank you for your trust."

"Wow, the great Nicholas Stone is thanking a common witch." We both chuckled at her attempt at a joke. After a few moments of silence, I asked, "What part does Kai have to play in this war?"

She took too long to reply, so I turned and saw that tears were rolling silently down her face. I pulled my hand from hers and wrapped it around her shoulders so I could pull her close to me. She leaned her head on my chest, and I wrapped my other arm around her and tightened my hold. We sat like that for a while until her sobs slowed and she was able to get her breathing back under control.

"Kai can never return to Farrarie. He doesn't know. The spell I used cancelled out any remaining fae blood that may have lingered in his system. Kai thinks the spell killed him and then brought him back. In part he is right, except the spell killed his fae side. Kai is full vamp now."

"Kai has seen himself as a full vampire for a really long time now, love. He will not be mad at you."

"You don't understand, Nico. The spell my father told me to use has a failsafe against our kind." She said *our kind*. Hearing those words made something in my heart flutter. I was beyond proud.

"What are you trying to say, love?"

"If Kai ever steps foot in the fae realm again, he will go up in ash."

"No, love, I cast the spell on my realm to burn all vamps aside from Kai."

"Kai was made from Randall's blood, correct?" I nodded. I had a feeling I knew where she was going with this story, and I didn't like it. Farrarie was Kai's home. "The spell wiped all remains of *Kai's* blood from his system, so the only blood that remains in Kai's system is Randall Cane's." *Oh fuck.*

Chapter Thirteen

RYAN

I felt Nico tense. Now he understood what I was trying to say. I knew Kai had hoped to return to his homeland after Randall was defeated, but now he could never go home. I abused his trust in me, and Kai was never going to forgive me.

"The spell you cast, though—Kai said he told you what spell to use. He would never use a spell that would block him from returning home."

"I didn't use the spell Kai told me to use."

"What? *Why?*"

I could hear the anguish in Nico's voice; he was devastated his brother could never go home. Even after their big falling out, Nico made Kai exempt from the spell he cast in Farrarie after Randall kidnapped Sophia.

"Because my dad told me the spell Kai wanted me to use would never work."

"There has to be more to it than that, love." Nico was smart enough to know I was hiding something else. Blowing out a breath, I forged on.

"We needed Kai to turn fully. When Randall falls, Kai is now a true heir to the vampire king. No one will be able to contest his claim to the throne. Melakai will be named King of all Vampires, through blood." I felt Nico stiffen, and his arms dropped from around me. I moved away from him and sat up straight, staring out at the lake. I was a coward and didn't want to face him.

"What have you done?" The sheer disbelief in his tone made me flinch.

"I did what I had to in order to ensure Kai returned to us."

"You took away his choice! Kai hates being a vampire, and now you have gone and made him a true heir to the race he despises most!" Nico was shouting now, and I wanted desperately to run away, but I couldn't.

"You wanted me to be open and honest with you, Nico, and that is what I am trying to do."

"I know, love—it's just a lot to take in. I think I just need time to process what you have told me." That was fair enough. I mean, I did just drop a bomb on him. I just needed to make sure that he didn't tell Kai before I had the chance to.

"Can you please not say anything to Kai? I will tell him, but I just need to find the right time."

"You have my word, love, but you need to tell him soon, before this war breaks out. I would hate for him to be blindsided by the news."

"I promise I will tell him soon."

"Can I ask you something?" I had been waiting for him to ask this question; I knew it was only a matter of time.

"Of course."

"What happened between you and Melakai? You seem different toward him now." There it is—Nico was very perceptive.

"That is a bit of a long story."

"I have nothing but time when it concerns you, love, in case you haven't noticed. After all, I did leave my realm to be run by my second in command so I could be here with you." I hadn't even thought of that. Nico was a king, yet here he was, in my world, trying to help me save his world.

"Nico, I'm so sorry. I hadn't even thought about what you've given up to be here."

"You're most welcome. Now can you put my curiosity to rest, please?" With a laugh, I began to tell him the truth.

"When Kai came to me in those daydreams I told you about, he said he may not make it and that I deserved to know the truth. He told me that he used his power of emotional control in the beginning of our relationship to manipulate my feelings for him. Don't get me wrong—I was attracted to Kai the moment we met." Nico started growling. He did that so often that I was starting to wonder if he was a shifter as well. "Kai only tried to manipulate my feelings for him because he wanted me to choose him."

"Why?"

"Because if I chose him, he would have taken me away from my sister and all this supernatural stuff, so I would remain oblivious to all this and I would never know what I was. If I didn't know what I was, then I could never be used by anyone."

"I get his reasoning, but I don't agree. You can't hide from what you are; you would have figured it out eventually."

"Kai also told me now that I know the truth, he and I could never be."

"You would never be his, love. You have been mine since we first met ten years ago." I ignored the fact that he was referring to when I was eight years old, because that was just creepy. "I can see the look on your face, and no I did not mean it like that. What I meant is that you would never belong to Kai because you are my *hug*—"

Nico was cut off by a portal opening behind us. He jumped to his feet so fast and yanked me up by his arms, positioning himself in front of me so whoever it was would have to go through him to get to me.

"Relax, brother, it's just me." How the hell did Dom know where to find us? Sensing there was no danger, I moved to stand beside Nico and smiled at Dom. "Hello, love," he said with his usual rakish grin.

"What is it? Why are you here, brother?"

"I thought you might like to know that Kai is up and moving about. We're all gathering in the mess hall to catch up before we call it a night. He said he has some things to tell us about Randall." Nico looked down at me with a regretful smile. Our little bubble of peace had just been burst. We both quickly put our shoes back on and Nico clasped my hand once more and we stepped through the portal.

After exiting the portal, the three of us went directly to the mess hall. Nico still had my hand firmly planted in his, and I didn't protest. I liked the feeling of him touching me. The whole team was here: Jax, Aurora, Sophia, Alex, Chase, and Kai, as well as two others I hadn't seen before. Once we made it to the table where they were gathered, the two newcomers bowed their head at Nico. Obviously they knew who *he* was.

"Ryan, this is Maverick, my right-hand man and commander of my army." Nico gestured to the burly man that had long, straight black hair and the most beautiful bright green eyes, they almost seemed like they were glowing. This guy was freaking huge—his arms were the size of a bear's. I smiled shyly and waved; this guy scared the shit out of me. Nico gestured toward the second man; he was tall and lanky, he looked like he was built more for speed and agility than brute strength. He had short-cropped brown hair that was shaved on the sides, and yellow eyes. I am guessing all fae had different colored eyes to humans, it would explain why I have a ring around my pupils. "Ryan, this is Larick, he is our spell master. He helps train our people in defensive and attack magic." That piqued my interest immediately.

"Hi!" God, I wanted to slap myself. I meet these guys, who are obviously important to Nico and the fae realm, and all I can do is squeak out a lame ass *hi*. Everyone chuckled at my obvious awkwardness.

"It is a pleasure to meet you, Your Majesty." Hold up— Larick just called me *your majesty*.

"Oh, I'm not a queen; my sister is the queen of our coven."

"I was referring you being the queen of Farrarie, Your Majesty." *Oh!* Before, when I felt embarrassed, that was just a taste of what I was feeling now. Now I was just awkward as fuck. What does someone even say to something like that? Nico saved me from responding by engaging the two in conversation about why they were here and not back in the fae realm training. I tuned them out and pried my hand from Nico's, taking a seat next to Kai. From the corner of my eye I could see Nico glaring daggers, but Kai either didn't see Nico's look or chose to ignore it.

"How are you feeling?" Kai looked much better, and a lot of his cuts had already healed. Kai still seemed down, though. I could tell he still had a lot on his mind.

"Much better now." Then crickets. Okay, so he wasn't in a talkative mood. I knew I had to witch up and tell Kai the truth about the spell, but right now didn't seem like a good time. So I chickened out and went with small talk.

"I'm glad you're back with us."

"Me too, mi amor." I felt weird hearing Kai call me *mi amor* now. I wasn't his love. Well, maybe I was, but he wasn't mine anymore. I felt a pain in my chest at the thought of losing another person.

Kai had been a huge part of my life, even before I knew he was real. Kai gave me someone I could talk to when things at home with my mother were bad.

Each night, when I went to sleep, I could escape to my dreams and be somewhere else, become *someone* else. My relationship with Kai has always been different to the one I have with Nico. Kai was the one who would listen and was gentle. Nico, on the other hand, would demand things and make me forget through the euphoric bliss of orgasms, until I forgot my own name. I could see now that the times in my dreams when Kai and I were intimate, that the spark and burning desire I felt for Nico was just not there. Don't get me wrong—I always felt need for Kai but only a base level, almost like I just wanted to feel good, so we would fuck.

When Nico and I have sex in my dreams, it's soul shattering and all consuming. Nothing else exists in that moment aside from the two of us. I'm embarrassed to admit that having sex with Nico became like a drug to me; I would crave the feeling of him each night and would find myself disappointed sometimes when I would arrive in my dream land to find Kai and not Nico. I am such an idiot that I did not realize sooner. A thunk on my head pulled me out of my thoughts. The culprit was a bread roll. I snapped my gaze across the table to glare at my cousin.

"I called your name like three times and you ignored me."

"I didn't freaking mean to ignore you, Chase, you big baby, I was thinking!" At my outburst, everyone around the table erupted in laughter.

I must admit it was nice to see everyone smile and laugh. It seemed to break the ice a bit, and we all started to talk about mundane things.

The girls wanted to know what it was like living in New Zealand and what foods we had there. We sat there for a few hours chatting and eating dinner and dessert. It was so nice to get to know these guys better; they may be a shifter, vampire, fae, or whatever else, but they were still people, and it was humbling to hear their stories of how they grew up and all that.

I tried to hide my fourth yawn, but Nico, the ever observant stalker, noticed and gave me a stern look which said *"go to bed."* I reluctantly stood and bid everyone good night. I was beat from the long-ass day.

Chapter Fourteen

NICO

After Ryan left the mess hall, everyone continued to chat amicably about their lives. I noticed Kai had been very quiet for most of this. It was strange, considering he normally added his version of events when I, Jax, or Dom told a story of our youth. However, I didn't have time to worry about his salty-ass attitude —this might be my only time to ask Ryan's cousins some things about her. I made my move when there was a break in the conversation.

"Were Ryan and her sister close, even though they lived apart?" Both of the warlocks' faces dropped at the mention of Ryan's twin sister. Chase was quicker to recover from the shock and answer my question.

"Stevie and Ryan were closer than anyone I know. Even though they lived apart, they would always find a way to see each other or talk on Ryan's hidden cell phone. It would destroy Stevie when she couldn't speak or see Ryan because her mother was on one of her tantrums. Stevie and Uncle Ralph tried many times to rescue Ryan,

But Nina would always threaten to expose what we were to the humans. Uncle Ralph thought he had more time, and that when Ryan turned eighteen, she would be free to leave and go live with him and Stevie. But obviously that's not how it went." I hated myself more than I ever have, hearing her cousin recount her fucked-up childhood. I knew firsthand what she had gone through and never lifted a finger to fucking help her. Ryan was a beautiful person, and so forgiving. Even after she knew Kai was meant to kill her, she still saved his life and made sure he was okay. And I know she's suffering guilt at the loss of Farrarie for him. I mean, who fucking does that? A question from Aurora pulled me from my inner turmoil.

"If they were so close, why would they part now?" This time it was Alex who answered.

"Ryan didn't have a choice. She knew nothing about supernaturals. All she knew was that we were taking a family trip to Alaska for three months. The truth is we were supposed to arrive here and tell her about what we are and what she is, then introduce her to our coven and that was it."

"What changed?" Ahhhh, so Kai *was* paying attention, he just didn't want to talk.

"*You* happened, Melakai." Kai snapped his eyes up to look at Chase. "On our way from the airport to the cabin, Ryan had fallen asleep and had a dream, and she was calling out your name! That's when we knew we were too late, if you were already visiting her." Chase sounded pissed, and I couldn't blame him.

"I was never visiting her to hurt her—" Alex cut him off with a hand raised.

"All you do is hurt people, Melakai; it's what the King has trained you to do!" In response, Kai slammed his fist on the top of the table, the two of them locked in a glaring match.

"You think you're so noble because you went to see her every couple of months or called and text when you could? No, you are not noble! You are all fools. She would tell you she was fine and her mother wasn't home or she was studying in her room for a test. She fucking lied to you all!" I could feel the anger radiating off Kai, and I was starting to get the feeling I was going to hate the ending of Kai's story. "She was never alone; if her mother was out, she made sure one of her dealers was there to keep an eye on Ryan. If they got bored, they would beat her or humiliate her. Every night she went to sleep I would go to her to help heal her wounds; I could never fully heal her or her mother would have noticed. I only gave her enough of my blood to heal the worst of her injuries. I was her escape, not either of you or her fucking good-for-nothing cunt of a sister." Kai turned his glare my way then. I knew he was angry and he was about to unleash his anger on me. "As for you, Nico—you are the worst of them all. Your lies are catching up quick, brother. I suggest you start telling her the truth. I don't give a fuck what she is to you! I will always protect her, even from you!" I jumped to my feet. He'd gone too far now.

"You ever fucking threaten to take her from me again, Cane, and I will kill you where you stand you—" Kai cut me off.

"I never hid her worst nightmare from her and lied about it. You are a spineless piece of shit. Tell her the truth or I fucking will." *Holy shit, Kai knew.* I looked to Aurora, who had the same look of shock I did. We were the only two who knew about it, and now Kai does too. I am so fucked if he tells Ryan. I need to man up and go to her. "You have till the day of your wedding to tell her the truth, or I will tell her before she walks down that aisle."

Her cousins are both now fixated on our conversation. "What the fuck are you talking about? What are you hiding from my cousin?" Great, now her annoying ass cousins are gonna be sniffing around too. Dom and Jax were both shaking their heads. They knew I did something bad; they didn't know what it was, but they knew it wasn't good based on Kai's reaction alone.

"Say nothing to her, Melakai. I will go to her now and tell her everything." I didn't wait to hear any of their replies. I stood and left the hall, making my way to Ryan's room. I was dreading this conversation with her. I regretted what I had done, but I can't change it or go back in time. I need to own my mistake and try making it right with her. Perhaps if she lets me explain, maybe then she could forgive me, in time.

As I was nearing her room, I started to feel a familiar pulse in my chest. I was more accustomed to these feelings now after having to deal with them for years.

When I arrived at her room, I stood outside her door and strained to hear any sounds. All I could hear was her steady breathing; she was asleep.

I tried to open her door but it was locked. *Oh, little one, that won't keep me out.* I placed my hand over the knob and chanted an unlocking spell, and the door clicked open. I stepped inside, shutting and locking it behind me. She was lying on her side, with one leg in the covers and the other over the top. She looked so peaceful. As I moved closer to the bed, I noticed she was just in a shirt and panties, and my mouth watered. Her ass was so plump and ripe that you wanted to just take a bite out of that beautiful, round peach. I stood there, staring at her for a moment, while the pain in my chest intensified. I knew what she wanted, but I was trying to be a gentleman. I leaned over and moved a stray piece of hair that had fallen over her beautiful face, but she started to stir at my touch, so I quickly pulled my hand back.

"Mmmm...Nico." She was dreaming of *me*, and the last of my restraint snapped. I quickly removed my shoes and socks and threw my shirt next to my jeans. I lay down in just my boxers and spooned her, gently sliding one arm under her head and wrapped the other around her, pulling her flush against my body. She started to move, trying to get comfortable again. Every time she moved, her ass would grind against my cock. After the third time she moved, I wrapped my arm tighter around her so she would quit fucking moving. My dick was hard as stone now.

"Hmmmm...Nico....you...so good...need you." Fuck, there was only so much I could handle, and little Nico wanted to play. I closed my eyes and chanted the spell that would take us both to our dream land.

As soon as I opened my eyes and moved out from behind a tree, I saw her standing there in the clearing. She seemed shocked that she was once again back in her dream land. I waited patiently for her to call out or make any sound. Her long brown hair was loose around her shoulders and flying around her body every time she would spin in a circle, and the white night dress she wore didn't leave much to the imagination.

"Nico! I know this is your doing." She was very perceptive. Not wanting her to wait any longer, I slowly made my way over to her. As soon as her eyes landed on me, they started to travel down my naked chest. I could smell her desire from here. I stopped just a foot in front of her. She craned her neck back so she could look me in the eye.

"Hello, love."

"Why are we here, Nico?" I couldn't admit my own weakness so I focused on hers.

"Because you are not ready for me in the real world, but here I can tend to your needs." I saw the blush start at the base of her

neck and make its way all the way to her cheeks. My little vixen was embarrassed.

"Things have changed. We can't do this anymore. You're real and it would complicate things. I mean...You...I...we...can't...." Not wanting to give her a chance to talk herself out of this, I closed the space between us and gripped the back of her head, tugging her hair so I could angle her face perfectly.

She released a breathy moan and that was it. I smashed my lips to hers and began pushing my way into her mouth. She didn't fight me; she opened like she always had for me. She tasted like the sweetest, most addictive drug in the world. I released her hair and pulled back, and the small pout on her face made me smile. Don't worry, love, I am nowhere near done with you.

"Why did you stop?"

"I need to make sure that you're okay with this, love." I didn't want her to wake up tomorrow and hate me for this; I came to her room to tell her something important, but then my other head took over and now here we are, me wanting to fuck her seven ways to Sunday. She dropped her eyes from mine and nibbled on her lip for a moment. I thought she was about to back out, but instead she surprised me by standing on her tiptoes and wrapping her arms around my neck.

"I want this, Nico." I had to make something perfectly clear before we continued, though.

"I will give you whatever you want, love, but on one condition." She groaned.

"What is it?" I slid my arms down her body and placed my hands on her ass and squeezed, and she gasped. I lifted her off the ground and she wrapped her legs around my waist.

"You never let Kai back into your dreams, only me."

She didn't respond straight away and almost looked like she was about to protest, so I distracted her. I started nibbling on her ear and kissing my way down her neck. Her head lolled back and gave me better access, so I made teasing bites down her collar-bone and started sucking on the top of her breast. She was moaning now.

"I need you to answer me, love." I continued to tease her, laying her on the grass and positioning myself between her thighs. I sat back on my heels, running my hands up her parted thighs, stopping before I could push her dress up further.

She wanted me to push her dress up to reveal her most intimate part, but I wouldn't give into her until she gave me what I wanted. I leaned forward and pushed the straps of her dress down so I could expose her tits. They are big and full, her nipples pebbled and ready for my sucking. I didn't make her wait. I lowered my head and began to suck, hard, just how she liked it. She cried out, wanting more, so I used my hand to pinch and twist her other nipple, eliciting another cry from her.

"Nico, please, I need you." This is exactly where I wanted her, begging and ready to give me whatever I wanted. I released her nipple with a pop.

"Agree to my terms, love, and I'll make you come so hard you will be screaming my fucking name!" This time she didn't hesitate.

"I swear, I promise...only you...no Kai. Now fucking make me come!" She didn't have to ask me twice. I kissed my way down her body, pulling her dress with me. Once I reached her hips, she lifted her ass so I could pull her dress off. I chucked it to the side and stared at her sweet glistening pussy. Fuck, I love her cunt.

She was always so wet and ready for me. I used one finger to run through her slick folds and started to rub her clit. She arched her back off the ground and started to moan.

With a smile, I withdrew my hand and positioned myself between her glistening thighs. I opened her with one hand and blew on her enlarged nub; she was squirming and getting agitated. I loved working her to the point where she was begging for me. I leaned forward and ran my tongue from her opening to her clit, pulling a deep moan from her. Stopping at her clit, I began to suck and lick that hard little jewel.

"Nico, more I....need." I pulled back and looked directly into her eyes.

"I know, love." I returned to my task and began eating her sweet pussy again, slipping first one finger and then another in her channel then pumping in and out of her tight sheath. I kept at a fast and hard pace while sucking her clit into my mouth, and before long she was a writhing mess beneath me. I could feel she was close; her walls were gripping my fingers, coaxing me for more.

"Come for me, love." I sucked her clit back into my mouth as she let out a loud cry, screaming my name. The sound of it nearly brought me to completion by itself.

Letting her come down slowly from her high, I withdrew my soaked fingers and traced patterns with them on her soft thighs while I made my way up her body so I could kiss her before I fucked her into oblivion.

RYAN

Oh my God! I felt like I was floating on a cloud. Nico made me come so hard, and fuck did it feel good. He nestled himself between my legs and leaned down to capture my lips in a searing kiss that felt like he was branding me. I could taste myself on his tongue, and I'm not shy to admit that I loved the taste of me mixed with the taste of him. I felt his hard bulge nudging my pussy as he was grinding his pelvis into me. I needed him inside me now.

"Nico, I need you inside me now, please" The smug bastard loved it when I begged.

"You want me to put my cock in this beautiful wet pussy, love?" I loved his dirty talk, it always made me more needy and wet.

"Yes!" It was the only reply he needed before he was stripping himself of his jeans and lining the head of his cock at my entrance. I lifted my head so I could get a better view.

His cock was beautiful, thick and velvety smooth. I know a lot of people think cocks are ugly, but not Nico's; it was a glorious sight to see. I started biting my lip in anticipation, knowing that soon enough he would have me soaring through another orgasm, screaming his name. He ran the tip of his cock from my opening to my clit, bumping slightly against the sensitive nub, making me moan. He kept rubbing the tip of his cock up and down, making me more wild for him. I was about to start begging when he lined himself up with my entrance, looked me in the eye, and slammed into me. The sudden pleasure forced a cry from my lips. I felt so full and complete having him inside me. I felt whole.

"You like that, love?"

"Fuck yes! Fuck me Nico" He was slowly pumping into me and driving me insane; I needed him to fuck me hard and deep, just how I liked it.

"Ask me nicely."

"Please, Nico, fuck me hard so I can come again." With the magic word, he began to slam into my body over and over again. I felt so full, every muscle was strung tight with need. I was close to coming, again.

"Nico, don't stop, please! I'm so close." He never eased his pace, if anything his pace quickened.

"I am going to destroy this pussy, love. You are mine and so is this cunt." As usual, his dirty words were my undoing, and I shattered beneath him, screaming his name.

"Tell me you're mine, tell me this pussy is mine!" I couldn't think straight, and I was still seeing stars. "Tell me now or I won't make you come again, and you can suck my cock instead."

"I'm yours, my pussy is yours. Just yours, Nico, now make me fucking come again, please." He made me come again before he finally found his release, roaring my name. He collapsed on top of me, keeping his full weight from crushing me by resting most of it on his forearms on either side of my head. We lay panting, looking into each other's eyes. I lifted my head and kissed him like my life was depending on it. I was done lying to myself. I was in love with Nicholas Stone and had been for years, even before I knew he was real.

Nico broke our kiss and rolled over, taking me with him, my head resting on his chest. He wrapped both his arms around me, tracing patterns on my bare back. I did the same on his chest, drawing small circles with my fingers. We stayed like that for a long time, neither of us talking, just both enjoying each other's company and embrace.

As I lay there listening to his breathing and the beat of his heart beneath my ear, I started to wonder if we could make this whole marriage thing work. I knew that I loved Nico, and I know a part of him must at least care about me. Together, we could be strong, and in this moment I had no doubt Nico would help me control my powers and wouldn't let me get hurt when we did unlock them.

All the fear I had about my powers disappeared in this moment; I knew I could do this if Nico was by my side. I didn't know how to tell him, so I would show him instead. I pushed away from him and sat up, I saw a look of hurt and confusion on his face—he thought I was trying to leave. No, big man, I plan to show you with my body what you mean to me. He must have read the look on my face, because he relaxed and dropped his head back down. I threw my leg over him so I was now straddling him, and felt his cock come alive beneath me. I couldn't hide my smile. I loved that I had this effect on him.

"Do you plan to ride my cock or sit on it and tease me, love?" His words sent a rush of liquid to my core. I could feel how wet my pussy was. I decided to tease him a bit and started to rub my wet pussy up and down his cock, feeling it harden beneath me. He was ready for me, but I wasn't done playing with him yet.

"Either stick my cock in that beautiful pussy or suck it," he growled, and I shivered at his words. God, it was such a fucking turn on hearing him speak to me like this.

"This time I'm in charge, big man. I get to fuck you how I want." His eyes widened and started to glow a deep purple. I have never taken control like this in my dreams before; Nico was always the one calling the shots.

I could tell my words had shocked him as he kept opening and closing his mouth, not sure what to say. After another minute of rubbing my wet pussy on his cock, I slid down his body and settled myself between his muscular calves.

His eyes lit with fire. He knew what was about to happen. He pushed forward and leaned back on his elbows so he could watch the show. I bent forward and licked the tip of his cock, tasting, teasing. He groaned loudly, and that was all the encouragement I needed. I wrapped my lips around the tip of his cock and began to suck him into my mouth. He was too big to take all the way in, so I used my hand to stroke the base while I sucked and licked the top half.

"Fuuuuccccckkkk, that feels so good, baby. Yeah, just like that." I kept sucking and pumping him into my mouth, and I could taste his pre-cum and still a bit of me on him. It was delicious. "Baby, your mouth feels like fucking heaven, but I need inside you now!" He didn't have to ask me twice, I released his cock with a pop and straddled his hips, lining his cock up with my opening.

I wanted this hard and fast, so I slammed myself down onto his shaft, both of us crying out at the same time. I began to rock my hips. He felt so much deeper with me being on top. Within just a few moments I was close already, my pussy was pulsing and he was thrusting upward every time I moved back, hitting just the right spot. God, I wouldn't last much longer.

"Nico, I'm coming!" As soon as the words were out of my mouth, I tipped over the edge, and he took over, wrapping both his arms around my waist and pounding his cock inside me. I was screaming his name to the heavens. In one swift move he had me pinned on my back and he was on top, back in control.

"That was fucking hot, baby but now it's my turn, and I'm

out of patience." My only response was to moan; I was spent. That last orgasm took it out of me. True to his word, Nico fucked me hard and fast and ripped another orgasm from me. Once he reached his peak, he collapsed to the side of me and pulled me into his arms. I couldn't keep my eyes open any longer...I was bone tired after so many orgasms.

I must have drifted off, because next thing I knew, I woke to Nico's face between my legs, eating my pussy. He made me come all over his face and then fucked me senseless. He woke me two more times after that, taking me from the back the first time, and then the last time was very different.

I woke to him scattering kisses all over my tired, naked body. He had positioned himself between my legs and then kissed me. This kiss felt different—there was so much emotion behind it that it stole my breath. He wasn't fucking me this time, he was...he was making love to me. Nico and I had never done the whole slow, make love thing...we liked to go hard, deep and fast. He broke the kiss and pulled back so he could look me in the eyes as he was slowly working his way in and out of my body.

"You are everything to me, my love. You are the sun on my darkest days and the light on my darkest nights. You, my love, are my queen." I couldn't hold my tears back. They started rolling down my face, but he didn't say anything or stop moving inside me, instead just leaning down and licking and kissing away my tears, murmuring how much he loved my body and how beautiful I was.

His thrusts started to pick up speed, and I wrapped my legs around his hips and pulled down, pressing him deeper inside me.

"What do you need love?"

"I need you deeper and harder, Nico, please." He gave me more of his weight as he picked up speed and began punishing me with his hard thrusts. It was so right.

"Don't stop, please!" And he didn't stop, until we were both screaming our release. I felt so sated and relaxed. As soon as Nico pulled out of me, I felt his essence leaking down my thighs, and he watched as his cum slid out of me with a satisfied smile on his face. Once more he lay down beside me and gathered me in his arms. I was drifting off to sleep when I heard him whisper.

"Please forgive me when you learn what I have done. I cannot lose you, baby. You are my hugacko." I tipped into the darkness before I could respond, and slept soundly for the first time in weeks.

Chapter Sixteen

NICO

As soon as she drifted off to sleep, I chanted the spell to bring us back to her bedroom in Jackson's compound. The sun was already rising, and I knew sleep would evade me. I had never felt like this for anyone in my many years of being alive. I laid there, just looking at her sleep in my arms. Her tiny body was nestled in the same position as it was before I took her to our dream land, and I ran my hand up and down her side, just needing to feel her. As soon as she learned the truth about what I had done she would hate me.

I am the reason she is here. I don't have the balls to tell her the truth, but I know I need to find a way before Kai tells her. I lay there watching her sleep for so long that I must have drifted off too, jerked awake some time later by a constant knocking on her door. Before I could untangle myself, the door smashed open and slammed against the wall. Ryan sat straight up, ready to scream, until she saw it was Kai, Dom, and Jax in the doorway. I didn't bother to move off the bed; I just sat up and wrapped my arms around her waist and rested my chin on her shoulder, glaring at the three bastards who disturbed us.

"I have a key, dumb ass, there was no need to break my

fucking door." Jax was clearly pissed that Kai was busting up the place.

"You weren't fast enough," Kai snapped at him.

"Both of you shut up. Clearly she's fine, judging by the way she won't make eye contact with us and is blushing so hard you would think she was sunburnt. I think she had a great night's rest, aye love?" I couldn't hide my smile.

Instead of answering Dom, I placed a kiss on Ryan's cheek, which caused her to blush even more. I loved watching her blush.

"How about we give you guys twenty minutes and then you meet us in the mess hall? We need to finalize these wedding plans." With that reality check from Dom, I unwrapped my arms from around Ryan and stood. I stopped moving and turned toward Dom when he whistled. I realized then that I was only in my boxers. Ryan turned her head and looked at me, her mouth was hanging open so I leaned over and used a finger to close it for her.

"You're drooling, baby," I said with a wink. She shook her head and snapped herself out of it.

"You slept in here with me, like that?" I laughed, after everything that happened last night in our dream, she was worried that I slept next to her in boxers.

"Baby, if I recall, I spent more time naked and inside you than I did in these." She blushed a dark shade of red and dropped her eyes. My little sex devil was shy in the light of day.

"You fucked her?" I snapped my gaze to Melakai, who was shaking with anger. Dom and Jax were holding him back. Ryan flinched at Kai's outburst, which made me furious. She had nothing to feel guilty about.

"Kai, I..." I cut Ryan's reply off, we didn't need to explain ourselves to him. We were about to be married!

"That is none of your fucking business. She is about to be

my wife, and what we do and don't do in the confines of our bedchamber is not your concern. Oh, and from now on, you will stay the fuck out of her dreams." I heard Ryan gasp, and she turned her angry glare my way.

"You do not get to tell me what to do, Nico!"

"Actually, love, yeah, I do. You promised me!" She was seething now, I could see the fire in her eyes, and damn that look alone was starting to wake my cock.

"You can't fucking hold that against me! Of course I would say whatever the hell you wanted when you wouldn't let me FUCKING COME!" As soon as the words flew out of her mouth, she slapped a hand over her lips and quickly looked back to where the three guys were standing in the doorway, looking varying degrees of shocked and furious. Ryan quickly dropped her head and stared at her lap; even I was shocked at her outburst. I never expected that to come out of her mouth, no pun intended.

"So, yeah, we're just like gonna go to the hall mess. I mean mess hall. And wait for you guys to come. I mean get there." I wanted to laugh at Dom, I had never seen him so out of sorts. All three men quickly left, even Melakai didn't make a fuss as he was ushered out of the room by Dom. Jax closed what was left of the door, and I made a mental note to make sure he got that fixed by this evening.

"Please don't say a word, Nico, just go and I will meet you at the mess hall." She flopped back on the bed and pulled the covers over her face. I couldn't leave her like this. She was so adorable when she was shy and embarrassed. I jumped back on the bed and ripped the covers away from her. Before she could protest, I hopped on top of her and wrestled my way between her legs. She tried to fight me, but she knew she would lose. With a groan, she opened them for me and I settled there. I leaned down so I could kiss her cheek, then her neck, and eventually found my way to her mouth. I thought she might turn away or try pushing me off, but she didn't, opening for me as soon as I prodded her mouth with my tongue. She tasted so sweet; I wanted to stay here and do this all day and hopefully bury my dick inside of her while we were both awake. But I knew if we both didn't get our asses up and to the mess hall, the whole gang would come to us. I pulled back and smiled down at her, and to my surprise, she didn't blush. I saw the desire burning in her eyes. With a groan, I quickly jumped off the bed and told her I would be back after a quick shower to get her, and she should get ready before the others came back.

After a quick shower and shave, I made my way back to Ryan's room to collect her. Just as I rounded the last bend, I saw two guys at her door already pulling the old door off and had a new one leaning against the wall. As soon as she saw me, she made her way out of her room and stood in front of me, chewing her bottom lip. I reached out and tugged her lip so she would stop chewing it; at the rate she was going she would chew the damn thing off.

"Sorry, nervous gesture, I always seem to do that or pace."

"Nothing to be nervous about, love, and by the way, you look beautiful." She blushed at my compliment; she was wearing skin-tight black jeans and a snug white V-neck shirt. That reminded me— she was wearing Aurora's clothes. I would organize Larick to go back and retrieve her and her cousins' belongings. I also needed to give her the letter from her father that she didn't know I had.

"Thank you." She grasped my hand and began to pull me

along, and when I finally snapped out of my shock, I took control and took the lead. She laughed, knowing that I was always the one that had to be in control. I may have let her have her moment last night, but not today. We made it to the mess hall in record time, and both of us had smiles on our faces as we entered. As we walked past the buffet, I saw her tense and drop her head. I strained my hearing and then I heard the whispers.

"Isn't she the Alpha's mate?"

"I thought she was fucking the Day-walker."

"Eww look at her, next thing you know she will be fucking the half-breed." I turned to put an end to this gossip when she stopped me with a hand on my arm.

"Don't, Nico. Let them think what they want. You jumping to my defense only makes it worse." At her request I let it go, but as we made our way through the tables to head toward the guys, the whispers intensified. There was one woman bold enough to even shout out her insult, which had Ryan freezing in her tracks and me glaring over her head at the woman.

"You're the Alpha's mate, but you fuck a leech and the king of the fae. You are trash! I don't know what they see in you." I waited for Ryan to drop her head or cry or something, but she shocked me when she replied to the bitch.

"They see a woman who can handle three alpha males all at once. Jealousy will get you nowhere, sweetheart." I turned to see the guys at our table with their mouths hanging open in shock; even my sister and Aurora looked taken back by Ryan's reply.

"You're a vile, disgusting bitch."

"And you're a jealous whore, but you don't see me standing here complaining about it, do you? Just so were clear, sweetheart, who I fuck is none of your concern." With that said, she made her way over to our table with her head held high. I felt like a dog following its master. I was so turned on by the way she finally stood up for herself. When we made it to our table, everyone was still staring at her.

"Close your mouth, Dom, you'll catch flies." Dom quickly shut his mouth then opened it. I wasn't sure which was worse.

"You are amazing! Marry me, not that good-for-nothing king." I was so close to punching Dom in the face and I hadn't even had breakfast.

"I guess I could add you to my *apparent* harem." Aurora and Sophia burst into laughter. I, on the other hand, was pissed. No way in hell would any of these guys be going near her. It was bad enough that fucking Kai has already been with her. She took a seat between Aurora and Chase and began to eat her breakfast. I was still standing, glaring at her. When she looked up and our eyes connected, she frowned.

"What's your problem big guy? Your mood swings are giving me whiplash." I could hear Jax and Dom snickering and that fucked me off more.

"He's just pissy because you said you wanted to add me to your harem." Fucking Dominic!

She just rolled her eyes and joined in on the conversation her cousins were having about our upcoming marriage. I begrudgingly took the last seat available, which just happened to be next to Kai, lucky me. He shot me a glare when I sat down, and his behavior didn't go unnoticed by Ryan.

"Why do you both look like you're about two seconds away from throwing hands?" Neither of us responded to her questions as Aurora began to shake next to her. The only time Aurora really touches anyone is when she is viewing their past; other than that, she avoids contact as much as possible.

A hush falls over the mess hall as everyone waits and watches Aurora. She is revered for her visions. She has saved this pack more times than any wolf shifter. Her visions allow Jackson to see any threat before it happens. After a couple of minutes, Aurora slumps forward and catches herself on the table. She's panting hard and fast. Jax quickly jumps from his seat and makes his way over to her, handing her a glass of water.

"It's okay, you're okay. Deep breaths, babe." Even now Jackson doesn't touch her, he just reassures her with his words. "Take your time." After another few moments, Aurora's gaze turns to me and I gulp—this can't be good.

"You have the letter?" *How the fuck...*of course she knows I took the letter Ryan's dad wrote her. Reluctantly, I nod.

"What letter?" Fucking Dom. I swear I am going to stitch his mouth shut. I wait for Aurora to answer, knowing Ryan is going to go off.

"The letter Ryan's father wrote her; she needs to read it." Before Ryan or anyone can answer or yell at me for having the letter, I ask,

"Why?"

"Because it will help Ryan understand what happened to her sister."

"What do you mean?" Ryan's concern is evident in her voice.

"Read the letter now, you have until sundown to figure it out."

"What happens at sundown, Rora?" Chase asks the question that is on everyone's mind.

"Stevie Knox will arrive here at sundown, at the northern border, to see her sister." You can hear Ryan's sharp intake of breath and both her cousins gasp.

"She will not breach our borders! I will—" Aurora cuts Jax off before he can finish.

"You will let her through! She will not harm Ryan. Nico, you need to be ready. She is coming to speak to her sister, but she is coming for your blood!" *Fuck me.* What is it with these Knox women and wanting to kill me?

RYAN

Stevie's coming, Nico hid something from me *again*, and Stevie wants to kill Nico. I keep running those words through my head on a loop. What did Nico do? Why would Stevie be coming here? Has she had a change of heart? Oh my God, Kai will have to face her. I didn't even think of Kai. As soon as Aurora finished telling us her vision, I left the mess hall and returned to my room, needing some time to sort my head out and prepare for my sister's arrival. Now I had to read the letter from my dad that Nico somehow has. Why does he keep breaking my fucking trust? Speak of the devil. The man himself has just walked through my bedroom door, without knocking.

"When a door is shut it means you need to knock!"

"I didn't knock last night, and it seemed to work out well for the both of us." The fucking *cheek* of this arrogant asshole!

"I was asleep, Nico!"

"Still, you can't tell me you didn't enjoy that dream." He was teasing me, and I was about ready to skin him alive.

"What do you want?" At my question, the carefree look on his face dropped, and he reached into the back pocket of his jeans and pulled out the letter from my dad. I didn't move, I just stood there staring at him. After a beat, he sighed and closed the distance between us. He lifted my limp arm and placed the letter in my hand. I wasn't ready to read this, but now I was out of time and had no choice. After a moment, I closed my fingers around the letter and pulled my arm from his grasp. He turned to leave but stopped when there was a knock at the door.

"Come in," he said.

"This isn't your fucking room—" I stopped talking as soon as I saw Larkin enter, carrying my suitcase and duffel bag that I left behind at the cabin we were staying in when we first got to Alaska. "How did you get those?" Larkin didn't answer, he simply deposited my bags by the foot of the bed and left the room, closing the door behind him.

"I sent Larkin to retrieve them this morning; I thought you might like your belongings back. I also got him and Maverick to retrieve your cousins' belongings. You should also know that the cabin is empty. Your sister isn't staying there." Where the hell was Stevie staying, then? Nico turned to leave, but I stopped him.

"Thank you for getting our stuff, but I need to know two things, Nico." He stiffened but wouldn't turn to face me. After a long sigh, he responded.

"Ask away, little one."

"How did you get the letter my dad wrote?"

"I snuck into your room one night at the cabin and took it, in case it held information that your sister could use against us." That was...that was actually smart.

"Did you read it?"

"No, now ask what you really want to know, love."

"Why is my sister coming after you?"

"She thinks I killed your father." See, I thought that at the start, when Aurora told us, but now I think it's something else.

"I don't believe you."

He didn't answer, just shook his head and left the room. After hearing the door click shut, I quickly made my way over to the door and locked it. I know it was dumb to think a lock would stop him from getting in, but it made me feel more secure. With a few deep breaths, I walked over to the single chair by the window and sat down. It was time to woman up and read this damn letter. I sent up a silent prayer to my dad, asking him to help me make sense of this whole shit show that has become my life. With another deep breath, I ripped the envelope open and pulled out the letter that was actually two pages. Seeing my dad's handwriting brought tears to my eyes. I knew reading this letter was going to hurt and open up old wounds of never having my father in my life. After a few more deep breaths, I began to read the letter.

To my dearest Ry,

If you are reading this, it means I am no longer alive. I would have given anything to have you in my arms one last time or just to be able to tell you that I love you. You are so special, Ryan. You are more than I could have ever hoped for.

I may not have been able to see you or protect you from the horrors you have lived through, but believe me, my dear, I know all about them.

The woman you live with now is not the woman I married.

You having this letter means Stevie has told you about what you are, but your sister doesn't know the full story. Stevie will take you to our coven in Wonder Lake, and you will learn about your gifts.

I need you to find a man named Jackson Marshall. He is the Alpha of the Alaskan Wolf pack, and he has a seer within his pack that will help you. The seer will tell you everything else you need to know. She will tell you where to find a man named Nicholas Stone; he is the king of the fae and a good friend of mine. He is the key to help you unlock your gifts.

Once you have done all this, there is something else you need to know, daughter. I have done something that you will not be happy about. You have powers that are beyond this world. I didn't know about your gifts till it was too late, and I am sorry that I have failed you, my dear.

In order for you to survive the release of your powers, you need to wed a man from another realm. When two worlds merge as one, you will be released from the confines of the block he placed on you.

I had to change the original spell the king performed so he could never use you without your consent. You must agree and want to wed in order for my spell to break. I added this failsafe in case of my death, so you would have to be willing and not forced. It was the only way I could protect you without someone trying to use you for your gifts.

I am so sorry for all of this. I wish I was there to guide you, my dear girl. You are stronger than any other supernatural; your power is what can lock the fae realm, not your blood, like the legend has foretold. Your blood is the key, though, to grant vampires the ability to walk in the daylight. I know this must be a lot to take in, but I have more to say yet.

The day I turned you away, when you came to the house, I had no other choice! Your sister is changing, and the day you came was one of her bad days. You see, the legend left out the part that one twin would be born pure of heart and good, while the other would be born of darkness.

Your sister is losing control faster than I could have imagined; this darkness inside her needs to lead and craves power and destruction. She wants me to step down and let her lead the Knox coven, but I can't have that. She is not the true heir to the throne, you are! She will try to take the throne from you, Ryan, and you cannot let that happen. You need to go to the Knox coven and find a lady named Mya, she will help you, and you can trust her.

You need to save your sister! She needs you. Once you learn to control the power you wield, you can banish the darkness inside her. This will come at a cost, but I haven't been able to find out what that cost is. Mya may have been able to find this out in my absence.

Your mother was also cursed, my dear; her mother's spell backfired. She thought she cast a spell that would conceal the child from anyone who wished to harm her—that wasn't the case. She messed up somehow, and your mother paid the price for your grandmother's mistake. Mya can tell you this story when you find her.

Your sister has just arrived home, so I need to go now, my dear. Just remember that you are strong and you are worthy. You can do this, daughter. I know you can, as my blood runs in your veins. I love you to infinity and beyond Ry-Ry.

Love always and forever,
Dad xx

I burst out into uncontrollable sobs, my heart breaking and begging for my dad. He fucking loved me, and that bitch kept me away from him. I hated my mother more than I ever had in this moment. I felt the power inside of me building and heating my blood. I didn't try to stop it or calm down; I needed to release the pain inside of me. I screamed out, and as I did, a blast of blue light shot out from inside me. I slumped back into my chair, sobbing. When I felt two strong arms wrap around me, I didn't scream or flinch. At this point, whoever it was could kill me and it would hurt less than the pain in my chest. I was lifted from the chair and then cradled in someone's lap; my eyes may have been open, but they were so cloudy from all the tears rushing from them that I still couldn't see.

"I got you, love. You're okay." Dom was the one holding me and stroking my hair while I broke apart in front of him. I didn't feel embarrassed or ashamed, just numb and shattered. "Let it all out, babe. I promise I'll hold you through it all." His kind words made me cry harder. I cried for the loss of my dad, the loss of the life I could have had, and the loss of my sister to this darkness that was eating her alive.

"I....I...I....didn't...say...bye." I couldn't form a proper sentence; I was hiccupping and sobbing too much.

"You didn't say bye to who, love?"

"D...D....Dad." I cried harder, the guilt was killing me. I

never said goodbye to my dad, I never went to his funeral. I was too angry at him, because I thought he abandoned me.

I thought he chose my sister over me. He thought I would be safe with my mother, so he took the child that he thought needed his help more. I turned in Dom's lap so I was pretty much straddling him and wrapped my arms around his neck and buried my face in the crook of his neck. He didn't say anything, just moved my legs so they were on the outside of his thighs; he used one hand to stroke my hair and the other to rub up and down my back. I don't know how long we stayed like that, but it must have been a while, because I dozed off and woke to the sound of voices.

"Now is not the time for this fucking conversation and your jealousy, Nicky boy." I smiled internally at Dom calling Nico *Nicky boy*. "She needed me to hold her while she broke; she is hurt and angry. You need to start telling her the fucking truth. I will not sit by any longer and watch this beautiful girl be destroyed by you." Dom was sticking up for me, a notion that had my heart warming.

"She is not yours to hold! She is mine. What is it with you three and constantly telling me how to deal with her? Stay the fuck out of my business, Dominic."

"Fuck you, Nicky boy. If she wanted you here, she would say it, but she isn't, is she? We know you're awake, love, and if you want me to swap with Nico I will, if not I'll kick the bastard out." I didn't lift my head or say a word, just shook my head. "Well, there you have it, Nico. Get out and send someone to fix her door again. I broke it down getting in here to her." The room was silent for a moment, all you could hear was loud breathing and I am assuming *that* noise was coming from Nico.

"Fuck. Fucking fuck. Ryan, I'll be outside waiting." I didn't acknowledge Nico's words, just remained buried in the crook of

Dom's neck. "Just know that I am sorry and that I am here if you need me." I heard the sound of footsteps and then the door squeaking shut.

"He's gone now, babe." I slowly started to untangle my arms from around his neck and lean back, so I could look at him. I expected to see pity in his eyes, but all I saw was understanding. That shocked me. How could he possibly understand what I am going through?

"Do you want to talk about it?" I sat and pondered his request, my eyes skipping to the door that is just hanging on by the hinges at an odd angle. Dom understands what I am saying without words. "I cast a spell as soon as he stepped out; he can't hear us." Wow, Dom really was a powerful warlock. I didn't even hear him utter any words. I made a move to get off Dom's lap, feeling awkward for the position were in. His arms shot out and locked around my waist; I snapped my eyes to him in confusion. "How about I take you to your favorite place and we can chat there?"

"Okay," is my only reply, Dom helps me from his lap. My legs feel numb from being crammed into the chair for so long. Dom bends down and retrieves the letter from my dad. I don't say a word as he folds the note up and puts it back into the envelope.

He hands me the letter, and I quickly shove it into my back pocket, not wanting to see my dad's handwriting again. Dom turns away from me and starts to chant.

I guess he's opening a portal to Lake William. Once the portal is open and Lake William is visible on the other side, Dom grasps my hand in his and starts to lead me toward the portal. Just before we enter, I hear loud noises coming from outside.

"Dominic! Un-bar this fucking door now! I can feel your

power and know you have opened a portal." Dom starts laughing. I look to him, confused as fuck.

"I also spelled the door so no one else could break in." I smile at his deviousness. *What a bloody clever warlock you are, Dom.* "Hang on, I need to remove the sound spell." Dom says a few words under his breath that I don't understand and then shouts, "Be back soon, Nicky boy, we have three hours to kill before the wicked witch gets here." With that said, he grabs my hand again and we step through the portal.

Lake William is beautiful, surrounded by mountains and trees as far as the eye can see. The old jetty sways as the wind blows the lake's water. I make my way down the pier and sit, Dom joins me and dangles his feet over the edge as well. We don't speak for a while, just stare out at the beauty that is Lake William. This place has brought me so much happiness over the years; I can't explain, but I feel like this place is a part of me.

"You know Nico is probably going to beat my ass when we get back." Shocked, I turn and look at Dom to see if he's joking, but he's not.

"Why?"

"Because Nico isn't the only one who can hide his tracks. When a portal opens, it leaves a magic signature behind, just like every magic user has a different signature." I nod my head, not really sure where he is going with this. "Well, I made sure that my portal left a trail to follow to South America." At his admission we both start laughing knowing Nico would be furious and trying to find us.

"He doesn't scare me."

"I know he doesn't love, sometimes he wishes you were afraid of him so you wouldn't keep running from him."

"I will never fear him, I only run because..."

"You run because you're feeling more than you want to for the angry bastard, and *that* scares you." Well, fuck me with a silver spoon, Dom was more intuitive than I gave him credit for.

Chapter Eighteen

I avert my eyes from Dom's face so he can't see the truth; the truth is Dom is right. I am scared of what I am feeling for Nico.

"Take it from someone who has been where you are, babe—don't run, embrace it."

"How have you been where I am?" I sound like a bitch, but come on. Look at Dom; what stupid woman would run from him? He's beautiful, with those violet eyes, sun-kissed skin and shaggy silver-blond hair that you wanted to run your hands through. He was a handsome man, but he was also kind and caring. He would give you the shirt off his back if you needed it.

"I was in a similar situation many years ago, and I was too much of a coward to admit my feelings. I lost my chance with the one I crave, but you haven't lost Nico, there is hope for you two. I see the way my friend looks at you, and I see the way you look at him. You are both stubborn fuckers, and sooner or later one of you has to give in."

"Who broke your heart?" What can I say, when in doubt, deflect the attention to someone else.

"I know what you're trying to do and it won't work. We're

here to talk about you, not me." Well, there goes that plane of deflecting the attention from me and my fucked-up love life.

"I don't want to talk about me, though. I swear I'm not really that interesting"

"I beg to differ, love, you are an anomaly, and have been fated to marry my best friend but loved my other best friend, and then he died and now he's back and now you don't want to jump his bones." Well, when he put it like that, I sounded like a fucking hussy.

"I don't want to talk about Kai."

"Okay, how about you tell me why you are so upset, reading a letter from your father, but you're fine when you have daydreams about him?" Okay I guess we were getting into the heavy shit.

"How do you know about me seeing my dad?"

"I may have done a little spell so I could listen in on you and Nico the other day when you were here." Fucking wanker! He heard me confess everything to Nico, and now he wanted to sit there with a fucking smug look on his face.

"You fucking bastard, how dare you—"

"I did it in case Nico lost his cool and I needed to step in. I never meant to hear all of that, I swear. I would never have done it if I didn't worry Nico would go ape shit. I didn't hear everything, I stopped listening after that."

"Why would he go ape shit?" Dom turned and looked out over the lake for a moment. I waited patiently knowing he would eventually tell me when he was ready.

"Nico is jealous and overprotective of you because you are his *hugacko*."

"What is a hugacko?"

"Werewolves have mates, as you know. Their soulmate, if you will. Werewolves, after they turn, can scent out a mate. They will travel the world to pick up on the scent of their mate.

Well, for a fae, it is much more complex. There is no scent to follow; they physically have to be in the presence of the person to find their hugacko. The last time a fae found their hugacko was over a hundred years ago."

"Why didn't Nico tell me?"

"Because when a fae finds their other half, normally they understand the feeling and accept the bond straightaway. Your fae half hasn't been unlocked yet, so he is hoping that when it is unlocked, you will feel the bond as he does."

"That doesn't answer my question, Dom." I could tell he didn't want to answer me but we have gone too far into this conversation for him to pull back now.

"Nico didn't want this discovery to have any sway over your decision to marry him. He wanted you to marry him because you have feelings for him and not out of duty to a bond you don't even know about."

I sat there, stunned for a long while, mulling over what Dom had just said. Nico is an asshole most of the time, but him keeping this from me isn't his normal asshole behavior. Him keeping this from me is one of the sweetest things he could have done. He didn't want to pressure me.

"What if I flat out refused to marry him and say to hell with the fae realm?" Dom laughed.

"He would have tried fucking hard to convince you to change your mind. Nico is a controlling prick and expects people to yield to him, but when it comes to you he's different."

"How so?"

"He would have let the love of his life—his soul mate—leave him and his people to die, if that is what you really wanted. He would never force you to stay, Ryan, even if it broke him to let you leave." This new discovery about Nico was doing weird things to my heart. I cared about Nico so much. I didn't want to lose him, but I still couldn't trust him. He has lied to me so many times.

"How about a change of subject?" It hit me that Dom could help me find Mya.

"I need your help."

"I have a feeling helping you with this task is going to get my ass kicked by the broody bastard who's trying to track our whereabouts." I giggled at Dom's description of Nico. He wasn't wrong; Nico really was a broody bastard.

"I need you to help me find someone." Dom turned and stared at me, like he was trying to decipher my deepest secrets.

"Who and why?" Here goes. I need to be honest with him. I owe him that much if he is going to help me.

"A lady named Mya; she is from the Knox coven. She is the lady that can hopefully help me save my sister." The look Dom gave me told me how skeptical he was—he didn't think my sister was savable. I wasn't sure, myself.

Chapter Nineteen

NICO

"I'm going to kill that fucking bastard!"

"Calm down, Nico, you know he will keep her safe." I turned to pin Jackson with a fucking death glare. The look I had on my face had him shutting his mouth real quick. That smug fucking bastard masked his trail and sent me on a fucking wild goose chase through South fucking America. I was going to kill him.

"They have been gone for fucking hours!" I was going out of my mind, worrying and wondering if she was safe. What if her sister got to her or even fucking worse what if Randall managed to ambush them?

"Brother, they have only been gone for just under two hours, Dom said he would be back before her sister arrived, correct?" I looked to Sophia, who was occupying the single seat by the window in Ryan's room. I knew she was right. Dom would bring her back before her sister arrived, but it didn't stop me worrying though.

"What if they got ambushed or something?" I voiced my fear to the group. Jax, Kai, Aurora, Sophia, and Ryan's cousins came running when they heard me threatening to kill Dom when I felt him open a portal. Kai and I tried to break the door down, but couldn't break through Dominic's magic. I had to ask her fucking cousins to help me break the seal. I hated how strong Dom's magic was. It hurt my pride so much having to ask those bags of dicks for help. They may be Ryan's cousins but they were annoying assholes.

"Dominic would lay down his life for hers." I pinned Kai with a look that told him out of everyone in this room he was the last person I wanted to answer my question. "Hate me all you want *king,* but I will always protect her and so would Dom. We know what she is to you now." Hearing him admit that he knew Ryan was my hugacko filled me with a sense of relief; he knew he could never have her or take her from me. She was made for me.

I felt the whoosh of a portal opening behind me and spun around to see Dominic walk through with Ryan's hand clasped in his. I saw red, already moving toward him, ready to beat the fucking bastard till he was begging. As soon as I was within striking distance, I cocked my arm back, ready to hit the prick, when Ryan rushed in front of him and screamed at me.

"Stop!" I dropped my arm to my side, glaring over her head at my best friend.

"He has it coming! Now move, love." I was seething and so ready to unleash my pent-up rage on Dominic's face.

"Step aside, babe, I got this." He just fucking called her babe! That was it—he was losing fucking teeth for that. Shaking her head and looking at me, she said.

"I promised Dom I wouldn't let you hurt him. Don't make me break that promise, Nico." The way she was looking at me was like a mother telling her toddler he couldn't have one last cookie before bed.

"I didn't promise shit!" Fuck, now I was starting to sound like a toddler.

"Nico, stop acting like a fucking child and sit your ass down." Fucking Jackson was next on my "beat the shit out of him" list. I growled and made my way over to her bed and sat on the end next to Aurora.

"Where have you two been?" Jax asked, but Melakai answered for Dom and Ryan.

"Lake William, I presume?" Both Dom and Ryan shared a look then nodded.

"How did you know that? I masked my trail so no one could follow us." Fucking Dom turned and winked at me, and I rose from the bed, ready to beat the shit out of him, when Ryan started to shout at us both.

"Nico, sit the hell down now! Dom, stop antagonizing him, you know he's brooding. Don't make the old man have a heart attack before we make it down the aisle." With that they both started fucking laughing. She called me brooding and old! What the actual fuck. Well, two can play at this game, sweetheart.

"My brooding old ass still managed to have you screaming my fucking name last night." She stopped laughing immediately. Everyone was silent, you could of heard a pin drop, it was so fucking quiet in the room.

"Wow, that was a dick move, brother." Dom wrapped his arm around her and whispered something in her ear. I was trying so hard to bite my tongue and not make an even bigger fool of myself. She blew out a long exhale and then turned her hazel eyes to me.

"You need to stop saying shit like that, Nico. This isn't a dick measuring contest. I am pretty sure everyone in this room knows our history. We're about to get married tomorrow, so you don't need to be so overprotective, okay?" I released the breath I didn't know I was holding. She was right; I had to stop lashing out. But this bond between her and I was making me crazy. I needed to have her in my sight at all times just to ease this ache in my chest.

"Look we're running out of time before Stevie arrives. Aurora, do you have any idea what she wants?" Alex asked.

"Only that she wants to speak to Ryan. I'm sorry, Alex, but that is all I could see. Well, that and Ryan needed to read the letter her dad had written her." Shit, I really needed to know what that letter said; seeing how broken she was in Dom's arms earlier nearly broke me. I could tell the letter had some hard truths in it. Ryan clammed up at the mention of the letter, obviously not wanting to discuss it with anyone. That notion burned a little, knowing that she didn't want to share it with me. "Ryan, is there anything you want to tell us." I could feel it in my gut that Aurora saw more in her vision, but she didn't want to betray Ryan's trust.

"Squirt, is there something you want to tell us?" Ryan turned to her cousin and then looked back to Dom; he gave her a curt nod and an encouraging smile. With a loud exhale she turned back to Alex.

"I don't want to go into details, as that letter was something private between my father and I, but there was something in the letter. There is a way we can save my sister, maybe." Alex and Chase exchanged a look of disbelief. I can't blame them; there was no cure for crazy.

"I don't think there is a way to save Stevie from herself, Ry..."

"You're wrong, Chase. *'The legend left out the part that one twin would be born pure of heart and good, while the other would be born of darkness.'* That's what my dad said, if I can learn to control my powers, I can banish the darkness from inside her. I need your guys help, please." Both Alex and Chase reluctantly nodded.

"We'll help you however we can, Ry." She seemed relieved that Chase and Alex were willing to help her try to save her sister, but I could feel there was more she wasn't telling us.

"I will meet with Stevie today, and while she is distracted with me, Chase, I need you and Alex to go with Dom."

"What? Go where?" Chase took the words right out of my mouth.

"I need you to go with Dom back to the Knox coven and find a lady named Mya." It was clear both her cousins knew who this Mya is. "You know her?"

"Yeah, Ry, everyone knows Mya." Alex cut Chase off then and took over the conversation.

"She was the second in command to your father. She ran the coven while your dad was back in New Zealand. She is very old and wise, and if she went missing, everyone would notice."

"Then ask her nicely to come with you and let her know the true coven queen needs her help." To say I was shocked at my sister's input would be an understatement. Since when did she get so wise?

I really needed to sit down and have a talk with my sister. She was continuing to not only surprise me, but Jax and Dom as well. Kai seemed like he was accustomed to this new Sophia. It pissed me off more that he knew my sister better than I did.

Everyone started making a plan on what was to happen. Ryan would meet Stevie, with Jax and I there, as well. Dom and her cousins would go find this Mya. Kai, Aurora and Sophia would finish the arrangements for the wedding tomorrow.

We needed to make sure Kai stayed out of sight, we couldn't let Stevie get wind of him being alive, yet. I felt for Kai in this moment; Kai always thought we would find a cure for him so he wouldn't be a vampire for all eternity.

He hated that he had to drink the blood of others. Dom and I had searched for years for a potion or a spell or something to return Kai to his fae form. Kai was the first fae to ever be turned into a vampire. We learned from Kai that a fae's blood remains pure in their vampire form; it doesn't dilute and disappear like a witch's or a humans. Because of that, we thought we had a chance to save him. But his fae blood is gone, taken by the spell that brought him back to life.

Ryan, Jax, and I made our way to the boundary gate where Aurora told us Stevie would be. Just before we cleared the edge of the woods to enter the clearing, Jax started growling. That immediately set me on edge, and I reached for Ryan, pulling her behind me.

"What's going on?"

"Your sister isn't alone; she brought the traitor with her!" Oh, that's what Jax could smell. He must have caught the scent of Tyler. I released Ryan's arm and stepped aside. She took a deep breath and straightened to her full height and held her head high. Jax and I walked on either side of her. We weren't trusting of Ryan's sister, so we made sure to have Jax's best wolves stationed around the area in case of an ambush. I wouldn't take any unnecessary risks with Ryan's life. She knew there were wolves stationed in the trees, as we told her the plan before we left the compound, and surprisingly she didn't argue with us.

We walked for a few more minutes and then finally emerged into the clearing. Ryan's step faltered at the sight of her sister but recovered quickly and continued to walk toward her sister. I was so fucking proud of Ryan. She was growing stronger by the day. A few weeks ago she would never have been able to do this. She has grown within herself, and the change was so noticeable now. She walked taller and with more confidence; she spoke her mind and wouldn't let others speak down to her. She was still scared and timid, don't get me wrong, but she hid it better now. She was going to be the greatest queen Farrarie had ever fucking seen. I was one lucky son of a bitch.

Chapter Twenty

RYAN

As soon as we emerged from the woods and into the clearing, I stumbled. Seeing my sister for the first time since everything happened was hard. Stevie had changed, physically. She had cut her hair shorter now, into a pixie cut, and her eyes seemed dull and dark now. Her face had hardened. Gone was the carefree look she used to have. Stevie wore jeans and a simple black shirt that was cut to show off her midriff. She wore black Chucks on her feet. How the hell was she not freezing? The temperature had dropped significantly. We stopped a few feet from her. I couldn't stop staring at my sister, and she was staring right back. I felt inadequate in her presence; Before we left I had changed and dressed in my own clothes. It felt good to have my own things again. I was wearing black skinny jeans and my favorite Joker and Harley Quinn shirt, which was covered by my thick jacket. I wasn't used to this type of cold; Alaska was kicking my ass. You could smell in the air that it was about to snow. The weather here changed so suddenly; it was warm and sunny yesterday, and today it was freaking cold.

It was starting to get awkward, just standing here between Jax and Nico while staring at my sister and Tyler. Tyler seemed like he wanted to be anywhere but here, and I found that strange. He betrayed his pack and his sister to help *my* sister and Randall. Why would he do that? I cocked my head to the side, staring at him, trying to figure out what his motive was for betraying his friends and family. Tyler started to squirm under the pressure of my gaze.

"Stop staring at me like that!" Tyler clearly didn't like having the attention on him, which urged me to continue. He started shuffling from foot to foot.

"Why are you doing this, Tyler?" The question flew out of my mouth before I could stop it. I couldn't let him or my sister see that I rattled my own cage by having no control over my vocal cords; Stevie would see it as a weakness and prey on it.

"We are not here to discuss him, sister." The sound of Stevie's voice sent ice down my spine. Her voice had changed. I know it sounds stupid, but it was deeper and sounded raspy. The girl standing in front of me wasn't my sister anymore. The darkness my father spoke of has clearly taken a hold over her faster than he thought. Were we too late to save her now?

"What would you like to discuss, then, coven queen?" Stevie snapped her gaze to Nico. Gone was the indifferent look she had been wearing; she was now glaring and shooting daggers at Nico with her eyes, her lips pulled back in a snarl.

"You do not get to fucking speak right now, you fucking bottom feeding cockroach." Ouch! That was fucking rude.

"That's no way to talk to your future brother-in-law, now is it?" if Stevie was shocked by Nico's admission, she didn't show it. Instead, she started laughing. I looked to Jax and Nico, confused, but they seemed no more in the know than I.

"My sister will never marry you, once she finds out what you did." I could see Nico out of the corner of my eye, and he didn't so much as flinch or react in any way to my sister's words.

His lack or reaction made me suspicious; an innocent person would have some form of reaction.

"You know nothing, witch; get to the point of your unwanted visit."

"I will speak to my sister privately."

"Yeah, that's not gonna happen."

"No one asked your opinion, Alpha; this is between me and my sister." I wanted to hear what my sister had to say, but I knew it would be difficult to get Nico to give me some space and time alone with her. I knew Nico was the more difficult of the two so I looked to Jax, pleading with my eyes that he give me some time with my sister. We stayed staring at each other for a long moment before Jax broke our little staring match.

"You have five minutes." I mouthed a silent *thank you* to Jax.

"Like fuck!" I knew Nico would make this difficult.

"Stone, give them five minutes." Now Jax and Nico were in a bloody stare off. Jax stalked over to Nico and gripped him by his arm; they were whisper arguing, and after that they took a step away from each other.

"Five minutes and not a second longer." I didn't verbalize my response to Nico, I only nodded, and they made their way back to the forest, with Nico turning back every couple steps like he wanted to change his mind and insist on staying with me.

I loved his protectiveness; it made me feel cared for, and I haven't felt like that before. Once they disappeared into the forest and I could no longer see their retreating forms, my sister finally spoke.

"Well, well, look at you, little sister." Stevie was looking me up and down with a disgusted look. "I see you are surviving well with the mutts and the fairies." I hated how Stevie was referring to the Pack and the Fae like they were beneath us; she was so wrong.

"One, you're older than me by a few minutes. Two, don't

speak about the Pack and the Fae like that. They're good people, Stevie, and they're innocent. Why do you hate them so much?"

"Because they are beneath me and need to learn their fucking place, like you do, sister." I saw Tyler flinch at the way she spoke about the pack; his reaction was disturbing. Why the hell would he care, when he was the one who turned his back on them to start with? Shaking myself out of my thoughts, I focused my full attention back on my sister.

"They are not beneath us, Stevie; they are just as important as the coven and the vampires."

"You are so fucking naïve, Ryan. No wonder mother dearest loved beating you." Her words fucking pierced me; Stevie knew what saying things like that did to me, and she was enjoying hurting me.

I couldn't let her see how much her words affected me. I took the advice she gave me the first night we arrived in Alaska: fake it till you make it.

"Get to the point of why you are here, Stevie." A sly smirk graced her face.

"Well, look who finally found their backbone." Wow, what a bitch. "You need to stand down and stop this fucking game you're playing. You will help us seal the fae realm. Those disgusting bastards killed our father. I guess you forgot that part, since you're marrying the king of fucking murderers!" My sister was so delusional; Nico didn't kill our father. I was starting to believe what my cousins said was right: maybe my sister was the one to end my father's life, or at the very least she had a hand in it.

"You don't get to tell me what to do, Stevie. I am not a child, and who I marry is none of your concern."

"Look at you, spreading your legs for anyone. First it was the leech, and now you're fucking the king of the people who killed our father. I'm sure Dad would be so proud of you, fucking his killer and all."

Fierce anger coursed through my veins. *How fucking dare she!* I have never wanted to hurt my sister physically except when I thought she killed Kai. And she thought she had the right to speak about Kai, after what she did to him? Stevie had no right to speak about our father, when she had no idea what the truth was. I started to feel really hot, and I could feel my magic rising within me.

I looked down and saw my hands glowing. This time I didn't freak out or try to calm down, I embraced the power running through my veins.

I walked toward my sister, leaving a foot of space between us. She didn't react to my display of power, and she seemed almost gleeful.

"You don't fucking ever speak about Kai, or *my* father again, you lying twisted bitch." She had the audacity to smile, and I lost it. I only meant to shove her back to release some of my pent-up anger, but instead I sent my sister sailing through the air. The wooden fence didn't stand a chance against the blast; the remains were mere splinters and my sister landed with a thud about a football field length away. Tyler ran to Stevie, but I didn't give a flying fuck if she was hurt.

She needed a taste of her own medicine. She liked to hurt and boss people around. I wouldn't let her do that to me anymore. No one was going to control me; I was finally free. I heard footsteps pounding the ground behind me, and I spun around to see Jax and Nico running toward me. I didn't want them to stop me; I wasn't done with my sister yet. I closed my eyes and called to the magic inside me, I envisioned a bubble so I could trap them inside of it.

I was shocked when I saw a dome of glimmering blue surround me, Tyler, and Stevie, but grateful that my power was starting to work with me instead of against me. I turned and started walking toward my sister and Tyler; the dome started shrinking as I drew closer to my sister. Once I was a few feet in front of her, I saw that her leg was at an odd angle and she wasn't moving. Tyler was checking her for a pulse, and it was then that I started to realize what I had done. Stevie wasn't the only monster now. I nearly killed my sister! The rage inside me was slowing and starting to ease, the more I looked at Stevie. What the fuck have I done?

Chapter Twenty One

RYAN

"Oh my God, Stevie." I rushed over to her and knelt down beside her. Tyler started growling, but that didn't deter me. I rolled her over so she was lying on her back and put my ear to her mouth so I could hear if she was breathing. I didn't hear anything, so I started to do CPR. I kept pushing on her chest then blowing air into her mouth, but it wasn't working. I killed my sister! "You don't get to fucking die, Stevie, wake the fuck up now." She wasn't responding. Tears were running freely down my face, and I was sobbing so hard I could barely continue to perform CPR.

"Let him in." I looked to Tyler, confused.

"L-let w-who in?" I could barely talk past the lump in my throat. Tyler raised his hand and pointed behind me, and I turned to see who he was pointing at and gasped. Behind the dome I had erected stood Jax, Nico, Kai, and about twenty other men, who I was assuming were the shifters Jackson had stationed in the trees in case my sister ambushed us. Why the fuck was Kai here? I turned to Tyler.

"If you say anything to Randall about Kai..."

"You have my word Ryan, I will say nothing." I didn't trust

Tyler as far as I could throw him. The expression on my face must have conveyed what I was thinking.

"His blood can heal her. If she doesn't heal soon, she will die. She has internal bleeding." I looked down at my sister and saw no clear sign that she was bleeding internally. "I can feel her life draining."

"How?"

"You are not the only anomaly, Ryan. Your sister is my mate." Oh my God. That's why he left and betrayed us—he didn't have a choice.

"That's why you left, isn't it?"

"Yes"

"You have to help me stop her Tyler, she cannot do this. She will kill a whole world."

"What the fuck do you think I am doing? I don't want to fucking help her or Randall kill the fucking fae. Going against my pack and Jax is the hardest thing I have ever fucking done. My sister is back there, and I can't even fucking see her! If Stevie finds out I am trying to help you, she will not hesitate to kill me. Wolves don't mate outside of their race, but apparently I am the exception. Unfortunately, your sister doesn't feel the bond the way I do."

"She can't help it, she's changing."

"We don't have time for this. *She is dying.* Now will you help me or not?"

"Of course I will, she is my sister."

"Fucking break it down now," I snapped at Kai.

"I can't." Why the fuck was he here then if he couldn't help?

"You got near her last time when she blasted Randall's office; no one else could, but you did." It burned my tongue to say that shit out loud. I hated watching him be able to go to her while I was spying from the forest outside Randall's office.

"Her power has grown; she doesn't want us near her, so we can't penetrate the force field until she lets us. Maybe Dom can breach it?"

"Dom's not fucking here, Kai." I was about to lose my shit.

"Can you open a portal next to her?"

"You don't think I fucking tried that, Jackson? I can't breach the dome, nothing I have tried has worked!" I know I was being an ass, but I couldn't control my temper; Ryan was stuck in a force field of her own making with her evil fucking twin and the traitor. Tyler could hurt her, and there wasn't a fucking thing I could do about it.

"Alpha." All three of us looked to Lucas; he was Jax's go-to for war strategies.

"What is it, Lucas?" Jackson was using his alpha tone, which meant his wolf was in more control than he was.

"Maybe Lady Sophia can help?" *How the fuck does he know about my sister?*

"How do you know about my sister?" I saw Lucas tense and looked at the other pack members around him.

"Lady Sophia is very powerful and she helped us." *What has my sister been up to?* Before I could answer, Jackson spoke.

"I linked one of the pack members to bring Sophia here immediately." No sooner had Jax finished talking a portal open five feet from us. My sister walked through the portal with not a care in the world.

"So, I hear you need my help, brother."

"How can you help if I can't even breach the fucking force field, Soph? How did you open a portal?"

"I see you still doubt me, Nico. Dom opened the portal for me; he and the boys are back from the coven. Dom will join us shortly after they get Mya settled." I saw a look of hurt cross her face before she masked it. "Kai, you and I need to move to the northern side of the dome so she can see us. She will let us through."

"You're not fucking going anywhere, Sophia, and he sure as fuck isn't going anywhere with you."

"You either trust me or you don't, Nico" Sophia was looking me dead in the eyes, I couldn't get the words out of my mouth. I trusted my sister, right?

"Fuck, we don't have time for this, Sophia, let's go." I stood there stunned as Kai gripped my sister's arm and led her to the other side of the dome. Why the fuck couldn't I tell my sister that I trusted her?

"You just royally fucked up, your majesty." *Tell me something I don't already fucking know, Jackson.*

Chapter Twenty Three

RYAN

"Drop the force field."

"I don't know how Tyler."

"Are you fucking serious?" I flinched at his tone; I felt so stupid right in this moment. I made the damn fucking thing and now I couldn't even drop it.

"Figure it out fast, because they have reinforcements now." I turned to see a portal open and Sophia step through it. Oh no, this can't be good.

"Fuck, okay, give me a minute."

"We only have about a minute, so fucking hurry or your sister dies." Fuck, I closed my eyes and started to envision the dome going away, but every time I peeked an eye open, it was still there.

"You need to hurry, Ryan. If she dies, I will lose control over my wolf, and I will kill you." Oh God. I gulped so loudly I'm sure everyone outside of the dome heard it.

I closed my eyes and tried to concentrate really hard on the dome disappearing, but every time I opened my eyes, it was still there.

Tyler growling constantly didn't help the situation. I closed my eyes again and said a silent prayer to my dad, asking him to help me.

"Ryan!" I snapped my eyes open at the sound of Sophia's voice. She was outside the dome, behind Tyler.

"I can't drop the dome! Sophia, what do I do?" Sophia turned and whispered something in Kai's ear.

"Mi amor, I need you to focus on me and envision a small tear in the dome. Sophia is going to cast a spell to tear an opening in the dome, but you need to help her." I took a deep breath and nodded. Closing my eyes again, I envisioned a small tear in my mind's eye. I tuned out Tyler's growling and every other noise in the clearing, focusing only on causing a rip in the dome. "Keep going, mi amor, you're doing great." A moment later I felt a hand land on my shoulder and shrieked; I looked up to see Kai staring down at me. "You did great, mi amor, Now I need you to move so I can save your sister's life." I know this wasn't easy for Kai, after all my sister had done to him.

Chapter Twenty Four

NICO

We watched Sophia and Kai from our position on the other side of the dome. I had no idea what my sister had planned or how she was going to get through the dome, but I had to trust in her; she asked me to trust her, and that is what I am doing.

"What the hell is taking them so long?"

"Sophia said to trust her, Jax, so that is what I am doing. You should trust her too."

"She's changed, you know; she seems so different now." I couldn't agree with Jackson more, my sister isn't the same girl she was before she was taken many years ago. Every move she made now was well thought out and calculated. She was stronger and more fierce. There was something else, as well; I just couldn't quite put my finger on what it was exactly. "She did it! She and Kai are through."

I took off to the side of the dome where my sister and Kai had just gone through. Once we reached the side they had gone through, we felt around the dome for the opening.

"I can't find the entrance, Alpha."

"Me either, Alpha." I, Jax and his pack members were feeling everywhere for the opening but couldn't find one.

"She closed it." I turned and bared my teeth at one of the men; I didn't know who he was, but I didn't like his insinuation that Ryan had locked me out but allowed Kai entry. "I meant no disrespect your majesty."

"Don't worry about it, Kane, Nico is just on edge." Jackson was right; I was on edge and I needed to calm down. I looked back to Ryan and saw Kai place a hand on her shoulder. I could see their mouths moving but I couldn't hear shit. Ryan moved from her spot beside her sister and let Kai take her place. What the fuck are they doing? I didn't realize I had voiced my thought until Jackson answered me.

"Kai is saving her sister." I turned to Jackson and then back to the others in the dome. He was right. Kai is saving Ryan's sister—but why?

"Why the hell would he save the bitch that tried to kill him?" Jackson sighed and then placed a hand on my shoulder.

"For someone so old and apparently wise, you really are thick, aren't you?" I turned to glare at him, only for him to chuckle. "He may have manipulated her feelings for him, but his feelings for her are real."

"What the fuck does that even mean, Jackson?"

"It means that he loves her enough to save the life of the woman that tortured him and tried to kill him." Well, fuck, Kai is a bigger man than I. I don't think I could do what he is doing right now. Thinking back to the state he was in when Tyler brought him back sent a shiver down my spine. I don't know anyone else who could have withstood that type of torture and not snitch like a rat. I really needed to get over my jealousy with Kai and Ryan. What he did for her I can never repay; he was there for her when I wasn't. He tried to protect her as best as he could, and that made him the better man. He may be the better man, but I was the right man, and I would never give her up, no matter what. When he finds out what she did to bring him back, I wonder if he will still feel the same way about her then?

Chapter Twenty Five

RYAN

It feels like hours have passed since Kai bit his wrist and fed his blood to Stevie, but in reality it was mere minutes.

"We need to reset her leg so it doesn't heal wrong." I didn't even think about her leg, but Tyler was right—it was at such an odd angle that there was no way it would heal right.

"How do we do that?"

"It's okay. I can cast a small spell to set it straight."

"Thank you, Sophia." I then turned to Kai, only to find him staring straight back at me. "Thank you for doing this; I know this can't be easy for you, and I appreciate you doing it. I owe you for saving my sister, Kai."

"I owe you as well." Both Kai and I turned to face Tyler, shocked at his admission. "You didn't have to save her after everything she did."

"I didn't do it for her or for you."

"I know, Melakai, but I still owe you a debt." Kai didn't respond verbally to Tyler, but gave him a curt nod.

"Okay, I'm going to move her leg now and then cast the spell before Kai's blood starts to heal it." We all nodded and followed Sophia's direction on how to move my sister's leg. I winced when I heard a crack as we straightened it. "Okay, that's fine, now step back." We did as instructed, and Sophia started chanting a spell under her breath. Tyler moved to sit by Stevie's head so he could place her head in his lap. Minutes passed before Stevie even started to stir, and I released the breath I didn't know I was holding. *What happens now? I think I just made everything worse by hurting my sister; I doubt we're going to have a peace talk now.*

"What happens now?" I didn't ask anyone in particular. I was just voicing my inner thoughts.

"Once she is conscious, I will take her home."

"Tyler, you need to help me convince her; what she is doing is wrong and you know it."

"She won't change her mind, Ryan."

"You underestimate your importance to her, wolf." Tyler snapped his eyes to Sophia. He was shocked she even knew about him and my sister.

"How did you know about Stevie and me?"

"I see others love lives—long story. Anyway you need to stay by her side." Okay, so now Sophia was being cryptic as shit. All conversation stopped when I heard shouting from outside the dome. I turned to where the guys were standing and saw Dom and my cousins had joined our audience. I gave them a small wave. What can I say? I'm an awkward fucker.

"So, how do we get out of this thing?" I was looking between my three companions, seeing which one of them would have an idea. By the looks on their faces, they had no fucking clue. Great. "Can we try doing that tear thing again?"

"My magic is low at the moment. I used a lot to help you open the tear and then heal your sister's leg." Oh right, Kai couldn't do magic, so he was out of the question. Tyler was a shifter, so he was out to. I guess we needed my cousins or Dom. Wait—why wasn't Nico helping us?

"Why didn't Nico break through the dome? I mean, I am glad you both did, but I thought he would have busted in here by now."

"Nico can't penetrate your dome." I started blushing and giggling at Sophia's words. Yeah I know, I needed to get my head out of the gutter. I heard Tyler muttering something about being real mature, but I ignored him. Clearing my throat, I looked to Sophia and asked,

"What do we do now?"

"I think we may need to ask your cousins and Dom for help." Sophia seemed reluctant to have to involve Dom, but everyone knew there was a story with them. I wanted to figure it out. They would make the cutest couple. I walked past Sophia with Kai hot on my heels, heading toward Dom and my cousins. Before we reached them, I turned to Kai.

"Thank you for saving my sister, Kai. I know that must have been hard for you." Kai didn't stop or look at me; he just continued walking toward the group outside of the dome.

"I didn't do it for her."

I felt like a piece of shit asking Kai to save Stevie, but I didn't have another choice. My sister was dying, and I knew Kai could save her. I was a fucking terrible person. As we reached the edge of the dome, my steps faltered, seeing Nico looking so angry. His body was tense and his face was contorted in harsh lines. His violet eyes were so dark they were almost blue, and his lips were pulled back in a snarl. Right. So clearly Nico was pissed he was outside the dome and not inside of it. Whoops.

"So on a scale of one to ten, how mad are you right now?" I tried for humor, hoping that would ease some of the anger coursing through Nico.

"You think this is funny, little one?" Okay, I guess my humor didn't work. Nico was *pissed.*

"It's not her fault." Nico turned to Kai, glaring. If his eyes could shoot laser beams, I'm sure he would have done it. Wait, *can* he shoot laser beams?

"You—" Nico stopped talking and then yelled to the heavens, no one spoke as we watched him pace a small line back and forth for a moment. I have never seen Nico this worked up before, it was quite scary. "You are trapped in a fucking force field of your own making with your bitch of a sister, who wants to kill you and nearly killed my best friend, and you think this is a fucking joke?" I reassessed my need to leave my protective bubble. Nico was *hot*.

"Nico, calm down, this isn't helping anyone." At least Dom was thinking straight. "Melakai, how did you and Sophia get in?"

"You men are so dumb." I turned to look over my shoulder to see Sophia had joined us. Fuck, she was quiet. I didn't even hear her approach.

"What the fuck is that supposed to mean, Sophia?"

"It means, brother, none of you have done the simplest thing."

"What *is* the simple thing then, little dove?" Soph turned her gaze to Dom and smiled.

"I simply *asked* her to let us in." Well, technically Kai asked. All the males outside of the dome turned to look at each other like Sophia had said the most outrageous thing in the world. Chase and Alex just laughed; my cousins knew I hated it when I was told to do something instead of being asked. I think Sophia's answer had merit; my power seemed to be so in tune with me at the moment. She did ask me to let her in, and my power allowed it. Nico, on the other hand demands everything, and I hate that, so of course my power wouldn't allow him entry. I needed to get this power thing sorted ASAP. So much shit was riding on me, and it was starting to weigh me down. My power was the key to stopping Randall, because he had ingested the blood of the previous alpha and coven king, my dad. My power was the only thing to save my sister from the darkness inside of her. My blood was the key to grant vampires the ability to walk in the daylight without ever having to feed off another fae. One drop of my blood and they were set for life. My whole life was a cluster fuck at the moment, and I couldn't see an end in sight. Nico's voice pulled me from my inner turmoil.

"Little one, can you let me in now, please?" I could tell it hurt his ego to have to ask such a thing and I must admit that made me feel quite triumphant.

"Yeah, that's easier said than done." Nico was glaring at me now. "Stop looking at me like that; it's not like I have a fucking manual on how to navigate these powers."

"You let my sister and *him* in." Called it. He's jealous.

"Stop getting pissy, Nico. Give me a second to think." I turned to Kai and Sophia. "When you asked to come in, I thought of a tear in the dome and then suddenly you both were inside. Is that what I do again?"

"I cast a spell to help the tear open. My magic is low so you would have to—"

"We'll do it." I turned back to face the others and saw it was Chase who spoke. "We are capable of doing it, Ry. Dom can't at the moment." Wait, why couldn't Dom do it? What was wrong with him?

"Dom, why can't you do it?" Dom wouldn't meet my eyes, and I had a sinking feeling something had happened when he went to the Knox coven to retrieve Mya.

"We're running out of time! Stevie is starting to wake, and if you don't get this fucking thing down she will go ape shit, Ryan." Oh fuck, I could hear the panic in Tyler's voice, I needed to hurry.

"Okay, Chase, what do you need me to do?"

"I need you to think of the dome disappearing, Ry. Alex and

I can only help you shrink it, but we can't make it go away. It's too strong." I followed Chase's instructions and closed my eyes, envisioning the dome disappearing. It was hard to concentrate when I could hear Jax, Dom, and Nico talking among them.

"If you three can't shut your cake holes for five fucking minutes, you need to leave! You are distracting her." I was starting to like Sophia more and more; she was my kind of girl. I closed my eyes and started to think of the dome disappearing. Sweat broke out across my brow. I could feel something was happening inside me, my body was starting to warm. I couldn't open my eyes to see if it was working, afraid if I did it would stop.

"That's it, mi amor, keep going, you're doing great." Kai's words of encouragement helped boost my confidence. I focused harder on drawing the magic back inside me.

NICO

She was doing it! The dome was getting smaller and smaller. I could see by the strain on her face it was taking a toll on her. She was doing fucking amazing. I just wished I was by her side instead of Kai. I should be the one there holding her hand and whispering words of encouragement instead of him. I know she doesn't feel the same way about him anymore, but my jealousy knows no bounds. She was my ever after, and he was a threat to that. What if I told her the truth and she chose him? I wouldn't survive that. She was mine, and I would make her see that. I had to show her that I was the better man and the right choice. She was my *hugacko* and nothing would change that.

"Keep going, Ryan, you're doing it." Jackson's voice snapped me from my thoughts. The dome had shrunk; it was only covering Ryan now, and Sophia and Kai moved back a step. I don't think they wanted to be trapped in the dome again.

Moving my gaze from Ryan to her sister and Tyler, they were surrounded by at least ten of Jackson's men in wolf form.

Shifters were at their strongest when they were in their beast form.

"Keep going, love, nearly there," Dom encouraged her. I watched as the last of her force field shrunk inside of her. She opened her eyes, looking around, and then started to sway. I shot forward and caught her just as she collapsed in my arms.

"I got you, baby." I kept one arm wrapped around the base of her neck while scooping her legs up with the other, cradling her against my chest. She looked so worn out.

"What should we do with her sister and Tyler?" Dom posed a great question, what do we do with them?

"Jax, do you still have the holding cells I made for your father?" Many years ago, I made Jackson's father some holding cells; they were strong enough to hold a shifter, and the iron bars I used muted fae magic. I also cast a powerful spell to mute any witch's or warlock's magic, as well.

"Yeah, but do you think it's a good idea to hold them, though?"

"Do you really think letting the bitch that tried to kill Kai and oh, hang on, wants to kill my whole fucking world, go free is a good idea, Jackson?" Seriously, Jackson was working my last fucking nerve. Jax started growling and baring his teeth. As much as I would love to throw down with Jackson and release some pent-up anger, now wasn't the time with Ryan passed out in my arms. "If you want to hit the gym later and spar, I will be happy to oblige, Jax. Right now isn't the fucking time, though."

"Nico's right, Jax." At least Dom was seeing some fucking sense. "We need to question her sister and find out what the fuck she and Randall are planning."

After leaving the others to deal with Stevie and Tyler, I made my way back to the compound. I laid Ryan down in her bed and sat next to her, gently stroking her hair.

"When you find out what I have been hiding, please don't hate me, little one. I only did it so I could protect my people. I thought giving Randall your mother would grant my sister's freedom and put an end to this war, but I was wrong. I didn't know you back then; I didn't know then what I know now." I heard someone gasp behind me and quickly stood so I could face the intruder—or intruders, in this case. I stood there staring at both Ryan's cousins.

"What the fuck have you done, Tink?" Shit. They heard. Fuck.

"I can explain..."

"You better fucking start explaining now!" Alex was yet to say a word. Chase, on the other hand, had no problem hurling insults at me. "You are a fucking lying piece of shit. Our father told us that fae were honorable people and couldn't lie; clearly he was wrong."

"Technically we can't lie." I was trying to stall so I could come up with a good excuse, anything was better than the truth at this point.

"All you have done is lie to her." Chase had a valid point, I haven't exactly been very honest.

"Nico, I have heard nothing but good things about you from our father and our uncle. You are starting to make me regret ever believing a word they said." I felt guilt at Alex's admission; this wasn't who I am as a person.

"I never meant to hide these things from her, but the more time that passed, the harder it got to tell her the whole story." I felt exposed admitting my feelings to the warlocks.

"She is more understanding than you give her credit for.

She has been through hell at the hands of her mother. It is going to destroy her when she finds out you lied to her, again. What did you do with Nina?" Fuck, I had to tell them now.

"Nina left on her own accord, I swear. I just intercepted her. I thought that taking her and trading her to Randall would grant my sister's freedom."

"Why would Randall want Nina?"

"Because, Chase, he didn't know about Ryan then. I thought if I could give him the child of the queen, that would be the end of it."

"Why do you look like you just ate a lemon, Tink?" I really hated that fucking nickname from Chase. I glared at the bastard. "Stop stalling and spill now!"

"Nina sang like a canary and told Randall she had twins. Randall knew about the prophecy. He had planned to take Ryan from you at that party but couldn't. He saw how strong she was. He also knew when Kai was able to get her when she blew his office apart that Kai had feelings for her. He couldn't rely on Kai to control her emotions. Stevie made it easy for him when she had planned to lock you three up."

"I get what you're saying, but Ryan won't be that mad. It's not like she loves her Mom." Alex really was the smart one; he knew I was holding back. Ryan is going to hate me.

"When Randall realized Ryan was real, he cut the deal off and wouldn't let Sophia go. He changed the terms of the deal and said I had to give him Ryan in exchange for my sister." Both Chase and Alex looked like they wanted to kill me, but I wasn't finished yet. "I told Randall I couldn't do it, and I was gonna figure out a different way to get my sister back. Randall started sending parts of Ryan's mother to me for my betrayal. I swear, I have been trying to get her mother back, I know she hates her, but at the end of the day, that is still her Mom."

"You bastard. You were going to trade Ryan, weren't you?" I can't directly lie when someone asks me a question. I took a deep breath. It was time I admit how much of a piece of shit I am.

"The thought did cross my mind. I had searched for my sister for years, and no matter what I did, Randall was always a step ahead somehow. You have to understand I didn't know Ryan well when I considered Randall's new trade."

"You lying piece of shit!" I spun around to see Ryan sitting up in her bed shooting a death glare my way. "You planned to trade me for Sophia?" I started shaking my head, ready to try explain myself, but she wasn't having that. "That I do understand, but taking my mother and lying about it? I have looked for her for months, and this whole fucking time you knew where she was! I don't like my mother, but she is still my mother, and you handed her over to the fucking devil himself."

"I...I...sorry." Fuck, I couldn't even put a sentence together. She was never supposed to find out like this.

"Sorry? I can't with you Nico. You have lied to me for the last fucking time. You knew where my mother was and never told me. Wait. My mother was at Randall's mansion when I was, wasn't she?" I didn't bother to speak, I just nodded. "Get the fuck out and stay the fuck out of my sight, Nico." I lowered my head and stood rooted to the floor for a minute, after a long inhale of air I turned and started to leave the room. Just as I opened the door ready to step out, she spoke. "You were right, you know." I turned and looked back over my shoulder.

"I was right about what?"

"Kai was definitely the better choice and better man." Well, fuck me, hearing that felt like a dagger to the heart.

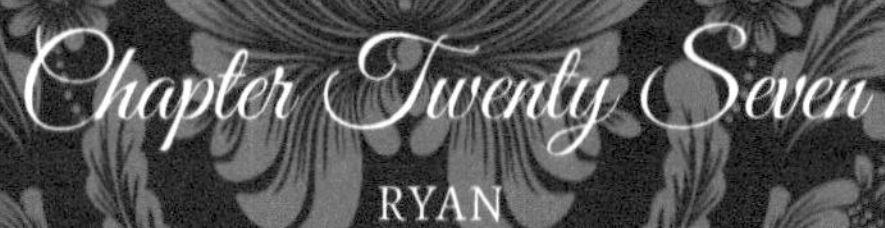

Chapter Twenty Seven

RYAN

I asked my cousins to leave as soon as Nico did. Once again I needed time alone to process the information that had been kept from me. I could understand Nico wanting to trade my life for his sister, that wasn't the problem. I was angry that he lied about it. He knew where my mother was the whole time. He never once mentioned while I was at Randall's mansion that my mother was there, that she was being tortured. I am so beyond hurt and angry. I just started to trust him and then he goes and pulls this shit. How am I supposed to forgive him? Once a liar always a liar.

I was sitting in the single chair by the window, looking out at the beautiful Alaskan scenery. It was so beautiful here. I loved the cool, crisp air in the morning. I could live here. I started thinking that I might actually do it, after all this shit is over with that dick Randall.

I might just move here. I knew Nico wanted me to live with him in the fae realm, but that wasn't going to happen. We would get married as planned, unlock my powers, finish this fight with Randall, and then go our separate ways.

Why did the thought of leaving Nico and never seeing him again cause an ache in my chest?

I knew I had feelings for him, that much was obvious, but you couldn't build a relationship on just feelings. You needed communication and trust. I didn't trust Nico, and we sure as shit didn't really communicate. I still found it gross that Nico was supposed to marry my grandmother. I mean, come on, that is fucked up, right? I knew Nico and the other three guys were way older, but how much older than me are they?

Questions like these are banking up. I know they're trivial, but there are things I felt like I should know. I need to find someone who could answer these questions—maybe Sophia?

I was pulled from my thoughts by a knock at the door; I didn't bother to move, just told whoever it was to come in.

Holy shit, did I somehow mind link her or something? Sophia and Aurora walked in, closing the door behind them.

"So is this how you plan to spend your last day as a single woman?" I hadn't actually thought about that.

"Um...no?" I didn't mean to sound so unsure, but what were my options, really? It's not like I actually had any friends that would want to throw me a party. I saw a look of pity on Aurora's face, but Sophia's held a look of determination. Oh no, that could only mean trouble. Sophia made her way over to me and grabbed my wrist, pulling me to my feet in one fluid motion. "What are you doing, Sophia?"

"Well, you're not going to sit around here and wallow in self-pity. My brother's a dick. Get over it, you're still marrying him." Wow, she really didn't mince words, did she? At least she agreed that her brother was a dick. I decided right here and now that I like Sophia, a lot.

"We have a suggestion." I looked past Sophia to see Aurora; she seemed hesitant.

"Okay, why do you look like you ate a lemon, Aurora?"

Sophia sighed, I turned to look at her, waiting for her to answer instead of Aurora.

"Fine! We're taking you to see your sister." Wait, what?

"Where the hell is my sister?"

"In the cells. Now, if you want to see her, you need to hurry up." I nodded to Sophia and quickly followed both the girls out of my room and down a zigzagging maze of hallways. We emerge from the building to a side of the compound I had never seen. It was barren and dark from the shade of the huge trees, and I felt uncomfortable being on this side. There was no warmth to be found from the sun, only darkness. "Hurry up and stay behind me." I nodded. We began walking toward an old shack; it looked really old. If a strong gust of wind came, it would probably blow it over. When we reached the front of the shack, Sophia knocked on an old, wooden door.

"Who is it?" Hey, I know that voice.

"Open the fucking door, Dom, it's cold as shit out here."

"How cold does shit get, little dove?" I could hear the humor in Dom's voice. Sophia didn't answer Dom, she growled instead. Holy shit, she could give a shifter a run for their money with that growl. You could hear laughter coming from the other side of the door before it was opened. Sophia pushed past Dom and made her way inside, and, not wanting to freeze my ass off, I quickly followed. Dom shut the door as soon as Aurora entered. The room is tiny; with just four of us inside, it was a tight fit. Looking between my three companions, I asked.

"Where's my sister?"

Dom just smiled and said, "Hold on love, she's below us."

Huh?

Dom placed his hand on the side of the wall and we started to descend. Oh my God, the room was a secret elevator. "If we had prisoners sitting above ground, anyone could try setting them free. Doing it this way, the elevator only works with certain magic signatures and palm prints." That was freaking smart, no one could break in and try stealing the prisoners.

"So, who can get to people below us?"

"Jax, Nico, Kai, and two of Jax's trusted guards, and well, of course, me." I didn't respond as the elevator came to a halt. Dom opened the wooden door we entered through above ground and exited. We followed Dom out, and I was shocked.

There was proper lighting down here and the walls weren't made of dirt or rock but rather concrete.

Walking further along, I saw quite a few cells, the bars on them seemed thicker than normal prisons—well, ones that I had seen on TV, and they were a darker color as well. We walked another minute and turned a small corner, and I stopped dead in my tracks. The cell at the end of the hall held my sister. She was sitting on a makeshift bed made out of a concrete slab. Her brown hair was a tousled mess, and her posture showed me how defeated she felt. I rushed past Dominic and stopped right in front of my sister's cell. She didn't lift her head or even acknowledge our presence.

"What's wrong with her? What happened to my sister?" The person that answered wasn't one that I expected; I turned my head to look at the cell next to my sister and saw Tyler.

"She draws her power from nature. Being so far underground and surrounded by concrete blocks that off."

"Open the door, I want to go in." I needed to make sure she was okay. I know Stevie has done some fucked-up shit, but she was still my sister.

"I can't do that, love." I turned to glare at Dom. How fucking dare he bring me down here and then deny me a chance to sit with my sister and try fix things?

"Open the fucking door Dom, I want to—" I stopped speaking immediately and spun around to face my sister when I heard her voice. She was still sitting in the same place, with her head hanging low.

"You can't come in here, Ryan."

"Why not, Stevie? I want to help you."

"You can't help me!" She snapped her head up and locked her gaze on mine. That's when I saw it—the darkness I saw in her eyes earlier had receded. Her being down here was a good thing, I think. She was cut off from all magic, which meant the darkness inside couldn't get to her down here.

"Stevie, I need to explain things to you, Dad told me..."

"You think I don't know about the darkness inside me? I have known all along, Ryan. Dad tried to hide it from me. Mya told me the truth. Oh and don't think that I don't know you took her from the coven." I gasped. How the hell did she know that? If Stevie knew all along why didn't she try to get help?

Chapter Twenty Eight

NICO

After leaving Ryan's room, I wandered around the compound for a while, trying to sort through my thoughts. I had no idea where I was going, I just couldn't stay in one place at the moment. I don't know how I wound up outside Jackson's office door. I was kind of glad that I did, I could use someone to talk to. I knocked, waiting for him to invite me in. When he did, I opened the door and entered. Jackson wasn't alone; Melakai was sitting on one of the couches, gazing out the window.

"I'll come back later." I turned to leave, only to be stopped by Kai's words.

"I'm sorry." I thought I might have misheard him, I turned to face him. "I shouldn't have tricked Ryan. I thought if I did, I could save her from all of this." With a long exhale, I made my way over to the other couch and took a seat. Jackson moved out from behind his desk and sat in one of the single chairs.

"I get why you did it, I just don't like that you did it."

"I didn't know what she was to you back then." I turned to look at Jackson;, he at least had the decency to look sheepish. "Don't blame Jackson, he told me the truth so I would back off and leave you and her be." I was shocked, to say the least.

"Thank you?"

"Don't sound so shocked Nico, if you had of told me from the start she was your hugacko, I never would have continued what I was...doing."

"Don't lie to me, Kai—you would never have stopped." He finally pulled his gaze from the window to look at me. Kai had changed since he came back; his eyes told you how haunted he was on the inside.

"I love her, Nico, but you are my brother. I would never try to destroy your bond with her. She is yours, not mine." I heard the pain in his voice. He didn't want to admit that Ryan was mine. I respected Kai so much right now, I know this can't be easy for him.

"Okay, both of you, do know she is not an object? She can't be owned." Both Kai and I snapped our gaze to Jax. "Don't look at me like that, either of you. This is why she is always pissed at the pair of you." I looked to Kai, who looked just as confused as me.

"What do you mean, Jax?"

"My God, Nico, you are thick. She hates that you both talk about her like she can be owned. She has lived through a horror story, her mother wanted to own her and control her. Her sister tried to control her. She finally got away from her mother when you kidnapped—"

"I didn't kidnap her, I just borrowed her." Both Kai and Jax glared at me. Yeah, okay, that was a piss weak attempt at sticking up for myself. Jax, Dom, and Kai knew what I had done with Ryan's mother, I told Dom and Jax after I realized Kai knew.

"Anyway, she was finally free, then all this shit happened and you two dicks are trying to do the same thing her mother did to her."

"Fuck." Yeah, what Kai said. I was doing the thing she hated most. Jackson had a satisfied look on his face as he saw realization dawn on our faces. Fucking smug prick, I'll give him a taste of his own medicine.

"So Jax, how are things with Aurora?" Jackson's expression changed immediately.

"Fuck you, Nico, you don't get to ask me about her." Yeah, that was a dick move on my part.

"Jax, I really am sorry. I only wanted to help Aurora."

"Help her, why?" And he said I was thick.

"Because she said you would fucking die, dumb ass." He recoiled at my outburst, but a look of understanding crossed his face. He knew I cast the spell to try and save him, not hurt him.

"I understand, Nico, but don't interfere with my love life again. You have enough interference in your own to worry about." Bastard was bloody right, but that didn't mean I liked to hear it. We sat there talking about good memories and mending bridges between us that were damaged from our time apart.

Shit might suck right now because Randall discovered Ryan, but I will always be grateful, because her coming here brought me and my brothers back together again.

It felt so good to sit here and have a few whiskeys with my brothers and laugh about dumb shit. Just as I started to pour our third glass, I stilled at Kai's confession.

"I wish you well tomorrow, brother, but I cannot be there." I finished pouring our drinks and carried them over to the guys and sat back down.

"Why can't you be there, Kai?"

"I will not face Randall until I am at full strength. I will not be able to tame the urge to kill him if he is in my sight." I could feel the anger radiating off Kai—now that he was free from his blood oath to the vampire king, he wanted vengeance.

"I understand, brother."

"No you don't, Nico, you have no idea how hard it was to stand by and not be able to do a thing while he hurt Ryan's grandmother and then to watch and not be able to help Sophia. That killed me every day." I tensed as soon as he mentioned my sister. Soph wouldn't disclose any information about what happened to her. She was with Randall for seventeen years and suffered untold torture. "She is not the same woman who was captured, Nico. Sophia is stronger than you could ever imagine." I knew he was right; So-So was definitely stronger.

"You're right, I won't sit here and say that I am heartbroken over the queen's death. She knew the risk of leaving the fae realm with Randall and what it would mean for her people if she didn't go through with the marriage to me. I know, deep down inside of me, she was the one who told Randall how to enter my realm.

Her doing that caused my sister to be taken. I will kill that son of a bitch for what he did to Sophia. I'm getting married tomorrow, Kai, and I really wish you would change your mind and be there with me; I want my brothers by my side."

I could see Kai was torn; he wanted to be there for me, but wasn't sure if he could control his urge to kill Randall. I did something that I don't normally do to sway his decision.

"Please."

"How could I say no when you asked so nicely?" Fucking prick.

"Okay, guys, I don't mean to break up this heart to heart, but one of my guys has just told me he saw Ryan, Sophia and Aurora enter the cells."

"It won't matter, Jax, they can't get down there."

"Actually, Nico, they already have."

"How the fuck did they get down there?"

"Dom" That one name from Jax's lips sent my blood boiling. Fucking Dominic. I was going to beat his fucking ass. He was going too far these days and needed to be taught a fucking lesson.

Chapter Twenty Nine

RYAN

"Stevie, if you knew this whole time, why didn't you say anything? We could have tried to help you!"

"I don't want your fucking help, Ryan! I am the queen of the Knox coven."

Is she fucking serious right now? That's all she cared about—being queen.

"Everyone knows you're the fucking queen, Stevie! I don't care about that, I care about you! I'm trying to save you from yourself, not take some fucking crown from you!" Stevie jumped to her feet, glaring at me, and made her way over to the cell door, where I stood.

"You will never get my crown, Ryan!" Okay, so maybe I was wrong. Her being down here didn't completely take away her psycho side. I leaned in closer, so we were nearly nose to nose through the bars.

"If me taking the fucking crown from you is what is going to save you, then I will. I will find a way to help you, Stevie. Dad told me there's a way. This darkness inside of you is going to kill you. I will not let you hurt yourself or anyone else again! What you did to Melakai fucking disgusted me!"

A cruel smile graced her face, a face that I knew all too well. I saw that face every time I looked in the mirror. Her eyes started to darken; they weren't green anymore but rather a muddy brown. She straightened up and looked down her nose at me; The way she was looking me sent shivers down my spine.

"I enjoyed breaking him. I loved hearing his screams." I recoiled at her words, and Dom surged forward and put his arm through the cell bars and gripped my sister around her throat, lifting her off the concrete floor. Tyler was shouting for him to put her down and hurling death threats at Dom.

"Dom please put her down." I was begging him to listen.

"You vile, fucking bitch. I will fucking kill you for what you did to my brother! I would love nothing more than to submit you to the pain you caused him. You're a fucking cunt!"

"Dominic! Put her down now!" Dom dropped Stevie immediately, and we all spun around at the sound of Nico's voice. Nico looked so angry. "What the fuck are you doing down here?"

"Calm down, brother."

"Don't fucking tell me to calm down, Sophia. That bitch has tried to kill Ryan, and you bring her down here, for what?"

"We brought her down here so she could deal with her demons, Nico."

"Shut the fuck up, Dominic! You and I are fucking going to have it out for this stunt!" Dom just smiled at Nico, almost like he had been waiting a long time for this showdown to happen.

"Fuck....you....all." I spun around at the sound of my sister's voice; she was still gasping for air and rubbing her throat. "Randall....and....I...will...kill..you all."

"Randall is a liar, Stevie!" She was so blinded by rage and this darkness inside her that she couldn't see the truth.

"He hasn't lied about anything, Ryan."

"He has Mom, Stevie." Stevie smiled a cruel smile. Holy

shit, she knew all along. I took a step back, shaking my head. She knew this whole fucking time and said nothing? She knew I was still searching for our mother.

"You think I didn't know, sister? Of course I knew. When Randall offered me the chance to side with him and seal the fae realm, I took it. Then he told me he had that cunt that gave birth to us, and I told him I would join his crusade if he let me torture the bitch! How'd you like those body parts, Your Majesty?" Stevie started laughing like a maniac. Fuck, I think I was going to be sick. I turned to the side and gripped the bars on a vacant cell and started to dry heave. I felt a hand rub up and down my back. I didn't turn to see who it belonged to. "Oh my, look who it is, Melakai fucking Cane, prince to the vampire race."

"You don't get to speak to him, you bitch!"

"Oh, Sophia Stone, princess of the fae. You seem quite fond of the vampire, are you fucking him too? You seem to have recovered nicely since we last saw each other." Dom started growling, and I turned my head to see it was him rubbing my back. I straightened and cleared my throat. I knew what I had to do now; I could only save one of them, and the one I wanted to save the least was probably the only one I could save. That realization nearly broke me, but I wouldn't give up hope that I could save them both. I looked toward Tyler's cell, seeing Aurora cling to her brother's arm. Tyler's gaze met mine, and he was begging me to help him save my sister, and I nodded.

"We need to leave now."

"Come on Ryan, don't leave now, we were just getting to the fun part. Don't you want to know how mommy is doing? You know she asks for you, sister. Come visit her while she's still breathing, at least then you can say you saw one parent before they died." I turned and glared at my sister. I was fighting so hard to hold my tears back. I would not let my sister see me break.

"I will find a way to save you from yourself, Stevie, and when I do, you will be on your own." My sister's manic laughter followed us all the way to the exit.

Once we left the cells and made it back to Jackson's office, there was a small slender woman with white blonde hair sitting in the single chair by the couches.

"Who the hell are you?"

"That would be Mya, Squirt." I turned to see both Alex and Chase sitting on the other couch. I was shocked that this lady was Mya. "She's not what you expected, is she Squirt?" I had no words, I just shook my head. Mya wasn't old like I thought her to be.

"The joys of immortality, Miss Knox." She has a Southern accent, and she was so not what I had pictured. She had long, white blonde hair, a color girls these days were paying huge money to achieve, but it was her natural color. She had muddy brown eyes that radiated kindness. "Do not let my appearance fool you, Miss Knox. I am as old as these four men." I raised my brows in surprise; she appeared so youthful and put together.

"Ryan, meet Mya." I looked to Chase and then back to Mya, still in shock. Mya smiled and made her way over to me. She extended her hand and I stood there like a stunned deer, staring at her hand. "Ry, you're supposed to shake the poor woman's hand."

"Right." I placed my hand inside hers and shook it. "It's a pleasure to meet you, Mya."

"The pleasure is all mine, Miss Knox." She released my hand and stepped back. "It is a pleasure to meet you all."

Everyone said hello and introduced themselves, but Mya seemed to know everyone. We all took a seat on the couches and stared at each other. I don't think anyone knew what to say. Mya cleared her throat then looked to me. "Would you like to tell me why I am here, Miss Knox?"

"Um...I got a letter from my dad that said you could help me."

"Ask me what you wish to know, Miss Knox." She was so formal.

"Please just call me Ryan."

"Okay, Ryan, what would you like to know?"

"I want to know about my mother and about my sister and I...I want to know how to save my sister." Mya nodded her head and looked around the room.

"Would you like to have this conversation in private?"

"No," snapped Nico. I turned to glare at him and he backed off.

"I mean, I think you would like us to stay for support, right?" Nico was looking at Jackson, who was nodding his head like he was encouraging a toddler. These guys are fucking ridiculous.

"Squirt, if you want to have this conversation alone, we will all leave, even the fucking fairy." Nico turned to glare at Chase.

"It's fine, Mya, please continue."

"Okay, so I'll start from the beginning. It's a long story, are you sure you want to hear all of this the night before your wedding?" it wasn't even a hard question for me, I needed answers. I knew it was getting late and everyone would be tired but I didn't care, they could leave but I was staying.

"I need answers Mya, please. If any of you want to leave and get dinner or go to bed, you can." There was a chorus of *no* and *no thank you*. Jackson said he would get some pack members to deliver dinner to his office, which I appreciated, as I was starving. I needed food as soon as possible or I would start to get hangry, and no one needed me acting like a bitch during all this.

We decided to wait till dinner arrived before we started our chat, filling the time with chit chat about the coven and general catching up. Dinner arrived ten minutes later and we all polished off our plates within a few minutes.

"Okay now that we are all full and Ryan isn't gonna hulk out on us, we can start I raised my middle finger to Chase but smiled sweetly at Mya and said, "Shall we begin?"

Chapter Thirty

NICO

I had never met Mya before; I was just as shocked as Ryan to see her youthful appearance. Mya's eyes held so much wisdom and knowledge.

"Right, your father came to me fifteen years ago, so I could help him find a way to save your mother, and help him find a way to save you and your sister." This was news to me. "He figured out that your mother was cursed not long after she had given birth."

"The child was never cursed!" Mya didn't look pissed off or angry at Kai's outburst, she almost seemed like she expected it.

"Ryan's grandmother didn't intentionally curse her own daughter Melakai, it was an accident."

"The queen put a spell on the child to protect it from harm."

"Yes, Melakai, she did. Somehow the spell backfired when the queen's daughter had children of her own, I'm not sure how or why it happened."

"So you're saying my mother changed, because she had children?"

"Yes Ryan that is exactly what I'm saying."

"How did my dad figure this out?"

"He didn't at first; your mother was fine and happy. Then over time she started to get worse and your father grew concerned. He came to the coven to seek answers. I offered to help my king. We went through so many books and legends and came to the conclusion that your mother was the long-lost child of the queen. It was a story most of us knew but didn't believe it held any merit, until one day it did."

"How did you figure out that the spell my grandmother cast backfired?" Ryan was asking great questions, questions I think we all had.

"We don't know for sure how it backfired, but our guess is that the cell that she was held in was spelled by a powerful rogue witch, and when she cast her spell to protect her child, the witch's spell must have held some sort of failsafe. I don't really know how to explain it; sometimes when you cast a powerful spell there is a price to pay. If the spell the witch cast was powerful enough, and your grandmother cast her own, maybe the two different types of magic didn't agree and caused a ripple of some kind."

"Kai did tell me that my grandmother's cell was spelled." I looked over to Melakai to see him nodding. So that's why Kai could never break her out. Everyone called her queen, but the truth was she was only queen of the vampires, not the fae, as we never married.

"How do we save Stevie from herself?" Chase asked.

"That question, Mr. Knox, is a hard one to answer. I have searched high and low for years trying to find a sure way to save Miss Knox from the darkness inside her."

"So you're saying that there isn't a way?"

"I am saying, Mr. Knox, that there is a way to save her." I saw Ryan's eyes start to glisten; she had hope now that her sister could be saved. "If Stevie has accepted the darkness and embraced it, then no, she cannot be saved. If Stevie is still inside, fighting it, then yes, I believe she can be saved." Ryan's shoulders dropped and her face deflated, the tiny hope she had just got squashed.

"My dad told me that if I can control my powers, I can blast the darkness out of her."

"That is what we originally thought, Ryan. I kept looking into it after your father left, There is no research or books on this. We have never had something like this come about, before now." Ryan looked crestfallen; she thought Mya would give her directions and a map to save her bitch of a sister.

"That's not all of it, though, is it Mya?" Everyone turned to look at Aurora, surprised by her comment.

"Oh, you are good, Miss Evans. I left that part out to see if you were as good as Ralph hoped you would be." Huh, how the hell did Ralph Knox know about Aurora and her gifts? He never met her.

"How did Ryan's dad know about me?"

"That I honestly don't know. Ralph never disclosed that information. He knew Ryan would cross paths with you somehow. I used to think that Ralph was a seer himself."

"Are you going to tell them, or should I?" Mya smiled at Aurora; clearly Mya was fond of Aurora's abilities.

"I'm sorry, Ryan." Mya took a deep breath and looked Ryan directly in the eyes. I could see from the look on Mya's face she was finding it hard to disclose her news to Ryan. "Stevie accepted the darkness fully into her about three days ago when she held a ceremony on the mountain of our ancestors." Both Alex and Chase gasped; Ryan looked to both her cousins, confused. "Your sister ruled that the coven must fight in the upcoming war." Fuck, now the vampires had the witches on their side.

"How the hell did she do it? There is no way Gregory would have let her accept the throne on the mountain in front of the ancestors. The elders wouldn't have allowed it either! They know Ryan exists now!"

"I am sorry, Alex—Gregory is dead. Stevie was able to complete the ceremony after she murdered him. She took a loved one from each of the elders to force them into aiding her crusade."

What the fuck has that crazy bitch done? I had known Gregory. He was a wise man and an elder. He guarded the mountain path to ensure that no one could access the power of the ancestors without elder approval. Alex and Chase both seem shattered. They turned their backs on their coven to help Ryan and now there coven members were being killed at the hands of their cousin.

"Stevie will answer for her crimes! Blood must have blood!" I have never heard so much venom and hatred come from Alex, there was no coming back for Stevie in his eyes.

"Alex, please, Stevie is sick, she needs our help." Ryan had tears trailing down her face, pleading with her cousins to understand and help her save her sister. Judging by the look on both the guys faces, they wouldn't spit on Stevie if she were on fire.

"She killed an elder, Ryan! A fucking elder. Gregory was a defenseless old man, and she fucking killed him. I am sorry, Ryan, but she has murdered a coven elder and taken our elders' loved ones hostage. It is the Knox coven way, cousin—blood must have blood." Ryan broke out into sobs at Chase's harsh words, and Dom wrapped an arm around her and rubbed his hand up and down her arm, trying to soothe her.

Chapter Thirty One

I was sobbing into Dom's chest, and I didn't care that the others were watching me breakdown.

"I am sorry, Ryan, but Chase is right. Even if you do save your sister, she will need to answer for the crimes she has committed." I couldn't look at Mya, I know it wasn't her fault, but I was banking on her being the one to help me save my sister. Instead she told the whole room that my sister was pretty much doomed.

"Hang on—our dad is one of the elders, Mya." I turned to look at Alex, wondering what he was getting at, and then it hit me.

"I'm sorry, Alex, I don't know where your mother is. She was taken with the rest of the elders loved ones."

"No! My parents are back in New Zealand." Chase was grasping at straws now.

"Stevie called all coven members back to Wonder Lake the day you, Alex, and Ryan fled. Your parents came as soon as they heard you and Alex went rogue."

"Where is our father, Mya?" Mya dropped her gaze to her

hands in her lap, and I had a sinking feeling her answer was about to hurt my cousins.

"All elders are being held at Randall Cane's mansion. Stevie made sure that she had a get-out-of-jail-free card before she came here to meet Ryan." Alex jumped to his feet and started pacing. Chase did the same and then punched a hole in the wall, screaming. My sister was always one step ahead of us. She had a backup plan in case something went wrong, and that's why she wasn't pissed or angry that she was held in a cell—she knew she wouldn't be stuck in there for long.

"I will fucking kill her!" Chase was glowing purple and his whole body was vibrating with rage.

"Chase, you need to calm down, we will get Mom and Dad back, brother. I swear." Alex was trying to reassure Chase and help him calm down. Chase was taking deep breaths, trying to control his rage.

"How do we get the elders back, Mya?" It was the first time Jackson had spoken since the start of this powwow.

"You need to return Stevie to Randall Cane tomorrow evening at the wedding."

"Evening? The wedding is happening at noon tomorrow." Nico took the words right out of my mouth.

"No, brother, the wedding will happen at night so the vampire king can bring his soldiers with him. Now that Kai and I are no longer with him, he has no fae blood to feed his men." That slimy fucking bastard.

"We played right into his hands. My sister was a distraction. He knew you wouldn't let her go, Nico, he even banked on it. That's why Stevie never fought back. She wanted to be captured so that we would have to change the time of the wedding and play by their rules." Everyone started talking at once, trying to make a plan on how we proceed. I was still stuck on the fact that Stevie knew we would capture her and that Mya would be here to tell us. I jumped to my feet and yelled.

"Everyone shut up!" Silence fell, and I turned my attention to Mya. "How did my sister know that we would come for you?" I know my dad said I could trust her, but something wasn't right.

"Because I told her you would come for me" I recoiled at her admission.

"You sold us out!" I was going to wring her fucking neck.

"It's not what you think, Miss Knox, I swear."

"You have no fucking idea what I am thinking! My father told me I could trust you, and yet you sit here telling us that you are the one who told my sister that we would come for you. How did you know, Mya, and don't fucking lie to me!" I must admit I respected her more when she stood and came to stand directly in front of me, never breaking eye contact. What she said next had me staring at my cousins for confirmation.

"I am a witch, but I am also blessed with the power to see into the future. I saw you coming for me months ago." My cousins looked as shocked as me.

"The Knox coven has no seers, Mya."

"Yes, Alex, they do. I am the only seer, and no one knows of my ability aside from the elders and Ralph Knox." I stumbled backward and plonked down next to Dom, and Mya reclaimed her seat. She was looking at me, waiting for me to piece it all together, but when I did, I wish I hadn't. Sorrow filled me, he knew what was coming.

"My father knew he was going to die, didn't he? You saw it?" I could see the pity in her eyes, telling me all I needed to know.

"Yes, that is why he made sure all his affairs were in order and that the coven knew of the crowning of the new queen. The Knox coven knows of your existence and that you are the true queen. That is why Gregory and the elders forbade your sister from claiming the throne on the mountain of the ancestors."

"Stevie knew, didn't she? That's why she made sure I made the trip to Alaska, so I would renounce the throne to her. It was the only way the elders would let her lead, wasn't it?"

"I believe she did know, yes. If you renounced your claim to the throne, the elders would have to let the next heir in line rule the coven." That's why Stevie was uptight and snappy when I first arrived at her home and even after we arrived here. I knew something wasn't right with my sister, I could see it in her eyes when we got here, but I didn't know any better. The darkness inside her is what is driving her need for power, and that's why she hates me. I'm a threat to her power.

"How did I not see this coming?" Aurora murmured. She seemed annoyed that she didn't see this turn of events.

"Because you are too close to this, your feelings are too far involved. You are the most powerful seer to walk the lands, Aurora Evans, do not doubt your ability."

"What happens now?" Melakai asked the million dollar question.

We all sat around for the next few hours and made a plan to change the wedding from noon to the evening and made sure that we notified everyone of the change of plans. I was shocked to learn that Dom's dad would be here for the wedding tomorrow. It would be cool to meet the alpha of the New York pack. I hated that we had to let my sister go, but I couldn't let my love for her cloud my judgment. Others' lives were at risk here. We agreed that after breakfast we would all go and see Stevie and try to get the information we needed out of her. The guys wanted to torture it out of her, but I quickly shot that idea down. The worst part was that Chase and Alex were on board with hurting Stevie.

After leaving Jackson's office, I went straight back to my room. I was exhausted and needed a solid eight hours of sleep.

After finally getting showered and into bed, I laid there staring up at the ceiling thinking about the past few weeks and how my life had changed so much. I went from being unwanted, unloved, and abused to the girl who had her sister and cousins by her side. I thought we would travel the world together and I would finally be happy.

Then arriving in Alaska changed everything. My whole life had been a lie. I wasn't who I thought I was, and my mother wasn't supposed to be the monster that she is now. My dad was killed, my sister was evil and possibly unredeemable, and I had to marry a guy I thought for years was a figment of my imagination. Oh and let's not forget that the other guy I have been fucking in my dreams is real and tricked me into loving him, and is also best friends with the guy I have to marry. My life is a fucking disaster. I let out a long exhale of air and closed my eyes, I needed to clear my mind and get some sleep. Tomorrow was going to be a long as fuck day. If what we discussed tonight is true, as soon as Nico and I made our vows and sealed it with a kiss, the lock he placed on my powers would shatter.

Nico would help me control them and stop me from dying, hopefully.

According to Mya, my powers needed another life force to help stabilize them in the beginning. Nico would hold some of my power until I could control it and then it would return to me. I felt like Thor and his hammer, *if he should be worthy he will possess the power.* I need to make sure I was worthy! I had to stop my sister, kick Randall's ass, save my aunt and uncle, and as much as I hated to admit it to even myself. I needed to save my mom.

Chapter Thirty Two

NICO

After leaving Jax's office, I made my way back to my room. I knew it would be hard for me to sleep. The words Ryan said to me earlier played over and over in my mind. *"Kai was definitely the better choice and better man."* She was right. Kai was the better man and the better choice. She needed to choose me, though, or this wouldn't work. I *wanted* her to choose me. A thought crossed my mind then. She may not talk to me here, but she was always more compliant in her dreams. I whispered the chant to take me to our dream land.

I opened my eyes and turned around to see I was near the dock at Lake William—strange. I was sure I chanted to take us to the forest, not this place that she came with Kai.

"You just gonna stand there or?" I turned to the left and saw her sitting on the grass by the edge of the lake. I made my over to her and sat next to her with my legs extended in front of me. She *had her long brown hair down and it was blowing slightly in the breeze. She wore the same white summer dress she always wore in her dreams. She wasn't looking at me, though. She was staring straight ahead at the lake. "Why are we here Nico?"*

"Because I am a complete ass and I'm sorry." She didn't turn to look at me and didn't say anything for a few moments.

"Am I your hugacko, Nico?" I whipped my head around so fast I heard my neck crack. How the fuck did she know that? She slowly turned her head so she could look me in the eye, but she gave nothing away with her expression.

"Who told you that?"

"A man told me." What the fuck!

"What fucking man?"

"Brown hair, deep green eyes and I think he was a king." She was toying with me, the smartass.

"Your dad told you?" She just nodded and smiled a sad smile. "I can't control who I...it just happens, and I—" She cut off my rambling by placing her index finger on my lips. I was dying to suck that digit into my mouth, and she must have read my mind because she quickly pulled her hand away.

"I'm not mad, Nico, I just don't understand why you didn't tell me. Before you get mad, Dom also told me about me being your hugacko."

If I had any chance of her ever trusting me again, I needed to be honest with her. I also needed to remain calm and not lose my shit over Dom telling her. He was really starting to piss me off with all his meddling.

"Because I didn't want you to feel like you had to choose me." Her features softened at my admission.

"That is the most selfless thing I have ever heard you say, Nico. I appreciate you trying to respect me enough to let me choose, but I must be honest with you as well." My shoulders dropped, and I turned to look out at the lake. She was about to tell

me she didn't want me. "Today when I told you Kai was the better man and the better choice, I wasn't lying." Just dig that dagger in deeper, love. "But he isn't the right choice for me, or the better man for me." I swung my gaze back to her, trying to read her meaning.

"What are you saying, love?" She giggled, and by God, if that wasn't the best sound I heard in a long time.

"I'm saying as soon as Kai lifted his control over my emotions, the love I thought I had for him vanished. Don't get me wrong—Kai will always be important to me. I am truly embarrassed to say this, but I fell in love with a guy who I thought was part of my imagination, only to find out that he was real. When I first saw you in the fae realm, I couldn't believe my luck.

"I have loved you for years, Nico, and never in my wildest dreams did I ever think you would be real and that I would get to love you properly. It was never a question of whether or not I would marry you, Nico. I would always choose you."

I sat there, staring into her beautiful hazel eyes with the peculiar yellow ring, utterly speechless. My hugacko loved me back, and that made me swell with happiness. I know we have fought and hurt each other, but she loved me, and that was all that mattered. I was the luckiest son of a bitch.

"I have loved you since the first time I invaded your dreams. When your fae side is unlocked, you will feel the bond as well."

"I think I already feel it, Nico. It's like a string is always pulling me toward you. It's like I can feel where you are before I even see you." Holy shit, that is exactly how the bond works.

"You are an extraordinary being, love." I gripped the back of her neck and pulled her toward me so I could kiss her, and after a moment she pulled back.

"I need you to promise me something, Nico."

"What is it, love?"

"Don't ever break my heart, and don't ever lie to me again,

please. It's hard for me to trust people, and I have tried everything to push you away and not let you in, but you are very persistent." We both chucked at the truth of that, and when our laughter subsided, she looked at me, waiting for my answer.

"I promise I will cherish your heart for the rest of our days, love. I promise to protect you and love you till my dying breath. I have waited over a century for you, Ryan, and I will never let you go. You are my reason for existing. I will never lie to you again. I will come to you and speak to you about any matters that concern you from this day forth."

Tears were trailing down her cheeks, and I pulled her onto my lap so she was straddling me. She pulled my face to hers and kissed me like I was the oxygen she needed to live.

We stayed in the dream land for hours, fucking and then making love. We both came to the realization that we didn't like slow and calm. We liked hard, deep, and messy sex. She was like a drug that called to me, an addiction that I never wanted to cure. Ryan Knox was my own personal drug. Finally we both agreed we needed to return to our bodies and rest before tomorrow.

"Nico, wait."

"What is it, love?" She started twirling her hair around her finger and wouldn't meet my gaze. I smiled. After everything we had just done, she was embarrassed. I could see the blush on her cheeks.

"Could you...I mean, only if you wanted to, you don't have to—"

"Just ask me, love." I was trying so hard not to laugh at her awkwardness.

"When we get back, can you come to my room and sleep with me?" I couldn't help it—I laughed, and she glared at me.

"You were just sitting on my face not ten minutes ago, telling me to eat your fucking pussy, and then you get shy asking me to sleep next to you." She was blushing so much and glaring daggers *at me. "I'm sorry, love, of course I will come sleep with you." As I started chanting to get us out of the dream land, I swear I heard muttering about me being a dick face and needing to be punched.*

As soon as I returned to my bedroom, I got up and made my way to Ryan's room. I knocked on her door, and she opened it for me, and we made our way over to her bed and sunk down under the covers, holding each other. I can't wait to go to bed with her every night and hold her like this.

"Goodnight, big guy." I smiled at her nickname for me.

"Goodnight, my love."

Not five minutes later she was sleeping again. I peered down at her and marveled at her beauty. I would never let anyone harm her. I would kill her sister and Randall both if I had to. I would never let anyone hurt her again, and I sure as fuck wouldn't be a gutless coward and stand by and watch this time. She is to be my wife and, one day, the mother to my children. I would die before I ever let any fucker try and take her from me.

Chapter Thirty Three

RYAN

I felt like I was burning up, I tried to move to get away from the heat without opening my eyes, but I couldn't seem to move. I opened my eyes quickly and looked down to see an arm around my waist and a leg over my thigh, and that's when it hit me—the heat I was feeling was coming from Nico's body. Memories of the night before came flooding back, and I felt the blush heating my cheeks. I admitted that I was in love with Nico last night, and to top it all off, he told me he loved me too, many times, while he was doing unspeakable things to my body.

"I can feel you overthinking, love." I fought the smile that tried to break free. "Go back to sleep. We don't have to be up for a while." But I couldn't go back to sleep; I wanted to explore Nico while I was awake. I turned so we were facing each other. Nico still had his arm wrapped around me and his leg over mine, and his eyes were still shut. I began to run my fingers across his chest and down his arm. "If you keep doing that, love, there will be no sleep happening." This time I did let the smile break free.

Would it be like this every morning when we woke? Me wanting to jump his bones and him holding me like he never wanted to let me go? I was pulled from my thoughts when Nico suddenly had me pinned beneath him. He looked so beautiful first thing in the morning. His jet black hair was tousled from sleep and his violet eyes were burning with hunger, though he wasn't hungry for food— he was hungry for me. I leaned forward to capture his lips, but he pulled back before I could kiss him. I pouted and he chuckled.

"I know we have done things in your dreams, love, but I want our first *real* time together to be as man and wife." This man could melt me with his words. I could already feel the tears threatening to spill from my eyes. "I didn't mean to upset you, love. Of course I have wanted to do this for a long time but I just thought it might be better to wait, till after the wedding." He looked so crestfallen I reached my hand up to stroke his cheek.

"You didn't upset me, big guy, you just surprised me is all. What you just said means a lot to me, and I appreciate you wanting to wait till after we're married." Nico didn't get a chance to reply as my bedroom door opened with a resounding thud when it hit the wall, I jumped and Nico groaned. What is the point of having a fucking door?

"Does locking a fucking door mean nothing these days?" I laughed at Nico's irritation; every time we seemed to be alone someone always seemed to burst in without knocking.

"Well, that is a sight I could have gone my whole life without seeing." Nico quickly scrambled off me and back to his side of the bed at the sound of his sister's voice.

"What the actual fuck, Soph!"

"Sorry, brother but you both need to get ready for breakfast so we can get this meeting with the evil witch over with, and then we need to get Ryan ready for tonight, so chop-chop."

"How did you get in here?"

"I used magic, of course." Right, of course, Sophia didn't even seem like her not knocking was a big deal. What did I have to do around here to get to some sort of privacy? Not wanting to cause a delay or have Sophia just standing there staring at her brother and me, Nico left the room to shower and change and I did the same thing while Sophia waited for me on the chair.

After showering and changing into jeans and a long-sleeved shirt, I grabbed my sweatshirt from my bag and threw it on, trading my faithful Chucks in for my combat boots. It was starting to get really cold here, so I'm guessing winter was approaching. Due to the weather, we decided to hold our wedding in the chapel at the back of Jax's compound instead of outside. After lacing my boots, I turned to tell Sophia that I was ready to go meet the others in the mess hall, but she didn't hear me. I called her name three times before she finally heard me.

"Sorry."

"Is everything okay, Sophia?" I had never seen Sophia so down and dare I say, sad.

"The man that beat and tortured me for seventeen years is coming to watch my brother get married. Of course I'm okay." I flinched at her dry tone; I didn't even think about how Randall being here would affect Sophia. I am such a shitty person.

"If I could have done this wedding without him being present, I would have Sophia, I swear. I hate that man for what he has done to you and Kai. He has my mother and my uncle now. I have to get them back, and when I do, I promise we will take that bastard down." She didn't answer, and my heart hurt for her and what she had gone through at the hands of that monster. We left the room and made our way toward the mess hall, but I had a question to ask her that was burning a hole in my mind since first meeting her. Clearing my throat and steeling my spine, I blurted it out. "Why is there a painting of you hanging in Randall's office?" Sophia never faltered or paused, just continued walking. I didn't think she was going to answer my question, but as the mess hall doors came into sight, she finally did.

"My painting hangs on his wall because Randall Cane believes he is in love with me." My jaw dropped, but she kept on walking as if she'd never said a thing.

After meeting everyone in the mess hall and quickly eating breakfast, we made our way to the cells. We went down in two groups, as the elevator wasn't big enough for us all to go down together. Once we were all safely down and in the cell block, we made our way over to my sister and Tyler's cells. As we rounded the corner, I saw my sister pacing her cell, muttering under her breath like a crazy person. Tyler was sitting on the cot in his cell with his head clasped between his hands.

"Someone looks like they're going a bit stir crazy." I cut my gaze to Dom, warning him to rein it in; now wasn't the time for jokes. I stopped directly outside my sister's cell with Nico on my side.

"I need you to tell me where the hell you put the family members of the elders you have imprisoned at Randall Cane's manor." My sister continued to pace her small cell, but she didn't bother to hide her smile. She loved every minute of having the upper hand.

"If you had just done as you were told and not fucked every-thing up, none of this would have happened." Great, now she wanted to blame me for all her problems.

"I'm not the one at fault here, Stevie, you are." My sister stopped pacing and turned to face me, I gasped. Her eyes had changed color— they were black. I could see black lines dancing across her face. Mya was right; I was too late to save my sister.

"Oh, don't look so sad, sister, you knew this would happen. I just didn't let you see the real me yesterday. I will kill everyone you hold dear. I will make you watch as I torture and kill them, and then when I am satisfied that you have suffered enough, I will then kill you." I felt the tears start to build, but I wouldn't let my sister see me cry or show her how much her words affected me. I would be strong and fight till my dying breath. The thought of her touching any of my friends or my cousins sent my blood boiling.

"How the fuck does she have access to magic down here?" Jax hissed, and I turned to see what Jax was talking about, but he wasn't looking at Stevie. I followed his gaze and saw my hands glowing blue. I'm guessing no one was supposed to be able to access magic down here, based on Jax's outburst.

"Because she is the only one who can save us from the darkness that lives inside her own sister." I turned to look at Mya, confused at what she was saying.

"Ahhhh, Mya, my trusty advisor." Mya's upper lip pulled back into a snarl. "Don't be like that! We had fun together, didn't we?" Stevie was smiling at Mya like there was a secret between them.

"Go fuck yourself, Your *Majesty*." Stevie laughed and it was a horrible sound, I can't explain it, but it sounded half like a dog bark and someone having a coughing fit. Stevie stopped laughing after a minute and snapped her gaze back to Mya.

"I, Stevie Lee Knox, hereby banish you, Mya Skye, from the Knox coven. You will not be returned to the mountain of the ancestors when you die, and you are forbidden from any and all contact with any Knox coven member." Mya clutched at her chest right above her heart; there was so much pain etched across her face. "Don't worry, though—my sister isn't a member of the coven, and my cousins are now rogues, so you can still speak to them."

"You can't fucking do this to her, Stevie! You will kill her!" I turned my gaze to Chase, who was making his way over to Mya. She was about to collapse before he got to her but Kai caught her and cradled her to his chest. There was an interesting look on his face, but. Alex's outburst pulled me from my thoughts.

"You fucking bitch! You just condemned our whole coven! Why would you do that?"

"Because she didn't tell you the best part, did she?" Everyone was looking between Stevie and Mya, waiting for one of them to speak and fill in the missing piece of the puzzle. "Oh fine, then I'll tell them, shall I, Mya? She must have forgotten to tell you that in order for you to save that murdering bastard's world, you must kill me, dear sister." What the ever loving fuck is she talking about? "The only way for you to beat me is to unlock those precious powers of yours and learn to control them. You will not succeed at this task, sister; I will kill you before you have a chance."

My knees nearly gave out, but Nico wrapped an arm around my waist and pulled me into his side. My sister just admitted that she would kill me and feel no remorse. How am I supposed to deal with that? All I wanted was to save her from this darkness, and she is too far gone. I can see the blackness running through her veins, and her eyes are a soulless pit. How did my sister become this monster? How did my dad let this go on for so long and not try to stop her? I let my tears fall, not from fear of my life but for heartbreak for my sister. Gone was the girl who used to sit on the phone with me and tell me I was going to be okay, and that she loved me more than anything in the world. My best friend is gone; my other half is dead. The person standing in front of me now isn't my sister. The person standing in front of me is a monster.

"I am so sorry, Stevie." I could hear the others murmuring behind me, clearly they were shocked I was apologizing. "Dad should have tried harder to save you. I should have known about all of this supernatural stuff so I could have helped you."

"You truly are fucking dumb." Nico growled in warning beside me. "Dad couldn't fucking save me! He was a gutless bastard."

"Don't fucking talk about him like that! He loved us, Stevie."

"You stupid, naïve bitch! He found the answer to saving me; he just couldn't go through with what he needed to do." I turned to Mya, trying to read her face for any deceit. She was still in Kai's arms but she had a puzzled look on her beautiful face. Clearly my father hadn't told her about this.

"What do you mean, Stevie?"

"*In order to save one from the fate of darkness, you must kill the light it was born with.* To save me, dad had to kill you." I gasped. That can't be true, can it? "He chose you over me! He deserved his death!" My knees did give out this time, and Nico picked me up and cradled me to his chest like Kai had done to Mya.

"We're done here, you will be released in exchange for the elders return. If you do not meet these terms, you will be executed." As soon as Nico finished speaking, he turned and started to walk away, but before we rounded the corner I saw a look of devastation and panic on Tyler's face.

Chapter Thirty Four

NICO

We left the cells and went straight back to Jackson's office. This place was starting to seem like our headquarters. I took the single chair by the window with Ryan still cradled in my arms. I watched as Kai gently deposited Mya on the other single chair. Kai was looking at her with so much confusion etched across his face, why the hell was he confused? He was so different now. I needed to get my head out of my ass and be there for my brother. Ryan started to sit up and try move to the vacant seat next to Jax, but I wasn't having that. I wrapped my arm tightly around her waist and whispered in her ear.

"You're not going anywhere, love." At my words she relaxed back into my chest, and I could tell from the look on her face she was pushing her emotions down and refusing to deal with them. I knew if she tried to deal with what she had just learned now it would break her, and we wouldn't be having a wedding today or saving any elders.

Her cunt of a sister pretty much just admitted to killing their father, and as soon as Ryan registered what her sister was saying, she collapsed. My strong little spitfire was trying so hard to hold it together.

"We are royally fucked, and I feel like we're missing a key piece to this puzzle." Dom was right—something wasn't adding up. Ryan turned slightly in my lap and faced Mya who looked shattered.

"What happened to you back there, Mya?" Mya continued to stare at her lap. Just when I thought she wasn't going to respond, she quietly said,

"Your sister exiled me from my home." I felt Ryan tense.

"I don't understand what that means, I'm sorry."

"What it means, Ryan, is the place I have called home for nearly a century is no longer my home. As the coven queen, she has the right to banish anyone she wants. I can never return to the coven." I hadn't heard of that ever happening before, so this was all news to me. I was also shocked to hear how old she was, I had never known a witch to live this long before. When Ryan gently moved my arm from around her waist I gave her a stern look, but she nodded her head in Mya's direction, and I let her go and comfort the woman that had just lost everything. Ryan walked over to Mya and knelt down in front of her, grasping both her hands in her own.

"I am so sorry for what my sister has done to you, Mya. I can't comprehend the pain you are going through. Just know that we are all here for you, and you will always have a home with me. I will take back the coven from Stevie, and I will make sure you come back to your home."

Mya started shaking her head. She lifted her gaze to Ryan's and I could see the tears in her eyes.

"You will be a great queen, Ryan Knox, both here and in Farrarie. But you cannot undo what has been done."

"What do you mean?"

"What she is saying, Squirt, is once you are banished or exiled from the coven, you cannot come back. Stevie pulled the bonds from Mya that tie her to the Knox coven, and once they are gone, they're gone." I didn't know that's what happened to witches; in my realm, if you are banished, the king can change his mind and bring you back.

"I am so sorry Mya, what my sister did is...." Mya jumped to her feet, causing Ryan to fall on her ass. I stood and so did the others in the room. Mya was fuming and glaring down at Ryan.

"Your sorry does not fix anything! If your father had just done what he should have, none of this would have happened. You and your sister have ruined everything!" Mya rushed out of the room, and I stood there stunned at her outburst. Kai offered Ryan his hand to help her to her feet.

"She didn't mean what she said; she just lost her home and is lashing out." Why the fuck was Kai defending this witch?

"I'm not angry at her, Kai, my heart hurts for her and all that she has lost at the hands of my sister." Ryan looked past Kai to the clock that said it was half past ten and sighed. "The wedding is at eight tonight, and we are running out of time, what the hell do we do?" Aurora spoke before anyone else could.

"We send Tyler back to Randall with a message to release all your coven elders and to find the loved ones your sister has hidden." Is she out of her ever loving fucking mind?

"Rora, your brother is a traitor and can't be trusted." Finally something I can agree on with Alex.

"He will do as he is asked."

"How do you know this for certain?" I asked Aurora.

"Because he will do whatever it takes to ensure his mate's safety." Everyone in the room except for Ryan seemed shocked at Aurora's admission. After a second, Jax started pacing his office.

"That's why my best friend did it, isn't it? He betrayed me because he mated with that psycho bitch." Aurora nodded and Ryan still said nothing—why?

"Love, why don't you seem shocked about your sister being a

werewolf's mate? You do know that a wolf has never mated outside of their race before, right?" Ryan took a deep breath before looking around the room and then settling her gaze on me. I saw the answer before she even said it.

"I knew Stevie was Tyler's mate." Everyone started shouting.

"When?"

"How long have you known?"

"Why didn't you say anything?"

"Silence!" Everyone stopped talking and turned to face me. I guess I wasn't the only one who had hidden things. "How long have you known about this, love?" Ryan squared her shoulders and lifted her head staring directly into my eyes.

"Since the day they arrived here, Tyler told me she was his mate." She has known for a couple of days and still said nothing to anyone?

"Why didn't you say anything, Ry?" I could hear the betrayal in Jackson's voice. Tyler was his beta and his friend. Jackson thought he betrayed him because he liked Stevie, only to find out it was deeper than that.

"Because Tyler asked me not to. I know you will all think I'm crazy, but I believe Tyler is trying to help us stop Stevie. He doesn't want to hurt anyone or seal the fae realm. He just wants to fix my sister. He has been trying to guide her to do the right thing, but the more he pushes the more she pushes him away."

"I knew my brother wouldn't leave me, I just knew it."

"But you knew, as well, didn't you, *mate?*" Jax spat the word *mate* at Aurora like it burned his tongue. She flinched at his cold tone and dropped her gaze to the floor.

"I didn't have a vision, if that's what you're insinuating, Jax. Tyler told me while you were all distracted with Stevie and Mya." You sneaky little devil, Aurora.

"What else did your brother say?" Jackson was being so cold toward Aurora, as if she had betrayed him as well.

"He said that he would help us get the coven elders back and try to help us find their loved ones. He believes Stevie has their loved ones locked in the basement at her cabin."

"He fucking tricked you! He is a liar and a rat bastard, Aurora." Aurora started shaking and began to cry. Dom cut in front of Aurora to block her from Jackson's view. Jax started growling, his eyes turning yellow.

"She may be your mate, brother but you will not fucking speak to her like that again!" Jackson didn't respond. His growl started to intensify and his eyes started to change to his wolfs. "She lost her brother and you lost your friend, do not take your anger out on her for loving her brother! She has done nothing wrong, Jackson." Jax's eye slowly started to return to their normal chocolate brown color, and once he had himself under control, his shoulders sagged. He knew he fucked up.

"Aurora, I'm sorry. I should never have lashed out at you; it's not your fault. My wolf is starting to pick up your faint scent, and it's driving him crazy that he can't fully scent you. It's no excuse, but I'm on edge and so is he. He's jealous that Tyler found his mate." I dropped my head in shame at Jax's quiet admission; I felt like a piece of shit for my hand in helping Aurora conceal herself from him.

"I'm sorry, Jackson, but now isn't the time to deal with us, I want to ask your permission this time, though." Jackson lifted his head and Dom stepped aside to let him see Aurora.

"My permission for what?"

"To let Nico conceal my scent again." Jackson recoiled like Aurora had slapped him. "You need to understand, Jackson. Right now, I need my abilities to help us. As soon as all this is over, I swear we will sit down and talk about this and sort something out." Aurora was pleading with Jackson to understand her logic, and she was right, we needed her seer abilities now more than ever.

Jax looked around for a moment and then his hard, untrusting gaze landed on me. He was contemplating whether or not I would betray him and go behind his back again. I wouldn't, not this time, and plus, if I did, I am ninety-nine percent sure Ryan would hurt my balls.

"I will not do anything without your consent, brother. I swear to you that you have my word. I will not go behind your back again." Jax moved his gaze from me and then turned to Kai and Dom and asked.

"What would you do?"

"I would do what was best for my people; I would want to save the lives of my family and friends first." Dom was so political in his response, Kai was still silent.

"Kai?" At the mention of his name, Kai looked to Jackson and then Ryan, sighing before answering.

"I would claim the love of my life before I had a chance to lose her. There is no guarantee we will all survive this battle, so I would want to claim what is mine and love her while I had the chance." I looked around the room and noticed the three women had tears glistening in their eyes, while the guys stood there mouths hanging open and staring at the huge blond haired, blue-eyed vampire. I think we were all in shock at Kai's confession; I have never heard him talk like this before. Ryan was staring at him in awe, and it made me fidget and feel slightly irritated. she has never looked at *me* like that before. Ryan made her way over to Kai and grasped his hand in hers. I couldn't hold my grunt in even if I tried. She turned to glare at me and then focused her attention back on Kai, who was looking down at her with a look of longing and hurt.

"You will find the one for you, Kai, and when you do, she will be the luckiest woman in the world. You are a beautiful man with a kind heart, and I will always be here for you. The world is a better place with someone like you in it. I love you, Kai." Kai didn't reply, he just continued to stare at her. I needed to break their moment apart stat!

"Okay, so back to Jax and Aurora now. Do you want me to cast that spell?" Everyone in the room turned to glare at me, except for the fucking two warlocks, who started laughing at my expense. I was really getting tired of those bastards.

"You are such a dick, Tink. She is marrying you in like"—Chase looked at his wrist to check the time—"nine hours, and you're still jealous over her talking to Melakai." The fucker had the balls to burst out laughing again and was quickly followed by his brother and Dom. I glared at Dom, the fucking bastard, who's side was he fucking on?

Chapter Thirty Five

RYAN

After the guys got their laughter under control, we all sat down and agreed to let Tyler go back to Randall with our message. Nico and Dom were going to tell him the terms and what was at stake. I didn't want to go and see my sister again. I couldn't. If I did, I knew I would have to deal with what she told me, and right now I didn't have any time for a breakdown. We needed to wrap up this meeting, as Sophia said I had a lot to do before my wedding this evening. I had no idea what she meant, but she was adamant that I had a shit load to do. Who was I to argue with the princess of Farrarie and my future sister in law? I was pulled from my thoughts when Jax spoke.

"Okay, if this is what you want, Aurora, I will do it for you." Jax and Aurora were staring at each other, and it felt intimate. Aurora seemed shocked that Jax would agree to her request.

"Thank you, Jackson."

"I have one condition though." Aurora took a deep breath and then nodded to Jackson. "I want you to move into the room next to mine. You being near will calm my wolf." Aurora tilted her head to the side, clearly at a loss.

"But your wolf was fine before."

"My wolf and I didn't know you were our mate then. This spell will mask your scent so my wolf won't claim you, but it won't stop him from knowing you're his mate. Grant me this one thing, Aurora, and I will agree to the spell. I will hold you to your promise, though, that as soon as all this is over you and I will talk."

Aurora agreed and said she would move into the room next to Jax's first thing tomorrow. Nico cast the spell soon after Jax agreed. We all said our goodbyes and filed out of the room. I was walking down the hall with Sophia and Aurora on either side of me when Nico called out.

"Can I talk to you for a moment please, love?" I turned back to tell the girls that I would meet them in my room shortly.

"What's wrong, big man?" He seemed nervous and kept moving from foot to foot, he put his hands in the pockets of his jeans and looked down. His hair fell forward and hung over his face so I couldn't see his eyes.

"I just want to make sure that...you know...you're okay with...and that you were sure?" What the hell was he saying?

"I don't understand what you're asking me, big guy." I was keeping my tone light so it would help put him at ease. He blew out a long exhale and then lifted his head so I could see his eyes.

"Are you sure you want to marry me?" Oh my God, I swear to fucking whoever was listening I just swooned so fucking hard for this man. I grabbed his face between both my hands and pulled his face down to mine so I could kiss him. The kiss was slow and unhurried. I was trying to tell him with this kiss that I was sure, and I was ready to marry him. I was literally marrying my soulmate, and tonight, when my powers were free, my soul would merge with his as his hugacko. I pulled back and looked him in the eyes and smiled.

"Of course I'm sure, big guy. I want to do this with you. We're gonna fight and we're both going to piss each other off while we get to know each other better, but we'll make it through, I promise." He smiled his signature panty-melting smile and pecked me on my lips again.

"You better go, then, before my sister comes looking for you." I gave him another kiss and quickly made my way to my room. As soon as I opened the door, I wished I had stayed in Jackson's office. My room was full of beauty products that were scattered everywhere; there were at least four dress racks that held different colors and types of dresses. There were flower arrangements all over the room, and Sophia and Aurora were sorting through the dresses. When I closed the door behind me, they both looked up, and Aurora squealed.

"Ryan! Come on you have to choose your dress and what flowers you want, and we need to do your hair and makeup." Aurora was talking so fast I could barely make out what she was saying, I think she was more excited about the wedding than Nico and me.

I didn't get a chance to answer, as someone knocked on my door, thank God. I quickly turned and went to answer the door to buy myself some time before I was subjected to trying on dresses. I opened the door and standing on the other side was Mya. She looked so remorseful. I stepped aside and invited her in, her eyes were as wide as dinner plates when she saw my room and all the stuff scattered everywhere.

"Sorry, you're busy, I'll go." I put my arm out to stop her and said.

"Please stay." We stared at each other for a long moment and that look alone conveyed everything we hadn't said, that she was sorry for what she said and she didn't mean it. I was saying I was sorry for everything my sister had done to her. We were both wiping the moisture from under our eyes and then hugged, letting bygones be bygones.

Chapter Thirty Six

NICO

After leaving Ryan and making sure she wanted to go ahead with the wedding, I made my way out to the shack to meet Dom. When I arrived, Dom wasn't alone—Jax and Kai stood beside him.

"I thought you two had other plans that you needed to deal with?" None of them answered me, they just turned and opened the door. Alrighty then, I guess we're not talking now. Once we made it to the bottom, we all exited the elevator and made our way toward the back cells that housed Stevie and Tyler. As soon as we rounded the corner, the evil bitch was standing in front of her cell with her arms hanging out of the bars. Jax growled, and she smiled. They may be twins, but they were nothing alike. Ryan was kind and caring, and Stevie was dark and power hungry. She didn't care if she hurt people.

"Back on your own, are we, boys?" I ignored the bitch; I had nothing to say to that vile murdering waste of space. Tyler was standing at the front of his cell, looking between the four of us and Stevie, trying to figure out what we had planned.

"Why didn't you tell me, Tyler?" Tyler looked to Jax, and I saw a crack in the mask Tyler was wearing; he didn't want to hurt Jackson. Ryan and Aurora were right—Tyler hated what he was doing but wouldn't give up his mate.

"Because you didn't need to know. You chose your side and I chose mine!" Tyler's words were lacking the bite you would expect from someone who hated you. Jax didn't respond, just nodded his head and pulled the key for Tyler's cell from his pocket.

"You fucking touch him and I will kill you! I will rip your bride apart." Fuck it, I spun around and pulled every bit of energy I had in me and released an energy ball that hit her in the chest and sent her crashing into the back wall of her cell. Holy shit, I never expected it to work. How the fuck did I do that?

"How the fuck did you do that down here, Nico?" I turned and just shook my head; I had no idea how I had access to my magic down here. Was Ryan's magic already starting to merge with mine?

"You fucking prick! I'll rip your fucking head off!" Tyler was angry and spewing insult after insult at me. Jax opened the cell door and he and Kai wrestled Tyler's arms behind his back and attached some cuffs that were iron infused with silver, and led him out the cell toward the elevator. He was fighting against their hold, trying to check on Stevie.

"If you stopped fucking yelling and struggling, you would hear her heart is still fucking beating!" Tyler stopped struggling against Kai and Jax's hold and listened like Jackson told him, and after a moment he relaxed in their grip and continued to walk to the elevator without a fuss.

Once at the top, we walked around the compound to the front of the property, garnering dirty looks and insults from pack members. Their insults and dirty looks were for Tyler, not us. They saw him as a rat and traitor. They didn't know he left to be with his mate. Tyler hung his head in shame; he knew his pack hated him right now.

"Keep your head up and don't let them see you as weak." Tyler turned to look at Jax, who refused to meet his beta's gaze. Tyler held his head high and straightened to his full height. Insults were still being thrown his way, but he didn't falter, and continued to walk with his head held high. Jackson was a great alpha. As soon as we reached the front of the property, we made our way into the woods, away from prying eyes. We continued to walk until Jax told us we were far enough away from his pack that they couldn't hear or see us. Jax released his hold on Tyler and stepped in front of him.

"We are releasing you to return to Randall, to pass on a message." Tyler nodded his head. "You will tell him that he is to bring the Knox coven elders with him tonight to the ceremony; he obviously knows we changed the time of the wedding to suit his fucking needs." Tyler just nodded again.

"If you betray us and try something stupid, Tyler, we will kill your mate." At Dom's declaration, Tyler turned and glared at him, growling low in his throat. "You obviously know this trail well, pup. You will pass the cabin where you believe your mate has imprisoned the elders' loved ones. You will set them free before returning to Randall." Tyler started shaking his head.

"She will never forgive me if I do this. She knew you would send me back to Randall to free the elders, but she will hate me for going against her and freeing her bargaining chips. If they're even in the cabin." The four of us shared a look between ourselves. We didn't care about Stevie and Tyler's relationship; that was his problem. We did, however, care about the wellbeing of innocent coven members. Jax pulled a burner phone from his pocket and placed it in Tyler's front pocket.

"When you reach the cabin, and *if* they are there, you are to set them free and then call me. After that, you go to Randall and bring the elders back tonight. The ceremony starts at eight, so don't be late." Jax uncuffed Tyler and sent him on his way, and we stood there and watched until he disappeared from view.

"Do you think he will actually go through with it?" Dom voiced the question we were all wondering.

"Yes, because the alpha of all alphas is his sister's mate." We all spun around to see who spoke. I knew he was coming, but it was still a shock to see him after so many years. "It's good to see you all back together again."

"It's good to see you too, sir." Jackson was such a kiss ass. Dom and I rolled our eyes.

"It's good to see you too, Dad," said Dom, as the two men hugged. He pulled back and looked at his son.

"Would you look at that, my baby boy has gone and grown up on me."

Kai, Jax, and I laughed at Dom's dad's teasing. Dom got his quick wit and smartass mouth from his father. Ian Silver was a beast of a man, standing well over six feet tall, with broad shoulders. He had tanned skin like Dom and the same silver-blond hair. They could have been twins, except Dom had violet eyes, the same as his mother's, and Ian had green eyes. We don't speak about Dom's mom; that was a touchy subject still nearly seventy years later. Dom pushed his dad away and started to try and fix his hair since his dad ruffled it. The rest of us shook hands and welcomed Mr. Silver back to the homeland. Jax may be the alpha of all alphas but we all respected Mr. Silver, he is wise and kind and also helped Jax as much as Ralph Knox did when he first took over being Alpha of his pack.

"What did you mean, sir, when you said he would do it because of his sister?"

"He will do as you ask, Jackson, because even though the witch is his mate, he still loves and cares for his sister. He won't risk your wrath against his sister; he would rather take the punishment his mate gives him than hurt Aurora."

"How did you know Aurora was my mate, sir?"

"My word, you boys should know by now that Dominic can't keep his mouth shut about any gossip." We all turned to Dom, who refused to meet our stares and was focusing his attention on his nails like they were the most interesting thing in the world.

"Dominic!" Dom sighed and then finally turned to Jax and shrugged his shoulders.

"What do you want me to say, Jax? It was fucking hard! I tried, I swear I did, but then dad asked if I knew anything new and then it poured out like diarrhea after a night on the booze." We all busted out laughing at Dom; he could never keep a fucking secret. If your life depended on a secret, don't ever tell Dom. You would be dead within minutes. "Stop fucking laughing at me!"

"Dominic, language!" We all laughed harder at Mr. Silver telling his son off. Oh he's going to be in for a treat, Dom had the mouth of a sailor these days.

RYAN

Aurora had run me a bath and told me I had to soak in the oils she had put in and wash my hair and shave. I wasn't going to argue; I had been dying to try out the massive claw foot tub in my bathroom but hadn't found the time to do so. After soaking for a bit and washing my hair with the amazing passionfruit and mango shampoo and conditioner Aurora had given me, I shaved everywhere. Sophia insisted that I should get waxed, but I flat out refused to let anyone wax my coochie. After my bath, I wrapped myself in my robe and put my hair up in a towel. I was now sitting on a chair that wasn't in my room before, with Aurora putting cream on my face that she swore would make me shimmer in the light of the moon.

She moved on to doing my hair and makeup next. I wasn't allowed to look until I was done and in my dress. The dress I picked out is a dress I would never have ever thought I would wear, but I just knew that Nico would love it.

My fingernails and toenails were waiting to be painted.

I felt bad Aurora was doing all this work while I sat here.

Sophia and Mya were sitting on the couch, watching Aurora do her thing with my hair and face, neither of them had done anything aside from drink the champagne that was being brought in. Every time they neared the bottom of the bottle, someone would knock and bring in a fresh bottle.

After hours of sitting here in the same spot, my ass started to protest and go numb. I was also nearing the end of my patience. I had been plucked and shaved, and my hair had been pulled every which way. My face felt like it was covered in mud. My fingernails and toenails had been scrubbed and soaked then scrubbed again. I wasn't a girly girl, so having to endure all of this for hours might be some other woman's idea of fun, but for me it was pure fucking hell. Sophia and Mya kept giggling every time they saw the look on my face. They were enjoying my discomfort, the assholes.

"Okay, Ry, I'm nearly done, and then you can put your dress on."

"Aurora, it's still early. Can't I wait till just before the wedding?"

"What are you talking about, Ryan?"

"What's the time, Aurora?"

"Ryan, it's seven. You get married in an hour." What the actual fuck? Where has the time gone? I started to panic. Holy fuck, I'm getting married, and I'm only eighteen. I'm going to be a teen bride. What's next, kids? I'm not ready to be a mom; I haven't even lived yet. Fuck, and I will have to move to Farrarie with Nico? What about the coven? What about my cousins? I started to hyperventilate; Aurora placed both her hands on my shoulders, trying to get me to look at her. My vision was going foggy.

"Ryan!" I looked up to see Sophia and Mya were now standing next to Aurora. "Snap out of it, now! You're going to blow this whole fucking room up otherwise." I looked down to see I was glowing; I couldn't get enough air into my lungs. All I could hear was my own heartbeat in my ears, like a drum.

Everything else was white noise. I was being shaken, and I managed to lift my gaze and then my eyes locked onto beautiful violet eyes.

"I need you to calm down, love, before your groom breaks down your door. I don't think Jax wants to replace that door for a third time." I couldn't communicate, no words were coming out of my mouth. "It's okay, love. Deep breaths. I guess you're probably freaking out about getting married, huh?"

I nodded my head, still struggling to calm myself. "Will it help you to know that my dad is here, and I am constantly being yelled at for swearing, and if I make a crude remark the old bastard just slaps me up the back of the head?" Listening to Dom was helping me get my breathing under control. He kept talking about mundane things to try and distract me, and it worked. After a few minutes I could finally breathe properly and the pounding in my ears had stopped.

"Thank you, Dom."

"How about you thank me by telling me what had you so freaked out?" I was a bit embarrassed to admit what set me off.

"It just hit me that I'm getting married, and I'm only eighteen. I'm going to be a teen bride like something out of an after-school special! Will Nico expect babies from me straight away? I don't want kids! I would be a terrible mother, and I'm going to have to move to Farrarie. What about my coven? What about my cousins?"

"Wow, hang on a second love and take a deep breath for me." I did as I was asked and took a deep breath. "Okay let's start from the beginning. Yes, you are getting married and no Nico doesn't expect babies from you immediately. You are not your mother, love, and you will be a great mother when the time does come. Yes, Nico will have to return to Farrarie. He is the king, after all. I'm sure you and Nico could work out together what happens with your coven. Nico doesn't expect you to give everything up, love, him being here as long as he has shows me how much you mean to him. He has never stayed away from his realm longer than a full day. He is choosing you over his people and over his duty to those people. He would never force you to do anything you didn't want to do." I could feel the tears building behind my eyes, and I quickly tried to blink them away for fear of ruining my makeup. Dom was right; Nico was a good man, and he understood me. We could work all this out together, I looked up to see my cousins enter the room. "Now why don't you tell me the *real* reason you freaked out?" How did he know? I felt my bottom lip start to tremble; I took a few deep breaths and then told him the true reason I had a panic attack.

"My dad isn't here to walk me down the aisle. He isn't here to give me away and tell me how beautiful I look." A tear snaked its way down my cheek, and I quickly brushed it away. Dom placed his hand under my chin, lifting my head so he could look me in the eyes.

"I never want to give you away, but I will, if that is what you truly want. You look more beautiful than I have ever seen, Ry. If you will accept us, Alex and I would both love to walk you down the aisle. Uncle Ralph may not be here physically, but he is here in our hearts and in spirit, Ry." Fuck, hearing Chase's speech broke the dam; tears were rolling down my face. I couldn't talk past the lump in my throat, so I just nodded my head and quickly pushed past Dom to hug both my cousins. I would be so fucking lost without them; they have been here for me through all of this shit.

"Okay, I'm sorry, but all you boys have to leave now so I can re-do her makeup and get her in her dress. We will meet you there, Chase and Alex, please be at the front of the chapel by five to eight." Alex and Chase gave me a hug before they left, Dom made his way toward the door but stopped and turned back to me and placed a small kiss on my cheek.

"You look beautiful, love. Nico is a very lucky man to have such a fierce and loving woman by his side."

"Right, come on, were running out of time." Aurora was barking orders at Sophia and Mya to hurry up and change while she touched up my makeup and helped me into my dress. I could do this. I *want* to do this. I mean, who can actually say they get to marry their dream man?

Chapter Thirty Eight

NICO

I still wanted to throttle my three best friends. Jax and Kai had held me back while Dom went to comfort Ryan. We were all sharing a drink with Dom's dad after we got ready, when I felt a sharp pain in my chest and knew straight away something was wrong with Ryan. I ran from the room with my friends hot on my tail, and right as I was about to open her bedroom door, I was tackled to the ground by Melakai. He and Jax restrained me while Dom went in. Mr. Silver was telling me to calm down and trust Dom. I did trust Dom, with my life, but Ryan needed me. I wanted to blast these bastards for holding me back, but I knew even if I did get them off, Mr. Silver would still be there blocking the door, and I could never hurt him, I respected him too much.

Mr. Silver told me it was bad luck for me to see my bride before the wedding, so I had to calm down and let Dom handle this. When Dom finally left her room after her cousins, I hit him straight across the jaw. He deserved way worse. The bastard had the cheek to just laugh and rub his jaw.

After pulling myself together and calming myself down, we made our way to the chapel, which was out the back of Jax's compound. It wasn't a huge chapel, but it was big enough to seat a hundred people. By the time we got there, it was nearly seven-thirty. Just as we started to walk up the stairs, I felt the hairs on the back of my neck stand up and spun around quickly. Walking straight toward us was none other than the bastard Randall Cane. He walked with his head held high. He was a short, plump bastard. He wore a suit and tie like us, except his suit was blood red. How fucking cliché.

His blond hair was slicked back, and he was surrounded by his soldiers. It is an ancient law that when a member of royalty from any of the races marry, all the heads of the leading covens and clans must attend. We were not allowed to harm each other at these events; it was forbidden. For the first time in my life I wanted to break that law, but if I did, the elders from each clan would make sure that I paid the price for my insubordination. King or not, no one was above the elders.

What was the point of having elders, when they never fucking did anything anyway? Each supernatural race had elders; they were the ones who upheld our laws. They wouldn't intervene now, though, even with Randall trying to kill my fucking realm. Stevie might have been onto something with manipulating her elders to do as she said. Randall was standing on the bottom step below us. He wasn't looking at me, though—his gaze was fixed on Kai. It felt great to see the shock on this old twat's face: he thought he killed his greatest weapon, yet here Kai stood.

"You're supposed to be dead." Kai smiled an evil smile; he had no emotion displayed on his face other than his hatred for Randall. Kai made his way back down the stairs to stand in front of Randall. Randall's soldiers moved to block Kai, but Dom quickly erected a shield to hold them back. Randall's eyes were darting everywhere, trying to find an escape route, and found there wasn't one. He was fucking pathetic. Kai wouldn't harm him. He knew the rules, and he also knew we needed him alive for the exchange of Stevie and the Knox coven elders.

"Before this night is done, I will fucking kill you! Fuck the elders' laws...I would gladly take their punishment just to see you fall." You didn't even need to be a shifter to hear how loudly Randall gulped. Kai turned and made his way up the stairs, continuing into the chapel to take his place.

"Put him on a leash, king." I smiled. Kai had rattled Randall and made him flustered. Before Dom dropped the shield holding Randall's minions back, I spoke.

"Melakai will never be on a leash now that he is free of your vile ass. You ever come for my brother or try in any way to harm him, and I will burn your fucking mansion to the ground with you in it, you gutless leech." Dom dropped his shield and he and Jax followed me inside to take our places at the front of the podium. Jax, Kai, and Dom were my witnesses.

After talking among ourselves for a bit, the minister announced we were five minutes out from the ceremony starting. I turned to thank the minister and stopped when I saw who the minister was.

"What are you doing here, Gabriel?" The old man smiled at my surprise.

"Did you really think I would let anyone else marry you?" Gabriel was the leader of the fae elders and my father's best friend; he married my mother and father.

"I tried to get in contact with you to see if you could do the ceremony, but Larick said he couldn't find you."

"I was in the Southern kingdom on elder business, but as soon as I heard you were to be married, I dropped everything and came. Thanks to you blocking all the portals, it was a bloody hard job getting here. I had to sneak through with Larick and Maverick and some of the other elders." I smiled at his devious ways. As old as he was, Gabriel was still a mischievous shit. "Are you ready, my boy?" I didn't hesitate to answer.

"I am beyond ready."

As soon as I finished speaking, music began to play and everyone quieted down and took their seats. A minute later, the doors opened, and Mya walked through carrying a bouquet of purple flowers. She wore an off the shoulder purple dress that matched the flowers she held. She made her way down the aisle and stopped on the opposite side from where we stood. Sophia walked through the doors next, her beautiful curly black hair up in an intricate bun.

She didn't have access to her fae magic, but she had the violet eyes of a fae. She wore a yellow dress that matched her flowers, and as she was approaching the front row, her step faltered when she saw Randall there smiling at her. She didn't move, she just stood there staring.

Dom raced over and placed his hand on her back, guiding her to her spot on the other side of the church. I tried to catch her gaze, but she wouldn't look at me, Dom whispered something in her ear that had her nodding and then he returned to his place behind me. The next to walk through was Aurora; she wore a blue dress that matched her eyes and the flowers she held, and she was searching the pews for someone, but I didn't know who. When she reached the end of the aisle, she deflated slightly, clearly annoyed whoever she was looking for wasn't here. Strange.

The music changed, and the small band in the back started a slow song. My eyes were fixed on the double doors, my breath stuck in my throat. The anticipation of seeing Ryan was killing me. If she didn't hurry her pretty little ass up and walk through those doors soon, I would go and get her myself.

My breath caught in my throat as soon as she came into view. Her long brown hair was done up in some sort of braid-bun, with little blue wildflowers placed throughout her hair. The dress she was wearing hugged her luscious curves in all the right ways. It was low cut in the front, and even I could tell from this distance that there was no way she could wear a bra with that dress. The sleeves hung off her shoulders, and the dress flowed behind her. The dress was an ivory color and had an intricate lace overlay. When she stopped at the start of the aisle, it was then that I noticed her cousins were on either side of her. Her gaze was locked on mine, and she was begging me with her eyes to give her strength to do this. I gave her a small nod and saw her exhale.

RYAN

Standing at the top of the aisle, looking at Nico in his suit, caused me to pause. He looked so handsome, with his hair slicked back, and his suit fit him like a glove. I was scared. I looked to him, hoping he could see me begging him with my eyes to loan me some of his strength. When I saw his small nod, I released the breath I was holding.

Looking around the small chapel, I saw so many people sitting in the pews that I didn't know. I would give anything to have my dad and sister here with me. There were thousands of candles lit throughout the chapel, and there were wildflowers hanging from the pews and the chandelier. It was beautiful. It felt like we were in the woods, and that is what I really wanted —to be married outside—but due to the weather and it being too open in case of an attack, we moved the wedding to the chapel.

"Deep breath, Squirt. You can do this." I looked to Alex and nodded, placing my arm through his. I then turned to look at Chase, who was looking down at me.

"If you want to bail and not marry the fairy, I'm all for that too." At the sound of someone growling, I quickly looked to the front of the chapel and saw Nico, Jax, Kai, and Dom glaring at my cousin. Okay, I guess the growl was one of them.

"Chase, I want to do this." He smiled and kissed my hand before I placed my arm in his.

"That's all I needed to hear, Ry."

We made our way down the aisle. I refused to look at the people here. I focused all my attention on Nico. Seeing him standing there, waiting for me, gave me the strength I needed to make it down this aisle and stand before all of these people. Nico made me feel like I could do anything. I pulled my gaze from Nico's when the minister cleared his throat.

"Who gives this woman to this man?" The minister was looking at my cousins with kind eyes; he seemed like a nice man, and clearly he was a fae, as his eyes were violet.

"I, Alexander Knox, from the Knox coven, give Ryan Knox to Nicholas Stone." I was so emotional; I wanted to burst into tears at how proud Alex sounded.

"And I, Chase Knox, also from the Knox coven, give Ryan Knox to Nicholas Stone. Who I know will treat her well and love her like she deserves." I looked to Chase, shocked, and then back to Nico, expecting to see anger on his face, but instead all I saw was respect. He respected Chase for protecting me.

"You have my word, Mr. Knox, that I will love her till the day I die and treat her like the queen she already is." Oh my God, I swooned, and the crowd murmured their hushed approval. The minister motioned for Nico to take my hand, which he did, and Alex and Chase took their seats in the front pew. I couldn't focus on anything else except for Nico. I was one lucky woman. Even with heels on, I had to crane my neck back to look him in the eye.

"We are gathered here today to celebrate the union of the king of Farrarie, Nicholas Stone, and the queen of the Knox coven, Ryan Knox." I heard murmurs around the chapel and grunts of disagreement at my title. I dropped my gaze only for Nico to put his finger under my chin and lift my gaze back to him.

"Never look down, love. You *are* queen, and they will fucking know it soon enough." Nico spoke quietly so only I could hear. I gave him a stiff nod and continued to hold my head high as the minister continued to speak. I was shaken from my daze when the minister called Nico's name. I looked at Nico, confused, but he just smiled and winked at me.

"You can read your vows now, son." What? Nico wrote his own vows? Shit! I didn't write anything for him. Why am I always awkward like this?

"Shhhh, love, it's fine." Clearing his throat, he spoke louder so everyone could hear.

"Ryan Knox, you are an amazing, talented, and strong woman with a heart of gold and the purest soul I have ever encountered. I met you by chance many years ago. I didn't know then that you were to grow and become my hugacko." Murmurs broke out across the chapel again, people clearly shocked at Nico's admission. Judging from the smile on his face, that is what he was aiming for.

"You, Ryan, are my better half. You are the other half to my soul. Without you, there is no me. I promise to love you from this day forth, and I promise to stand by your side and fight beside you through every battle. I promise to adore you till the end of time. Ryan Knox, I have been in love with you since the first time I came to you in your dreams two years ago, and I am the happiest and luckiest man alive to be able to be standing here in front of you today. I cannot wait to be able to call you my wife. I love you, Ry." I was crying. I could feel the tears rolling down my cheeks. I couldn't wait any longer; I stood on my tiptoes and pulled his face down to mine and kissed him. After a minute, I heard someone clearing their throat.

"Cut it out, you two, we haven't gotten to that part yet" I pulled away from Nico to see Dom grinning at me and wiggling his eyebrows. I couldn't help but blush.

"Okay, well, let's get to that part already, shall we?" I chuckled at the minister and so did a few others. "Do you, Ryan Knox, take this man to be your husband?"

"I do."

"And do you, Nicholas Stone, take this woman to be your wife?"

"I do."

"Then by the powers invested in me by the elder council in Farrarie, I now pronounce you husband and wife. Nico, you may *now* kiss your bride." Nico leaned down to place his lips on mine, but I felt a sharp pain in my chest and gasped.

"What is it, love?" I couldn't talk past the pain, it was excruciating. I felt like someone was ripping my chest open.

"Everyone out now!"

"Get the fuck out!"

I didn't know who was shouting and telling everyone to get out. I was too consumed by the pain in my chest. As another wave of pain hit, my knees gave out, and I landed with a thud. Nico quickly grabbed my head before it could hit the stairs. The pain was getting worse. I screamed out as another wave of pain ripped through me.

"It's the bounds on her power. Dom, put up a force field to minimize any damage now. Alex, Chase—I need you both to help him maintain the blast. There are too many people outside if this goes sideways; they will get hurt." I closed my eyes, trying to focus on not screaming. My body started to feel hot. I could feel myself getting hotter and hotter, from the tips of my toes to the tips of my fingers.

"What do we do?"

"I have no idea."

I couldn't hold it in anymore. I screamed out, in agony. I felt like I was being burned alive.

I was clawing at my dress, trying to rip it off. I needed to get all my clothes off to try cool myself down, but I couldn't focus.

My head was pounding and felt like it was going to burst any minute. Fuck, right now I would welcome death if it would just make this pain stop. My veins felt like they were filled with liquid lava, and I couldn't hear or see anything now. It was all just fire and fury.

Chapter Forty

NICO

"What do we do?"

"We have to help her!"

"I don't fucking know how to help her!" I shouted.

"We need to figure it out and fast, because she is dying!"

"You don't think I fucking know that, Jackson?"

I was scared. I never got scared, but seeing the woman I love writhing in pain in front of me and screaming out to make it stop, begging for me to help her? I felt useless. I didn't know how to make it stop, and I didn't know how to take the pain away.

"Nico! It hurts, it hurts so fucking much!" She was starting to glow blue, and a blue mist started coating her body, starting at her feet and making its way up slowly. Out of the corner of my eye, I saw Aurora drop to her knees; I turned to her, prepared to try and catch her if she fell, but Jackson stopped me.

"Don't touch her! She's having a vision." Sure enough, Aurora's eyes were white. This vision didn't last long, maybe a minute, if that. As soon as Aurora's eyes turned back to their normal color, she turned to me.

"Kiss her, Nico!"

"What?"

"You never sealed the exchange after the vows; she kissed you before them. You must kiss her and accept her power into you." Fuck! Right now I would try anything. I leaned my head down toward hers and whispered.

"I'm gonna make it stop, baby. I'll take the pain away." I plastered my lips to hers, and as soon as I made contact, she stopped shaking and stilled beneath me. I pulled back so I could see if the mist stopped moving, but instead it was making its way up her body faster now. I turned to the others to see if they knew what to do and how to stop it. None of them were looking at me—they were all focusing on Ryan.

"Dominic, you, Alex, and Chase are going to need to hold that force field tight. Nico, move away from her, everyone needs to move back near the chapel doors now."

I turned to my sister, who had a serious look on her face. I don't know why, but in this moment I trusted my sister's advice, and we all moved to the back of the church and huddled in close. "Mya, I need you to help me make a barrier around us. When she expels that power, we are gonna need a shield. Nico can't help us; his power is locked in with Ryan's."

I was staring at my sister in awe. How did she know all of this? Mya and Sophia didn't waste any time. They both quickly started chanting, and a yellow and purple barrier started to shimmer in front of us. My sister wasn't a weak witch anymore; she was strong and powerful, a force to be reckoned with. My attention was pulled back toward Ryan when she let out a gut-wrenching scream. I really hope these force fields the guys had up would mute the sounds from traveling outside.

We all watched, transfixed on the sight before us. Ryan was completely covered in blue mist now. It was like a cocoon wrapped around her. Her groaning and screaming stopped. We all waited with bated breath to see what would happen next. Is it over? Is she okay? I looked to the others, seeking out their thoughts, when I heard someone gasp. I turned back toward where Ryan was and saw the mist had lifted her into the air. She was floating, arms stretched out wide, her dress rippling like it was blowing in the breeze. There was no wind in the chapel.

Chapter Forty One

I felt weightless and free, like a missing piece from inside me had been finally put back. I was whole for the first time in my life. My worries and fears weren't so troubling anymore. I felt like I was strong enough to take on the world. I didn't want to open my eyes and ruin this moment or the feelings I had; I knew I couldn't keep my head buried in the sand forever.

I reluctantly peeled my eyes open and frowned in confusion. I could see Nico, Jax, Kai, Dom, Alex, Chase, Mya, Aurora, and Sophia all standing at the back of the chapel. There was a bubble around them that was shimmering yellow and purple.

Why were they behind the bubble? I looked around to see all the walls shimmering as well; it reminded me of the dome I had made the other day. Why were they looking up at me?

I looked down, and that's when I noticed, I was floating mid fucking air with a blue mist surrounding me!

What the actual fuck is going on? I started to panic. I could see Nico's mouth moving, but I couldn't hear what he was saying from this side of the dome. What's happening to me?

Why couldn't I get back down to the ground? I felt heat creeping its way up my body, making me panic more, thinking I was going to start burning from the inside again.

I looked to the others, asking them to help me. Jax and Kai were holding Nico back. I was really starting to freak out when the heat intensified and worked its way down my arms. I stretched my arms open wider, and instead of fighting the burning sensation, this time I chose to embrace it.

I leaned my head back and let out a shriek from deep within. It wasn't from the magic, but me letting go of all the pain I had suffered in my life. I felt pressure build in my chest, and that's when it happened—a force so strong it burst out of me, and all I could see was blue light. The more I was pushing whatever this was inside me out, the more I felt free and less constricted.

It was so freeing to release all this pent-up energy from inside me. I felt more in control now. As the pressure inside me lessened, I felt myself slowly float back down to the ground. As soon as my feet hit the ground, I dropped to my knees, exhaustion suddenly taking over my body. The chapel was ruined.

The pews were a splintered mess on the ground, and the windows were smashed. The flowers were burned to a crisp, and even the chandelier was broken.

I leaned over, placing my hands on the ground in front of me so I could try to stabilize myself. I was panting hard, trying to catch my breath. After a couple of minutes, I saw someone kneel down in front of me and then two hands were placed on my shoulders. My head felt so heavy I could barely lift it, but I pushed through and lifted my head to see who was in front of me. Two violet eyes stared back at me, concern evident on his face.

"Are you okay, love?" Nico moved his hands from my shoulders to cup my cheeks, and his touch was like a balm warding off the heat inside me. At his touch I started to feel relaxed and content. My body felt like it was being pulled toward him, and a voice inside my head was telling me he could make it all better. Call me crazy, but I believed that voice. Nico didn't waste another second. He scooped me up and cradled me in his lap, stroking the hair out of my face. "You're okay, baby, I've got you." I couldn't get my voice to work, so I nodded instead. Looking around, I could see the others had formed a circle around us, displaying varying looks of awe, shock, concern, and worry. I didn't have the energy to try and decipher those looks. Mya and Sophia looked like they were ready to pass out. The most concerning thing for me right now though is why Dom, Alex and Chase looked like they had seen a ghost. What the fuck happened?

"Are you okay, Ry?" I gave Aurora a smile and nodded my head. Truth was, I felt like I could sleep for days.

"Soph, are you okay?"

"I feel like I am going to pass out, brother, I don't know how Mya and I managed to hold that shield against that blast."

"I agree, I am wiped out. I have never in my life stood against a force as strong as that. I am very grateful Sophia and I were able to hold the shield, or we would all be dead right now." I cuddled deeper into Nico at Mya's foreboding tone. I felt free in that moment, and alive, while my friends and *husband* were fighting for their lives against my power. Nico was rubbing my back and holding me tighter, trying his best to comfort me.

"The true heroes are you three guys; you've done amazing holding the blast. You guys saved a lot of lives here today." I turned my head to see Dom and my cousins with their heads down. Chase started shaking his head from side to side. Why are they so down? They had done so well. I owe them so much for what they had done. I owe all of these guys so much.

"We didn't, Jackson...we tried, but..." Dom cut in and spoke for Chase, looking at me and making eye contact for the first time.

"We couldn't hold the blast, love. I'm sorry."

Speaking for the first time since the incident, I asked, "What do you mean, Dom? What happened?" Dom dropped his gaze, and I felt Nico tense beneath me. I looked to both my cousins for reassurance, but both their heads were still hanging down.

"Answer her, Dom! What happened?" Nico was trying hard to contain his frustration. Dom opened and shut his mouth a few times but said nothing, and a pit of dread was starting to form in my stomach. Then out of nowhere, Jax dropped to his knees and started gripping his hair with both hands.

"No, no, no—we did everything right! How the fuck did this happen?" I saw tears rolling down Jackson's face, and he seemed like he was in pain.

"Dominic, what the fuck happened?" Sophia shouted. Dom wouldn't make eye contact with anyone. Alex spoke, and fuck my life—I really wish Alex let me live in my naïve bubble for a bit longer, because what he had to say changed everything. I was royally fucked, and I deserved everything coming my way for what I had just done.

"We couldn't hold the force field. The reason why yours and Mya's shield held was because Dom, Chase, and I helped you hold it. In doing so, the force field weakened, and Ryan shattered it to smithereens. We fucked up, and they all paid the price." Alex had tears leaking from his eyes.

"How many, Jackson?" I looked to Kai then, who was waiting for Jackson's answer.

"At least fifty." Oh my God, I killed fifty people! I'm a murderer. I am no better than my sister. I'm a killer.

"We need to run now! I have to take her to Farrarie, where they can't get her. I'll convince the elders it was an accident." Why did Nico want to hide me? Who was going to take me?

Everyone started talking at once, trying to make a plan, while I sat there cradled in Nico's lap with silent tears rolling down my face.

I deserved everything that was coming my way. Everyone stopped talking as soon as the chapel doors banged open. Nico stood with me cradled in his arms and turned to face the doorway.

Kai, Jax, and Dom moved to stand in front of us to block me from the view of whoever entered. Alex and Chase moved to stand in front of Mya, Aurora, and Sophia. Their tense posture put me on edge, and I strained my neck to see around the guys so I could see who entered and put everyone on guard, but they were too bloody big and wide, and I couldn't see around them, even with the added height of being in Nico's arms.

"Alpha, as this is your land, we are asking you to step aside quietly. This does not need to get out of hand; we just need the girl."

"She will be returning to Farrarie with me, Lachlan; there is no need for your presence here." Nico's voice held so much authority that even I would have obeyed him. Whoever this man was, Nico sure as shit didn't like him. His arms tightened around me, securing me closer to his chest.

"She will remain here in the custody of the vampires. She is your wife, so she cannot return to the fae realm." I was really starting to get scared now; this Lachlan guy wasn't backing down. What was going to happen to me?

"Then she will remain here with me and my pack."

"She will not. You are too close to the accused and her husband; therefore she will be remanded into the care of the vampire king." What the fuck! I am not going anywhere with Randall fucking Cane.

"Fuck that. She can be held at the Knox coven until her

hearing." What the hell, Chase? Stevie would kill me if I went there.

"No, Mr. Knox, she will not return to her coven. I am tired of this conversation. Hand the girl over or we will take her from you!" I looked up at Nico, trying to convey to him with my eyes that I didn't want to go, I wanted to stay with him.

NICO

Looking down at her, I can see the fear in her eyes, and I would rather die than hand her over to those fucking leeches. I look around the chapel, trying to find a way to escape. I've been trying to access my magic since I learned the guys didn't contain the blast. I don't know what the hell is going on. If I can't access my magic, I can't even open a portal. Where the fuck are Maverick and Larick? I saw them here earlier, and they should be here right now, helping there fucking queen.

I can see Dom's lips moving, and I start to hope. My brother is opening me a portal to run and take Ryan away from here. I'll deal with my magic problem later. Dom's lips start moving faster. What the fuck is taking him so long?

"Are you going to do this the hard way or the easy way?" No one says anything. Lachlan sighs and shakes his head. "I figured it would be the hard way, pity." Lachlan calls out to whomever to come in, and when I see who they are, I know we are fucked.

I have to find a way out of this; I am the king of the fucking fae and married to the most powerful supernatural on the planet, so why can't I access my fucking magic?

"Dad?" I follow Chase's line of sight toward the Knox coven elders and see a tall muscular man with black hair and blue eyes. The man cuts his gaze to Chase and then Alex, and a private conversation must transpire between them, because Alex starts nodding. The Knox coven elders are here in the chapel—all of them.

"Bring the girl to me or the elders will take her from you." Fuck, I lean forward slightly to whisper in Kai's ear. I need more time to think of a plan.

"We will bring her outside." Ryan turns to stone in my arms at Kai's words. Lachlan nods and turns to exit the chapel with the elders following him. "Make a fucking portal and leave now!" Kai whisper-shouts at me as we slowly walk toward the exit.

"I can't. I don't know what's happening, but I have no access to my magic." At my admission, Ryan starts to tremble in my arms. Fuck, she's scared, and I can't even protect her right now.

"I can't access mine either. I tried to before, because you were taking too long." That's why Dom was chanting faster; he was getting pissed, his magic was muted for some reason. As we were nearing the end of the aisle, Chase spoke.

"No one can access their magic right now, not even Ryan."

"What are you talking about?" Dom took the words right out of my mouth. We all stopped and stared, waiting for him to answer. "My dad and the other elders are wearing the moon stones around their necks. I don't know how they found them or where they got them from, they were supposed to be a myth or a legend."

"What is a fucking moon stone, boy?" Shit, Kai was at the end of his patience now.

"The moon stone can mute all magic. It can stop the cravings of a vampire and stop a wolf from shifting. They are the most powerful stones, and they are supposed to have been destroyed centuries ago." How the fuck did Mya know about this and I didn't?

"Hurry up, boy." I tensed at the sound of Randall's voice. He was outside waiting with the elders, fuck. Looking around our group, and seeing everyone here prepared to fight with nothing but our fists, to save my wife, meant so much to me. Each one of them gave me a nod, telling me that whatever I decide to do, they are with me. We reluctantly and cautiously exit the chapel and descend the stairs. Standing in front of us is none other than Randall fucking Cane. On either side of him is the elder council from the vampires, led by Lachlan, and then on the other side is the Knox coven elders.

"I can't access my pack through our mind link."

"You can't use your link or magic of any kind, Jax; the moon stone prevents it." Fuck, Mya was just full of good news tonight, wasn't she?

"Hand her over, boy, and I promise I'll take *real* good care of her." I'll snap that slimy cunt's neck the next chance I get.

Looking down at Ryan, seeing her eyes so vacant, nearly broke me. She has been through so much and pushed her emotions down so far to help me and my people. After what happened tonight and the deaths of so many on her hands, she couldn't lock away her emotions any longer. I leaned down and kissed her lips and then whispered in her ear.

"I love you, Ryan, and I will fight for you always, my love. When this is over, little one, I will help you get through the guilt of tonight, and I will help you get vengeance for your father as well." I moved toward Dominic and placed Ryan in his arms; he looked shocked, but what he must see on my face snaps him out of it, and he quickly cradles her to his chest. I lean in to whisper in his ear. "If this doesn't work, you take her and you run. I will buy you as much time as I can, but you run and you take her home as soon as you have access to your magic." I pull back and look Dom in the eye.

"You have my word, brother." Turning around I face the elders and Randall.

"What transpired here tonight was an accident; we were unaware that our union would be the key to unlocking my wife's fae magic." I heard a couple of the elders gasp. I was lying through my teeth, and then I noticed that wolves and witches were starting to gather around. I hope they were on our side and not against us. "My wife never meant to hurt anyone."

"But she did, so hand her over now!"

"Fuck you, Randall. You killed Jackson's father and you are trying to seal my realm so my world will die. You should be the one standing trial." I can hear the wolves and witches around us gasp. The Knox elders and vampire elders don't seem shocked. Why isn't Lachlan shocked, did he know?

"You are a liar and have no proof, boy. I am not the one who has locked the *true* queen of the Knox coven in a cell." At Randall's outburst, Lachlan turns his gaze to me.

"Is this true, Nico? Have you got Stevie Knox locked in a cell?" Fuck, I want to slap that sly smirk off Randall's fucking face. Where the fuck are the fae elders? I nod my head.

"Release her now!"

"You can't release her, she is dangerous."

"The only dangerous person here is the woman you all are so intent on protecting! Now release her." Jax turns around, looking for someone, and then proceeds to tell them they have to find one of the two guards who can access the cells and bring Stevie to us. We wait until Luther, Jackson's guard, comes back with Stevie. She is smiling from ear to ear and almost skipping. That bitch is crazy.

"Miss Knox, I wasn't aware that you were held captive."

"Since when do elders get involved in shit like this, Lachlan?"

"Since two leaders have died so close together and both of them have the scent of fae on them, that's when, Dominic!" I winced at his outburst. Lachlan was angry, and he was also a very fucking powerful vamp. I don't blame him, but he had it wrong. It wasn't us, it was Randall and Stevie, and we needed to prove it. "Hand the girl over, Nico." Yeah, that's not gonna happen.

"The girl can remain here in the custody of the shifter elders." I turn my head to see Mr. Silver limping toward us; he's leaning heavily on a cane, trying to hold himself up. I turn my gaze to Dom, who is shocked and then that look turns to anger. His father can't use his shifter healing because of the moon stones.

"Ian, a pleasure to see you, old friend."

"And you, Lachlan."

"The girl cannot remain here, Ian. she is too close to the alpha. She must be held by the vampire elders, as we are the only neutral clan."

"Randall has her mother imprisoned and is actively trying to kill her, and so is that fucking psycho coven queen."

"You have no proof, my dear Sophia." Sophia starts to tremble at the way Randall is speaking to her.

"I have had enough!" Stevie shouts, and then I'm sailing through the air and hitting the front of the chapel, I look around to see that the rest of our group has been thrown against the chapel, as well. Aurora seems to be hurt badly, as she's not moving. Jackson starts growling, but there is nothing he can do. We have no magic. We all dropped to the ground, but still held there by magic. How the fuck can Stevie use magic and we can't? I'm struggling and fighting as hard as I can. I have never been subdued by anyone else's magic before, except for Dom.

Something is seriously wrong with Stevie; if she had that much power, she could have broken out of those cells easily. I can feel the power radiating off her, she feels as strong as Ryan.

She starts walking toward Dominic with a huge smile on her face.

"Stop right there and stay away from my son!" Stevie turns toward Mr. Silver and smiles, with a flick of her wrist, Mr. Silver is sent flying. Dom immediately starts to shake, torn between going to his father and protecting Ryan.

"Ooops, I hope your daddy is going to be okay." The crazy bitch laughs, and everyone around the clearing is standing there in shock., I notice now a few of my people are gathering, and some vampires are here now too. The witches look terrified, and the shifters are torn, wanting to attack and protect their alpha but waiting for his orders. The vampires are bloodthirsty and want to fight, disgusting fucking leeches. Scanning the clearing, I spot Maverick. He sees me looking at him and I shake my head, telling him with my eyes to hold off on an attack. We're far too outnumbered.

"You're a crazy fucking bitch, you know that? You will never win. Ryan is ten times the woman you will ever be. Enjoy your reign while it lasts, because your sister is coming for *her* throne." Stevie slaps Dom clean across the cheek, making his head snap to the side. Sophia starts going nuts, fighting against the magic holding her in place.

"I'll fucking kill you! Stay the fuck away from him, you evil bitch!" Stevie ignores Sophia's outburst.

"Hand her over now, or I start hurting your friends. Starting with the mouthy fucking fae bitch." No! not my sister! Dom turns to look at Sophia and then back to me. I can see he's torn, and fuck, so am I. I can't lose my sister again, but I can't lose Ryan either.

"Take me instead!" I shout.

"Aww that's so cute, but no." Stevie raises here hand and Sophia starts to float toward her. As soon as Soph is within her grasp, Stevie grips her by the throat and starts to choke her.

"Lachlan, do something!" The fucking bastard stands there watching on in horror at what he is seeing. He needs to stop this. Everyone is frozen in place except for the vamps and witches. We underestimated Stevie, and now my sister will pay the price. Soph is struggling to breathe.

"Stop! I'll do whatever you want. I'll seal the fucking fae realm if I have to!" I hear gasps all around at Dom's outburst; Soph is starting to turn purple. "Let her go and I'll seal it, I swear."

"Enough!" Stevie releases my sister, who drops to the ground, gasping for air and clawing at her throat. Ryan wiggles out of Dom's arms to stand on her feet, and Dom rushes to Soph and picks her up, moving back toward the chapel stairs near the rest of us.

"I was having fun, Ry. You're a party pooper." Stevie's eyes are pitch black, you can see black liquid swimming beneath her skin. I can see Ryan is shaky on her legs and trembling. She exerted so much power tonight that she is weak. "Come with us now and none of them will be harmed. If you delay any longer and try something stupid, I will do something like this." She clicks her fingers and then I hear Aurora scream. Looking over at her, I see it now, blood is dripping down the front of her head. She must have hit her head hard against the chapel wall, and on top of that, Stevie just broke her arm. "Or this." Now Chase is screaming out; Stevie broke his leg, and it's hanging at an odd angle. His father steps forward for the first time tonight, but pauses when he sees Stevie is looking at him. "Or..."

"Stop! You have my word I will come with you without a fight." Ryan turns to look back at me. I'm stuck on the ground fighting against my restraints like a worthless dog while my wife is standing in front of a deranged killer. Ryan smiles a broken smile and mouths *come for me*. I see the tears in her eyes and the doubt, but I will never stop until I find her. I harden my facial features and nod. I'll come for you, baby, and I'll kill everyone in my fucking way.

Epilogue

RYAN

I've been sitting in a cell for nearly two weeks, beaten and barely lucid. I am injected with something three times a day. I don't know what's in the injection; not five minutes after they inject me, I black out. Randall comes to me every day and withdraws blood from me. I don't know what he needs the blood for, and I would have thought he would have killed me by now. Every time the darkness takes over, I try to reach my dream land with Nico. I have even tried to reach Kai, but nothing happens. I held out hope for the first few days that Nico and the guys would come for me, but they have left me here. I knew it was too good to be true.

"Are you awake?" I turn my head slowly; it's such an effort to move even my head. Every bone in my body is aching and sore. I am beaten three times a day, after every injection; they beat me before I pass out. I heard the guards talking. There is a big elder meeting. All four of the elder councils are coming here today."

"What..." Clearing my dry throat, I try to speak again. "What does that mean?"

"Something big is going down." I wasn't holding out hope. If Nico was coming for me, he would have already been here. I felt used. He married me and then left me. Well, I left him, really, but I did it to save their lives. Stevie enjoyed hearing Nico scream out for me as she dragged me by my hair all the way to the car the night of my wedding. Randall has tried to get me to use my powers when I'm brought to him in his office, but for some reason I can't use them. Normally all it took was for me to be angry and then I would blast shit, but now, I can't even do that.

"I think they're coming for you."

"Trust me, no one is coming for me. My husband left me here to rot, my cousins haven't come, and my friends haven't shown up either. They all probably think I'm dead and are celebrating that the fae realm can live on." I could hear the bitterness and heartbreak in my own voice, but I wouldn't shed another tear for what I had lost.

"Don't say that, Smurfy." I hated the nickname as soon as he had come up with it; I told him I glowed blue when I used magic, and ever since he had been calling me Smurfy. We can't actually see each other, as it's pitch black in the cells. We have no lights down here at all.

"If I ever get to blow this joint, I promise I won't leave without you."

"Yes, you will. Everyone leaves me."

"Not me, Smurfy, I got your back all day. I swear." The stupidest and weirdest part is I believed him.

Changing the subject, I ask my jail buddy, "You still haven't told me why you're in here?"

"My mom was a prisoner here for many years and died, apparently. The king told me I had to live out the rest of her sentence. I was born here, so I know no other life. For nearly seventeen years, this is all I have known."

"I swear to you, if *I* ever blow this joint, I will not leave without you, Lucian."

Nightmare
CURSE OF FATE BOOK 3

Chapter One

RYAN

I was at my breaking point. They're torturing me—daily. Vampire blood may heal my bones and wounds but it doesn't take the pain away. Which basically means they know they can make me suffer as much as they want without ever allowing me to just die.

I thought my mother's treatment was bad, but oh God, how wrong I was. Living with my mother was a picnic in the park compared to this.

They draw my blood three times a day and inject me with something; it knocks me out for God knows how long. When I wake, I always wish I hadn't.

Lucian, my jail buddy who is in the cell across from mine, tries to draw the guards' attention so they will focus on him, instead of me. Sometimes I think it just gives them twice the fun.

I'm lying here on the cold hard ground, nursing what I'm sure is a broken arm. No doubt they will be down soon to give me blood to heal my broken bone. I can't take deep breaths either, so I guess my ribs are broken—again.

"Are you awake?"

"Unfortunately." There is nothing I want more than for everything, especially me, to just be over. But I deserved all this pain for what I did at the chapel. I was a coward and getting weaker by the day. What you see on TV isn't what happens in real life; you don't drink vampire blood and become a superhuman. All the blood does is heal your wounds and bones.

They give me the blood daily, so I'll heal, and then they torture me again. It's a cycle I have been living for weeks now. I can't do this for much longer.

"Don't say that, you can't die! You owe me a trip around the world." Lucian and I spend our days—when I'm not being beaten or unconscious—talking about what we're going to do when we get out of here.

He has never seen the outside world, except for once when he was about ten.

Lucian was raised in the cells by a woman who died when he was ten years old; he doesn't remember who she was, but he says she was kind and cared for him. The first and only time Lucian was able to be outside was to watch Randall Cane kill the only mother he'd ever known. She was trying to set Lucian free and got caught.

I sighed. Lucian was trying to keep my spirits lifted, but they were wearing me down. I hurt all over, breathing was becoming a chore, and no one was coming for me or Lucian. We were stuck here at the mercy of the vampire king and my sister. "Don't give up Smurfy, please."

I could hear the panic in Lucian's voice: he wanted me to fight and make it out of here. I didn't want to let him down; he needed me just as much as I needed him. We were each other's only saving grace in this fucking nightmare of a place. I may be physically hurt, but Lucian has had it a lot harder than me. His mother died giving birth to him, he doesn't know who his father is, and the woman who raised him was killed trying to help him.

I need to woman up and think of a plan to save myself and Lucian; I couldn't leave here without him.

"I won't give up, Lucian, I swear. We will make it out of this hell hole, even if it's the last thing we do. I refuse to die down here." Lucian didn't get a chance to answer. We heard a creak and bang; that meant someone opened the door at the top of the stairs. We both remained quiet as we listened to the stairs groan. My stomach sank. I couldn't handle another round of torture, not this soon and not without the vamp blood to heal me.

I knew they weren't coming for Lucian. They never did. Whoever was making their way down the stairs wasn't very big. I could tell from the sound of the creaks. When the big guards came down, it sounded like a tree splitting.

I held my breath, waiting for whoever it was to make themselves known. You couldn't see shit down here. You could make out the silhouette of a person, but that was about it. It was another kind of torture, being in complete darkness all the time.

I pushed myself up into a sitting position and bit back the scream that wanted to tear out of me. I was in so much pain. Clenching my teeth, I scooted back along the ground until my back was against the wall and waited to see what was coming next. After a beat, a shadowy figure appeared in front of my cell.

"Well, well, how the mighty have fallen." I flinched at the cold, malicious tone. "Being beaten and bloody suits you, sister." I counted to three in my head before answering.

"I'm glad you are enjoying this, Stevie. I had thought I would see you sooner. I guess Randall has you on a tight leash," I wheezed out. I may not be able to see her properly, as there were no lights down here, but I swear, I saw her body stiffen, and I smiled a bit. I had hit my mark.

"You think Randall runs the show?" Stevie sneered. Clearly I was missing something here. A feeling of dread washed over me.

"Oh dear sister, you really are fucking stupid."

"Don't speak to her like that!" *Oh no, Lucian shut up.* I saw my sister's dark figure turn away. She must be in front of Lucian's cell. If I said or did anything in his defense, she would use him against me, like she did the others.

"Oh, so you can speak, mutt?"

"Fuck you, leave Smurfy alone." My heart swelled at Lucian's protectiveness; he has never seen me or met me properly, but he was loyal to me. Call me dumb, but that made me trust him more, than anyone.

"Oh, so you think you can save my dear sister? Why would you want to save a murderer?" I felt a pang in my chest at the mention of what I had done. Stevie knew what she was doing; she was trying to turn my only friend here against me. I never told Lucian about what happened on my wedding day. I couldn't. I pushed thoughts of that night so far out of my brain they were probably in my toes. I was in denial and I planned to stay that way, until I had a private place to sort through my emotions.

Lucian responded. "Because she is a good person! You, however, seem like a royal bitch!"

"You will watch your mouth, you vile mutt" How dare she? I had to distract her without letting her think I cared for Lucian.

"What are you doing down here, Stevie?" A minute passed before Stevie's shadow came into view again. It looked like she was leaning on the bars. I guess she wanted to keep both Lucian and I in her eyesight now.

"I came to gloat, of course, sister."

"Gloat about what, Stevie?"

"Well, you see, it's a bit of a long story, but a good one, I swear. Anyway, since I took you from your sham of a wedding, your vile cunt of a husband has been trying to get you back." My heart skipped a beat or two. I thought he gave up on me.

"It is delaying our plans, with the fucking elders now involved. Randall is to fucking gutless and won't go against his elders like I did. Now we have the fucking fae elders and the shifter elders wanting to make a trade."

My mind was reeling; Nico has been trying to save me! He didn't abandon me, nor did the others. This new piece of information gave me a renewed sense of hope and determination.

I could keep doing this, with the knowledge that one day, it would end.

"What kind of trade?" I was scared to hear her answer, but I had to know.

"Melakai Cane, for you." My heart stopped and bile rose in my throat. I was working hard to swallow it back down. Kai can't do this; they will kill him this time. Why did they want Kai though?

"Why, Melakai?"

"We know the spell you used made him Randall's blood heir. Randall wants to make an example out of him and obviously can't risk Melakai having a claim to his throne. This time, I promise you, he will die at our hands. Plus, the bonus is that his death will hurt you all over again."

"You're not taking her anywhere!" Lucian yelled. Stevie chuckled, and the sound put me on edge. I was missing something.

"Of course she's not, we're trading her cunt of a mother for Kai. Randall doesn't know that though, so shhhhh. It can be our little secret." What the fuck was Stevie up to?

"Why, Stevie?"

"Because you still need to seal the fae realm. I'm going to make Kai pay for your betrayal, and you'll watch every moment of his suffering. Then I will kill you. You will never be free again, sister."

Chapter Two

RYAN

Stevie left after she dropped the bomb that Kai would be traded. I couldn't let him go through with this! Kai wouldn't die for me.

I had to figure out a way to get the fuck out of here. Kai and the others had no idea it was all a trick; Nina was to be traded not me.

I knew I didn't have long before someone came down here and took my blood, injected me, and then beat me.

I had to think while I had the chance—what the hell was I going to do? I can't access my magic, and I don't know why. I thought it might be because of the cell I am in, but it won't even work when I'm taken to Randall's office. Lucian said he doesn't even know if he has any magic, he doesn't even know what type of supernatural he is, but Stevie's comments about him being a mutt certainly were a hint.

Soon after I got here, I had tried screaming, reasoning with guards, and I even tried bribing them. Nothing worked.

I don't know where Nina is, but she was here somewhere in this mansion.

Stevie is so far gone now that I don't think there is any coming back for her. As the days dragged on, I have grown to resent my sister even more. I estimate that I have been here for roughly six weeks now. I smell like I have been here for years.

"Psssst, Smurfy." I smiled at Lucian's attempt to whisper; that boy is louder than a fog horn.

"If you're trying to whisper, you're doing a shit job." We both chuckled, and I winced. Laughing was out of the question while my ribs were broken. It was silent for a moment before she spoke again.

"Who's Melakai, Smurf?" I sighed; I regretted sighing straight away when a searing pain hit me in the side. Clutching my ribs to try easing the pain, I took some slow and shallow breaths.

When I finally got my pain under control, I answered Lucian.

"Melakai is a friend of mine."

"Okay?" I could hear how reluctant Lucian sounded; he knew I had a chance at being rescued and couldn't understand why I wouldn't take it.

"Kai and I have a complicated history; just know that I will not leave here without you. And if there is a way for me to stop Kai from exchanging positions with me, I will do it." I heard his sharp intake of breath; he must think I'm crazy.

"Why would you do that?"

"Because I owe Melakai, and he deserves to have his life. He nearly gave his life for me once; I won't allow my sister to trick him. If they do make an exchange then it would be for nothing, Nina would be free, not me. And of everyone involved, Nina is least deserving of freedom."

We sat in silence for a long time. Something was wrong. No guards have come to inject me, and Randall hasn't come to draw my blood.

"Lucian, something's wrong."

"I didn't want to be the one to say it, but you're right. The guards are always here by now."

"Do you think it's that big elder meeting you were telling me about?"

"Maybe?" We didn't get to finish speculating. The door opened and banged, the stairs started creaking and groaning, but there were so many footsteps pounding down the steps that my alarm only escalated.

A moment later a shadow appeared in front of my cell, but I didn't move from my position. If they were here to beat me, it was better to remain still and just get it over with. The more I fought back, the more they enjoyed it.

"Get up, you're coming with us." This can't be good.

"Where?" I know it was stupid to ask questions; it usually just pissed them off.

"You don't get to ask questions, bitch, now move." I wouldn't leave here without Lucian, I promised him.

"I won't leave without Lucian."

"Smurf, no! I'll be okay. Do what you need to do."

"Quiet! You're both coming. Now get the fuck up!" I didn't argue any further. I used the wall to help me stand and forced myself not to make a sound. My ribs were killing me and my arm hurt like a bitch. I wouldn't give these bastards the satisfaction of seeing me crumble.

Once I was on my feet, the cell door opened, and shadowy figures entered. They gripped both my arms and pulled them behind my back, I couldn't hold my scream back. The pain was crippling and my knees buckled. I remained standing because of the grip the two guards had on me.

"If you fucking hurt her again, I swear to God, I will fucking kill you!" I heard the sickening sound of a crunch come from Lucian's cell. "Is that all you got? What a fucking pussy!" I heard more sounds and a scuffle, then a moment later dark figures passed by me.

Cuffs were placed on my wrists, and I was dragged from my cell. Tears were streaming down my face from the pain. I had to block the pain out; something big was happening. I hadn't seen Lucian leave his cell the whole time I had been here.

I was dragged up the stairs and stumbled more than a few times. I couldn't fucking see anything. As we neared the top of the stairs I closed my eyes knowing that the light was going to hurt like a bitch after being in the dark for so long. They yanked me through the door, and I screamed out in pain, but the guards didn't give a fuck. After being dragged for a while, I braved the light and slowly started to open my eyes. It stung at first, and my eyes started to water. Once I got my vision under control, I started to look around, but nothing was familiar.

"Smurf!" Oh God, where is Lucian? I couldn't see him anywhere. Where the fuck have they taken him?

"Lucian!" I was swiftly punched in the face by the guard on my left, but I didn't black out, thankfully. My face was now throbbing and felt like it had a pulse; I slumped in the guards' hold, letting them drag me to wherever we were going. We rounded a corner and then the front doors of Randall's mansion came into view. What the fuck was going on? I saw a group of six guards standing by the front door holding a man who was slumped forward, unconscious.

That wasn't just any man—it was Lucian. With a new sense of purpose, which was to make sure Lucian was alive, I started to struggle in the guards' hold; I got my feet under me finally and started to pull away, the pain in my arm, ribs and face forgotten for the moment.

"Cut it out before you get knocked the fuck out!" Left guard snapped at me. I turned and glared at the ugly bastard.

"Fuck you!" Lefty cocked his arm back, ready to hit me again, when

a hand appeared out of nowhere and stopped him from landing the blow to my face.

"Touch her again and I will rip your fucking head off, feel me?" I leaned forward so I could see around Lefty and was shocked; the last person I ever thought would save my ass just did.

"Tyler?"

"Don't look so shocked, Ryan." Tyler had changed in the weeks since I had last seen him. His ginger beard was gone and his rust-colored hair was cut short on top and shaved on the sides now. His brown eyes were dull, and he had dark circles under his eyes. Tyler looked like shit.

"What's going on, Tyler?"

"Shut the fuck up!" Oh, so now Righty wanted to speak up. Great.

"Bring her to the car out front, and bring the boy as well."

"You don't tell us what to do, dog!" Righty had grown some balls in the space of a few seconds.

"When Randall and my mate are not here, I am in charge! Now do as I fucking say and hurry the fuck up!" What the hell was going on? Why was Tyler acting weird?

Tyler's eyes kept darting around the room like he was watching for something or someone. We were dragged outside, and Lucian and I were placed in a blacked-out SUV after the guard removed our cuffs. No guards were in the SUV with us, and Lucian was still out cold.

Tyler jumped behind the wheel of the SUV and sped away from Randall's mansion.

"Tyler, what the fuck is going on?"

"Well, I believe I just saved your life and ensured my own painful death at the hands of my mate. Any other questions?"

Chapter Three

NICO

It had been weeks since our wedding—since the day everything went wrong. She was taken from me, and there was not a fucking thing I could do about it.

I was banished back to Farrarie the night of our wedding. The fae elders called a mandatory meeting that night which led to me being banished from Earth.

The vampire elders made sure to declare that I cannot go back to the Earth realm until the trial. They say I can't be trusted, because Ryan is my wife. They're right. I won't stop trying to get her back; the look on her face that night has haunted me every time I close my eyes. She was begging me with those beautiful, strange eyes to save her, and I couldn't. Something was going on with the elders; I could feel it. Lachlan was being shady, and Victor was having council meetings without me present. The witches had no choice but to listen to Stevie. The shifter elders were the only ones who were being open and honest with us.

"Your majesty?"

"What is it, Cyrus?" I snapped.

"The alpha and Dom are here." I sighed, I had a feeling they weren't coming here to give me good news.

"Send them in, Cyrus." With a nod of his head, Cyrus left my study.

I started pacing, too anxious to sit still while I waited for the guys. After what felt like hours but was more like ten minutes, Jax and Dom strolled through the door.

"Nico." I walked right over to them and embraced each of my brothers. "It's good to see you, too, brother." Dom seemed taken aback by my embrace.

"How's everything going? Is there any news on Ryan?" Jax dropped his gaze to the floor, and Dom gestured for us to take a seat on one of the couches. I reluctantly followed them and sat down. Neither of them would make eye contact, and an uneasy feeling settled in my gut. What the fuck has happened?

"One of you two need to start talking!" I ground out through clenched teeth. Releasing a breath, Jax finally spoke.

"The shifter elders have been trying to get a trial date set since Ryan was taken. Ian has been pushing them to hurry but—"

"But what?" I snapped, and Jax flinched at my tone. I know this wasn't his fault, but I needed him to hurry the fuck up and get to the point.

"But they say there is no rush, as Ryan left willingly."

I couldn't sit still anymore; I stood and started pacing my study, again. I needed to release my pent-up anger. If I didn't, I was going to blow this whole room apart with the magic raging inside me. Having Ryan's magic inside of me was making my own magic slightly unstable.

I needed to save Ryan. She probably thought I had given up on her.

"Nico?" I turned to face Dom, who wouldn't meet my eyes.

The somber tone in his voice had me on edge. I released the breath I didn't know I was holding and took a seat, again.

"Dominic, in all the years we have known each other, you have never avoided eye contact. Why are you starting now?" Dom and Jax exchange a look that I couldn't decipher. "Seriously, start fucking talking!"

"Okay, let me get this all out before you go bat shit crazy, okay?" I took four calming breaths before agreeing to Dom's terms. Dom shook out his arms out and started cracking his neck from side to side, like he was gearing up for a fight. Dear God, what is he about to say?

"My dad managed to convince Lachlan to have a meeting, just the two of them. When dad got back, he said that the vampires' terms for Ryan return were simple—"

I cut Dom off, needing to know what we had to do in order to get my wife back. "What are the terms? What are you waiting for?"

"Randall wants Kai in exchange for Ryan."

Fuck me!

"Melakai is prepared to make the exchange." I snapped my gaze to Jackson in shock. *What the actual fuck?*

"Why, why would Kai do that?"

"Because he loves her, and he knows what she means to you." I couldn't ask this of my friend. No—not friend. Melakai was my brother. I couldn't trade his life for another; he had nearly given his life for Ryan before. What the fuck am I going to do?

"The elders need to lift the fucking ban on me not returning to the Earth realm. I need to see Kai."

Jax glared at me. "Kai wanted to come with us today and tell you himself, but the fucking portal blocked him." *Oh, shit.*

"What Jax is trying to say is why the fuck have you blocked our brother—our best friend—from returning to his home, Nico?

Are you that caught up in your own jealousy? He is trying to fucking help you and Ryan—" I cut Dom off before he could finish his rant. They had a right to know why Kai could never return to his home. They weren't going to like it, but they had to know.

"If he comes back here he will die!" Both of my brothers reeled back in shock.

"The spell Ryan used to bring Kai back wasn't the spell Kai told her to use."

"What the fuck are you saying, Nico?" Jax growled.

"Ryan has been having daydreams of her father, and he told her the spell Kai was going to use wouldn't work. She used the spell her father gave her, and that spell cancelled out his fae blood." Both of my brothers looked confused.

"So?"

"So, Jax what that means is—"

Dom cut in before I could finish. "Melakai is full vampire now."

"So? You and the elders cast the spell on Farrarie to burn any vamp aside from Kai." Jax wasn't getting what I was saying.

"The spell cancelled out his fae side, which meant the only blood that remained was vampire blood. Kai was turned by Randall Cane. I blocked Kai from entering Farrarie so he wouldn't die." Jax still looked confused, but Dom got it, and by the look on his face he was fucking livid.

One second I was sitting on the couch, next thing I knew I was sailing across the room and pinned to the wall behind my desk. Dom was glowing; his eyes changed to the color of his wolf, gray eyes that were glaring daggers at me. Jax sat there in shock.

"Your fucking wife tricked him! You fucking bastard! Do you have any idea what this news is going to do to him?" Dom raised his arm, and with a flick of his wrist, I was sent sailing into the corner of the room and hit the wall with enough force to rattle my bones. This is an old castle, so the wall I hit was three-foot-thick stone. Fuck, it hurt.

I didn't get a chance to recover because Dom used his magic to lift me from the ground and pinned me against the wall. I was done taking his shit. *My turn to play, brother.* I let my magic build and felt the heat of it in my veins. With a roar, I released a blast of my magic, the hold Dom had on me broke, and the blast sent everything in the room sailing. Dom was fast to act and quickly erected a shield around him and Jackson so they weren't hit by anything in the blast.

I wasn't done yet. I gathered more magic in my hand, making a purple energy ball, and threw it straight at Dom's shield, shattering it. I didn't give him a chance to retaliate, immediately lobbing another energy ball at him and sending him sailing through the window.

Hearing the glass shatter and seeing him fly through the window made me feel better. The next time that bastard wanted to fight, he better be prepared.

"Are you fucking crazy? He could be seriously hurt, Nico." I didn't give a fuck about Jackson's anger. That asshole insulted my wife and tried to best me.

"He needs to learn that this is my fucking realm. He may not have been born here, but as a fae himself, he should know better than to ever challenge the fucking king!" As soon as I finished putting Jackson in his place, a huge yellow orb appeared through the shattered window. The yellow orb stopped a few feet away from me then popped, and Dom stood before me.

Well, fuck me. That was a neat trick. I had never seen him do that before. Dom scowled at me. He was vibrating with anger, fists clenched at his sides.

"The next fucking time you throw me out a window, dick

face, I will fucking end you! I won't hold back next time, Nico. You may be the fucking king of this realm, but you are not my fucking king!" Maybe I did go a bit far by throwing him out of the window.

"Don't ever fucking talk about my *wife* like that again, and I won't throw you out a fucking window."

"Take it down a notch, boys." We spun toward the door to see my sister strolling into the room. She was dressed the same way she did before she was taken: jeans and a crop top, with Chucks. She surveyed the damage and turned to the three of us, glaring.

"I had nothing to do with this, Soph." Fucking Jax, the brown nose kiss-ass, was nudging his head to Dom and me.

Chapter Four

NICO

"I don't give a shit who started it, Jax," Soph snapped. I covertly gave Jax a smirk.

Sophia walked further into the room and started whispering under her breath.

A moment later, everything in the study was returned to how it was before the incident—even the window was fixed!

I stared at my sister in shock.

"Little dove, how did you just do that?" Dom took the words right out of my mouth.

"Wouldn't you like to know? I don't have time for this shit. I just received word from Larick; he is escorting Aurora to the castle now." *What the hell is she doing here?*

I wasn't the only one in the dark. "Why is Aurora here, Soph?"

"I have no idea, Jax, but she should be here shortly."

Sure enough, twenty minutes later there was a knock on my study door and both Larick and Aurora walked in. Aurora's gaze landed on Jax straight away, and he immediately started scenting the air. *Fuck, the spell is wearing off way too soon, and*

Jax was going to lose his shit and claim her if I don't get a new one laid down immediately.

Dom went for the proactive approach. "Jax, are you going to be okay?" Jax turned to Dom and started growling, and Dom immediately backed away from Jax with his hands in the air.

Jax viewed Dom as a threat because he was a wolf.

Aurora quickly made her way over to Jax and placed her hand on his chest.

"I'm right here with you, Jax. Look at me." Jax reluctantly pulled his gaze from Dom back to Aurora. After a beat, he started to calm.

"Right, well, that shit is starting to get awkward as fuck. Soon as this shit is over, you both need to either except the mate bond or fuck it out of your system." Fucking Dominic, that bastard needed to learn how to filter his fucking thoughts.

Soph apparently agreed. "Dear God, you really need help with that mouth of yours." Dom turned his gaze to my sister.

"Are you volunteering to teach me, little dove?" Sophia sneered at Dom but didn't answer him. I was going to get to the bottom of this shit between Soph and Dom one day *very* soon.

"Could we all have a seat, please? I need to tell you all something."

We all did as we were instructed and sat down. "Melakai went to make the exchange..." My stomach dropped. *Kai, you fucking idiot!*

"We have to get him back!"

"Let me finish, Dom. When Kai got there, he could tell something wasn't right. They brought Ryan in with a bag over her head." My anger skyrocketed. *How fucking dare they do that to her!*

"Dom's dad halted the exchange. He said that the scent of the prisoner the vampires brought didn't match Ryan's."

"Who was it?" I had a feeling I knew the answer to this question.

"It was Ryan's mother, Jax." *I fucking knew it.*

"What happened after that?"

"Mr. Silver demanded that Nina Knox be released into the care of the shifter elders. Randall tried to play it off like it was a mistake. Kai was supposed to make the exchange alone, but Dom's dad wouldn't allow it, thank God. The elders granted the shifters care of Nina."

"I don't give a fuck about Nina Knox. Where is Ryan, Aurora?"

"I don't know, Nico."

"You're a fucking seer, how can you not know?" Aurora flinched at my harsh tone.

"Calm the fuck down, Nico!" Jax was right, I shouldn't be taking my anger out on her; she has been trying for weeks to pinpoint Ryan's location. Everyone has been trying their best to find my girl since she was taken. I was going out of my mind with worry. I detested not having control.

"We'll get her back, brother." Sophia's words didn't reassure me. She couldn't know that for certain, and God knows we hadn't made a bit of progress in these long weeks.

"There's something else." I looked to Aurora and could see she was torn about whether or not she should tell me.

"Please, Aurora, I need to know everything." I begged. She took a deep breath and sat up straight.

"I did have a vision just before I got here. I saw my brother." Jax started growling at the mention of his former beta. Aurora's brother had mated with Ryan's sister, poor bastard.

"What else did you see, love?" Dom asked.

"I saw Tyler making plans to break Ryan out while Randall and Stevie were distracted with the elders. I don't think they ever planned to trade Ryan; I think it was always going to be

Nina. I also saw that Randall and Stevie can't locate the main portal to Farrarie to seal off this realm." I was shocked, hearing Aurora's confession. I never expected Tyler to go against his mate; I just hoped that he succeeded in his plans to get Ryan out.

Now I knew why they haven't made Ryan close the portal that stabilizes my world—they couldn't find it. I congratulated myself for my foresight on this; I had set up many decoy portals across the world over the years. The real portal was hidden in Alaska and very few knew of its location.

"That's good news; if your brother succeeds, then Ryan will be free. Better still, those fuckers have no idea where the real portal is." Dom's excitement was contagious. The others were smiling, and for the first time in weeks, I had hope.

"We still need to keep guards stationed at the portal; I won't rest until Ryan is returned and the threat against my realm has been eliminated." Since being back in my realm, I have been training each morning with my men, and Larick and Maverick have been meeting with me each afternoon to go over battle strategies. We have also been planning for worst case scenarios, in case they did find the portal.

"I need you guys to help me convince the elders to remove the ban on me returning to the Earth realm." Dom started grinning from ear to ear. "Why are you smiling like that Dominic?"

"Did we forget to mention that when we got here?" I started growling low in my throat. "My dad got the elders to remove the ban on you returning to the Earth realm. There are terms, though, Nico." *Aren't there always?*

"What are the terms, Dom?" I snapped.

"You are to be confined to Jackson's compound, and you cannot, under any circumstances, go after Randall or Stevie." I didn't like the terms, but I agreed all the same. I would agree to anything as long as it got me closer to my wife.

"There is one other thing." I looked to Jax, waiting for him to elaborate. "Ryan's cousins are gone."

"Where the hell have they gone?"

"I don't know, Nico. They were at the compound two days ago and then they vanished." What the actual fuck? Where the hell could they have gone? And why?

RYAN

We have been driving for hours, the daylight fading to darkness. My ass is numb from sitting for so long. Lucian has slept the entire time. I have no idea where we are going, or if Tyler is even telling the truth. Why would he help me? That's the one question that has been burning a hole in my mind the whole time we have been in the car. "Are you hungry?" It's the first time Tyler's spoken since we left Randall's mansion. My stomach grumbles before I can even answer. "I'll take that as a yes. We're nearly there."

"Nearly where?" I noticed that the pain from my arm and ribs has subsided a little bit, which is a bit alarming. "Why am I not hurting so much now?"

"To the airfield. While you were unconscious this morning, I came down and injected you with vampire blood." What the actual fuck? How did he get vampire blood, and why were we going to an airfield?

"If you're planning on killing me, at least let Lucian go. He's innocent and hasn't done anything wrong." Tyler's gaze met mine in the rearview mirror, a look of remorse on his face. I won't be fooled into trusting him; he betrayed us before. I am grateful for him giving me the blood, though; my arm and ribs were killing me this morning,

"I'm not going to kill you Ryan; I'm trying to help you. If I was going to kill you I wouldn't have given you the blood to help you heal." Smug prick, I still needed to know why he was helping us.

"Help me how?"

Tyler let out a long sigh before answering.

"By taking you to someone who can help you control your magic. My sister's visions are not always correct." Wait, what? As far as I knew, Aurora's visions were always accurate.

A short time later, Tyler turned down a dark, uneven road, and I started to question whether he was telling the truth about not wanting to kill me.

Lucian was leaning against the door, with his head resting against the window. I hadn't been able to see Lucian's features before, as we were held captive in complete darkness. Looking at him now, I could see he was painfully thin and dirty. I don't even know if he had ever showered; I know I smelled like I hadn't showered in years. Lucian had his hair piled on top of his head, from what I could see in the dim light of the car, it looked silver, with black streaks running through it.

Lucian sat up so fast I jumped back and bumped into the door. It's a strange feeling—he was my comfort when we were locked up, but now, I felt....unsure. We didn't really know each other. Was I being stupid by trusting him?

He whipped his head from side to side. Seeing how tense and unsure he was, I remembered he'd spent all but a few moments inside that dungeon, and knew immediately that Lucian needed me.

"Shhhh, it's okay Luce." He stopped whipping his head from side to side and turned toward me. I still couldn't see his facial features in the car's dim lighting.

"Smurfy, where the hell are we? Why are we moving like this?" Oh my God, Lucian was freaking out because we were in a car! I reached across blindly, feeling for his hand, and as soon as I touched his hand, he gripped onto mine for dear life.

"We're heading to an airfield, we're in a car. A car is something people use to get them somewhere faster." I felt like an idiot explaining what a car was, but Lucian was like a toddler. Everything was new to him.

"Okay...what's an airfield? Tyler saved me from answering Lucian's question.

"It's a place where planes land and take off; a plane is something that lets you fly through the air. You're about to see for yourself, we just arrived."

I looked out my window, and sure enough, there was a small plane sitting in the middle of a vacant field. The only lighting was the lights on board the small plane.

Tyler drove us right up to the steps that descended from the aircraft. I gripped Lucian's hand tighter; I was scared of the unknown, and where the hell was Tyler taking us?

"Tyler, I don't want to get on that plane." I could hear the fear in my own voice.

"I figured you would say something like that, that's why I brought them." I looked out my window again toward where Tyler was pointing, and that's when I saw them. I released Lucian's hand and threw my door open, leaping from the car like it was on fire and running up the stairs. I was lifted off my feet and embraced in the best hug ever.

"God, it is so good to see you, squirt." Being in Alex's arms never felt better; I was almost immediately tugged away from Alex to be bear-hugged by Chase.

"You have no idea how worried we have been."

Tears leaked out of my eyes; once they started, I couldn't

stop them. Horrible sobs wrecked my body, and I clung to Chase, afraid if I let go, he would disappear.

"I...I...missed...you, I thou-thought y-you l-left m-me." Chase squeezed me tighter.

"We would never leave you, Ry; we have been trying to get you back for weeks." Hearing that they didn't give up on me meant more than they would ever know. A throat clearing behind us interrupted my sob fest; I quickly pulled away from Chase and wiped away my tears as best as I could. Once I had myself under control, I turned around on the stairs and faced Tyler, who had a scared-looking Lucian standing next to him.

I made my way down to them and stood directly in front of Lucian. The lighting still wasn't good, so I couldn't see the color of his eyes, but I could tell Lucian was at least six feet tall. He stood there, tense and staring down at me; he needed me to help him find his way in this new world.

"Thank you for keeping me alive. I owe you my life, Lucian." I heard my cousins gasp behind me. "I promise you, I will never leave you. I will help you find your way in this world and make sure you are cared for and loved."

Lucian placed both his hands on my shoulders. He may only be sixteen, but his next words were those of a grown man.

"I pledge my allegiance and life to you, Smurf. I was giving up hope when you arrived. You have my loyalty from now and until the end of my days." I couldn't talk past the lump in my throat, so I pulled him in for the most awkward hug ever. Lucian clearly had no idea what a hug was or how to even return the gesture, so he stood there, arms raised, until I started to giggle.

Chapter Six

RYAN

We were all seated on the plane with our belts fastened; Lucian was sitting next to me, gripping my hand. I turned to look at him and gasped. Now that we were able to see, thanks to the lights in the cabin, I finally got to look upon his handsome face and saw his unusual eyes. They're violet, with a gray ring around the pupils. He had a ring just like mine! He had the sculpted cheekbones of a magazine model and a perfect straight nose. He appeared to have a similar skin tone as Dom, but I couldn't be sure with the amount of dirt caked on him. Lucian looked down at me and smiled. His teeth were beautiful and straight, and even more strange was the fact that they were gleaming white, I am quite sure he didn't brush his teeth every day.

"We're about to take off. Captain is just loading the last of the bags." I turned away from Lucian to look at Tyler, who had just taken the seat opposite us. He looked so tired and thin. What he did for me today, I could never repay. He went against his own mate to save *me*.

"Thank you, Tyler." He turned to look at me but quickly turned away, staring out the plane window. I knew why he couldn't stand to look at me.

"Thank you for helping me when you didn't have to." I heard Tyler snort from beside me; I turned to glare at him.

"Was something Lucian said funny, Tyler?" Without turning to look at me, he answered.

"Yeah, actually. I knew there was no way in hell you would leave willingly without the trifecta."

"What is a tri-trifecta?" I turned back to Lucian, I had no idea what the hell a trifecta even is. I was saved from answering when the plane started to move.

Lucian gasped and yelled, "What's happening? Why are we moving?"

"It's okay, mate. The plane needs to move in order for us to gain enough speed on the ground so we can launch into the air to fly." My heart swelled at how kind Alex was being toward Lucian. He didn't talk to him like he was a stupid kid but rather with respect . I looked at Chase, who had a look of pure fury on his face.

"Chase, what's wrong?" I asked.

"I swear to fucking God, we are going to kill that fucking leech king for what he has done to you, Ryan. We are also going to fucking torture him first for what he has done to Lucian. I swear to you, bro, Alex and I will make sure you know everything you need to know about the world, we will also make it our mission to help you find out what kind of supernatural you are."

I loved my cousins so much. I told them briefly about how Lucian grew up when we first boarded the plane, they were pissed to hear how he has been a prisoner his whole life. I knew Alex and Chase would help Lucian as much as they could.

"Can I ask you something, Lucian?"

"Yes, Master Chase." Chase glared at Lucian; to Lucian's credit, he didn't flinch.

"Don't ever call me master! You are not a fucking slave!

You're free now, Lucian, don't ever submit to anyone again." I smiled at my cousin. I was so proud of his protectiveness. Lucian nodded his head.

"Okay. thank you, Chase." Chase smiled at Lucian in return.

"So, my question was, why do you call Ryan 'Smurfy?'" I groaned. They are going to fucking mock me about this.

"Because she told me her powers are blue. The lady who raised me told me stories about the blue people called Smurfs." Chase and Alex started laughing so hard that they were both clutching their stomachs; I even saw Tyler's shoulders shaking from the corner of my eye.

Fuck. My. Life.

After a few hours of catching up with my cousins and hearing what they and the *others* had been planning, yes—I was calling them the "others" because I was still salty as fuck that they hadn't come to my rescue.

I was shocked to learn that Nico had been banished back to Farrarie and wasn't allowed back to the Earth realm until the council deemed it was okay.

"We're about to land."

"Land where, exactly, Tyler?" Tyler still wouldn't look at me, and my heart hurt for him. I wish I could comfort him but my appearance just made everything worse.

"Look, I wish I could tell you, but I can't." What the actual fu—. Alex cut off my thought.

"We have been spelled, squirt. We literally cannot tell you. All we can say is that where we are going is the best place for you." I was too exhausted to fight them or try to pry information from them.

After we landed, we all disembarked the aircraft and collected our bags. My cousins took my bags from Jax's compound for me. We didn't go through any security or customs, which I found strange but didn't comment on.

We walked along the tarmac for a few minutes and toward an aircraft hanger, and entered through a side door. Waiting inside was a big SUV. Tyler clicked the key fob in his hand and the car beeped. We loaded our bags in the back and then climbed inside. I was in the backseat, sitting between Chase and Lucian, while Alex rode shotgun and Tyler drove.

After being in the car for roughly four hours, Tyler pulled off the highway and took us to a McDonalds drive-thru. Lucian's eyes lit up at seeing the fast food restaurant. I had to explain to him how it all worked and how to order food from the menu. Lucian couldn't decide what to order, so Chase ordered for him, and after collecting our food, Tyler continued to drive us onto our destination.

"Oh my God, this is so good." I chuckled at Lucian's facial expressions. He was biting from random items and moaning and exclaiming in delight in between. Chase ordered him two Big Mac combos, four cheeseburgers, twenty-four nuggets, and three different flavors of thick shakes. Lucian was in food heaven.

After eating the best food I have had in weeks, and finally feeling full, I relaxed back into my seat. My eyes kept drifting shut, and I didn't fight the pull of sleep anymore; I let it lull me into a dreamless slumber.

Chapter Seven

Jackson's compound felt cold and empty without Ryan here. I stood in the room she had been staying in, and noticed all her belongings were gone. Did Jackson move them? Did some low life steal her stuff?

A knock on the door pulled me from my thoughts; I turned around to see Melakai standing in the open doorway.

Kai looked the same physically, but I could see in his gray-blue eyes that a war was going on inside him. He ran his hand through his blond hair, making it stick up haphazardly. We stood there staring at each other for a long while, neither of us saying anything. We used to be so fucking close; he was my right hand man growing up, but now, it felt like we were worlds apart.

Kai entered the room and closed the door behind him; I sat on the single chair by the window while Kai leaned against the far wall with his arms crossed over his chest.

"Are you going to tell me why I'm blocked from entering the portal?" I could hear the hurt lacing his tone, and I felt a flash of anger at Ryan for leaving me to explain this to Kai. He is going to go ape-shit, and I don't blame him.

"I did it to protect you." He scoffed and rolled his eyes.

"Don't fucking bullshit me, Nico, am I banned because you're angry at me?"

"No." I said, shaking my head.

"Because you're pissed that I'm still a vamp?"

"No."

"Okay, is it because I fucked your wife?" Son of a fucking bitch, I jumped to my feet, shocked to find that Kai and I were nearly nose to nose, I didn't hear him move. "Why am I fucking locked out of my home, Nico?" Kai was yelling in my face.

"I can't—"

"You fucking spineless prick, answer me!"

"I...I..." How do I tell him that my wife betrayed him in the worst possible way?

"Fucking tell him!" Both Kai and I turned our heads toward the doorway to see both Dom and Jax standing there. Taking a deep breath and steeling my spine, I looked Melakai in the eyes and the truth spilled out.

"Ryan changed the spell that brought you back. She wiped all your fae blood out so you would be full vamp. Which means only Randall's blood remains inside you, so if I let you into Farrarie, you will die."

Kai's face changed. There was no look of anger or sadness... just acceptance. My heart broke; I would have rather him be angry and lash out than just accept what was done to him. I loved Ryan and missed her so much, but right now I was so pissed at her for doing this to my brother.

"Why?"

"Why what, Kai?"

"Why did she change the spell?" he gritted out through clenched teeth, his tone was flat and emotionless.

"Because the spell you wanted her to use wouldn't have worked. Her father told her to change the spell in a dream; he said that you needed to be king of the vampires, and this way, being Randall's blood heir, no one can contest your claim to the throne." Jax and Dom haven't said a word—the one time Dom chooses to stay quiet is the one time I wish he wouldn't. I see the moment it all sinks in: his eyes mist and I have never seen such a broken look grace Kai's face before, not even when he was turned into a vampire. I place my hand on his shoulder to try and comfort him, but he shucked it off and retreated back to the other side of the room, sliding down the wall, cupping his face between his hands.

I have never felt like a worthless piece of shit more than I do now; I have not only shattered his dream of returning home but also taking away any hope he had of ever being returned to his true form.

"Melakai, brother we are all here with you, no matter what." Dom was trying to comfort Kai.

"You will always have a home here, with me and the wolves." Dom glared at Jax. The last thing Kai wanted was to be told he could live here when all he wanted for decades was to return to the fae realm and be among his people again instead of being the "day walking leech."

"I will find a way to fix this brother, I swear. I will not return to Farrarie until you are able to as well."

What the fuck is Dom saying? He couldn't make that kind of promise. "Dominic..."

Dom turned to glare at me, his eyes flashing to the gray of his wolf's.

"You do not get to speak right now. You may not have been the one to do this to him, but you will still bear some of the blame." I hung my head in shame. He was right. If I hadn't skirted around the truth so much with Ryan, she might have come to me and asked for help.

"Lift the spell on Farrarie, Nico, so he can go back."

I wish it was that simple. "I can't Jackson. I wish I could."

"What the fuck does that mean?" Jax snapped.

"It means that when he cast the spell he drew on the power of the elders and the power of the harvest moon. The elders may be the strongest of our kinds, but that spell cost the elders a great deal of power. It took them years to recover."

"Can Ryan do it? She is supposed to be the most powerful supe." That was an intriguing thought; Jackson might be onto something.

"She could. She would need someone to balance her, though." Ryan would need someone to stabilize her power in order for her to remove the spell. If she were to do it on her own, it could kill her.

"Why can't you do it?"

"I can't do it, Jax; the power inside me that is linked to Ryan has to be returned so she is at full strength. I hate to admit it, but I'm not strong enough on my own to stabilize her." I was ashamed to admit that out loud, even to my brothers.

"I'll do it." I turned to look at Dom, shocked. He wasn't strong enough either, to hold that amount of power back from consuming Ryan.

Before we could debate more, there was a knock on the open door, and Lucas, one of Jackson's pack members, stood there.

"What is it, Lucas?" Jax asked.

"The elders have requested your presence in the mess hall, Alpha. All of you. The vampire and witch elders are here, as well."

What the fuck was going on? Why were the elders here?

Chapter Eight

RYAN

When I woke from a dreamless sleep sometime later, the sun was up and it was a glorious day. I looked either side of me and saw that Lucian and Chase were both still asleep. Looking to the front of the car, I saw that Alex was now driving and Tyler was sleeping soundly in the passenger seat. Yawning and stretching my arms over my head as best I could in the cramped space, I cringed. I really needed to pee. I always had to go as soon as I awoke.

"Alex, I really need to pee," I whined. I met his eyes in the rearview mirror, and he looked exhausted. How long had he been driving?

"Okay, Squirt, I'll stop at the next gas station." I hoped that wasn't to far, because my bladder was about to burst.

Twenty minutes later, I was bouncing my knee and gritting my teeth.

"Alex just pull over, I need to go now!" Alex grumbled about tiny bladders, but did as I asked and pulled over near some bushes and trees. It feels like we're in the middle of nowhere, no other cars or housing to be seen. Alex hopped out of the car so I could crawl over the center console, not wanting to wake Chase or Lucian to get out.

As soon as my feet hit the pavement, I ran behind the bushes and quickly went about my business, sighing at the instant relief.

After finishing, I made my way back to the car, only to notice the others were awake and standing outside the car, stretching.

"You are such a lady, peeing in a bush and all," Chase said, chuckling.

"She's probably the first queen to ever pop a squat in the bush." At Tyler's comment, all four of the guys started laughing, and my cheeks flamed red. I was going to beat the shit out of Tyler one day—very soon, hopefully.

"Well, some of us can't turn into a wolf and cock our leg to pee!" I snapped at Tyler, which only made them laugh harder. Gritting my teeth, I stomped back to the SUV, shoulder checking Tyler on my way past. The fucker just laughed.

We drove a couple more hours before we stopped at a local convenience store to grab some junk food for our breakfast. Tyler had a fast metabolism due to being a wolf, so he had to eat often. My left butt cheek was numb, and I was getting restless sitting in the car for so long. The confined space of the vehicle only emphasized how bad Lucian and I reeked from not showering. The smell had to be worse for Tyler, with his enhanced senses, but he didn't comment on it. He just kept his window down so he got fresh air.

"How much further, Alex?" I whined.

"Squirt, you have asked me that like ten times in the past three hours. It's a nineteen hour drive from Toronto to where we are going. We had to take the long way in case your husband and his band of misfits tried to follow us." Hearing Alex call the others misfits stung a bit; I was pissed at them, but they were good people. They were my only friends, and I cared about them.

"Just so you will shut up, we have like two more hours and then we'll be there!" I poked my tongue out at Tyler, but I was glad to have a time frame. He still didn't need to be a dick about it.

Upon entering the mess hall with my three brothers, we stopped in the entryway. I haven't seen all the elders together like this since my crowning as king.

"Boy's come join us." Looking to Mr. Silver, who was nodding toward four vacant chairs that were front and center. I released the breath I was holding and made my way over. We sat down and looked to the elders, waiting.

They all wore their traditional black cloaks, most of them with their hoods up except for the main elders. Mr. Silver was the main elder for the shifters. Jax, Kai, and I were all on the elder council but we weren't the leaders; we were given a seat among them but the truth was our votes didn't mean shit. Dom wasn't on the elder council because he wouldn't choose which race he wanted to represent. Dom may be a shifter and fae, but his powers were a cross between warlock and fae. Dom was an anomaly, just like Ryan. I have no idea how he is able to cast and wield magic like a warlock but still open portals and manipulate the elements like a fae.

Lachlan stood in front of the vampire elders with his hood

down, Standing in front of the witches was Ryan's Uncle David, Chase and Alex's father.

I felt a pang in my chest when I turned my gaze to the fae elders, knowing that Gabriel wouldn't be among them.

He died in the blast at the chapel the night of my wedding. Victor now led the fae elders, and he was a power-hungry son-of-a-bitch. I noticed the witches weren't wearing the moon stones they had on the night of my wedding. Interesting.

"Why aren't Stevie Knox and Randall Cane here?" Jax asked the elders.

"We'll explain that shortly, son. We need to ask you boys a few things first." All four of us nodded our heads at Mr. Silver. "Lachlan, did you want to fill the boys in or should I?" I still found it comical how Mr. Silver called us boys; I am 104 years old. Kai and Dom are both 102 and Jax is the youngest at age 98. We weren't boys anymore.

"I will tell them," Lachlan said, nodding his head to Mr. Silver. "The reason we are here without the queen of the Knox coven and the king of the vampires is because we believe there is more to this story than they have shared. As you can see, the number of elders here are less than normal. Some died at your wedding and some cannot be trusted." I looked over the number of elders and was shocked that Lachlan was right—over half were missing. The elder council was made up of thirteen members for each clan, the vamps had six, the witches had nine, the shifters had ten and the fae had eight elders present.

"What do you mean *can't be trusted?*"

"What we have to say, young alpha, could cost us our lives. The queen and king believe we are here to bargain with you." What the fuck? I saw Kai tense next to me.

"We are not trading our brother!" Dom growled.

"Son!" Mr. Silver snapped at Dom.

"Nah, Dad, fuck that! We are not trading Kai for Ryan.

Has he not suffered enough for her? We were lucky they tried to screw us over with Nina; if not, Kai would be dead, or worse!"

"Watch your language Dominic!" To Dom's credit, he didn't shy away or flinch at his father's alpha tone; he just sat there glaring at his father. I had to break the tension in the room—the way Dom was looking at his father and holding eye contact for so long would be seen as a challenge for the alpha of the New York pack.

"Okay, let us speak like grown folk. Dom, calm down, we are not trading Kai." I looked directly at Lachlan when I spoke.

"Correct, we do not plan to take Randall's heir from you. We told them we had come here to try and convince you to trade the location of the portal for your wife." Kai growled low in his throat at the mention of being Randall's heir.

The only elder that knew of the real portal's location was Gabriel. Something felt off with Victor and Lachlan. I couldn't explain the feeling, but I just knew in my gut I couldn't trust them with the location.

"We have come to try and help you."

"Help us how?" Jax asked the vampire elder. I noticed Jax kept scenting the air; he was trying to pick up on any lies.

"To help you stop the coven queen and vampire king. We, as elder members, have sat back too long and let them get away with too much. We learned a lot about our king recently. We still do not have proof that he is indeed trying to seal the portal to your realm. We also have no proof as of yet that Stevie Knox is trying to help him do it, either."

"Well, if you have no fucking proof, why the hell are you here, then? We gave you all the proof we had! They openly admitted it to us; Stevie Knox has even said herself that she wants all fae dead and blames them for her father's death, when in fact she killed Ralph Knox!" Jackson was vibrating with anger. He was right—we had told all the elders this before and none of them believed us.

"How the hell do you know she killed my brother?" David Knox was glowing purple; I forgot we only told the shifter, fae, and vampire elders about Stevie killing her father.

"She told us. Well, she told Ryan, but we were all there and heard it."

"What exactly did she say, boy?" David snapped at Jax, who started growling.

"Ian Silver may get away with calling us boys, but you will not! I am the fucking alpha of all alphas, and you will show me some fucking respect while you are on my land!" Holy shit, I have never seen Jackson so alpha-ed out before. David Knox bowed his head.

"Forgive me, alpha. As you can imagine, I was told that the fae had murdered my brother, and now I find out it was my niece." David hung his head in sorrow. Ralph Knox was his only sibling, and he had known Stevie her entire life.

"I can assure you, Mr. Knox, my people and I had nothing to do with your brother's death. Ralph Knox was a good man. I would never have hurt him in any way." David nodded his head but didn't comment.

"We don't have time for this, I'm sorry—" Dom cut Lachlan off.

"Where are your sons, Mr. Knox?" I hadn't even thought to ask the coven elder that, go Dom for being on point. David tensed at the mention of his sons.

"I-I don't know." I didn't believe him for one second.

"Lie!" Jackson growled, and David snapped his gaze to Jax. "I can hear your heartbeat. It skips a beat when you lie. I can also scent a lie, so do you wanna try that answer again?"

"He can't tell you, Alpha. He has been spelled to secrecy. We are here because we believe that David being spelled and not able to disclose his son's location is because they are with Ryan." *What the actual fuck?*

"What do you mean?" I ground out.

"I'm sorry to have to be the one to tell you, your majesty, but your wife is no longer in the care of the vampire elders."

"Oh, shit!" Yeah, you could say that again Dominic.

Chapter Ten

RYAN

Finally, after so many hours traveling, we arrived at our destination. We drove down a long gravel driveway, lined with huge pine trees on either side. After a few minutes, we came around another bend and a massive—I mean *massive*—log cabin came into view. It was at least three stories and looked well-tended. It had huge log pillars and broad windows that would allow you to see the beautiful view, with an A-frame roof that allowed for plenty of shade.

If this house looked this good on the outside, I couldn't wait to see the inside.

"Where are we?" I whispered.

"Welcome to the Yukon, Ry." I had no idea where Yukon is, but I would live here if I could have this cabin.

Alex finally stopped the SUV in front of the stairs that lead up to the porch, and we all shuffled out of the car. I looked to the side and noticed a six-car garage situated behind the house. Who the hell needed six cars?

I turned to look back the way we came and all I could see was trees and mountains. This place was freaking beautiful; the air was so crisp and clean, the sun was shining down on us, and even though there was a chill in the air, I was just grateful to be outside and free.

I heard a throat clearing behind me and turned. Standing on the top of the steps was an elderly man and woman. When the woman's gaze landed on me, her hand came up and covered her mouth. She was shocked? Who the hell are these people?

Alex and Chase both dashed up the stairs and embraced the man and woman, happy sounds coming from both pairs.

The old man looked familiar. He was tall, but not as tall as my cousins. He had salt and pepper hair that was slicked back, with high cheekbones and a straight but narrow nose. He wore a flannel shirt with dark blue jeans that matched his eyes.

The woman next to him was petite; she only came up to the man's chest. She had gray curly hair that came down to her shoulders, and she wore a sweater and black leggings with knee-high boots. She had good style for an old lady. I lifted my gaze to her face. She had plump red lips and a small button nose. My gaze met hers and I gasped—they were a deep green. I stumbled back and smacked into something or someone. I turned to peer over my shoulder and saw it was Lucian I stumbled into. I quickly turned back toward the porch to see both my cousins standing behind the man and lady, the man and woman were both staring straight at me. The woman had tears trailing down her face, but the man looked unfazed.

"Smurfy, are you okay?"

"I-I think so," I answered Lucian.

"Who are they, Smurf?" I didn't know how to answer that. I am pretty sure I know who the man and woman are, but I didn't want to say it out loud and be wrong.

"Come here, child," the old man said.

Lucian came around beside me and gripped my hand, leading me to the bottom of the steps. I craned my neck back and looked up.

"She looks just like him, Marcus," the old lady said with a warble in her voice. As soon as she said his name, I knew I was right. I steeled my spine and looked at the man.

"Hi, I'm Ryan. I believe you are Marcus and Bethany Knox, my grandparents, who I thought were dead."

Bethany dropped her hand from her mouth and made her way down to me. She cupped my face between both her hands and leaned forward till she was resting her forehead against mine.

"I have been waiting a long time to finally meet you, my dear. I am so sorry for all of the secrecy, but we couldn't afford for anyone to find out that I am alive."

"What do you mean?" I asked.

"We had to run and hide so you would live. I am a seer, Ryan, and so was your father."

Chapter Eleven

NICO

I clenched and unclenched my fist so many times to try and quiet the anger inside of me. Where the fuck was Ryan?

"What happened?" I growled.

"The day that Randall and Stevie went to trade Nina for Melakai was the day Ryan escaped." That was nearly three days ago. "Randall and Stevie have been trying to find her ever since."

"How did she escape, Lachlan?" Dom asked.

"We believe Tyler Evans helped her escape." I clutched my head between my hands. Where is she? Why didn't she come back to me?

"Why do I feel like we are missing something?"

I turned and looked at Kai. This is the first time he has spoken since we began this meeting. Lachlan sighed, and David, Victor, and Mr. Silver all shared a look with each other before Victor answered.

"Stevie and Randall found all the decoy portals. They are closing in on the location of the real one."

"That doesn't matter, though, if they don't have Ryan, right? They can't close it without her?"

"We don't know. With the new power the Knox witch now wields, we are unsure. If she does find the portal, she may not have the power to close it, but she does have the power to poison our world." Victor was right; Stevie didn't need to enter my world to kill it. She could stand on this side of the portal and rain hell on my kingdom.

"Shit, okay. If Stevie does find the portal, how long do we have before our world is beyond saving?" I asked Victor.

"I estimate they will find the location of the portal in the next two or three months, sire. They have been relentless in their search. She could kill our world within a month or two of finding it."

"Okay so what you're saying, Vic, is that we have about five to six months, tops, to try stop these fuckers and then find Ryan and train her to kill her sister. Is there anything else?"

The way Dom put it made it sound so fucked up. We didn't have much time at all. I need to try and find a way to stop Randall; if we can take Randall out, then Kai will rule the vamps, and that would leave Stevie on her own. All Ryan would need to do is take the coven back and then get rid of her sister. I wouldn't let my world die no matter what.

"Maybe if you could tell us where the portal is we could help you?" I gazed up at Victor, who wore an unreadable expression. I turned to look at my brother's; each of them had a look in their eyes telling me not to do it.

"If the time comes for you to need to know the location, then I will tell you." Victor seemed annoyed at my response but quickly masked the look on his face.

"Why aren't you wearing the moonstones?" Jax asked David.

"The moonstones have been returned to where they belong. There is no need to worry about them, Alpha." David's answer felt like it had a double meaning.

The four of us and the elders sat for hours, making plans. Get Ryan back, kill Randall, and then destroy Stevie.

I thought it was a bloody good plan, but the hardest part was trying to find Ryan.

The witches had tried doing a location spell already; it was like she had fallen off the face of the Earth. My stomach sunk; what if Tyler killed her? My stomach was in knots with worry. She was finally mine, and now I may have lost her forever.

Chapter Tweleve

RYAN

After my grandma dropped her bomb, we all made our way inside the cabin. Tyler had yet to say a word but simply trailed inside behind the rest of us. As soon as we entered the cabin, I gasped. I was right, it was just as beautiful inside as it was outside. There were antlers and huge timber beams, and gorgeous indigenous blankets hanging on the wall. I saw a sitting room to the left and stairs that led upstairs, but we didn't get a chance to stop or look at any of the other rooms.

My grandpa led us straight into the kitchen, which was freaking huge. I mean, this is the type of kitchen Gordon Ramsey would have in his house. I stopped looking around and followed the others over to a massive rectangular table that could seat twelve. It looked like someone had carved it from a tree trunk. The chairs were handmade, and no two were the same. The backs of the chairs were tree branches, all interlaced. I took a seat on the opposite side of Chase and Alex, and Lucian sat on my left and Tyler took the seat on my right. I was shocked he would even sit next to me. Grandma and Grandpa sat at each end of the table.

I looked from my grandparents and then to the others and

cringed. Lucian and I were filthy and covered in so much dirt and blood. The blood Tyler had given me may have healed my broken bones, but residual pain remained.

I schooled my features so the others wouldn't know I felt weak; when I had a moment to myself I would inspect my injuries properly.

My Grandpa cleared his throat and then spoke, looking directly at me.

"I know this is all a shock, but we don't have the luxury of time to sit here and hold your hand. Your grandmother has seen what needs to be done in order to save your husband's world. I will train you and so will she—"

I cut Grandpa off, which earned me a scary as fuck glare from the old man. Whoops. "I thought Dom, Aurora and Nico were the only ones who could help me?" Grandpa shook his head.

"No dear, the young seer let you believe that," said Grandma. I turned to Tyler, and the look on his face told me all I needed to know. He knew.

"I don't understand why Aurora would do that," I stated.

"She did what needed to be done. My sister is a powerful seer and knows she cannot *ever* interfere with her visions. She had to lead you to believe that she, Dom, and Nico would train you, when all along she knew you would need to be trained by your grandparents. Dom and Nico are not equipped to help you." It was the first time Tyler had spoken since we arrived. My mind was reeling with this new information.

"She knew Stevie would take me, didn't she?" I looked from Tyler to both my grandparents. They all nodded. I felt so betrayed; she knew what would happen to me at the hands of Randall and Stevie and still let it happen.

"The young seer has much to learn, dear. She was only doing what she thought was best, do not blame her." I looked to my grandmother and got lost in her eyes for a moment. My father got his eyes from her. I felt my tears building, I took a few deep breaths to stop the tears from falling. Lucian clasped my hand under the table and gave me a reassuring squeeze, letting me know he was there for me.

"Did you even go?" Both my grandparents wore looks of confusion.

"Go where, dear?" my grandmother asked.

"To my father's funeral, or did you both hide here?" My grandmother gasped, and my grandfather pounded his fist on the table and leaned forward, scowling at me, I glared back at the old man. Tyler growled low in his throat as a warning to my grandfather. Why the hell was Tyler trying to defend me?

"You may be blood of my blood, but you will not disrespect me or my wife in our home! You have no idea what sacrifices we had to make in order to keep your father alive as long as we did!" I sighed and gave a short nod. He was right, just because I was hurting didn't give me the right to lash out.

"Grandpa, she's been through a lot." I appreciated Chase trying to stick up for me.

"She doesn't need you all handling her with kid gloves. The more you coddle her, the weaker you make her. She needs to fight her own battles; she cannot win this war if you all try and fight it for her."

I got what he was trying to say. I have never been on my own. After Mom disappeared, I went straight to my sister. When I ran from Stevie, I had my cousins and the guys with me.

"She doesn't need to be on her own, sir. I refuse to let her fight on her own. She is not weak! She is so strong. I don't know any of you, but I do know Smurf, and she is stronger than you all think." Tears trailed down my cheeks, and Lucian's sweet words had warmth spreading through my chest. I squeezed his hand in silent thanks for having my back. I saw Grandpa's sly grin out of the corner of my eye. He lifted his gaze to my grandmother.

"You were right once again, Bethy, the boy will balance her." Huh?

"What do you mean, Grandpa?" Alex took the question right out of my mouth.

"Lucian is the *real* key to helping Ryan stay alive in this war."

Chapter Thirteen

RYAN

After Grandpa dropped his cryptic as fuck bomb, he insisted we were all shown to our rooms. On the second floor, there were five rooms. Grandma and Grandpa occupied the third level by themselves. My room was at the end of the hall. Alex and Chase had the rooms on the left, and Tyler and Lucian had the two rooms on the right side of the hallway. My room was stunning, with a king-sized bed in the middle of the room. It wasn't as big as the one I was staying in at Jax's, but this one felt more homey.

There were side drawers on either side of the bed, topped with lamps. My bags sat at the foot of the bed, and I walked past them to peer out the window. The view was gorgeous. All you could see were mountains and trees covered in snow. Yukon was a stunning place.

I moved away from the window to inspect the rest of the room. There are two doors on the other side of the room, I found that one led to a walk-in closet and the other led to my own private bathroom.

I could not wait another second to clean the filth off my body. The tub looked so inviting, but a glance down at myself told me it was best to shower rather than sitting in my own muck. Quickly, I shucked off my clothes and turned to the mirror over the sink.

Underneath the filth that covered my body, I could see countless bruises and cuts. It looked like I had gone five rounds with Mike Tyson. I had two black eyes, my upper lip was split, and I had dried blood on the side of my temple. Vampire blood will keep you from dying but it isn't like traveling back in time. And it definitely doesn't remove the memories.

I shook off the encroaching memories and worked on figuring out the faucet.

Once the steam was billowing inside the shower stall, I finally stepped in and sighed. The water felt amazing cascading down my body; the shower had the perfect amount of pressure.

After a few moments of standing under the spray, my joints and muscles started to relax. After standing there for a solid five minutes, just letting the hot water wash over me, I decided it was time to wash away the grime covering my body. I shampooed my hair twice and conditioned it a couple times. I used the bar soap to scrub my body, then I used the pump soap for one final wash. I found a razor in the shower that looked new, so I used it.

By the time I stepped out of the shower, my hands were prunes and my skin was an angry red, but I was truly clean.

I quickly dried myself then wrapped one towel around my body and used another to wrap my hair.

In my suitcase I found a comfy pair of sweats and my brush. God, did my hair need a good brushing. I couldn't find an acceptably comfortable shirt in my suitcase, so I switched over to the duffel bag. I pulled out the first shirt I found, but I saw what shirt it was, I dropped it to the wooden floor like it burned me.

I stood there staring at the damn shirt like it was going to talk to me or something. It was the black shirt Nico had worn the night he stayed with me in my room, after our dream together.

Taking a deep breath and giving myself a mental pep talk, I quickly bent down and plucked the shirt off the floor. My brain was telling me to chuck the shirt out the window, but my heart was telling me to sniff it and see if it still smelled like him. My heart won, and the shirt still held Nico's faint scent.

My eyes began to water, and then a second later, tears fell in a rush. I crumpled into a heap on the floor, clutching my husband's shirt to chest, wishing he was here with me.

Nico would hold me and tell me everything is going to be okay. He would stand by my side. I missed him so fucking much. I even missed Dom, Jax, and Kai. I missed the girls as well. I wanted to go *home*.

I snapped out of my thoughts when I felt two strong arms come around me and lift me off the floor, I quickly blinked away the tears so I could see who it is, and was surprised at my rescuer.

"W-what a-are y-you doing, Ty?"

"If you're gonna break down, at least do it somewhere comfortable." Tyler placed me on top of my bed then made his way over to my bags. Within a second, a shirt hit me square in the face.

"Put that on, would you." Oh my God, I was practically naked in front of Tyler. I quickly pulled the shirt over my head, while Tyler's back was to me, I slipped the sweat pants on next. I can feel the blush heating my cheeks. Not trusting my voice, I clear my throat to indicate that I am decent.

Ty doesn't face me, but instead he makes his way over to the window and stands there staring out. I see he has showered and changed as well. He looks better than when I first saw him at Randall's.

"You know, when I first met you, I didn't like you." I wish I could say I was shocked. "But as time went on and I got to know you through your sister, I realized that Stevie was the bad twin, not you." Ty hung his head. He still wouldn't turn and face me.

"I betrayed my mate by saving you."

"Why did you do that? Why did you save me?"

"Because I have known from the start about my sister's vision. I had a part to play in making sure that you would live and escape Randall's mansion. I just didn't bank on falling in love with my mate. It hurts so much to be away from her. My wolf is trying to break free and run back to her. It is taking everything in me to not shift right now."

My heart hurt for Tyler. He gave up his pack, his sister, his friends, and his mate to help save me. I stood from the bed and made my way over to him, wrapping my arms around his waist and resting my head on his back. He stiffened at the contact, but after a minute relaxed.

"I am so sorry for everything you have gone through, Ty. I wish I could change it, but I can't. Thank you for saving me and for everything that you have done to make sure you were where you needed to be in order to save me."

Chapter Fourteen

RYAN

After Tyler left, I quickly brushed my hair and then stuffed Nico's shirt under my pillow to cuddle tonight when I slept. I exited my room and quickly went to the first door on my right and knocked.

"Come in!"

I opened the door and then stopped in my tracks. Holy fucking shitballs! Lucian was H.O.T. He wore a pair of jeans that hung low on his hips and a white T-shirt that clung to him. Lucian was thin from years of starvation, but fuck me, if that shirt was tight now, wait a few months and it would be bursting at the seams.

I continued my appraisal of my friend and saw that he didn't have as many bruises and cuts as I did, which I was glad for. It was still so weird seeing him face to face. Lucian's hair was washed and back up in its man bun, and his silver black hair was gorgeous. His eyes were so captivating, too—violet with a gray ring around the pupil. I'm not totally certain, but I have a feeling that he is fae or part fae.

"How did you like the shower?"

Lucian grins like a kid in a candy store. "It was the best

thing I have ever done in my life. The water never fills! It just keeps going down the hole. I was dirty before, and then after washing with some liquid stuff, I am now clean. I even saw what I looked like in the mirror." He sounded so happy, and it warmed my heart. I made my way over to the big guy and wrapped him in a hug, which he returned this time. A throat clearing had us pulling apart. I turned to see who was at the door and groaned. Both my cousins stood there with shit-eating grins on their faces.

"How fucking cool would it be if our cousin divorced the king of the fairies?" Alex and Chased both laughed and I groaned, and Lucian just frowned.

"Your husband is from Farrarie?" How did Lucian know about Farrarie?

"Uh...yeah. He's the king of the fae." Lucian's face lit up like a Christmas tree. He gripped me by my shoulders and leaned down so we were eye to eye.

"The lady that raised me told me that my mom and dad came from that place. Maybe your husband could help me find out who my parents were." Oh my goodness, I was right. Lucian is a fae!

"You have my word, buddy. I will make it my mission to help you find your parents."

We are all sitting around the dining room table in the same seats we sat in this morning, having the most awkward dinner of my life. No one said a word except for me explaining to Lucian how to use a knife and fork. The only sound in the room was cutlery scraping across plates. My eyes kept darting between my grandparents, waiting to see which one of them would break the awkward silence.

"Oh, for heaven's sake, Marcus! Stop acting like a child." I snapped my gaze to my freaking badass grandmother. She was awesome, standing up to Gramps like that.

"What would you have me say, Bethany?" Grams continued to glare at her husband; I saw his eyes flicker from side to side to see if anyone was going to jump to his defense. Chase and Alex kept staring at their plates like they were watching a movie in them. Lucian continued to inhale his food, totally oblivious to the tension, and Tyler and I both stared openly at my grandparents.

"Speak to her Marcus! She is your granddaughter for God sake. Stop blaming her!" What the hell was Gramps blaming me for? What did I do?

"I can't! She is the reason my son is dead!" Oh God, Gramps blamed me for my father's death. I felt five pairs of eyes on me, and I was struggling to hold myself together. I cleared my throat and pushed back from the table.

"Thank you very much for the delicious dinner, Grams" My grandmother smiled at my nickname for her, but her eyes radiated sadness. "I think I'm just going to go take a walk."

I rushed from the room and headed for the door we entered through today, snagging a random jacket off the coat rack and slipping into my shoes that I left there earlier. I ran as fast and as far as I could, tears falling freely down my face. My grandfather hated me; he blamed me for my father's death. Gramps was right, if my dad had just killed me, he would still be alive today.

Chapter Fifteen

RYAN

I've been sitting next to this stream for hours; the only lighting out here was from the moon. I refused to go back to that cabin. I would make Tyler take me back to Nico. I tried screaming Nico, Kai, and Dom's names when I first found this stream. I thought maybe Nico would feel me through our *hugacko* bond. I was so upset and angry earlier, and I thought my magic might spark back to life.

I haven't felt or even had access to my magic since the night of my wedding. The only person who knows this is Lucian. I couldn't save or destroy a world if I didn't have any magic, and at this point, I was counting that as a win.

I heard a branch snap behind, but I didn't turn. I didn't need to. I just knew it was him.

"Your father would come out here as a child. It was his favorite spot to think." I heard Gramps sigh behind me, but I didn't move. "Ryan, I'm sorry. It isn't your fault my son lost his life."

"You're right, though; he did die because of me." My father lost his life because he wouldn't kill me. If he had killed me,

Stevie wouldn't have had any darkness inside her and the fae realm wouldn't be at risk.

"He died *for* you. Your father knew his end was coming, and he made sure he was ready for it. Your father died a warrior and a king. Do not dishonor his memory by quitting."

I balled my hands into fists and jumped to my feet, glaring at my grandfather. How fucking dare he!

"You have no idea what I have been through, or what I have had to live through. I gave my word that I wouldn't quit, and I never break my word. I will end my sister for what she did to my dad, and I will save the fae realm. Now you can either help me or step aside." Wait, could he even help me? I still didn't even know why the hell we were here, honestly. A small smile graced Gramps's face.

"There's that Knox fire! That attitude right there is what is going to win you the war. I will help you wield your power, and your grandmother will teach you spells. I will not coddle you or hold your hand. You will train from sun up to sun down every day. We have three to four months to get you ready and back to Alaska to save *your* realm and end that sister of yours." Holy shit, Grams and Gramps were going to train me? I had a few terms of my own to list first before I agreed.

"I have some conditions." Gramps raised his brows, but I continued. "You have to help train Lucian as well. I'll agree to your four-month training but no longer. And when we leave for Alaska, you and Grams have to come too." I saw Gramps tense. "Please, if I am to lead the Knox coven, I need your help, Grandpa." Gramps chuckled and started shaking his head.

"You truly are your father's daughter. He could always get me to agree to anything. I agree to train the boy. If your grandmother agrees, then we will return to Wonder Lake. We will remain there for three months to help you, then we will return. This is our home now, and this is the house where we brought our sons for vacations. The memories here are precious to us." I didn't know that. There was so much I didn't know about my family, and it was starting to fucking annoy me. I stuck my hand out and Grandpa shook it, sealing the deal.

"Uh, Grandpa? I forgot to mention that I can't access my powers. I haven't been able to access them since the night of my wedding." Gramps smiled down at me and winked. He fucking *winked*.

"That's what happens when you have a neutralizer for a cellmate."

Chapter Sixteen

RYAN

The next morning, Gramps woke us at dawn, as promised, banging on our bedroom doors. Groaning, I rolled over and slid my legs over the side of the bed. I moved to stand but tripped over something on the floor and face-planted.

This was not my morning!

Groaning, I sat up and reached for the object that I had tripped on. My bad mood evaporated when I saw Lucian sleeping on the floor next to my bed. I had tripped over *him*.

He looked so peaceful. He didn't deserve the life he had lived. Lucian was sweet and kind. I heard Gramps shouting that we had better move our asses, so I leaned forward and shook Lucian till he woke. When his eyes opened, I smiled.

"Morning, sunshine. We have to get up and start our training today." Lucian didn't complain or comment on why he slept on the floor next to me. He got up, took his blanket and pillow, and left. I quickly got dressed, brushed my teeth and then made my way downstairs.

I met Gramps, Tyler, Lucian, and my cousins in the huge sitting room. I dropped down next to Lucian on one of the couches and waited for Gramps to speak.

"You will be up and ready at this time every morning and that includes feeding yourself." It was *five-thirty in the morning*! That means I would have to get up at five each day just to get fed and dressed before it was training time.

"Today we are going to work on basic hand-to-hand combat. If for some reason you can't access your magic or you have depleted your power for a short time, you will need to be able to defend yourself in combat." This made perfect sense. My magic was so unpredictable that I definitely needed to learn hand-to-hand combat stat.

"You will all train and help each other. Ryan, Chase, and Alex—you three will work together on combat training. Lucian, you and I will work together to try to figure out how your power will work."

"Ah, sorry, sir. I don't even know what I am or who I am." Lucian hung his head in shame, and my heart broke for my friend. I felt so protective of Lucian, and right now I needed to help him by taking the attention off him.

"So how about you all tell me how Tyler knew about you and Grams, and why Alex and Chase couldn't tell me about you?" Gramps looked to the other three males, who wouldn't meet his gaze.

"I'm not one to mince words, so I'll get right to it. Tyler has known from the start because of his sister. Why he kept quiet is a mystery to even me. Alex and Chase have been spelled from a young age to never mention us. We left the Knox coven after your grandmother had a vision; the only way for you to be born and for your father to live as long as he did was because we left." Okay, straight to the point and no mucking around, noted.

Gramps led us all outside and sent the four of us to train while he and Lucian made their way into the woods. Anxiety churned in my stomach. I didn't like Lucian being away from me. Ever since we escaped Randall's, I have felt this need to keep Lucian close to me. I trusted that Gramps would keep him safe, but my anxiety wouldn't let up until Lucian was beside me again.

I followed the three guys over to the huge garage, where Alex pushed a button on the remote and one of the six roller doors lifted, revealing a home gym set up inside. Alex turned the lights on, and with a clearer view, I saw that there was only one car parked inside—the rest of the space was used as a gym.

There was so much gym equipment in here: weight benches, treadmills, exercise bikes, and more. We bypassed all of the machines and moved over to the gym mats that were set up on the floor, which took up two of the parking bays. The three boys started removing their shoes and socks, so I followed their lead and did the same. Tyler made his way to the middle of the mats, and Chase followed. Alex led me over to a couple of plastic chairs. I sat down and turned to ask Alex what the hell was happening but Tyler spoke.

"Okay, Ryan, Chase and I are going to spar, and we'll show you a few self-defense moves. When you can master these moves, we will then progress to attack training." I had nothing to say to that, so I just nodded and settled back into my seat to watch them go at it.

Tyler and Chase began to circle each other, hands raised in front of their faces.

Alex told me to watch their foot work and to keep an eye on

how they kept their guard up constantly and never lowered their hands. Tyler was circling Chase like he was hunting, and Tyler watched Chase with keen eyes, just waiting for Chase to make a move or drop his guard so he could attack. Chase stepped toward Tyler with his fist out, ready to strike, but Tyler was so quick on his feet that he spun in a circle and ended up behind Chase.

Tyler didn't stop there; he landed three blows to Chase's back. Chase spun and threw his left arm out to clock Tyler on the side of his head, and Tyler grabbed Chase's arm and spun him so his back was facing Chase and then used Chase's own momentum to throw him over his back. Chase landed on the mat with a loud thud.

I gasped. Tyler was a badass!

"You did good. Next time keep your guard up and your elbows closer to your chest," Tyler said while offering Chase his hand to help him up. "Alex you're up."

Alex and Chase swapped places. Alex wasn't even on the mat for two minutes before Tyler had him on his back.

"Stop dropping your hands! I could have knocked you out five times in the first minute. You need to move your feet and not stand there waiting for the attack. Every time you try to attack you tense, it's your tell," Tyler snapped at Alex while helping him to his feet.

"Ryan, your turn." Oh dear Lord, help me.

Chapter Seventeen

RYAN

I traded places with Alex and stood in the center of the mats facing Tyler.

"Okay, put your hands up like they did." I tried to mimic my cousin's position, but clearly Tyler didn't like that. He sighed and then showed me how to hold my fist properly.

"Don't tuck your thumb into your fist. If you hit someone like that you'll break your thumb." Oh, okay, didn't know that. "Stand with your legs shoulder-width apart, knees slightly bent, left foot turned

to point toward your opponent. Make loose fists, and hold your right hand by your chin, left hand in front of your face. Chin down, eyes up." Holy shit, it's a lot to take in, and I haven't even done anything yet. I tried to do as he instructed, and after watching me on Struggle Street, Tyler finally took pity on me and positioned my body the way he wanted.

"Okay, you saw how I flipped Chase and Alex?" I nodded.

"That is the first move you are going to learn. It's going to be a lot to take in. You need to create muscle memory, so that your body will automatically assume that stance when a fight breaks out." I nodded again. "You're going to attack me and then I'm going to throw you on your back." Uh—what?

Tyler circled around me; I did the same, so my back wasn't turned to him. I was smart enough to know that you never turn your back on your enemy. Tyler told me to try to hit him. I listened and then before my fist could even connect, I squealed as I was thrown onto my back. It happened so freaking fast. I laid there and groaned. These mats didn't soften your fall much, and my body was still sore from the beatings it had taken.

Tyler offered me his hand, which I accepted, and once on my feet, he said, "Channel your pain, don't let it limit you. I know you're still hurting, but you need to push through it. Pain can be your enemy or it can be your savior. The choice is yours, Ryan."

Tyler's words stuck with me for the rest of the day. My body ached, but I pushed the pain out of my mind. Tyler set us all up on the equipment and told us what to do and for how long. The treadmill sucked balls; I was lazy and I hated that I had to walk on this stupid freaking machine until Tyler said stop. While two of us were using the equipment, Tyler would spar with the other; we had no down time. The only break we got was when Grams brought us some drinks and food for lunch.

Gramps and Lucian still hadn't shown back up when Tyler finally told us we could call it quits for the day. I dragged myself out of the shed and was making my way over to the woods where I saw Gramps and Lucian disappear this morning. A hand clamped on my arm, pulling me back. I spun to see who the hell it was and was met with Tyler's fierce gaze.

"He can help the boy, Ryan. You need to let him. There is more to that boy than even he knows. He is the *trifecta*" *Fuck that.*

"I won't leave him, Tyler. He needs me."

"No, Ryan, *you* need him." What the hell did that mean? I

pulled my arm from Tyler's grasp and turned away. Relief flooded through me as I saw Lucian and Gramps making their way to us. He was okay. I waited at the bottom of the porch steps for them, but when they got to me, Lucian walked straight past without a word and went inside.

"What the hell did you say to him?" Gramps spun around and glared down at me from the top of the stairs.

"Do not question my motives, granddaughter. The boy had to be told some harsh truths. Stop babying him like everyone babies you, and maybe he just might live."

After showering and changing, I thought about going to see Lucian but I stopped myself. What if Tyler and Gramps were right? Did I baby him? Did I need him? Of course I needed him —he was my friend—but I didn't want him to feel like he *had* to stay with me. He wasn't bound to me, he had his freedom now and he could leave anytime he wanted. The thought of Lucian leaving me hurt more than I wanted to admit. I shook myself out of my thoughts. I would not throw myself a pity party.

I joined the others for another silent dinner. After last time, I wasn't going to say a word. Quiet was better than Gramps being a douche.

We all helped clean up and then made our way back to our rooms. It was only six at night, but I was ready to crash. I changed into my sleep shorts and pulled Nico's shirt on. Pulling the collar of the shirt over my nose, I inhaled his scent. It calmed me.

I missed Nico so much. I haven't ever gone this long without seeing him, one way or another. I wanted him to hold me and tell me everything was going to be okay.

I knew I needed to woman up and learn how to fight and to control my magic. I only had a few months to learn all of this, and when I did master my combat skills and my magic, I was going straight for my sister and then Randall. Stevie would fucking pay for what she did to my dad and for everything she has done since. Randall, the ugly piece of shit, would die slowly, if I had any say in it. I went to bed that night with a smile on my face and more determined than ever to train and master my craft.

Chapter Eighteen

RYAN

I awoke the next morning to Grandpa banging on all our doors again. Groaning, I rolled over and sat up. Out of the corner of my eye I saw something on the floor and leaned over. It was Lucian, sleeping on the floor, again.

I hopped out of bed and gently woke him. He didn't say anything; he just grabbed his stuff and left the room. What the hell is going on with him? I fretted about it while I got changed then pushed it out of my mind and went downstairs for food.

I ate quickly with the others, then Lucian and Gramps went to the woods again and the rest of us went to the gym. We went through the same motions as yesterday.

Tyler told us we would keep doing this every day until we could master the simple move of flipping him over. Apparently that was a standard self-defense move. It made me feel better that Chase and Alex hadn't been able to flip Tyler either.

The day dragged on, switching between the machines and sparring with Tyler. The only break we got was for lunch when my sweet Grams would bring us our sandwiches and muffins.

I wished I had some time alone with her, to get to know her better. I didn't know shit about my grandparents. I tried to ask

Stevie about them when we first arrived in Alaska, but she didn't know about them either.

They were a mystery. I needed to get some time alone with my cousins and pump them for some info. A thought struck me while we were eating lunch.

"Where do your mom and dad think you two are?" I asked Chase and Alex.

"I think dad knows where we are; he would never tell anyone, though."

"Why do you sound so sad about it?"

"We have never been able to discuss our grandparents, Ry. Alex and I have only met them twice. We are spelled to never speak of them; they are both very strong. This is our first time here as well. Grandpa is the most powerful living warlock known."

"I thought Dom and Nico were?" I asked. Both Alex and Chase chuckled.

"They are the strongest fae, Ry. They are not warlocks." Now I got what Chase meant, but before I could ask more questions Tyler barked that lunch was over and back to training. Great, it was my turn to train with Tyler now. Yippee.

Sparring with Tyler sucked; I have been flipped on my back more times than I can count. He keeps barking at me to hold my hands this way, strike this way, look for an opening, stop rushing, move your feet. All his fucking orders were giving me a headache! I was exhausted and sore as fuck, but he just kept pushing and pushing.

I know he was trying to help us, but fuck me, it's harder than it looks to flip someone twice your size! All the guys were bigger than me. I don't understand how he thought I could do a move like that. Sighing, I walked to the center of the mats again and got into the position Tyler had been grilling me to remember, which apparently still wasn't good enough, as he adjusted my stance and hands.

By the end of the day, I was still no closer to flipping Tyler. I made my way upstairs, showered, and changed into my sleep-wear, scenting Nico's shirt as soon as I put it on.

Lucian didn't look at me or even acknowledge my presence during dinner or even when we were cleaning up. I was starting to get annoyed at the silent treatment. I decided that once we were upstairs, I would go and speak to him.

After doing dish duty, I made my way back to my room and lay in bed, waiting for when Lucian would sneak in and sleep on my floor.

I was fighting to keep my eyes open, and just as I was drifting off to sleep, I heard my door open and then close. I closed my eyes, feigning sleep, so Lucian wouldn't bolt back out the door. I was shocked when he sat on the side of my bed. I remained still. Opening my eyes slightly, I could see how tense he was.

"I'm sorry, Smurf. If I don't figure this shit out, I could lose you," he whispered. The sadness in his voice was nearly my undoing. I sat up. Lucian didn't flinch. He knew I was awake.

"What does that mean, Lucian?"

"I am your neutralizer." What the hell is a *neutralizer*?

"I don't even know what that is."

"Your Grandpa is helping me understand what I am and how to access my power. I know why they left and hid for so many years; if they didn't, you and your father would have veered off the path fate had intended for you, and you and I would never have met."

"Don't get me wrong—I am so glad I met you, but I'm still not following, Lucian." He took a deep breath and then sighed before speaking.

"I have to access my magic, and fast. I still don't know what I am, and your grandfather won't tell me, as it will alter your grandmother's vision. I need to control my magic in order to help you stabilize Farrarie so it doesn't need a portal to survive." Holy shit!

"I-I don't even know what to say to that. Why are you so sad, though?"

"Because if I don't learn to control my magic and learn how to neutralize your power, you will die! The reason you have no access to your magic is because I am blocking you, somehow. I am your shield, Ryan; I am the one who has to help stabilize your magic so it doesn't consume you."

Chapter Nineteen

RYAN

I was up and ready before Gramps knocked on my door this morning. My grandfather owed me an explanation. I quietly snuck out of my room and went down to the kitchen and waited for Gramps to get up and have his coffee before waking the others. I sat at my usual chair at the dining table and waited. Five minutes later Gramps strolled into the kitchen and froze.

"I'm going to need coffee before getting into this conversation."

Gramps poured us both some coffee and told me to follow him out onto the back patio. We sat on the back steps, staring out at the forest. The air was chilly this morning, which made me glad I wore leggings and a sweatshirt. I turned to look at my grandfather; he looked tired and stressed. Seeing this big strong man look like he had the weight of the world on his shoulders worried me.

"Gramps, what's going on?" He exhaled loudly and slumped forward slightly before answering me.

"Lucian told you he is your neutralizer?"

"Yes, not that I know what that means."

"I knew that boy wouldn't keep his mouth shut." I smiled, Lucian and I had a bond that I couldn't describe.

"You need him, Ryan. Without him, you will die. The power you hold is too much for just one person." Okay, then. Don't sugarcoat anything, Gramps.

"I need you to explain it to me. Lucian is all in knots. I will not ask him to put himself in harm's way for me."

"You don't have a choice. Your grandmother had a vision years ago, before you and your sister were born. If we stayed in Wonder Lake, Ralph would never have been king and wouldn't have had the time with you or your sister that he needed. It was the hardest decision for your grandmother and me to make. We left both our sons and grandsons behind. I haven't seen David in years; it kills your grandmother to be away from her only living child. I know you have had a hard life, Ryan, but the finish line is in front of you now. End this fight and save your people, then you can be free."

Gramps had me stumped; I had no idea what to say. The sacrifice he and Grams made for me and my dad was so selfless. I could never repay them for what they had done. I don't think I could ever give up my children, especially for a granddaughter that didn't even exist at the time they left. I respected my grandparents so much more now that I knew why they left.

"Gramps, what happens if I don't want Lucian to be my shield?"

"You will die. Stevie has the power to kill off the fae realm; she doesn't need to close the portal. The only way to stop the fae from dying is if you stabilize their realm and make it so they don't need a portal on Earth to sustain their world."

"I don't even know if I am capable of doing that, Gramps." I didn't want to lie to him and say I could do it when I didn't even know how to make an energy ball on demand. The fate of the fae realm was resting on the shoulders of a novice hybrid.

"I will train you and help you. You have to do it, or the fae realm will die, and so will you." Well, when he put it like that, I really didn't have a choice, did I?

"There is one other thing."

Seriously? "What's that, Gramps?"

"You need to end your sister, Ryan. No prison can hold her, and she will not stop. The Knox coven will demand her demise. Blood must have blood. That is our way."

I knew it had to be done, but hearing it out loud was a harder pill to swallow than I thought. I knew my sister was so far gone that she couldn't be saved, and she had done so many unspeakable things. I was the only one who had enough power to destroy her, and I had to find the strength inside myself to end her reign of terror.

"You have my word, Grandpa. I will set Stevie's soul free."

"You need to help Lucian understand that *you* need him. You need him to shield you from your power. If it's unleashed at full capacity, you won't be able to call it back to you without his help. Everyone in life has a destiny, and his is to help you. Finish your combat training with Tyler and then you and Lucian will train with me."

"What about Alex, Chase, and Tyler?"

"Your grandmother will train your cousins, and Tyler isn't a warlock. Tyler will continue to work on his control over his wolf. The mate bond is strong for him; he needs to fight it or he will lose control of his wolf when he scents your sister." A thought struck me; Tyler had once said that he would lose control of his wolf if Stevie died.

"Tyler's training to control his wolf so he doesn't go mad when Stevie dies, isn't he?" Gramps turned to look at me with a sad smile on his face.

"Yes, when a wolf loses their mate, they go mad." Oh my God.

"Gramps, what happens if Tyler doesn't control his wolf?"

"Then I will need to be taken out." I jumped to my feet and spun around at the sound of Tyler's voice. He didn't look scared or worried; he just seemed to accept his fate. But I couldn't let Tyler die, not after everything he had done for me.

We may not have always gotten along, but I could tell he was a good guy and he didn't choose her as his mate. I walked over to Tyler and grasped his hand, giving it a small squeeze.

"I will not let you die, Ty. I will do whatever I can to help you." Tyler looked down at me, shocked.

"Why would you help me? I betrayed you and my pack, for my mate. I helped them take your coven elders and their loved ones. I am not worth saving, Ryan."

"The fact that you don't believe you are worth saving is the very reason why you are worth saving. You did all of those things because of the bond you have with my sister. You will not be judged by your actions any longer; you will only be judged on what you do to make up for your mistakes."

We trained harder today than we did the previous days. I learned a few moves that were easier to pick up, including how to do a groin kick effectively against the guys. I also learned how to do a hammer strike, though if you have car keys on you, it helps.

The next day I mastered a heel-palm strike. It took me a few attempts to get that move right, but it proved effective when I sparred with Chase and got him in the nose. He crumpled to the mat after that hit and I dropped with him, feeling so guilty. Tyler just rolled his eyes and told us to do it again.

Chapter Twenty

RYAN

As the days turned into weeks, I made progress with my hand-to-hand combat. My body had its own internal alarm now, and I woke without needing Gramps banging on my door. Lucian slept on the floor next to my bed every night. We didn't speak about why he did it, it just became a routine. He didn't sneak in anymore—he would come with me to my room after dinner with a stack of books.

Grams has been teaching him how to read, and Lucian was like a sponge; he absorbed any and all information. I was learning new things too. I had learned a lot about where my family came from and that my Gramps was the strongest warlock until my dad came into his powers.

Grams is a seer, and her gift passed onto my dad. No one in the coven knew about Dad or Grams's gift of being a seer. Gramps told me that it would have made them a target; seers are desperately sought by all the clans. That explained why Jax always made sure Aurora's identity was kept a secret, and no one out of the pack really knew she existed.

Grams had shown me photos of my dad as a kid, and she let me keep one of the albums.

Dinner time wasn't awkward and quiet now. We had settled into a routine and I looked forward to it every evening, the sharing of stories and our shared history. Lucian had gained weight and was starting to fill out; he would go with Gramps in the morning and then come to the gym in the afternoon to learn some combat moves. I'm embarrassed to say he picked the self-defense moves up quicker than the rest of us.

I was the last one left to master the flipping move, and Gramps said once I did that I could move on to magic training.

By week seven I noticed that I was starting to develop some muscle definition, and my fighting position was automatic.

Tyler was right; the more I did it, the more my body would remember it.

I now know how to do an elbow strike, alternative elbow strike, I know how to escape a bear hug, my hands being trapped, and a headlock. I had given myself a deadline: I had to master this flip before the end of week eight.

Eight weeks of training, and I was on my last day for my personal deadline. I was standing in the middle of the mats with Tyler.

Gramps and Grams were in here; they had started coming to the gym more often now to check on our progress. I had to block out the fact that I had five sets of eyes on me. Everyone knew I had set a deadline for myself and today was D-day.

"Okay, you have trained your ass off for weeks, Ryan. You need to master this so you can move onto magic training. You have smashed everything else, you just need to master this move." I nodded. Tyler was right; we were running out of time.

We had been working on attack training as well, because apparently, I was holding everyone else up with my lack of being unable to flip Tyler.

"Okay, let's begin."

I took a deep breath and blocked everything out. I just focused on Tyler. I watched how his body shifted and how his left hand would twitch. Tyler had been telling me for weeks that everyone had a tell; if you found it then you would know when they would make their move.

I haven't been able to find Tyler's yet.

We circled each other. Both our guards were up. Tyler struck out his left fist, I spun right to dodge, and I lashed out with my fist and made contact with his ribs.

I didn't celebrate; Tyler was a wolf and he could take a lot of hits. We kept doing the same dance for five minutes.

I knew Tyler was getting annoyed and just wanted to end this sparring match, but I kept evading his attacks. He had nearly got me when he had me in a headlock, but I used my training to get out of it.

Tyler threw his right fist out, and I was too overwhelmed with the fact I just found Tyler's tell to move out of striking distance. His fist connected with my face, but I blocked the pain out. I would deal with that later. Tyler thought he had the upper hand, and I encouraged his mistaken belief, lowering my hands, faking that I was hurt.

As soon as Tyler moved forward and placed both his hands on my shoulders, that's when I saw it again: his left eye twitched. He was going to attack! I quickly placed my hands on his shoulders, turned around while maintaining my grip. I took a step forward and pulled Tyler in to my side and bent at the knees. Using his own momentum against him, I rolled him over my hip.

Tyler landed on the mat with a thud. I looked down at him,

shocked it actually worked. Even Tyler looked surprised. I did it! I just fucking flipped Tyler! I was elated.

A strong pair of arms wrapped around me and spun me around in a circle. "You did it, Smurf! You fucking did it!" Lucian placed me back on my feet and gave me a side hug while we watched Tyler climb to his feet. I moved out of Lucian's hold and went to stand in front of Tyler with my hand extended; he shook it with a smile on his face. He looked so proud of me, and that warmed my heart.

"Thank you, Tyler, for everything." I owed Tyler so much. No one would ever have the chance to hurt me again, thanks to him.

"Don't mention it, little hybrid." Tyler had given me that nickname a few weeks ago; he still called Lucian *trifecta*. The only other person who knew what *trifecta* meant was gramps and he refused to tell us. He said knowing the meaning behind the name would alter Lucian's path.

Gramps gave us the rest of the day off. It was our first free afternoon in two months.

It was snowing outside, so there wasn't much we could really do. We all made our way back inside the house, where the fireplace was lit and the cabin was so freaking toasty.

I remembered something I had been wanting to do—try out the tub in my room. I haven't had time to even consider using it. I raced up the stairs to my room and slammed the door shut behind me,

turning on the faucets while I stripped out of my clothes. As soon as the tub was full, I hopped in and sighed.

I leaned my head back and closed my eyes, trying to clear my mind.

My thoughts drifted to Nico, as they always did. I haven't seen Nico in over three months and wouldn't get to see him for at least another two. What would he think when he saw me again? Would he still want me the way I want him? Did he hate me now?

My heart started to ache. I still slept in his shirt every night, but his scent no longer lingered. Wearing the shirt to bed every night made me feel like he was wrapped around me. I missed my husband so fucking much. We have been married for months, and I haven't even been able to call him my husband to his face. I haven't had any dreams, which worries me daily. Did he use me? Was any of it real?

Chapter Twenty One

RYAN

We were two weeks into our magic training and fuck me—I thought Tyler was a hard-ass, but Gramps is ten times worse!

We were gathered outside in the freezing snow, standing in a circle. Alex, Chase, Lucian, and I had been doing this dance for two weeks now; my cousins could access their power, but I couldn't access mine until Lucian learned how to release his shield. Apparently Lucian's fear of losing me was causing his magic to block mine.

Gramps had told us that Lucian's and my path would have always crossed; he was my savior. He was the only one who could help me control my magic. If he had been there the night of my wedding then no one would have died. He would have been able to neutralize my magic. I still felt sick about that night and all the lives I had taken. I would be held accountable for what I had done after this war, and I should be.

"Lucian! Release it now!" Gramps shouted.

"I can't, sir! I'm trying, I swear!" Lucian shouted back. He was frustrated. We all were. I couldn't do shit until Lucian released his hold on my magic. I didn't blame him, but we were running out of time, and I needed to train.

Alex and Chase were both holding purple energy balls in their hands. Lucian was, as well, except his energy was yellow. Gramps was trying to get him to focus on his own magic so he could release mine.

"If you don't learn how to release her magic, she will die!" I saw Lucian tense; this was a lot for him, and I felt terrible. I had to do something.

"Luce, I'm right here. No one here is going to hurt me. I need you to trust me." I was pleading with him.

"Alex, you and Chase are to train with your grandmother for the rest of the day," Gramps snapped. Both my cousins strode out of the forest as fast as they could without breaking into a sprint. Lucky assholes got to train with the *nice* grandparent.

"Smurf, I am trying, I swear." I saw Gramps look out into the forest and then back to us. He had a sly smirk on his face.

"Let's see if we can scare the control out of you." In the next second, Lucian was lifted off his feet and pinned to the closest tree with his arms stretched out wide.

"Gramps what the hell are y—"

I didn't get a chance to finish yelling at Gramps. Something slammed into me from behind, and I landed face-first on the hard-packed snow. I quickly rolled and jumped to my feet, getting straight into my fighting stance. Tyler was right; muscle memory was the shit.

I gasped when I saw what had knocked me down: in front of me stood a huge, rusty-colored wolf, with bright yellow eyes.

"Tyler?" I asked the wolf, and the wolf growled in response. I was taking that growl as a *yes*. The wolf jumped at me again, and I quickly stepped out of the way.

"Gramps what the hell?" I didn't take my eyes off the wolf; I didn't trust Tyler not to attack me while my focus was elsewhere.

"Release her magic, boy; she doesn't stand a chance against a shifter without her power." Gramps was fucking nuts. "You can't stop her from becoming what she was meant to be! She needs to learn to control it now! When she gets back to Alaska, the other half her husband holds will return to her." Lucian didn't get a chance to answer Gramps. Tyler lunged for me again, and this time, I wasn't fast enough to move.

His sharp teeth sunk into my arm and I screamed as I felt his teeth pierce through my skin. I tried to pull my arm away, but Tyler kept his jaws clamped.

"Let her fucking go!" Lucian yelled.

"NO! Release her magic now!" I turned to Lucian and saw the fear on his face. Tears were flowing down my cheeks freely, my arm was burning like it was on fire.

I pulled my focus back to the wolf and started punching it in the head as hard as I could, trying to get it to release my arm; I saw blood—my blood—trickling out of its mouth.

"Tyler, stop!" I begged. I saw a hint of recognition in the wolf's eyes. I knew Tyler could have ripped my arm off if he wanted to. He kept his jaws clamped on my arm, but didn't bite any harder than he had already.

Tyler released my arm, and my bloody limb dropped to my side. The wolf backed up, and I knew he was gearing up to attack again. My right arm was useless; I had to block the pain out or I would never make it out of this forest in one piece. I resumed my fighting stance again, but I only had one arm up.

"Look at her, boy! She only has one arm to defend herself. She will die if you don't let her go!"

Tyler launched himself at me. I quickly spun and used my leg to kick him in the side. He skidded on the snow-covered ground and came straight back at me. I was screwed. Tyler wouldn't stop coming for me until Lucian let my powers go. If this was the only way, then so be it. I dropped my good arm to my side and stood up straight. I looked the wolf in its eyes and nodded my head. I knelt down on the cold, icy ground and exposed my neck to the wolf.

"Smurf, No!" I saw Tyler run toward me and closed my eyes, praying that this was the incentive Lucian needed. If it wasn't, then I would be dead in the next minute.

I felt a whoosh of air and knew Tyler was in front of me, about to end my life. Before his jaws could connect with my neck, I felt heat in my toes. My body started to warm, and then the warmth turned into liquid lava in my veins.

My magic was back!

I snapped my eyes open just as Tyler was about to bite my exposed neck. I channeled enough power into my good arm to throw him; I didn't want to hurt him, but I needed him away from me.

I swung my good arm toward his chest, and a blue light burst into him, sending him sailing through the air into a nearby tree. Tyler yelped when he hit the tree and landed on the snow-covered ground with a thud.

Oh my God, what the fuck did I do?

I rushed over to the wolf, knelt down beside him and started to stroke his face with my good arm.

"Ty, I am so sorry." He was still breathing, so I took that as a good sign, I watched as the wolf shifted back to a very naked Tyler. I sagged in relief as Tyler looked at me with a huge grin on his face. "Next time, when you throw your enemy into a tree, don't run over and make sure they're okay, little hybrid." I smiled at my friend. We stood and I made sure to avert my eyes so I didn't see little Tyler flopping in the wind. Just as I turned back to face the others, I saw a fist connect with Tyler's face and shrieked.

"You ever fucking do that to her again, wolf, and I will kill you!" I grabbed Lucian with my good arm to stop him from hitting Tyler again.

"Luce, stop, please!"

"It's okay, Ry. I deserved the hit."

"No you didn't, Tyler!"

"Look at your fucking arm, Smurf. It's bleeding." I looked down at my arm and saw that my jacket sleeve was torn to shreds and blood was dripping from the tips of my fingers onto the snow. The pain started to register then, and I cradled my bleeding arm to my chest.

"That's it for today. Go get your arm cleaned up. Grams will help you dress it." I turned to glare at Gramps. He didn't even look remorseful; he looked like a smug asshole.

"Don't look at me like that, Ryan. I tried it the nice way and it didn't work. You should be thanking your dear old Gramps." I scowled at him as I walked past heading back to the cabin, but the old fool just chuckled as he followed us back.

NICO

It's been nearly four months since I have seen Ryan. I have tried every night to enter our dreamland, but I can't find her. I am so desperate I even asked Kai to try and access her in her dreams. He can't find her either. It's like she's blocked from us. I thought she might be dead, but Mr. Silver told me that if she was I would have felt it through our *hugacko* bond.

For weeks all I have done is travel back and forth from Farrarie and Earth for elder meetings and training my army for the war. There were tents up all over Jax's land; many of my soldiers have come to Earth in case our timeline is off when the war will start.

I have been asking Aurora for weeks if she has had a vision of Ryan. All she has said is that we need Ryan back or we will never win. Stevie is stronger than five thousand fae soldiers. We found out from the vampire elders that Randall's strength has grown. He ingested the blood of Jackson's father, Ryan's father, and now he has ingested Ryan's blood.

Lachlan told us that he was collecting Ryan's blood and injecting his men so they could all now walk in the daylight. There is nothing worse than having thousands of vampires walking around all hours of the day and night. Randall was now stronger then we could have ever imagined.

Jax, Dom, Kai, Sophia, Aurora, Mya, and I were all sitting in Jax's office with somber looks on our faces. We all knew we were fighting a losing battle. Without Ryan, we have no chance of winning this war and saving my people.

I failed as king. I failed as a leader. My world was going to die because I found my *hugacko*. My soulmate was the reason my world was going to die. I couldn't kill Ryan, and nor could Kai; our love for her weakened us. Even still, I would never regret loving her. She deserved so much more than the life she has had.

I would feel a lot better about death if I knew she was okay, but I couldn't blame her for hiding and staying away. I missed her so fucking much that I physically ached for her. I would give anything just to see her one last time.

"We have just over two months before this war is supposed to break out. Aurora, have you seen anything that would change this timeline?" Jax asked.

"No, as far as I have seen the timeline is still accurate." That was a relief to hear. I have started evacuating those of my people who are too young or too old to fight to other parts of the realm. I know this won't save their lives if Farrarie falls, but at least they can live in peace for now.

"Have you been able to reach Ryan, Nico?" I looked to Dom and saw he was hesitant to ask me about Ryan. Every one of them knew speaking about Ryan was a sore subject for me.

"No, I have been trying every day and still I can't reach her." I lowered my gaze, not wanting to see the resignation on my brother's face. Dom had been spending a lot of time with his father and the New York pack, who came here to help aid us. From the intel we have gathered, we were evenly matched with numbers in this war, but the vamps had Randall and the witches had Stevie. Even with Kai, Jax, Dom, and I going for Stevie, she was still stronger than the four of us.

"Wherever she is, I hope she is happy. She deserves to be free. This was never her fight."

"How can you say that, Soph? Without her, we're all going to be slaughtered." I knew my sister was trying to make me feel better, but of course Jax didn't see it that way. He took Ryan's disappearance hard.

"I know this is hard for all of you, but Ryan has had nothing but misery from the supernatural world. She had eighteen years of misery at the hands of her mother—which we could have prevented—and five months ago she found out she was a hybrid and that she was the only one who could save a world she didn't even know existed. That is a lot for someone so young to deal with," I said.

"She won't abandon you, Nico." I turned to Kai, shocked.

"What makes you say that?"

"I have seen the way she looks at you brother. Even before she knew we were real, she would always talk about you and how you made her feel. It was never a question of whether or not she would choose you, *you* were always her first choice. She will come back for you Nico; you just need to give her time."

Kai's words hit me deep. He has never given up hope that Ryan will return, in spite of her betrayal. She has a lot to make up for with him.

"Thank you, brother."

"Stop it, you're both going to make me cry."

"For the love of God, Dominic, get a fucking filter," Sophia snapped at Dom. Those two have been at each other's throats even more in the past few weeks. I just don't have the energy at the moment to get involved in their shit.

"I've had a vision." We all turned to stare at Mya.

"A vision about what?" Dom asked her.

"I didn't see much—all I saw was Stevie lying in a pool of her own blood."

"Was she dead?"

"Was she breathing?"

"Does that mean we won?"

Everyone was barking questions at Mya; the poor woman couldn't keep up.

"Shut up! Let her fucking answer one question at a time!" Kai shouted. Everyone stopped speaking and sat there quietly. We were all stunned at Kai's outburst.

"Look, all I saw was that she was lying in her own blood, and that's it. I don't know any more than that."

Hearing this gave me a sense of hope. Maybe we weren't all doomed after all. Maybe, just maybe, we might live.

Even with the other half of Ryan's magic inside me, I couldn't use it to help us win the war. It just lay dormant inside of me, waiting for its master to call it back.

"How's her mom doing?" Jax asked me. I had taken Nina back to my realm. I took her there initially to question her and get answers about what had happened at Randall's mansion or if she saw Ryan.

I thought the woman was fucking nuts! She ranted like a mad woman and then was found weeping in the corner. It took weeks to even get a coherent sentence out of her. After weeks of being in my realm, I saw a change in her.

"I don't know how to explain it, but she's changed. The woman doesn't want to drink or do drugs anymore. She swears she can't remember most of her life. The last thing she remembers is Ralph leaving her; she said everything else is blank. I think whatever this curse is was broken the moment she entered my realm."

"How is that even possible, brother?" I looked to Kai; I knew it was hard for him, because he made a promise to save Nina and make sure she was safe, but he couldn't have known that the queen's spell would have backfired.

"I have no idea, Kai. Nina has changed so much. She helps the women with their young children, and so many of the fae love her." I still found it strange; I saw what she was like over the years, and I saw what she was like with Ryan. That woman doesn't exist anymore. Nina is actually kind and caring now.

"Have you told her about her past?"

"I told her some of it, Dom. She broke down and locked herself in her room for days, bawling her eyes out. She doesn't understand why Ryan even tried to look for her; she said Ryan should have killed her." Nina Knox was a changed woman, and I wanted to help her get better. I had to—it was my fault the woman was beaten and starved and missing a finger and toe. The least I could do was try to help her build a better life.

Chapter Twenty Three

RYAN

We had two weeks left before we had to leave and head back to Alaska. Gramps was training me and Lucian while Grams helped Alex and Chase hone their power.

Alex and Chase were improving so fast and doing so good! I was so proud of my cousins. I know they were eager to get back and see if their parents were okay.

We were outside in the forest, freezing our asses off. My arm was finally starting to scab over, and I know Tyler felt bad, but without that fear, Lucian might never have released my power. The bite mark was going to scar, but nothing could be done about that now.

"Okay, you both have done great work with accessing your power on demand and throwing energy balls. Your levitation has been amazing, Ryan." Gramps was so proud that I could levitate; no one else here could do that except for me and Lucian. Lucian hadn't quite mastered that skill yet, but he was getting better.

I preened. "Thanks, Grandpa."

"Kiss ass." I turned to glare at Chase, him and Alex were cackling like a pair of school girls.

"Ignore him, Smurf, he's just angry his magic glows a girl's color." Chase stopped laughing and scowled at Lucian. In the time we have spent here, Lucian has come out of his shell and developed a sense of humor and quick wit to rival even Dom's. Chase hated that Lucian had quick comebacks now. He just couldn't seem to best my friend with jokes.

"Enough, you boys go back to your grandmother and train. Lucian, I need you to try pull Ryan's power back when she releases it." Gramps has been making us practice this over and over again to make sure Lucian was prepared for the real deal. Lucian knew it would be harder when the other half of my magic came back to me.

I closed my eyes and focused on pushing my power outside of me. I was better at doing this now; the first time I did it I nearly leveled a part of the forest from the force of my magic. That scared me because I only had half of my magic—imagine what I could do when I got the other back from Nico.

"Okay, Ryan, hold it there." I opened my eyes and saw the blue bubble that surrounded me; it was amazing how I could use my magic at will now. It didn't scare me anymore; Gramps said if I let fear and anger control my power it would always be unpredictable. I needed to embrace it and trust it, so it would listen to me.

"Lucian, I want you to pull it into you and hold it inside as long as you can." Lucian nodded his head and pulled the bubble to him. It disappeared inside of him in a flash.

"Good man, hold it for as long as you can."

Gramps was trying to see how long Lucian could hold my magic in case I needed some time to recover after stabilizing the fae realm and taking care of my sister.

Ten minutes later, my magic was back inside of me. I sighed in relief; I hated not feeling my magic inside. It's become a part of me now, and I couldn't live without it.

"That was great, son. For the rest of the time we have here I want you both and Chase and Alex to spar with your magic." We had been practicing dodging and blocking energy balls, as well as throwing them at each other.

Let me tell you something, those fuckers hurt if they hit you. It was like being electrocuted from the inside and there was nothing you could do to stop the pain. Needless to say we all learned how to block them pretty fucking fast.

Chapter Twenty Four

RYAN

Two weeks passed in a blur. It was our last night here in the snowy Yukon. We all gathered in the sitting room, sipping hot chocolate and watching the flames dance in the fireplace.

No one had said a word in ages, each of us lost in our own thoughts. I had something to say to my grandparents and had been working up the courage all day to say it.

Taking a deep breath, I blurted it out.

"Thank you both for everything you have done for us. I love you both so much, and because I love you, I don't want you to come with us tomorrow." Grams's eyes welled with tears, and Gramps was swallowing repeatedly.

Did I just stun Gramps speechless?

"We love you too, sweetheart, and we are so proud of you all." I smiled at Grams. She was such a sweet and kind woman. She has helped me get to know my dad better through the stories she has told me and pictures she shared. She taught me about how witches draw power from the elements. I'm very thankful for the time I have been able to spend with them both.

"Why don't you want us to accompany you, Ry?" Gramps asked.

I took a deep breath and looked around the room. Tyler and my cousins gave me a curt nod and Lucian gave my hand a squeeze; they knew why I didn't want them to come with us.

"I don't want you to come because I couldn't bear to lose either of you. I want you to stay here and be safe. Please, Gramps. Don't follow us back to Wonder Lake. Stay here with Grams and enjoy your life. When this war is over, then come and visit us."

Both my cousins agreed with me, and I could see that having all three grandkids gang up on them wasn't something they were prepared for. Lucian and Tyler voiced the same concerns we had, and five against two is good odds.

"What if you lot need us?"

"Oh Grams, we will always need your love and support, but not if it could cost you your life," I said while wiping tears from my cheeks. Gramps remained stoic in his seat, looking at all of us. He could tell from our expressions that we wouldn't let him come with us; we were just hoping that the stubborn old fool wouldn't follow us as soon as we left.

"I couldn't be more proud of the men you four boys have grown into. Each of you has come into your own and that swells me with pride. Ryan, my sweet granddaughter." Oh my God, the tears were falling faster now. Gramps had never spoken to me or looked at me like this before. "You have overcome so much in your life and still you come back swinging. I see so much of myself in you; you will make an amazing queen to both the fae and the Knox coven. Give them hell, my dear, and take no prisoners."

I jumped up from the couch, hastily put my cup on the side table, and then ran over and hugged my grandfather. He hugged me back, and I whispered in his ear.

"I have never had a father figure in my life, Gramps, but you have been that for me for the past four months. Thank you so, so much." I pulled back and saw Gramps had a stray tear trailing down his cheek, he quickly swiped it away and acted like it never happened.

I smile at the stubborn old man.

I couldn't sleep. I had been tossing and turning for hours. With a groan, I sat up and tucked my long hair behind my ears so it wasn't in my face. I heard Lucian stir beside me. When the temperature dropped, it was too cold for him to sleep on the floor so I decided to just let him sleep next to me in the king-sized bed.

It felt awkward at the start, but now it just felt normal having him sleep beside me.

"Smurf, I can hear you over thinking from here." I chuckled. Nico had said the same thing to me once.

"I'm nervous about tomorrow, Luce."

"Are you nervous about seeing *him?*"

"Yes! What if his feelings for me have changed? What if he doesn't want to be with me?" Lucian chuckled and I glared at him. I knew he couldn't see my glare in the dark room, but I felt better about doing it anyway.

"So you're not nervous about fighting for your life? You're nervous in case your husband has changed his mind?"

"Yes," I snapped.

"Smurf, he is one lucky man to be able to call you his wife. More than that, you are his soulmate. You don't ever stop wanting or loving your soul mate; you *always* need the other half of your soul." Lucian's words brought tears to my eyes. He was right; I was being silly. I knew deep down that Nico wouldn't have moved on. I also knew he would be worried and wondering where the hell I have been.

Lucian cuddled me and told me everything was going to be okay. After that, I settled back down in bed and finally fell into a dreamless sleep.

Goodbyes sucked! Grams bawled her eyes out when we left, and even Gramps looked a little dewy around the eyes. I was so beyond grateful for everything Grams and Gramps had taught me. For the first time in my life, I had a family. I hated leaving them.

I made a deal with Gramps: when the war was over, he and Grams would come to Alaska and help teach me the ropes of being queen of the Knox coven.

Lucian elbowing me in the ribs pulled me from my thoughts. I turned to him and smiled; my beautiful friend had cut his hair shorter. I was shocked when I saw it this morning. It was just above his shoulders now. Lucian had filled out and bulked up a lot in the four months we were in Yukon. Gone was the skinny boy. The man before me now was broad, clean, and healthy. I loved Lucian like a brother, and I would do anything for him. He was strong, and Gramps had even said he hasn't tapped fully into his own magic yet.

"How are you feeling?" Lucian asked.

"I'm okay. Sad to say goodbye to Grams and Gramps but keen to get back to Alaska." I had butterflies in my stomach about seeing Nico again. I know Tyler was nervous about returning to his pack, too. I just hoped Jax would forgive him.

If Jax didn't let Tyler come back to the compound, I don't think I would be able to stay there. Tyler and I had grown close over our time in Yukon, and he was an amazing guy.

The drive was long. We left at five this morning and arrived at the air strip in Toronto just after midnight. We only stopped twice for food and kept the bathroom breaks minimal, and I was exhausted. I hadn't been able to sleep a wink in the car—my nerves wouldn't let me.

We quickly grabbed our bags and made our way onto the small plane, placing our bags in the overhead compartments and then taking our seats. I sat next to the window so I could stare at the night sky. When the plane took off, I reclined my seat, intending to get some shut eye. I managed to get a few hours in before Lucian woke me.

I rubbed my eyes and quickly excused myself to use the restroom and freshen up. I made my way back to my seat and fastened my belt, hoping my nerves would calm the hell down.

"We land in twenty minutes, guys; it's early in the morning here."

"Thanks, Alex, I can't wait to stretch my legs." I said.

"We're gonna land in the same place we left from; it's safer than the commercial airport." That made sense, but I probably wouldn't have thought of it. I'm glad Alex and Tyler were in charge of our travel plans.

Lucian grasped my hand and interlocked our fingers; I turned and smiled at my sweet friend.

"I'll be with you the whole time, Smurf." Hearing that warmed my heart. I knew Lucian would have my back.

We landed somewhere near Fairbanks in a large open field. I was beyond glad to be able to walk around and stretch my legs.

After twenty minutes of walking around in circles, we all piled into the waiting SUV and began another long-ass drive to Wonder Lake.

Chapter Twenty Six

NICO

"We have just over a month, your majesty. We will be ready."

"Thank you, Maverick. Make sure Larick and Cyrus are briefed about the plan and continue to move all the others to Chicago." Maverick bowed before me and then left the room. I looked at the clock on the wall and cursed; I was late for the elder meeting. I quickly left my room and raced to the mess hall. All eyes turned to me as I burst through the doors. I apologized and quickly took my seat next to Dom.

"Your majesty," Victor said and bowed low. I gave him a nod and told them to continue. "We were just saying that we have received word from Lachlan. The coven elders are being held prisoner on the coven lands. Lachlan and the other elders are being watched, so they won't be able to meet with us anytime soon."

Fuck, this wasn't good news. It sounded like Randall or Stevie knew their elders were betraying them and were making sure to keep them close, but how?

The elders are the strongest of us, and the only reason Stevie can control her elders is because of the power she holds. She doesn't need to take their loved ones from them anymore. I couldn't shake the feeling that Victor was hiding something, but maybe I was just being paranoid.

After the meeting ended, we all made our way back to Jackson's office. I couldn't stop pacing. I was running out of fucking ideas of how to save my realm.

Stevie was too fucking strong, and Lachlan had told us that her power just kept growing. I don't understand why she didn't just attack us now, and then search for the portal. What was she waiting for?

"Brother, sit down before you wear a hole into the floor." I sighed but did as Sophia suggested and plonked down into the single seat.

"I just want to say that no matter how this ends, I'm glad we were all able to be together till the end." Fuck no. Jackson could fuck right off with his goodbye speech.

"Don't do that Jax, this isn't the end."

"How do you know that, Dom?"

"Because I'm too fucking pretty to die." Everyone started laughing at Dom's answer, and it surely did us good. I loved my three brothers and my sister. Aurora and Mya were growing on me, as well.

"I needed that laugh, thank you Dom."

"Anytime Rora—"

Dom's reply was cut off when Jax jumped to his feet and growled out, "Stevie's here, by the chapel!" I envied the link Jackson had with his pack.

Everyone raced out of the office and toward the chapel. Jax

said Stevie had only come with four others. She wasn't here to attack, so what the hell was she here for?

We burst out the back door and ran across the snow-covered ground to where the chapel was. Jackson's pack were scattered throughout the trees in case they were needed. I saw some of my soldiers with their weapons drawn; we were ready if she tried anything. We all stopped running when we saw who three of the guys were; there was a stranger with them, but I couldn't see Stevie anywhere.

I felt like my body was being pulled toward the four men, and I only ever had this feeling when Ryan was around.

"Tyler?" Aurora said, shocked at seeing her brother back on pack lands.

"Hello, little sister." Jax stepped slightly in front of Aurora to shield her from Tyler's view and started growling at his former beta. I saw a look of hurt cross Tyler's face before he quickly masked it.

"What the hell are you doing here, Tyler? And why are Chase and Alex with you?" Jax snapped.

"We're here to help you, Jackson." Alex answered.

"W-who are you?" Sophia said, pointing to the stranger with Tyler and Ryan's cousins. Sophia looked pale, almost like she had seen a ghost. What the hell?

"I am Lucian; I am here to help the queen."

"I'll fucking kill you before that bitch ever wins!" Dom growled at the stranger.

"You will not lay a single finger on him, Dom." Oh my God, that voice. My legs nearly gave out.

Chapter Twenty Seven

RYAN

I push between Lucian and Chase and saw all my friends staring at me with looks of shock and confusion.

I turned to Jax's right, and that's when I saw him—his beautiful jet-black hair was a mess and long on top now. He had a five-o'clock shadow, and his piercing violet eyes burned holes into me. He was just as shocked to see me.

Nico took a step forward, and Lucian stepped in front of me to block Nico's path.

"Unless you want me to remove your fucking head, boy, you will move!" Nico growled.

"You can try to move him, *Tink*, but without him she dies." Nico paused his movements and looked to Chase. He tried to peer around Lucian to see me. I gave Lucian a pat on his shoulder, indicating it was okay for him to step aside, and he moved to stand next to me again. Then I was facing Nico, who was closer than before.

He smiled, and I swooned a little bit. I didn't know what to do. I darted my eyes around, shocked to see so many people in the trees. It made me uncomfortable.

Lucian grabbed my hand and interlocked our fingers.

"Unless you want to lose that fucking hand you will release my *wife* now!"

"Nico, stop!" I turned my gaze to a tear-stricken Sophia, completely befuddled at her demeanor. Why the hell was she so upset?

"Little dove, what's wrong?" Dom asked her.

"No one is to touch him, do you all understand me?" Sophia was pointing to Lucian. Why the hell was she protecting Luce?

"Everyone calm down. Let's go back to Jackson's office; we have a few things to discuss." Everyone turned to Aurora. I smiled at her, letting her know that I held no anger toward her anymore. The five of us didn't move an inch; we waited for Jackson to say the word and invite us in.

"For God's sake, Jackson, invite them in!" Nico roared.

"The four of them can come, but not the traitor." I felt my magic surge inside of me. I took a step in front of the guys so I could protect them if need be. I heard rustling come from the trees all around us, and I knew the soldiers in the trees were getting ready to attack. I heard bones cracking; some of them had shifted into their wolf form.

"Stand down! No one is to touch her!" Nico yelled. He never took his gaze off me; I let my power run through me and levitated a few feet off the ground until I looked down at my friends. Their eyes were wide.

"If any of you or your men lay a single finger on Tyler, you will have me to answer to. Tyler is my pack, and where I go he goes. Same for Alex, Chase, and Lucian. They stay with me at all times. If you will not welcome him into your home as a courtesy to me, Jackson, we will leave!" I spoke loud enough so those hiding in the trees could hear. Jackson kept opening and shutting his mouth in consternation.

"As the leader of the Shifter elders, I, Ian Silver, grant you, Ryan Knox, and your friends entrance to the compound. No harm will come to you or your friends, you have my word." I turned and saw Dom's dad standing by the trees. I smiled and thanked him. I brought my power back inside me and slowly made my way back down to the ground. Then I turned to Tyler.

"Thank you, little hybrid, you didn't have to do that."

"Ty, you're family now. I told you I wouldn't leave you, and I meant it." Tyler smiled and engulfed me in a hug, and I heard someone growling behind me. I just knew it was Nico.

"Clearly he doesn't like any man touching you," he whispered in my ear.

To say the atmosphere in Jackson's office was awkward would be an understatement. We were all so divided, and I hated it.

Nico stood to one side with Dom, Kai, Jax, Sophia, Mya, and Aurora, while I stood on the other side with my four guys. Kai still hadn't said a word to me. He hadn't even *looked* at me. I knew in my heart that Nico had told him what I had done. I wish I had been the one to tell him the truth, but I couldn't change that now.

"Okay, this is just awkward as shit. Come here, love." Dom opened his arms wide and walked to the middle of the room, and I walked into his embrace without any hesitation. Being wrapped in Dom's arms again felt great.

I missed him and all his smart-ass comments. We stood there hugging each other until Nico pulled him away and stood directly in front of me, looking down into my eyes. We stood there, lost in each other's gazes for a long moment. There was so much emotion swirling in the depths of his eyes.

"Hello, little one." The dam broke, and tears slid down my

face. I wrapped my arms around him and buried my face in his chest. His arms came around me and squeezed me so tight. I felt safe, and being in his arms again felt like home.

"I missed you, love." I couldn't talk past the lump in my throat. I clung to him while tears silently leaked from my eyes.

"I don't think she's gonna divorce the king of the fairies, Luce," I heard Chase say with a sigh.

"Did you really have to bring him back with you?" Nico grumbled. I chuckled. Nico clearly hadn't missed my cousins. I pulled away from Nico and wiped my eyes. Being back with him felt so right.

"I think we should all have a seat and talk," I said. Nico nodded but stuck close to me as I said hello to the others. I saved Kai for last.

Standing in front of the giant of a man who had starred in many of my dreams, I saw the mistrust and disappointment on his face and it crushed me. I held his gaze, because I needed to own my shit, and answer for what I had done to him.

"I'm so sorry for what I did to you. I should never have gone behind your back. I have no excuse except inexperience. I know I hurt you, Kai, and I will spend the rest of my life trying to make it up to you, if you will let me." Kai averted his gaze above my head, and what he said next struck so deep I almost fell to my knees.

"You condemned me to hell, Ryan, and took the last hope I had left. I will stay and fight with my brothers, but I will *never* lead the vampires."

Chapter Twenty Eight

NICO

I could see the devastation in her eyes as Kai spoke. She chose to sit between Tyler and her new friend, instead of sitting next to *me*.

I could see how her body curved into the new guys' side for comfort. Who the fuck was this guy, and why was my wife so dependent on him?

"Who is he, love?" I asked, pointing to the new guy.

"Oh, this is going to be good." Chase the dickhead said, fist-bumping his brother. Fucking immature dumbasses.

"Lucian is important to me," she said, looking directly into my eyes.

"That didn't answer my question, little one." She looked to Lucian, who nodded his head. *She needs his permission to answer me?*

"Lucian is my neutralizer." Her what? Before I could ask, my sister butted in.

"Where did you two meet?"

"Lucian and I were both prisoners at Randall's mansion," Ryan answered.

"Why were you held there?" Dom asked Lucian. A storm of

emotions passed through Lucian's eyes: remorse, shame, anger. Ryan clasped his hand in hers, and he relaxed at the comfort she offered him. I started taking deep breaths as my fury rose. She wasn't his to touch, she was *mine*.

"I was born at the vampire king's mansion." I saw tears gather in Sophia's eyes. What was up with my sister today? I have never seen Sophia so emotional.

"How old are you?" my sister asked.

"I don't know exactly, I think I'm around sixteen." Sophia gasped and covered her mouth with her hand, her eyes darting to Dom.

"Soph, what the hell is going on?" I asked. She tore her gaze from Dom and stared at me. She looked...scared. She started shaking her head, got up, and raced from the room. I turned to Dom to see he was staring at the closed office, looking befuddled.

"What the hell aren't you telling me, Dom?" I snapped.

"I honestly have no idea what the fuck just happened, Nico. I don't know what is going on with her." Dom turned and glared at Lucian. "Why is she acting so strange toward you?" he snapped at the kid.

"I-I don't know"

"Don't lie to me boy, I have known her most of her life and have only seen her cry twice! Why is she continuously crying when she looks at you?" Dom was seething with anger.

"Don't talk to him like that! Lucian has done nothing wrong. There is no way he knows Sophia!"

"How can you be sure of that, love?" Dom asked Ryan.

"Because I spent my whole life in the mansion until four months ago. I have lived my whole life in a prison cell, in the dark. I didn't even know I was a supernatural until I met Ryan. I have never seen that woman before in my life, I swear." I could hear the truth in Lucian's voice, and I actually felt sorry for the boy. I turned to Jax, who nodded his head, indicating that the boy wasn't lying.

"We didn't come here to talk about Lucian. We came here to help fight. Lucian isn't a threat to any of you." Ryan spoke like a true queen, she sounded so much more confident in herself now. She even dressed differently: she wore tight black jeans, a black shirt that showed off her midriff, and a black leather jacket. She looks badass, and my blood heated as I scanned her tight and toned body.

"First though, I think Aurora has a few things to set straight." Everyone shifted their gaze to Aurora. To her credit, she didn't shrink back. She straightened up in her chair and met our gaze, determination in her eyes.

"I will not apologize for keeping things from you all. I did what I had to in order to ensure everyone, *especially* Ryan, ended up where they needed to be." Aurora's tone left no room for argument.

She turned to Ryan. "I am sorry for all that you have endured. I couldn't help or alter your course. If I interfered in any way, you would never have met Lucian."

Ryan didn't look angry or upset, but rather smiled at the seer. I could see my wife held no ill feelings toward Aurora, but I wasn't too happy that Lucian was the cause of all this lying.

"I understand. I am not mad at you. I would go through it all again if it meant that Luce would be free."

I bit my tongue, knowing if I lashed out because I was jealous it would make me look like a fool.

"Wait, you knew where she was and what was happening this whole time?" Jackson asked. Aurora nodded. "Why didn't you say anything?"

"Because Nico would have gone after her. Ryan needed the time to train, and she couldn't have done that with you four males breathing down her throat. Jax, I know you are angry and hurt about my brother leaving you, but he had a part to play as well." Jax reeled back in his seat like Aurora had just hit him.

"What was his part to play, *mate?*" Jackson snapped at Aurora.

"Okay, I am getting tired of you using the word 'mate' like that. I have never interfered with any of my visions before, *except one.*" Jackson hung his head in shame. "Tyler needed to be on the inside so he could set Ryan and Lucian free, should the opportunity arise."

I looked at Tyler. He betrayed his pack and his best friend just to save my wife's life. I could never repay that debt. I stood and crossed the room to stand in front of him. Ryan looked like she was ready to intervene at any moment if I should try anything. I extended my hand to Tyler.

"Thank you." He looked at me with confusion. "I treated you like shit. What you did for Ryan is something I will never be able to repay. Thank you for saving my wife's life. I, Nicholas Stone, King of Farrarie, am in your debt." I bowed my head to Tyler.

Where I come from that is *the* highest honor, to have a king bow before you. Tyler jumped to his feet and clasped his hand in mine and shook it.

"There is no debt to be repaid; I did what I had to in order to ensure my pack would live. Training Ryan was my honor, Your Majesty." I snapped my gaze to Ryan, shocked that Tyler had been the one to train her.

Dom huffed. "Okay, I am tired of this back and forth. Ryan, start from the beginning, love, and fill in all the missing pieces for us, please."

Chapter Twenty Nine

RYAN

I watched as Nico returned to his seat, checking his ass out. I'm not even gonna lie or try and deny it; he had a great ass, plus he is my husband, so I should be able to check him out whenever I want.

"Eye-fuck your husband later, love." Dom said in a stage whisper while winking at me. I didn't even blush. I just smiled at him and winked back.

"Okay, here goes. After I was taken from the chapel, I was thrown in a cell at Randall's. I was beaten three times a day." I heard a lot of growls and grunts around the room; the guys clearly didn't like that. "I was given vampire blood to heal my wounds and then injected with something that would knock me out. Randall would come and draw my blood three times a day. I don't know what he did with my blood; maybe he drank it or gave it to his men, who knows. Lucian and I bonded as he was in the cell across from me. When Randall and Stevie left the mansion one day, Tyler set us free and took both Lucian and I to meet up with my cousins."

Sophia re-entered the room, looking more composed now. She sat in the seat she occupied before.

"We chartered a plane. Before we continue, I need you all to swear to me that what I am about to tell you will not leave this room."

After everyone gave a verbal agreement, I continued.

"We flew to Toronto and then drove to the Yukon, to my grandparents, Marcus and Bethany Knox." I heard gasps around the room; they too believed my grandparents were dead.

"Once there, they took us in and cared for us. Gramps trained Luce, while Tyler trained me, Alex, and Chase in hand-to-hand combat and self-defense. After training with Tyler, we then moved on to magic training with Gramps. It was then that we learned that Luce was my shield, or neutralizer. Lucian is the only one that can help me draw my magic back inside of me so I don't die. Lucian and I are bonded and must remain together in order to save—"

"Have you fucked him?" Nico blurted out.

I turned to him and glared. I could tell from the look of shock on his face that he didn't mean to say that out loud. Chase, Alex, Tyler, and Lucian all began to laugh, and Nico jumped up, obviously embarrassed and ready to defend his dignity.

"For the love of all that is holy, Tink. You really are stupid." Nico growled at Chase and I could see his pulse pounding in his forehead.

"Nico, Lucian is very important to me, and I love him dearly."

Nico turned his eyes to me, and the look of heartbreak on his face nearly broke me. He thought I had replaced him.

"Don't look at me like that, big guy."

"Look at you like what, love? I have been here worrying and searching for you, while you've been off fucking some kid! How am I supposed to feel, huh?"

I jumped to my feet and we stood there glaring at each

other, neither of us willing to back down. Lucian stood and tried to step in front of me, but Nico lashed out and blasted Luce with a purple energy ball. Sophia screamed, and I didn't hesitate to launch my own energy ball at my husband and send him sailing into the wall. He crumpled to the ground.

He sprang up and made his way back to me, where I stood waiting, in a fighting stance.

"So, this is how it ends, is it?" Nico sounded so angry and betrayed. I tried to formulate a response but nothing would come out.

"It will never end for you and her." I turned to see Lucian climbing back to his feet with Sophia's help.

"The whole time we were held captive all she wanted was you! When she did manage to get some sleep, it was you she called for. When we were free, she would sleep in *your* shirt every night. She was worried sick that you didn't love her anymore. You are a fool if you think she would ever love another man like she loves you!"

Lucian's words brought tears to my eyes. I didn't know I called out for Nico each night. Lucian really was the best; I loved that guy so much.

"How do you know she called out to him every night?" Fuck, only Dom would pick up on that bit of info. I turned back to Nico and saw a look of hurt cross his beautiful face.

"Because I couldn't bear the thought of sleeping alone again. Plus everything was new and scary. I couldn't sleep without Ryan."

Nico started growling and so did Dom. I quickly cut in to try smooth things over.

"He slept on the floor, Nico. Then as it got colder, we did share a bed." Nico's expression darkened and he looked like he wanted to murder Lucian. "We have never had sex, I swear."

Nico took a menacing step forward. We were so close I

could feel his body heat. My body wanted to lean into him and have him hold me, but I could see we were still at odds.

"Am I just supposed to believe you, little one? You have changed in your time away, you even dress differently now. Wouldn't be the first time you fucked someone else while being with me."

Wow! That was a fucking low blow, and he knew it. I chose to be the bigger person and let his dumb-fuck comment go.

"You should believe me because I am telling you the truth." Nico reached up with his hand and pushed my hair behind my ear. I shivered at the feel of him. He leaned down to whisper in my ear.

"I. Don't. Believe. You."

I feel her shiver at my touch. As I stand here, staring down at the woman that has stolen my heart, I want nothing more than to believe her words. A part of me doesn't trust that the boy kept his hands to himself. She stands there looking up at me with desire and longing swirling in her eyes. I groan internally. I want her so bad, but I have to know the truth first.

I also want to know what else happened while she was away and why we couldn't locate her. I pull my gaze from hers and look over her head at the boy. My sister is fussing over him, checking for any injuries. What the hell is wrong with her?

"Soph, leave the kid alone, he's fine," Dom snaps.

"Shut your mouth, Dominic." Shit, my sister is in a mood. A hand wraps around my neck and another on my cheek. My face is turned and pulled down, so I'm looking into my wife's eyes again.

"I swear to you, I never betrayed you. Lucian and I have found it difficult to sleep on our own since Randall's. We both have nightmares. That's *all*, Nico. I love Lucian like a brother." Her words had me slumping and the anger draining from my body. I rest my forehead against hers and just breathe her in.

Her eyes flutter shut, and I wrap my arms around her and pull her against me, resting my chin on top of her head. My gaze meets Lucian's, and he smiles and nods his head. I see it in his eyes that he loves Ryan like a big sister.

"Why couldn't I locate you?" I pull away from Ryan and wrap one arm around her waist so she is tucked into my side.

"Luce, do you want to answer that question, buddy?" Huh, why would he answer for her?

"Oh, right. Because I am Smurf's shield or whatever, as long as I am with her, you won't be able to track her or locate her." Well, Lucian might just come in handy after all.

"That's a nifty little trick. I wondered why I couldn't find her. I knew she was alive, but I couldn't pinpoint her location." Mya looked impressed with Lucian's abilities. That reminded me...I turned to look over my shoulder at Lucian.

"What kind of supernatural are you?"

"I think we should all sit down for this one." Tyler sounded ominous, so we all listened and sat. Ryan was tucked into my side. "Okay, so—" Jax cut Tyler off.

"You don't get to speak!"

"Jackson, how many—"

Aurora's scream cut her brother off and shut everyone up. "I have had enough! Jackson, stop behaving like a fucking child. Tyler, make a formal apology, then we can move on. If you two can't sort your shit out there will be no family reunion or no chance of talking about being mates!"

Holy shit, Aurora just went Hurricane Sophie on their asses. Both men looked—or rather glared—at each other, neither moving.

"I swear to God, I will move out of the room next to yours, Jackson, and Tyler, I will not speak to you again."

"Fuck you, Rora!" Tyler yelled. "I did all of this for you! You told me about your fucking vision, and I went along with it because you told me it would *save* the pack. Now look, I'm two minutes away from being pack-less and out on my own, and my wolf is driving me half-mad over my betrayal."

"Tyler, you will never be on your own. I told you this. Where you go, I go," Ryan snapped at Tyler. Tyler turned to her, and the anger in his eyes started to dissipate. "I mean it, Ty. We're in this together, remember?"

Tyler smiled sadly and turned to Jackson. "I'm sorry, Jackson. I never meant to betray you. I thought I would be strong enough to fight the mate bond. I was never meant to fall in love with Stevie Knox. I got sucked in, and when the time came to choose a side, I hesitated, but in the end I kept up my part and set Ryan free. I was always the one meant to train her, and Gramps was always going to be the one to help her train to use her magic. I did what I did to save the pack."

I could hear the truth in Tyler's words, and I saw Jax scent the air to see if he could detect any deceit.

"As alpha of the Alaskan pack, you are forgiven and welcomed home." Aurora and Tyler were both smiling at his words. "As your friend, I can't forgive you....yet. Once more, though, my mate has lied to me, again! Vision or not, Aurora, you need to stop lying to me!" Aurora and Tyler weren't smiling anymore. They both had a lot of work to do in order to win Jackson's trust back.

"Can we get this talk over with? I'm starving." Fucking Dominic needed a muzzle. Ryan giggled beside me, the sound sending warmth coursing through my body. I missed her so much while she was gone.

"I tried to come to you every night, love. I even asked Kai to try." Ryan stiffened at my words and glanced at Kai then quickly back to me. After a long sigh, she finally spoke.

"I tried for weeks to reach you. I even tried to reach Kai." My jealousy surged at the mention of her trying to go to Kai. I took a few deep calming breaths to control my jealousy. "I didn't know what was up until Gramps told me that Lucian cancels out any magic that tries to get near me." That little fucker was blocking me! I snapped my gaze to him and glared.

"Hey, it's not my fault. I don't even know what the hell I am, dude. It wasn't something I did intentionally."

"What do you mean?" Sophia asked Lucian.

"Look, all I know is my parents were fae, that's it." Sophia hung her head and wouldn't meet the kid's gaze. There was something going on with her and I needed to find out what it was, soon.

"Look, this has been a long-ass day, and I'm hungry as shit." Tyler, Lucian, and her cousins started laughing, and she flipped them the bird.

"All I have to say is we're here now, and we're ready to fight. I have learned how to master my magic, and I can fight now. Tomorrow morning I will take the other half of my magic from Nico, and Lucian and Tyler will help me manage the new power."

Like fuck would they be the only ones helping her. Ryan has another thing coming if she thinks I will sit back and let her do this on her own.

Chapter Thirty One

RYAN

After leaving Jackson's office, we all made our way to the mess hall. We all gathered our food from the buffet and sat down to eat. I'm sitting between Lucian and Nico, and Alex and Chase keep sending me sly smirks and winks from across the table. I want to slap both their stupid faces right now. Everyone is talking and catching us up on what we have missed and what the battle plan is. Dom continues to scowl at Lucian, because Sophia can't seem to stop staring at my friend. I have no idea what her fascination is with Lucian, but clearly Dom doesn't like it.

I didn't realize how much I had missed these guys until now. It's been great catching up with them and laughing, but I do miss Grams and Gramps.

"Hey does anyone have a phone?" All eyes turned to me.

"You can use mine, little hybrid. The number is already saved." I thanked Tyler and grabbed his phone.

"Who are you calling?" Nico asked, and before I could answer, Alex cut in.

"You need to get a handle on your trust issues. She spent the past twenty-two weeks trying to figure out a way to get back to you, Tink. To save you and your world. Give her some breathing space, and for the love of fucking God, at least trust her."

Before Nico could go ape-shit on my cousins, I placed my hand on his forearm and said, "I'm going to call my grandparents, big guy."

I didn't wait for a response. I stood from my seat and made my way out of the mess hall. I walked toward my old room, hoping it was still empty. As I opened the bedroom door and stepped inside, a sense of nostalgia hit me. I had missed this room.

"Didn't think you could leave me behind, did you?" I spun around at the sound of Lucian's voice and smiled.

"Sorry, Luce, I didn't even think."

"Don't sweat it, Smurf. Let's call Gramps and Grams." Lucian shut the bedroom door and we made our way over to the bed and sat down. I scrolled through Tyler's contacts until I found Grams and Gramps, saved as "Secret Knoxs." I chuckled at Tyler's silly name for them and hit the green button. It rang four times before someone picked up.

"Hello?"

"Grams, it's Ryan!"

"Marcus, it's Ryan, come here. Hello, my dear, how are you? Did you get there safe?"

"Let her talk, Bethy." I smiled at Gramps telling Grams to slow down on the questions.

"I'm fine, we're all fine. We're here now, Grams, and we're all safe."

"Thank heavens, we have been so worried about you all."

"We're fine, Grams, I swear."

"Is that trickster husband of yours treating you right? If he isn't, send one of those boys to deal with him!" I chuckled at Gramps's overprotectiveness, but I also loved it. This is what I had missed my entire childhood.

"He's been fine, Gramps. He was shocked to see us and to meet Lucian." Gramps laughed, I knew he was laughing at Nico's expense. Alex and Chase had told Gramps how jealous Nico could get. Gramps wanted payback for Nico using a glamour on himself when they first met many years ago.

"Good, serves him right for the shit he put you through. How is the battle planning going?" I filled them in on the plan and how we were going to meet with the elders tomorrow. I was nervous about seeing the elders and how they would react to me after what I had done the night of my wedding. I had taken so many lives, and I knew I had to face the consequences for my actions. But that would happen after the battle and after I saved the fae realm.

"You keep your head held high, you hear me? You are the queen of the Knox coven, and you come from a strong line of witches and warlocks. You are also the queen of the fae. You bow to no one, granddaughter."

Gramps's words made me feel proud. I felt like I could take on the world with them behind me.

"If you need anything, you call us, dear. We will be there as soon as we can." I thanked them both and told them I would call again soon. I missed them so much already, but I had to end this war in order for them to be free. Stevie would use them against me if she found out they were alive.

"It was good to hear their voices."

"Yeah, it was, Luce. I miss them so much already."

"I know you do." Lucian pulled me into a side hug, and I rested my head on his chest. The bedroom door burst open and Nico stalked in with a vile look on his face.

"Get the fuck out, *boy!*"

Chapter Thirty Two

NICO

As soon as she left, her lap dog jumped to his feet and followed her out. I scowled at his retreating form then sat there quietly seething. How fucking dare he go after her? *I'm* her husband.

"Calm the fuck down, Tink, it's not even like that with them." I snapped my gaze to Chase and glared at the bastard.

"Nico, he is a child, and lost. He needs Ryan to help him, they care for each other like siblings." Tyler's words did nothing to ease my jealousy. She was eighteen, and he's sixteen. They were close in age and probably had more in common than she and I did. I'm over a century old and had lived a life full of adventure while she was just starting hers.

"Brother, he is of no threat to you, I swear it." I turned and looked at my sister with brows raised.

"How would you know that, little dove?"

"I just do, Dominic. He cares for her, but she loves you. I told you I saw that you and she would be together."

"I never saw him coming! I didn't even know he would play a part in her life," Mya said to Sophia.

"Fuck this." I stood from my seat and marched out of the mess hall, the guys' laughter following me out. I could feel through our bond where she was. I stopped in front of her bedroom and tried to calm down. I heard them talking, and then it went quiet, and I couldn't stop myself. I burst through the door and froze at the sight of her in his arms. I saw red.

"Get the fuck out, *boy*!" I snapped. Ryan pulled away from him and frowned at me. "Tell him to leave now!"

"Don't tell her what to do!" I lashed out and wrapped him in my magic, lifting him from the bed. Ryan jumped to her feet, and her hands started to glow blue.

"Smurf, no!" Ryan looked to Lucian and then her hands stopped glowing. She glared at the boy, who was suspended off the ground, and made a small, angry screaming sound that almost distracted me, it was so cute.

"I got this, trust me." What the fuck was this boy on about?

"Lucian, don't, please. Nico, put him down now before—" She didn't get to finish. The boy let out a deafening roar, and my hold on him snapped.

My magic returned to me, and the boy stood there, glowing yellow, his eyes morphing from gray-violet to pure violet. I underestimated the boy; he was stronger than I thought. I could feel his strength. He was part fae, but there was something else.

He was another hybrid! How could that be?

Besides Ryan, Sophia and Dom were the only two hybrids we knew. Sophia couldn't access her fae side. Dom could access both his sides, but I have never heard of another.

"I have been beaten, starved, and treated like shit my whole life. I will never let another treat me that way again—or anyone I care about." I heard noise behind me and saw the whole gang was here— great. Ryan never took her gaze off the boy.

She moved to stand in front of him, and I took a step forward to stop her when I was blasted by a force so strong it sent me sailing into the others.

We all crashed to the ground, and with a groan I quickly

stood and helped Dom and Jax to their feet. They both looked pissed that they were the ones to break my fall. Whoops, my bad. I glared at Lucian, and watched as my wife stood in front of him.

"He has a force field around them, I-I can't breach it." Dom was the strongest fae I knew, but if he couldn't breach this force field, it meant that this boy was stronger, strong like Ryan.

"He won't let you breach it. Lucian is strong, one of the strongest fae I have ever met. Unless he wants you near him or Ryan, you will never enter his field." I could hear the awe in Alex's voice.

"Luce, look at me, please, buddy." Ryan was trying to calm the boy. "It's okay, Luce, I'm right here. Nico would never hurt me, I swear. He was just being an overbearing jackass. It's kinda his thing." I opened my mouth to protest but Dom pinched me, hard.

"I will not let him treat you that way, Smurf."

"I know, Luce. Thank you. I need you to drop the shield now, buddy. I promise Nico won't hurt me." I would rather die than ever cause Ryan physical harm, and the fact that Lucian thought I would ever harm her made me angry. I loved that girl more than anything.

Lucian started to draw his magic back into himself, and as soon as the last of it disappeared, Ryan engulfed him in a hug.

"He may be her shield, but she is his anchor." I heard the truth in Tyler's words. There was more to this boy, and I had a feeling my sister knew what that was.

"I'm sorry, Smurf."

"Don't be, buddy. I love that you protected me. Nico and I have a lot to sort out, and until we do that, he is going to be an ass."

"You know I can hear you, right? I'm standing right here!" I snapped at my wife, and she and the boy both chuckled.

"Do you think you would be okay to hang with Ty and my cousins for a bit while I talk to Nico?"

"Yeah, Smurf. If you need me, just call out. I won't be far." I growled.

"Boy, you are overstepping your place and need to back the hell off," I snapped.

"I will back off when you can prove you can keep her safe! Until then I will not leave her side, *Tink*" I heard the others snicker behind me at the use of the nickname Ryan's cousins had been calling me.

I was going to lose my shit soon!

"All of you, out!" Everyone started to file out of the room, and I could hear them all giggling like a pack of assholes.

Lucian hugged Ryan one last time before making his way out of the room. I slammed the door as soon as he left and locked it—not that locking it ever stopped any of them from entering before. I took a deep breath before turning around and facing my wife.

"Hello, love." She started laughing, and I couldn't help but laugh with her.

"After all of that macho display, you go with 'hello love?'" I shrugged my shoulders.

"I thought it might be a good ice breaker."

"Touché, big man" I sighed and ran a hand through my hair. I could feel how awkward things were between us, and I wanted to fix that.

"Can we sit down and talk, love, please?" She nodded her head and made her way over to the single seat by the window, and I sat on the edge of the bed. We sat there, staring at each other for a while. I had dreamed of those beautiful, strange eyes every night while she was gone.

"I missed you." Her admission shocked me. "Don't look so shocked, Nico."

"I can't help it, love. I just never thought you would say that out loud. You really have changed. You're not so shy anymore."

"I have changed. I didn't really have a choice, though. I went through a lot; I needed to be stronger and learn to stand on my own. I couldn't reach you or Kai, and I'll be honest, if it wasn't for Lucian, I would have given up while I was stuck at Randall's."

"Don't say that. Don't ever say that, love."

She smiled a sad smile. "It's true, Nico. I gave up hope that you would come for me." I stood and stalked over to her, placing my arms on either side of the chair, caging her in. I leaned down so we were nearly nose to nose and said, "I will never not come for you. I will burn the whole fucking world down for you, Ryan Stone."

Chapter Thirty Three

RYAN

Him being this close to me was intoxicating, and his words didn't really register until he said *Ryan Stone*. I never thought about my name changing when we got married.

"What's wrong, love? You look scared." I started shaking my head, and Nico clasped my face between both his hands so he could look into my eyes. "What's wrong?"

"M-my name."

Nico smiled a cocky smile; he knew what I was talking about. He loved the fact that he shocked me about the name change. He wanted to mark me as his in every way possible.

"Of course your name has changed, love, we're married." I batted his hands away and pushed to my feet. I needed to pace.

"I know we're married, it's just a shock to hear my name come out of *your* mouth." Nico's arm snaked around my waist, and I was pulled flush against him, my back to his chest.

He kept one arm wrapped around my waist and used his other hand to push my hair away so he could run his nose up and down the side of my neck. I stilled, unsure what was happening.

"Relax, love," he whispered in my ear. He continued to run

his nose up and down my neck, and I gasped when he licked the same trail with his tongue. He stopped licking, only to start sucking the side of my neck. I craned my neck to the side so he had better access.

He stopped sucking, and then started peppering kisses over my neck and then my cheek. I turned my head toward him and captured his lips in a searing kiss.

He spun me around without breaking our kiss and ran his hands down my body, gripping the back of my thighs and lifting me. My legs wrapped around his waist, and I locked my arms around his neck. Being here like this with Nico felt right. I've missed him so much. He walked us toward the bed and laid me down gently.

He pulled back and looked at me, so much love and desire swirling in his eyes.

"I have missed you every day, little one. I couldn't think straight without you, and it killed me when I couldn't reach you in your dreams. It hurt more and more each day when I couldn't find you. Now that you're back, I won't ever let you go, love...I can't." I could see from the hard lines in his face it was hard for him to admit this to me.

"I'm sorry I didn't call you when I got to the Yukon. We had to be so careful not to tip anyone off as to where we were, not just for us, but for my grandparents, too. I tried to reach you in my dreams every night. I didn't know Lucian was subconsciously blocking my dreams. Please don't be mad at him."

"Can we not talk about him while I'm standing between your legs with a fucking boner, love?" I gasped, and as if my eyes had a mind of their own, they trailed down Nico's body and landed on the hard bulge straining against his jeans. Nico started chuckling, and I quickly jerked my eyes up. I was busted! I felt the blush creeping up my neck. I don't know why I was embarrassed. It's not like I haven't seen it before—I just haven't seen it in real life.

"Why do you look sad, love?"

"I'm not sad, I-I'm just nervous, I guess." The smile dropped from Nico's face.

"Nervous about what?"

"You and me and you know?" I said, gesturing between us with my hands. He started laughing again and I groaned; I was beyond embarrassed now. I used both my hands to cover my face. I was inexperienced, and he had nearly a century of practice.

What if I wasn't good enough?

Nico pulled my hands away from my face and leaned down so he was hovering above me, resting his hands on either side of my face.

"Don't hide from me, love. Tell me what's going through your mind right now." I knew I needed to be honest with him. I took a deep breath and then said.

"Nico, you know I have never done this before. I mean, I have, but—"

"What the fuck do you mean *you have*?" I could see the anger brewing in his eyes. Dear God this guy and jumping to conclusions was like a moth to a flame.

"Stop interrupting! I meant you know I have only done this in my dreams. I've never done this while I was *awake*." I saw the moment Nico registered what I was saying. He leaned down and captured my lips, and I opened for him as I always did. He slipped his tongue inside my mouth and started exploring.

I relaxed into the bed and started to run my hands down his back and under his shirt, scraping my nails along his spine. He moaned into my mouth and started to rock his pelvis into mine. The friction of him grinding into me, and my jeans rubbing me in the right place, had me writhing beneath him. I needed more. I wanted him inside me *now*. I bunched his shirt in my hands and pulled it up, and Nico helped me pull it off and chucked it to the side. I shrugged my jacket off and lobbed it across the room. Nico immediately slid his hands under my black crop top and peeled it right off my body. I lay there beneath him in my jeans and my red lacy bra, chest heaving.

His gaze turned dark as he looked down at me, lust swimming in the depths of his eyes. That look bolstered my confidence, knowing I was the one who put that look on his face and caused that bulge in his pants.

"I want you, love." I could tell from the raw huskiness of his voice that his restraint was about to snap. I wanted him; I have *always* wanted him to be my first. He said he didn't want to have sex until we were married, and now that we are, and we're finally together again, there is nothing stopping us from making love. I looked him in the eyes and ran my hand down his cheek.

"I want this. I want you." He kissed me while he undid my jeans, only breaking the hold on my lips to pull my jeans off. His hungry gaze rakes over my tiny red thong and I shiver. He's looking at me like I am a feast after a long fast. The anticipation of what is to come is killing me.

"You're so fucking beautiful, love...I can't wait to taste you." Goosebumps break out over my skin as Nico runs his hands up my legs and over my stomach. When he reaches my breast, he pulls the cups of my bra down and exposes both the girls.

My nipples are rock hard already, and I can feel the liquid pooling between my legs.

Nico leans down and captures one of my nipples between his teeth and starts to suck, hard. I moan loud and arch up off the bed so I can force my breast further into his mouth. His other hand comes up, and he begins to twist and pull my nipple. I buck beneath him, desperate for him to touch me elsewhere.

"Nico, please." He releases my nipple with a pop and peers up at me through his long lashes.

"Please what, love?" He loved doing this shit to me in my dreams. He got off on me begging.

"I need you to touch me." He began to tweak both my nipples between his fingers.

"I am touching you, love." I groaned. He knew what I meant but he wanted me to say it.

"I want you to touch me down there." The smug bastard smirked at me.

"Touch down where, love?"

I growled. "I want you to touch my pussy, Nico, and make me fucking come!"

"Well you don't need to shout, love." I wanted to slap that smug look off his face. Before I could reply with a smart remark, he began to make his way down my body, trailing kisses across my stomach and then down my thighs.

He was torturing me with how slow he was moving. He kissed all the way down my leg and back up, then started nibbling on my inner thigh and slowly making his way to the apex of my thighs. He leaned in and inhaled.

"I can smell your arousal, love." I couldn't find it within me to be embarrassed.

Chapter Thirty Four

NICO

It turned me on, scenting her arousal. I pulled her thong down her legs and discarded it to the side. I had seen her sweet pussy so many times, but seeing it for the first time while not dreaming was something else. I couldn't hold back any longer. I wanted to draw this moment out, but my restraint was about to snap. I dove in and started to feast on her sweet pussy, swirling my tongue around her enlarged nub. She cried out, and I licked and sucked her even more vigorously.

"I-I need more, Nico!" I didn't make her beg like I normally would, I wanted her first time to be different. I slowed down and licked her while I slid a finger inside her wet pussy. Fuck, she was so tight. I groaned; my dick was straining against my jeans, painfully.

I started pumping my finger in and out of her, and she moaned loudly, her moans spurring me on. On the next push in, I added another finger so I could get her ready for me. I wasn't small, so I needed to stretch her as much as I could to make this first time easier for her.

I picked up the pace and ate her like she was my last meal,

all the while pumping my fingers in and out of her. She was thrashing beneath me and grinding her pussy against my mouth.

"Nico, I-I'm gonna come."

"Come all over my fingers, baby." I sucked her enlarged nub into my mouth and pumped my fingers inside her pussy faster. Within a minute she was screaming my name, her tight channel pulsing, squeezing my fingers.

I slowed my movements to let her come down from her climax gently. Aftershocks wracked her body. I pulled my fingers out of her and kissed her inner thigh before making my way up her body. I pulled her up so I could unclasp her bra, chucking the garment to the side. I laid her down gently and began running my hands down her body. I was mesmerized by her beauty. She's a goddess. Looking down at her beautiful face and seeing how flushed her cheeks are from her orgasm made my dick twitch. Her long brown hair is fanned out around her, her eyes are staring at me with wonder, excitement, and fear. I want to make this special for her.

Chapter Thirty Five

RYAN

I can see the torment on his beautiful face. I reach down and unclasp his jeans pushing them and his briefs down, I don't break eye contact with him. I'm trying to tell him with my eyes that I'm ready and I want him.

He helps me by removing his jeans and then settles between my thighs. I lie there, looking up at him, and I see so much love and devotion in his eyes. I reach up with my hand and run it through his hair, pulling it lightly so he'll bend down to me. When he's halfway, I sit up and capture his mouth in a kiss. He starts grinding his hips and I moan, feeling my center once again warming at his touch.

I pull back and smile at my husband. He is so beautiful, with his jet-black hair, violet eyes, and a body to kill for. I am one lucky woman to be able to call this man my husband. He steals my breath away every time. I never thought I would ever be lucky enough to ever find someone like Nico. He literally is the man of my dreams.

"I love you, Nico." His eyes soften at my words.

"I love you too, Ryan." He lines himself up at my opening.

"Are you sure you're ready? We have the rest of our lives together to do this. We can wait."

I pull his face down to mine and look him straight in the eyes as I say, "I want this, Nico. I am absolutely ready."

He nods his head and slowly, he starts to push inside of me. I feel a slight sting and I tense and try to take deep breaths. He stops pushing and I can see the strain on his face. It's taking everything inside of him to not slam inside of me.

"Relax, baby, I'm halfway there." I nod my head and try to relax, but if he was trying to reassure me, that wasn't the right thing to say. Only halfway! It's never felt like this in my dreams. He waits for me to adjust to his size, and after a few moments, I give him another nod.

"Keep going." This time he doesn't go slowly; he slams the rest of the way inside me, and I feel the moment he snaps my innocence. I feel so full, yet complete, like my final puzzle piece has been put into place.

"Are you okay, love?" I can hear the strain in his voice, and I see sweat dotting his brow. I know it's hard for him to be still and let me adjust to him being inside me, but I just need a minute to breathe through the pain.

I nod my head after the stinging starts to abate, and he begins to move, the pain giving way to pleasure. I moan loudly and rake my nails down his naked back.

"You're so fucking tight love," he pants, picking up the pace and pounding into me. I can feel a storm brewing inside me... I'm so close to coming.

"Nico, I-I...oh, God. That feels so good, gonna come." I couldn't form a proper sentence. He slams into me so hard, I start to see stars, then I shatter beneath him, screaming his name. He continues his relentless assault on my body, tipping over the edge himself just moments later.

He collapses next to me, both of us panting. That was the

most incredible experience of my life. Nico pulls me against him, both of us lying on our sides, staring at each other. I open my mouth to talk to Nico, but before I could say anything, Nico jumps off the bed and saunters into the bathroom. Holy shit, he just left me here. Before I could continue to spiral down my rabbit hole, Nico returns with a washcloth in his hand and his boxers back on.

"What's the cloth for?"

"To clean you up, my love. You didn't think I just left you did you?" I want to shake my head and tell him no, but I don't want to lie, so I nod my head instead. He looks hurt that I would think so little of him. He opens my legs, and I blush immediately, I know he was just inside me, and his face was down there, but come on.

Nico gently wipes me then takes the cloth back to the bathroom before rejoining me on the bed again.

He reaches over and gathers me in his arms, then tugs the comforter over the both of us and places a gentle kiss on the top of my head.

I sigh in contentment and snuggle into him.

"I know you still don't trust me fully, love. One day I hope that you will, though." I hate to admit it, but he's right. I may be in love with him, but I don't trust him fully. Things between us moved very quickly, and we have a history that has not helped develop that mutual trust.

"I don't want there to be any secrets between us, love."

Holy shit, does he know? I push the thought out of my mind; there is no way he could know.

"Why do I feel like there's a *but* coming?" I mumble into his chest. He takes a deep breath and starts rubbing my naked back. I hope what he has to say doesn't ruin this moment. I want this to be a happy memory, one I can hold onto.

"Your mother is in Farrarie," he blurts out. I tense, and he stops rubbing my back. We're both as stiff as boards, waiting for the other to say something or do something.

If I'm honest, I was more worried he knew about *my* secret. Here I am, letting him think he needs to earn my trust back, when in reality whatever progress we make I will shatter when the time comes. I don't want him to know the truth; I want to enjoy these last moments we have together before everything blows up in our faces. I know he will be hurt and angry, but I have to pay the price for the sins I have committed.

"Why is my mother in the fae realm?" I whisper. I feel Nico deflate; he was waiting for me to go off and lose my shit. Glad I could surprise you, big man.

"After you went missing, I had her sent to my realm so I could question her. The elders had me banned from this realm, because they knew I would come for you. The only way the fae elders could ensure peace was to lock me in Farrarie."

Holy crap, that's why Nico didn't come for me? He was literally a world away. I felt guilty for thinking less of him. I thought he had given up on me but the whole time he was trying to get back here so he could come for me. I held him tighter and kissed his chest. This man never ceased to amaze me.

"Did my mother tell you anything?"

"No, love, her memory is blank. She doesn't remember much about raising you. I filled her in on some of it, and she was devastated. She hates herself for what she has done to you. I believe being in my realm is helping her and taking away the curse that was placed on her years ago. She is...well, a very different person."

"I...I don't know what to say. I mean, as a child, I always wished my mother would change, but now I don't know if I could view her as anything but the star of my nightmares."

Chapter Thirty Six

NICO

Ryan finally drifted off to sleep. We laid there talking for hours. She told me about her training and how close she had gotten to her grandparents. I filled her in on what she had missed out on here. We spoke about other mundane things, and I felt like we were becoming closer. We used to talk like this all the time, before she knew I was real. I missed these talks. I would never let her go again, not after what we had just done. She willingly gave me a part of herself that no other man would ever have.

My love for this woman just keeps amplifying. I don't know how I stayed away from her for so long. My cock starts to stir inside my boxers at the thought of how amazing it felt to be inside of her.

Having sex in her dreams was nothing compared to the real thing. She fit me like a glove, and watching her come apart beneath me while we were both awake was the most beautiful thing. She is my beautiful dream, come true.

A knock at the door pulled me from my thoughts. I looked down at her to make sure she was covered properly under the blanket before telling whoever it was to come in. I groaned at the sight of Lucian entering the room. He scanned the room, his gaze landing on my wife's sleeping form. I cleared my throat to draw his attention to me; I didn't like him looking at her, especially because she was naked under the covers.

"What do you want, boy?" Lucian smirked at me and made his way over to the window to gaze out at the scenery.

"You know, if you weren't such a dick, I might actually like you." I smiled at his back; the kid had balls, I give him that.

"You do know I am a king and can have you punished for speaking to me like that." He chuckled quietly and then turned to face me; his eyes were downcast and his shoulders tense.

"I actually came to ask you a favor."

"Oh, this should be good. Give me a minute and I'll meet you outside?" Lucian nodded and left the room. I untangled myself from Ryan and quickly dressed, dropping a light kiss on her shoulder before leaving the room. I closed the door quietly behind me, finding Lucian was leaning against the wall in the hallway.

"What's the favor, Lucian?"

"So you do know my name." he said with a smirk. I narrowed my eyes at him. He straightened and steeled his spine. I respected him more in this moment; he met my gaze and never wavered. "I was told my parents were from your realm; I want to find out about them."

"What exactly are you asking me?"

"I want your permission to enter your realm after the war. I want to search for answers and find out what my mother did to become a prisoner of Randall Cane's." Well, well. The boy wanted to do some digging and find out where he came from. If I denied him, my wife would be pissed, if I granted him entry, he would be close by when Ryan moved to my realm. Having him there with her might help her settle in better, though.

"I don't want Smurf to know about this, though."

"Why don't you want her to know?"

He averted his gaze from mine and mumbled, "I need to do this by myself. She needs to live her life. If I tell her, she will want to help me." He's not wrong—Ryan would want to help and wouldn't rest until she got answers for her friend, but I also wouldn't lie to her again.

"You have my permission, but I won't lie to my wife, Lucian." Our conversation was cut short when the bedroom door opened behind us and Ryan walked out, back in the clothes she arrived in. She glared at Lucian.

"All you had to do was say that to me, Luce, and I would have left you be. Asking Nico to hide shit from me is low." She shouldered past Lucian but didn't get far before he gripped her arm and pulled her back. I growled. I was ready to put this bastard down if she said the word.

"Don't, Luce, let me go now!"

"Smurf, please—I'm sorry, but I don't want you to put your life on hold for me. You deserve to be happy and live a life with your husband, not chase ghosts with me." I saw her eyes soften and her body deflate at his words.

"Luce, you are family to me. I would chase ghosts for the rest of my life if it meant you were happy. Please don't ever shut me out again, or ask Nico to hide things from me, just talk to me." They embraced each other in a quick hug, Lucian whispering a promise to never hide anything from her again. I nearly puked at how mushy they were being.

Fuck, I really needed to get a handle on my jealousy.

Chapter Thirty Seven

Lucian, Nico, and I made our way to the mess hall to grab some dinner. After the workout Nico and I had just completed, I needed some fuel for my body—and a shower.

We entered the mess hall, and I must say for the first time it was actually refreshing to see and hear all the hustle and bustle in here. We made our way over to the food station and loaded our plates full of delicious food before getting a table toward the back of the room.

We ate in comfortable silence. Halfway through our meal, I looked up to see Dom, Jax, Aurora, Mya, Sophia, Tyler, and my cousins join our table. Kai was nowhere in sight. My heart sank; he was so angry with me. I knew he would be pissed off and hurt, but I didn't think he would cut me off completely.

"The mosquitoes must be bad around here," Dom said, laughing, I looked around the table, confused. The only people not laughing were Nico, Lucian, and I.

"Here I thought Kai was the only biter." They all started laughing harder at Jackson's comment.

What the hell are they all on about?

"I don't understand what is so funny?" Sophia's gaze softened as she turned to face Lucian.

"We're laughing because clearly my brother has a thing for biting the hybrid." Sophia was trying hard to not laugh again, I turned to face Nico and saw a frown marring his beautiful face.

"What do they mean?" I asked. He pulled my hair over my shoulder so it covered the side of my neck and leaned down to whisper in my ear.

"I may have *accidentally* marked you." Oh for the love of all that is holy, did he give me a fucking hickey?

"Nico did you....did you give me a fucking hickey?" I gritted out between clenched teeth. The smug fucker just grinned at me. I was going to kill him. Now everyone at the table knew what we had just done. I slouched in my seat and kept my head down while pushing food around my plate, my appetite was long gone now. I was so embarrassed.

"Come on love, don't be mad." I turned and glared at the prick I had to call my husband.

"Your stupid jealousy just had to let everyone know what we were doing. You are a dick, you know that?" I could see he was trying hard not to smile, and I knew I was blushing. I glowered. Jackson cleared his throat and spoke.

"Wolf shifters have great noses, love. Dom and I could smell him on you."

"And. in you," Dom added. I froze. Oh, for the love of mother Mary. They could smell him inside me. Fuck my life. I jumped to my feet and marched out of the room, their laughter following me as I high- tailed it out of there.

I ran all the way to my room, slamming the door shut behind me. My suitcase and duffel were sitting at the foot of my bed, thank you Lord. I quickly pulled out my sleepwear and went straight into the shower.

After the shower warmed, I quickly stripped my clothes off

and stepped under the spray. I scrubbed every inch of my body to try get rid of Nico's scent.

Fucking overbearing asshole knew what he was doing and wanted everyone else to know it as well. I shampooed my hair with the wonderful shampoo Aurora had given me for my wedding day, but quickly shook thoughts of that day out of my head. I would deal with those when the time came. I rinsed the shampoo out and started to lather conditioner in my hair and closed my eyes.

Two hands landed on my waist and I shrieked, ready to attack the bastard with a ball of energy. One hand left my waist and quickly gripped my wrist to stop me.

"Calm down, love. It's only me." Nico stood there, staring down at me, with droplets of water falling down his face. He was naked!

"You're naked." The bastard cracked up laughing while I stood there and glared at him.

"Yeah, babe, I'm naked."

"Why are you in here?" I felt self-conscious all of a sudden. He had seen me naked plenty of times in my dreams, and he saw me naked today, but I couldn't help but feel less than him. He was beautiful, with a body carved by the gods. I was average height and average looking; what he saw in me I don't know. I dropped my gaze to the floor, but he was having none of that. He released my wrist and tipped my chin up so I had to look at him.

"What's wrong, love?"

"Nothing, I just don't think we should shower together," I lied.

"Why shouldn't we shower together?"

"Because I, I thin—I mean, like..."

"Spit it out, love."

"Because you're beautiful, and I'm not, and now that we're

both standing here in our birthday suits, you can see all my flaws —and you might not like what you see. You might think I'm yuck and not want to be married to me anymore." I blurted all that out so fast I was panting, trying to catch my breath.

Nico's face took on a serious look, and he gripped my waist with his hands and pushed me back until my back was against the tiled wall. He glared down at me. Why was he angry?

"Don't ever, I mean ever, fucking say that shit again! I don't ever want to hear you talk about yourself like that. You are not something to be replaced, Ryan! You are my wife, my *hugacko*. I would die without you; you are my reason for living. You are the most beautiful creature I have ever seen in my life." He didn't give me a chance to reply. He slammed his mouth against mine, forcing my lips open and slipping his tongue inside.

Chapter Thirty Eight

I take my time exploring her mouth, moving my hands and using one to fondle her nipple while I grip her hair with the other. I continue to kiss her like she is the air that I need to live. When I pinch her nipple between my fingers, she groans in pleasure, and the vibrations send a shiver down my spine. I release my grip on her hair and move to cup her sex. She gasps when I run my index finger through her folds, gripping my shoulders for balance as I push my finger inside her. Her sheath tightens around my finger immediately, and this time I'm the one groaning.

I know she is probably still sore, but I need to be inside her again. She's like a drug to me; I can't seem to get enough of her. I break our kiss and look down at her, all hooded eyes and flushed cheeks.

"Are you too sore?" She shakes her head. "I need to hear the words, baby."

"No, I'm okay," she murmurs. I pull my finger out of her and she pouts; I love this look on her. She's looking at me like she needs me inside of her as much as I need to be in her. I drop to my knees in front of her, and she gasps at the sight of me, understanding the significance; I'll never kneel before anyone, except her.

I hook one of her legs over my shoulder and dive in, feasting on her. She cries out as I lick up and down her slit, and then I suck her nub into my mouth. She tastes so fucking good.

"Oh my God!"

I pull back and gaze up at her. "How about we try 'Oh my Nico?' God won't ever get to taste this pussy, baby." I don't wait for her response, I dive back in and lap at her folds, swirling my tongue around her clit. I insert two fingers inside her and pump in and out of her while I suck her clit into my mouth.

"Holy fuck, Nico." She grips a handful of my hair and rides my face like there's no tomorrow. A minute later, she screams out my name, and I pull my fingers out and jump to my feet, lifting her up and slamming her down on my hard, waiting cock. She cries out, and I know I should be gentle, but fuck me, I just can't.

I step forward so her back is against the shower wall and start to move inside her.

"Fuck, your pussy is so tight."

"Mmmmhhhh. Don't stop, Nico. I need more, please." Her words shatter any restraint I had left. I slam into her over and over again, using her body weight to keep her firmly against the wall as I pound inside her until we both find our release in one fantastic crescendo. As we come down, I rest my forehead on her shoulder, panting. Not ready to let her go, I turn us so my back is against the wall and slide down until I'm sitting on the floor.

She doesn't attempt to get up, instead wrapping her arms around my neck and snuggling into me. It's in this moment, with her cuddled against me, and straddling my lap with my dick still inside, that I realize she owns me. I am unconditionally in love with Ryan Stone. I grip her long hair in my hand and pull until she stares up at me, looking annoyed that I interrupted her snuggle session. I release her hair and push the stray strands behind her ears as the water continues to beat down on us. She looks breathtaking, rosy cheeks and glassy eyes, rivulets of water pouring down her body.

"I love you," I blurt out. She places a kiss on my lips before leaning back.

"I love you too, Nico."

Chapter Thirty Nine

RYAN

Nico and I made love in the shower once more before getting out. I say made love, because it was slow and passionate and fucking beautiful. I was losing my whole heart to him and no part of me wanted it back. I wanted him to have my heart forever. I was going to miss him so fucking much.

After changing into my PJs, I hopped into bed, waiting for Nico to get back. He needed clean clothes from his room, and he said he would bring all his stuff into my room tomorrow. We were both too tired to even attempt to do that tonight. My bedroom door opens, but it wasn't Nico that walks in—it's Lucian.

Shit, how the fuck could I have forgotten that Luce was my bed buddy?

Lucian must have showered somewhere, because he was in sweats and a shirt now. He made his way over to the empty side of the bed and drew the covers back. I didn't have the heart to tell him Nico would be back soon. He climbed into the bed and rested his head against the pillow. I had to say something, but what could I say?

Hey, Luce, now that Nico is here, you can't be? Or hey, Luce, back to the floor you go so I can snuggle my husband.

"Smurf, I can hear you overthinking from here. What's on your mind?" I released the breath I didn't know I was holding and laid down on my side so I could face Lucian.

"I don't know, Luce...I didn't expect today to go how it did."

"You mean you didn't expect to fuck your husband six ways to Sunday?" I giggled and hid my face for a moment.

"Who the hell taught you that saying?"

Lucian shrugs his shoulders and says, "Chase has been teaching me some slang." We both laugh, knowing Chase was the worst person to teach Lucian slang.

"Don't listen to my cousin, he will lead you astray."

"He's good people, Smurf. Now stop stalling. What's got you so worried?" Lucian reached over and clasped my hand in his. Being here with Lucian like this felt familiar and safe. I knew I could confide in Lucian with anything; well, except one thing.

"I love him, Luce, and that scares the shit out of me."

Lucian's eyes softened. "Why are you scared?"

"Because one day, something might tear us apart." A look of confusion crossed Lucian's face, then understanding.

"What aren't you telling me, Smurf?" Lucian was great at reading me, so I had to steer this conversation in a different direction before he clued in. He had an inkling about what I had planned, but Gramps and I wouldn't confirm his suspicions.

"Nothing, I'm just scared that after the war I have to leave this place behind. I've only ever been to the fae realm once, and soon I'll have to live there. Not only that—I just found out my mother is there too." Lucian sucked in a sharp breath; he knew what happened to me and what my mother had done to me.

"Fuck me, Smu—"

Lucian was cut off when the bedroom door slammed open

with a loud thwack. A seething Nico stood in the doorway, glaring at us and then at our joined hands.

Fuck, could this situation get any worse?

"*Fuck me?* Did you just ask my fucking wife to fuck you, boy?" Well, that answered my question. Nico launched an energy ball at Lucian, who deflected it with the flick of his free hand. Nico stormed over to my side of the bed and ripped my hand out of Lucian's. Lucian jumped to his feet, and they stood on either side of the bed glaring at each other.

"Calm the hell down, Nico!" I snapped.

"Calm down? Calm down? I open the door and see you in bed with another man, and you think I should calm down?" He was blowing this way out of proportion.

"Seriously? Nico, you're being a dick, let go of my arm." He didn't release my arm immediately, until I started slapping his hand that was gripping me. I shifted to the middle of the bed, not wanting to be near Nico right now. He was being an absolute drama queen.

"How would you feel, Ryan, if you walked in on me with another woman?" I flinched at his tone. Nico was past the point of being angry, he was livid. I hate to admit it, but he does have a point.

"Nico, I..."

"No! You don't get to turn this on me, not this time, love." Fuck him, how dare he. Lucian was there for me when he wasn't; Lucian was my savior in the night when I would wake, screaming.

"Fuck you! He was there when you weren't. He kept me alive while they broke me each and every fucking day for *weeks*. He stopped one of the guards from raping me! He took a beating that day just so they wouldn't rape me—*me,* a stranger he didn't even know. You do not get to come in here and compare our situation to you in bed with another woman. This is different, and you know it!"

I needed to calm down; I could feel my magic surging inside of me. I was too angry to do it myself, and I quickly turned to Lucian.

"Luce, help me, please." Lucian leaned across the bed and gripped my face between his hands. He closed his eyes, and I mimicked him.

"Deep breaths, Smurf, and release it to me," Lucian commanded.

"What the fuck are you doing?" Nico snapped at us.

I couldn't see him; I couldn't risk opening my eyes. I had control over my magic, but it seemed like whenever I was around Nico, all my training went out the window.

"I'm saving her from blowing this whole fucking place up. Shut up or get out. You're making it worse." I kept taking deep breaths, blocking Nico out and focusing on matching my breathing to Lucian's. After a few minutes, I felt calm and my magic receded. I let out a deep breath and opened my eyes. Lucian smiled, and I leaned forward and rested my forehead against his.

"Thank you, Luce."

"Don't thank me, Smurf. I'll always be here to help you."

NICO

Standing here, staring at the two of them, I feel out of place. He's kneeling on the bed, cradling her face between his hands, while resting his forehead against hers. I have never felt so unneeded in my life. He's the one she needs. Maybe fate fucked up and chose wrong; maybe he was meant to be her *hugacko* and not me. What if she chooses him?

I thought everything would be okay after the whole Melakai thing. He told her the truth and admitted to using his emotion control on her to make her love him. Now I have to go through it all again. I can't, not again, not after what we had shared today.

"You good now, Smurf?" he asked her. Why the fuck does he even call her that?

"Yeah, I'm good." They didn't break apart, they were still resting their heads together. I can't take it anymore. I turn on my heel and pretty much run out of the room. This is total devastation, not jealousy; this was me being honest with myself. I wasn't what she needed—Lucian is. He is the one who can save her from herself.

I exit the compound and keep walking until I find a creek in the middle of the woods. The moon is the only lighting out here.

I pull my knees up to my chest and wrap my arms around my legs. I peer out into the darkness, listening to the running water in the stream.

What has my life become?

Before her I was a fearless king who ruled his people fairly, now I was a mess. I don't know which way is up or down. I've shirked my duties as king a lot lately; I've spent more time in the Earth realm than need be. I should be in Farrarie. My soldiers should be in Farrarie training, not sleeping in tents on Jackson's land. What the hell is wrong with me?

I'm more angry at myself for letting my feelings over cloud my duty to my people. My world is on the brink of dying, my people are at risk of losing their life—hell, *I'm* at risk of losing my life. All because I fell in love with a hybrid who has the power to kill my world. Imagine that, my *hugacko* is the only person in the world strong enough to seal the portal that grants my world life. I am so fucked.

A branch snapping from behind me pulls me from my thoughts. I didn't need to look to see who it was, I could feel them coming. A second later, Dom, Jax, and Kai appeared. Kai had two bottles of whiskey in his hands, and Jax and Dom both had bottles with them, as well. I smiled at my brothers as they sat beside me.

"So, why the hell are you sitting out here in the dark and not banging your wife?" I couldn't hold my laughter back; Dom was always great at breaking the tension in serious situations.

After I got my laughter under control, I snatched one of the whiskey bottles from Kai's hand, unscrewed the top and raised the bottle in cheers to my brothers. They each opened a bottle and raised theirs. I took a few big gulps and shuddered as the whiskey burned its way down my throat.

"Do you wanna tell us what's going on? Ryan's running around the compound looking for you." I released a long breath and looked up at the night sky. I took a deep breath and then answered Dom's question.

"I don't think we're meant to be." Admitting the truth to my brothers felt like a weight had been lifted off my shoulders.

"Why do you say that?" Jax asked. I filled them in on what just happened and how it made me feel to see my wife with another man, a man who could help her.

"That's fucked up." I couldn't agree with Dom more.

"Have you tried talking to her?"

"Yes, Jackson I have, but she's different now." Jax and Dom agreed. Kai had been quiet this whole time.

"What are you gonna do?"

"I don't know, Jax." Kai released a loud exhale.

"Do you have something to add, Melakai?" I snapped, irritated that he was huffing and puffing next to me. I didn't ask him to be here, so he was free to leave whenever the hell he wanted.

"Actually, yeah I do."

"Oh pray tell, Kai, we're all dying to hear this," Dom remarked dryly.

"Okay, smart-ass." Kai said tartly. "Ryan is different. She has changed a lot since being here in Alaska. She has been through a lot."

"No shit!" I sneered.

"Let me fucking finish before cutting me off, Nico! Before coming here she thought she was human, now she has learned she is a hybrid. She has the power to end a world she didn't even know existed. That is a lot for any one person to deal with. To top it all off, the one person she thought she could rely on is a psycho bitch and wants to kill her. She meets two guys she thought were part of her imagination. Then one of the guys she *thought* she loves nearly dies. She then starts seeing her dead father and then marries the other dream guy she actually loves, only to end fifty or so people's lives *the night of her wedding*. She then gets taken prisoner and is tortured for six weeks. Every day while she is beaten, there is one saving grace. Her cellmate, the one person who was there for her at the hardest time of her life. She then flies to a whole new country and meets her long lost grandparents, whom she thought were dead. She trains for four months, learns to master her magic. Comes back to Alaska to help save a world she doesn't even really know. She was free, Nico—she could have run and left us for dead, but she didn't. She came back to help us...to help you!"

Well, fuck, when he puts it like that, it is a lot. I never really sat back and thought of it like that. Kai was always the best of us at reading people and looking beyond the mask people wore.

I understand what Kai just said, but it doesn't change the fact we are too different. I hadn't realized I had drunk the whole bottle until I went to take another drink, only to find the bottle empty.

Jax offered me his other bottle while he and Dom shared Dom's spare one. I think it was safe to say we were all getting a bit tipsy. We sat in silence for about ten minutes until I spoke; well, slurred is probably a better word.

"I get what you're saying, Kai, and you're right. It just doesn't change the fact that she needs *him* more."

"She doesn't need me more."

What the fuck? I turned my head and saw Lucian standing behind us. Fuck, we must be drunk. I turned to Jax and Dom, and by the looks on their faces, they didn't hear him coming either. I turn to Kai and squint in the low light to see his bottle is still nearly full. The fucker heard Lucian coming and never said a word.

Chapter Forty One

NICO

Lucian walks around to stand in front of us. I glare up at the little bastard. I'm pissed Kai didn't even give us a warning that the shithead was coming. I lean over and snatch the mostly full bottle from Kai's hand and the fucker just laughs as I pass it over to Jax.

"Why are you here, young one?" Kai asks.

"Because my best friend is out of her mind with worry." Fuck him. I don't give a shit that Ryan is looking for me right now. That woman is doing my fucking head in.

"Why don't you go comfort *my* wife then?" Saying those words hurt me more than I wanted to admit. I was drunk and angry, and I didn't mean it, but it was too late. I said it. The little fucker scowled down at me.

"You know what? You can hate me all you want, Nico, but don't take this out on her." If I could have stood without falling over I would have. Instead, I stayed sitting and glared at him as best as I could.

"Fuck you! You don't get to tell me what to do, you little shit. You have fucked everything up!" I snap.

"Nah, man, you're doing a good job of that yourself."

I went to stand so I could attempt to hit the smug prick, but Kai placed his hand on my shoulder and pulled me back down. I landed on my ass with a thud.

"Dude, were having a bro sesh. If you're here to fuck with that, just leave," Dom said to the kid.

"I'm not here to do that, *dude*, I'm here to try help him understand," Lucian said, pointing to me.

"Just say what you have to say and then leave, kid." Jax sounded irritated.

"Look, she doesn't have feelings for me. Smurf and I.."

"Why do you call her Smurf?" I cut in.

He smiled down at me before replying. "Because she glows blue." We all started laughing—a full-on belly laugh. Kai was even laughing, and that the kid managed to get the giant stone statue to laugh was an achievement. After we managed to get ourselves under control, I told Lucian to continue with his story.

"Smurf and I bonded while we were locked up. She wouldn't even speak to me at first—it wasn't till the day one of the guards tried to... you know."

I nodded my head, Jax and Dom growled, and Kai was breathing fast. They knew what Lucian was insinuating.

"Anyway, they never used to beat me, but they came to beat Smurf everyday like clockwork. That one day, I screamed and yelled and did everything I could think of to get his attention off her and on me. Long story short, he beat the shit out of me instead of hurting her. After that day, she talked to me and we bonded. I tried as much as I could to get them to beat me instead of her. A couple times it worked, most of the time it didn't. Once Tyler broke us out, we formed a different bond.

"Look, I know you don't like me, but I love her like a sister— at least I think that's how you say it. All I know is I don't think Smurf is someone I want to kiss." Hearing that made me feel a bit better.

"Why do you insist on sleeping next to her?"

Lucian dropped his gaze and looked at the ground while he answered.

"I don't like to be away from her, because I'm afraid she will leave like my mom and the woman who raised me did. I can't sleep on my own. I have never slept through the night until I slept next to Ryan at her grandparents. I may be able to help her with magic, but her just being near me is helping me heal. I'm not used to people and living outside of a cage, you know? Smurf is helping me deal with this, and so are Tyler, Alex, and Chase. Smurf just helps me on a deeper level; she gets me. Anyway, I just came to say that if my presence is causing you two trouble, I'll stay away and keep my distance until she needs me.

"I've never met you until this morning, but I feel like I know all of you, from how much she has talked about you all. She loves you so much, Nico. Don't let my problem of not wanting to be alone tear you away from her. She won't survive losing you."

"How do you know she won't be better off without me?" I ask. He lifts his gaze to meet mine, and I see sadness in his eyes.

"She told me you were the Yin to her Yang, her better half. She lost her dad, her sister, and she thought she lost her mom— not that it sounds like that was much of a loss. But she said losing you would end her. You are her everything, but she won't tell you that because she has been hurt so much in her life. She would lay down her life for yours."

Maybe this kid wasn't so bad after all. I respected him for being willing to face me and admit his own insecurities, for Ryan's sake. He has had a shit life, and I didn't want him to suffer any more than he already had. Ryan needed him, and he needed her. I was going to have to get used to that.

Because I couldn't let her go.

I managed to climb to my feet after three attempts. By the time I stood on my feet, the others were already standing. Fuck, I was drunk as a skunk. I reached my hand out to Lucian, who stood there staring at my hand like it was going to bite him. After a minute, he placed his hand in mine and shook it.

I held onto his hand and looked directly into his eyes.

"I'm sorry about the life you have had. I will keep my word and help you find your parents after this war. I also won't push you away from her, but don't ever let me catch you in the same bed as my wife again." He shook my hand again and nodded his head. "You sleep on the couch or the floor, you get me?" He smiled at me and nodded. The floor or the couch was the best compromise I had.

"I feel like a proud dad! Nicky boy is all grown up and acting like a big boy now!" We all chuckled at Dom's smart-ass comment and made our way back to the compound. Okay, fine —I stumbled most of the way back.

Chapter Forty Two

I have searched for Nico everywhere. He took off like a bat out of hell. I can't find Dom, Jax, or Kai either; I asked some of Jackson's pack members, but they just said they didn't know, which I knew was bullshit. They could mind link him if they wanted to help, but it's typical behavior for the pack. Tyler, Alex, and Chase wouldn't help me look. They said to leave Nico have his tantrum. Lucian was MIA as well.

I have been pacing a path in my room for over an hour. What if he left and went back to Farrarie?

Tears started to gather behind my eyes. I couldn't lose Nico. I needed to get out of this room. I decided to go search for the girls and try to take my mind off my husband.

I found Sophia, Aurora, and Mya in the game room. I made my way over to them and plopped down on the couch next to

Sophia, resting my head on her shoulder. She tensed immediately.

"Soph, what's wrong?" Aurora asked. Sophia shook her head and then turned her gaze to me.

"What's happened between you and my brother?" I reeled back, shocked.

"How do you know something happened?" She smiled sadly.

"I can see peoples love lives, remember?" Oh, that's right, did she have a vision when I touched her?

""Did you just see something?" I asked.

"I can see that Nico's heart is hurting and that so is yours. Why are you both hurting?" I released a loud exhale before answering her.

"Nico's pissed at me. He walked in on me and Luce talking and got the wrong idea. I love your brother more than I love my own life, but I can't give Lucian up." Sophia's eye's softened and began to glaze— was she about to cry? What happened to Sophia while I was away?

"I think I respect you even more now. My brother can be an ass, and Lucian is of no threat to him. Be patient with Nico. He loves you, and I don't need a vision to tell me that. I can see it in the way he looks at you. Nico has never been like this before, with anyone."

Her words warmed my heart. Nico and I could work this out. He was my soul mate, and I wouldn't give him up without a fight.

The girls and I left the game room and headed to the mess hall to get some dessert before heading off to bed. It was late, but I wasn't about to turn down the chance to have some sugar. I knew sleep was going to evade me tonight, so I might as well hang out with the girls to keep my mind busy and off Nico.

We each grabbed a bowl of pie with some ice cream and sat down at one of the tables. We chatted about mundane things and how they had been the past few months. I told them about my time while I was away.

"When will you take your power back?" Mya asked, but I didn't get a chance to answer as Alex, Chase, and Tyler sat down at the table. Tyler answered Mya's question.

"As soon as possible. She needs to learn how to control her whole power before the war." It was like a bucket of ice water had been dropped over me; my good mood evaporated immediately. Here I was, obsessing about my argument with Nico, when his whole world was at stake—*his life*. How fucking petty could I be? I needed to get my head into the game. I guess it is true what people say—sex really does change things. Maybe I should have waited till after the war before losing my V-card to my husband.

Shaking myself out of my thoughts, I spoke to the group. "First thing tomorrow we will begin the exchange. After that I will continue to train daily with Tyler, Alex, and Chase in combat and then train with Lucian in the afternoon to hone my magic skills. We've got to get this show on the road."

I returned to my room ready to fall into bed. I was mentally drained and my coochie was feeling the after effects of losing my V-card. I needed an ice pack for it, but I wasn't about to try find someone and explain why I needed it. Sighing loudly into the empty room, I decided I needed to just go to bed and then deal with Nico tomorrow. I climbed under the covers and switched the bedside light off, staring up at the ceiling and thinking about how shit my first day back in Alaska had been. Of course I was happy to see everyone again and be with them, but I didn't expect to lose my V-card and then fall out with Nico all in the same day.

With a sigh, I forced the fears from my mind. I knew I needed to stop overthinking and try and get some sleep, or tomorrow I would be a bitch-a-saurus.

Chapter Forty Three

NICO

I didn't bother to shower or change after the guys brought me to my room. I lay down on my bed and closed my eyes, hoping sleep would claim me, but it didn't. I laid there for so long thinking about how the day went from being the best moment of my life to one of the worst. Ryan and I have fought in the past, but this felt different. I don't know how I am supposed to breach the gap between us.

She has changed so much and is a different person now—a person I didn't know. My feelings for her haven't changed in the slightest; she is still the center of my world.

Moving forward, I think it best that I keep my distance and then after this battle is over we can try work on us. My feelings for her are clouding my judgment. I would help her release the power inside of me and then I would return to my realm and take my men with me, so they could train at home and not live in tents.

My soldiers deserved to be home with their loved ones; it might be their last chance to be with them. I fucked up so much these past few months, and I needed to get my head on straight and be the king I have always been instead of this lovesick dog.

Sighing, I turned over and decided to just deal with everything in the morning. I couldn't change how the day went today, but I could change the outcome of tomorrow, hopefully.

I awoke with the worst headache known to man or beast. I showered and changed then made my way to Jackson's office for our morning briefings. I opened the door, but the office was empty. I look to the clock on the wall: seven-thirty, I'm not late. Where the hell are they?

I shut the door and made my way to the mess hall; maybe they decided to grab breakfast first, without me.

The mess hall is bustling with activity this morning, as usual. I scan the room, peering over the top of people's heads, and spot Dom's silver hair. The bastards *were* eating without me.

I grab a plate and load it with all the greasy food available: bacon, eggs, sausages, steak, toast. My stomach growls as I make my way over to the guys.

Just before reaching them I pause. Ryan, Tyler, Alex, Chase, Lucian, and the girls are all at the table with Dom, Kai and Jax. The fuckers ditched me to eat with Ryan and her groupies? I curse under my breath and plonk my ass on the seat between Dom and Kai.

I refuse to utter a single word or make eye contact with any of them. Their conversation quiets down as soon as my ass hits the chair. I can feel the awkward tension in the air, but I refuse to acknowledge it. I'm going to enjoy my breakfast before getting into a verbal sparring match with my wife.

I decided last night that I was going to keep my distance and let her come to me. I haven't told the others yet that I plan to return to Farrarie today.

"Well, this breakfast went from being enjoyable to plain old awkward." Trust Dominic to make a wise-ass comment about the situation.

"I feel like a butter knife could cut through the tension." The table erupts into laughter at Chase's remark. After their laughter subsided, I could feel *her* gaze on me. I continued to eat like I didn't notice the hole she was burning into me.

"Nico, can we talk please?" All conversation around the table stopped. I finished my mouthful and then took a drink of my juice before meeting her gaze. I could see so much remorse and shame in her eyes, but I couldn't let her emotions change my mind. Sitting up straight and clearing my throat, I answer her.

"I think we should go ahead with you taking your power back this morning, straight away." She reels back in shock at my emotionless response. I made sure to keep my face blank.

"W-why?" she stammers out.

"Because I need to return to my realm." Everyone around the table gaped at my confession. I was a king, for fuck's sake, and I needed to run my kingdom. I couldn't shuck off my job for love, that wasn't how it worked.

"Why are you leaving?" Jax asked. I never took my eyes off Ryan while I answered him.

"I have a kingdom to run, and I have spent enough time away from my realm. I need to return with my soldiers and train them back home. They have lived out of tents for months, I owe them more than that. They should be with their families, in their own homes, in case shit goes bad."

Ryan's eyes start to mist with unshed tears, and I can't take it. I stand and tell them I will meet them outside in an hour to begin the transfer of power. I exit the mess hall with Kai hot on my heels.

Chapter Forty Four

RYAN

I swallow past the lump in my throat, blinking my tears away. Nico is leaving. He was really going back to his realm. My chest feels like it's about to break in half. I waited *months* to be with him again. Now, so close to D-day, he wanted to run away.

I couldn't let him leave. I raced out of the mess hall and down the hallway that leads to the back of the compound, hoping and praying this is the way he went. I round the last corner and pause at the sight in front of me.

Kai had Nico by the scruff of his shirt, pushed up against the wall. Nico didn't even try to fight back; they stood there nose to nose glaring at each other.

"Why are you running away?"

"I'm not, Kai."

"Don't fucking lie to me, Nico! We need you here. *She* needs you here."

"Nah, you guys will be fine. I have a kingdom to run! I need to go home. If everything turns to shit, I need to make sure that I have everything in order. She will be fine, won't you, love?" Nico's gaze turns to me, and I gasp. There was no love in his gaze, no warmth. He looked at me like I meant nothing to him. My heart splintered in my chest.

"Don't do this, brother—don't you dare self-sabotage. You deserve this, Nico, let her break down those walls." Kai was pleading with Nico, trying to make him see that he was needed here, that I needed him.

Nico pulls his gaze back to Kai and scowls. "I don't deserve shit, Melakai. You know nothing! I married her, and I did my duty. She has made her choice. She doesn't need me. Now, get your hands off me so I can go and tell my people we are leaving." As soon as Kai releases Nico, he barges out the door.

I stand there stunned and rooted to the floor. *I did my duty, I married her.*

His words keep playing on repeat over and over in my head. Nico only married me out of duty to his people? Did he even really love me?

I was such a fool! I was in love with a man who threw me aside as soon as he got into my pants. I was so lost in my dark thoughts that I didn't even see Kai approach. I craned my head back and looked up at his beautiful blue-gray eyes, full of so much pity.

"He doesn't mean it. He has been through a lot, and seeing you so close to another man hurt him. Give him some time." I felt awkward having this conversation with Kai; he has barely said two words to me since I got here yesterday and now the first real conversation we have is about my love life, great.

"He meant what he said, Kai. I don't know what I have done to make him think I have feelings for someone else." Kai has a sad smile on his face, I didn't want him to pity me.

"You are *everything* to him. He thought he didn't deserve love."

"Why would he think that?"

"When Sophia— the only woman he ever truly loved—was

taken, it destroyed him. He searched everywhere for her. It broke him when he found out Randall had taken her, and no matter what he did, he couldn't get her back. Nico only started to find peace when he began visiting you in your dreams. Nico doesn't know this, but Dom and I kept in contact over the years, and Dom would give me updates on how Nico was coping. He thinks he doesn't deserve happiness or love because he couldn't protect the person he loved most when she needed it. Just like he couldn't protect you from Randall, either."

My heart hurt even more now after hearing that. Nico blamed himself for Sophia being taken...Oh my God.

"Nico isn't really angry at me, is he?" Kai shook his head. "He's angry at himself because I was taken and there was nothing he could do about it." Kai nodded his head. "So this is some kind of trigger for him, his old doubts and feelings are coming back from when Sophia was taken."

Kai nodded again. "He is using sarcasm and jealousy to throw us all off track. I know him too well, though, and he wants you to think he is leaving because of Lucian. He is really leaving because he is afraid of losing you, and there is nothing he can do about it."

Tears dripped down my face, but the tears weren't for me. They were for Nico and all the pain he has suffered. Kai grasped my hand and led me out the door Nico had just left through. I didn't protest or try to fight; I let Kai lead me to wherever we were going.

Kai stopped in front of a large tent pavilion, pushing the flap open and leading me inside. There were eight men and Nico inside. Nico glared at Kai.

"Get out, Melakai, I am meeting with my generals," Nico snapped.

"All of you get the fuck out now." No one moved. "I said NOW!" Kai roared. The men looked to Nico, who hadn't taken his gaze off Kai. Nico gave a stiff nod and they quickly stood and exited. As soon as the flap shut behind the last man, Nico snapped.

"How fucking dare you. You do not get to come in here and tell my men what to fucking do!" I moved out from behind Kai and released his hand. Nico briefly looked at me then averted his gaze. "What is *she* doing here?"

I paused and looked at Nico; his words and derisive attitude hurt. I needed to put my feelings aside and help him. He looked so stressed and tired, and his black shirt was wrinkled and his jeans had grass stains on them, he looked a hot mess.

"She is not Sophia, and you are not the same person anymore. You will keep her safe, and she will remain with you." With that said, Kai turned and left. Nico and I stood rooted in place, avoiding eye contact. I have never felt so out of my element before. I loved Nico, and he was my fucking husband. I needed to bridge this gap between us and fix things.

I took a deep breath and then made my way over to him, stopped directly in front of him. With a loud exhale, I closed the gap between us and wrapped my arms around his waist. He just stood there, stiff as a board.

"I wasn't taken from you. I left. I didn't have a choice, Nico; Stevie was hurting our friends. There is a huge difference. If there was another way, I would never have left you. I love you, and I want to spend my life with you. Don't push me away, please. I couldn't handle losing you. If you have to leave, I understand, just don't run away from me. Let me fix this between us first."

Chapter Forty Five

I stood there with her arms wrapped around me, stunned. Listening to what she was saying didn't make me feel any better. If I was honest with myself, I *am* running away. I'm so scared of losing her like I lost Soph. I couldn't handle her being taken from me, again. I nearly lost my mind when Stevie dragged her out of here. I wrap my arms around her and rest my chin on top of her head and she relaxed in my hold. King or not, I couldn't live without her.

"I love you too."

"Then don't leave me, Nico. We are stronger together. I'm so sorry about yesterday. I will talk to Luce and see if we can work something out with his sleeping arrangements."

I smiled. The boy hadn't told her about our conversation last night. "I don't want to lie to you; Luce did stay in my room last night." I growled. The little prick was going to get it.

"He slept on the floor, I swear." My smile was back in place. The boy would live to see another day.

I knew I owed her an explanation, but I didn't want to talk about it here. I released her and took a step back, and she frowned at the space I put between us.

"Let me just set my guys up and then we'll talk, okay?" She smiled, but it didn't reach her eyes. I placed both my hands on her shoulders and bent down so we were eye to eye. "I'll be back shortly; I promise I'm not running away."

"Okay." I placed a chaste kiss to her forehead and left the tent.

I returned to the tent from giving my generals their orders; they were to return home. Ryan was sitting in one of the high-backed chairs, and I slumped into the twin chair next to her. She was going to be upset that I was still leaving, but I had to put my people first, and they needed their king.

"Ryan, I—"

"I know, Nico, you're still leaving." I was stunned that she knew.

"How?"

"I heard people talking as they walked past. Why are you leaving?" She looked so crestfallen, and the light in her eyes had dimmed. She may look different and act different, but she was still the same on the inside, scared to lose anyone she loved.

"I'm not leaving because of *us*. I need to return home to rule my people. I have let my emotions control my judgment since you arrived here. It's not your fault, it's mine. I moved my men here as soon as the ban was lifted from the elders. I have taken them from their home and their families, because I wanted to be here for you. But you're back and safe, and my people should be able to spend their last weeks in their own world."

I see resignation in her features, she knows my mind is made up. I know the timing of my leaving her world isn't ideal, but I needed to rule with my head and not my heart. She leans across and places her small delicate hand on my arm, her eyes meeting mine. I see turmoil shining in her eyes, and I swallow past the lump forming in my throat. I hate that I am the one to put that look on her face. I never want to hurt her, ever.

"I understand. I just wish there was another way. You're right, though, your people need their king. When this battle begins, they need you to have a clear head and not have your judgment clouded by your emotions."

I stood and pulled her to her feet, wrapping my arms around her and holding her tight. For a few minutes we just stood there, holding each other.

"Nico, I need you to tell me that we're okay. I need you to tell me you will never stop fighting for us." I felt her tears on my shirt, and I felt the lump in my throat return. She really had no idea how much she meant to me. I pulled away to look down at her; I can see the uncertainty in her gaze.

"I will never stop fighting for us—for you. I told you before, I would burn this whole fucking world down before I let you go. I thought yesterday that maybe you wanted something else, someone else. I see now how wrong I was. I let my fear of losing you cloud my clarity. You mean everything to me. You, Ryan Stone, are the beginning and ending of my life story."

Tears leaked out of her eyes and slowly trailed down her cheeks. I wiped them away and bent down to kiss her. She tasted so sweet. I groaned. I knew she would be sore from losing her virginity yesterday, so before I lost my self-control and took her, right here, right now, I pulled away from the kiss.

"Why are you stopping?" She looked annoyed; fuck me in the ass for trying to be a gentleman around here.

"I know you're sore, love; I'm trying to be considerate." I smiled down at her, and she glared back.

"Since when have you ever cared about being a gentleman?"

I grinned, she had me there. I wasn't known for being sweet or gentle, but for her, I wanted to try.

"Since now, and don't make me fail on my first day of trying, love." She burst out laughing, and I joined her. It felt so good to laugh with her again, and I knew, in this moment, we were going to be okay. We have faced our fair share of downs, but now it was time for us to have our *up* moments.

Chapter Forty Six

RYAN

Nico and I made our way through the forest to the same place we had met Stevie and Tyler all those months ago. Being here again brought back mixed emotions. The others were gathered near the fence. I gripped Nico's hand, and he stopped his movements to turn and face me.

"I just need a minute." Nico's eyes softened, he knew why I needed a moment. He wrapped me in his arm and stroked my back, and his embrace helped stop the pounding in my chest. I took some deep breaths and gave myself a mental pep talk before stepping back from Nico. I gave him a nod, and he gripped my hand again, leading us toward the others.

"Took you love birds long enough." I smiled at Dom; he was so good at easing tension and helping people relax with his outlandish comments.

"We had some things to sort out," I told him. I didn't want to lie. They all knew Nico and I weren't on good terms yesterday.

"Oh, so you were doing the horizontal dance while we were all here waiting for you?" I blushed immediately and tried to use my long hair as a curtain to shield me from their gazes.

"Nah, I can't smell him on her. Plus he looks too tense to

have just blown a load." I could hear the laughter in Tyler's voice. I was going to kill him for that comment later.

"Wait, you're more scared of us knowing you had sex than when Tyler bit you?" Lucian remarked; I heard gasps and growls erupt around me. I quickly lifted my gaze and gripped Nico's hand tighter, trying to hold him back.

Dom, Jax, and Kai had murderous looks on their faces. The three girls looked shocked. I had to make a quick decision. I released Nico's hand and quickly stood in front of Tyler. I would not let them hurt him. Alex and Chase moved to stand either side of me, and Lucian stood next to Chase.

It felt like a Mexican standoff, with Nico and the others on one side with me and my crew on the other side.

"Step aside now, love," Nico gritted out between clenched teeth. Oh boy, this wasn't going to end well. Dom was glowing yellow, Jax's eyes had changed, and Kai was snarling with his fangs out. Nico's hands started to glow purple, and their display of power caused a reaction from my side, Alex, Chase, and Lucian had their power on display as well. I wouldn't display my magic unless I had to.

"Step aside, little hybrid. I knew it was wrong when I did it." I turned to look over my shoulder so Tyler could see the look in my eyes. He sighed, clearly accurately reading the expression on my face. I would never let him fight this alone.

"Jackson, please, he's my brother!" Aurora was trying to reason with her mate. Why were they all so uptight about a bite?

"He knew the rules, and he also knows the punishment for what he did." What the hell?

"What the fuck are you all going on about? I'm fine." I even showed them my arm, the one Ty bit. There was a scar, but it didn't bother me. I was proud of my battle wound.

"You don't understand, Ryan; it is forbidden to attack someone's mate, or in this case, *hugacko*. The punishment is death."

I reeled back at Mya's admission—what the actual fuck! No way in hell was Tyler dying for something my grandfather had told him to do. Jax and Kai took a step forward, and I released my magic and my hands started to glow blue. They both paused at my power display.

"If any of you—yes, Nico, including you—try to harm him in any way, you will need to go through me first!" I growled to the group of men.

"And us!" Chase chimed in.

"He bit you, Ryan! He could have killed you!" Jax shouted.

"He was doing as he was told. If he hadn't done what he did, Lucian would never have released his hold on my power!" I snapped at Jax.

"Who told him to bite you?" Dom asked.

"My grandfather. He had Lucian pinned to a tree and made him watch as I battled Tyler with no magic. The only way Lucian could get over his fear of losing me was to watch me nearly die." I mumbled the last bit out, I didn't want to put Lucian in the hot seat, but I didn't have a choice right now.

"Your grandfather is fucking crazy!" Kai shouted.

"Watch the way you speak about our grandfather, Cane," Alex sneered.

"Why the hell wouldn't you release her power *before* he bit her?" Dom asked Lucian, looking perplexed.

"Because she told me when we were locked up that her power consumed her. When the seal was broken on her power, it took control of her and *that thing* happened that night. I was scared that if I gave it back to her that she would be lost to the power inside of her." The three girls looked touched and awed at Lucian's admission, but the guys looked conflicted. They didn't know whether to be angry with him or shake his hand. Nico stopped glowing and so did Dom. Kai stopped snarling and retracted his fangs. Jax was the last to calm down, but his eyes finally changed back to chocolate brown after a few moments. As soon as I saw Jax relax, I pulled my power back and so did my three guys.

"I kind of want to find any reason to hate you, but I just can't find one good enough yet," Nico ground out to Lucian. I smiled.

"So, am I still on death row....or?" Jax looked over my head at Tyler, glaring.

"This is your final warning. You step out of line or break any more rules, and your sister being my mate will not save you." Jax pulled his gaze from Ty and looked directly at me. "I am the Alpha of all wolves, Ryan. It is my call on how I punish my shifters, and you will not interfere again." I glared at Jackson. How fucking dare he?

"You may be the Alpha of Alphas, but she is the queen of the Knox coven and the queen of the fae. I think she outranks you, *Alpha*."

I looked at Mya in shock. I never expected her to come to my defense like that.

"Okay, enough of this shit. Nico and I need to leave and go back to our realm soon. We need to do the transfer of power now, we're wasting daylight."

Oh my God, Sophia was going back with Nico. I loved having Soph around and it made me sad to think of her not being here.

"Don't look so shocked, Ryan. I need to help my brother lead *our* people. We will be back before the war, I swear." I nodded my head in understanding. It still sucked that they were both leaving, though.

Chapter Forty Seven

Ryan and I walked out to the center of the empty field. I had no idea what I was doing. She looked confident enough for the both of us, so I was taking that as a good sign. The others spread out around us, making a circle.

"So, how do we do this?" I asked, and she smiled.

"Trust me, big guy, I got this." I nodded my head, but I was still a bit nervous.

"Luce, come on, buddy." I opened my mouth to ask what he had to do with it, but she anticipated my question.

"Lucian will help me control the power coming from you. He will filter it to me in doses, so I'm not overwhelmed with it all at once." I nodded my head again. That was actually fucking smart. I didn't trust Lucian as far as I could throw him, but Ryan trusted him, and that had to count for something, right?

"Are you ready, Smurf?" Lucian asked as he approached us in the center.

"As ready as I'll ever be. You got this, Luce." She turned to face him and clasped both his hands in hers. I stood there watching their strange interaction. He seemed to relax at her touch—why?

"I trust you, Lucian. I know you won't let anything bad happen to me." He was looking at her with such intensity, and I could see the war raging inside of him. He was scared to fail her.

"Your Gramps isn't here to coach us this time, Smurf. What if I stuff it up or what—"

"Don't do that, Luce. I believe in you. You need to believe in yourself, you're so much stronger than what you think, buddy." She released his hands and then pulled him in for a quick hug, and he sagged in her arms. His lack of confidence wasn't exactly awe- inspiring for me.

"Can you do it or not?" I didn't mean for it to come out sounding so harsh, but Lucian flinched none the less. Ryan shot me a death glare. Whoops.

"He can do it, I know he can." I looked past Ryan to Lucian, who was nodding his head. He still didn't seem confident, and suddenly I wasn't okay with this plan.

"Little one, maybe we—"

"No, Nico, we are doing this now. I trust Lucian, and I know he can do this." All righty then, I guess we were doing this whether I liked it or not.

Ryan stood in front of me, and Lucian stood to the side between us. He placed one hand on my shoulder and one on Ryan's.

"Okay, Nico, I need you to release your hold on Smurf's power, and I'll pull it into me." I nodded my head, closed my eyes, and concentrated. I reached deep inside of myself to feel for her power; once I located it, I began to push it outward. I didn't know if I was doing this right, but I just had a feeling this was how I was supposed to do it.

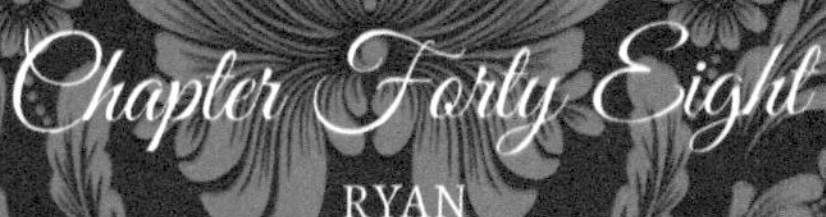

Chapter Forty Eight

RYAN

I stared at Nico in awe; his whole body was covered in blue light, my color, and it was a beautiful sight to see. Nico opened his eyes and I gasped—his eyes had changed. They were no longer violet; they were now the same color blue as my power. Lucian's shaking pulled me from my thoughts; I turned my head slightly to see sweat had broken out across his brow and upper lip.

That wasn't a good sign at all.

"Luce, start channeling it into me now. It's too much for you to hold onto." Lucian gritted his teeth and nodded his head. I didn't feel anything at first, then suddenly I began to feel warmth spread from my shoulder where Lucian was touching. The warmth spread like wildfire, and within a second my whole body was warm. Once Lucian started funnelling the power back into me, he couldn't stop. The magic wasn't responding to him like Gramps said it would.

It knew who its master was and wanted to be back with me. I wasn't ready for that, my body started to grow hot, I felt sweat drip down my back. I tried to focus on my breathing and remain calm. Magic was ruled by emotions, and if I freaked out now, all hell would break loose.

"Why is she shaking?" Nico snapped. I couldn't answer him. If I did it would break my concentration, and I couldn't risk that. I needed to focus; I closed my eyes to block everything out.

"D-don't t-touch h-her. Y-you need to move back by the others." I could hear the strain in Lucian's voice. I knew this was taking a huge toll on him, but we couldn't stop now.

"I am not leaving her!"

"Y-you need to go, Nico! I can withstand her blast if she loses control. You can't. Leave for her—if she hurts you, she will never forgive herself." Lucian was right, I would never survive hurting someone I cared about. Nico was muttering curses underneath his breath, then I heard him leave. I felt Lucian move from beside me to stand in front of me, and he placed his other hand on my shoulder.

"I can't hold it much longer, Smurf." Lucian's voice was trembling, and I opened my eyes to see him struggling. An idea came to me, quick as a flash.

"DOMINIC!" I screamed out, and not a moment later Dom is standing beside me.

""What is it, love?" He looks between me and Lucian, seeing the struggle on both of our faces.

"You are the strongest magic wielder I know, and Lucian is just as strong." Dom nods his head, but I can see in his eyes he's confused. "Lucian is going to release my power, and I don't know if I can handle it all at once. Can you help him funnel it?"

I don't know if what I am asking is even possible. Dom is my last resort, or I will level this whole forest and kill everyone within the vicinity, and I can't go through that again. Nico is too emotionally attached to me and wouldn't risk my safety; he would try to make Luce and I stop the transfer.

"I-I think I can...I will have to do it through him, though."

Dom turned to look at Lucian. "Will you allow me to do that? I will need to push through your bonds and help you stabilize the power inside of you." Lucian gritted his teeth and nodded. Dom moved to stand behind Lucian and placed both his hands either side of Lucian's head.

"I need you to let me in, don't fight it. If you do it will hurt you." Luce nodded. "Hurry, I can't hold it much longer," he ground out.

"How much power could she really have?" Lucian and I didn't find Dom funny at this moment. Dom shook his head then closed his eyes.

"*Tereso tereso calulu calide, Tereso tereso calulu calide, Tereso tereso calulu calide entaly!*" I had no idea what the hell Dom was saying, but whatever he was doing was helping Lucian. I felt Lucian relax his hold on my shoulders, and his face lost some of the strain he was sporting minutes ago. I even felt warm now and not like I was burning up. At the rate Dom was helping Lucian funnel the magic into me, I would be able to handle this.

Chapter Forty Nine

NICO

It took everything inside of me not to run to her when she called for Dominic. Well, that and my sister pulling me back, telling me to trust Dom. I *do* trust Dom; I just didn't understand why she called for him and not me. I stood on the sidelines and watched as Dom placed his hands on either side of Lucian's head.

The blue light started to dim between Lucian and Ryan. Whatever Dom is doing is working; he's slowing the speed of the transfer.

"He's doing it!" I could hear the awe in my sister's voice. The others started to migrate to where Sophia and I stood by the edge of the forest.

"Well, isn't that a blow to your ego, Tink?" I turned to glare at Chase. I hated that fucking nickname.

"Why would Nico's ego be hurt?" Mya asked, and Chase and Alex chuckled before Chase answered. "Because Ry wanted Dom and not him."

I growled.

"Let's be honest, though, you may be king, but Dom is better at magic than you." Alex was really enjoying this. I was not weak, but even I had to admit Dom was powerful. Dom may only be half fae, but he trained harder than anyone I know to be the best.

He was one powerful son-of-a-bitch. Before Ryan and Stevie came back to Alaska, Dom was the only person who could rival me in the power department. That said, I didn't like having my shortcomings announced in public like Ryan's cousins had just done. Dicks.

My attention was pulled back toward Ryan and the two guys. It seemed like the transfer was taking hours, but in reality only about ten minutes had passed.

I could see the strain on all three of their faces from here. I could tell Ryan was fairing okay with the transfer, but the two guys weren't.

It wasn't often that you saw Dom struggle with magic and seeing it now was not reassuring. Lucian was trembling and gritting his teeth. They needed to hurry before Lucian lost his hold.

"The boy is losing control," I said to the group.

"He'll be fine. He is stronger than even he knows." I looked at my sister from the corner of my eye.

"How do you know that, Soph?"

"I just know, Nico. He will not let any harm come to her." My sister was being cryptic, and I wasn't in the mood for her games.

"Ever since that kid has shown up, you've been acting weird. Why?" My question came out harsher than I intended, but I was sick of never being able to figure her out.

"All of you shut up! I can't fucking concentrate," Dominic screamed at us. I flinched at his tone; I could hear the strain in his voice. Sometimes I forget how good his hearing is, being half shifter. Everyone shut their mouths and watched.

RYAN

I could feel my magic come alive as it came back to me. I didn't realize how incomplete I felt until the other half of me started to come back. My magic felt like a warm caress, almost like the waves of the ocean swaying inside of me. It was a feeling I couldn't explain...euphoria was probably the only word that could best describe this feeling.

"Hold on, kid, we're nearly done," Dom gritted out through clenched teeth. I pulled myself from my inner bliss and focused on the two men in front of me, both wore looks of fatigue. I hadn't realized how much of a toll this was taking on them.

"Luce, I need you to let go of the rest now!" Lucian started shaking his head. "Lucian, listen to me, you're turning gray. If you hold it any longer, it will kill you." I felt tears gather. I couldn't lose Lucian, he was too important to me.

"Do it, kid! I can feel your life force draining." Lucian wasn't listening to Dom, and he started swaying on his feet. I felt his hands start to go slack on my shoulders, and my tears fell without my consent. I could see his eyes starting to dim.

"Luce, please!" I choked out.

"Release it now!" I have never in the months that I have

known Dom ever heard such authority and control in his voice like that. His tone reminded me of Jackson's in alpha mode. Lucian's eyes widened, and his trembling stopped.

Without warning, I felt it all rush in to me, like a tidal wave. I stumbled back a few steps as it crashed against me.

I saw, from the corner of my eye, the others running toward us, and I quickly erected a shield around myself. I needed to calm down and not have everyone in my face or I would explode. I looked to Dom and saw that he had his arm wrapped around Lucian's waist. Lucian's head was hanging down lifelessly.

I snapped my eyes closed and blocked my emotions out. I would deal with the guilt later.

"Ryan, let me in. Let me in, love." I refused to open my eyes and look at Nico; if I let him in I would lose control. I sat down and crossed my legs. Keeping my eyes closed, I began to take deep steadying breaths.

Calm as the trees, calm as the sky. Think of the ocean and how it moves as one with all its different currents.

I kept thinking of the phrase Grams had told me over and over again, until I felt my blood start to cool down and my magic stop warring inside of me. I remained seated for a few more minutes, just to make sure I was in control. When I was certain, I pulled the shield down and brought the magic back into me. Within a second, Nico's arms wrapped around me and lifted me off the ground. I didn't have a chance to protest before he was marching us back toward the forest.

"Nico, I'm fine. You can put me down." He glared down at me. Why the hell was he fucking angry?

"We'll meet you in the mess hall, little hybrid." I leaned my head back over Nico's arm to see Tyler and Dom carrying Lucian and the others following them toward the compound. If the compound was that way, where the hell is Nico taking me?

"Nico, I need to go check on Lucian! Put me down now." He didn't answer me.

"*Portaly awa wiremu opeinga.*" I know what *portaly* meant; he was opening a portal to somewhere, great. I get to be whisked off to God knows where with the brooding king of the fae. Yay me.

Chapter Fifty One

NICO

I couldn't look at her right now; she had just shut me out again. Why does she keep doing this? As soon as we passed through the portal to Lake William, I deposited her on her feet. Once I was sure she was steady, I removed my hands from her shoulders.

I moved away from her and walked to the end of the dock. I stood there, staring out over the lake and the mountains, and felt myself relax. This place had a calming effect.

"Nico, why are we here?" I felt her standing behind me, but I refused to turn and face her. I couldn't, not yet, my anger was still burning inside of me. She reached out and touched my arm, and I flinched away from her.

"Why did you bring me here, if you're just going to ignore me?" I wheeled around to face her, and she stumbled back a step. I narrowed my gaze on her; how could she not know?

"You keep blocking me out, why?" She flinched at my tone. I didn't have it in me to care that I had upset her.

"I-I don't intentionally do it," she stammered out.

"Bullshit!" I yelled, and she moved back a couple of steps, a look of hurt crossing her face. "You blocked me out back there, again." She glowered back at me and closed the space between us, craning her neck back so she could look me in the eye.

"You dumbass! I put the shield up in case I couldn't hold the power inside of me. I didn't let you in because I was scared I might hurt you!"

"Stop being scared of hurting me! I want to help you, but you keep shutting me out." She dropped her gaze and moved back a step, and I took deep breaths, trying to control the rage inside of me, but it wasn't working. She released a loud sigh and then spoke.

"I don't mean to do it, I swear. I'm scared, Nico. This is all new to me, and the last time, I hurt so many people." My resolve started to falter; how could I be so dense?

"I didn't think, love. I know you're scared. I just want to help you through this so badly." She reached out and clasped my hand, looking me in the eyes.

"I'm trying to deal with this as best as I can, Nico. I hate that so much of this battle rests on me. I'm not special, yet I am the only one with the power to save a world."

Couldn't she see it? I closed the gap between us and peered down at her.

"You were *born* special, Ryan. You were never meant to be ordinary. You're the most extraordinary being there ever was, embrace what you are." I cupped her cheek with my free hand, and she nuzzled into it.

"Don't fight what you are, love; if you do, it will only make wielding your power harder." Tears started to glisten in her eyes. She released my hand then gripped the back of my neck to pull me down for an earth-shattering kiss.

The taste of her was driving me insane. I wanted inside of her now, but we didn't have time. I pulled away from her reluctantly and gazed down at her. Her strange eyes held so many conflicting emotions.

"We don't have time, love; we need to get back."

She nodded and leaned forward so her forehead was resting against mine and whispered, "I know you have to leave, but I don't want you to go."

I wish I didn't have to return to Farrarie, but my soldiers deserved to spend whatever time they had left in their own homes. And I knew she couldn't come with me; she needed to be here and train.

"And I wish you could come with me, but you must remain here and train with the others. I wish I could be the one to train you, sweetheart, but I could never push you past your limit like the others can. I love you, Ryan Stone." She smiled so wide at the sound of her new last name, and her smile warmed my heart. Before she could reply, I pulled back and clasped her hand in mine and began to walk us back toward the forest, opening a portal that led us back to Jackson's compound.

Shit, I didn't mean for us to arrive at *this part* of the compound. Her gasp said it all—she was devastated at the sight of what remained. I unintentionally opened the portal right by the chapel.

I turned to shield her from the charred remains of the building, but it was too late. Jackson had ordered the chapel to be destroyed; he said it was too hard for everyone to look at.

"Deep breath, love." She looked up at me, and my heart splintered at the look of utter devastation on her face. I cupped her face between my hands. "It wasn't your fault, and the elders aren't pursuing this, love. They know it was an accident."

Chapter Fifty Two

RYAN

Guilt weighed so heavy on me. I couldn't escape the ghost of my past. Nico had no idea...no one would get over what I had done. Fifty-two people lost their lives that night, all because I came into my powers. No matter what anyone said, I was the one to blame for the events of that night, no one else.

I didn't have the time right now to ease Nico's worries. I would deal with the fallout of my deceit later.

"I'm okay, can we just go inside now? I want to check on Lucian." Nico nodded his head and released his hold on my face. I clasped his hand in mine and led him toward the compound.

We entered the mess hall, searching for the others; I spotted them near the back and was relieved to see Lucian awake and upright.

I made my way over quickly, with Nico following. As

soon as we neared the table, I went straight for Lucian. He saw me coming and stood. I wrapped my arms around him and rested my head on his chest, and his arms were like a vice around me. After a moment, he pulled back and looked me in the eye.

"I'm sorry, Smurf, I thought I could handle it." I could see remorse and regret warring in his gaze, and I was having none of that.

"Don't you dare apologize; you did amazing, Luce. I am so proud of you, and I know Gramps would be proud as well." Lucian smiled and we both sat down, and the others resumed their conversation. Tyler was sitting on my other side and nudging me with his elbow. I turned to glare at him.

"Now that I have your attention, I think we should start training tonight." I groaned internally. Tyler liked to train at all hours; he wanted us to be prepared in case Stevie decided to attack at night. I hated night training, and I sucked at it.

"Come on, little hybrid, you have like three weeks max to learn control." I slumped in defeat. He was right, I needed to use every spare moment I had to train. I looked to Luce to see if he was listening to Tyler and me, and he nodded his head. I guess we're doing night training.

"I must be going now. Maverick and Larick are waiting for me." I turned toward Nico, it had slipped my mind for a moment that he was leaving. I took a few deep breaths and told myself to woman up. I wasn't going to sit here and cry. Nico was a king, and he had a job to do. We all stood and followed Nico out of the compound toward the forest where Maverick and Larick were waiting for their king. As soon as we neared the portal, Nico began to bid everyone goodbye, and everyone wished him well.

I waited for him to reach me. I couldn't meet his eyes. I had a lump the size of a boulder in my throat. I tried to swallow past it and not cry, but it was fucking hard. I just got him back, and now we are about to be apart again!

When would we ever get to just be together and not have a threat of imminent death or destruction hanging over us? Nico cupped my face and used his thumbs to wipe away my tears. He lifted my face so I was looking at him.

His violet eyes softened, and he looked over my head to whoever was standing behind me and said, "Look after her. If anything happens to her, you will have me to deal with. Believe me, you may think Dominic is strong, but *I* was the one to train him!"

"You don't need to threaten us, *Tink*. We would die to protect her." I pulled out of Nico's hold to turn around, and Chase, Alex, Tyler, and Lucian all stood behind me, nodding their heads. Out of the corner of my eye, I saw Dom, Kai, Jax, and the three girls nodding their heads as well, and my heart swelled.

"You have our word, brother. We will protect her with our lives." I turned and faced Dom; he wasn't looking at Nico, he was looking at me. I nodded my head and mouthed a silent *thank you.*

Nico turned to me so I was facing him, brushing the pad of his thumb across my lips. I lifted my gaze to his, and I could see he was torn between his duty to his people and staying with me. I had to be a queen in this moment, and not a wife.

"I'll be okay, I promise. It's only a couple weeks, and then you'll be back." I tried to keep my tone light, hoping to ease some of Nico's tension. He tried for a casual smile but it didn't reach his eyes. He dipped his head forward to avoid my gaze, and his jet-black hair fell over his forehead.

No way—he was not going to avoid looking at me. I needed to show him that I could do this. He needed to know that the woman he married was strong enough to last a few weeks without her husband. I wasn't weak anymore; I would be strong for him. I cupped his face and lifted it till his gaze met mine.

"We can do this. You have a world to run, and I need to stay and train with the guys. We're going to be apart now so we can be together forever." Nico's smile was blinding, and I knew had appeased his doubt with my words.

"You are going to be the best queen Farrarie has ever known." It was my turn to smile now.

"I don't think Farrarie is ready for a queen like me." His face turned serious.

"Well, they had better be ready, because I am." His words boosted my confidence. If Nico thought I could do it, then I would. He leaned down and kissed me, sending fire through my body. I kissed him back like it was the last time I would ever touch those lips. A throat clearing had us pulling apart, and Nico grinned down at me while I stood there panting and trying to get my racing heart under control.

"Be safe, love. If you need me, or if anything happens, go to the place you love the most, and you will find your way to me." Cryptic much? What did he mean? Before I could ask, he turned and walked toward the portal. Just before entering, he turned to look over his shoulder and smiled at me. A second later, he was gone. Sophia bid us all goodbye and followed her brother through the portal. Larick and Maverick nodded their heads at me before following their king and Soph through the portal. As soon as Maverick's second foot cleared the threshold, the portal closed with a popping sound.

As we all made our way back to the compound, it hit me—I know what Nico meant. I know where the portal that stabilizes Farrarie is. Was that why I was so drawn there? I always knew that place was magical.

Chapter Fifty Three

RYAN

"Put your shield up!"

"I'm fucking trying, Tyler!" I snapped. We have been doing this every day for the last five days. Morning, noon, and night, we trained. I do hand-to-hand combat in the mornings with Alex and Chase. After lunch, I work with Lucian and Dom on magic and control.

Every night I train with Tyler in the clearing of the woods. Jax, Dom, Kai, Aurora, Mya, and Lucian joined us tonight. Alex and Chase have been busy studying up on coven law. I assigned them the task under the pretense that they would teach me how to rule the coven after the war.

"Try harder! Do you think your sister will stop attacking you because you ask her to? Suck it up buttercup and let's go again!" I glared at Tyler. Whenever we trained, my friend Tyler was gone and in his place was a drill sergeant.

"Ty, cut her some—" Tyler turned and glared at his sister.

"If I had gone soft on you, Aurora, you wouldn't be who you are today." What the hell? Tyler trained Aurora? How did I not know that she could fight?

"But Ty, she is—" He cut his sister off once again.

"No, Aurora, I told all of you, if you can't stay out of her training then don't come out here. She can handle it; she just needs to believe she can." I didn't have time to process his words, because within a second, Jax was on his feet and crowding into Tyler's space, growling.

"She may be *your* sister but she is *my* mate! Watch how you speak to her." To Tyler's credit, he didn't flinch or shy away from Jax.

"My sister doesn't need you to fight her battles, *Alpha*. If you pulled your head out of your ass for more than a minute you would see that," Tyler snapped back.

Before they could bash each other's brains out, Kai quickly stood and pushed them apart.

"That's enough, Jackson. We don't have time for this shit. Ryan needs to train, and you are taking up that time." Thank God for Kai, he was the best at diffusing tension-filled situations. Once Jax and Kai were seated again, Tyler turned back to me, a look of determination on his face.

Oh boy, I know that look.

"You will not leave here until you can either shield yourself from me or push me away." I didn't get a chance to prepare. Tyler charged at me, and I tried to build a shield quickly, but I was too late, and Tyler knocked me on my ass—again. He didn't help me up. He just looked down at me, disappointed.

"I'm trying, Ty," I protested.

"Try harder, Ryan. If you can't even push me away in my human form, how do you expect to push a vamp away?" He was right. I don't know why my magic wasn't doing what I wanted.

"We're running out of time. You need to be able to take down your sister and stabilize Farrarie all in the same day."

You know, take down my incredibly powerful twin sister

and stabilize an entire world, all before bed. The elders had ordered it all be done in one day; I knew why, but the others didn't.

"Tyler, if I may?" Dom stepped forward and made his way over to us. Tyler looked him up and down and then reluctantly nodded and made his way over to the others.

"Hello, love, you seem like you're in a bit of a pickle."

I chuckled. "Yeah, you could say that."

"What seems to be the trouble, love?" That was the problem; I didn't know what was wrong or why my magic wasn't responding to me.

"I don't know. I had it all figured out before I got the other half back from... you know." I couldn't say his name. I missed him too much. I hadn't seen or heard from him since he left. No dreams, nothing.

"Ahhhhhh, I see what the problem is." I cocked my head to the side— what did he get?

"Our magic is tied to our emotions, love." I nodded. "You miss him. You're blocking your feelings, so your magic is blocked."

"Wait a second, are you saying my magic won't work because I refuse to think about Nico?" Dom nodded his head and smiled at me. Fuck my life.

"You need to let yourself feel, love—all the anger, hurt, everything. The more you suppress it, the more your magic will fight you." That was a lot easier said than done. I didn't want to re-live all the hurt and anger I had been through. Once was bad enough.

"Believe me, love, the more you block yourself off, the more potent the magic becomes and the harder it is to control." Is that why I lost control *that* night? Because I refused to feel and then it all came rushing out when I got my power unlocked? Nico wasn't the only one occupying my thoughts, though.

"Okay, I need you to do me a favor."

"What is it, love?"

"I need you to take me to Nico." Dom looked taken back, and I heard the others murmuring behind us.

"Why, love?"

I sighed. "I need to speak to my mother."

Chapter Fifty Four

NICO

"Sire, the queen is here." I spun away from the bookshelf and faced Cyrus.

"What do you mean?"

"The queen isn't alone, sire." I rushed out of the room with Larick, Maverick, Cyrus, Sophia, and a few guards taking up the rear and picked up speed as I went.

"Drop the bridge, NOW!" I yelled to the guards at the guard tower. The bridge wasn't all the way down before I was sprinting across it and jumping off the end. As soon as my feet hit the ground, I was running toward the forest, where I saw four figures emerge. I scanned the group for her, catching sight of her long brown hair blowing in the breeze.

My breath caught in my throat. I stood in the middle of the open field, waiting for her to come to me.

She looked gorgeous in her trademark Chucks, dark wash jeans, and a form-fitting plain black shirt. She lifted her gaze, and I saw her scanning my group, looking for me.

When her eyes found mine, a smile so bright and wide graced her beautiful face. She broke away from the others and started running. When she was a couple steps away from me, she launched herself into my arms. I caught her, she wrapped her legs around my waist, and before I could say anything, she leaned down and stole my breath with a kiss.

"I think the queen of the fae wants to bone the king of the fae." Just as I pulled back from Ryan, I heard the distinctive sound of flesh being slapped.

"Why the hell did you hit me, Soph? To think I actually missed you!"

"Because you can be such a dick, Dominic."

I grinned up at my wife, who was smiling down at me. She wiggled in my hold, and I reluctantly set her on her feet. I pulled her into my side as I greeted Dom, Tyler, and Lucian.

"This place is so...unreal." I could hear the awe in Lucian's voice at seeing my home for the first time. "Oh my God, Smurf, he lives in a fucking castle!" I chuckled, the others joined me.

"Yeah, Luce, he does."

"He really is a king." Lucian turned to face me with a look of fear on his face. "You know how I called you a dick and said some dumb shit? I really didn't mean it, so please don't, like, order for my head to be removed or any—"

I cut off his mindless rambling. "It's fine, don't worry about it. Welcome to Farrarie. My home is your home." Lucian grinned, and I felt Ryan snuggle in closer into my side. She was happy to be here. I looked down at her and kissed the top of her head. I missed her so much.

"Okay, this is gross watching you fawn all over her. I'm going to your office; I need a drink." I chuckled at Dominic. Even though it's only been six days, I missed him as well.

We all followed Dom back to my office. Larick and Maverick greeted their queen as she walked passed them, and Ryan blushed then nodded hello. She pulled out of my hold briefly to greet my sister and hug her. She was still finding it hard to accept that she was a queen. What she didn't know was that she was the only one who didn't.

Dom, Soph, Tyler, Lucian, Ryan, and I all stood around my office with drinks in our hands I could feel the tension pouring off Ryan in waves now that we were inside the castle. What the hell was going on with her? She was standing by the window that I had thrown Dom out of. I stood beside her, slipping my hand in hers.

"What's wrong, love?" The others ceased their conversation. I looked around the room, but their faces were unreadable. My gaze landed on my sister, who gave a small nod of encouragement.

I turned my gaze back to my wife and tried again. "Did something happen?"

She took a deep breath and looked me in the eyes. "I can't access my magic fully until I deal with all my emotions."

"I don't quite understand what you're saying, my love." She let out a sigh before steeling her spine and standing taller. I reached out with my free hand and cupped her cheek. She nuzzled into my hand and closed her eyes for a moment, enjoying my touch.

As soon as her eyes opened, I saw determination in them.

"I need to see my mother, Nico." I dropped my hand. I didn't expect her to say that. "In order to control my magic and use it properly, I need to deal with my emotions. I thought I was struggling because of how much I missed you, but it wasn't you. I did fine training with Gramps. My magic has been funny since you told me that my mother was here, and I'm pretty sure she is the cause of the block, and I need to fix it."

I had no words. I nodded my head like an idiot and turned toward my desk to retrieve a key from my desk drawer then motioned for her and the others to follow me.

I had put her mother in the east wing. At the request of Nina herself, after I told her what she had done to Ryan, I had the east wing locked off so no one could enter and she couldn't leave. She was terrified of losing control of her mind and hurting someone again. After a five minute walk, we finally arrived at the double doors that led to Nina's suite. I placed the key in the hole but stopped and turned to look at Ryan.

"Are you sure you're ready for this, love?" She took a steadying breath and nodded her head. I turned back and unlocked the doors, and with a deep breath, I pushed the handles down and opened the doors.

"Nina?" A moment later, Nina popped around the corner from her sitting room with a wide smile on her face.

"Nico, I'm happy to see—" She stopped speaking as soon as she realized who was standing next to me. Nina's hand came up to cover her mouth.

Chapter Fifty Five

RYAN

There she was, standing right there. She was right in front of me, but she didn't look the same. She didn't look like a monster anymore.

Her face wasn't hollow, and her eyes weren't sunken into her face. She had put weight on. She looked...healthy. I ran my gaze over her. She was in a beautiful yellow summer dress. Her hair was out and flowing around her, the blonde much more pronounced. Her rich brown eyes were filled with tears.

If I didn't know any better, I would swear this woman wasn't my mother. She was clean and healthy and looked normal. She wasn't drunk or high. I have *never* seen my mother sober. Completely overwhelmed, I turned to leave.

"Please...Ryan." I spun around and glared at her. How fucking dare she!

"Please, you fucking think you have the right to speak to me?"

I felt myself growing warm, and I could feel my magic surging inside of me. Oh, *now* my magic wanted to work. I felt a hand land on my shoulder and turned to glare at the owner of the hand, but stopped when I saw it was Lucian. He was siphoning my magic so I didn't hurt anyone. I pulled my gaze from him to turn back to face the star of my nightmares.

"You're right, I don't have a right to speak to you, but I want to." Tears rolled down her face freely. I shrugged Lucian's hand off my shoulder and moved toward Nina. I felt Nico and Lucian behind me but refused to acknowledge them.

I stopped a foot away from her and looked her right in the face. This woman broke me in so many ways.

"Do you have any idea what you put me through?" I didn't realize I was crying until I felt the tears rolling down my face. I have to give Nina credit; she didn't avert her gaze or look to the others for help.

"No, I don't. I have no idea what I put you through. Nico—"

"You don't get to say *my* husband's name!" I screamed, and she stumbled back a step.

"Dom, why don't you Soph and Tyler go get something to eat?" Nico said.

"Nah, man, I think I want to stay and—" I heard a *thwack* and flinched; someone had just hit Dom across the head, I would bet money on it.

"Fuck, Sophia, are you this frisky in bed now?" Nico growled, a moment later I heard the doors close behind us.

Nico came to my side and clasped my hand. I felt the tension drain from my body at his touch.

"Why don't we go into the sitting room and talk?" Nico suggested. Nina—I refused to call her mother—lead the way to her sitting room.

I sat on one of the two couches, and Nico and Lucian sat on either side of me. Nina sat on the other couch with her hands clasped in her lap, her eyes downcast.

Good. How did she like being the weaker one in the room now? I relished in the feeling of her being inferior and afraid.

"Why are you here, Ryan?" Nina murmured, and I gritted my teeth. How fucking dare she ask me what *I* was doing here.

"You are in *my fucking home*, Nina!"

"Ryan, that's enough." I turned to glare at Nico; he didn't get to tell me what to do with *her*.

"Don't you dare, Nico—"

Nina cut me off. "It's fine, Ni—. It's fine. She has every right to be angry with me."

I turned back to Nina. "You don't know anything about me, let alone how I am feeling! You fucked up my life!"

"Yes, I did! I didn't mean to; I didn't know what I was doing. You want to be mad and treat me how I treated you, then fine, do it. Trust me, it won't make you feel any better. I punish myself every day since being here and having a clear head.

I hate myself for what I did to you, my own daughter! To make it worse, I don't even remember it. You are my daughter, and I hurt you. I will spend the rest of my life trying to make it up to you and trying to fix the wrongs I have done.

I am so, so fucking sorry for what I put you through." Nina burst into gut-wrenching sobs, and all the anger leaked out of my body like a pinhole in a balloon.

What the hell is wrong with me? Nina was sick, and here I am condemning her for something that was out of her control. She was a victim, as well.

I stood and walked round the coffee table and plonked my ass down on it in front of her. She dropped her hands from her face and met my gaze, tears running down her cheeks. I took a deep breath and faced the woman who gave me life. I had to let this anger go. Not for her sake, but for mine.

"You're right, you weren't in control. But I can't forgive you." She dropped her gaze and twiddled her hands in her lap. "Maybe one day I will, but right now, I can't. I would like to sit down with you one day and talk. I don't have the time for that right now, but soon I will, hopefully." Her gaze met mine again, and I saw fear in her eyes.

"You have to fight your sister don't you?" I nodded. "W-will she survive?"

I wouldn't lie to her. "No. I wish there was a different way, but there isn't."

Chapter Fifty Six

NICO

Lucian and I left Ryan and her mother alone, at Ryan's request. We made our way back to my study, and as we rounded the corner we both stopped at the sound of shouting.

"How the fuck could I breach his mind if he isn't related, Sophia?"

"I don't know, Dominic!"

"Don't fucking lie to me, Sophia—not about this. Who is he to *me*?"

"I don't know!"

"Stop fucking lying! You know more about that kid than anyone. You recognized him the day he turned up with Ryan. Who. Is. He?"

"How am I supposed to know, Dom? He told you himself he was raised in a cell." Lucian rushed around the corner, and I followed after him. Dom and Sophia stood outside my office, glaring at each other. As soon as they realized we were standing there, they both turned toward us. Dom looked pissed while Sophia looked fearful. Before I could ask them what was going on, Lucian spoke.

"How do you know me, Sophia? I saw the look on your face, as well, the day I arrived with Smurf."

Sophia dropped her gaze to the floor. "I don't know who you are, y-you just reminded me of someone."

"I don't need Jackson to be here to know you're full of shit, Sophia! Tell me the fucking truth!" I snapped my gaze to Dom, who was glaring down at my sister.

"Don't fucking talk to her like that!" I roared.

"Stay out of this, Nicky boy," Dom warned.

"What the fuck is going on between you two?" I looked between my sister and Dom, waiting for one of them to answer me.

"Dom and I, we kind of—"

"SIRE!" I spun around to see Cyrus and one of the other guards running toward me.

"What is it, Cyrus?"

"The alpha sent word; they are under attack *now* sire. The queen's sister has located the portal." Fuck, the war at Jackson's was a distraction, I just knew it.

"Ready your men, take them to the alpha, and do as he says until your king gets there, Cyrus. Eric, go retrieve the queen from her mother and bring her to the king's study."

Fucking hell, Sophia was like a drill sergeant. Both men stood there, looking at me, waiting. I nodded, and they both took off to fulfill their tasks.

"Nico, we need to go now. If she's found the portal, we don't have long!" I could hear the panic in Dom's voice. He was right; we would need to split up.

"I'll go with Ryan—" Dom was shaking his head before I could even finish.

"Randall has the blood of Jackson's father, Ryan's father, and Ryan's blood. You need to be at the compound to help us take him down if he's there. Ryan has to go to her sister on her own." I was already shaking my head.

"She won't be alone; I'll be with her." Dom and I turned to face Lucian. I knew the kid was powerful, but I didn't trust anyone aside from myself with Ryan's safety.

"Trust me, I will keep her safe, I swear it."

"I'll go with them."

I turned to my sister. "You can't, Soph. We need as many magic wielders as we can get to stop the witches." My gut filled with unease. I needed to be at Jackson's to help with Randall and the witches. I had no choice but to trust Lucian to keep Ryan safe.

The sound of footsteps pounding the floor drew all our attention. Ryan and Eric rounded the corner.

"What happened?" she asked, panting.

"Your sister. We need to go, now!"

Chapter Fifty Seven

RYAN

We all ran from the castle like it was on fire. Once we breached the forest and made it to the clearing, Nico stopped me. He looked down at me with such anguish.

"I'm sending you to your sister, love." He wasn't coming with me. "Lucian will go with you to help, but we must go to Jax and Kai and help them." I nodded my head, this was it. "Stay alive, Ryan, do you hear me?" He clasped my face between his hands.

"I will. I'll save Farrarie, Nico. I promise." He leaned down and kissed me then pulled back and leaned his forehead against mine.

"Come back to me, love."

A stray tear leaked out the side of my eye. "I swear it."

Nico pulled away and released me reluctantly.

"I'll open a portal to your sister, love," Dom said, and began chanting. A portal opened beside me. Sophia gave Lucian and me a quick hug. I turned and smiled at Nico, who looked like he was two seconds away from saying fuck it and coming with me. Before Lucian and I could enter the portal, Dom stopped us.

"Trust in yourself, Ryan. You can do this. Lucian will help

you, but you need to trust him to be able to bring you back from the brink." Dom then turned to look at Lucian. "I don't know who you are kid, but don't die."

Lucian didn't reply, he just grabbed my hand and led me through the portal. I turned back just before we disappeared and saw Dom and Sophia holding Nico back.

"I love you!" I yelled. I hoped he heard me.

Lucian and I exited the portal in the middle of the woods. I knew these woods so well. I can't believe I never put it together before.

"Where the hell are we, Smurf?" I smiled. Kai told me years ago this place was the closest he could get to being home.

"Follow me." Lucian and I quietly made our way out of the woods, which was no small feat given the heavy underbrush. I resigned myself to the fact that my sister would know we were here.

I turned to Luce and said, "She would already know we're here, may as well just get this over with." We tromped through the rest of the woods, and when we emerged, Lucian gasped.

"Welcome to Lake William, Luce." I scanned the area and spotted Stevie standing at the end of the dock. Her back was to us, and I made my way down to her. I motioned for Lucian to stay back. He reluctantly nodded and waited on land.

As I walked toward Stevie, I noticed how thin she had gotten. She had leather pants and shit-kicker boots, with a black tank top. Her bones protruded in ways I'd never seen on her before. I cautiously approached her and stood beside her at the end of the dock, looking at her out of the corner of my eye.

She had her eyes closed. I could see black lines dancing under her skin. This darkness was killing her from the inside out. I couldn't think of her as my sister right now; if I did, I would never be able to do what needed to be done.

"I didn't think you would be ballsy enough to come, sister," she sneered.

"You plan on killing my people and harming the ones I care about. Of course I would come."

"You should have run while you had the chance, you stupid fool. Now you will die."

"It doesn't have to be this way, Stevie. If you let me, I will try to banish that evil inside you." My sister laughed, the sound like nails on a chalkboard. I turned to face her, and when she turned toward me, I gasped. There was no white around her pupils; her eyes were inky black.

"You and all those you hold dear will die today."

I wasn't prepared for what came next: a blast that hit me straight in my chest. I went sailing through the air and crashed into the water of the lake. I felt like a bowling ball had torn through my chest, and black spots were dancing in my vision.

The pain was unbearable. I focused on trying to push past the pain and get myself to the surface, I broke the surface of water, gasping and coughing. I had no time to recover; magic wrapped around me like a rope and pulled me from the lake.

Black swirls of magic were wrapped around me, and my arms were anchored to my sides. I looked down and saw my sister at the end of the dock with a cruel smile on her face. I jerked my eyes to the shore and icy dread went down my spine. Lucian was being held down by at least five vampires, and there were many more on the shore, at least fifty.

"You stupid bitch, did you really think I would come here alone? You really are naïve." Stevie was right; we had banked on them sending all their soldiers to Jackson's and her coming here alone. We were fools, and our stupidity had cost us greatly. I could barely breathe, let alone fight. The magic that held me immobile began to squeeze, and I gasped.

It was getting harder and harder to take a breath. The black spots were spreading throughout my vision, and I could see Lucian struggling against the hold of the vampires.

I was going to pass out.

"You will die in the place that you hold so dear to your heart," my sister hissed.

The magic tightened around me, and the pain in my chest intensified.

"Smurf! Fight it! You're stronger than her." I turned my heavy head toward Lucian and smiled a sad smile. I wasn't strong enough to beat my sister. One hit from her and I was down already. With one last deep breath, I blacked out and began falling toward the lake.

Sophia, Dom, and I emerged from the portal at the back of Jackson's land. There were people everywhere; some of them were dead on the ground, and others were fighting to get the elderly out of here. Jackson was supposed to evacuate his compound the week before the attack: all elderly, and children or pregnant mothers were to leave here and go to safe houses until the attack was over. My blood began to boil when I looked down and saw a young boy with his throat torn out. He couldn't have been more than eleven years old and here he was lying at my feet dead. I growled and ran toward the fight, Sophia and Dom behind me. I launched an energy ball at a vampire attacking a shifter, launching him a few feet away. Dom and Sophia were throwing balls of energy at anyone who wasn't a fae or a shifter.

"We need to find Jax and Kai!" Dom yelled, and we took out as many witches, warlocks, and vamps as we could as we made our way toward the back of the property.

We huddled close to the building, and I peeked my head around the corner. There were witches and vampires every-where. I couldn't see Jax and Kai among the warring supernaturals, but what I did see had my blood turning to ice. Without waiting or warning the others, I took off toward the four vampires who had Dom's father on his knees. The vampire with the black hair was going for the kill shot. I built the biggest energy ball I could in my hand and launched it at the unsuspecting vampire, who was knocked off his feet. Energy balls whizzed past my head, and I knew Dom and Sophia were behind me.

"Get the fuck away from him!" Dom roared.

I was throwing energy balls at one of the vamps, but he kept dodging. As I neared Mr. Silver, the blond head vamp engaged me in hand-to-hand combat. He was fucking strong, I give him that. I dodged his fist that was coming straight for my nose and landed a blow to his gut, but he recovered quicker than I would have liked. We traded hit for hit for a few moments before I called on my magic and punched him as hard as I could in the chest. My magic exploded out of my hand and blew the blond vamp to pieces. Vampire juice coated me from head to toe.

"Dad!" At the sound of Dom's panicked voice, I turned to see he and Sophia had taken out the other two vamps and were now kneeling in front of Dom's dad. "What happened? Are you okay?"

"If I was okay, Dominic, I wouldn't be on my fucking knees." Dom gave a half-hearted chuckle at his dad's attempt to lighten the mood. "They took Jax and Kai."

"Who?" I demanded.

"Randall Cane and his minions. He took the shifter and fae elders as well." How the hell did he manage to overpower the elder council?

"Why?" Sophia asked.

"I don't know, sweetheart, I feel like we're missing something. They attacked out of nowhere. Almost like they knew Ryan wasn't here. I think we have a rat." Mr. Silver sounded so weak; I have never seen this bear of man ever look as defeated as he did now. I looked around us to see the battle still raging on. These vampires were stronger than any I have ever encountered before.

"Where are Tyler, Aurora, Mya, and Ryan's cousins?" I asked.

"They were heading toward the lake; Tyler said there was something different about these vamps. They're stronger than any I have ever fought." I could hear the anger lacing Mr. Silver's tone.

"They drank her blood."

"Drank whose blood, Sophia?" Dom snapped.

"Ryan's! She said they were taking her blood three times a day. Randall gave her blood to his vamps so they would be stronger. That's why they're here during the day; her blood gave them the ability to walk in the daylight as well as extra strength." Oh my God, she was right. It hadn't even registered to me that it was daylight and vampires were here. They have Ryan's blood in their system.

"We need to find Kai; he will know how to stop them." They all nodded their heads. Dom and I helped Mr. Silver to his feet, then he waved us off and told us to go.

Dom was reluctant to leave his dad. "Go, son, go help the others. I have it under control here, the other packs were notified. They will be here as soon as they can." Dom nodded to his father and followed me and Sophia back toward the woods.

I knew where Randall would be taking Kai and Jax. I opened a portal to Lake William as soon as we entered the woods. I guess I would fight side by side with my wife after all.

Chapter Fifty Nine

RYAN

I felt weightless and free, and I didn't feel any pain. It's a bit of a relief, honestly. I thought dying would hurt.

"*Ryan, wake up.*" I knew that voice.

"Dad, is that you?"

"*Yes, darling, I need you to wake up now.*"

"I can't do it, Dad, I'm not strong enough."

"*You are strong enough, daughter. You just need to believe it. Trust in yourself and your power. If you don't wake now, you will die! Many have lost their lives today, don't let your fear cripple you.*"

"She's too strong, Dad. One hit and she already took me down!"

"*Remember your training, remember what your grandfather taught you. The whole supernatural race is counting on you Ry, now WAKE UP!*"

My father's scream jarred me awake. I was smart enough to not drag in a lungful of water. I scrambled to swim to the surface, my lungs burning from lack of oxygen. I broke the surface of the water, gasping, and pulled in lungful after lungful of air.

My head was cloudy from lack of oxygen and I tried to quiet my breathing so I wouldn't be noticed. Stevie was on the docks, arms outstretched, shooting black magic into a portal that wasn't there before I blacked out. I turned away from her to search for Lucian. He was on his knees with his arms behind his back. I looked past him and gasped.

Kai and Jax were kneeling behind Lucian. Randall-fucking-Cane stood behind them with a smug smile on his face.

"Don't pout boys, the half-blood bitch didn't stand a chance." I could hear the laughter in Randall's voice from all the way out here.

"Fuck you! I will kill you." A guard rained blow after blow on Kai for his outburst.

"You will all die for what that crazy fuck did to Smurf!"

Stevie stopped shooting her power into the portal and turned around, shooting a lighting-shaped blast into Lucian's chest. I screamed out as his eyes went wide and he collapsed into a heap.

All eyes spun toward me. Stevie glared. I released all the pain and anger I had been holding onto for years. Stevie reached out to shoot me with her magic but was knocked off her feet by an energy ball. I turned to see Nico, Dom, and Sophia walking out of the forest. I didn't have the time to process their arrival or deal with fallout that their arrival would bring.

"You are strong enough, daughter, you just need to believe it. Trust in yourself and your power."

I replayed what my dad had said to me. I could do this. I forced the cage open that I had locked all my feelings inside; it was time to let them out. Pain, anger, hurt, love, joy, happiness all warred inside of me. I chose to focus on anger. I channeled my magic and used it to propel myself out of the lake, levitating over to the dock. My sister was on her feet, scowling at me. My body was thrumming with power. I could feel my own strength, and it was *intoxicating*.

"You little bit—" I didn't let her finish. I blasted my sister with my magic. She went flying to the end of the dock and landed with a thud. She was back on her feet in an instant; my blow hadn't even hurt her. I needed to channel more magic. I focused on anger and hurt and let those feelings come to the surface, then threw another blast of magic at her. She dodged and reached her hand out, sending a blast of inky black magic toward me. I quickly erected a shield to stop the attack but I skidded back a few steps. Stevie was fucking strong.

She didn't stop her attack but increased her efforts, lobbing one blast after another, blow after blow. Sweat broke out across my brow. We circled each other, my back now to the woods. I was getting tired, and I could feel the magic inside of me slowing. Stevie moved toward me, throwing black balls of energy, and I threw my own balls of energy back at her, both of us dodging the other's attack.

I heard a scream come from behind me, and I averted my gaze from my sister to see Sophia screaming at Randall. Randall had Dom's head clasped in his hands, ready to break his neck. I had a choice to make; I saw Stevie out of the corner of my eye, ready to launch another energy ball right at me. I could block her attack and save my own ass, or I could save Dom's.

I chose to save Dom. I released the energy ball in my hand that was meant for my sister and hurled it at Randall.

I prayed that my aim was on point, and it was. It hit Randall in the side of the head and he stumbled back. His hold on Dom dropped and he collapsed to the ground.

I spun back toward my sister to see the ball of energy coming straight for me. This blast would kill me, but I was at peace with the decision I made to save Dom.

Everything was happening in slow motion. I could see the

elders were here. On my right I could see Nico screaming out to me, but I couldn't make out what he was saying. I smiled at my husband and mouthed *I love you*. I returned my gaze back to my sister and gasped at the site in front of me.

What the fuck?

NO!

Chapter Sixty

RYAN

No, no, no!

What the fuck was he doing? He sacrificed himself for me—*for me*. Why the hell would he do that?

The blast hit him in the chest, and he staggered a couple steps back and then dropped to his knees.

My sister let out a gut-wrenching scream. Black magic exploded from within her, and I jumped in front of Tyler and prepared myself for the blast. I pulled all the magic I had inside of me and released it, creating a shield around everyone on the shore. I didn't want to protect the vampires, but I didn't have a choice. In order to save all of my friends, I had to save everyone on the shore.

My sister's blast of magic rattled my shield, and the power of her blast had me gritting my teeth. Stevie's pixie-cut hair was whipping around her face. The amount of power she was releasing would weaken her greatly. The trees around us began to crack and break. Stevie was leveling the forest with her power. I felt someone approach and saw it was Nico, he was covered in blood and panting. His shirt was no longer white and was barely hanging on by a thread.

"You need to take her out now, love. Her power is traveling through the portal to Farrarie and killing our home." I turned back toward the dock; I could see black magic traveling through the portal.

"You have to do it now!" I looked down toward Tyler, his head resting in his sister's lap, Jackson beside her.

I knelt down and gripped Tyler's cold hand in mine.

I could see his life slowly draining from his eyes. Tears began to gather in my own.

"You got this, little hybrid," he wheezed out.

"Why did you do it, Ty?" I choked out.

"I lied. There was never a cure for me surviving my mate dying. Now go, before she kills your world and ours." I let my tears fall freely as I leaned forward and placed a kiss on his cold, clammy forehead.

"Thank you for being our alpha when we needed you most. You are the brother I never had, Ty. I love you, and we will meet again someday. You have my word that I will look after our pack. Run free and run wild Ty. I got this." A smile tugged at his lips, but I didn't wait for him to respond. I stood and walked away.

Just as I was about to pass through my shield, Nico's hand clamped down on my wrist.

"Let me help you," he begged. I didn't have time to waste. I turned and placed a chaste kiss to his lips and then sent a shock of electricity through him when I placed my hand on his chest. He dropped to his knees, a look of betrayal crossing his face. I would deal with his anger later. I pushed through my shield, knowing it would still stand without me in it, but I kept a piece of the shield around myself.

I pushed against my sisters magic; it felt like I was trying to move a boulder. Stevie was strong, stronger than any of us thought. I needed to get her and stop her before she destroyed both worlds. Focusing on my emotions, I sifted through them. I focused on my happiness. A voice inside my head was telling me my darker emotions wouldn't stand against my sisters darkness. I was light, and Stevie was dark. I focused on happiness and how happy I have been to be with my cousins, finding Kai and then Nico. Having Dom and Jax in my life as well, I met the girls through them and found friends. I found Lucian and Tyler. I loved all of them, and they loved me. Nina was getting help, and getting better. My dad loved me and wanted me to succeed. I married the man of my dreams, and I wanted to save the lives of all the people I cared for and loved. For the first time in my life, I had a family. And a future.

The weight I had felt on my chest earlier started to dissipate. My chest still hurt from Stevie's blow, but I would deal with that pain later. I started to feel weightless, relishing the thrum of the power inside of me, begging me to let it take control. Resigned to the fact I couldn't kill my sister on my own, I let the power inside of me take control.

It didn't burn; I didn't even feel warm. I just felt...content. The power coursed through my body, and I felt like a battery that was just recharged.

I didn't protest or fight the feeling, I embraced it, and I accepted the power inside of me.

I finally accepted who I am and what I am.

I leaned my head back, stretched my arms out wide and roared to the heavens. A blast so strong, stronger than the night of my wedding, shot out from within me. I snapped my head forward and stared at my sister. She was glaring right back.

My blue light was fighting and pushing against her black magic, against her darkness.

I moved one foot in front of the other and pushed with everything I had in me. My sister began to do the same and was making her way over to me. She wore a look of determination and rage.

We were closer to each other now. I felt sweat dripping down my brow and spine. Pushing against her magic had worn me down a bit.

"You will pay for what you have done, you bitch."

I smiled at my sister. I had gotten under her skin.

"I will walk away from this sister, but you will not."

Stevie grinned from ear to ear, she looked so deranged. "You are weak, and I have nothing left to lose. If I am to die today, I will make sure I take your precious fae realm with me."

Chapter Sixty One

NICO

I'm still on my knees, watching her fight against her sister's blast. She has blue energy encompassing her. I'm pulled from my thoughts by Aurora's screams. I turn to see her clutching her brother's lifeless body. Tyler's gone.

Stevie killed him. He sacrificed himself to save Ryan. I heard what he said to her, that he lied to her about being able to save himself after she killed Stevie.

Tyler spent the past few months training *my* wife to kill *his* mate. Tyler was selfless, and he didn't deserve this end.

"She is using too much power, we need to find Lucian." Kai's voice pulled me from my thoughts, and I nodded. He was right. Ryan was pushing waves of power out, and I knew she needed to exude more power than she ever has, but I was worried now that she wouldn't be able to rein it back in. I jumped to my feet and looked around for Lucian, but I couldn't see him anywhere.

"There, he's out there!" Dom said, appearing at my side like a ghost. Lucian lay on the ground by the docks, and he wasn't moving. Stevie and Ryan were both using so much power that I wasn't even sure he would be able to withstand the amount of energy out there.

We were all trapped inside this dome. Without Lucian, we were all fucked. He was the only one who could bring Ryan back.

"What the hell are we going to do? She can take Stevie out, but if Lucian doesn't wake the fuck up, Ryan could take us all out!" Dom was right, but I didn't have a plan. I didn't know what to fucking do because my wife had, once again, left me behind.

RYAN

Stevie and I were so close that the only thing separating us was our magic. Black smoke surrounded her, and I assumed I looked the same but blue. Stevie had a murderous look on her face, a look that promised pain.

"Stop your attack, Stevie, it doesn't have to end like this." A manic laugh escaped her, the black lines slithering beneath the surface of her skin like worms. I shuddered. I knew in my heart Stevie was too far gone; there was no saving her. I had to give her a chance to surrender, though. My conscience wouldn't allow me not to.

"You're fucking pathetic! I would rather die than live in your shadow; I have been second to you my whole life. That changes now!" Stevie launched a ball of fire at me—actual fucking fire!

I deflected it using my magic to push it aside. How the fuck could she throw fire?

We began to circle each other. I was now with my back to the dock, and Stevie had her back to the armies fighting behind her. I could see Nico, Dom, and Kai standing there, staring at me. Dom was furiously pointing to something near me, but I couldn't afford to look without Stevie attacking me.

Thank God I didn't risk it. Stevie hurled fire ball after fire ball at me. I needed to do something, now. I focused on my connection with nature; I was surrounded by it. Grams had told me all witches draw their power from the land. I was half witch, so I needed to focus on that side of my being.

"Help me...help me fight her." I didn't know if asking Mother Nature for her assistance would work, but I had to try.

Stevie was stronger than we had all anticipated; I needed to use both sides of my power in order to beat her.

"Call the water to you, Ry." I heard my father's voice inside my head, and I didn't hesitate or question it. I stretched my arms out wide and commanded the lake water to come to me. In a flash, balls of swirling water were hovering over my palms. I didn't stop to dwell on it.

I launched them at my sister's fire balls.

I needed something stronger than these water balls; they may be extinguishing Stevie's fire but they weren't slowing her down.

"I need more, I need you to shoot water." I sounded like a mad woman, talking aloud to myself, but I had no idea how else to ask the elements for help.

Water shot from the lake like a cannon, the pressure so hard it knocked my sister back a few steps. She tried to dodge the blast to no avail. Stevie's black magic stopped pulsing out of her; she tried to erect a shield to shelter her from the blast, but the strength of the water broke through her shield.

I knew this was the moment—while she was down and distracted, I needed to make my move and end this once and for all.

I called all of the magic inside myself and channeled it into a bright blue orb. It hovered over my palm. The more magic I pulled from within myself, the more unstable I felt. I was losing control.

I needed Lucian, but he was nowhere to be found, and I didn't have time to waste thinking about how to bring myself back from the brink. I walked toward my sister with purpose. She was struggling to her feet, and when she finally stood and spun around, I was directly in front of her.

I could see the shock on her face, which quickly turned to rage.

"I'm so sorry, sister." I said as I pushed the magic orb into her chest, tears rolling down my cheeks. Stevie's eyes rounded like saucers, pain reflected in her eyes. She stumbled back several steps, screaming. Blue light illuminated under her skin, and it was like a rat race, blue chasing black. Blue was winning, for a moment, but the black worms inside my sister started to fight back.

I reached out with my hand and sent a stream of blue light into her chest. She screamed in agony, but I didn't stop pushing my magic into her until she dropped to her knees.

Tears were flowing down my cheeks freely as I watched my sister shake and shiver on her knees. I knelt down in front of her, cupping her face between my hands. When my gaze connected with hers, a sob broke free. Hazel eyes now stared back at me. The darkness inside of her was gone, and tears rolled down her cheeks. She was gasping for air.

"Stevie, I am so sorry. I'll fix this, I swear." I looked around for someone to help me—anyone. They were trapped behind the shield I had created. I pulled the magic from the shield back into me and it disappeared, just like popping a bubble. Nico came running, falling to his knees beside me and looking between me and my sister.

"She's dying Nico, help her, please." Nico looked to my sister, and she started to shake her head.

"I...can't...b-be...saved...Ry." She was in so much pain, I could see it in her eyes.

"I can take the pain away." I looked up to see Mya standing next to us, and I nodded without hesitation. She placed one of her hands on top of Stevie's head and whispered in some language I didn't understand.

"I have made her comfortable, but she doesn't have long, Ryan, her heart is slowing."

"Thank you, Mya." I turned back to my sister, who still looked weak and pale but no longer in agony. "I am so sorry, Stevie, I didn't want this to happen—"

Stevie cut me off. "Shhhhhhh, it's not your fault, Ry. I have been fighting against this power for so long. The darkness consumed me and I let it." I could hear the embarrassment in her voice. "I need you to know, Ry, I did not kill our father. Randall Cane did and blamed the fae." Stevie turned to look at Nico, so much regret and shame shone in her eyes. "I am sorry for all the harm I have caused you and your people. I let my grief consume me and blamed the wrong race."

"You are forgiven, coven queen." My heart bolstered at the respect and kindness in Nico's tone. He didn't have to formally address my sister, not after everything she had done, but he did it anyway, for *me*.

Stevie turned her gaze back to me, tears clouding her vision, she smiled a smile that didn't reach her eyes, she lifted her hand and cupped my cheek, I could see how taxing it was for her to hold her arm up.

"Don't cry, little sister, I am finally free. It was always going to end this way. I tried to fight as long as I could against it, but I was tired and—"

Stevie started coughing, blood spluttered out of her mouth. I brushed her hand away and shifted us so her head was resting in my lap. I knew deep down she didn't have much time left.

"Live your life, sister. Live for both of us." She coughed again, this time more blood spluttered out and her breaths came in short pants. "L-love...you...Ry," she choked out, then her eyes went wide and she sighed.

I watched the life leave my sister's eyes. A crushing weight slammed into me. My heart felt like it was on fire, and power like never before surged within me. I felt like a bomb, ready to explode.

"GET THE BOY, NOW!"

Chapter Sixty Three

NICO

I can see her struggling. If we don't get Lucian to her now, she will level this whole place and take out everyone in it. Dom and Kai pretty much carried Lucian toward us.

"No, no, no, no! What have I done? Stevie, please come back, please!" Tears are falling down her face like rain. Her grief is palpable, and it's crushing her. I try to comfort her by placing a hand on her shoulder, but she shrugs my hand off and glares at me.

"This is your fault!" I reel back; how is this my fault?

"Little one, I never wanted this to happen." Her glare turns from anger to rage, and I dart my gaze past her to search for Lucian. They're nearly to us, I just need to keep her occupied for a bit more. She gently places her sister's head on the ground and stands. She looks down at me with hatred. I don't get time to process that look before her magic wraps around me like a vine and I'm lifted into the air. I am man enough to admit that my wife scares the shit out of me right now.

I'm suspended at least five feet off the ground, hanging there like a limp noodle, my arms trapped at my sides. The magic wrapped around me starts to tighten its hold.

"You could have stopped all of this! You could have killed me as a child. My sister would still be alive if you did!" she screamed. She launched a ball of energy, and it happened so fast I didn't even have time to prepare for the attack. I went sailing through the air and landed on the hard ground with a bone-rattling thud. *Fuuccckk,* that hurt.

I had no time to process or calculate if I had any other injuries, because magic wrapped around me again, lifted me into the air, and pulled me back toward her.

This time she deposited me on the ground in front of her, her magic still wrapped tightly around me. I flinched as the magic squeezed me tighter.

"I blame you, I blame you for everything!" I couldn't bear to stare into her eyes any longer, the hatred and disgust in her gaze broke me. I hung my head in shame. She was right. I couldn't kill her, even after I knew Kai had failed. She is my *hugacko* and killing her would mean killing my soul. I saw a blue orb hovering in her hand, but I didn't protest or plead. I just waited for her to attack.

"Don't do it, love! You're angry and you're hurt. Killing him won't take the pain away." My head lifted to see Dom, Kai, and Lucian standing behind Ryan. Dom was trying to appeal to her humanity, but right now it looked like she had none. Her gaze was burning holes into me. If she needed someone to blame I would be that person, but I couldn't stand by and watch her lose herself to the power inside of her. She was glowing blue, but this time it was different, it was like she was encompassed in flames.

"If you need to hate someone or hurt someone, I will be that person. I love you, Ryan Stone."

"I am not Ryan Stone, Nico. I am a fucking Knox." She let out a scream so powerful it knocked everyone at Lake William to their knees; her power was like a wave of destruction. Wave after wave of power battered us. I Looked to Lucian, and his gaze met mine. We both knew if he didn't stop her, she would kill us all. Lucian closed his eyes and shouted out a spell I had never heard of before.

"*Braka incontinu faylinga prowess, bundunu!*" Lucian never hesitated; as soon as he was free of Ryan's power, he jumped to his feet and tackled her to the ground. The barrage of power stopped immediately. Lucian flipped her over so she was on her back then straddled her and clamped her arms by her sides.

"Get the fuck off me, Lucian."

"Never, Smurf. I can't let you do this, so don't fight it. It will only hurt the both of us. Just let me take it away. Let me take some of the pain away. The power inside of you is intensifying your pain. Let me do this for you, Smurf, please," Lucian begged.

"It hurts so much, Luce. Stevie is dead…my sister is dead." She broke into uncontrollable sobs.

Sophia, Alex, and Chase now joined us, all three of them heartbroken at her grief. I don't think any of us would have been able to do what she did today.

I moved toward my sister and wrapped my arm around her shoulders, grateful that I had her back in my life. Ryan made a sacrifice today that I understand all too well.

"I'm gonna take it away now, Smurfy. let it go. Release it to me." Ryan nodded her head, tears still streaming down her face. Minutes that felt like hours ticked by as Lucian funneled her power into him.

Finally, Lucian released his hold on her arms. A couple more minutes passed, and her head lulled to the side. She passed out. Lucian looked around to all of us, his strange eyes glowing brighter. "I can't hold this inside of me for long; the hit I took from her sister has weakened me. When she wakes, I need to start funneling the power back to her."

"Is there no way you could hold it longer?" Dom asked.

He shook his head sadly. "The longest I have ever held it was ten minutes." We all nodded. Lucian was injured, and we were all asking him to hold a bomb inside of himself.

"I hope she has calmed down by then. I mean, look around," said Kai. Lake William was destroyed. The dock was pretty much wood chips now, the forest was broken and bent, trees littering the ground. Bodies were all over the place, some injured, but most of them dead. So many had lost their lives today, all for the greed of another. Stevie was a victim of darkness, and I understood her part of this attack. Randall Cane had started all of this for power.

"Where the hell is Randall?" I asked the group. Everyone begun to spin in circles to see if they could spot the vampire king who had wreaked havoc on our lives for years.

"I haven't seen him since Ryan blasted him in the face," my sister answered.

Chapter Sixty Four

RYAN

I woke in a strange land, one I had never seen before in my dreams. I was on a beach, with crystal clear water lapping at the sand. I looked down and saw I wasn't in my usual white dress. I was wearing shorts, flip flops, and a yellow camisole. Where the hell am I? I heard a noise behind me and spun around.

"Daddy?" I choked out. My father smiled and walked toward me with open arms. I ran, slamming into him and wrapping my arms around him. He held me while I sobbed into his shirt. This must be heaven. I must have died, right? I don't remember dying.

"You're not dead, sweetheart. Your mind just needed to take a break." I pulled back from my father and stared at him. His soft green eyes held nothing but love and contentment.

"How am I here? Where are we?"

"You tell me, Ry, this is your dream, after all." I had no idea how I had called my father to me or where the hell we were. I wasn't going to look a gift horse in the mouth, though. I would enjoy this moment.

"Dad, I did something today, I—"

"Shhh, Ry. I know, and Stevie isn't mad. You freed your sister from a lifetime of misery." Tears began to fall from my eyes, and my dad wiped them away.

"I didn't want to do it, I didn't have a choice." A sob broke free, and I wrapped my arms around myself, trying to hold myself together.

"Ryan, you did what you had to do. Stevie is okay. She hated what she had become."

"You said I could blast the darkness out of her, but it didn't work! I killed her, Dad." My dad's face softened, and he cupped my cheek with one of his hands.

"It was too late, daughter, she had accepted the darkness inside of her. There was nothing you could have done, Ry." Wait —if my dad was here, then did that mean...?

"Is Stevie here?" My dad sucked in a breath before he answered.

"You're not ready to see her yet, sweetheart. When you are, she will come to you. Just trust me when I tell you that your sister is free now, thanks to you. She loves you, Ryan, and doesn't blame you." I broke out into uncontrollable sobs. I wanted to see my sister and tell her I loved her one last time.

"Ryan, I won't see you again, my dear."

"What, why?" Dad smiled down at me, but the smile didn't reach his eyes.

"I was granted the power to come to you from the elders of the past, to help you in this battle. Now that the battle is over, you must live and not dwell on the dead." I tried to butt in, but dad raised his hand signaling for me to shut up and wait.

"You have a long life ahead of you sweetheart, a long, happy life. When you return to your reality, let all the anger and pain of the past go. Your power overrode you today because you have never truly let go of your past. You cannot live in the past, Ry. Look toward your future and focus on that." Dad was right, but it was easier said than done.

"For you, I will try. I promise to try letting my anger go toward Mom and be happy." When Dad smiled down at me again, this time it did reach his eyes.

"I am so beyond proud of you, my daughter. I am sorry you had to do what you did today. I would never have been able to choose between my daughters. Because I was too weak to do what needed to be done, you were left with that burden." I wrapped my arms around my dad and hugged him. I didn't want to say goodbye.

"Go now, my daughter, live your life and be happy. We will meet again one day." Dad placed a kiss to the top of my head.

"I Love you, Daddy." As soon as I said that, everything went dark.

Chapter Sixty Five

RYAN

I awoke back at Lake William, with Lucian still straddling my legs. I turned my head from side to side to see everyone except Mya and Aurora staring down at me. I couldn't bear to meet Nico's gaze for longer than a second. What I did and said to him was disgusting. I let my pain and grief cloud my judgment, and I took it out on him.

"Smurf, I need to give it back," Lucian gritted out, and then I could see the strain on his face.

"I'm okay, Luce, I can take it," I said, smiling up at him. Lucian blew out a loud exhale and placed his hands on my chest. Power seeped into me at a slow pace, and I didn't feel any heat this time. It didn't hurt to have my power inside me now that I accepted it.

Once the transfer was complete, Lucian stood and helped me to my feet. Dom engulfed me a hug as soon as Lucian stepped back.

"Thank you for saving my life, love." I returned his embrace and smiled.

"It was never a choice between you or me, Dom." Dom held me tighter for a moment before he stepped back and nodded his head then turned on his heel and left. I turned to face my cousins, both of whom hugged me and then left, saying they were going to help clean up. Sophia and Lucian followed after them. I was to chicken to turn around and face Kai and Nico.

"You can't avoid us forever, you know?" Kai was right; it was time to face the music. I turned around slowly and kept my head down, not having the balls to look either of them in the eye.

A hand lifted my chin, and I looked up to see the most mesmerizing gray-blue eyes.

Kai smiled down at me, but I couldn't return the gesture. Because of me, Kai now had to lead the race he hated most. Randall was gone, so now Kai was the king of the vampires.

"I'm so sorry, Melakai," I choked out.

"Don't be sorry for being a queen and making the hard decisions, *mi amor*." He called me *mi amor*! He hadn't called me that since he found out what I did to him. The words brought a smile to my face.

"You are going to be an amazing queen. The fae and witches are lucky to have you." Kai leaned forward and placed a kiss on my cheek. It wasn't enough for me, and I wrapped my arms around his waist and rested my cheek on his chest. Kai held me to his chest.

"Thank you for everything, Kai. Thank you for being my escape, my friend, and my protector. I love you." I felt his body soften at my words.

"I will always be here for you, Ryan. You will always hold a special place in my heart. If you should ever need me, all you need do is call." Kai and I broke apart, Kai bid Nico and I goodbye, and then left to help the others. It was time to face the music. I turned my gaze to Nico. He was looking at me with so much pity and shame in his gaze. None of this was his fault, and I was wrong to blame him.

"Nico—"

He cut me off. "You were right, you know, I could have stopped this. I could have killed you, saved my world and saved you from this pain. I couldn't do it, though, even after I knew Kai had failed. From the first moment I entered your dreams, I fell head over heels in love with you. Killing you was never an option after that; I would risk everything for you. You can be Ryan Knox or Ryan Stone. I don't really give a flying fuck as long as you are mine. I will never let you go, Ryan, you are mine. I am a selfish bastard, and I won't apologize for that.

"I'm sorry you had to go through what you did today, but I still wouldn't go back and change a thing if it meant I couldn't have you—"

I didn't let him finish his rant; I launched myself at him. We held onto each other and whispered words of love into each other's ears. We stayed like that for ages and only broke apart at the sound of someone calling my name. I turned around to see it was Victor, the leader of the fae elders.

It was time.

Chapter Sixty Six

NICO

I thought closing the portal and stabilizing Farrarie would be a lot harder. I mean, it looked easy from where I was standing, but in reality it was probably hard as shit. Ryan made it look so effortless. She didn't even need Lucian this time to help draw her power back. I honestly thought she would have been spent after exhausting so much power to stop her sister, but clearly I was wrong.

Farrarie now didn't need a portal to Earth to stabilize it. It could sustain itself now, thanks to Ryan. She truly was a gift to all of Farrarie and the strongest supernatural I have ever encountered. Many have tried to find another way to help my world, but no one succeeded but her.

I left Cyrus and Larick back at Lake William to help with the cleanup and to bring the lost fae back to our realm so they could be buried with their loved ones. I carried Stevie back through the portal with Ryan at my side. She wouldn't look at her sister.

I didn't blame her; Stevie's chest had a charred hand print right where Ryan had pushed her magic into her.

Jackson's compound was in utter turmoil. Parts of the compound had been burned, and bodies littered the ground. So many had lost their lives today: fae, vampire, shifter, and witch.

I sent Maverick to retrieve all the fae we had sent over the world to let them know it was safe to return home. Half my soldiers were sent back to my realm to help with the burials while half remained to help restore order and clean up.

Ryan refused to send Stevie back to the coven until she had met with the witch elders. The witches didn't want her buried on the mountain with her ancestors. Ryan was not having any of that. We learned from her uncle that the witch elders' loved ones were being set free, thanks to Kai ordering the vamps to release them. Ryan also learned that her father wasn't buried in New Zealand; he was buried on the same mountain the witches refused to let her bury her sister.

I placed Stevie's body in the same room Kai had been in when Tyler first brought him back. Ryan and I were turning to leave the room to meet with all the elders in the mess hall when Jax and Aurora walked in. Jax was carrying Tyler, and at the sight of him, Ryan broke out into sobs and raced over.

She stroked Tyler's cheek softly and whispered, "Thank you for all that you have done, Ty. I hope you find peace now." Ryan leaned forward and placed a kiss on his forehead. Aurora cleared her throat and looked to Ryan. Ryan stiffened, and I know she was waiting for Aurora to lash out for her brother's death.

"I would like for Tyler to lay with his mate. I would also like to ask that she and Ty be buried together. Shifters are always buried with their mates."

"O-of course," Ryan stuttered out. She moved aside to let them place Tyler next to Stevie on the bed. Ryan went rigid when Aurora walked to the other side of the bed where her sister lay and placed her hand on Stevie's.

"I wish you peace, Stevie Knox. I hope that you and my brother find each other in the life to come." Tears leaked from Ryan's eyes. Ryan caught Aurora's arm as she went to leave the room.

"What you just did, I know it wasn't easy."

"I didn't do it for your sister; I did it for my brother."

Chapter Sixty Seven

RYAN

As we entered the mess hall, I saw all the elders standing against the back wall. I swallowed past the lump in my throat. Before Nico could move further into the room to join the others, I stopped him. He looked down at me with concern.

"I just want you to know, everything I have done I have done because I love you. I need you to remember that, okay?" Fear passed through his eyes.

"What have you done?" he whispered.

"Miss Knox, would you join us, please?" I looked past Nico to see the leader of the vampire elders motioning us forward to stand with the others.

"It's Mrs. Stone," Nico growled.

"Of course, please forgive me," Lachlan muttered. Nico and I made our way over to stand with Kai, Dom, Jax, Sophia, Aurora, Lucian, and my cousins. Where was Mya?

"Let's not waste time, old friend, we have a lot to do and a lot to fix before this day is over," Dom's dad said to the vampire elder.

"Very well, first on our list. Melakai Cane, it has been brought to my attention that you are now a true blood heir of the late king?" I stiffened next to Kai, and Nico gripped my hand in his, offering me his silent support. I looked to Kai and heard him release a loud exhale.

"What you have heard is true. I am the rightful heir to the throne of the vampires." I could hear the strain in Kai's voice at having to say that out loud. My chest constricted at the pain I had caused him.

"Very well. I, Lachlan Inkwell, leader of the vampire council, accept your claim to the throne. You will be initiated as the king once we return to the mansion." Kai gave a stiff nod but said nothing.

My uncle David stepped forward next, a look of pity in his eyes. The elders were the only ones that knew the truth aside from me. We had to go through all of this political bullshit before we got to the truth.

"Ryan Knox, descendant of Ralph and Nina Knox, granddaughter of Marcus and Bethany Knox, do you accept the role of coven queen to the Knox coven?" I released Nico's hand and stepped forward, looking my uncle directly in the eyes.

"I, Ryan Knox-Stone, accept the crown and the role." Uncle David bowed to me and stepped back. I followed his lead and moved back between Kai and Nico. Next to speak was Victor.

"Do you, Ryan Knox-*Stone,* accept the role of queen of Farrarie?" The doors behind us opened, and I heard footsteps of many soldiers, guards from all four races surrounding the room. It was time for the truth to come out.

"What is the meaning of this?" Nico demanded.

"Dad, what the hell is going on?" Dom asked his father.

I turned to Nico and gripped his hand in mine. He looked down at me, and I could see it in his eyes—he knew what I had done.

"No." he whispered. I released his hand and stepped forward to face the council. I wrapped my magic around my friends, making them immobile. Lucian stepped forward to stand by my side. Luce now knew what I had planned. The look on his face told me he didn't like it, but he would stand by me.

"Ry, what the hell are you doing?" Chase shouted at me, but I ignored him and focused on the council.

"I, Ryan Knox-Stone, reject my claim to the throne as queen of the fae." I heard gasps and growls sound behind me, but I pushed on. "I Ryan-Knox-Stone, queen of the Knox coven, hereby abdicate my claim of the throne to my cousins. Alex and Chase Knox. Both have been studying the laws and the politics of the coven for months and have grown up knowing who and what they are. The Knox coven would be lucky to have them as their kings!"

"I don't fucking want it, Ryan! What the hell are you doing?" Alex shouted at me. I turned to face my cousins and then looked to my friends and my husband. Nico had a look of utter betrayal on his face and was looking around the room frantically.

"I have to answer for the crime I committed, Alex. You and Chase will lead the Knox coven as it should be. I was never going to be a good queen. All I ask is to please allow my sister to be buried with respect and honor. Stevie was as much a victim in this as anyone else who died today. Please let her be buried with dignity. I am sorry to all of you for lying to you about this. I knew none of you would let me go through with it, but the elders offered me a deal, and I took it to ensure all of your safety."

"Safety from whom?" Sophia asked.

"She took the lives of fifty-two supernaturals and some of those were elders. She must answer for her crimes." I lowered my head in shame at Victor's words.

"If any of you so much as *think* of harming her, I will kill every single one of you myself. Fuck your laws and fuck your rules! She is my wife!" Nico roared, and I flinched at the rage in his voice. Mr. Silver stepped forward to address the room.

"The elders will take some time to discuss the punishment and reconvene when we have made a decision. Your actions today and saving the fae realm will be brought into consideration, Ryan." Mr. Silver approached me and gestured with his hand to follow him out of the room.

"Dad, I swear to God, if you take her out of here—" Dom snapped at his father. Mr. Silver didn't falter in leading me out of the room as he spoke.

"I'm sorry, son."

Chapter Sixty Eight

NICO

Betrayal didn't come close to how I was feeling right now. How could she do this? As soon as she left the mess hall with Mr. Silver and Lucian, her magic evaporated from around us, and we sprang into action and fought our way out of the mess hall. The guards were no match against all of us. We ran through the compound, searching for her everywhere. She was nowhere to be found. I tried to feel for the bond she and I shared, and I deflated when I couldn't feel her presence anywhere. Lucian being with her is blocking her from being found.

"Where the hell did they take her?" Kai gritted out.

She gave up on me—on us. We would have helped fight the elders, what the hell did they have over her? In order for us to find a way out of this, we had to figure that out, and we also needed to find out what they planned to do to her.

"We need to find your father, Dom."

Dom was a picture of anger, just vibrating with rage, and his fists were clenched at his sides.

"Yeah we do. He and I need to have a little chat as well," Dom gritted out.

Hours had passed. We all congregated in Jax's office after we helped clean up. All of the people that lost their lives were returned to their pack, coven, or clan. Kai had to return to the mansion with the vampire elders to be announced as their king. Jackson had announced to his pack that they would do their burials tonight.

I refused to allow Stevie to be buried without Ryan present, so with Aurora's consent and Alex and Chase's okay, the witches cast a spell to preserve their bodies until that could happen. I thought it weird to have two dead bodies lying in a room, so we arranged for two caskets to be brought here and for their bodies to be cleaned and prepared for burial. Alex and Chase had to return to their coven, but they refused to take over leadership until they spoke with Ryan. I respected them for that; most people would jump at the chance to be a king, but not those two. They were loyal to my traitorous wife.

Dom, Sophia, Aurora, Jax, Mya, and I sat around Jackson's office, all lost in our own thoughts for some time. I got so lost in my spiraling emotions that I didn't even hear the door to Jax's office open. I was pulled from my thoughts by the sound of Lucian's voice. I turned to face him and Mr. Silver, who were now standing by the door.

Dom immediately strode over to them.

"I know your angry but—" Lucian didn't get a chance to finish what he was saying before Dom punched him straight across his jaw. Sophia shrieked and jumped up to stand between the two glaring males.

"It's not his fault, Dominic!"

"He knew what she was doing, Sophia! He could have told us, but he didn't. He is a fucking traitor!" Dom roared.

"I never betrayed anyone. I told you all I would always be loyal to Smurf. You knew that, Dom. I did what I had to in order to find things out. Now are you ready to listen, or should your father and I leave?" Lucian snapped.

"You have our attention, boy," I ground out. Lucian nodded and stepped away from Dom and Sophia. Mr. Silver remained quiet this whole time, which was unsettling. Lucian looked to Mr. Silver, who nodded his head.

"Is this room okay to talk freely?" What a peculiar question.

"Yes," Jax answered.

"Good, because I shouldn't be telling you any of this. I swore to always be loyal to Smurf and to always have her back, and I'm about to break that vow." I looked around the room to see everyone wore looks of shock. We all knew how loyal this boy was to Ryan, so for him to betray her meant something big was at play here.

"You should have a seat," Mr. Silver said.

"Smurf made a deal with the council when we were in Yukon at her grandparents. Her grandfather told her it was the only way. She contacted the leaders of the council. They told her if she didn't turn herself in they would come after all of us. She didn't even want me to know, but I was listening to her conversation with Gramps."

What the fuck.

"I would like to see them try!" Jackson said, his voice dripping with malice.

"Calm down, son, I was there when she called. Victor and Lachlan told her as the leaders of the fae and vampires, they would de-throne Kai and Nico and arrest them. They tried to get David and me to agree to do the same. They wanted David to arrest his own sons and for me to take over as head alpha and lock my son and Jackson away."

Those conniving bastards. I wanted to elect new council leaders at the next meeting.

"Mr. Silver is right. Smurf did what she had to in order to make sure you lot didn't pay the price for her mistake," Lucian confirmed.

"What do they plan to do with her, Dad?" Dom asked.

"Victor and Lachlan want her powers bound and her to pay with her life." The room erupted in chaos, everyone was shouting.

"QUIET!" Mr. Silver's voice boomed throughout the room, and the screaming trickled off. "David and I won't agree to that, and we are at a stalemate. They promised Ryan that she would stand a fair trial, and Ryan was under the assumption that she may face jailing. She has no idea they plan to bind her power. I personally believe that Victor and Lachlan always planned to kill her."

"What do we do in the meantime, then?" Mya asked.

"We wait for back up to arrive." Lucian had an evil grin on his face. What ace did the boy have up his sleeve?

"What back up?" Dom queried.

"They will be here shortly," Lucian smugly replied.

They?

Chapter Sixty Nine

RYAN

I couldn't shake the look of betrayal on Nico's face from my mind. I agreed to leave with Dom's father in order to not upset the others more by staying in the mess hall. Mr. Silver had driven me to a remote cabin in the mountains; he said this place was warded, meaning no one could track me or find me here.

He said there were clothes and food inside, and I should be comfortable enough until he returned. Lucian refused to stay; he was angry and felt betrayed. I couldn't blame him, but I had to answer for the crime I committed. Many good people had lost their lives because of me, and my conscience wouldn't allow me to run and not face my punishment.

After Lucian and Mr. Silver left, I wandered through the small cabin. There was a single bed with a metal frame, and a worn recliner that had seen better days. There was a small fireplace, a kitchen which was the size of a closet, and an equally small bathroom.

It was so quiet here, and there was nothing here to distract me from my thoughts. I tried to feel for the bond Nico and I shared, but felt nothing. I wish I didn't decide to do this on my own. I was here alone with my grief, which was overwhelming. I needed a distraction, I grabbed a coat from the end of the bed and left the cabin.

I walked around the woods aimlessly, and after a while I stumbled upon a small stream. It seemed so out of place, seeing this stream on a mountain. I sat down on a large rock, pulling my knees up to my chest and wrapping my arms around them, resting my chin on my knees. I sat there, staring out at the running water, tears leaking from my eyes.

I cried for my dad, at never getting to know him. How could you miss someone you didn't really know?

I cried for Nina. I felt for her. I wish I didn't, but I did. She had no control of her life for so long. She and Stevie were so much alike in that aspect. Neither of them had a chance to be themselves; they were ruled by a curse placed upon them. Thinking of my sister opened the dam and tears streamed endlessly down my face.

My heart felt like it had split in half. I looked up to the heavens and screamed. Why did it have to be me? Why did I have to be the one to end my sister's life?

"Why me?" I screamed to the sky. No one answered me, not that I expected a reply. I thought being a mystical hybrid might have its perks, but so far the only perk was finding my soulmate. A soulmate who I ridiculed for hiding things from me and yet here I was doing the same to him.

I kept making decisions on my own. I kept hurting him. I jumped to my feet, stretched my arms wide, and roared, a blast of power shooting out of me.

Screaming and releasing my power didn't make the pain go away or even lessen it. I dropped to my knees and sobbed on the forest floor, alone.

I couldn't blame anyone. I did this to myself. I chose to leave my friends and husband in the dark. This was my fault. I deserved to be alone and broken.

By the time I pulled myself together and wandered back to the cabin, it was getting dark and cold. I hoped I was going the right way. I would hate to get lost in this forest and starve or freeze to death. How ironic would that be?

I could see a dim light through the trees. Huh. I'm sure I didn't leave a light on when I left. I froze—did the elders find me here? Shit, what if it was one of the vampires, and they still held a grudge about what I had done to their former king?

"I know you're there, Ryan. I promise I come in peace."

Chapter Seventy

NICO

Everyone left Jackson's office after Lucian and Mr. Silver told us to meet back there after the burial of the shifters. I made my way back to my room and showered. I felt a minute amount better after showering. I sprawled across the bed. I had an hour before the burial started, but I didn't feel like meeting the others in the mess hall. I couldn't stomach the thought of food.

Lying here looking up at the ceiling, my thoughts got away from me. I wasn't angry with Ryan for doing what she did; given the same choice, I would have done the same thing. I was just pissed that she cut me out again. I would have helped her fight against the elders. I was, however, pissed as fuck that Victor and Lachlan were wanting her dead. What the hell was their end game?

What would they gain by killing her?

I hate that I can't feel her through our bond; I just wanted to know she was okay. Was she safe? For fuck's sake, I am 104 years old, and I have an eighteen-year-old woman reducing me to a teenage boy whose emotions are out of control. I smiled to myself. I have lived for over a century and not once in my life have I ever felt like this. Two years ago, when I decided to infiltrate her dreams, I did it for my own gain, and then that quickly changed. She changed me.

She didn't have a single bad bone in her body. She was selfless and kind. She would never hurt anyone intentionally. I know today had taken a huge toll on her. If I was exhausted from no sleep she must be wiped out.

All I wanted was to lay here and hold my wife in my arms and tell her we could be free and happy now. Most of all, I just wanted her back with me.

I met Jax and the others on the east side of his property; it was a half hour walk from the compound to where they hold their burials. Shifters didn't return their dead to the earth like the witches and fae; they burned their dead on a pyre.

There were so many dead shifters lined up on row after row of pyres. Cyrus was still tallying the lives of the fae lost in the battle, so far we were up two hundred and something. Jackson had lost nearly the same amount. Shifters from other packs had come to aid us in this battle and lost their lives.

I know from the message Jax had received from Kai that the vamps had lost nearly six hundred, and the witches had called covens in from over the world to help fight as well, under their queen's command.

Alex and Chase were dealing with the fallout of that. We didn't have a number yet for how many of the witches had lost their lives, but we did know that many of their kind had died as well.

I stood next to Dom, near the podium that Jax stood on,

with Dom's father at his side. I looked around for the others, but couldn't see them.

"Where is Mya, Lucian, Aurora, and my sister?" Dom didn't turn to look at me. His silver hair was blowing in the wind and his eyes seemed so bright, but I could see anger lingering in the depths of them.

"Lucian is meeting the *backup* and Aurora refused to come. She wanted to stay with her brother. Mya was summoned back to the Knox coven, and Chase and Alex are trying to find a way to make her part of the coven again."

"What about Sophia?" Dom tensed at the mention of my sister, but he wouldn't meet my gaze.

"She left. I don't know where she went." His clipped tone pissed me off; he was being vague on purpose.

"I am asking you as my best friend, Dominic. What the hell is going on between you and my sister?"

This time, Dom turned to meet my gaze.

"It's my fault your sister was taken seventeen years ago. Randall never came to the fae realm. Sophia fled Farrarie to get away from me." I reeled back in shock.

"Why was she running from you, Dom?" I had a feeling I knew what his answer would be, but I needed to hear it from him. Dom's gaze held so much regret. I swallowed loudly. His answer was going to change things, I just knew it.

"Because I fell in love with her. Tyler and Stevie aren't the first to mate from separate races. Sophia and I are...your sister is my mate, Nico, and I...rejected her."

Chapter Seventy One

RYAN

I knew that voice. I raced through the forest and emerged from the spot I entered through. On the steps to the cabin sat Sophia Stone, my sister in law. I made my way over to her.

She looked beautiful as always, long black hair tumbling around her shoulders, vibrant violet eyes focused on me. She looked so sophisticated, even wearing plain dark jeans and a long-sleeved shirt.

"You look shocked to see me." Laughter was clear in her voice.

"Well, yeah, Lucian and Mr. Silver told me no one would be able to find me here." Sophia laughed and I tilted my head to the side, confused.

"Oh, Ryan, you forget I can see peoples love lives. I saw you at the stream earlier in a vision, and I could see you in pain. Your heart is calling for my brother. Plus I know this cabin and that stream well, very well."

She sighed and then turned to look ahead. I leaned on the railing at the bottom of the stairs, looking at her, *really* looking. I could see so much sadness in her eyes, and I didn't like seeing that look on her face, Sophia was one of the strongest women I knew, so whatever has her looking this way must be bad. I climbed the stairs and plonked down beside her. She rested her head on my shoulder.

"You know, when I first learned about you and what you were to my brother, I was jealous." I looked down at her in shock, her gaze still facing forward. Darkness was in full effect now, the only lighting the porch light and the moon. It was a beautiful night.

"Sophia, why the hell would you be jealous of me?" She chuckled.

"Because you have your *hugacko*."

"You will find yours one day, Soph, I just know it." She shook her head.

"I already found mine." I pulled away, shocked, and she turned to look at me, a sad smile on her face.

"Who?" I felt excitement for Sophia bubble up inside of me.

"It doesn't matter. I'm here to talk about you, not me. My brother is hurt by your actions today. We all are."

I hung my head in shame. "I did what I had to do." I was proud that my voice didn't waver.

"We know why you did it; Lucian told us. We just don't understand why you did it alone. I know we have only known each other for a short time, Ryan, but I consider you a friend—a sister, even. I didn't have an easy upbringing. Mother didn't want me, and father couldn't stand the sight of me. Nico raised me. We are closer than most siblings. He would do anything for those he loved. He will stand by your side, Ryan, and weather any storm for you, because he loves you."

I could hear the truth in her words. Sophia loved her brother and thought the world of him. Here I was constantly hurting the man she loved so dearly. I didn't deserve her as a friend. I wrapped my arm around her shoulders and pulled her to me, and she came willingly. We sat there in silence for a long while, both of us lost in our thoughts. Then a thought struck me, and I looked around the front of the cabin. I didn't see a car anywhere.

"Soph, how did you get here?" She pulled away and grinned at me, a devilish glint in her eye.

"Promise not to tell anyone?" I nodded my head, eager to hear her answer. "My *hugacko* is a fae, so I can siphon some of his power. Meaning, I can portal myself anywhere." My mouth dropped open in shock. How fucking cool was that? Did that mean Nico and I could do the same? Sophia pushed my mouth shut with her hand, and we both giggled.

"The way I see it, you can stay here in isolation and wallow in your own self-pity. Or you can come with me back to the compound and help us find a way out of this situation you have landed yourself in. We will not allow the council to end your life, Ryan, with or without your consent."

What the fuck?

"What do you mean *end my life*?"

Sophia looked taken back. "You don't know?" I shook my head. "Lachlan and Victor are asking Ian and David to join them for a majority vote to have your life ended. David and Ian refused, so the elders have to include the other members for a vote."

Holy shit, what the fuck have I done? When I spoke with the elders, Lachlan and Victor didn't mention any such thing to me, those lying bastards. I stood and looked down at Sophia, who had a triumphant smile on her face. She knew she had me hook, line, and sinker with that bomb she just dropped.

"Let me get my things. I have a group of people to suck up to, a husband to beg for forgiveness, and a couple of asshole elders to deal with." Sophia stood and placed a hand on my shoulder, smiling at me.

"You are going to shake my brother's world upside down; I

can't wait to watch you drive him mad." We both broke into fits of laughter, and I quickly shut off the porch light and locked the cabin door. I made my way over to Sophia, who had a portal open and waiting for me. She clasped my hand and we stepped through the portal.

Chapter Seventy Two

NICO

The burning of the shifters passed in a blur, I couldn't focus on anything aside from what Dom said. As soon as the service was over, I bee-lined it back to Jackson's office, I needed something to distract me, or I would go postal on Dominic.

I barged through the office door and came to a screeching halt. Lucian was there, with an older couple next to him. The man and woman looked so familiar, but I couldn't quite place them. I moved into the room and closed the door behind me. Lucian stood and the couple followed suit.

"Nico, I would like to introduce the backup, Ryan's grand-parents, Marcus and Bethany Knox. Gramps, Grams, meet Nico, king of the fae and husband to your granddaughter." I swallowed hard. I just fought a fucking battle for the life of my people and my home, and yet I was more nervous facing my wife's grandparents—well, her grandfather, to be more precise.

I walked over and extended my hand toward Marcus. His blue eyes held a challenge in them. We were nearly eye to eye, me just an inch or two taller. Marcus lowered his eyes to stare at my outstretched hand, and he had no intent of shaking my hand, I could see it in his body language. We worked together once, and now that I was married to his granddaughter, he couldn't stand me. Great.

"Oh for heaven's sake, Marcus!" Ryan's grandmother placed her small delicate hand in mine and shook it; I met her kind, deep green eyes and smiled down at her. She seemed like a sweet woman.

"Please excuse my husband's manners, he doesn't get out much." I smiled wide at her attempt to lighten the mood.

She released my hand and reclaimed her seat, pulling her husband down with her. I sat across from them on the other couch.

I felt Marcus's gaze burning holes into me. The silence stretched in the room; it was awkward as fuck and the tension was worse, so much alpha male blood in one room wasn't good. I refused to back down to Ryan's grandfather. I was a king, and I would not show weakness in front of someone I once considered a friend. Well, in his defense he met me as someone else. I used a glamour when I met him many years ago. I helped Marcus gather all the intel he needed to make the first treaty.

"You tricked me!" There it was, the real reason he was glaring at me. He was still angry that I never revealed my true identity to him.

Before I could answer, the office door banged open and Jax and Dom walked in. Each of them looked from my couch to the other, a question clear in their gazes. With a sigh, I answered their unasked question.

"Meet Ryan's grandparents, Bethany and Marcus Knox, Founder and first king of the Knox coven." Marcus sneered at my introduction. Okay, so sucking up wasn't going to work. Dom and Jax bid them hello, and the old bastard smirked at me as he shook each of their hands. Jax and Dom took a seat next to me.

"So, what did we miss?"

No one answered Dom, so in true Dom fashion, his filterless mouth got away from him. "May I just say how beautifully stunning you are, Bethany. I know where Ry gets her hotness from now." Bethany turned a shade of red, and Marcus glared at Dom, his upper lip pulled back in a sneer. Lucian used his hand to cover his smile.

"Boy, I have heard stories about your smart mouth. If you wish to keep your tongue, you will not speak to my wife like that!"

The office door opened once again and in walked Dom's father, wearing a grin from ear to ear. He looked straight toward Marcus and said, "I have been telling him that for years to no avail, old friend." Marcus smiled his first smile since being in here.

Mr. Silver and Marcus embraced each other; clearly it had been a long time since they had seen each other. After they pulled apart, Mr. Silver embraced Bethany. He pulled back and looked down at the older woman, a soft smile on his face.

"You know the offer still stands; you could still run away with me."

"Piss off, Ian, and stop hitting on my wife."

"Pity, she could have done so much better than you." The three of them chuckled at their little banter. Dom glared at his father.

"Clearly your son takes after you, Ian. I think I may have to fill him in on some of our good old days." Mr. Silver paled. Oh, so he had some skeletons in his closet.

"My son doesn't need to hear about our glory days. Surely he has more important things to do than listen to stories about his father." "Actually, no, I don't. I have a lot of free time these days. Whenever you're ready to spill the beans, Grandpa, let me know." Jax and I both groaned. Dom was such a dick. Marcus pinned deadly eyes on Dom.

"It's Mr. Knox to you, boy, and when you learn some respect maybe then I will share with you." Dom didn't miss a beat, he just grinned at Marcus and winked. He fucking *winked* at my grandfather-in-law. I didn't know what to call him, so I was sticking with that.

Mr. Silver claimed the single seat, and I looked around the room, waiting for someone to speak. I didn't have to wait long.

"Marcus, Bethany, we need your help. Your granddaughter's life is on the line. I called you here because I found out a couple days ago what Lachlan and Victor were planning." So Mr. Silver was the one to call her grandparents here. Good to know.

"Why do they want to kill, Smurf, sir?" Lucian asked.

"Because she is stronger than all the elders, dear. Those two power-hungry knuckleheads don't want a being stronger than the elders around." Bethany's voice held a harsh edge; clearly she didn't like the elders very much.

"So you're saying Ryan is stronger than the elder council in their entirety?" Dom was awed by this fact.

"Yes, son. If what you saw today wasn't clarification enough, then I don't know what is. That girl stabilized a whole world in less than five minutes. She accomplished what many before her could not. Ryan Knox is not someone to be underestimated."

"It's Stone, not Knox," I blurted out. I didn't mean to, but it just flowed out of my mouth like verbal diarrhea. Marcus lent forward and rested his forearms on his thighs, glaring at me.

"You should have been named Loki with all the tricks you play, boy. My granddaughter is a Knox and will remain one." Hell no, he didn't get to try and push me around. I helped the old fool and thought highly of him, and now he wanted a pissing contest over my wife? Fuck that.

"You can hate me all you want, Marcus. I helped you at the risk to my own people. We all got what we wanted from that treaty. As for *my* wife, she wants her name hyphenated: Knox-Stone. She is mine, Marcus. Think of me what you will, but don't ever doubt my love for her. I risked the lives of my people and my world because I fell in love with Ryan. Do not question me about her again!" Marcus leaned back and stretched his arm across the back of the couch. He smiled wider than the Cheshire Cat.

"That's exactly what I wanted to hear, boy. I was never truly angry with you for deceiving me—annoyed, yes. I let that all go the moment my granddaughter told me what you meant to her. I had to test you, to see if you were worthy for her, and it seems you passed."

I exhaled a breath I didn't know I was holding. This whole fucking thing was a test. I see now where Ryan got her cunning-ness from. And also her temper.

Chapter Seventy Three

RYAN

Sophia and I arrived at the back of Jackson's compound. I looked down at my watch to see it was ten at night. I was wiped out. I needed to see the others and say sorry, then go to bed. I would deal with the rest of this shit tomorrow.

We made our way across the yard and entered through one of the many side doors. Sophia led the way, thank God, because I had no idea where I was going. I knew how to get to Jackson's office and the mess hall from my room, but that was about it. A few minutes later we stopped outside a familiar door. Sophia didn't wait or knock, just opened the door and strolled in, and I followed my sister-in-law's lead.

Seven pairs of eyes turned toward us, each and every one of them wore looks of shock.

"Surprise!" Sophia announced to the room, I moved toward my grandparents immediately, shocked but thrilled to see them here. They both embraced me in a three-way hug. Grams checked me over to make sure I had no injuries and was really fine. Gramps clamped a hand on my shoulder and told me to fill him in on what happened later. I nodded.

I embraced Luce quickly and then waved hello to Mr.

Silver. He didn't seem annoyed to see me here, which was good. I took a deep breath, steeled my spine and then turned to face the three alpha males sitting on the couch.

None of them would meet my gaze. Sophia gave me a nudge. I walked toward them and plopped down on the coffee table in front of them, and still the three of them avoided looking at me.

I turned back to Sophia, and she gave me an encouraging nod. I needed to suck up my pride and ask for their forgiveness and help. I looked from Jax to Dom and then settled my gaze on Nico, who found looking at the side of Dom's head more interesting.

"I know you're all mad at me." Jax scoffed, but I pushed on. "I did what I did to help. Well, I thought I was helping. I didn't mean to block you guys out. I thought you would have tried to stop me. I'm sorry." Jax glared at me, and the heat of his gaze made me jerk back.

"You *chose* to make this decision without us! We would have helped you, Ryan. You didn't just hurt Nico, you hurt all of us. We all fought together just hours ago and risked our lives together and then you go on a solo mission of your own? We wouldn't have stopped you; we would have helped you find a better way."

I blinked my tears away. I wouldn't cry, I needed to be strong right now. I turned toward Dom, who reluctantly faced me. Gone was my carefree friend. Instead his look had changed to one of sadness and hurt.

"*We* would have stood by you. *We* would have helped you, *we* would have protected you. Instead *you* chose to go it alone, and now we're all left picking up the pieces on how to save your life." Dom didn't give me a chance to reply; he just turned to gaze back out the window. I turned to the last of the three men, the one I dreaded facing the most. When he met my stare, my resolve cracked. No emotion was displayed on his face, his eyes gave nothing away.

"You chose to leave me—to leave us—again. What did you think would happen? You would come back and we would be happy? Of course we're happy to see you, but were all pissed as hell at you as well. Now if you would excuse me, I would like to turn in for the night." Nico stood from his seat and left the room without so much as a look back, and Jax and Dom followed suit.

I sat there in shock. That certainly didn't go how I thought it would.

I couldn't leave things like this with the guys. I went to follow them but was stopped by my grandmother's words.

"Can you take us to see Stevie please, dear?"

I agreed to take them to my sister. It was Lucian, Grams, Gramps and me. I paused outside the door to the room we laid my sister in with Tyler.

I didn't know if Gramps and Grams knew about Tyler. I took a deep breath then pushed the door open. I paused as I entered the room. They weren't on the bed anymore. There were two caskets, both a dark wooden color, and neither had lids on.

I had to be strong for my grandparents. I couldn't break down, not right now.

"Why are there two caskets?" I looked at my Grams. Her eyes were welling with tears. They didn't know Stevie, but she was still their blood. I opened and closed my mouth several times but no words would come out.

"Tyler is laid in the other casket." Lucian saved me from

having to say that out loud. Gramps didn't hesitate; he made his way over to one of the caskets with the rest of us trailing behind him.

I peer over the edge to see it was Ty in this one. He had been cleaned and changed into his signature shirt and jeans with his Doc Martins. He looked so peaceful that I could almost be fooled into thinking he was sleeping.

"You foolish boy." I flinched at the anger in Gramps' tone. How could he be so callous?

"Gramps—"

The old man cut me off before I could scold him. "How did he die?" I didn't hesitate to answer; Tyler was my hero.

"He died saving my life. He knew he wouldn't be able to live if his mate died." Gramps tore his gaze from mine to peer down at Tyler once more.

"I always knew you had it in you, son. You are a savior and a hero, and you will be laid to rest on Knox Mountain with your mate. I will make sure of it."

Tears welled in my eyes at hearing Gramp's declaration. I knew if anyone could get Stevie and Ty buried up on the mountain, it was Gramps. Gramps clasped Grams's hand in his and led her over to the other casket, where my sister laid. Lucian gripped my hand and towed me toward where my grandparents now stood, peering down at my sister's body.

Anxiety tore through me the closer I got to the casket.

I was the reason she was laying in there.

I took several deep breaths before looking at my sister. Tears fell immediately, because my sister looked so calm and peaceful. She had been cleaned and re-dressed in her favorite style, jeans and a T-shirt.

"I hope you find peace and happiness now, blood of my blood." I looked to Grams and saw tears rolling down her cheeks. "I didn't have the pleasure of seeing you grow. I vow to you now, Stevie Lee Knox, that I will not make that mistake with your sister. You have my word, I will protect her and care for her until my dying breath."

I choked back a sob at Grams's declaration. She leaned forward and placed a kiss on my sister's forehead. I looked out the corner of my eye to see Gramps blinking rapidly; he was trying not to cry.

"What happened shouldn't have happened. Your death will not be in vain, granddaughter of mine. Many will tell stories of your sacrifice, and you will live in the hearts of your family and in the memories of those you love." Gramps leaned forward and placed a kiss to my sister's forehead. "Until we meet again, little warrior," Gramps whispered as he pulled back.

I couldn't speak. There just weren't any words to follow that.

NICO

No sooner did I enter my room and plonk down on the bed did my door open again. Jax and Dom waltzed in and joined me on the bed. Each of us sat there quietly in our own thoughts until the door opened again. This time my sister walked in with a smug look on her face. I looked from her to Dom, wondering how I had missed the signs. Was I so self-absorbed that I didn't know my best friend was in love with my baby sister?

"Okay, so you're all angry and pissed off. I get it, but she did what she thought was right to save you three. She didn't want you to give up any more than what you had already given. She was trying to protect you. If you ask me, Kai got the raw end of the deal, not you." I glared at Sophia. She could be a real pain in the ass at times.

"Who died and made you queen?" Dom snapped.

"Nico's sister-in-law," she deadpanned. I flinched at the reminder of Stevie's death.

"Cut her some slack, brother, she loves you—"

"She has a funny way of showing it!" I snapped at my sister, who just grinned at me.

"You are over a century old and here you are pouting with

your cheer squad in your room. How pathetic. You are a fucking king, Nicholas, start acting like one! Jackson, you are the alpha of all alphas, pull your head out of your ass and act like it. Dominic...well, you really don't have a job, so stop fucking sulking like a child." Dom glared daggers at my sister.

"What would you have us do then, sister?" Her grin turned conniving, I knew that look. Whenever my sister had that look in her eyes, heads always rolled.

"Listen up and listen good, boys."

I awoke the next morning feeling more refreshed and more like myself. I didn't go to Ryan or try to find her last night, and she didn't come to me either. That's a good thing; we needed her away from us if we were to pull off this plan of my sister's.

I went about my morning ritual of showering and changing before setting out to find the others at the mess hall. No sooner had the doors opened then my ears begun to ring from all the noise. I loaded a plate full of food and made my way over to the others. I sat next to Dom. Our group had shrunk. It was only Dom, Jax, Aurora, Sophia, and me now.

We all ate in silence until another body joined us at the table. I peered up from my plate to see it was Lucian. I bit my tongue so I didn't demand he tell me how she was or what she was doing. He must have seen the unasked questions in my stare.

"She slept on the floor next to her sister. She isn't doing too great. Her Gramps has placed her on house arrest while he and Grams go to the Knox coven to try and help David and her cousins come up with a plan."

"I feel for Ryan, this must be so hard for her." We all turned our gaze to Aurora. She wouldn't meet any of our stares, and that's when it hit me.

"You knew what she was going to do, didn't you?" She still wouldn't meet my gaze, even when she answered.

"Yes, yes I did. It had to play out like this in order for a different ending."

"What the hell does that mean?" Jax demanded. She kept her eyes down, focusing on her untouched plate.

"If you had intervened, she would have died. Her doing it the way I told her to is what is going to save her life." We all sat there, mouths agape, while Aurora stood and left the room. I shook myself out of my stupor to face Lucian.

"Did you know about that?" I queried.

"No, I guess you're not the only ones Smurf left in the dark." Lucian sounded hurt that Ryan had left him out of the plan.

"She's doing what she thinks is right." Four heads turned to Sophia, but she didn't cower under the pressure of our gazes.

"You knew, too, didn't you, little dove?"

Sophia held her head high, and looked Dom directly in the eyes as she answered.

"Yep, sure did."

Chapter Seventy Five

RYAN

Three days had passed, and I had been holed up in my room for most of that time. The only time I left my room was to visit my sister and Ty. I didn't eat in the mess hall; Gramps said it was too risky in case the elders sent someone to try and take me out. I had two guards that followed me wherever I went. I had two more guards stationed outside my door. Having them here made Gramps feel better, so I just put up with their presence.

I'm sprawled out on my bed, bored out of my mind. I can feel myself going down the rabbit hole of grief and shame. Before I can get lost further in my own mind, a knock sounds at the door.

"Yeah?" I call out.

"You have a visitor," one of my guards shouts back. I sit up and stare at the closed door.

"Who is it?"

"D!" I smile. I know that voice.

"D who?" I call back.

"Deez nuts in your mouth!" I burst out laughing then stop when I hear a hard thump.

"What the fuck was that for?"

"That's my fucking wife you're saying that shit to!" I jump from the bed and run to the door, swinging it open in one fluid motion. Standing on the other side of the door is none other than Dom, Jax, and Nico. Nico looks delicious in his white shirt and skin tight jeans. I run my gaze over him. Fuck, he is gorgeous. A throat clearing snaps me out of checking out my husband.

"We're standing right here! Can you make those fuck-me eyes when were not around, please?" I grin up at Dominic; he smiles and shoots me a wink.

"Can we come in?" I look to Jax and nod my head, stepping aside so they can enter.

The three giant alpha males step inside my room, and I close the door behind them and lean against it. I feel nervous and unsure now that they're here with me. They all stand at the end of my bed, facing me. I can feel each of them looking me over, for what I'm not sure. I chance a glance up at Nico to find his gaze locked on me. I sucked in sharply.

He has desire and anger swimming in the depths of those beautiful violet eyes. I pull my gaze from him to stare at Jax, and his eyes soften toward me. Those beautiful chocolate brown eyes can lull you like no other. I look to Dom and gasp—he cut his hair! It's short on the sides and longer on the top. His beautiful silver locks are gone. His eyes still hold a hint of mischief in them, though.

I look to Nico and see a smirk on his face. He was waiting for his turn to be checked out.

His jet-black hair is slicked back, not a hair out of place. His eyes are burning into me with intensity.

"Let's get this over with so they can fuck. The sexual tension in here is making me horny." Both Jax and Nico turn to glare at Dom. He shrugged his shoulders and winked at me. I smile at his teasing. I have missed his humor. I've missed Jackson's smarts, and Kai's brooding, and I've just missed Nico, plain and simple.

"I'm sorry," I blurt.

"Sorry for what, love? Come on, be more specific now. We're grown ass men and were reduced to putty in the hands of an eighteen-year- old woman. Stroke our egos a bit, aye?" Jax and Nico's features soften at their friend's words. I straighten up and do as Dom said.

"I am sorry for cutting you all out. I am sorry I went behind Kai's back and did what I did. I'm sorry I didn't bring you guys in on the plan. I didn't want you all to give more up than you already had. If I could go back and change it, I would. Please forgive me." Each of them looked at each other, their expressions unreadable.

"Did you know the council had planned to kill you?"

"No, Jax, I didn't, I swear."

"What did they tell you?" I looked Jackson in the eye and answered.

"They told me that if I came back and turned myself in, you would remain alpha, Nico and Kai would still be king of their races, and Dom would be free. They also promised that I could hand over leadership of the coven to anyone of my choosing. They told me I would stand trial, and if found guilty, I would be sentenced to jail." I let out a whoosh of air, it felt good to get this all out in the open.

"You would risk your freedom—your life—just so we could go on living as we always have?" Dom sounded so surprised that I would do this for them.

"Of course I would. If I didn't Sophia would lose her brother. Aurora would lose Jax. Kai would be a slave, and you would be forced to become alpha of your father's pack."

"And what would you lose?" His voice sent shivers down

my spine. I pulled my eyes from Dom to stare at the man of my dreams. I wouldn't lie to him, he deserved the truth.

"You." My voice didn't waver, and I mentally high fived myself.

"Thank you, Ry. We'll leave you two alone now, Dom?" Jax looked to Dom expectantly.

"Oh come on, we're just getting to the best part!" Dom whined.

"For fuck's sake, Dominic, grow up. Let them have some privacy!" Jax growled.

"They don't mind if I stay and watch, do you Ry?" Dom was going to get slapped again, I could feel it.

"So help me God, Dominic, I haven't beaten the shit out of you about my sister, but I will gladly do it now if you don't fuck off!" Nico ground out.

Jax and Dom made their way toward me, Dom pouting like a child. I stepped aside and opened the door for them, and Jax gave me a hug and left. Dom stopped and looked down at me with a mischievous smile on his face.

"You know, there are other ways you could thank me, love?" I burst out laughing again while Nico yelled.

"GET THE FUCK OUT, DOMINIC!" Dom's laughter followed him as he left the room, closing the door behind himself.

Wow, the tension in the room just went up by several thousand notches.

Nico and I stood there staring at each other, neither of us willing to back down.

I didn't want to fight with him. I didn't like this tension between us. I sucked up my pride and made my way over to him. I clasped his hand in mine and led him over to the single chair by the window. He didn't protest when I pushed him down into the seat.

As he looked up at me, I could see the smile in his eyes. I didn't want any space between us, so I sat across my man's lap. He wrapped his arms around me and pulled me to his chest.

I sighed in contentment. He ran one of his hands through my long hair, and I moaned at the feeling of him massaging my scalp.

Chapter Seventy Six

NICO

This was proving harder than I thought. Holding her to me and rubbing her hair had turned into me massaging her scalp. Her moaning was driving me *and* my cock crazy. She's so relaxed in my hold, and her eyes are closed, her full kissable lips on display. I couldn't hold it any longer. I leaned down and claimed her mouth. She opened for me instantly.

God she tasted like honey and home. I missed her. I missed *this.* I lifted her so she was straddling my lap and cupped her face between my hands, looking directly into those beautiful green eyes with that peculiar yellow ring.

"No more hiding from me, no more blocking me out. I can't and won't go through this shit again. You're my wife, my part-ner. We're a team." Tears shone in her eyes, and she brushed my hands away to lean forward and place a quick peck on my lips before meeting my gaze again.

"I swear on my life, Nico, no more. I promise. These past few days without you have been hell. I need you." That's all I needed to hear. I wrapped my arms around her waist and stood. I carried her to the bed and laid her down, crawling slowly up her body, taking my time.

"Oh, I have missed you, little one," I said as I popped the button on her jeans. A second later I pulled the jeans from her body and helped her out of her shirt. She laid there beneath me in a blue lace bra and panty set. Fuck me, my cock sprang to life. I kissed my way up from her bellybutton to her mouth, then I trailed kisses back down to her plump, luscious tits. I pulled the cups of her bra down to expose them, and her nipples pebbled as I blew across them. I sucked one of them into my mouth and squeezed the other. She was a writhing mess beneath me, just how I like her.

"Nico, please." I released her nipple with a pop and gazed up at her. Her cheeks were flushed and her eyes glassy.

"Please what, love?"

"I want you."

"Want me where?"

She growled. "Don't fucking make me beg, please."

"Please what?" She leaned on her elbows, glaring down at me as I toyed with her nipples.

"Please fuck me. Dick inside me. Is that clear enough?" she snapped.

"You didn't need to shout, babe." I leaned back and smiled down at her.

I made quick work of shucking off my pants and shoes. I didn't bother to peel her panties off; I tore them from her body instead.

"Are you wet for me, love?"

"Fuck yes!" was all the answer I needed before I slammed my hard, aching cock into her pussy.

We both cried out. Her pussy was fucking heaven. God, I missed being inside her. I pumped in and out of her while I used my thumb to rub her clit. Not two minutes later, I felt her pussy start to tighten around my cock.

"Ohhhhh, God," she cried out.

"Not God, love, just me." I wasn't going to give that bastard the credit for making her feel good.

"Nico, I'm gonna come."

"Come all over my fucking cock, baby, I want to feel you on my dick." She screamed my name as she climaxed, and a few pumps later, I joined her in ecstasy, calling her name as I came undone. I was a little embarrassed that I didn't last longer, but we had the rest of the night to make up for that. I flopped down beside her and pulled her into my arms, and we lay there both panting for the longest time.

I felt content to just lay here and hold her.

"I could stay like this forever." I chuckled at her lustful tone. This woman was a little vixen under the covers.

"We have the rest of our lives together, love. I plan on fucking you every night before we sleep and every morning when we wake." She giggled, a sound that had my heart soaring.

"I can't wait." I turned my head and captured her lips. My cock started twitching; the little devil was ready for round two.

Chapter Seventy Seven

RYAN

Nico and I made love for hours. My muscles were aching and tired, but in the best way. We finally fell asleep in the early hours of the morning. I thought I would fall into a dreamless slumber since I haven't been having any dreams for months now.

That was about to change.

I woke on the same beach I had seen my dad on days ago. I spun around looking for him; he said I wouldn't see him again. I turned back toward the ocean, confused. Why was I here?

I saw something...no, it wasn't something, it was someone coming out of the ocean. I squinted against the sunlight to see who it could be, then I cried out and then took off running to the water's edge. I slammed into her, wrapping my arms around her neck, and she wrapped her arms around my waist. I clung to her like my life depended on it. Sobs wracked my body. She was here! I thought I would never see her again.

"Shhh, little sister. It's okay." I pulled back to look at Stevie. Her wet hair clung to her face, and she was in a polka dot bikini. She smiled at me, and she looked...happy.

"Are you okay?" I choked out between sobs.

"Yeah, Ry, I am."

"I'm so sorry, Stevie, I—"

"Shhh, none of that now. You did what you had to do, Ry. I don't blame you, I'm thankful for what you did." Huh?

"Why are you thankful?"

She sighed and stepped back, gesturing behind me. I spun around to see two beach chairs with an umbrella in the middle of them.

They weren't there a moment ago. I followed Stevie to the chairs and sat down on one while she sat on the other. She met my gaze and smiled a sad smile.

"I grew up with an evil inside me. I fought it as long as I could. The older I got, the harder it was to ignore. Losing Dad and thinking that the fae were behind his death was when I gave up the fight. I need you to know the things I said and did, I never meant. I was a passenger in my own body; I could see and hear everything, but I had no control. All I felt was the need for death and power."

"Stevie I know you would never hurt anyone intentionally. I just wish I could have done more for you."

She reached over and grabbed my hand.

"You gave me the greatest gift of all, Ryan. You set me free. I am able to be me now without fighting something inside of me every day." Tears continued to trail down my face. My heart ached at the daily battle my sister faced her whole life.

"I-Is Ty, with you?" Stevie's smile reached her eyes, and a blush coated my sisters cheeks. Oh my God, Stevie is blushing!

"Yeah, he's here with me. He is fucking aaaamazing, Ry, and don't get me started on what he's like in bed. His di—"

"Stoooooppppp. Please, Stevie, I look at Ty like a brother. I don't want to be picturing his manhood, thank you very much!" Stevie broke out into a fit of laughter. Hearing her laugh and seeing how happy she is gave me a form of relief. I was still heartbroken I wouldn't see her every day, but seeing her now and how she is, lessened the burden of what I had done to my own sister.

"I needed that laugh."

"I didn't think I would see you." Her expression sobered and turned serious in an instant. I tensed.

"You weren't supposed to see me for years, but your grief called me to you, Ry. I'm here because you need me."

"What? I didn't call you."

"Your subconscious did, sister. I also needed to come to you and tell you some hard truths."

"What happened, Stevie?"

"Randall Cane isn't dead. Lachlan and Victor are planning to kill you and take the four guys out so they can lead with Randall. Randall promised them that he would make them head of each of their chosen races if they helped him take you out.

"The reason Randall's body was never recovered the day of the battle was because Victor sent him through a portal to somewhere. Victor and Lachlan must be dealt with, Ry. I know some things that will help you." My sister and I sat there for hours talking over what she had learned about the elders and how fucked up they really were. The sun had started to set when Stevie stood and pulled me to my feet. We stood there holding each other's hands, tears shining in both our eyes.

"I don't know how I'm supposed to say goodbye to you, Stevie."

"Then don't say goodbye, say see you later." She tried to smile but failed.

"I'm gonna miss you so fucking much!" We wrapped our arms around each other and held on.

"I'll never truly leave you, Ry, I'll always be here watching over you. Go be great, sister, and kick some ass. Show those old fuckers what Knox women are really made of. Oh, and tell that husband of yours I'll be checking in to make sure he treats you right." I laughed at her attempt to scare Nico.

"I love you, Stevie," I sobbed.

"And I you, Ry, now go. I can hear that brooding king calling for you."

Chapter Seventy Eight

RYAN

I woke to Nico looming over me and shaking me awake. I blinked up at him and saw worry lines across his forehead.

"What the hell happened, Ryan?" I pushed away from Nico and sat up, clutching the sheet to my chest.

"I saw it all last night love," he replied at my need to shield my body. I poked my tongue out in response.

"What happened, love? You were screaming and crying. I couldn't break into your dream." I smiled. My sister told me she blocked him out.

"I was with Stevie." Nico cocked his head to the side, confused. I quickly filled him in on what had happened and everything that Stevie had told me.

"We need to find the others and tell them." Nico jumped off the bed and started picking up his clothes off the floor. He chucked my clothes at me, and I growled.

"I am showering before we meet with the guys; I am not going near them without washing *you* off." Nico spun around and grinned at me, still naked as the day he was born.

"Fine, you shower, and I'll call Kai and your cousins. I'll

send Dom to collect them, it will be faster." I agreed and kissed Nico goodbye before he left. I headed for the shower to prepare myself for Operation Take Down the Lying Asshole Elders.

Nico returned to collect me from my room and we made our way to the bat cave. I chuckled at my new name for Jackson's office. Nico peered down at me like I was losing the plot, and I shrugged my shoulders.

I didn't knock or wait for Nico I just opened Jax's office door and walked right on in like I owned the place. Two seconds inside the bat cave and I was plucked off the ground and bear-hugged by none other than my cousin Chase. After he was done he passed me over to Alex, who didn't squish the life out of me when he hugged me.

"Don't you ever pull another stunt like that again!" Being scolded by Alex was like being told off by your parents.

"Yes, Dad." I tartly replied and moved away from him to say hi to Mya. I looked around to see Kai standing by the window. I didn't even think or hesitate; I made my way over to him. He opened his arms as soon as he saw me approaching. I ran to him, clinging onto his shirt. I missed this. I missed him.

"You really didn't have to come, you know," I mumbled into Kai's chest.

"When Nico told me it was urgent and you needed my help I dropped everything. I told you I would always look out for you. Plus, my skill set will come in handy today." Oh my gosh, how could I have forgotten? Kai had the power to control people's moods and emotions. He really was the perfect person to have with us today.

"You know, Tink, I'm proud of ya. Not once have you growled or thrown a tantrum about *your* wife being in another man's arms." I groaned, Chase really was an ass to Nico.

I pulled out of Kai's embrace to see him smiling down at me. He was enjoying Chase teasing Nico.

"Awwww, my baby is all grown up. I feel like a proud father." Chase cracked up laughing at Dom, and Nico glared at both of them. I made my way over to my husband and huddled into his side. He wrapped his arm around my shoulders, pulling me in closer.

"And I feel like a proud brother, knowing you have finally come out of the closet, Dom. You and Chase will make an amazing pair." Dom jumped away from Chase like he had shocked him, and everyone broke out into fits of laughter. Dom glared at each and every one of us.

"I'm enjoying seeing Dom squirm just as much as the rest of you, but I have to ask: Why are we here, brother?" Kai asked.

Nico looked down at me. "Would you like to tell them or should I?" I looked around the room and smiled. These guys weren't my friends; they were my family. Dom, Jax, Kai, Alex, Chase, Aurora, Mya, and Sophia. Wait—

"Where is Lucian?" I asked.

"He's collecting Dom's dad and your grandparents. They will join us momentarily." I nodded. I didn't want to have to repeat myself, so I turned to Aurora. She deserved to know how her brother was. She looked so lost, and she had dark circles under her eyes.

"Aurora, I need to tell you something." She lifted her broken eyes to me. I smiled, trying to ease her discomfort.

"I'll explain how I know all of this when Luce gets here, but I need you to know Ty is happy." She looked shaken and taken back.

"H-how do you know?" she stammered out. I didn't get to

answer, as the office door banged open. In walked Luce, Grams, Gramps and Mr. Silver. I guess it was showtime.

NICO

Everyone claimed a seat and listened intently as Ryan explained everything her sister had told her about the elders. To say everyone was shocked would be an understatement. Her grandparents were livid to find out the elders had ulterior motives; we needed to be smart about this.

We would only get one shot at bringing down the leader of the elders. The elders were made up of the strongest of each race; no one has gone up against them and lived to tell about it. I was beyond aggravated to learn about Victor's involvement in this. I thought Lachlan was one of the good ones, as well. Clearly I was wrong.

We were to meet with the elders in two hours; they had finally made a decision. We needed to come up with a plan and fast. If we failed, they would take us out. Dom and I weren't strong enough to take on the elders, not even with half of them being dead. We learned from Ryan's grandfather that her uncle had told him the elders were recruiting new members, and they would be with them today. David also told his father that the witches had spelled all council members so Kai's *gifts* wouldn't work on them.

I didn't like our odds; we had no other choice, though. If we had an eyewitness to the leader of the fae and vampire elders' nefarious dealings that would help, but we didn't. All we had was the word of a ghost who tried to kill us.

"I don't mean to but in, but when you saw your sister, did you see my brother?" Aurora's bottom lip was trembling, and she was on the verge of tears. Ryan straightened in her seat next to me and met the seer's gaze.

"No, I didn't see Ty. Stevie told me they were together and that they were happy. She tried to fill me in on what they had been up to, but I didn't need that mental picture." Everyone around the room let out a light chuckle.

"Stevie wanted me to pass on a message to you, though." Aurora steeled her spine, and her lip stopped trembling. Stevie was her least favorite person. "Stevie told me to tell you, look to the night sky, look two stars to the left and there you will see—"

Aurora cut Ryan off, finishing the sentence for her.

"The star that will lead us to Neverland." Aurora broke out in tears. She was smiling, though—did she have a mental breakdown?

"A-are you okay?" Ry cautiously asked. Aurora nodded her head vigorously.

"That message wasn't from your sister, it was from Ty. He used to tell me that when we were kids. It means he found his happy place." There was not a dry eye in the room. Hell, even I felt choked up.

We all left Jackson's office as one.

No one spoke as we made our way to the back of the property where the chapel once was. How cliché that the elders wanted to meet there. We knew they had asked for the leaders of each race to come; alphas from all over had flown in. Leaders of each sub coven had come. Vampire leaders from different seethes were here as well, and they were given fae blood from the elders so they could be outside for the meeting. The only faes that would be here would be Cyrus, Maverick, and Larick, as fae didn't have sub clans; we all lived as one and only had one ruler—*moi*.

The closer we got to the back door, the clammier Ryan's hand became in mine. She was nervous. I couldn't fault her for what she had done to save us. What she didn't know is that when she left earlier to go to the bathroom, we had staged a coup behind her back, in case things didn't go our way.

We stopped in front of the door that led us to the back of the property. Mr. Silver turned back to look at Ryan, and after taking a deep breath, she nodded her head. She was ready to face this shit, and we all had her back. She saved all our asses and sacrificed so much; we all owed her a debt.

She didn't expect anything from us. Hell, she tried to talk us out of coming with her to this meeting. She didn't want her grandparents to be outed, as all the elders, aside from Mr. Silver and the witch elders, thought they were dead.

Her grandfather refused to stay hidden any longer. There was no need for them to hide now that Stevie was no longer a threat.

Mr. Silver and the others were at the front of our group. Lucian and I stood on either side of Ryan, while her grandparents walked behind us.

Hopefully the shock of seeing her grandparents would make Lachlan and Victor back down. Marcus Knox was one powerful warlock, a warlock you didn't want to get on the wrong side of. He may be old, but he was far from weak.

Dom's dad pushed the door open and walked out with his head held high, his son on his right and Kai and Jax on his left. Chase and Alex moved to walk beside Dom. Soph, Mya, and Rora remained behind the guys and in front of us. I gave Ryan's hand a reassuring squeeze as we made our way outside.

Chapter Eighty

RYAN

I gasped at the sheer number of people here—there must be over a hundred at least!

Why did so many people need to be here for this? I began to regret my decision; I never should have agreed to their terms. Gramps had told me the elder council were honorable people and upheld the supernatural law, and that they could be trusted.

I bet Gramps was regretting telling me that now. I should have trusted the others enough to go to them as soon as I arrived, and come clean about the deal I made. I thought I was saving them, but in reality all I did was piss them off and sign my own death warrant.

As we walked toward the chapel, I felt dozens of pairs of eyes on me; it made my skin crawl.

I knew some of these people had lost loved ones the night of my wedding. I didn't blame them for hating me, and I didn't think badly of them for wanting my death.

In the last seven months, my whole life has been flipped upside down. I left my home to be with my sister. Flew to a new country, met new people, got married. Got locked up and beaten, found my grandparents, fought a war, and lost my sister. My life was out of control.

I looked to Nico and whispered, "I'm so sorry for not coming to you with this. I should have brought you in on this from the start. Whatever happens today, just know I love you." His steps never faltered as he looked down at me with determination in his gaze.

"Don't do that. This is not goodbye; I will not live without you. I will fight till my dying breath if need be."

"Preach, brother!" came from Lucian, and I smiled at both of them. The closer we got to the chapel—well, the charred remains of what used to be the chapel—I noticed the shocked and confused looks on people's faces.

I followed their gazes, and that's when it clicked. They were shocked to see my grandparents alive and well.

A minute later we came to a stop. I couldn't see the elders as the guys had formed a wall in front of us.

"Ian, what is the meaning of this show of force?" one of the elders asked.

"No show of force, just leading the young lady out is all." Mr. Silver answered.

"Where is she?"

"She is here, but first I think David of the Knox coven has something to say." Mr. Silver nodded his head, and I assume that was my uncle's cue to speak.

"Yes, thank you, Ian. I, David Knox would like to hand over leadership of the witch and warlock elders to its rightful leader —" That same voice cut my uncle off. "You cannot do that!"

Chase stepped forward to address the elders.

"Actually, yes he can. If you look in the bylaws, it states that if a leader has not been removed or relinquished their role, they may return to said role at any time."

"There is no other leader, boy!" a new voice roared. I was

ninety percent sure that voice belonged to Lachlan. Gramps moved from behind us and walked to stand beside Chase. A collective gasp sounded from the elders in front of us.

"I think you should watch your tone on how you speak to my grandson, Lachlan. It is my right to lead the elders, and my son David has graciously offered to step down."

"Very well," Lachlan gritted out. "Now, step aside so the accused can be seen by the elders."

The wall of bodies in front of me reluctantly moved aside so I could step forward with Lucian and Nico either side of me. Before me stood all the elders. They had added more members. I counted each faction and saw that there were thirteen in each group. Lachlan, Victor, Gramps and Mr. Silver all stood in front of their council members. Gramps gave me a small nod; he was with me till the bitter end.

"Ryan, queen of the fae and rightful heir to the Knox coven, you stand before us today on trial for the murder of fifty-two supernaturals." Victor spoke so robotically that he sounded gleeful at speaking the number of lives lost. "The elders have met and come to a decision that—"

"I wasn't part of that meeting, so I regretfully have to say that the witches and warlocks cannot back your decision," Gramps smugly replied.

"I must agree with Marcus, I was not present either. So the shifters will not be able to back the fae or vampire's decision." Mr. Silver's facial expression gave nothing away. Victor growled at both of them.

"Your presence was requested four days ago for a formal elders meeting!" Lachlan snapped.

"Well, I couldn't be there four days ago. You see, I got a phone call from an old friend beseeching my wife and I to return to Alaska, because the elders wanted my granddaughter's life forfeited." I heard dozens of people gasp around us.

Lachlan darted his eyes around at the people gathered. He smiled sweetly at them, trying to placate them and their worries.

"A decision wasn't reached until late last night, Marcus. We took longer than we originally thought to reach a decision. Whoever you *dear friend* is, they were misinformed." Lachlan was trying to be diplomatic but was failing miserably.

"So the elders are not here to end my granddaughter's life then?" Gramps volleyed back.

"I cannot say at this moment, Marcus," Lachlan snapped.

"Why not?" Mr. Silver asked. Victor turned to glare at the leader of the shifter council.

"You know why Ian. Until we have reached that part in the trial, we cannot say."

"Oh so this is a trial, Victor? I thought it was a meeting?" Both Lachlan and Victor turned to glare at Mr. Silver.

"Enough of this, we are wasting time. *All* elders that were present at the meeting came to a decision—that you will pay with your life for the lives that you took!" I gasped. Lachlan's eyes held so much hatred toward me—why?

"Like fuck. She will not be dying for you or anyone else today. We know you have been planning this from the start," Nico yelled.

"Planning what, king?"

"Cut the shit, Victor, we know you and Lachlan planned to have my wife killed from the start of learning who and what she is. We also know that you two worked together the night of our wedding to make sure that not everyone got away from the chapel." Victor smiled at Nico.

"Do you have any proof of this? Was someone there to witness these heinous crimes you say we committed?" Nico tensed next to me. We didn't have any witnesses. I was going to sound mad, but I had to act fast.

"Yes, we do."

All eyes turned to me. Lachlan and Victor exchanged a glance between each other before schooling their features and facing me. I gulped. Everyone was going to think I'm crazy.

"And who might this witness be, my dear?" My skin crawled at his term of endearment. I pushed my shoulders back and looked directly at both men that were vying to have me killed.

"My sister." More gasps rang out around us, and Lachlan and Victor were visibly taken back.

"Your sister?" Lachlan queried, and I nodded.

"As far as I am aware, you killed her days ago, and her body lies inside the alpha's compound." I flinched at his cold and detached way of speaking about Stevie, like she was nothing more than a distant unpleasant memory.

"Y-yes." I cleared my throat and took a deep breath before continuing. "Yes, my sister is dead, but I have seen her and—" Lachlan cut me off with his boisterous laughter, and I looked to my friends to see them all glaring at the leader of the vampire council.

"So let me get this right. You have seen your sister's ghost, and she is the one who told you about this preposterous scheme?" I ground my teeth together.

"Yes, she also told me Victor was the one to portal Randall Cane out of the battle field so we couldn't kill him." That wiped the smile off both those asshole's faces. Just as I started to feel like we had the upper hand, they knocked us back down.

"Well, can Miss Knox join us now and tell us this herself?" Victor's smile was victorious and evil. They both knew I couldn't just bring Stevie out and have her defend me. They had me right where they wanted me. I had no other back up plans. I was fucked and probably going to die.

Chapter Eighty One

NICO

I saw her deflate, a look of defeat plastered across her face. I looked to my three brothers, and they each nodded.

It was time for us to try save my wife. If this failed we would battle our way out of here and run. My wife would not die by the hands of these lying, callous bastards. I released Ryan's hand. I felt her gaze on me but I couldn't look at her.

As I stepped forward, my brothers flanked me on either side. We stood there staring at the elders. The vampire and fae elders looked confused while Mr. Silver and Marcus looked proud.

I spotted a figure out of the corner of my eye trying to catch my attention. I squinted and saw it was Cyrus. He gestured to the person standing next to him. I was shocked, what the hell was she doing here?

"What is the meaning of this?" I pulled my gaze back to the elders and glared at the sons of bitches. Mr. Silver and Marcus moved to stand either side of the two dickbags.

"We want to make a trade," Jax bellowed loud enough for everyone around to hear. I heard a gasp behind me. I chanced a look back to see Ryan held back by Lucian and her Grams. I smiled at my wife.

"What kind of trade, Alpha?" I could hear the intrigue in Victor's voice from here. I don't know how I was fooled for so many years by these two. I thought they were trustworthy men —how wrong was I?

"For the life of Ryan Knox-Stone, I, Jackson Marshall, will step down as *the* alpha." Everyone gasped, and Lachlan looked gleeful.

"I, Melakai Cane, king of all vampires, am prepared to step down from my position, and allow the elder council to lead the vampires—*if* Ryan is freed of all charges!"

Kai sounded like a true king, brave and confident. I was beyond proud of my brother; he never wanted the title or to be a part of the vampires, but here he was falling into the role like a pro. Lachlan was grinning from ear to ear; this was what he wanted, to rule the vampires.

What I still couldn't figure out was where Randall was.

"Well, I don't have a fancy title, but, I, Dominic Silver, hereby swear that I will fulfill my destiny and claim the title of alpha of the New York pack. My terms are the same as the others: as long as Ryan goes free." Ian Silver stood taller and looked proud; his son has finally agreed to accept his fate, but why was there so much sadness in his eyes? Dom has never wanted to lead; he just wants to be free to live his life. It was my turn, and I took a step forward.

"Nico, no, please, you guys can't do this," Ryan begged. I turned and smiled at my wife.

"Isn't it obvious, love? We would give it all up for you, without having to be asked."

Love shone in her eyes, but so did shame. She was blaming herself for what we were doing, what the elders wanted from the start. I turned back and faced the four leaders of the council.

"I, Nicholas Stone, will renounce my claim to the throne and hand it over to Victor *if* my wife is set free." Victor's eyes said everything, he wanted the power and the title of *king*. I knew then we had the elders. Marcus and Mr. Silver's gaze's raked over us; they were proud of us.

They knew what we were giving up for Ryan. Jax and I were giving up our birthrights, Dom was finally falling into line, and Kai was going to be homeless.

"We will discuss this—" Lachlan cut Marcus off.

"There is no need for that, my friend. I am sure we all agree that this is a fair exchange."

"Yes, I agree, I think we can close this matter and release the girl from her crimes." Murmurs began to break out around us. The leaders that had gathered for the trial weren't happy. Either they wanted my wife's head on a platter, or they were pissed we had just handed over control of all our races to the council.

"Quiet!" Lachlan yelled, and everyone stopped talking. "Well now that the matter has been settled, we will need you four to fill out and sign over—"

"Actually, my son-in-law and his friends will not be giving anything up, and you will not be charging my daughter with anything!"

All eyes turned toward the slender woman walking toward us, her long hair billowing around her. The closer she got, the more I could see the determination in her brown eyes.

Nina Knox had an ace up her sleeve.

Chapter Eighty Two

RYAN

Nina looked like a badass. She held her head high and walked with purpose. She even looked the part, in shit-kicker boots, black skinny jeans, and a form-fitting white shirt. She looked ready to fuck shit up. I was shocked. I have never seen her look so put together, but what the hell was she doing here?

"How dare you interrupt us!" Victor shouted, and Nina smiled back at the uptight bastard.

"Now, as the mother-in-law to the king of Farrarie and mother to the queen of the Knox coven, I believe I have a right to speak." Nina looked toward Gramps and asked, "Am I correct, Marcus, may I speak on behalf of my daughter?" Gramps looked at Nina for a long moment.

"Yes, you may speak." Lachlan and Victor turned to glare at Gramps. Nina made her way over to stand by Nico and the guys. Nico looked down at her and whispered something in her ear, but I couldn't hear their private conversation.

When Nina whispered back in Nico's ear, his body went tense, then he turned to look at me. The look on his face was relief. What the hell was Nina up to?

"Get on with it then, woman!" Victor growled.

"Don't be like that, Victor. I mean, we were friendly once, weren't we?" The leader of the fae turned a shade of crimson, anger was evident in his eyes. "You should know, Victor; all those times you thought I was too high to understand or remember things, you were wrong." Nina moved to stand directly in front of Victor. He glared down his nose at her. Nina spun around, her hair slapping Victor as she did.

She looked around the clearing to each and every one gathered. Then her gaze settled on me as she spoke.

"What my daughter said is true! The leaders of the vampire and fae council wanted her dead long before the night of her wedding. They were working under the orders of Randall Cane. Randall promised them they could each lead their race if they helped him set my daughter up. Victor erected a shield around the fifty-two people that died. He told them the shield would protect them. When the blast from Ryan emerged outside of the chapel, he dropped the shield, killing those that were inside it. They knew the punishment for this would be death for my daughter."

"How do you know this?" Mr. Silver asked.

"Because Victor and Lachlan raped me while I was held at Randall Cane's mansion. When they were done with me, they would shoot me up with drugs, thinking that it would make me more compliant. They would make phone calls or discuss the battle while still in the room with me, and I heard every fucking word they said!" Nina spun around so fast then slapped Victor clean across the face.

He raised his hand to strike her, but before he could, a blast of purple light shot him backward and he landed on his ass. I looked around to see who had done it and gasped when I found the culprit.

"If you ever try to lay another hand on my daughter-in-law, I will fucking kill you where you stand, Victor! That goes for you as well Lachlan, you piece of shit!" Gramp's tone sent chills down my spine; I have never heard him so angry.

"There's the man I married." I looked to my side and smiled at my Grams. She loved seeing Gramps so riled up.

"Cyrus!" Nico called out, and a moment later Cyrus and four other guards appeared in front of Nico. "Arrest them and detain Victor and Lachlan in the alpha's cells."

"You cannot do this! We are the elder council leaders. That woman is nothing but a liar and a common whore!" Lachlan shouted, but Nina never missed a beat.

"A common whore who bit your dick when you tried to put it in my mouth? Or the common whore who was present when you and Victor made plans to eliminate my daughter?" Lachlan looked around, shocked, clearly expecting the other members of the council to help.

"You're right, Lachlan, as leaders we cannot arrest you." Lachlan smiled, and as soon as Victor was on his feet again, he had a triumphant smile on his face as well. "The only way we can do that is if the other members of the council agree with us."

My stomach sank. What if they didn't believe Nina? We would be back to square one with my head on the chopping block.

I looked to each of the council members to see them speaking in hushed tones among themselves.

"The shifter council is in agreement. We vote for their arrest and for their lives to be forfeited." Lachlan and Victor looked murderous at Mr. Silver's words.

"The covens are in agreement." Gramps spoke loudly so everyone could hear. I looked to the fae and vampire council members. A young woman from the fae council stepped forward and bowed her head to Nico.

"The fae council is in agreement with the coven and shifters." She looked to me and smiled, and I mouthed a thank you. All we needed was for the vampires to be on our side. It felt like it took hours but in minutes a young man from the vampire council stepped forward. The young elder gulped loud enough for everyone to hear before speaking.

"We agree with the other council members." At his words, Lachlan and Victor began to fight and struggle against the guards.

Uncle David looked to Kai and nodded his head, and Kai made his way over to Lachlan and Victor. He placed a hand on each of them, two seconds later both men stood there with confused expressions. They didn't struggle or fight against the guards as they led them away. Uncle David must have removed the spell that blocked Kai.

Nico spun around and plucked me out of Grams's and Lucian's hold. He spun me around in circles, stopping only when I threatened to puke on him. He placed me on my not-so-steady feet and cupped my face between his hands.

"We did it. We're finally free to live our lives, little one." I blinked away the tears that threatened to fall and stood on my tiptoes to place a kiss on his lips.

"Do I get a kiss as a thank you?" Nico and I pulled apart to look at Dom. I smiled and hugged him.

I thanked each and every one of my friends and my cousins. Without these guys, my ass would have been dead several times over. There was no doubt in my mind about that.

"Dominic, we need to talk." We all stopped talking and turned to face a solemn-looking Mr. Silver. Dom rushed over to his father.

"Dad, what's wrong?" Mr. Silver tried to smile but it didn't reach his eyes.

"I'm so sorry, son."

"Sorry for what, Dad?"

"What you did today—" Dom cut his father off.

"Don't sweat it, old man. I still get to be free and be me." I could hear the happiness in Dom's voice.

"No, son, you won't get the life you want." Huh. Why the fuck not?

"What do you mean?" I could hear the slight shake in Dom's voice.

"Son, you made a vow and swore it today. You can't undo what you have done. You have no choice but to return to New York with me and become alpha."

"Dad, no! I didn't mean to...I can't...I don't want to!" Mr. Silver had so much sadness in his eyes; he didn't want to do this to his son.

"I'm sorry, you made a vow, and if you don't honor it, your wolf will override you. Wolves are bound by honor, and you vowed here today to take over for me."

Chapter Eighty Three

RYAN

I left the others to go search for Nina. I found her around the side of the compound, speaking to my grandparents. I hid behind a tree to listen. Yeah, I know I was being nosy, sue me.

"I'm so sorry, I never meant to hurt Ralph. I loved him!" I could hear the anguish in Nina's voice.

"We know you loved him Nina, it wasn't your fault he died." Bless Grams for being so sweet.

"What you said back there—I didn't like hearing it, but I think you were very brave." Oh. My. God!

Gramps just gave Nina a compliment. She chuckled nervously.

"I'm glad I could help, I just wish I would have been brave enough years ago. My daughter may live, but she will always hate me, and I can't blame her for that."

Nina's words hit me in my heart. It was time to let go of the anger and the hate. Nina was sick, and I couldn't hold that against her anymore. My mother had just saved my life, after all. I didn't want to overthink this anymore. I moved out from behind the tree.

"Mom?" My mom spun around so fast she nearly lost her footing.

My mother stood there staring at me, mouth agape in shock.

"Y-you called me Mom." Her voice was shaky from trying not to cry.

I shrugged my shoulders. "Well, you did kind of save my life, so I thought I owed you one." Mom walked toward me and stopped directly in front of me.

"You owe me nothing! I did what any parent would have done for their child." She dropped her gaze, and I sighed. It was now or never.

"I'm so sorry for what those assholes did to you. I swear I will help you through it." She brought her gaze back up to mine, so many unspoken questions swirling in her eyes. "I'll never forget what happened to me as a kid, but I will move past it. You're all I have left. Dad's gone and so is Stevie. I want to make this work between us." My mom nodded her head vigorously and then crushed me against her, sobbing into my hair. After the shock wore off, I wrapped my arms around her. It felt strange to be hugging my mother. Right here, in this moment, all my anger and resentment toward her vanished. I knew she would do better and be better now. I was excited at the prospect of getting to know my mom.

The next day we all traveled in a convoy to Knox Mountain. Today was the day my sister and Ty were being laid to rest.

No one protested when Gramps said Stevie and her mate were to be buried with our father. Standing up here and looking at both caskets was a bittersweet feeling. I knew Stevie and Ty were together and happy, but I still missed them both. When a witch or warlock is buried, his or her power is taken from them and then passed onto their chosen one. I had no idea about this until Grams told me this morning.

"It is time; I will now say the sacred spell to transfer Stevie's power onto her chosen one." I looked around at all the people gathered here, wondering which one of them would inherit my sister's power. Would they inherit the darkness as well?

Nico's hand squeezed mine as he leaned down to whisper in my ear.

"So help me God, if you get any more power, I think it would crush my ego." I giggled at my husband's goofiness.

I gasped as I watched purple power rise from Stevie's casket, tears sprung to my eyes. That was my sister's essence, and now it would go to someone else. I hoped Stevie chose well.

"Seek your chosen vessel, granddaughter," Gramps whispered to the purple magic swirling above my sister's casket. The magic shot to the left of me, and I thought it was going to my mom, who stood beside me, but then gasped when I realized its target.

"Oh my God, Stevie chose you!" I said in awe as I looked at a shocked Mya. She was running her hands all over her chest in disbelief.

Stevie gave her power to Mya.

"Welcome back to the Knox coven, Mya. I couldn't have picked someone better to inherit my granddaughter's gifts." Gramps was happy to have Mya back in the coven. Mya opened and closed her mouth so many times, but words wouldn't come out.

I guess Mya was going to be one strong-ass witch. Mya looked to me; she looked scared, like I was going to be mad. I leaned around my mom and gripped Mya's hand.

"I am so glad it's you; this is my sister's way of righting her wrong. I know you will do her proud, Mya." Mya relaxed at my words.

"I swear, Ryan, I won't let you or Stevie down. I'll use this new power to help the others track Randall."

It had become a mission assigned to a select few from the council to track down Randall Cane. Kai, Jax, Aurora, Mya, Alex, Chase, and a few others were dead set on justice being served.

Dom wasn't able to join them, as he would have to leave with his dad to go to New York. Sophia and Lucian were returning to Farrarie with me, Mom, and Nico. Sophia had promised to help Lucian find his parents.

Epilogue

RYAN

Standing here in my empty pink room at my father and Stevie's house was bitter sweet.

I only spent a couple days here, but it had a feeling of home. I had put off packing and selling my sister's house for as long as I could. My sister's childhood home was now sold to a family who would make their own memories here.

I smiled at the thought of my dad and sister playing and laughing in this house. I took one last look around the room that was supposed to be mine. I would have loved living here. Growing up with my mother was traumatizing, but it also made me the woman that I am today.

My mother had been speaking to a healer back in Farrarie who was helping her; it was a long road for my mom, but she was prepared to put in the work. I even saw a healer as well, to help me heal from the trauma of my wedding night. Nightmares still plagued her, and she said it was karma's way of punishing her for what she had done to me. I didn't blame her anymore for my childhood; I managed to get past all of that. The healer was helping her deal with what those bastards did to her.

After the council bound their power and banished them to the human world, my mother finally started to relax, and she knew then that they could never hurt her again.

Victor and Lachlan were banished from the supernatural world, never allowed back again. Nico, Jax, Kai, and Dom, with the help of Gramps and Mr. Silver, had both the traitors placed inside a human prison where they would live out the remainder of their days in solitude. I don't know how they managed to pull that off, but I was thankful.

"Are you ready, love?" I was pulled from my thoughts and turned to see my sexy-ass husband by the door. Nico still took my breath away. He stood there in dark wash jeans and a form-fitting black shirt that clung to his skin. His jet-black hair disheveled, like he had just run his hand through it, and those violet eyes always made me weak in the knees.

He sauntered into the room and stopped in front of me. I craned my head back so I could see his eyes. He smiled down at me. I know that look.

"If you keep looking at me like that love, I'll have to defile you in your childhood room."

I shivered at the huskiness in his voice, and the desire in his eyes sent liquid pooling between my thighs. He leaned down to capture my lips in what I'm sure was to be a heated kiss but stopped his descent at the sound of Lucian's voice.

"Eww, you two were about to fuck, weren't you? Do it when you're dreaming or something." I stepped back and smiled.

I moved toward the door where Lucian now stood and patted him on the chest. "You really need to find yourself a girl-friend, buddy. Your always cock-blocking me, and it's not cool for me or my coochie." Lucian reeled back like I slapped him, and I grinned. Nico and I learned that Lucian was the reason

Nico couldn't come to me in my dreams. After returning to Farrarie, Lucian learned to control his power and removed his hold on mine, completely. Nico had a hunch that he was blocked because of Luce; that night Nico tried and managed to enter my dreams. It felt good to have him with me again in my dreams. It was like the final piece had been put back in place.

"I could have gone the rest of my life without knowing what your lady bits needed." I burst out into a fit of laughter. Living with Lucian has been an experience. We have been trying for months to track down information on his parents, but have had no luck. Sophia is with us in Farrarie, as well, and she has been nothing but amazing toward Lucian. She has been teaching him to read and write, and she was even the one to help Lucian to sleep on his own, in his own room.

Sophia hasn't smiled a full smile since Dom left for New York six months ago. Those two needed to sort their shit out and admit that they loved each other. I don't know what the history is between them, but I know there is a story there; Sophia just won't spill the beans.

We don't hear from Dom much. We've seen him twice since he left. Nico has tried to reach out and ask if we could visit, but he always has some excuse as to why we can't.

Dom is being weird and cagey, and I don't like it. Mr. Silver has even reached out and said he was worried about Dom. Nico and I are planning to visit him very soon and get to the bottom of whatever the hell is bothering him.

"All right, you two, let's lock up and get out of here. We still have to stop in Wonder Lake to see Jax and Aurora and get an update." Nico's words pulled me from my happy moment. Kai and Mya were in Chicago; they got a tip from one of the packs there that they had spotted Randall.

Kai is still king of the vamps, and Mya was welcomed back into the coven. With Stevie's power transferring to her, the link to the coven was restored.

Kai was doing great at being king, and he was even more happy now that I managed to break Nico's spell on Farrarie that wouldn't allow vampires to enter. All this power was finally able to heal something instead of hurt it.

Alex, Chase, and Lucian helped me with that—it took us a couple weeks to figure it out, but with the help of my brainiac cousins, we did it.

Chase and Alex agreed to take on the role of kings of the Knox coven. Gramps and Grams stayed with them for a few months to help them settle in before returning back to the Yukon. I speak to Grams and Gramps at least twice a week. Everyone was doing well, even Jax and Aurora, who were starting to take things slow. Aurora still refused to mate with Jackson until the threat on his life was dealt with.

"I'm ready to blow this joint; what about you, Smurf?"

We made our way down the stairs and I paused to look at the wall that used to have photos of my dad and sister all over it. I was taking all the photos with me back to Farrarie, along with a few other things. The rest I donated to charity. I lived in a freaking castle now, so I had no need for any of the other stuff.

I pulled my gaze from the wall and smiled down at Nico and Lucian, who were waiting at the bottom of the stairs for me. A sense of déjà vu hit me: falling down these stairs over a year ago is where my adventure really started. I wasn't that same naïve eighteen-year-old girl anymore, that's for sure.

"Yeah, Luce, let's get out of here." I made my way down the remainder of the stairs and clasped Nico's hand in mine. We passed through the foyer and out the front door. Once we were at the car, I stopped before getting in and turned to take one last look at the house.

I smiled.

So much has changed since I first arrived at this house. I was not that same girl anymore. I'm a queen, a wife, a granddaughter, and a friend. I thought my life would always be ***A Beautiful Nightmare,*** but with a bit of luck and ***A Twist of Fate,*** my life has become ***A Beautiful Dream.***

Click the link below to continue reading Dom and Soph's book Redemption

Thank You!

Thank you for reading Den Of Nightmares!
Holy shit, I haven't touched these books in over three years.
This trilogy is what made me an author and honest to God I am still in awe of Ryan and how much of a badass she is!
This trilogy has taken me on a journey, it has taught me so many different things and shown me dreams are achievable!
This trilogy isn't just words on paper for me, this trilogy is the start of a career I never thought I would be blessed enough to have.
Amazon, Bookbub or Goodreads, it would mean a lot to hear your feedback.

Acknowledgments

Honestly, Where the hell do I even start?
To my amazing husband, Mark. You are the fucking best thing that ever happened to me, I wouldn't be who I am or where I am without you and that glorious dick of yours!
My babies, my demon spawn I fucking love you both like there is no tomorrow. You are my reasons for everything, you teach me how to be everyday.
Last but certainly not least, my amazing readers!
Without you, all of this wouldn't have been possible. There are no words to describe how important you are to me. You make this dream of mine possible and allow me to live the life I have always dreamed of. I love you all dearly.
Xxxx
Sam

About the Author

Samantha Barrett is originally from Auckland, New Zealand but living in Brisbane, Australia.

Sam writes all things dirty dark and delicious with a side of twisted mind fuck.

She is a lover of all things red flags and an anti-hero is a must.